FROM BITTER ROOTS, THEY WOULD BUILD A MIGHTY NATION . . .

JENNY TAGGART—A brave, strong-willed beauty, she would face shame, betrayal, and torment sustained by the courage born of an enduring dream.

TIMOTHY DAWSON—Handsome, enterprising, he would turn a squatter's plot into a vast estate. But his passionate love for Jenny would be threatened by a dark barrier from the past.

JOHN BROOME—The dashing naval hero had been separated from Jenny by the violent turmoil of the times. But his love and honor would impel him to find her—to renew their eternal pledge.

FOR THEIRS WAS THE DESTINY, THE SACRED TRUST OF . . .

THE SETTLERS

Also by William Stuart Long

THE
SETTLERS

Volume II of THE AUSTRALIANS

William Stuart Long

A DELL BOOK

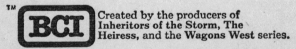

Created by the producers of Inheritors of the Storm, The Heiress, and the Wagons West series.

Executive Producer: Lyle Kenyon Engel

*For Kim and Lee, William, Simon, Edward and
Marjorie...my most affectionately regarded
Australian family*

Published by
Dell Publishing Co., Inc.
1 Dag Hammarskjold Plaza
New York, New York 10017

Dell ® TM 681510, Dell Publishing Co., Inc.

ISBN: 0-440-17929-7

Printed in the United States of America
First printing—August 1980
Tenth printing—April 1985

Acknowledgments and Notes

The author acknowledges, most gratefully, the guidance received from Lyle Kenyon Engel in the writing of this book, as well as the help and cooperation of the editorial staff at Book Creations, Incorporated, of Canaan, New York: Marla Ray Engel, Philip Rich, and particularly Rebecca Rubin, who traveled a long way in order to work on it.

Also deeply appreciated has been the aid in the field of background research so efficiently given by Vera Koenigswarter and May Scullion in Sydney, Australia.

The main books consulted were:

The English Colony in New South Wales—Lieutenant-Colonel David Collins, reprinted by Whitcombe & Tombs Ltd., 1910; *The Macarthurs of Camden*—S. M. Onslow, reprinted by Rigby Ltd., 1973 (1914 edition); *A Colonial Autocracy*—M. Phillips, P. S. King & Son, 1909; *A Picturesque Atlas of Australia*—Hon. Andrew Garran, Melbourne, 1886 (two volumes, kindly lent by Anthony Morris); *The First Twenty Years of Australia*—A. Bonwick, 1882; *Rum Rebellion*—H. V. Evatt, Angus & Robertson Pty., 1938 (reprinted 1975); *A Book of the Bounty*—G. Mackaness, J. M. Dent & Sons Ltd., 1938; *Mutiny of the Bounty*—Sir John Barrow, Oxford University Press, 1831 (reprinted 1914); *My Love must Wait*—Ernestine Hill, Angus & Robertson Pty., 1941.

These titles were obtained from Conrad Bailey of Sandringham, Victoria, and through the York City Public Library and the recently retired City Librarian, O. S. Tomlinson. Maps were made from copies obtained from various sources, including the Mitchell Library, Sydney.

Because this is written as a novel, a number of fictional characters have been created and superimposed on the narrative, but the basic story of Australia's early years is factually and historically accurate. When real life characters' actions, adventures, and misadventures are described, they are true and actually took place as nearly as possible as described, having regard for the novelist's obligation to tell a dramatic story against a factual background. In the light

of hindsight, opinions differ as to the merits or otherwise of
Captain John Macarthur and also of Governor Bligh—each
has his admirers and his critics, just as each, being human,
has his vices and his virtues. Both are shown here, warts
and all . . . but it is a fact, which the author freely
acknowledges, that John Macarthur played a very prominent and valuable part in rendering the colony prosperous
by establishing its wool industry. He also, as Book Three in
this series will illustrate, came perilously near to destroying
it. . . .

The author spent eight years in Australia and traveled
throughout the country, from Sydney to Perth, across the
Nullabor Plain, and to Broome, Wyndham, and Derby,
Melbourne, Brisbane, and Adelaide, with a spell on the
Dutch East Indian Islands and on a station at Toowoomba,
having served in the Australian Forces and the British XIV
Army during World War II.

PROLOGUE

Captain Edward Edwards, commanding His Majesty's twenty-four-gun frigate *Pandora*, completed the entry in his journal, and as he waited for the ink to dry he read it through once again, a frown drawing his beetling red brows together in an ill-humored pucker.

Under the date—Saturday, August 28, 1791—he had written:

> Passed numerous islands and cays. Coast of New Holland sandy and barren. At noon, in latitude 11° 18′ S, longitude 144°20′ E, sighted what I conceived to be Cape York. A boat was sent to search for the opening in the coral reef, marked on Mr. Cook's chart as leading through Endeavour Strait and into the Gulf of Carpentaria.
>
> This being discovered and soundings taken, I altered course, intending to come to anchor off the entrance to the strait during the hours of darkness, passing through it to double the north part of New Holland at first light.
>
> The reef—designated the Labyrinth or Great Barrier Reef by Mr. Cook—runs along the greater part of the eastern coast, and being extensive and much of it uncharted, it presents a grave hazard to navigation. Mr. Bligh gave the corrected position of Cape York as 141°15′ E but I consider his reckoning—made in an open boat—to be 3°05′ wrong.

Captain Edwards's frown deepened. William Bligh's epic voyage, in a twenty-three-foot launch from Tofua in the Friendly Isles to Timor in the Dutch East Indies, with survivors of the *Bounty* mutiny, had made him a popular hero in England. Any criticism of Bligh might therefore be misunderstood when Edward's journal was presented to Their Lordships of the Admiralty for perusal. He sighted and, reaching for his quill, stroked out the last three lines, wondering yet again what lapse of vigilance or discipline on

Bligh's part had permitted his first lieutenant, Fletcher
Christian, to lead more than half his ship's company to rise
in mutiny against him and deprive him of his command.

Reassured by the sounds reaching him from the deck
above that all was well, the *Pandora*'s captain started to
riffle through the earlier pages of his meticulously kept
journal. The *Bounty* mutiny had taken place on April 28,
1789: Bligh had reached Timor on June 14 with eighteen
loyal members of his crew, and had returned to England
on March 14 of the following year. His account of the
piratical seizure of his ship and the consequent sufferings he
had endured had roused not only the Board of Admiralty
but the whole country to anger—which was the reason, Edwards reflected wryly, that he was here.

Cleared by a formal court-martial at the end of October
and promoted, William Bligh had urged that a British ship
of war be sent to apprehend the mutineers, and the *Pandora* had been charged with this mission. Edwards had
sailed from Portsmouth on November 7, his orders to proceed to Otaheite. Should he fail to find the *Bounty* or any
of her crew there, he was to make a search of the Society
and Friendly Islands and bring home as many of the mutineers as he might apprehend.

He had discovered fourteen of the villains—two of them
were midshipmen—in Otaheite. With impatient fingers Captain Edwards flicked through the pages of his journal in
search of the entry. Slowly he read aloud, "Matavai Bay,
Wednesday, March twenty-third, 1791 . . . the armorer of
the *Bounty*, Joseph Colman, attempted to come on board before we had come to anchor. He was followed, after we had
done so, by George Stewart and Peter Heywood, late midshipmen of that ship, before any boat had been put
ashore . . ."

His mouth hardened as he recalled that first meeting.
They had faced him, looking, with their half-naked bodies
and heavy tattoos, more like natives than English seamen,
claiming that they had had no part in the mutiny. Young
Heywood, in particular, had attempted to play the innocent, insisting that he could vindicate his conduct. He had
had the effrontery to ask to see his one-time shipmate of
the *Bounty*, Thomas Hayward—now third lieutenant of the

Pandora—but Hayward had treated him with the contempt he fully deserved.

Captain Edwards passed a hand through his thinning red hair and sighed as he recalled the scene. He had scant sympathy with mutineers having, in his first command, been called upon to suppress an attempt to seize his ship, and he had ordered all three of the *Bounty*'s rogues to be taken below and put in irons. Later, the rest of the scurvy crew had given themselves up, but four—Ellison, Muspratt, Millward, and Burkitt—were captured only after a chase by the *Pandora*'s pinnace and launch. They had endeavored to make their escape in a small schooner they had built themselves, but were compelled to abandon their ill-constructed vessel at Paparre, on the far side of the island, and surrender to a landing party led by his first lieutenant.

Again Captain Edwards turned back the pages of the journal, to refresh his memory, this time as to his orders. Yes, there it was, in plain black and white, the entry copied from the Admiralty Commissioners' official instructions.

> On their being apprehended, you are charged to keep the mutineers as closely confined as to preclude all possibility of their escaping having, however, proper regard for the preservation of their lives, that they may be brought home to undergo the punishment due to their demerits.

The punishment for men found guilty of mutiny when serving in the Royal Navy was death. They were hanged from the yardarm in view of the whole fleet, to serve as an example to any who might be tempted to rebel against naval discipline. He had carried out his orders to the letter, the *Pandora*'s commander thought with grim complacence.

Edwards had had a roundhouse built on the afterpart of the quarterdeck, eleven feet in diameter, to which entrance could only be made through a scuttle, some eighteen inches square, on the roof. The prisoners were confined there in fetters, secured by leg-irons shackled to strong wooden bars. It was the healthiest place in the ship, according to the surgeon, George Hamilton.

No escape attempt was made, but since there was always

a danger of it, the captain had kept all fourteen of the mutineers in their wooden prison while, in obedience to his orders, he pressed on with his search for the *Bounty*. An abortive search, as it had proved. Captain Edwards gave vent to an exasperated sigh. Fletcher Christian and his piratical crew had seemingly spirited the *Bounty* into hiding in some far-off, uncharted part of the vast Pacific Ocean, and the prisoners—whether or not they were telling the truth—had, from the outset, professed ignorance of her destination.

They spoke freely of Christian's proceedings immediately after he had cast Captain Bligh and his people adrift, recounting in detail the unsuccessful attempts Christian had made to set up a settlement initially on the island of Tubuai and then at Tongatapu, in the Friendly group. Both had failed, owing to the hostility of the native inhabitants; in consequence, quarrels had broken out among them, which had culminated in the decision of the men he had apprehended there to return to Otaheite, in order, as they obstinately insisted, to await the arrival of a British ship.

"To which, sir," young Stewart had stated repeatedly, "it was always our intention to give ourselves up. We are not mutineers, sir. We were detained on board the *Bounty* because there was not room enough in Captain Bligh's launch for us to accompany him."

Rereading the page on which this statement had been punctiliously recorded, Captain Edwards swore under his breath. The damned young rogue! He and Heywood were king's officers, and whatever they might claim, they had both disgraced the uniform they had once been privileged to wear. They had made no attempt to regain possession of the *Bounty* from Christian; instead, they had permitted themselves to be set ashore at Otaheite and had lived there, as natives, for almost two years—in adulterous association with native women, most of them even fathering children!

From the deck above he heard a shout from the leadsman in the chains. He could not make out the man's words but, detecting a note of alarm in his voice, instinctively stiffened. Then, shrill and clear in the sudden silence, the masthead lookout hailed the deck.

"Breakers dead ahead, sir!"

The *Pandora*'s captain seized cap and glass and made at

a shambling run for the companion ladder outside his cabin. The second lieutenant, Corner, was on watch, and he acted with commendable promptitude, yelling to the quartermaster to put his helm down and attempting to back the fore-topsail to check her way. He was too late; before the startled men of the duty watch could haul taut the tacks, the ship struck with a shuddering lurch on the treacherous coral reef and was held there, as if in a vice. As Captain Edwards reached the deck the leadsman's call confirmed his worst fears.

"By the mark three, sir—an' shoaling!" Then, a moment later, "A quarter less two, sir!"

She was aground, Edwards knew, but there was a chance that he might get her off. If only her bow had taken the ground, she might break free, though heaven knew with what damage to her hull and the copper in which it was sheathed.

"Call the watch below, Mr. Corner," he rasped, as more hands tailed on to the sheets and braces in response to his shouted orders. "Mr. Saville, go below with the carpenter and report back to me if she's making water. Look lively, boy, I want the well sounded without delay!"

The off-duty watch turned up, First Lieutenant Larkin at their head, Hayward at his heels, and both in their shirt-sleeves, clearly just roused from their hammocks by the pipe.

Larkin said as he struggled into his watch-coat, "Wind's dropping, sir. Shall I—"

Edwards did not let him finish. Brace his yards and trim his sails as he might, the *Pandora* had not shifted a foot, and now she was listing heavily to larboard and must be relieved of the weight of her top-hamper, lest she capsize. Lieutenant Saville, hurrying to his side to report that the carpenter had found four feet of water in the hold, decided him.

"Send down to'gallant yards and masts, Mr. Larkin," he ordered brusquely, "and I want the launch and pinnace hoisted out. We'll send out an anchor and try to warp her off. Take charge of the boats, Mr. Hayward, and rig a transporting line to the kedge anchor. Jump to it! There's no time to be lost."

Apprehensively, Captain Edwards glanced astern; the

light was fading rapidly. In a matter of minutes it would be dark. Raising his speaking trumpet to his lips, he bawled an order to Lieutenant Corner to set all spare hands to man the pumps.

The topmen swarmed aloft, needing no urging, for all were aware of the danger threatening their ship and their lives. In these lonely, unfrequented waters, there was scant chance of aid reaching them from a passing ship. With the topmasts down and the guns of the larboard battery pitched overboard, the list became less acute, but the carpenter's next report, again delivered by Lieutenant Saville, sent the captain's briefly rekindled hopes plummeting.

"She's made eighteen inches in the last five minutes, sir, and the water's gaining fast. The bottom's been torn out of her for six feet or more on the larboard side and—" He was interrupted by a harsh, grating sound, and the ship lurched wildly, almost jerking the feet from under him. "I'm sorry, sir, I—"

The captain was not listening. He steadied himself, cursing. The swell was driving her farther onto the reef, he realized; there was no hope now that she could be warped off. The wind, which had dropped at the very moment when he had needed its aid most, had veered and was rising, its blustering force increasing the pressure of the swell on the frigate's exposed stern. He sent Saville below, with orders to set what men he could find to aid the carpenter to make repairs, and went grimly to consult with his first lieutenant as to what further measures might be taken to save the ship.

Larkin said, his tone guarded, "Sir, the prisoners—"

"What about the prisoners, Mr. Larkin?"

"They are alarmed, sir. Three or four of them have slipped their irons, and they are begging to be set at liberty to—to take their chance with the rest of us. They've all volunteered to aid us in working the pumps, sir, if you could see your way to releasing them."

"Release them?" Captain Edwards exclaimed savagely. "No, by God, I will not!" All the bitter frustration he was feeling at the prospect of losing his ship welled up like bile in his throat. But for the accursed scoundrels from the *Bounty* he would not have been in this precarious situation. Damn them, they were villains, for whom death was a fitting reward . . . here or in England, it mattered little to him where they met their fate. Besides—he stiffened as the thought suddenly occurred to him—were he to release them now, they might seize one of the boats and make their escape, leaving his own men without the means to preserve their lives should the ship go down.

The captain raised his voice to shout for the master-at-arms to attend him. When the man came, he said coldly, "I'm informed that some of the mutineers have broken out of their fetters. See to it that all are properly secured. The sentries are to shoot any man who attempts to break out of the roundhouse. Is that clear? Then pass the word to them."

"Aye, aye, sir," the master-at-arms acknowledged. He was a taut hand, accustomed to discipline since it was his duty to see it enforced; but unable to hide his shock at the harshness of the order he had been given, he ventured a protest. Captain Edwards wrathfully waved him to silence.

"Do as you are ordered, Master-at-arms. I shall hold you responsible if—"

Lieutenant Larkin put in urgently, "Sir, the for'ard pump has broken down—the piston's seized, sir. And I've no spare hands to relieve the others. Sir, the prisoners' help would be of great assistance."

The captain considered the suggestion, but before he could reply, he felt the deck cant steeply beneath his feet. The ship shuddered from stem to stern, and the crash of mangled timbers rang in his ears. . . . Wind and the incoming tide had beaten her over the reef. She steadied and then began to settle sluggishly in deeper water.

"Let go the small bower, Mr. Larkin!" Edwards ordered thickly. "Mr. Corner—I want soundings taken. Hail Mr. Hayward in the launch and tell him to row round to the larboard bow." He gave his instructions with a semblance of calm but with a sinking heart. It was of no surprise when Hayward reported the bow stove in below the waterline and fifteen fathoms under foot. With two anchors out the ship held, but when Saville came running breathlessly to tell him that there were now eight feet of water in the hold, he knew that there was little more that he could do to save her. More guns were hove over the side and a thrummed topsail prepared to haul under the ship's bottom, but the water was gaining at an alarming rate, the men at the pumps dropping with exhaustion. Reluctantly, Captain Edwards sent for the master-at-arms again.

"You may release Colman, McIntosh, and Norman and set them to work at the pumps," he rasped. "Are they all secured in irons?"

White-faced and tense, the master-at-arms inclined his head. "They are, sir."

"Then they are to remain so. The officers are not to be released, d'you understand?"

"They're pleading with you for mercy, sir," the petty officer said. "When Hodges and I were locking the irons on them, like you ordered, sir, before she went over the reef, they was begging us to intercede with you. Midshipman Heywood's only a boy, sir—Ellison too. And Byrne, the fiddler—he's almost blind and simple with it. Why—"

Edwards cut him short. In the dim light his expression struck chill into Master-at-arms Jamieson's heart, and involuntarily he stepped back a pace.

"Carry on, Jamieson," the captain's voice cut like a whip-lash, brooking no argument, "unless you want me to take your rate from you. We've not lost the ship yet."

"Aye, aye, sir," the master-at-arms responded woodenly. He summoned Armorer's Mate Hodges, and together they climbed onto the roof of the roundhouse, known to the lower deck as *Pandora*'s Box. The marine sentry posted at the scuttle greeted them with undisguised relief.

"Come to let them poor devils out, 'ave yer, Master-at-arms? About time too, I reckon."

Jamieson shook his head. "Only three of 'em. The rest are to stay here—captain's orders."

The sentry stared at him aghast. "But she's goin' down any minute, ain't she? I 'eard the first lieutenant order the other two boats lowered ten minutes since." He shivered. "Wish I was in one of 'em."

"The captain doesn't reckon she's lost, lad," Jamieson told him glumly.

Hodges had the scuttle open, and the two of them lowered themselves into the roundhouse in turn. Within its confines, the stench was appalling. The fourteen wretched prisoners had been kept there, chained hand and foot and deprived of exercise, since the ship had left Matavai Bay.

There they had remained during the four-month search for the *Bounty*.

Unwashed and verminous, they crouched semi-naked on the bare deck planking, wrists and ankles firmly chained. The tubs they used for their necessary bodily functions had been removed and emptied once weekly, but that was all. A few buckets of seawater, occasionally flung into the roundhouse, was the only concession to their hygiene Captain Edwards had permitted.

The poor sods were as weak as kittens, the master-at-arms thought pityingly. If the ship did go down they would stand little chance of swimming to safety, even if the captain relented and ordered their release. The nearest cay was about four miles distant. He jerked his head at Hodges and the armorer's mate started to strike off Joseph Colman's leg-irons.

"Are you letting us out, Mr. Jamieson?" Midshipman Stewart asked in a low, controlled voice. He was twenty-three, dark-haired and slender, with a large, gaudily colored star tattooed on his chest.

Jamieson, unable to meet his gaze, shook his head and answered gruffly, "Just Colman, McIntosh, and Norman—they're to help on the pumps. I've no orders for the rest of you."

"But she's foundering, for God's sake! Are we to be left to drown like rats in a trap?"

"And what about poor Byrne?" Midshipman Heywood put in bitterly. The fiddler crouched beside him, his blank, blind eyes moving this way and that, as if seeking in his own greater darkness for some clue as to what was going on beyond his ken. Heywood's hand clasped his, offering comfort. "You know he can barely see, Mr. Jamieson—give him some chance, can't you? Whatever the captain says, Byrne's no mutineer."

Hodges had released Norman, the carpenter's mate, and was ushering the three who had been ordered to the pumps up through the narrow opening of the scuttle. Jamieson sighed. He knew his duty and knew too, only too well, what any dereliction might cost him. Captain Edwards was a cold-blooded martinet, and in a British ship of war the captain's word was law, his orders—however inhumane—must be obeyed, on pain of flogging or worse. But in the

faint light of the lantern he carried, the master-at-arms
studied the two faces upturned to his and pity triumphed
over discretion. Heywood was not yet eighteen, his cheeks
innocent of stubble, a handsome, blue-eyed boy with all his
life before him. And as for Byrne . . . why, the poor fellow did not even know what time of day it was. Jamieson
bent and inserted his key into the lock of Byrne's wrist
fetters, aware that the man was so emaciated that he would
have no difficulty in freeing his bony ankles from the leg-
irons.

"I can't let you out, Mr. Heywood," he said. "The captain was most particular—the officers aren't to be released.
Those was his orders."

"What about *us*?" Thomas Burkitt demanded hoarsely.
He swore loudly and angrily, his pockmarked face con-
torted. "We ain't bleedin' officers, Mr. Jamieson, an' this
stinkin' ship's goin' down, as well you know!"

"*Mamoo,* Tom!" Midshipman Stewart warned, using the
native tongue of Otaheite. He turned to the master-at-arms
and asked gravely, "Mr. Jamieson, for the love of God, will
you come back and release us if she *is* going down? We
have a right to a trial. Captain Edwards cannot condemn
us out of hand. He—"

The tall petty officer bowed his head. "I'll come back,
Mr. Stewart," he promised. "I'll not leave you to drown."
Cutting short Burkitt's protests, he levered himself out of
the scuttle and slammed the grating shut behind him.

Left alone in their malodorous darkness, William Muspratt, who had been involved in the mutiny on board the
Bounty from its outset, started to weep.

"We should have gone with Mr. Christian an' the others.
We should've stayed with the old *Bounty*. Cap'n Bligh was
bad enough, God knows, an' we thought *he* was goin' out
of his mind, starvin' an' floggin' us. But this Cap'n Edwards, rot him—he's a bleedin' monster! Ain't he got no
pity, no feelin's at all?"

"It would seem he has not," Stewart said dryly. He was
cool and wonderfully calm, and young Peter Heywood
took courage from his stoicism.

"Do you suppose Jamieson will keep his word, George?"
Heywood asked, lowering his voice to a whisper.

George Stewart answered with conviction, "Jamieson is a good man. If the ship is in serious danger, he'll let us out if he can. And they may save her yet—you heard what he said to the sentry."

"Yes, but they've lowered the boats, lowered all of them, the sentry said so. If they've done that, then—"

"Edwards was just taking precautions. He hasn't ordered any provisions to be loaded into them yet, has he? We'd have heard if he had." Stewart was struggling with his leg-irons. "Lord, Hodges made a job of these when he put them back on! How are yours, Peter?"

"Tight," Heywood admitted ruefully. He tapped Byrne's knee with one of his manacled hands. "Try and work your legs free, Michael, and then see if you can pull the bar out for the rest of us. Go on, lad."

"We ought to be praying, Mr. Heywood," the blind man objected.

"We'll pray a whole lot better if we're free of these blasted irons!" Burkitt told him. "Go to it, yer little swab— you're the only one that can."

"I got to pray for forgiveness, Tom," Byrne answered apologetically. His misted eyes sought Muspratt. "I'll pray for you, Will, along with myself."

Will Muspratt swore at him. "Tell 'im ter do what Tom says, Mr. Heywood—he'll listen to you."

Hillbrant, the Hanoverian, said in his strongly accented voice, "It is of no use to ask him, Will—not until he is done with his praying. And he is right. . . . All of us should pray, for it seems to me only Almighty God can help us now. You are the senior officer, Mr. Stewart . . . will you be so good as to lead us in prayer?"

Thus appealed to, George Stewart did his best, reciting first the Lord's Prayer and then all he could remember of the prayer for those in peril of the sea. They all joined in, even Burkitt and Muspratt; then Byrne, still anxious to intercede for forgiveness, offered a prayer of his own, which went on so interminably that John Sumner—one of the hard core of the *Bounty* mutineers—who had hitherto maintained a sullen silence, struck the blind man viciously across the face with his manacled fist.

"Pipe down, yer pulin' little bastard!" he exclaimed impatiently. "And start workin' these bars so's we can get our leg-irons unhitched before this plaguey ship takes us down with her. You—"

"Leave him be, John," Heywood interrupted.

The note of authority in his voice annoyed Sumner; he sneered openly at the one-time midshipman, his scarred, heavily bearded face ugly in its resentment.

"And *you* c'n pipe down, Mr. Heywood! 'Cause you ain't an officer no more—you're a bloody mutineer like the rest of us."

"You know that's not true," Heywood protested.

"Accordin' ter Captain Bleedin' Edwards it is. He don't treat you no different from me or Burkitt or Muspratt, does he? He treats you worse than he does us."

George Stewart wearily intervened. He had been indulging himself in his usual daydream during Byrne's lengthy prayer—recalling happy, unforgettable memories of his life on Otaheite: the love of the native girl he had taken to wife and called Peggy, the birth of their infant daughter, the warm friendship and loyalty her family had given him, and, above all, the pleasant, undemanding existence he had led in a place that now seemed nearer to paradise than anything he had previously experienced. And it was gone, lost to him forever, as were Peggy and the child. . . . He smothered a sigh.

What the devil did it matter if the *Pandora* did go down and take them with her? It would be over; they would at least be spared the rest of the long voyage in this foul cage. They would not have to endure the humiliating ordeal of the court-martial that must, inevitably, await them on their return to England, and the shame it would bring upon their families if they were unable to prove their innocence.

"Have done, Sumner," he said sharply. "The lad's doing the best he knows how." His voice softened as he turned to speak to Byrne. "There now, Michael lad, you've made your peace with God, and I'm sure in His infinite wisdom He will know that you are truly repentant and will look upon you mercifully."

"Will He, Mr. Stewart?" the blind boy echoed eagerly. "Oh, thank you, sir. I was worried, see? But I'll get me legs out, like Sumner wants, and—"

With a harsh grinding sound, the stricken ship freed her

stern from the coral of the reef and began to sink, with a heavy list to larboard as the water rushed in through her lower-deck ports. Shouts and the pad of bare feet on the deck planking brought the prisoners' heads up, all of them listening intently in an effort to interpret the sounds reaching them from outside their cage.

The senior rating, a boatswain's mate named James Morrison, whose eyes had been closed in silent prayer long after Byrne had been called upon to desist, moved awkwardly to a split in the planks, through which a restricted view of the quarterdeck could be obtained.

"One o' the pumps ain't working," he said disgustedly. "And they're preparin' to hoist out them two native canoes the cap'n bought in Samoa . . . lashin' 'em together. It don't look good, boys. I reckon they're gettin' ready to abandon ship."

"What about us?" Burkitt growled. "Damn their eyes!" He started to call out to the sentry who bent, musket at the ready, to enjoin silence.

"Ain't you got orders ter let us out?" Burkitt demanded furiously.

"No, I ain't—only ter shoot you if you try ter rush me." The marine sounded frightened, though whether of them or of the situation of the ship it was impossible to tell. But he added, taking pity on them, "She's down by the head, but she's still afloat. Mr. Corner has a party tryin' ter haul a sail under her bottom ter stop the leak, an'—"

"A hell of a lot of good that'll do, wiv' 'arf her bottom torn out an' the pumps failin'!" Burkitt retorted bitterly. "Bloody Jolly—you'll be all right if she founders, but we shan't! Why—"

George Stewart again, almost with reluctance, intervened. "Stow your gab, Burkitt," he said curtly. And to the sentry, "Do this for us at least, lad—unless you want our deaths on your conscience—if the order comes to abandon ship, open the scuttle before you quit your post."

"I'll do what I can, Mr. Stewart," the marine conceded. He withdrew his head, straightened up, and, shouldering his musket, resumed his measured pacing on the roof of the cage.

The hours dragged past, with every sound from the deck adding to the prisoners' torment. Stores were being loaded

into the boats; Lieutenant Corner's party had abandoned
their efforts to haul the thrummed topsail under the hull,
but a loud crash from forward suggested that the foremast
had been cut away in an attempt to lighten her. Two
pumps were still working, but it was evident, from snatches
of overheard conversation between the men on the deck
and the swish of water across the forecastle, that they were
barely keeping pace with the inrush of water from below.

Byrne had at last contrived to free his legs from their
shackles. Urged on by Burkitt and Muspratt, he was vainly
endeavoring to lever out one of the two wooden bars to
which the leg-irons of the others were secured.

Moving closer to Stewart, Peter Heywood whispered,
"George, Captain Edwards *will* relent, won't he? Before she
goes down, I mean?"

His fellow midshipman shrugged. "Who knows?" He
sounded curiously resigned, almost indifferent, as if he had
ceased to care what fate had in store for them, and Peter
Heywood stared at him in open-mouthed dismay.

"Doesn't it matter to you?" he challenged. "Are you—
are you not afraid to die?"

Stewart shook his head. At that moment, he seemed
much older than his twenty-three years, and there was a
note of disillusion in his voice as he answered quietly, "I
think I prefer death to what would otherwise be in store for
us, Peter. If Edwards's treatment is an example of what we
may expect, then I want no part in it. Least of all do I want
to face a court-martial in England."

"But we're not mutineers, you and I—nor are most of
us, come to that. Bligh's boat would have been overloaded
if he'd taken us with him, and he gave his word—his sol-
emn word, George—that he would see that justice was
done to those of us who remained with Christian against
our will."

They had talked of those last moments—when Captain
Bligh's launch had put off from the *Bounty*—a hundred
times without reaching any useful conclusion, and Stewart
repeated his shrug. "Bligh must have changed his tune,
once he reached England—tarred us all with the same
brush, I fear."

"I *was* afraid to go with him," Heywood admitted
shamefacedly. "Even if I'd been given the chance to go, I

cannot be sure that I would have taken it. But that doesn't make me guilty of mutiny, does it? I never raised my hand against him." He waited, but when Stewart was silent, burst out, "Now, when I am facing the imminent prospect of death, I can tell you the truth, George. . . . I hated Bligh! He—"

"No need to speak of such matters in the hearing of others," Stewart put in gently, "even if we *are* facing death." He gestured in the direction of the boy, Ellison, who was craning his head in an attempt to hear what they were saying, and sharply bade him go to Byrne's aid. "Tom Ellison would have shot Bligh if Christian hadn't prevented it. He had good reason, too, you know . . . and Christian had the best reason of all to want Bligh dead."

Remembering the last words Fletcher Christian had spoken to him, when they had parted on the shore of Matavai Bay almost two years before, Heywood caught his breath.

When a British ship comes—as one surely will, Peter—give yourselves up at once, you and George. You are both innocent—no harm can come to you, for you took no part in the mutiny. It is different for me—I must run for the rest of my life, for William Bligh will never rest until he finds me. I must cover my tracks well. . . .

There had been other confidences, other admissions, together with messages for his family entrusted to him by Christian, before the *Bounty* weighed anchor and bore away, to leave Otaheite behind her forever. Heywood glanced uneasily at his friend. "George, I—"

George Stewart said in a low voice, deeply charged with emotion, "Captain Bligh is a madman. One day, if he is permitted to go on living, his madness will manifest itself for all to see. He'll no longer be able to conceal or control it, and then God help those who stand in his way! The pity of it is that for us—"

He broke off, a stream of orders shouted from the deck freezing the words on his lips.

"Abandon ship! D'ye hear there—abandon ship! All hands make for the boats!" The captain's voice, harsh with despair, echoed from end to end of the doomed ship. "Stand by to pick up swimmers, Mr. Hayward!"

Booted feet thudded on the roof of the roundhouse, as Edwards himself, with two other officers at his heels, used its elevation in order to ensure that his instructions were obeyed. The concerted cries of the prisoners, pleading desperately for release, met with a curt response they could not hear above their own clamoring, and a moment later, all three officers had gone, only Robert Corner pausing to call out to them that the order had been given to set them free.

The ship lurched over onto her larboard side, flinging them this way and that, and as they were picking themselves up, cursing and tearing at the chains that held them, the scuttle was unbarred and the face of the master-at-arms appeared in the aperture.

"Captain's orders, my lads," he told them. "Byrne, Muspratt, and Skinner are to be let out of irons. Make way, there—the armorer's coming down," he added crisply as Burkitt voiced an angry protest at his own omission and young Ellison, beside himself with fear, tried to thrust past the descending Hodges.

The armorer's mate cuffed Ellison out of his way and set stolidly about his task. Byrne, already free, was assisted out through the scuttle, sobbing his relief; Muspratt followed, but Skinner, too panic-stricken to wait for his fetters to be unlocked, was hauled up with his hands still pinioned.

And then, to the shocked dismay of those who were left, the scuttle was again slammed shut, leaving Hodges still imprisoned with them. He gave them a wry grin and went on knocking off the leg-irons of the men nearest to him, his stoical display of courage putting even Burkitt to shame.

"The jaunty's only obeyin' orders, boys," he offered reassuringly. "Waitin' till the captain's gone over the side."

"He has now," Morrison asserted, peering out through his accustomed spyhole. "I can see the bastard swimmin' out to the pinnace and the first lieutenant after him. Rot 'em, the scurvy swine!" Freed of his chains, he made for the space beneath the scuttle, and his voice took on a frantic note of urgency as he besought Jamieson not to desert them. "For God's sake open up an' let us out! The captain's gone—all the officers have, damn them to hell!"

"An' we need the key to our 'andcuffs," Burkitt yelled.

"Never fear, my boys, I'll not leave you—we'll go to hell together if we have to," the master-at-arms responded stoutly. The scuttle opened and he dropped his key into Morrison's eagerly waiting hands. "I'll have the lot of you out in—" his voice trailed off into a cry of anguish. The ship, her bows awash, turned over onto her larboard side, hurtling him into the sea, the sentry with him.

From the hovering boats there rose a shout calculated to strike terror into the hearts of all who remained, "There she goes! That's the end of her!"

Water was pouring into the cage now, and as the key was passed from hand to hand, even the freed men were struggling waist-deep in it, seeking to haul themselves out through the scuttle before it closed over their heads.

Unable to disentangle his leg-irons from the bar to which they were shackled, Peter Heywood resigned himself to certain death. He offered up a despairing prayer and then, as if by a miracle, it was answered. The bar slid away and he saw that one of the *Pandora*'s marines, a big, powerfully built corporal named Hawley, was beside him, tugging the bar through the shackles with the aid of a man who clung to the hatch coaming, up to his neck in water—Will Moulter, a boatswain's mate.

"Out you go!" Hawley urged breathlessly and thrust him in the direction of the open scuttle.

"God bless you, Hawley—God bless you both!" the midshipman managed hoarsely.

Moulter hauled him out into the sunlight he had thought never to see again and yelled to Hawley to follow him.

The deck was awash and deserted, but the boats, Heywood saw, were standing by, their crews picking men up from the water. He dove without hesitation over the stern to strike out for the nearest boat; but he was naked and weak from his long incarceration, and it was all he could do to keep himself afloat. He was thankful to see a plank, to which he clung with desperately clutching fingers.

All round him were bobbing heads, and the cries of men who could not swim echoed like a knell of doom in his ears. One poor fellow attempted to share his plank but went under before Heywood could put out a hand to help him. He reached the longboat and was lifted into it, to lie gasping and retching up seawater on the bottom boards, too weak even to murmur his thanks.

Recovering at last, Heywood sat up and turned to look apprehensively over his shoulder. There was nothing to be seen of the *Pandora* but her mainmast crosstrees, and now there were only a few bobbing heads in the water, all bunched together close to where the ship had gone down. The launch was pulling toward them, urged on by Lieutenant Corner, the crew pulling frantically at their oars, and he thought he recognized Corporal Hawley among the swimmers. The pinnace, almost on the point of foundering from the weight of the men crowded into her, was heading for the nearest cay, with the longboat, also crowded, just astern of her.

Lieutenant Hayward—his one-time shipmate and friend on the *Bounty*—motioned the newly rescued midshipman to join him in the stern sheets. Regarding him with more sympathy than he had hitherto shown, Hayward said, "You were fortunate, Peter. We have lost a lot of men—George Stewart among them. He—"

Peter Heywood stared at him, shocked. "You mean George *drowned*? But he got out of the Box before I did—I saw him. And he was a good swimmer, Tom. Don't you remember, he—"

Tom Hayward cut him short. "He and another of the prisoners—Sumner, I think—were struck by a grating which fell or was thrown from the ship. They sank before we could reach them. Perhaps it was for the best—who knows?" He shrugged and did not address Heywood again until the boat grounded on the cay.

The cay was small and devoid even of bushes, and as the sun rose, men—particularly those who had swallowed seawater—began to experience the torments of unassuaged thirst. Captain Edwards doled out water very sparingly from the casks contained in the pinnace and set a guard over these and over the surviving prisoners, who were permitted only half rations.

When the launch joined them, he ordered Lieutenant Larkin to call the roll, which revealed that thirty-four officers and men were missing. They included four of the *Bounty* prisoners—George Stewart, Sumner, Skinner, and Hillbrant—young Lieutenant Saville, and to Peter Heywood's heartfelt regret, the man to whom they owed their lives, the master-at-arms, Ben Jamieson. Light-headed and miserable as the sun beat mercilessly down on his naked body, Heywood crouched on the sand, taking no more than a cursory interest when the captain, having taken stock of the provisions brought ashore, announced that he intended to make for Timor in the boats as soon as the men were sufficiently recovered from their ordeal.

Boats were sent back to the wreck—more in the hope of salvaging provisions than in the expectation of finding any of her missing people alive—and they returned with only a few spars and scraps of sailcloth to show for their efforts. With these and a sail from the launch, Captain Edwards ordered shelters to be set up, but the ten *Bounty* prisoners were sternly forbidden their use.

"The bastard *wants* to put an end to us," Morrison asserted bitterly when even his plea for a tattered remnant of canvas, lying unwanted on the shore, was curtly refused. "Why don't he hang us an' have done?"

No one answered him, but Tom Ellison observed with equal bitterness that Hillbrant had gone down with the ship, still in his chains. "I reckon that was what the swine wanted to happen to the lot of us. Hodges says Edwards ordered the soddin' *hen* coops put overboard before he was sent in to let us out!"

Three days later, on September 1, the ninety-eight survivors of the wreck were divided among the *Pandora*'s four boats, and Captain Edwards set course for Timor, estimated at more than a thousand miles away.

Their provisions were meager—a few bags of ship's biscuit, three small casks of water and one of wine—the daily ration being the equivalent of two wine glasses of water a man, with the addition of a small quantity of biscuit, which most of them were too parched to swallow.

For the prisoners in the captain's boat, the sixteen-day voyage was well-nigh unendurable. Peter Heywood, as the only surviving officer from the *Bounty,* became the butt of Edwards's ill humor, addressed always as a "piratical villain" and kept with his ankles firmly bound, even when ordered to take his turn at the oars. Off the Mountainous Island they were attacked by natives and pursued by war canoes, and only on a few occasions were they able to land, to augment their supplies with shellfish and to top up their depleted water casks.

All were exhausted and near to starvation when, on the morning of September 16—having sighted the island two days earlier—the little procession of boats entered the Coupang anchorage. Captain Edwards went ashore, accompanied by the first lieutenant, to wait on the Dutch governor, and within two hours of his departure, permission was given for the *Pandora*'s people to land.

There were two Dutch soldiers with Lieutenant Larkin as Peter Heywood stumbled onto the quay. Larkin flatly told Heywood and the other prisoners, "You're all to be taken to the fort and held there until the captain can arrange transport to Batavia."

Heywood looked about him dazedly. The pleasant, white-walled houses of the Dutch settlement ringing the bay were, he saw, overshadowed by the towering fort; guns were mounted to cover its sea approaches, and doubtless it was furnished with dungeons, deep below its formidable walls, for the accommodation of prisoners such as himself. His head drooped as one of the soldiers grasped his arm.

"You'll not be the only British prisoners," Larkin told him, not unkindly. "Eleven escaped convicts from the penal settlement at Sydney Cove in New South Wales sought refuge here some weeks ago. They made the voyage in a twenty-three-foot lug-sail cutter, incredible though it may seem." He sighed, his expression relaxing a little. "Poor devils! Governor Wanjon has handed them over to our captain's custody, and he has ordered them to be confined with you and the other mutineers. Fitting company, I hope, Mr. Heywood."

He turned on his heel, and the Dutch soldiers took the weary party of *Bounty* prisoners up a long, sun-drenched road toward the fort.

Escaped convicts from a penal colony were, Heywood thought, indeed fitting company. Like his shipmates and himself they would face the death sentence when they saw England's shores again.

The judge, a dignified figure in his scarlet robes, took his place on the bench, his bewigged head briefly lowered in response to the bows of counsel and the body of the court.

The members of the jury resumed their seats, and then their concerted gaze returned to the five prisoners who, manacled and under guard, stood in the dock waiting for the charges against them to be read.

There were five of them—four men and a young woman of perhaps five-and-twenty in widow's garb. All were deeply tanned, lacking the prison pallor of most of those brought to trial at London's Old Bailey, but they were thin to the point of emaciation. The jurymen studied their faces with intense curiosity, aware—since it had been recounted at some length in the newspapers and talked of in the taverns—of the extraordinary story the prisoners had told following their arrival three weeks before. Committed to Newgate by magistrate's warrant, they had received a sympathetic hearing at Bow Street but were now on trial for their lives before judge and jury.

There was a slight stir, as the well-known Scottish advocate, Mr. James Boswell—his wig a trifle askew—entered the court, made his belated bow to the judge, and then took his seat immediately behind the young barrister who had been appointed counsel for the defense.

The clerk of the court, the charge sheet in his hand, named the accused in turn.

"If your lordship pleases . . . John Samuel Butcher, who now wishes to be known by his rightful surname of Broome, James Martin, William Henry Allen, Nathaniel Lilley, Mary Bryant, born Mary Broad."

The prisoners stiffened into rigidity, their faces devoid of expression. "You are charged with having, on the twenty-sixth day of March, seventeen ninety-one, absconded from the penal settlement at Sydney Cove, in the country of New Holland whither you had been sentenced to transportation for crimes committed in this realm, of which each and every one of you had been adjudged guilty by a properly constituted court of law."

Consulting his papers the clerk listed each of the previous sentences and the courts that had imposed them. With the single exception of William Allen—a tall, gaunt man in his mid-fifties who had been given life—their sentences had been for seven years.

After a brief pause the clerk went on, "You are further charged, severally and with others now deceased, with having stolen from its moorings in Sydney Cove a cutter, the property of His Majesty's government, for the purpose of absconding from the colony prior to the expiration, in each and every case, of the sentences previously imposed on you."

Again he paused and then, addressing each prisoner in turn, demanded, "How say you? Are you guilty or not guilty of these charges?"

John Broome faced him, blue eyes suddenly ablaze in his handsome, sunburned countenance. Taller than the others, he drew himself up to his full height and asked defiantly, "Is it a crime to seek freedom from tyranny?" The clerk did not answer him, and so Broome appealed to the judge, "*Is* it, my lord?"

"Reply to the learned clerk's question concerning the charges brought against you," the judge bade him severely. "Did you or did you not abscond from the penal settlement in New Holland before your sentence had expired?"

"I did, my lord," the prisoner admitted. Some of the jurors murmured sympathetically, and he turned to flash them a grateful smile.

"Then you must so plead, unless it is contrary to the advice given to you by learned counsel for the defense," the judge ruled. "You will be permitted to speak in mitigation at the appropriate time." He added curiously, "Was this your first attempt to escape?"

"No, my lord. It was my third. The first two were unsuccessful."

The judge's white brows rose. "For which, no doubt, you were tried by the colonial court and punished?"

Broome inclined his head. He answered, aping the lawyers' respectful parlance, "If it please your lordship, the colonial court sentenced Lilley and myself to two hundred lashes on each occasion. After receiving them, we were required to perform our public labor in leg and arm fetters for three months."

The picture his words conjured up again won a sympathetic murmur from the jurors, which the judge quelled with a withering glance. Aware that he had allowed his curiosity to override correct judicial procedure, he commanded brusquely, "Make your plea, Butcher. Are you guilty or not guilty of the offenses with which you are charged?"

Still defiant, the accused man did not lower his gaze. "Guilty, my lord," he returned. "If, in your lordship's view, my actions constitute a crime. And my name is Broome, sir. That is the name I was born to."

The other prisoners, sullen-faced, seemed about to echo his plea, but the judge intervened, advising them to consult their counsel. After a whispered exchange all declared themselves not guilty and were directed to sit.

Counsel for the crown began his opening address.

"Me lud . . . members of the jury . . . the prosecution will show that the accused persons—all of them convicted felons previously deported to New Holland—together with four others of the same kidney, William Bryant, William Morton, Samuel Bird, and James Cox, now deceased, absconded in a stolen boat, in which they voyaged to the Dutch Island of Timor, in the East Indies. Timor, me lud, is distant some three thousand miles from Sydney Cove, and the accused landed there on the fifth of June of last year. . . ." The barrister glanced at the jury, allowing time for his words to sink in.

Mary Bryant's thin cheeks drained of color as he went on.

"During the voyage they suffered no loss, but the husband of the prisoner Bryant and her three-year-old son—ah, Emmanuel—died subsequently of fever. On landing at Coupang, they endeavored to pass themselves off as survivors of a shipwreck, but the Dutch authorities, who had received them with kindness and compassion, became suspicious. When one of their number, in a state of intoxication, revealed their true identities, they were placed under arrest.

"On the arrival in Coupang of Captain Edward Edwards of the Royal Navy, whose ship—the frigate *Pandora,* me lud—had been lost in the treacherous Endeavour Strait, the prisoners were delivered into his custody by His Excellency Governor Wanjon, to enable them to be returned to this country."

"Is it your intention to call Captain Edwards to give evidence, Mr. Symes?" the judge asked.

"It is, me lud, should his evidence be required."

"Very well. Pray continue."

Mr. Symes bowed. "Captain Edwards, as your lordship will recall, was dispatched to the South Seas by the Board of Admiralty to search for and bring back the mutineers who seized His Majesty's ship *Bounty,* in April of the year seventeen eighty-nine, in order that they might stand trial. It was following the successful conclusion of his mission, with fourteen of the mutineers on board, that the *Pandora* went down with the loss of some thirty-four lives. Captain Edwards reached Timor, with the survivors of his ship's company and ten of the surviving mutineers in the *Pandora*'s boats, on the sixteenth of September of the previous year. . . ." The deep, resonant voice droned on, but now John Broome was scarcely aware of what was being said.

A bitter rage flooded over him and he clenched his manacled hands convulsively at his sides. Edwards, he thought, Captain Edward Edwards of the *Pandora*—that most cruel and vindictive of men!

Whatever harsh discipline Captain Bligh had imposed on the *Bounty*'s company paled into insignificance by comparison with the treatment Edwards had meted out to the unfortunates he had made captive in Otaheite. He had shared their imprisonment in the fort at Coupang and later in Batavia. Then he had made the voyage with them to the Cape in the Dutch Indiamen *Hoornwey* and *Horsson,* chained below decks on Edwards's command, in conditions far worse than those that had prevailed in Governor Phillip's convict fleet . . . The courtroom faded.

John Broome—who had called himself Butcher during his years of exile in New Holland—was back in the stolen cutter, reliving the long ordeal whose full story would not, he knew, be told here. He glanced at Mary Bryant, pale now beneath her tan but dry-eyed and wonderfully composed. She met his gaze and smiled, and he marveled at her courage.

Mary Bryant had endured the terror of storms that had come close to wrecking their frail craft; she had suffered near-starvation and the awful pangs of thirst without complaint, seeking only to spare her children from such torments. She had bailed with the rest of them when the boat had been swamped; had cooked when they ventured ashore

and were able to light a fire; and had eaten raw fish and
sea-bird meat when it had been too dangerous to show
themselves on land. She had remained silent when the native Indians had launched savage attacks on them, heralded
by a shower of spears or arrows from a pursuing war
canoe. And she had lived when death had claimed her little
son and then her stalwart husband, Will—who had planned
and made possible their escape, only to fall victim to the
endemic fever that was the curse of the Dutch East Indies,
his constitution undermined and his will to live snuffed out
by Edwards's calculated cruelty. For ten days, in Batavia,
while the *Pandora*'s captain had wrangled with the Dutch
officials over the price of their passages to the Cape, the
prisoners—convict and mutineer alike—had been confined
in the stocks, supposedly as punishment for insolence.

John Broome caught his breath in an attempt to fight
down his anger. On the voyage to the Cape, James Cox
had jumped overboard from the *Hoornwey* in the shark-
infested Sunda Strait, and Will Morton and Sam Bird had
died of the fever. But the cruelest blow of all had been the
death of the Bryants' infant daughter, Charlotte—ironically
on board H.M.S. *Gorgon*, when only a week's sail from
Spithead. (The prisoners had been transferred from Dutch
hired vessels to H.M.S. *Gorgon*, homeward bound from
Sydney, and brought to England to stand trial.) The *Gorgon*'s commander had treated all the prisoners well: Mary
Bryant had been freed of her fetters and allocated a cabin,
but the child had still died, and Mary, poor young soul,
had been prostrate with grief. . . .

"Wake up, Johnny—'e's talkin' about 'ow we made it to
Coupang an' 'e ain't arf pilin' it on! Makin' us out ter be
soddin' 'eroes!"

His eyes had been closed, Johnny Broome realized. . . .
He sat up, listening intently.

"It has to be conceded, me lud," the prosecutor was saying, "that these people miscarried in a heroic struggle to
regain their liberty, after having combated every hardship
and conquered every difficulty. Their voyage in an open
boat, which they navigated across three thousand miles of
perilous ocean, must rank with that of the much esteemed
Captain Bligh. For this reason, if your ludship pleases, the

crown is not demanding the death penalty that is usual in
such cases."

Mary Bryant expelled her breath in an audible sigh of
strained relief. It was the first sign of emotion she had
shown since entering the court, and Johnny Broome's heart
went out to her in wordless pity.

He found himself thinking suddenly of the girl he
had wanted to take with him when they made their escape—the girl he had wanted as his wife. Jenny Taggart,
the yeoman farmer's daughter who had toiled to bring a
few poor acres of alien land into production and who had
managed to see hope for Sydney's future, where he had
seen none.

In her own way Jenny had been as courageous as Mary
Bryant and perhaps—he smiled wryly to himself—perhaps,
after all, hers had been the right decision since, even if they
escaped the gallows, he and his fellow escapers could hope
for little more. It would be Newgate or the Hulks for them
if they were not sent back in chains to serve out the remainder of their sentences in the colony.

The judge was addressing the young barrister who had
been entrusted with their defense. Johnny had missed the
preamble but caught the words ". . . save the court's time,
to which end I am disposed to exercise the prerogative of
mercy. . . ." He tensed, uncertain of how to interpret the
implied suggestion and the young barrister advised the
others, "Change your plea to one of guilty. His ludship will
show you clemency, and no witnesses will be called."

They did as he asked, only Mary Bryant displaying any
hesitation, and the judge directed the jury to bring in a
formal verdict of guilty.

"May we do so with a strong recommendation to mercy,
my lord?" the foreman, a gray-haired man in the sober
garb of a merchant, questioned respectfully.

The judge inclined his head. "That recommendation
shall be recorded. I have already signified my intention to
concur with it." He turned his gaze on the five in the dock,
and they came to their feet in response to the hoarsely
whispered command of one of the jailers.

"Prisoners at the bar, you have pleaded guilty to the
charges brought against you—namely, that you absconded

from the penal settlement at Sydney Cove, prior to the expiration of the sentences under which you were transported there. I therefore direct that you be one and all committed to Newgate Prison, there to serve out the remainder of your original sentences."

This was clemency indeed, Johnny Broome thought, elated. They were not to be sent back to Sydney or even to the Hulks, and compared with the conditions they had endured when in Captain Edwards's custody, Newgate would be easily bearable. They would not starve or be flogged as they had been in Sydney, and when their time was served, they would be released—in his own case that meant in two years' time. He spared a thought in a brief, silent prayer for the *Bounty* mutineers, who could expect no such outcome from their court-martial unless they could prove their innocence.

The jailer tapped his shoulder and motioned to him to follow the others to the cells below the docks.

"You're goin' ter 'ave a visitor," he said gruffly. "Mr. Recorder Boswell, no less. Bin in court listenin' ter every word o' your trial, 'e 'as. Best be civil to 'im, 'cause 'e can 'elp yer. Might even get yer all pardons if 'e 'as a mind to."

"Pardons?" Broome stared at him incredulously. "For *us*?"

The jailer flashed him a gap-toothed grin. "An' why not, lad? There was writers—reporters from the newspapers—takin' it all down with pen an' ink. One young chap from the *London Chronicle* gave me a guinea." His grin widened. "Wants ter talk ter you after you've 'ad a word with Mr. Boswell. You tell 'im your story an' it'll be in the *Chronicle*. 'E specially wants ter know about conditions in Sydney Cove."

"I can tell him all he wants to know about Sydney Cove," Johnny Broome assured him. "I'll be only too glad to tell him."

He descended the steep stone steps, his smile as wide as the jailer's and a new lightness in his heart.

Under a banner headline, the edition of the *London Chronicle* for July 9, 1792, contained the full story.

On Saturday, James Martin, John Broome, alias
Butcher, William Allen, Nathaniel Lilley, and Mary
Bryant were brought to the bar at the Old Bailey.
They are all that survive of eleven persons who es-
caped from the settlement at Sydney Cove.

They said that Governor Phillip used them very
well, but that the soil did not return half the quantity
of grain that had been sown on it. Their cattle had
died from want of forage or been destroyed by natives
and famine was the consequence. They were reduced
to four ounces of flour and four of salt beef per day,
half of which was cut off if, from illness or accident,
they were unable to work. They therefore seized the
first opportunity of throwing themselves upon the
mercy of the sea, rather than perish upon this inhospitable shore—to which all declared they would
sooner die than return.

It then went on to describe the terrible privations they
had endured during their endless voyage.

It is understood that the late recorder of Carlisle, Mr.
James Boswell, who was much moved by the forego-
ing tale of their misfortunes, intends to prepare a petition on behalf of the five for a royal pardon.

The trial by court-martial of the ten surviving
Bounty mutineers who were brought to England
aboard HMS *Gorgon* is expected to take place at
Portsmouth in about a month's time. Captain Bligh,
who was in command of the ill-fated vessel, is absent
in the South Seas in command of a small squadron,
seeking to bring to completion the breadfruit trans-
plant mission on which the *Bounty* was engaged. He
is not expected to be back in this country in time to
give evidence at the court-martial of the officers and
men who so cruelly mistreated him.

BOOK ONE

The
Seed
Is Sown

CHAPTER I

Major Francis Grose, commandant of the New South Wales Corps and acting governor of the colony, stood at an upper-story window of Government House, a telescope to his eye as he watched the approach of a cutter under sail. The boat came about to make for the landing stage at the foot of the Government House garden, and he recognized one of his officers, Lieutenant John Macarthur, seated beside the helmsman.

It was early, the sun newly risen over the rows of white-walled huts and numerous public buildings that constituted the settlement at Sydney Cove. It had grown in the five years of its existence from a makeshift cluster of tents and flimsy brushwood shelters to the beginnings of a small but well-planned town. Many of the huts were, it was true, constructed of wattle and daub, and only Government House itself possessed a second story and glass for its windows. But locally produced brick was now in good supply, and granaries and storehouses—like the recently completed military barracks—were brick and timber-built with shingle roofs, giving the settlement an air of permanency—if not prosperity.

He intended to change that, Grose thought, buttoning his tight-fitting scarlet tunic over white cravat and waistcoat, preparatory to meeting Macarthur. What other reward could he and his officers hope for, save commercial profit, in return for their years of exile in this primitive and inhospitable land? Now that Governor Phillip had gone, the opportunities were there for the taking. So many opportunities that Phillip, in his misguided idealism, had denied to those who could best make use of them, in order that they might be given instead to the miserable felons he had emancipated, who—without capital or the incentive to work—had simply squandered them.

The commandant's round, red face was lit by a smile. He picked up his wig and then discarded it—the devil take it, he told himself, it was too infernally hot for such formalities! The convicts went barefoot and in rags, and his own soldiers were little better supplied with clothing, but that, too, he would change.

Ships were coming to the colony now, on speculative trading ventures—from America, as well as from England and India—and the syndicate he and the officers of the corps had formed had money with which to purchase their entire cargoes. In Sydney, where even such necessities as cloth and shoe leather were in short supply, there would be a ready market for years to come, with prices dictated by demand. The convicts could sell their labor if they lacked money or crops with which to barter for the goods they wanted. And liquor—with very few exceptions—was the commodity they wanted most of all.

During Phillip's governorship, convicts had been forbidden to buy or work for liquor. They had still obtained it, of course, but if found with supplies in their possession, they had been liable to severe punishment. Now, although officially still forbidden, the punishments were no longer imposed or searches ordered for illicit supplies. Idle, improvident felons toiled with a will when promised payment in spirits, and in any event, since Sydney was without currency, it had proved a convenient method of paying them for their work.

Francis Grose saw the cutter bring to alongside the jetty, and set down his telescope, his smile widening.

The master of the *Hope*, out of Rhode Island, had sold nearly eight thousand gallons of prime American spirits to the corps's syndicate at four shillings and sixpence per gallon and—with rum retailing at twelve shillings a gallon in Sydney—that purchase had shown a handsome profit, as would the next.

The signal flying from the lookout flagstaff on South Head had denoted the arrival of the first ship the corps officers had chartered on their own account and sent to the Cape of Good Hope—the *Britannia*—so long overdue that they had feared her lost.

A contrary wind off the heads had delayed her entry into the harbor the previous day, and John Macarthur, all impatience, had gone out to meet her in the cutter, in order to bring back the anxiously awaited details of her cargo and, it was to be hoped, mail and newspapers from England picked up at the Cape.

Containing his own impatience, Major Grose descended to his office on the ground floor. Seated at the ship's desk Governor Phillip had used, he was seemingly absorbed in the usual accumulation of official paperwork when Macarthur entered unannounced.

He said, omitting the customary greeting, "Captain Raven wasted much valuable time on his sealing venture and went to Rio as well as to the Cape but"—he laid a pile of cargo manifests on the desk—"he's brought us flour, sugar, tobacco, and a goodly consignment of spirits. Rum, porter, and half a dozen pipes of good Cape brandy for our own use. He did not forget the Russian duck either—a hundred and twenty bolts. But he's had devilish bad luck with the livestock."

Livestock—and, in particular, sheep—were, Grose knew, of much concern to his ambitious young subordinate, who was seeking to build up a breeding herd on the land grant he held at Parramatta. He asked gravely, "What happened to the livestock, John?"

Lieutenant Macarthur gave vent to a sigh of frustration, and his tone was harshly critical as he replied in detail to the question, "Raven bought thirty-one cows at the Cape, paying twenty dollars a head for them, and he's lost twenty-nine on the passage! He claims they struck exceptionally bad weather and were fourteen days hove to, under bare poles. He hopes to land five or six horses—three of them mares, purchased for us—and a dozen or so goats. He paid thirty dollars each for the mares, and they looked in very poor condition."

Major Grose pulled the pile of papers toward him. There were two newspapers among the cargo manifests, and he opened the first, studying its front page with furrowed brows as John Macarthur talked on, still angry with the *Britannia*'s master for the loss of his stock.

"Good God!" the acting governor exclaimed, interrupting the flow of complaints. "They let some of the *Bounty* mutineers off—only three are to hang! According to the *Chronicle* the midshipman—what's his name? Ah, yes, Peter Heywood was found guilty, but he's been reprieved and Lord Hood, who presided at the court-martial, is to give him an appointment to his own flagship. And the rest of the villains were acquitted. I can't believe it! Imagine the effect this will have on naval discipline."

"There's an even more incredible report, sir," Macarthur told him glumly. "On one of the center pages." He leaned forward to indicate the page. "The felons who stole Governor Phillip's cutter and made their escape to Timor have apparently been let off also—and made out to be heroes. There's a cutting from an earlier edition of the *Chronicle* that Raven gave me to show you." He produced the printed sheet from his pocket. "They were simply ordered to serve the remainder of their sentences—in England. They're not to be sent back here."

Major Grose read the report, two bright spots of indignant color rising to flood his plump cheeks.

"We shall have to make sure that word of this doesn't leak out. If the convicts hear of it, there'll be no restraining them. Damme, it's encouraging them to escape! Not that they need encouragement." He shrugged despondently. "What other news did the *Britannia* bring, John?"

"Little that augurs well, sir," Macarthur admitted. "There's talk of war in Europe. The French king and queen are virtually prisoners of the revolutionary mob in the Tuileries, and Raven said that several captains told him that the Royal Navy is hurriedly fitting out and commissioning more warships. It's expected that England will declare war on the French before long."

"And here we are," Grose observed, "removed from all chance to gain military glory! Did you bring the mail?"

John Macarthur shook his head, his pendulous lower lip drooping in disapproval. "No, Major—Raven insists he must deliver it to you in person. There's not much, I gather—only what he took from the transport *Halcyon*, which was dismasted in a storm and had to return to port. She was carrying some free settlers on their way out here. Three of them, with their servants, transferred to the *Britannia* at the Cape after buying sheep there."

"Free settlers?" the commandant questioned. "Did you speak with them? What manner of people are they?"

"I dined in their company last evening, sir," Macarthur answered. "That's to say, in the company of two of them— a father and daughter by the name of Spence, who will, I think, grace our society. Mr. Spence—Mr. Jasper Spence—

is a gentleman of means, a widower, lately retired from service with the East India Company. His daughter is a very personable young lady of, I should judge, eighteen or nineteen years." He sighed with more than a hint of envy. "Fortunately for Mr. Spence, most of the stock he purchased had to be left at the Cape, to be forwarded on by the next ship routed here, since all the *Britannia*'s cargo space was taken by ourselves. He may therefore hope that they will arrive without any serious loss. Ah . . . I've offered the Spences the hospitality of my farm, whilst they await the allocation of their land grant, sir. Miss Spence will be company for Elizabeth, which I am sure she will welcome."

"And what of the third?" Major Grose wanted to know. "You mentioned three settlers, did you not?"

"Yes—but the third is just a farmer. Dawson I fancy his name is. Young, single. He did not mess in the cuddy, so I did not meet him. Socially of no account." Macarthur dismissed the farmer with an indifferent shrug. "Oh, and there is a new ensign for the corps, I understand, but he was unwell and confined to his cabin, so I did not make his acquaintance. Brace, by name—a somewhat arrogant young fellow, of whom Captain Raven appears not to be greatly enamored."

"The Honourable Charles Windham Brace," Grose supplied dryly. "A younger son of the Earl of Dunloy and a protégé of Sir Evan Nepean. And his father's bought him a lieutenancy in the corps, as it happens, my dear John."

Grose pulled the cargo manifests toward him. "Is there anything else I should know before I start work on these?"

Macarthur shook his head. "No, sir, I don't think so."

"When does Raven expect to reach the anchorage?"

"Not before tomorrow, he said. The wind's southwesterly but he was hoping to come to anchor inside the heads before nightfall, if that's possible."

"Good," Major Grose approved. "That gives me a little leeway. I shall have to take men off the building gangs to unload the ship and that won't please George Johnstone or the chaplain! But at least the walls of the church are up." He sighed and went on thoughtfully, "I intend to propose to our syndicate that we send the *Britannia* to Bengal, John, as soon as we can empty her. You'll take a share, will you not? We're a little short of funds—and Raven can bring you sheep, of course."

Macarthur hesitated, his shrewd dark eyes narrowed.

"I don't trust Raven to carry livestock, sir. And I want Merinos to breed with my Bengal ewes. I can only obtain those at the Cape, as you're aware."

"I am," his commanding officer conceded, "but there are more profitable cargoes than your infernal sheep." He gestured to the pile of manifests, momentarily permitting his irritation to show. "Captain Raven owns the *Britannia*, which is a great advantage. And he's done very well on the whole, provided he can deliver most of this shipment undamaged. Put your money into liquor and trade goods, John—it will be safer than livestock and show a better return, you know."

Again John Macarthur hesitated, biting his lip in well-simulated uncertainty. "I'd like to, sir, but Elizabeth has set her heart on building up our farm. We need more land. The house is admirably situated, but it's too close to the township. I've no room to expand, build breeding pens and another granary. And I've only ten convict laborers assigned to me."

Major Grose eyed him skeptically. But he asked, his voice carefully controlled, "How much more land do you need? You've doubled your original grant already, with my award of a hundred acres."

"Which I earned, sir, by good husbandry—you must allow me that," Macarthur reminded him. He went on forcefully, "I've promised I'll buy Nepean's Bengal flock from him when he goes, and Raven tells me there's a Merino herd at the Cape up for sale. But, sir, what I really need is land with water, so that I don't lose half of them in the next drought. I want water on three sides of my land, sir."

"I take it you have a particular grant in mind?" the commandant inquired, relaxing a little. Macarthur, he knew, was obstinate and must be handled with tact. Although, damn his impudence, his property already bordered the river.

The younger man nodded. "Yes, sir. Unhappily it forms part of a grant made by Governor Phillip to a convict woman whose life sentence he saw fit to remit. Taggart, her name is—Jenny Taggart, I believe. She hasn't much stock."

His lip curled in contempt. "A mare and yearling foal, a few goats and hogs. Most of her land is under Indian corn, and it includes a creek. She doesn't need it, but I do, believe me. Sir, there's a parcel of land, about fifty acres, between my holding and Taggart's. . . . Look, sir." He picked up a quill from the desk and sketched out the area in a few deft strokes. "Allocate those fifty acres to me to include the creek and I'll let Taggart have some land I've recently cleared for sowing. She can keep her house—it's on the edge of my property, and the river's within half a mile."

Grose smiled thinly. "See the surveyor, Augustus Alt, about it, John; you shall have my authority. And presumably you will—ah—arrange the matter with the Taggart woman yourself?"

"Gladly, Major . . . and thank you. She knows I want the creek land—I've spoken to her about it."

"Keep the transaction within legal bounds," the major warned.

John Macarthur echoed his smile. "Of course, sir. And I shall be happy to take a share in Captain Raven's next trading venture."

It was the outcome he had wanted, Francis Grose thought, and stifled his momentary uneasiness. Few convicts made good farmers; they did not work hard enough or possess the resources to develop what they had, and probably the Taggart woman was like all the rest. At all events there could be no doubt that John Macarthur and his industrious and charming wife, Elizabeth, would make better use of the creek than she had. After all, he had had imported two plows, and he fed his family and convict laborers on game, thus costing the government nothing, save their clothing ration.

Parramatta had become a flourishing community since he had put Macarthur in overall charge in February, superseding Phillip's civilian administration. A penal settlement was best run on military lines and under military discipline.

Remembering his young subordinate's other request, he said crisply, "And you may have as many more convicts as you want, provided you accommodate and feed them."

"Thank you, sir," John Macarthur acknowledged. "Twenty will suffice."

"Then take them," the acting governor bade him. He heard voices from the adjoining room; Captain Collins, the judge advocate and government secretary, had arrived. Collins had been Phillip's man and still was. Grose jerked his cropped head in the direction of the outer office, and Macarthur rose at once, a resentful gleam in his eyes.

"You should encourage David Collins to follow his master, sir," he observed softly and took his leave.

The judge advocate, tall and good-looking, his faded marine uniform impeccably pressed, entered a few minutes later. "Sir," he said when his greeting had been returned, "I regret to have to remind you of an unpleasant duty. We have a man to hang."

"Yes—the mutineer from the *Kitty*," Major Grose returned. "You do not have to remind me, Captain Collins."

Jenny Taggart slipped to her knees on the springy grass at the edge of the creek and began slowly to empty the basket of woven reeds she had brought with her.

Like her dress, the basket was her own handiwork, and as she set out the homely provisions it contained, she reflected a trifle wryly that the five and a half years she had spent in New South Wales—if they had done nothing else—had at least taught her self-reliance.

Below her, splashing happily in the cool water, her little son, Justin, cried out to her in innocent delight, and she waved to him, calling a warning that he should keep to the shallows. Within a few months of his second birthday, he was a fine, sturdy child, blue-eyed and golden-haired, his small naked body healthily tanned. He looked as she imagined his father must have looked at the same early age but . . . Jenny bit back a sigh. His father would probably never see him. She knew from a letter she had received from him nearly a year ago that he had succeeded in his escape to Timor, with all the odds stacked against him; and it was unlikely in the extreme that Johnny Butcher would ever willingly set foot in New South Wales a second time. He would be wanting in intelligence if he did.

She rose and, collecting a handful of dry grass and twigs, set light to them and put the blackened spade she had been

using across the stones of her improvised fireplace to heat.
There had been times, not too long ago, when their rations
had not stretched to include a midday meal, but the situation had improved of late, with more ships coming to Sydney to trade, better harvests, and the building of a corn
mill at Parramatta. The mill was a primitive affair, worked
by hand, but a millwright had come out in the last transport—the *Bellona*—and it was said that he had begun work
on the construction of Sydney's first windmill. Whatever
the reason, the weekly ration of flour had been increased
and . . . Jenny smiled as she deftly prepared the mixture
they called "damper" and set it to cook on the surface of
her spade. Now they could pause in their daily toil and eat
while they rested.

She soon called to Watt Sparrow that the damper was
ready, and the little cockney pickpocket—who was her oldest friend as well as her assigned convict servant—
thankfully abandoned the irrigation ditch he was digging
and limped over to douse head and hands in the creek.
This done, he picked up the unwilling Justin and carried
him, squirming and protesting, to the fire.

"Gettin' above 'isself, the little rogue," Watt said, eyeing
the boy with a pride that belied his words. "Takes 'is poor
old gran'dad all 'is strength ter carry 'im now, 'e's that
strong."

Although in fact there was no blood relationship, Jenny
was happy that they kept up the fiction. She owed old Watt
a great deal. The little man—whose previous life had certainly not fitted him for agricultural labor—had shared the
work of the land grant with her and was, indeed, becoming
both skilled and knowledgeable. But . . . She studied his
lined face anxiously. He was not young, and there were
many occasions when she feared that he was overtaxing his
strength.

As if he had read her thoughts, Watt leaned his head
against the twisted roots of one of the gum trees at his back
and grinned at her with sly amusement.

"There's life in the old dog yet, Jenny lass," he told her.
"You've no call ter fuss, not over me you ain't. An' we're
doin' all right, the two of us. Once we gets the water
flowin' the wheat'll shoot up, an' we'll get twelve or fourteen bushels to the acre. An' as fer the maize, why it's the

healthiest I've seen in these parts—as good if not better than Mr. Macarthur's, an' that's sayin' somethin'. It's this creek as makes all the difference." He took the beaker of hot, sweet tea Jenny gave him and relinquished the remainder of his damper to the child. "Gotta build you up, young fellermelad, ain't we, so's you c'n do the work when yer old gran'dad finally gets past it."

Justin snuggled affectionately against him. A flock of brightly colored parakeets came swirling overhead to settle among the branches of the trees lining the creek bank, undeterred by the presence of the resting humans, and the little boy, to whom they were an unfailing source of pleasure, jumped up eagerly to watch them.

"Melia used to hate those birds," Jenny said pensively. "Do you remember, Watt, she always told us that she would give a hundred of them for the sight of one English sparrow?"

It was more than eighteen months now since the girl who had shared so many of the trials and tribulations of Jenny's first years of exile had won a full pardon and gone home, but to her own surprise Jenny realized that she did not envy Melia any more. Governor Phillip's hopes for the colony no longer seemed unreal—his promises made on the day when he had laid claim to this unknown land were beginning to come true. Slowly, perhaps, but the dream was no longer beyond the bounds of possibility—it could be realized.

She recalled his words, repeating them softly to herself. "*Here are fertile plains, needing only the labors of the husbandman to produce in abundance the fairest and richest fruits. Here are interminable pastures, the future home of flocks and herds innumerable. . . .*"

They were all here, the fertile plains and the pastures, with more being surveyed and settled with each passing year—at Prospect Hill, Toongabbe, and along the Hawkesbury River, and between Parramatta and Sydney Cove, at Northern Boundary, Ponds, and Kissing Point and the Field of Mars. A few adventurous convict settlers had taken up land grants to the south, where another river had been found, and yet more were venturing toward the hills to the southwest, beyond which, it was believed, lay acres of fertile land.

She had endeavored to tell Johnny Butcher all this, Jenny recalled, when he had sought to persuade her to throw in her lot with the Bryants and escape to Timor but . . . She leaned back and closed her eyes. Johnny had not understood her determination to remain here nor had he shared her belief in Governor Phillip's promises for the future. To him, her reluctance to return to England had been equally incomprehensible . . . yet what had England given her?

A few years of happy childhood, then poverty, drudgery, injustice—a cruel sentence for a crime she had not committed, the awful degradation of Newgate, and the final repudiation of exile as a convicted felon. These had been her thoughts when Johnny had begged her to go with him, she recalled, and her heart echoed the words she had said to him then: "My life is here. I will never go back. . . ." She stifled a sigh. She had made her choice, had come to terms with this new life, and God willing, in time her labors—and that of others like her—would produce in abundance the rich fruits, the flocks, and the herds of Governor Phillip's farsighted vision.

For little Justin, at all events, if not for herself—a low call, ending in a shrill, birdlike note, roused her to wakefulness, and she sat up.

"It's that Indian wench," Watt Sparrow told her unnecessarily, "Barangeroo, with 'er kids."

The aborigine girl, Baneelon's wife, came trotting toward them, white teeth bared in a widely welcoming smile, a boy of about four at her side, a baby slung on her hip. Baneelon, Jenny's first friend from among the native tribes that inhabited the area, had acted as guide and interpreter to Governor Phillip and had been a particular favorite of his during his term of office. He and a young hunter named Yemmerra Wannie had accompanied the governor to England in the *Atlantic* the previous December, to be exhibited—with other curious forms of antipodian life—to the king and members of the Royal Society, at the behest of Sir Joseph Banks.

Her husband's prolonged absence had left Barangeroo bereft, and in her loneliness she had frequently sought Jenny's company, usually in the isolation of the creek, for she went in terror of the soldiers. By aboriginal standards she was a handsome young woman, of slim and dignified bearing, expert with canoe and fishing line and an affectionate and devoted mother. Like all her kind she plastered her body and those of her offspring with mud, which dried to a dusty grayish color but afforded protection against flying insects and the heat of the sun. Watt Sparrow wrinkled his nose in disgust as the trio approached.

"I'll get back ter work, Jenny," he grunted, "an' leave you ter 'ave a chat wiv' yer friends. They stink too much for my likin'."

Jenny flashed him a reproachful glance but wisely said nothing, and little Justin, who had no such inhibitions as his adopted grandfather, leaped eagerly to his feet again, as pleased by their appearance as he had been earlier by that of the parakeets. In the manner of children, he and the older boy, Dilboong, communicated freely in some incomprehensible tongue of their own and, despite the difference in their ages, enjoyed each other's companionship—particularly when it entailed splashing in the creek together. They went off, hand in hand, to the water, and Barangeroo squatted at Jenny's side, shifted her infant to her outspread knees, and gave him the breast.

She had picked up a working knowledge of English from Baneelon, and from long practice as well as familiarity with many of the native words, Jenny experienced no difficulty in conversing with her. They talked of the baby, and then the aboriginal girl said, "Ship come *Weerong*."

Weerong was the native name for Sydney, and when Barangeroo indicated by signs that the ship was a large one, Jenny's interest was kindled.

"Maybe Baneelon come back?" the girl suggested hopefully. Jenny shook her small red head and Barangeroo's face fell. "He long time gone, Jen-nee," she protested.

"Ships take long time," Jenny told her. The fastest passage made by any ship from England had been four months—a record set by the *Justinian* storeship almost three years before. The average was five to six months, so that Baneelon and his companion could only just have set foot on English soil. She tried to explain this to Barangeroo, but the girl would have none of it. Dragging her nipple roughly from her baby's hungry mouth, she thrust him screaming onto her shoulders and demonstrated her angry disbelief by stamping on the patterns Jenny had drawn o. patch of sand to illustrate the passage of time.

"I go *Weerong*," she insisted shrilly. "Not find Banee-lon . . . take n'other *muree-mulla*." But her anger was short-lived: After a minute or two she hung her dark, crispy curled head and did not repeat her threat to seek consolation for her husband's absence with another. In-stead, as she saw Jenny putting out the cooking fire, she volunteered, "You go work. I watch little ones."

She was reliable, Jenny knew; she nodded her thanks and, picking up her spade, went to join Watt Sparrow at his toil. He said, a faint edge to his voice, " 'E wants this creek, don't 'e, Lieutenant Macarthur?"

"Yes," Jenny conceded. "He does. He's offered land in place of it . . . and it's good land, Watt."

"No good if there's a drought, though," the old man as-serted. He plied his spade vigorously, watching the water come flooding into the newly turned trench. "An' there is a drought most years—but this creek don't never dry up completely."

"No, it never has."

"Then you ain't goin' ter let 'im 'ave it, are you, lass?"

Jenny's chin came up. Lieutenant Macarthur was in command of the company of the New South Wales Corps stationed at Parramatta: Since the commandant had sus-pended the civil administration he had acted as chief mag-istrate, as well as being in overall charge of the convict superintendents. He was thus in a position of considerable power and influence, and clearly he would make a danger-ous enemy were she to offend him. But he had already dou-bled his initial land grant and built a substantial brick house four miles from here, with outhouses and fences and a fine garden, presided over by his wife, Elizabeth, after whom the farm was named. Her own grant was so much smaller—a mere fifty acres. Surely he would not insist if she refused his offer?

She shrugged. "No," she returned, meeting Watt Spar-row's questioning gaze. "No, he shan't have this creek if I can help it."

The little man grunted his satisfaction. They worked in companionable silence for the next hour and were prepar-ing to start on the construction of a second ditch when a high-pitched shriek from Barangeroo shattered the silence. She came running up to them, the baby astride her shoulders sobbing mournfully and Justin toddling behind her, his hand in Dilboong's muddy black one.

"*Gwee-un!*" Barangeroo cried, pointing. The word meant fire, Jenny's mind registered in swift alarm, and the girl was pointing in the direction of the cabin, hidden from them by a belt of trees. The gum trees were tinder dry—a spark would set them ablaze. From behind them, Jenny realized, a thin cloud of gray smoke was rising skyward. Barangeroo's sensitive nostrils must have smelled the smoke, because from the creek bed she could not possibly have seen it.

"Come on!" she urged Watt, and still clutching their spades they both began to run toward the spiraling smoke. For all his limping gait the little man outdistanced her, and reaching the brow of the slight slope he called back breathlessly, "It ain't the cabin—it's the grain store!"

Jenny was conscious of sick relief. The grain store was bad enough, heaven knew, but the cabin—built and improved with such labor over the years—contained all their worldly possessions, and its loss would have been infinitely worse. She quickened her pace, anxious now for the safety of old Reuben White, the other convict assigned to her, who occupied a small hut beside the store.

Reuben was in failing health and for some days past had suffered one of his periodic attacks of fever and kept to his bed. Even so, had runaway convicts or a band of marauding blacks attempted to rob the cabin or the store, Reuben would have stood up to them—for all his frailty, he was not lacking in courage.

"Where's Reuben?" she cried, cupping her hands about her mouth. "Reuben—are you there? Watt, we must find Reuben!"

They found him, without difficulty, stretched out in front of the smoldering ruin of the wooden grain store and his hut, which had newly caught fire. From twenty yards away Jenny could see the pool of blood in which he lay and the dreadful head wound that had felled him. Watt knelt beside him, feeling for his heart, then rose, shaking his head despondently.

"Dead," he stated flatly. "Dead as a doornail. Clubbed

ter death, it looks like . . . an' that means the soddin' Indians." He got up angrily and started to fling shovelsful of earth onto the blackened timbers. But the fire had done its work—the seed corn, carefully hoarded for planting in the newly irrigated land, was lost, together with their tools. And Reuben's hut was already crumbling into a shapeless heap of glowing ashes. Jenny caught her breath on a sob as she, in turn, bent over poor dead Reuben, covering his face with her kerchief.

Watt, she knew, disliked and distrusted the Indians, but it had been a long time since any of the local tribes had raided a settler's holding. Under Governor Phillip's influence, most of them were friendly, and Baneelon's people moved freely about Sydney Cove and Parramatta—they had even been given a hut on the northeast side of the cove in which to keep their canoes and fishing gear. True, the Botany Bay tribes had always given trouble, but this was a long way from Botany Bay, and although they all tended to wander, each tribe remained within its own territory.

Shocked and more than a little bewildered, she went to join Watt, and together they plied their spades until sheer exhaustion compelled a halt. Nothing could be saved from hut or store, but at least they had prevented the fire from spreading, Jenny thought wearily. She was reminded suddenly of a scene from her childhood, which she had believed buried in the past, hearing in memory the crackle of flames and the awful neighing of horses trapped by the blaze.

Lord Braxton's men had come, under cover of darkness, and set light to her father's barn. And he, without a moment's hesitation, had sacrificed his life to save his horses. His body had looked like a charred log when their neighbors had brought it out, unrecognizable as a human form to her childish eyes and infinitely terrifying.

Jenny wiped the tears away with the back of a smoke-grimed hand. Watt was swearing impotently as he examined the charred remains of the plow he had been making, its metal parts buckled by the heat.

"Filthy Indians! If the swine 'ad stolen the corn an' me plow, I'd not 'ave minded so much. But just ter burn it, plague take 'em! *And* kill Reuben!"

"I don't believe it was the Indians," Jenny said with conviction.

"Don't yer? Well, where's that bitch Barangeroo then, that you think so 'ighly of?" Watt challenged. "Made orf, ain't she? Jus' stayed long enough ter make sure we was out o' the way while 'er pals got ter work 'ere.'"

"Oh, dear heaven—Justin!" Jenny spun round, and her heart missed a beat when she saw that little Justin was trotting unsteadily down the slight slope, naked and bare of foot . . . and quite alone. Of Barangeroo, Dilboong, and the baby there was now no sign.

She ran to meet the child and gathered him into her arms. " 'E could've drowned for all she cared," Watt called after her, still angry. "Scurvy savages, the lot o' 'em!" He set down his spade. "I'd best go ter Parramatta an' report it, 'adn't I? They'll 'ave ter know."

"Yes," Jenny agreed dully. Her gaze went to Reuben's still body, and Watt took her arm, urging her toward the cabin.

"I'll put 'im under when I gets back," he promised. "Likely they'll want to see 'is body."

They probably would, Jenny thought. In normal circumstances, the death of an enfeebled old convict was of little importance, but Reuben had been murdered . . . and murder was a crime, whoever had committed it.

She carried Justin into the cabin, for once deaf to his pleas to her to stay with him, and taking a blanket from her bed, went out to lay it over Reuben's body. A crow alighted with flapping wings on the tall red gum tree growing at the side of the cabin—a bird of ill-omen, her Yorkshire-born mother had always claimed, warning of misfortune to come. Jenny lifted her spade in a threatening attitude, and the crow rose from its perch with a harsh croak, to take reluctant wing.

But it was back again when she returned from an anxious inspection of her livestock, none of which appeared to have suffered the attention of the marauders. And that, too, was odd, she thought. . . . The aborigines were always hungry. Why, if it *had* been they who had clubbed poor Reuben to death, had they fled without taking at least a young goat with them?

Still puzzled by this seeming incongruity, Jenny retraced

her steps to the cabin, noticing as she did so that the garden, with its crop of pumpkins and its carefully tended vines, showed no sign of damage. But perhaps Reuben had given his life to prevent this. . . . She sighed and held out her arms to her little son.

Justin beamed at her and then turned his head away. He had been playing with something, she realized—something forbidden, since he was unwilling to let her see what it was.

"What have you got?" she asked.

"Nuffin," the child evaded. Both his hands were tightly clenched, and weary and out of patience, Jenny said sharply, "Whatever it is, Justin—give it to me at once!"

It took a slap across the knuckles before he yielded up his prize. Lying on his small, grubby palm was a bright round object, and Jenny stared at it for a moment in bewilderment before taking it from him. It was a brass button torn from a military tunic, with the plumed insignia of the New South Wales Corps stamped on its polished surface.

"Where did you find this, Justin?" she demanded.

Justin indicated the floor, and hurt by her unaccustomed sharpness, his muddy little face puckered and he started to cry.

"There, love, there," Jenny soothed, instantly contrite. She gave him back the button and forced the suspicions its presence had aroused to the back of her mind, aware that—however strongly she might feel them justified—she would be powerless to prove them.

CHAPTER II

Timothy Dawson restlessly paced the *Britannia*'s upper deck, watching impatiently as her seamen lay out along the upper yards, taking in sail, and a boat was lowered to begin the slow and laborious task of warping the ship alongside the landing jetty.

The view from shipboard of the Sydney Cove settlement had long since ceased to interest him. There was little enough to see, in all conscience, apart from the rows of exactly similar wooden huts in which the convicts were housed, a few larger stone and brick-built officers' dwellings and administrative offices, a barracks and the reddish-brown brick edifice occupied—Captain Raven had told him—by the acting governor.

After the breathtaking magnificence of the outer harbor of Port Jackson—an immense vista of sapphire-blue water, hemmed in by tree-clad cliffs and golden beaches—Dawson had experienced the keenest disappointment of his life when the *Britannia* had entered the cove and he had caught his first glimpse of his future home.

Following almost six years of British rule, he had expected Sydney to be larger, with better roads, more impressive public buildings, eye-catching floral gardens, and waving palm trees, with the ships of all nations crowding the anchorage. But the *Britannia* was alone, and the people he could see gathering now by the quay to await the docking of the ship looked miserably poor and down-at-heel. And they were a silent, apathetic crowd for the most part, with a little knot of rowdies who, to Timothy Dawson's disgust, appeared, this early in the day, to be drunk.

He sighed, his interest momentarily rekindled as a convict working party was marched up, some of them in leg-irons, with two armed soldiers guarding them and a civilian—presumably a superintendent—shouting harsh orders that he reinforced with cuffs and blows from his cane. The convicts, Timothy had been warned, were the scum of the English jails, but even so, he was unprepared for the unhappy spectacle they presented.

"Oh, those poor creatures! Look at them, Papa . . . are they not a terrible sight?"

Timothy spun around. He had been waiting in the hope that Henrietta Spence would come on deck, but now that she had done so, he found himself, as always in her presence, wretchedly tongue-tied. She was a pretty, dark-haired girl, very small and delicate in appearance, with a tiny, pale face in which her brown eyes seemed to him enormous and infinitely appealing.

She had been brought up in India, which, he supposed, accounted for her pallor and the slight sibilance in her voice—the result, her father had explained, of having been cared for in childhood by an Indian *ayah*. To Timothy Dawson her soft drawl and her fragility added to her attraction, and big, husky countryman that he was, he had fallen willing victim to her charms within a few minutes of making her acquaintance when he had boarded the ill-fated *Halcyon* at Gravesend—now more than eight months ago.

Initially, Henrietta had encouraged his courtship; she had sought him out and seemingly taken pleasure in his company, assuring him laughingly that by the time they reached New South Wales, all his rough corners would be rubbed smooth and, thanks to her tuition, he would be able to hold his own in Sydney's highest society.

But then Lieutenant Brace—the Honourable Charles Brace—had joined the ship at the Cape, stranded there as they themselves had been after weathering an Atlantic storm, and when the *Halcyon*'s master, his repairs delayed, had arranged their transfer to the *Britannia*, Brace had accompanied them. His decision, Timothy reminded himself resentfully, had been made on Henrietta's account—the wretched fellow could have taken passage weeks earlier in a convict transport and, as an officer serving in the New South Wales Corps, it would not have cost him a penny. Instead, Brace had elected to pay his passage in the *Britannia*, and the hitherto gentle and affectionate Henrietta had left Timothy in no doubt as to whose attentions were more welcome to her. It had been a humiliating and hurtful experience.

Timothy Dawson's blue eyes were troubled as he stole a glance at her now, thinking how elegant and desirable she looked in her sprigged muslin gown and fashionably beribboned straw bonnet, leaning on her father's arm as they stood together at the rail.

He bowed stiffly. Henrietta affected not to have seen him, but Jasper Spence acknowledged the greeting with his usual courtesy and a faint smile that was almost—if not quite—apologetic. He reddened. He liked the older man, who had never treated him with the disdain his daughter had lately displayed toward him. Spence was a white-haired, energetic little man, full of eager plans for the farm he intended to establish in the new colony; aware of his own lack of experience in agricultural matters, he had sought Timothy's advice and paid heed to his opinions. Indeed, at one time there had been talk of a possible partnership, but the advent of Charles Windham Brace, with his military commission and his aristocratic connections, had put an end to any such prospect.

Jasper Spence was an indulgent father. He permitted Henrietta to twist him round her little finger; whatever she wanted he gave her willingly, and she had used her power to the full . . . in his own case, without compunction. It had been at her instigation, Timothy felt sure, that he had been relegated to the boatswain's mess instead of taking his meals in the cuddy—although Captain Raven had told him the arrangement had been made at the request of Mr. Spence.

Raven, although undeniably avaricious where his passengers and cargo were concerned, was a decent, God-fearing man. He had not liked what he had been called upon to do, and he had made this plain by inviting the young man to share his own meals on a number of occasions and by showing him many small favors. In spite of this the injury to his pride still pained Timothy.

"Oh, Papa—look!" Henrietta exclaimed. "There's Charles, do you see? He's come to meet us."

In spite of himself, Timothy's gaze followed the direction indicated by her pointing finger. Lieutenant Brace, despite his indisposition, had been ordered ashore to report to his regimental commander the previous afternoon when the ship had managed at last to work into Port Jackson, and a boat had been sent out to fetch him.

He stood now, a prominent figure in his well-cut scarlet uniform, easily picked out from among the ragged throng

of scantily clad women and fettered convicts, a hand raised
to his shako in languid salute. Studying him jealously, Timothy Dawson was forced to concede that he made a fitting
partner for the fashionably gowned Henrietta, whereas he
himself . . . He glanced down at his well-worn homespun
breeches and stained boots, belatedly recalling that he had
neglected to change or wash himself since earlier tending
his livestock in the hold. Small wonder if Henrietta found
him lacking in gentility, and no blame to her if she refused
to acknowledge his presence on deck in such a state.

He started to move away, but Captain Raven called out
to him from the lee side of the quarterdeck.

"Take my advice, lad," the portly master said earnestly,
"and have a good look around before you make an application for land. They'll fob you off with any old rubbish if
they can. Go up to Parramatta and Toongabbe—that's
where the best land is and where most of the officers have
taken grants. Mr. Macarthur among 'em—and *there's* a
shrewd gentleman." He grinned, forestalling Timothy's
question. "Parramatta's about fourteen miles from here,
and there's a launch that goes up there every other day.
But I'll put your horses and their gear ashore as soon as we
tie up—you can make it quicker overland."

Timothy Dawson thanked him, sincerely grateful for his
continued kindness.

"My first mate has some unfinished business from our
last trip to do for me in Parramatta," Captain Raven went
on, "and the sooner he gets there, the better. So if you'll let
him ride one of your horses, he can show you the way—fix
up accommodation for you overnight, too, if you wish." He
couldn't refrain from adding, with conscious malice, "Don't
worry your head about your lady love and her pa. . . .
Mr. Macarthur's promised to entertain *them*. Likely you'll
come across them in Parramatta while you're there and
. . ." He broke off to shout a stentorian order to his boat's
crew. "Pull, ye lubberly swabs! Put your backs into it!"

Timothy left him to his maneuvering and went below to
prepare his horses for going ashore. Both were saddle-
broken, a stallion and a mare from which he hoped later to
breed; and he had lavished great care on them during the
voyage, grooming and feeding them himself and standing
by their heads during the storms the *Britannia* had encoun-

tered between the Cape and Sydney. But inevitably both
animals had suffered from their long confinement below
deck, and he fussed over them anxiously, wondering how
they would stand up to a fourteen-mile ride so soon after
being landed.

Horses were his particular passion. Finding that he
showed little interest in farmwork, his father had apprenticed him at the age of ten to a bloodstock dealer, but the
experience had been brief. Young Dawson had grown too
tall and heavy to be put up on delicate thoroughbreds, and
the dealer had returned him ignominiously to his family.
Working once again on the Dorset farm—the youngest of
three sons—his ability to handle the fine Shire horses they
bred had been his sole claim to his stern old father's regard.

Yet when the old man had died just over two years ago,
he had left the farm to his elder sons and to Timothy himself had bequeathed only a small sum of money, with the
advice that he use the money to set up on his own "in some
other field of endeavor." But there had not been enough
money in cash to pay him his inheritance; to do so in full
would have entailed selling stock or land, which his brother
had obstinately refused to consider. So in the end—
Timothy fondled the bay stallion's handsome head, his
mouth hardening in remembered anger.

In the end he had simply taken what they could raise,
and since this was insufficient to enable him to set up on
his own in England, he had reluctantly made application
for a passage to New South Wales as a free settler. The
terms offered seemed favorable—even generous: a grant of
a hundred acres, free of taxes for ten years; an allocation of
tools and implements as well as of seed for the first year's
planting; an initial supply of provisions from the government store; and assigned convict labor, with assistance provided to enable the newly arrived settler to build himself a
house. Timothy's expression relaxed.

True, he did not much like what he had so far seen of
the settlement at Sydney Cove, but Parramatta was, by all
accounts, more promising, and Captain Raven's advice—to
go there now and see it for himself—was obviously good
advice. By the time the stock he had purchased in Cape
Town was delivered, Timothy could have pens and a house
built and some of the land cleared and prepared for sowing,

and all of it done without making serious inroads into his small remaining capital.

"We're alongside the jetty, Mr. Dawson," one of the seamen called from the hatchway. "Cap'n said ter tell you it'll be 'arf an hour 'fore 'e can get them 'osses ashore, but 'e thought as you might care to stretch yer legs a piece."

Timothy Dawson needed no second bidding. He went on deck, careful to avoid Henrietta and her father, who were still standing by the rail, and made for the gangway which now linked ship with shore. But scarcely had he set foot on the landing stage than he found himself surrounded and all but knocked over by a mob of ill-clad, clamorous women. They hemmed him in, talking to and of him in strident voices and clutching at his coatsleeves as he sought to push past them.

"Fine lookin' feller, this one!"

"Aye, that 'e is! Make some lucky lass a good bedfellow."

"You wantin' a woman, mister? Plenty ter choose from 'ere. Willin' too!"

Their wanton shamelessness shocked and confused him. He retreated a pace, but one, whom he judged to be little more than a child, contrived to clasp her arms about his neck. She was thin and dirty, her bony little body barely concealed by a ragged dress, and to his horror her breath reeked of spirits as she laid her cheek against his.

"For God's sake, take your hands off me!" Timothy bade her, struggling to free himself from her unwelcome embrace. He was conscious that Henrietta was a witness to his discomfiture but nonetheless could not bring himself to risk hurting the young wanton in his efforts to avoid her. She clung to him, laughing shrilly.

"A rare one, this—a *gentleman*! 'Twill be a lucky girl as catches 'im. Rally round an' 'elp me, the rest o' yer!"

"Have you no shame?" Timothy rebuked her, shocked to the depths of his being. Nothing in his strict upbringing had prepared him for such a scene as this. His austere old father, ever ready with quotations from the Good Book, had permitted little intercourse with young women in his home, unless they were of unchallenged respectability . . . and both his elder brothers had married respectable girls.

Wild cackles of laughter greeted his reproof, and the women surged round him, openly mocking.

Charles Brace was watching, Timothy realized, a disdainful smile curving his lips but—although undoubtedly a single word of command from him would have quelled the women instantly—Brace did not intervene. Instead he strolled in leisurely fashion to the gangway, paused for a moment at its foot, and then ascended to join Henrietta and her father on the *Britannia*'s deck.

Timothy silently cursed him. Angry now, he attempted to thrust past the encircling women, his face scarlet with embarrassment as their taunts became more lewd and, without intending to harm her, inadvertently pushed the girl who had sought to hold him, so that she lost her balance and fell heavily. Instinctively he begged her pardon and bent to help her to her feet. To his astonishment her thin little face was lit by a smile.

She accepted his hand and whispered as he lifted her up, "God's teeth, you *are* a gentleman! No offense, mister. . . . It's just that we don't get many o' your kind 'ere, see? Mostly they're like 'im."

She indicated Lieutenant Brace and then, turning to her companions with a shrug, bade them desist. "We'll all find what we're lookin' for on board the ship, girls. Leave this one be—got other things on 'is mind, 'e has."

They obeyed her, not without some banter, and Timothy returned to the gangway. His horses were unloaded a little later, and he led them off the landing stage and away from the crowd, the women waving him a not unfriendly farewell. The mate, a bearded, middle-aged man named Silas Porter, made no mention of the humiliating scene on the quay when he joined him, seeming to regard it as of less account than the fitness of the horses.

" 'Tis a tidy step to Parramatta, Tim lad. How are those nags o' yours? You reckon they'll carry us?"

"If we don't push 'em too hard, they will," Timothy assured him. "What sort of horseman are you?"

"Poor," the sailor confessed. He inspected both animals with appraising eyes. "Never seen these in daylight before, but they're quality, ain't they? Cost you a pretty penny, I'll warrant."

"They did that. But"—Timothy Dawson grinned, his

natural self-confidence returning—"this colony'll need horses, and I'm going to see it gets 'em. Oh, I'll farm sheep as well, but these two beauties are my stock in trade, and they've survived the voyage, thanks be to heaven! Up you get, Silas. We'll walk them on nice and slowly till the poor creatures find their land legs." He gave the bearded mate a leg up and mounted the stallion himself. "You all right?"

"As right as I'll ever be on the back of a horse! Steer hard a-larboard—that's the road over there."

They made the first part of the journey in easy stages, pausing at intervals to dismount and rest their animals. The road—narrow but well-constructed of hard-packed earth, with stone and brick-rubble covering its surface—followed the course of the upper harbor to its head, but at a distance of a mile or two from the southern shore to enable its numerous creeks and inlets to be skirted. At the head of these and at intervals along the road were the farms of government officials and some of the corps officers, clusters of huts for the accommodation of convict work-gangs, and a number of emancipist settlers' establishments, which Timothy studied with growing interest.

The soil improved as they drew nearer to Parramatta; it became clay instead of sand, and what he could see of its cultivation looked promising. In places, where the land had not been cleared, a variety of trees and shrubs flourished, many of the trees gnarled, hollow trunks that, although seemingly of a great age, still bore slim living branches, with pale evergreen leaves.

He caught his first glimpse of a kangaroo and exclaimed in wonder at the speed with which the strange creature leaped and bounded away from the approaching horses in swift alarm.

"They hunt 'em with dogs," Silas Porter told him. "And the Indians spear them. Make good eating if they're young, do them 'roos. But they can shift—without dogs you can't get near 'em. The Indians use wild dogs—dingoes, they call 'em, and they're real savage brutes. In their wild state they'll take lambs and even small calves . . . and they can't be properly tamed. Mr. Macarthur keeps greyhounds as hunting dogs and does pretty well with 'em, by all accounts. Like me to bring you a couple, next time I'm here?"

"Yes, that I would," Timothy assented without hesitation.

"They'll cost you."

"Never mind—I still want them."

"You mean to stay here, don't you, Tim?" the *Britannia*'s mate questioned, eyeing him curiously. "You really do intend to take your chances in this place?"

"Yes, that's right, I do."

"Wouldn't be my choice," Porter stated emphatically.

"I have no other, Silas. So I have to stay, have I not? And I have to succeed."

"You'll have your work cut out, lad," the older man warned. Seeing that Timothy clearly expected an explanation, he went on gravely. "The odds are stacked against the likes of you—you're free, but you'll not be greatly better off than the emancipated convicts. And you won't be treated much better than they are, when it comes down to brass tacks. It's the officers of the corps that'll do well out o' Sydney Cove . . . and they won't do it sweating their guts out on the land."

Timothy frowned. He pulled up. "Better give the horses a breather." When his companion followed his example and dismounted, he asked, "What are you trying to tell me, Silas? The officers all have farms, haven't they?"

"Most of 'em have, yes. But that's only to enable them to eat well. They're putting their money into trade goods—liquor and tobacco. I know, that's what they chartered the *Britannia* to bring here. If you've any capital, you'd be well advised to do the same, not spend it on livestock." The mate smiled wryly. "Livestock don't travel well—liquor does. And that's what the folk here want, what they'll sell their souls for, believe me."

For the second time that day Timothy Dawson was shocked. He thought bitterly of the woman who had accosted him, of the reek of rum on her breath, and of the drunken antics of the harridans with her and shook his head angrily.

"I'm a farmer," he stated. "That's all I know—farming and horse breeding. That's what I came here to do."

Silas Porter shrugged. "Have it your own way. But you'll lose that pretty lass you fancy."

"I've lost her already," Timothy retorted. He climbed

stiffly back into the saddle. "How much farther is it to—what's the place called? Parramatta?"

"Not above a couple o' miles." Silas Porter did not take offense. The lad would learn, he thought cynically—and learn the hard way. He had done his best to offer sage advice, as he knew his captain had, and they could do no more. As for the girl . . . well, she was best suited to become wife to an officer, with her airs and graces, and young Tim Dawson would realize that when he had been in this place a while longer. A New South Wales farmer needed a woman who wasn't afraid of hard work, not one who had spent half her life in India, waited on hand and foot by a lot of black slaves.

They rode in silence, each busy with his own thoughts, until the township of Parramatta came in sight. Timothy was pleasurably surprised by what he saw as they approached it through a parklike expanse of excellent grassland, fenced and well shaded by trees, beneath which cattle were grazing in healthy content.

The town itself was built in the form of a crescent on elevated ground, the convicts' huts in orderly lines, each with its own vegetable garden. Porter pointed out the newly completed barracks, the stone-built storehouses and granaries, and the governor's residence, which stood on the crest of a low hill, with a flourishing vineyard circling its foot and maize showing green on its under slope.

"They've got most everything they need here now," he observed. "Brick kilns, a pottery—the clay here is second to none, they say. There's the blacksmith's forge, over to your right, the carpenters' shop and covered sawpits and the superintendent's house opposite. The judge advocate's house, where the local court sits, is that stone-faced building ahead of us, and the chaplain's is just beyond. Better at raising corn than saving souls, they reckon the chaplain is. Up to now he hasn't bestirred himself to put up a church here, though I hear he's started to build one in Sydney Cove, which is where he spends most of his time."

"But they do hold church services here, don't they?" Timothy asked. "I was told they did."

"Aye—in the open air and compulsory for convicts." Silas Porter's tone was disapproving. "It's the Reverend Johnson one Sunday and the corps's chaplain the next, turn

about. You won't lack religious guidance if you settle up
here. And the hospital is to be rebuilt. That's it over there,
see . . . the long wooden shed with a thatched roof? I've
heard tell the new one's to be twice the size—and they
need it, 'cause there are more people here now than there
are in Sydney. Like your livestock," the *Britannia*'s mate
added dryly, "the poor devils they send out from England
don't stand the voyage too well. Half of 'em are sick before
they board the transports, by all accounts."

Timothy sat his horse, staring about him and trying to
take in all his guide was telling him. It was just after midday—the hour of rest for the convict laborers—and the
township appeared almost deserted, save for a pacing sentry guarding the stocks and two more in front of the barracks guardroom.

The road they had been following led on, he saw, skirting the government garden, and Silas Porter, following the
direction of his gaze, replied to his unvoiced question.

"That road goes down to the wharf about a mile away.
The Rose Hill packet—the *Lump*, the people call her—
loads and unloads there. She's a rum-looking craft—built
here, she was, by the carpenter of His Majesty's ship *Supply*. But she serves her purpose. She can carry passengers
and ten tons of stores, and so far she hasn't foundered. But
it'd pay some enterprising fellow to build a bigger and better craft to replace her."

"Why don't *you* do it?" Timothy challenged.

"No, not me." Porter closed one eye in an elaborate
wink. "I'm a seaman . . . and I'm doing all right with
Captain Raven and the old *Britannia*." He gestured ahead
of them. "Toongabbe's nor'east of us and Prospect Hill due
east . . . both about four miles distant. Likely you'll want
to look at both before you make up your mind where to
settle, but first we'll call on Tom Macrae. He'll find you a
lodging for the night and take care of the horses. He was
one of the survivors of the *Guardian*—the ship that struck
a berg on her way here from the Cape—and he's a good
man. Works here as a superintendent and master builder.
That's his house over there."

The house he indicated was worthy of a master
builder—a sizable half-brick cabin with a shingle roof and
an extensive and well-kept front garden. A few yards from

it stood the stocks, in which two men were doing enforced penance. Both were emaciated, their faces unshaven and their clothing in rags, and Porter said, jerking his head in their direction, "That's how they serve runaways here— seven days in the stocks, on bread and water, instead of the lash. It's mostly the Irish who try to run. They're rebels, the lot of 'em, and fools into the bargain. If they don't die of starvation in the woods, the Indians get them or they're forced to crawl back—but they won't be told."

Reaching the superintendent's house he slid awkwardly from the saddle and, giving his rein to Timothy, beat a loud tattoo on the roughhewn timber of the door.

"Tom . . . are you at home? 'Tis your old friend Silas Porter come to give you the time of day!"

A woman answered his summons. She was gray-haired, wearing a fresh white apron over her dark dress, and she had a thin but unexpectedly youthful, rosy-cheeked face, which lit with a welcoming smile when she recognized the caller.

"Silas . . . ah, you are indeed a sight for sore eyes! Tom is inside, eating his lunch. Come in, pray—he will be overjoyed that you are returned to us." Her gaze went in mute question to Timothy, standing beside the horses, and Porter introduced him as a newly arrived settler and the owner of their mounts.

"We do not see very many horses here, Mr. Dawson," the woman said. "And we have no stables but . . . there is an outbuilding at the back. Shall I take them for you?"

Timothy shook his head. Both animals were tired, and he was anxious to get the saddles off them.

"If you'll permit me, ma'am, I'd like to water and bed them down. They're just off the ship, you see."

"Then follow me," she invited. "If you'll be so good as to announce yourself, Silas."

Silas Porter, rubbing his stiff posterior, needed no second invitation. The superintendent's wife gathered up her skirts and led the way to a wooden shed normally occupied by a flock of plump, healthy-looking fowl, Timothy guessed as his hostess chased them clucking from their sanctuary. While he unsaddled and rubbed both his horses down with wisps of straw taken from some bales piled up at the rear of the shed, she fetched him water and a pan of coarse grain.

"This is all we have," she explained. "It is a mixture of Indian corn and barley, but the other stock seem to thrive on it well enough, so I do not think it will do these fine horses of yours any harm."

"Thank you, ma'am." He relieved her of the water bucket, touched by her thoughtful kindness. She had a pleasant voice, with a faint hint of Scottish accent and a warm and friendly manner that put him instantly at ease— Thomas Macrae was a fortunate man. "I'm much indebted to you."

"Out here, sir, we learn to help each other. It's a hard life but it's improving."

"Improving?"

She smiled. "We no longer go in daily fear of starvation. We are growing crops, breeding stock, finding better and more fertile land . . . and the ships are coming, bringing us what we cannot yet provide for ourselves. In the first years"—the smile faded and her thin face clouded over— "there were no ships and we feared we had been abandoned to our fate."

Timothy stared at her, letting the stallion drink more than he had intended in his astonishment. "You have been here since the beginning, Mistress Macrae?"

"Yes," she admitted without hesitation. "I came out in the first fleet, under Governor Phillip's command."

"Then you—that is—" Timothy broke off, scarlet with embarrassment.

Mrs. Macrae's smile returned. "I came out as a convict, sir, under sentence of transportation for life."

"But you're a—a respectable woman," he began incredulously and then broke off, conscious of his own clumsiness. "I do beg your pardon, Mistress Macrae. I—I did not mean—"

"I fear you did, sir," the Scotswoman chided him gently, cutting short his stammered apology. "But we are not all depraved and wanton, as you appear to suppose. You will have heard tales of the convict transports, no doubt?"

Timothy inclined his head, not trusting himself to speak, and she went on, her voice soft and devoid of bitterness. "Some of the tales are true—too many. But this was due to the kind of people who were sent here. Governor Phillip, it is well known, pleaded with the home government to send artisans, farmers, and craftsmen, women with nursing and housewifely skills, seamstresses and the like. But above all he wanted fit and healthy folk, capable of hard work. Instead they simply cleared the jails without giving a thought to his requests. More than half of those in the second fleet were old and ailing, and almost half died on the voyage or were dying when they landed." Mrs. Macrae bit back a sigh. She set down the pan of grain and laid a hand on his arm.

"Pray come to the house as soon as you have fed your horses. I will prepare some refreshment for you."

Chastened and still embarrassed, Timothy delayed his return to the house for as long as he could. *You live and learn*, he told himself—even about convicts. When he finally screwed up his courage to enter the superintendent's house, it was to find that Silas Porter had finished his meal, and that both he and his host were on the point of departure. Superintendent Macrae was a tall, balding man of about fifty, somewhat taciturn in manner, but his greeting was pleasant enough, delivered in a strong Scottish accent.

"I'll gie ye a bed for the nicht, Maister Dawson, and ye can leave your horses here in safety until they're rested. I maun be at ma work until sunset, and Silas has business tae transact, so maybe ye might care tae look around on foot. 'Tis the way maist folk have tae travel i' these pairts, and ye could get tae Toongabbe an' back before dark, if ye've a mind tae. The morn, if ye make an early stairt, ye could ride tae the Hawkesbury River. . . . I'll gie ye directions, an' there's a musket here ye may have the loan o', just in case ye see ony game on your way."

He nodded in dismissal, brushing aside Timothy's thanks. "Annie'll gie ye a bite now, and this evening we'll gie ye both a proper meal. Fresh pork—I killed a pig yesterday, so we're i' luck. Now, Silas—if ye're ready, we'll away."

After they had gone, Annie Macrae served him with some griddle cakes and goat's-milk cheese, and when he had eaten his fill, she found the musket for him and pointed out the direction he should take in order to reach Toongabbe.

Timothy set off at an easy pace, following a rough but
well-defined track that led northwestward. He passed more
convict huts, noting that while most of the gardens were
planted with vegetables or vines, others were badly neglected or given over to the ravages of scrawny chickens or
a few undersized pigs. To his left he saw a labor gang
working on a long, low building he decided must be the
half-completed new hospital of which Silas Porter had spoken; at the farthest extremity of the settlement he was unpleasantly reminded of the nature of its inhabitants by the
sight of a gibbet. From it hung the body of what must once
have been a man, and he stared with loathing at the grisly
relic, wondering what crime the dead man could have committed to cause his judges to deny him Christian burial.
For there was a cemetery—a small forest of white-painted
wooden crosses, ranged in meticulously spaced lines in a
tree-shaded square, met his questing gaze as he trudged on,
dust rising in his wake.

It's a hard life, Mrs. Macrae had told him. Evidently it
was, for the cemetery was proof of the toll it had taken—
no doubt of the fit and strong as well as of the sick and
ailing. And . . . He glanced back involuntarily at the gibbet. Also, it seemed, of those malefactors who had failed to
leave their evil ways behind them. Timothy shrugged and
plodded on.

He had covered about three miles, passing cultivated
land and glimpsing distant dwelling places and fenced stock
pens, when the dusty track curved round the head of a
small creek with a screen of trees growing along both
banks. The trees were the usual eucalyptus gums, their
grayish-white trunks and narrow, constantly moving leaves
now familiar to him, but the creek itself looked cool and
enticing. Conscious of a growing thirst he left the track and
slithered down the near bank. A flock of white cockatoos
rose from the branches that had been harboring them with
raucously protesting cries, and as he knelt to scoop up water with his hands, another bird—which he could neither
see nor identify—gave vent to a sound like demented human laughter, startling him more than a little.

But the water was sweet and pure, and he drank deeply
and gratefully before washing the dust from his head and
face. He rose, refreshed, to see that the farther bank was

almost on a level with the land beyond and that, between the trees, three or four irrigation ditches had been dug. Curious, he crossed the narrow strip of water by means of two gnarled and long-dead tree trunks that had been felled in such a way as to form a bridge. He found himself looking at a broad patch of dark, loamy soil that—with the ditches intersecting it—had been prepared with painstaking skill for the the sowing of the new season's wheat crop.

This was the first settler's holding he had seen at close hand, and he studied it with interest. To his left, several acres of what he judged to be maize was showing green, and ahead and to his right he saw a well-built cabin, surrounded by a fenced garden, with a thin blue wisp of smoke rising from its chimney. There were pens and a single outhouse, but between the cabin and its adjacent pens stood a heap of charred and blackened timber that momentarily puzzled him. Then realization dawned—the settler, whoever he was, had recently suffered the loss of some of his buildings, obviously by fire. It looked as if a storehouse had been destroyed, and he found himself wondering whether the fire had been accidental. Mrs. Macrae, when speaking of the new Hawkesbury River settlements as he ate his lunch, had warned him that a constant threat was posed there by raiding natives.

"Here they're well behaved and friendly enough," she had said. "We have a company of soldiers to make sure they remain so. But out at the river, with only a handful of grants taken up, they do much as they please."

Timothy instinctively tightened his grasp on his borrowed musket, then relaxed it again. This place was only about three miles from Parramatta and its company of soldiers, and it was surrounded by other, similar small holdings. The Hawkesbury was twenty miles or more away, out in the wilds, with fewer than half a dozen bold spirits seeking to make their homes beside its fertile banks. No doubt an overturned candle or a careless pipe smoker had wrought the destruction he was looking at. Or . . . His mouth twisted into a wry smile, as he remembered the women who had accosted him when he had landed in Sydney Cove that morning. A drunken quarrel between the settler and his wife was just as likely to have been the cause. Most of the small grants in this area were held by emancipated convicts; Mrs. Macrae had assured him that not all convicts were depraved and wanton . . . but that left plenty who were.

He sighed and was about to continue on his way when a movement among the animal pens caught his eye. A woman emerged leading a well-grown foal behind her. The young animal was skittish, but the woman handled it as though to the manner born; with only a head-collar and her voice she swiftly gentled it into docility and then, with the foal at her heels, began to walk toward him with the easy grace of one long accustomed to going barefooted over the rough terrain.

Timothy's gaze was concentrated initially on the foal as the two approached; then, realizing that he would have to explain his presence to her, he looked again at the woman. She was young, not much more than a girl, slim and well-proportioned, with a head of coppery red hair on which the sun glinted as she moved. Like Mrs. Macrae, she wore an apron over her dress, and the dress, of calico, was more practical than becoming, its sleeves rolled up to the elbow to display strong, tanned arms. A convict—or an emancipated convict—his mind registered, but clearly a hardworking and respectable one, with looks any woman might envy. And she was not barefooted. His first glance had deceived him. She was wearing leather-soled sandals held in place by leather thongs, evidently homemade, as were the foal's head-collar and leading rein. And the foal, a filly, was a beauty, a dark bay in peak condition.

He raised his hat and introduced himself.

"I trust you'll pardon my intrusion, ma'am. I am a new settler, just arrived from the Cape on board the *Britannia*."

"And you are looking for land, sir?" the young woman suggested. She held out a hand. "I am Jenny Taggart."

Her voice was educated and pleasant, her manner friendly, and she addressed him politely but as an equal. Timothy warmed toward her. He shook her hand and explained that he was acting upon the advice of Captain Raven in coming here before making his formal application for a grant of land.

"I rode to Parramatta this morning with the *Britannia*'s mate, and Superintendent Macrae is to afford me hospitality overnight."

"Then you are in good hands, sir," Jenny Taggart assured him. She hesitated. "Did you say that you *rode*?"

He grinned, delighted. "Aye, that I did. I've brought two horses with me from the Cape—a stallion and a mare—both broken to the saddle. I hope to breed from them. As I see you have done. May I? . . ." Receiving her nod of assent, Timothy subjected the foal to a knowledgeable inspection. His praise was sincere, but the girl rejected it with an honesty he had not expected.

"I only obtained her dam when she was in foal, Mr. Dawson. In the manner in which such things are done here—by barter. One of the Marine Corps officers imported her, like you, from the Cape." She went into breeding details, displaying an awareness of essentials that found an instant echo in his heart.

He said with enthusiasm, "Then we have a common interest, ma'am. Or is it your husband who—"

Jenny cut him short, her face suddenly shuttered and remote. "This farm is mine. I have no husband."

"But you have laborers, surely? Convicts assigned to you? I mean—" he reddened, puzzled by her expression. "A woman could not work this place alone. Not as it is worked. It's in good condition and—" He broke off, floundering, aware that once again he was being clumsy and tactless in his quest for enlightenment. "I ask your pardon, Mistress Taggart. My questions were not prompted by mere curiosity. I'm anxious to learn the ways here, what can be done on the land and *how* it can be done. It is evident to me that your farm is prospering." He waved his hand toward the irrigation ditches and the dark, newly turned soil and added with conviction, "It is also evident that you are well versed in husbandry."

"I have been here since the beginning," she told him quietly. "For five and a half years, with necessity as the spur. I have—had—two laborers assigned to this farm, both of them old men and old friends. But"—the quiet voice hardened into bitterness—"one of them was bludgeoned to death only yesterday, by whoever burned down the store and the hut he lived in, poor old man. We buried him this morning."

"I observed the ruins when I crossed your creek," Timothy said.

"Yes—they are an eyesore."

"You said 'whoever' . . . do you not know who did this terrible thing?"

She sighed and shook her head. "Not for certain. The authorities in Parramatta are satisfied that it was the work of Indians."

"But you are not?" he suggested, detecting a note of uncertainty in her guarded words.

She eyed him warily. "We are on good terms with all the Indians in this area and in Sydney. It's true that the wild tribes in the woods steal and kill but usually much farther afield. They attack men on the run and the isolated settlers between here and the river. The people who have taken land by the Hawkesbury suffer greatly from them. There is a chief from the Broken Bay tribe called Pimelwi who is particularly troublesome—it was he who wounded Governor Phillip some years ago. An expedition was sent after him, but he escaped capture."

"You seem to know a good deal about them."

Jenny Taggart repeated her sigh. "I believed I did," she admitted. "I believed I had friends among them. Now I am not sure what to believe." She changed the subject abruptly. The filly was becoming restive, and she gestured to the creek. "She wants to drink. I bring her down here most evenings, to get her accustomed to being handled."

"A good idea," Timothy approved. He led the way back to the creek. "Do you intend to work her when she's old enough?"

"I must." She let the filly's head-rope slacken, and the pretty creature lowered her muzzle into the sun-dappled water, sucking noisily and stamping her forefeet at her own reflection on its surface. "She will have to learn to earn her keep, as we all do. I had hoped to break her mother to the plow, but now—"

"Now?" he prompted when she broke off.

"The plow we were making was in the store—the fire ruined it. Our seed wheat was destroyed too—I can apply for that to be replaced, but I'll have to take whatever the government storekeeper chooses to give me. Ours was grown here, on this land, and had been carefully selected. But . . . I must not keep you listening to our troubles. I'm sure you have better things to do." Her shrug, Timothy noticed, was resigned, as if she were accustomed to set-backs and disappointments.

"I had planned to go to Toongabbe and return before dark," he admitted. "But I've been longer than I intended. Perhaps I—"

"Then I will not delay you," the girl said with finality. "The land there is good, but it's better beyond Prospect Hill and best of all near the Hawkesbury. You should try to see as much as you can before you apply for a grant."

"I will," he assured her. Having no further excuse for remaining, he thanked her gravely and prepared to take his leave, offering his hand after a momentary hesitation. She was a convict, he reminded himself and then, ashamed of the thought, added impulsively, "I'd like to show you my horses, Mistress Taggart, if you'd permit me to call here again."

She accepted the proffered hand, an odd little smile curving her lips. "If we are to be neighbors—even distant ones—you will be welcome, Mr. Dawson. And I should appreciate the opportunity of seeing your horses. My father bred horses—farm workhorses they were, Clydesdales. He was well known for the quality of his stock all over the Yorkshire dales."

"So that's where you come from, is it—Yorkshire?" Without realizing that he had done so, Timothy had retained her hand in his. He released it in sudden confusion and bent to pick up the musket he had propped against the hollow trunk of a tree at the water's edge. But his questing fingers never grasped the weapon. Something moved among the dry leaves lying in the tree's hollow shell—he glimpsed a slithering black shape and the next instant felt a sharp pain in his wrist, which almost instantly spread, as a dull ache, up his arm.

He swore aloud in shocked alarm. "A snake—God's blood, I've been bitten by a snake . . . a black snake!"

Jenny Taggart's reaction was swift. She tore off her apron and used its strings to bind his upper arm, pulling them so tightly that his whole arm went numb.

"This will hurt," she warned. "But it is necessary." There was a small knife in her hand, Timothy saw. Instinctively he flinched and then gritted his teeth. The point of the knife was plunged into his wrist, and despite the numbness, he became conscious of an agonizing pain. But he uttered no protest; a sort of lethargy was creeping over him, dulling his senses. Dimly he became aware that the convict girl had applied her lips to the wound she had made. She sucked at it vigorously, pausing only to spit blood from her mouth—*his* blood—and he felt her strong fingers pressing his arm to open the wound still further and encourage the blood to flow.

As if from a very long way away he heard her raise her voice to call someone by name, and a little later the sound of footsteps reached him. A man's voice demanded in a strong cockney accent to know what was wrong.

She answered breathlessly, "He's a new settler, Watt, just off the *Britannia*. A snake bit him, one of the black ones. It was in the hollow of that tree."

"Looks pretty far gone," the man said. He knelt, peering into Timothy's face, his bright, birdlike eyes full of concern. "Them black snakes is the most poisonous, ain't they?"

Timothy attempted to speak but found the effort beyond him; his jaw seemed to be frozen, and his tongue felt twice its normal size, filling his mouth. The girl said something he could not catch and then, in a louder tone, "Help me to get him to the cabin, Watt. I've done all I can."

Between them, with the filly following at the end of her rope, they half carried, half dragged him past the burned-out storehouse to the cabin he had seen from the creek bank. He slumped down on a couch of sacking, barely conscious of his surroundings, and Jenny covered him with a blanket. He felt the breath rasp in his chest, and the man said anxiously, " 'E can't 'ardly breathe, poor sod. Shall I see if I can get Doctor Randell ter come 'ere?"

"No." Jenny's voice was firm. "Even if you could find him, he'd never get here in time. Wait a little and see how he is in half an hour, Watt. We'll have to tell Mr. Macrae he's here, or they'll be sending out a search party—he told me he was staying overnight at the Macraes'."

They worked over him tirelessly: propping him up, bathing his wrist and his swollen right arm with warm water, and forcing a few drops of some raw spirit between his tightly clamped teeth. After a while it became easier to draw breath, and Timothy drew great gulps of air into his tortured lungs. But their voices still seemed to be coming from a great distance, and his desire for sleep was becoming almost irresistible. He heard the man say, "Well, 'e's still alive, ain't 'e, lass? An' that's a miracle—the only time I seen anyone get bit by one o' them black snakes, 'e was dead in 'arf an hour. You reckon 'e'll pull through?"

"I think so," Jenny answered. "I did what the Indians do when one of them suffers from snakebite. I watched Colbee do it once, and the man lived. His arm's very puffed up though. . . ." She caught her breath on a sigh and then went on more firmly, "Go to Parramatta now, will you, Watt, and tell them? And stay there—it'll be dark before you can get back. Time enough in the morning."

"I'd as soon not leave you on your own, Jenny," the man she had called Watt objected. "Not after what 'appened ter Reuben."

"I shall be quite safe. Mr. Dawson had a musket, hadn't he? Bring me that before you go, if you're worried."

The man grunted. Timothy let his heavy lids drop, unable any longer to ward off sleep. He heard a child's voice set up a plaintive wailing and Jenny say softly, "Hush, Justin—hush! Your grandpa's only going for a little while—there's no call for you to fret, love. And this poor gentleman is ill."

As the mists started to close about him Timothy felt her start to rise; filled with sudden inexplicable fear, he put out his left hand to grope blindly for hers.

"Don't . . . leave . . . me, Jenny. . . . I . . ." It took a great effort for him to get the words out, but somehow he managed it, and to his heartfelt relief she sank back on her heels beside him again.

"It's all right," she whispered reassuringly. "I'm here—I won't leave you. Try to sleep. You're not going to die, Mr. Dawson."

"God bless . . . you," he muttered hoarsely and lapsed at last into unconsciousness, her small, work-roughened convict's hand held tightly in his, as if it were a link between himself and the life he had so nearly forfeited.

CHAPTER III

Jasper Spence was well pleased with the outcome of his formal call on the acting governor of New South Wales. He reflected as he picked his way along the dusty road in the wake of his guide that Major Francis Grose was a man after his own heart.

A lifetime spent in the service of the Honourable the East India Company had taught him that commercial profit was the only real recompense for health-sapping toil in an alien land. It had soon become evident that Francis Grose shared this view and that he was more than willing to accommodate a settler with money to invest and plans for future commercial development. Grose had also made it clear to the new arrival that—while land would, of course, be granted to him—agriculture in the colony was rather a long-term than an immediate prospect, and that a share in Captain Raven's next cargo would, as matters stood at present, be a great deal more rewarding.

"Choose your land, Mr. Spence," the acting governor had invited. "It shall be surveyed and marked out for you—and I will see that a convict labor gang is set to work at once to build you a brick house and such farm buildings as you may require on the property. In the meantime take a look at a house, here in Sydney Cove, that I can put at your disposal until your own is ready for occupation. You may prefer such an arrangement to any other since it will leave you entirely free to inspect what we have to offer without—ah—any outside influence being brought to bear."

He had meant John Macarthur's influence, Spence presumed, a trifle puzzled. But clearly the acting governor was the man in authority and the one most likely to aid in promoting his interests, and probably wished to exercise his authority as lieutenant governor. Macarthur's offer of hospitality had been made with genial friendliness and, it had seemed, without any ulterior motive but . . . if Major Grose did not want him to accept it, he would make his excuses tactfully. Or perhaps accept for the few days it would take him to inspect the settlements in the Parramatta area.

No doubt his decision would please Henrietta. She had not wanted to stay for any length of time with strangers, she had told him in somewhat petulant tones, but her reason was evident. Young Charles Brace was to be appointed to the Sydney company of his regiment, and obviously he would not find it convenient to dance attendance on her if she were separated from him by fourteen or fifteen miles of ill-constructed road.

Horses were at a premium in the colony; few, even of the officers, possessed riding or work animals. Most made necessary journeys on foot or by boat. Baggage, government stores, and settlers' crops were transported by boat also, or in handcarts propelled by convicts. Even land clearance was done, in backbreaking fashion, by labor gangs wielding axes and hoes—there were no oxen or other beasts of burden, and only John Macarthur had had the forethought to import a plow. Probably he used chained convict laborers to draw that. . . . Jasper Spence smiled thinly to himself.

Young Timothy Dawson—the suitor his daughter now affected to despise—had made a wise choice when he had decided to buy his equine breeding stock at the Cape and bring them with him in the *Britannia*. They were good, strong animals, of some quality; if he could get them to breed, he would do well enough, although as Major Grose had so rightly pointed out, any form of livestock breeding must, like agriculture, be considered in the long term. For certain and immediate profits, the import of trade goods and spirits was undoubtedly a better proposition, and he could have no regrets concerning his decision to take a share in the *Britannia*'s next cargo.

She was going to Bengal, leased officially to the government this time. He had contacts there, and his offer to introduce Captain Raven to some of the Calcutta merchants who were well known to him had been well received by Major Grose. So much so, in fact, that the suggestion of a house in Sydney Cove had followed the acting governor's acceptance of it.

"I will arrange for you to be appointed and sworn in as a

magistrate, Mr. Spence," Grose had said. "It need not be an arduous task—my officers undertake most of the work of the Court of Criminal Jurisdiction, and the civil and admiralty courts seldom require to be convened. As a justice of the peace you would be entitled to a house and servants free of all charge, which, I daresay, you would find to your advantage."

Indeed he would, Jasper Spence had decided, on reflection—provided, of course, that the house proved to be well-positioned and comfortable. Many of the original officers' houses were in a state of dilapidation due, the acting governor had explained, to the lack of limestone in the colony. But now a plentiful supply of this essential commodity was being sent from Norfolk Island, where it had been found in abundance, and the houses were being rebuilt or repaired. They . . .

His guide, a soldier the acting governor had sent with him, came to a halt. "That's it, sir," he announced. "That's the house his honor said I was to show you."

Like all the colony's houses, this one was small and without an upper story—by comparison with the bungalow he had occupied in Calcutta, it was a wretched hovel. But, Jasper Spence saw as his escort unlocked the door, it had been carefully renovated and was built of sandstone, surrounded by a well-kept kitchen garden.

" 'Twas Captain Hill's house, sir," the soldier added, in explanation. "He embarked in a ship called the *Shah Hormuzcar*, on his way to England—him being in poor health and invalided from the regiment." The man put out a scarlet-clad arm to open the door wider, and Spence noticed with a sense of acute shock that his wrist bore the unmistakable scars of fetters worn over a prolonged period.

"Were you," he asked sharply, halting in the doorway, "a convict before you enlisted, my man?"

The soldier met his gaze squarely. "Aye, sir, I was. I come out in a hell ship called the *Neptune* three years ago."

"But how—"

The soldier smiled. "Men of good conduct, with previous military service, are permitted to volunteer for service in the corps, sir. We enlist for life, but our sentences are remitted and we're fed an' clothed, sir, an' housed out of barracks with our wives if we're married." While Spence was silently digesting this alarming piece of information, his escort went on, a note of bitterness in his voice, "I fought in America and was twice wounded, but I didn't desert, sir. Half my comrades in the corps are deserters from other regiments—they enlisted to save their necks." His mouth snapped shut, as if he were aware that he had shocked his listener, and standing aside, he gestured to the interior of the house and said woodenly, "It's a good house, sir. Four rooms, servants' quarters, and a kitchen at the back."

By Sydney's standards, Jasper Spence thought as he made a minute inspection of the premises, the American veteran was probably right. The rooms were cramped but quite habitable; when his furniture was brought ashore from the *Britannia* and installed, the place would be vastly improved. At present all it contained was strictly utilitarian—two roughly made wooden bedsteads, a table, and half a dozen chairs, but Henrietta would transform it, he knew, with curtains, carpets, and pictures. She had excellent taste and had spent much time and thought in the selection of the furnishings they had brought with them. Spence nodded his white head, satisfied. They could spend three or four days at Mr. Macarthur's farmhouse in Parramatta, which would allow time for their baggage to be unloaded, and then take up residence here.

He took a notebook from his pocket and, finding ink and a quill on the table, penned a brief note of his acceptance to the acting governor and gave it to the soldier to deliver.

On his return to the ship he found his daughter awaiting him, with impatience, in her cabin. The ship was a hive of activity as cargo was unloaded, the decks swarming with convict laborers and the seamen shouting loud commands, which they enforced with cuffs and kicks if the work parties moved too slowly for their liking.

"I cannot stay here an instant longer, Papa," Henrietta told him tearfully. "You can have no idea what is going on. They've permitted convict women to come on board and! . . ." She shuddered. "Their behavior is—oh, it is offensive to a degree! I daren't stir from my cabin alone, I . . ."

"I understand, my dear," her father assured her. He patted her hand, hoping to ward off the tears, and told her in glowing terms of the house he had been offered and how completely he saw eye to eye with the colony's acting governor. She interrupted him in midsentence.

"Can we not go to the house now, Papa?"

"It is scarcely furnished, child. It must be cleaned and swept before you can enter it. I have to arrange for servants and—"

"Then I suppose we shall have to go to the Macarthurs'?"

"Only for a few days, Etta my dear," Jasper Spence answered. He frowned, eyeing her thoughtfully. "Why are you so reluctant to accept Mr. Macarthur's offer of hospitality?"

"Because I did not like him," Henrietta admitted without hesitation. "But"—she shrugged her slim shoulders— "rather than remain on board this ship I would go anywhere. How are we to get to Parramatta, Papa? Does Mr. Macarthur expect us to walk?"

Her father shook his head. "No, of course not—he said he would send a boat for us. I will make inquiries— possibly it is here and we could leave this afternoon. I understand it only takes four hours or so by water and that it is scenically most beautiful. If you can be ready to leave after luncheon, my dear—"

Henrietta lowered her gaze, dabbing at her eyes with a lace handkerchief. "Oh, yes, I can be ready. But what about servants and the unloading of our furniture?"

"The servants will be allocated to us whenever we want them. And Captain Raven will, I am sure, arrange to unload all our belongings when I instruct him to do so. I shall leave O'Leary in charge."

Relieved by her acquiesence, Jasper Spence again patted her hand affectionately. The two men he had brought out with him as indentured farm servants could supervise the unloading of the furniture and prevent any pilfering by convicts. Seamus O'Leary, the shepherd, was a reliable man. Not as efficient or as devoted as the Indian servants to whose ministrations Spence had for so long been accustomed, but on the long voyage both O'Leary and his son, Patrick, had shown themselves to be sober and honest, and his wife had acted as lady's maid to Henrietta. Not, it was true, entirely to her satisfaction, for the poor woman was untrained in that capacity and lacking in manners, but . . .

"I do not think, Papa," Henrietta said, as if reading his thoughts, "that I will bring Mrs. O'Leary to Parramatta. Mr. Macarthur's wife will have trained maids, no doubt, against whom she would seem . . . well, a trifle uncouth. In any case she would be better employed setting our new house in order, would she not?"

Her father did not argue. "I'll tell O'Leary," he promised. "And now I must seek out Captain Raven. You'll stay here in your cabin until luncheon, won't you?"

"I cannot venture anywhere else, Papa," Henrietta returned tartly. "And I would advise *you* not to go within sight or hearing of the mess deck if you are wise."

Jasper Spence suppressed a smile. "Very well, my dear, I will do my best to follow your advice." He asked, almost as an afterthought, "Has Charles Brace called on you today?"

"No, he has not," his daughter returned, her tone icy. "He is too busy with his soldiers. It seems that they are flogging men at the triangles this morning, and Charles had to be there." She added with some reluctance, "From the way he spoke yesterday I thought he was . . . well, not averse to witnessing such things. Oh, Papa, this is a horrible place! I wish with all my heart that we were back in India."

There were moments when he shared her feelings, Jasper Spence thought wryly—although for very different reasons. He sighed. "Do not distress yourself, child," he pleaded. "This is a penal colony—you must always remember that. And once we have settled on our land grant and built a fine new house, out in the country, I feel sure that you will find there are compensations. The climate, for one thing, my prospects for another. I told you, did I not, that the governor intends to appoint me a justice of the peace?"

"Yes," Henrietta acknowledged without enthusiasm. "You told me that, Papa. But I still wish we could have stayed in India."

"India ruined your dear mamma's health, Etta," he reminded her bitterly. "It was for her sweet sake that I came home, as you know very well."

"Oh, yes, I know. But poor mamma died in spite of it,

God rest her soul. And we could have gone back, Papa—we could *still* go back now," Henrietta pleaded. "This ship is to go to Calcutta, and I am sure that Captain Raven would accommodate us and—"

Jasper Spence cut her short with unusual sharpness. "No," he said. "I shall never return to India. I have my reasons, Etta, and it is not for you to question them."

They were valid reasons, he reflected, feeling beads of perspiration break out on his brow—all too valid—but, please God, his daughter would remain in ignorance of them, just as his wife had. Although, perhaps, his beloved Margaret had suspected the truth when he had been summoned so peremptorily to appear before the revenue commissioners, six months before their departure for England. He mopped his brow hastily and became brisk.

"I must seek out Captain Raven. Mrs. O'Leary can sit with you or help you to pack, child, until I can escort you to the cuddy for luncheon."

He kissed her lightly on the cheek and went about his business, giving her no chance to detain him.

Three hours later, they were in Mr. Macarthur's boat, on their way up the harbor to Parramatta, and Henrietta, her earlier despondency forgotten, exclaimed in wonder at the beauty of the scene around her. And it was indeed beautiful, Jasper Spence decided, the prospect constantly changing.

Now blue, sunlit water lapped beaches of golden sand, next these gave place to tree-clad slopes and rocky inlets, to be in turn succeeded by acres of flat pasture land with small settlements dotted here and there, the huts and outhouses gleaming in the afternoon sunshine. They caught glimpses of dark-skinned aborigines fishing from their canoes—flimsy craft, fashioned from bark—which they handled with effortless skill, and, on the pasture land, small herds of goats and domestic pigs wandering at will.

Their boat, swiftly propelled by four convict oarsmen, entered a river, on either side of which the grass was green and lush and the settlers' dwellings more numerous. It soon narrowed, and they passed between high banks with timber growing up to the water's edge and brightly colored cockatoos and parakeets flitting from tree to tree with shrill, discordant cries of alarm. Once a flight of wild duck rose, and the coxswain bemoaned the absence of a musket as the birds winged skyward, their bodies dark silhouettes against the setting sun. Then the Parramatta wharf came in sight with a labor gang at work unloading a hoy, and as quickly as they had risen, Henrietta's spirits fell.

"It will only be for a few days, will it not, Papa?" she whispered, reaching out apprehensively to clasp her father's hand, as the men shipped their oars to let the boat glide alongside the wooden jetty.

"Yes, my dear, of course," Jasper Spence assured her. "Only for a few days."

The coxswain, hat in hand, assisted him to step ashore. "I'll send word to Mr. Macarthur that you are here, sir," the man offered and gestured to the guardhouse at the rear of the wharf. "The sergeant of the guard will give you shelter meantime."

As Henrietta crossed the wharf a young convict paused in his work to stare at her, mouth agape, until the gang overseer brought the thong of his whip across the lad's bare shoulders in a vicious, stinging blow. His cry of pain was echoed by Henrietta's sob, and cursing under his breath her father put a protective arm round her and led her to the guardhouse.

"There, there," he urged gently, "don't take on, my dear. The man is a convicted felon."

"But he's *English*," Henrietta protested. "We never treated the Indians like that, Papa."

It was true, her father had to concede. He sighed and walked on, tight-lipped and silent.

At eight o'clock in the morning the two companies of the New South Wales Corps mustered on their parade ground to witness the punishment of two of their number.

Both men, Captain Foveaux had told Charles Brace at dinner the previous evening, had been charged with being absent without leave, found guilty, and sentenced to be flogged by the five officers forming the court-martial.

"In fact," Foveaux explained, "the commandant would not have them tried on a capital charge, as he might well have done since, on their own admission, the blackguards intended to desert. They stole a longboat and arms, fled into the woods, and held some settlers to ransom before they were apprehended. They richly deserve what they're going to get. If it had been left to me, I'd have hanged them! It's one thing for convicts to try to escape but quite another, damn their eyes, for our soldiers to attempt it. They are well treated and accorded most generous privileges—so there's no excuse for these rogues."

Charles Brace, whose previous service had been six months' garrison duty with his father's regiment of militia, had never witnessed a military punishment, and as he stood stiffly in front of a line of scarlet-uniformed soldiers, he hoped fervently that his stomach would be strong enough to endure the spectacle. The sentences had seemed to him excessively severe, when Foveaux had replied to his questions concerning them. The drummer, Roberts, was to receive three hundred lashes; the corporal, Williamson, five hundred, in addition to being reduced to the ranks. But when he had asked whether such a sentence did not amount to one of death, his company commander had laughed.

"Good heavens no! Each man will be given as much as he can take. When the surgeon says he's had enough, we cut him down. He receives the rest when he's fit to do so. Admittedly we order more lashes here than we would at home, but this is a penal colony and discipline has to be severe—it's all these people understand. Sentences passed on convicts during Governor Phillip's time were, I understand, much less severe than those meted out to our predecessors, the marines. And the admirable Captain Phillip did not hold with women being flogged."

Something in his tone, an odd sort of resentment, had made Brace stare at him. Joseph Foveaux was younger than most of the others of his rank in the corps—twenty-seven or -eight, as nearly as Brace could judge. Of medium height, he was good-looking in a dark, saturnine way, with thin lips and glowing, almost black eyes. Like John Macarthur he had received substantial grants of land and was rumored to be farming even more successfully than Macarthur himself. Someone—Brace could not recall who it had been—had told him that Foveaux was the illegitimate son of the Earl of Ossory and that his mother had been a cook of French origin, employed at the earl's family seat in Bedfordshire. Certainly the name was French but . . . He glanced uneasily at the sternly set face of his company commander and decided to forget that interesting piece of gossip, lest it lead him into trouble.

Foveaux had been decent enough to him since his arrival, and in any event the officers of the New South Wales Corps were—like their men—what his father would have described as a "mixed bag." Captain Johnstone and most of his company had been marines who had come out to the colony with Governor Phillip; Captain Paterson he had not met, since he was in command of the Norfolk Island garrison, and Macarthur, Brace had learned, was known as "Johnny Boddice" because his father was said to have been in trade as a draper.

The commandant, on the other hand, had served with some distinction in the 96th Regiment of Foot; he had a brother in the Foot Guards, and his father, also named Francis Grose, was a well-known antiquarian and the author of several learned works. He . . .

"Parade . . . at-ten-shun!" The stentorian voice of the adjutant, Lieutenant Rowley, broke into his thoughts, and Brace came obediently to attention. A sergeant and two drummers marched across the parade ground to take their places in front of the triangle of halberds—which had been set up at its center, facing the hollow square of soldiers. The sergeant carried a red cloth bag that, Charles Brace knew, contained the cat-o'-nine-tails—a savage instrument with a handle eighteen inches long to which were bound nine lashes, or tails, of heavy cord, their ends knotted. He felt his stomach churn and swallowed hard.

The prisoners, stripped to the waist, were marched up under guard, and the provost marshal read out the charges and sentences. He was a short, broad-shouldered man in his mid-fifties, dressed in a naval uniform of faded blue cloth with the white patches of a midshipman on the collar and a dirk at his side, and Brace found himself watching him in some astonishment, unable to understand why a naval officer of any rank should be present at a military punishment. Neither Major Grose nor Captain Collins, the judge advocate, had seen fit to attend—Captain Foveaux, he realized, was in overall charge of the parade.

Foveaux took up his position within a foot or two of the triangle and nodded to the sergeant, who removed the cat-o'-nine-tails from its baize bag, and as the first man was being seized up to the piled halberds, Foveaux inspected the lashes, running them expertly through his fingers, his dark eyes bright.

"Do your duty!" he snapped, passing the cat to one of the drummers.

The man came briefly to attention and then, removing his shako, raised the whip in his right hand. The first few strokes, marked by a beat on the drum, raised livid weals across the prisoner's bare shoulders. He endured the first dozen stoically, without crying out, but as the lash bit deeper into his tortured flesh, a moan was wrung from him. After two dozen, Captain Foveaux jerked his head, and the second drummer relieved his comrade of the cat. He was left-handed, Brace saw, and he watched, sickened, as the lash descended once more, cutting a fresh pattern across the unhappy prisoner's back.

"One hundred!" the sergeant shouted. The assistant surgeon, a young man whom Brace had not seen before, made a somewhat perfunctory examination and then stood back, saying nothing. Foveaux snapped a command and the flogging continued, the floggers relieved at intervals and the assistant surgeon occasionally stepping up to nod his silent assent to the prolongation of the punishment.

The victim's back was reduced to a red, oozing pulp, but beaten now into insensibility he no longer uttered a sound. And Foveaux looked as if he were actually enjoying the ugly spectacle. . . . Brace shuddered. Would he, he wondered dully, would he ever become so accustomed to such brutality as to view it with indifference? He shut his eyes, forcing himself to think of something else, but his mind was blank, incapable of coherent thought, and he opened his eyes again to hear the sergeant bawl "Two 'undred and seventy-five, sir!"

This time, to his relief, the surgeon spoke.

"That's about all he can take, sir," he told Foveaux, and the unconscious prisoner was cut down and carried off by two of the escort.

Brace's relief was short-lived. The second prisoner was marched up to the halberds, his wrists secured, and the whole dreadful business began again. Brace could not watch it. He remained at attention, but now he kept his eyes firmly closed and directed his thoughts back to Henrietta Spence. She was a beautiful girl, he reflected, her trim figure and lovely eyes a delight to behold, and she had afforded him welcome distraction during the voyage from the Cape, it was true. He was grateful for the pleasure he had found in her company, yet here . . . He stifled a sigh.

Here in New South Wales, was she what his father would call socially acceptable? He had been banished to this outlandish place in order to avoid an unsuitable marriage to a young woman of whom his father had strongly disapproved. His involvement with her had caused a scandal of damaging proportions, and although he was not the heir—he had two brothers older than himself—his autocratic father had refused to listen to his excuses or even give credence to his promises that it would not happen again.

"You and George will have to marry money," the old earl had warned. "Everything I have must go to Henry when I die, and God knows, it isn't much. I'll buy you a commission in the New South Wales Corps and allow you a hundred a year, but after that you must fend for yourself, Charles. You may exchange into a better regiment in two years' time if you wish and are able to arrange it. With a war coming it should not be difficult. But don't expect me to keep you if you marry without my approval. Whilst a well-endowed girl is essential, she must be of good family. If she's not, then you will not be welcomed at Dunloy Castle and would be well advised to remain in Botany Bay."

Charles Brace repeated his sigh. Henrietta's father undoubtedly had money—he had brought servants with him and had bought expensively in the Cape Town livestock market. But . . . there was something about Mr. Jasper Spence that did not quite ring true. He had talked of his service with the East India Company freely enough during the long evenings they had shared in the *Britannia*'s cuddy, yet Spence had never specified the precise nature of his employment. Neither had he said why he had decided to

come to New South Wales to settle or why—with no experience whatsoever of agriculture—he intended to set up as
a farmer.

True, the men he had brought with him as servants were
of farming stock. The shepherd he had left behind at the
Cape to travel with his flock was a particularly good man,
a Scot, well versed in husbandry, who would be worth his
weight in gold when the sheep were delivered. All the same
it seemed odd that a rich and respected John Company
nabob should seek to exchange the luxurious life his kind
led in Bengal for the perils and hardships that must inevitably face free settlers in a penal colony.

The hiss of the cat-o'-nine-tails as its lashes descended on
the present victim's bloodstained shoulders brought Brace's
thoughts back to the immediate present. Reluctantly he
stole a look across the intervening stretch of sunbaked
earth and saw that Captain Foveaux had not stirred. But
then, suddenly, he moved. His hand came out to strike the
flogger a stinging blow across the face, and as the man
reeled back, letting the cat fall, Foveaux rounded on him
wrathfully.

"Damn your eyes, drummer!" he shouted. "Don't hold
back because this plaguey rogue is one of your own. Lay
on as you should, or I'll see *your* backbone! D'you hear
me? Then do your duty!"

The startled drummer recovered himself, bent to pick up
the fallen whip, and returned to his unwelcome task as the
sergeant called, "One 'undred and eighty-three, sir!"

Charles Brace swallowed the bile that rose in his throat
and dragged his thoughts back to Henrietta. She *was* lovely, he told himself, but of late she had become a trifle
possessive. Clearly she expected him to propose to her,
sooner or later, and perhaps his courtship conducted on
board the *Britannia* had been ardent enough to encourage
such expectations. Yet he had embarked on the chase initially with no other objective than to pass the time that
might otherwise have lain heavily on his hands. He had not
intended Henrietta to regard him as a serious suitor.

When he had joined the ship the oafish farmer's boy,
Dawson, had been casting sheep's eyes at her. Brace smiled
faintly at the metaphor. It had amused him to challenge

Dawson, and he had had little difficulty in outwitting him. Dawson had no social graces, and in his coarse homespun clothing, which reeked of the stockyard, he could hardly be said to have been a rival. Henrietta was, to say the least, fastidious in her tastes, and almost from the moment of his own arrival on board she had given the clodhopper his congé.

Nonetheless . . . Charles Brace's smooth fair brows met in a frown. Unless he played his cards very carefully, he might well find himself in the same awkward position as he had been in two years ago with Dolly Lightfoot. Dolly, of course, he could now recognize, *had* been impossible. She was an actress, talented and breathtakingly beautiful. He had been very young and she had bewitched him. Indeed, looking back, he could feel only gratitude to his father for having extricated him from her toils, bitterly though it had hurt at the time. He had been saved from a hideous social blunder, and it would behoove him to think long and hard before he allowed himself to be maneuvered into another, because the penalty would be—as his father had threatened—exile here, in a very inferior regiment, for the rest of his days.

Henrietta *might* be acceptable to his family; she had exquisite manners and a fine conceit of herself and, as the daughter of a John Company nabob, must be well-endowed—a condition his father had specified.

He thought of his eldest brother, Henry—Viscount March, a captain in His Majesty's 1st Life Guards—and of the pale, insipid little creature he had married, and he expelled his breath in a long drawn sigh. Nothing his father could have said would, he knew, have induced *him* to take the Lady Patience to wife, with her shrill, prattling tongue and her milksop ways. Henry would come into the title and what was left of the family fortunes, but God help him, he had had to pay the price. And as for poor George, fobbed off with an ensigncy in the 27th Foot and unable to buy promotion.

"Two 'undred and twenty-five, sir!" the sergeant called out from his post at the rear of the triangle of halberds.

"Cut him down," Foveaux ordered after a brief exchange with the surgeon.

Brace stiffened. Praise be to God, it was over—for today at least. It was not yet over for the two would-be deserters, though—the one-time corporal still had more than two hundred lashes of his sentence to receive, the drummer, now lying motionless on the ground, another seventy-five. Poor devils—no matter how heinous their crimes, he could find it in his heart to pity them.

The adjutant took over the parade; he ordered the officers to fall out, and Brace thankfully relaxed. His face and hands were wet and sticky with sweat, but at least his squeamish stomach had not betrayed him. He mopped his brow with his kerchief and was preparing to return to his quarters when a hand was laid lightly on his arm. He turned to see Foveaux beside him.

"Sir?" he acknowledged woodenly.

"I thought you might care to break your fast with me," his company commander said. "I've some coffee, by courtesy of the good Captain Raven, and we might take a glass or two of Cape brandy, if you've a taste for it."

The invitation, both unexpected and, at that moment, unwelcome, took Brace by surprise. He stammered something, seeking vainly for an excuse to refuse, but conscious that he could ill afford to offend a senior officer at this early stage in his career, he managed a smile.

"I—thank you, sir. I—er—I'll be pleased." He needed the brandy, he thought grimly, if only to take the bitter taste from his mouth. Foveaux was unmoved, even cheerfully expansive, talking away easily as they fell into step together to cross the parade ground.

"Not bad, are they, our new barracks?" He waved a hand at the timbered building with its shingle roof and the palisade of logs by which it was surrounded. On the far side a work gang was toiling to build a replica of it of which, so far, only the foundations were laid. "Until that block is finished," Foveaux went on, "half our men have had to be permitted to live in huts outside the barracks, and that's unfortunate. They hobnob with the convicts, drink with them and, of course, marry the women, which makes it well nigh impossible to maintain proper discipline. Most of the female convicts are whores." He shrugged his elegantly uniformed shoulders. "But Governor Phillip, as I fancy I told you, wouldn't have them whipped, more's the pity, no matter what they did."

"But surely," Brace exclaimed, the words wrung from him, "you cannot approve of flogging women!"

"My dear fellow . . . these women?" Foveaux's tone was contemptuous. "They are the scum of the London whorehouses, the vast majority of 'em. They do no public work if they can possibly avoid it, and they are often heavier drinkers than the men. They steal and incite riots. When you've been here a little longer, you'll cease to feel any pity for them, I promise you. Well"—he halted in front of a well-built stone house, with fruit trees and vines growing in its garden—"these are my quarters. In you go."

He stood aside to allow Brace to precede him and raised his voice to shout for his servant. "Bring us a pot of coffee and the brandy and bestir yourself, Sherwin! I have a guest."

Evidently Foveaux's return had been anticipated, for the coffee was brought in at once and the servant—a smartly turned-out soldier of the corps—set brandy and glasses on an inlaid table in the center of the room, moved this to his master's elbow, and silently withdrew.

Brace looked about him, envying the quality of the furnishings and the comfort with which his company commander had surrounded himself. A handsome Indian carpet covered the floor; the dining table was of polished walnut, the chairs, with their satin cushions, were obviously expensive, and the padded chaise longue, on which Foveaux settled himself with a contented sigh, looked like an antique. By comparison his own quarters—two rooms situated on the opposite side of the road to the barracks—were wretchedly appointed, all the furniture rough and locally made, the garden neglected and overgrown with weeds, and a thick layer of dust covering everything. He sighed, wrinkling his nose at the appetizing aroma of his host's coffee.

Foveaux splashed brandy into the two bulbous glasses with a lavish hand and thrust one in Brace's direction.

"You know," he observed, "we must stick together, Brace—support each other."

Charles Brace put down his coffee cup to stare at him uncomprehendingly. "Of course, sir," he answered, at pains to hide the dislike he felt. "I'm appointed to your company. Naturally I—"

"No, no, I didn't mean that," his senior interrupted. "Speaking confidentially, of course, you and I are the only two officers in the regiment with any pretensions to—ah—good breeding, as possibly you may not yet have realized."

"No, I—that is, I—" Brace sipped his coffee, uncertain whether he had heard aright. "Surely the commandant—"

Again he was cut short. "Oh, Grose isn't at all a bad fellow, and Abbott and Piper are decent enough in their way. Nepean, of course, is well connected, but he's had enough of this place and is going home—no doubt he'll get command of a regiment if there's a war. His brother will see to that. But as for the rest . . . dear God!" Foveaux spread his hands in a gesture of disdain. "They're the progeny of tailors and shoemakers, tobacconists, peddlers, and street hawkers. Macarthur's father was a stay-maker. That's why he's called 'Johnny Boddice.' Their sole aim, my dear Charles, is to make money—they are all confounded traders at heart."

Lost for words with which to reply to this tirade, Charles Brace downed his brandy at a gulp. During his resultant fit of coughing, Foveaux hospitably refilled his glass.

"Why in heaven's name," he asked curiously, "did you buy a commission in the corps? I mean, with your father's position and influence . . . were you in debt?"

It seemed easier to confess to this rather than to go into the real reason for his banishment, and Brace inclined his head wordlessly.

"That was my undoing also," his host confided. "It happens to us all at times. I was in the 60th and the infernal Shylocks forced me to sell out." He fell silent, scowling into his brandy glass, and Brace wondered how soon he could decently take his leave. The brandy, taken on an empty and already rebellious stomach, was having an alarming effect on him. He made to rise, mentally rehearsing the excuse he had concocted, when a pretty, buxom young woman entered the room. She was dressed in a neat gingham frock, with a white mobcap and a spotless apron, and she dropped a curtsy to him before addressing Foveaux.

"If you please, sir, Mr. Macarthur's gamekeeper is here. He has brought a kangaroo haunch for you, with his master's compliments."

"Has he, by George!" Foveaux threw back his head and laughed with genuine amusement. "You see, Charles, old Johnny Boddice is trying to buy himself into my good graces. Well, some fresh meat will be more than welcome." He turned to the woman. "My compliments to Mr. Macarthur, Ann—tell his man to say that I send my thanks to him. And we'll eat it tonight. You'll join me, won't you, Charles? Come now—I won't take no for an answer."

"Then thank you, sir," Brace responded reluctantly. The woman picked up their empty coffee cups and left the room. He followed her with his eyes, wondering what role she filled in his company commander's household. A servant, obviously but . . . Foveaux, still smiling, answered his unvoiced question.

"Ann's my cook and housekeeper, and as you can see, she makes an excellent job of it. She's married to Sherwin, my servant." His smile widened. "Not *all* the female felons we have here are whores, Charles, and having a respectable young woman to run your establishment would add much to your creature comforts, you know. Would you like me to procure you one?"

"I—that is—" Charles Brace reddened. He thought of Henrietta. God in heaven, what would *she* think if he took a personable young convict girl into his employ? Admittedly a woman's touch would greatly improve the bare austerity of his quarters; he would have someone to cook and mend for him, to sweep the dust from his two wretched rooms, and perhaps even . . . He swallowed the last of his brandy. It had been a long time since he had bedded a woman, and unless he married her he would have not the smallest chance of persuading Henrietta to enter his bed.

"Is it in order?" he asked uncertainly.

"My dear fellow, of course it is!" Foveaux assured him. "All the officers have female servants, and the convict women, I give you my word, are eager to take employment with us. You have to choose carefully, but I'll arrange to have one or two sent round to your quarters. Some of the late arrivals, who haven't been here long enough to become corrupted—Ann shall make inquiries for you."

"Thank you very much, Captain Foveaux." Brace rose a trifle unsteadily to his feet. It was odd, he thought confusedly, he had come here with the greatest unwillingness, believing that Joseph Foveaux was a heartless sadist and that he disliked him. Now—whether or not it was the effect of the brandy he had drunk—his feelings had changed. Foveaux was a good fellow, well disposed toward him, anxious to help him settle into these new and quite alien surroundings, offering him sound advice . . . even friendship. And if his brother officers were the social misfits Brace had inferred them to be, then Foveaux would be a valuable friend, perhaps the only one to whom he could unburden himself.

And it was possible that whoever had said Foveaux was illegitimate had made the claim maliciously, seeking to blacken his character. He had the air and manners of a gentleman, and if he had previously held a commission in the 60th Regiment . . .

Foveaux took his arm, and retrieving his shako, offered it to him gravely. "I shall walk along with you to your quarters, Charles," he said. "Perhaps we did start drinking a mite early—I confess my head's a little muzzy. But the air will clear it, so come on, my dear fellow—put your best foot forward! And do not forget that you are dining with me tonight on Johnny Boddice's kangaroo."

Brace suffered himself to be led out through the open door, but the air, far from clearing his head, caused him to stagger, and but for Foveaux's supporting arm he would have fallen. His companion laughed.

"Steady on, old son! Don't want to fall flat on your face in front of the soldiery, do you?"

"No," Brace returned thickly. He jerked himself upright and heard a voice, dimly recognized as his own, ask aggressively, "Did you ever have a woman flogged, Foveaux?" He had not intended to ask the question, but now that he had inadvertently done so, he waited tensely for the answer.

Joseph Foveaux gave it without hesitation, his thin lips twitching into a smile, "But of course, my dear fellow—and ordered their heads to be shaved, which they mind even more. It's necessary, don't you understand, if we're to maintain discipline!"

Reaching the door of his quarters, he released Brace's arm and made off, humming softly to himself.

Watt Sparrow picked his way carefully along the darkened road. The route was a familiar one; he traveled it at least once a week in order to draw rations from the government store in Parramatta, but tonight the moon was obscured by clouds, the shadows deep and oddly menacing.

It was his imagination, the little man chided himself; he was setting too much store by what had befallen poor old Reuben White. As Jenny had said, the local Indians were friendly—their friendship purchased, admittedly, by means of ration issues and the provision of axes and suchlike, which ensured their good behavior. But there were other, much less well-disposed tribes, and they were not all that far away. Only ten days ago, when a boatload of settlers carrying provisions to the Ponds had been swamped in a squall, the natives had watched them drown and had then, according to the single, wounded survivor, gone out in their canoes to salvage what they could of the boat's supplies, making off with them in the direction of the Hawkesbury River.

Watt shivered despite the warmth of the night. He did not hold with trusting the Indians, as Jenny did. A bunch of naked, treacherous savages, the lot of them, and as for the woman, Barangeroo . . . He snorted his disgust. She made a great show of grieving for her husband, Baneelon, but weeks before his departure to England with Governor Phillip he had taken a second wife, who was younger if not better looking, and Barangeroo had transferred her fickle affections to one of the other natives.

A shadow, deeper than the other shadows at the side of the track, caught his eye, and Watt halted, holding his breath. It had moved, taking human shape—and that had not been a trick of his imagination, he thought, eyes narrowed as he peered into the gloom. There was someone or something there, but in the plaguey darkness he could not be sure if it was human. He gripped the cudgel with which he had armed himself and padded cautiously forward, wishing with all his heart that he was back in London. There were perils in the London streets, it was true, but he had lived among them all his life, and they held fewer ter-

rors for him than did the nameless shadow he was facing
now.

He called out, his voice a harsh croak and, to his bound-
less relief, heard a grunt echo his challenge. The sow, his
mind registered—the sow and her litter! In the confusion
caused by the unexpected arrival of the new settler, Dawson, with his snakebite, both Watt and Jenny had forgotten
to drive the sow into her pen for the night, and the wily old
creature had taken advantage of their omission. Watt
grinned and, circling swiftly to his right, rapped on a tree
trunk with his cudgel, sending sow and piglets racing back
in the direction of their pen, shrill squeals charting their
progress across the uneven ground.

He cursed them without heat and returned to the track,
whistling softly between his teeth as a warning to the errant
sow that he was behind her. He wondered what he would
find when he reached the cabin, and found himself hoping
fervently that Mr. Dawson had survived the night and Jenny's native-inspired treatment of the bite he had sustained.
Both Superintendent Macrae and the mate of the *Britannia*,
when he had reported the accident to them, had been of
the opinion that if the newcomer lived through the night,
he would be in no further danger.

"Dr. Arndell's awa' on a kangaroo hunt," Macrae had
said. "They're no' expecting him back here until the small
hours. I will inform him, of course, but you had best go
back, I am thinking, an' gie yon lass o' yours what help
you can. I have heard tell that hot compresses, applied to
the bite, have a beneficial effect. Maybe you could try that
if the poor young man is still alive when you return."

Watt gritted his teeth as he stumbled over a tree root,
imagining for a moment that it was a black snake—this
miserable country abounded with snakes and ants and
other stinging insects. But the root remained reassuringly
immobile, and he limped on, in sight of the cabin now and
able to see that a lamp was burning in its interior. He
would pen the sow, he decided, and then seek out Jenny
for news of the young stranger.

It was as he approached the small, fenced-in stockyard
that he glimpsed the intruder, and this time he was left in
no doubt as to the shadowy figure's human form . . . or,

come to that, as to his intentions. The padlocked gate was open, the padlock—as the one on the burned-out store-house had been—was wrenched from the hasp to which it had been attached. The thief, whoever he was, had gone into the yard, and as Watt broke into a shambling run he again encountered the sow and her litter. Taking fright, they were fleeing back to the brush from which he had driven them only a few minutes earlier, and it would not be long, he thought despairingly, before the goats, the heifer, and Jenny's highly prized mare and foal followed their example.

He hesitated for an instant in indecision, knowing himself too old and frail to be a match for even a single native sneak thief; then, catching sight of a second dark figure, he turned and made a dash for the cabin. To Jenny's startled question he answered only that the Indians were raiding their stock, and snatching up the musket Dawson had brought with him, he stumbled back into the darkness, the cartouche box in his free hand.

It was the work of only a moment or two to prime the musket, despite the trembling of his unaccustomed hands; then he drew a long, shuddering breath and made for the stockyard again, guided to it now by the flickering flames that were rising from the nearest pen. And luck was with him—one of the raiders emerged from the darkness to stand silhouetted in front of the blazing thatch.

Watt did not hesitate a second time. The target was perfectly situated, the range almost point-blank. His finger curled round the trigger, and with a roar that almost deafened him the musket fired. At that range even so imperfect a marksman as himself could not miss. The raider sank to the ground with a strangled scream.

"Oh, Watt—where are you? Are you all right?"

Jenny's voice, high-pitched with alarm, came from behind him. She was carrying a lantern, running to him, her skirts held high. Watt took the lantern from her and moved slowly toward the man he had shot.

"Plaguey Indians!" he swore. "Damn their souls, they—" he broke off, stunned into silence. For the body lying on the ground in front of the stock pen was not that of an Indian. It was a soldier of the New South Wales Corps, in uniform, his face smeared with dark mud. "There were two of them, Jenny . . . two of the swine. I swear I seen a second."

"They were stealing, Watt," Jenny managed. She looked at the leaping flames, which were rapidly encompassing the nearest of the wooden pens, and choked on a sob. "The animals are gone—they drove them out and set fire to the pen. They had no right, they—"

"Listen, lass," Watt cautioned. The sound of running feet—booted feet—reached them, then faded, lost in the crackle of the flames. "That's 'im gone, the other sod. Makin' for Parramatta, an' when 'e gets there, what story d'you think 'e'll tell?"

Jenny looked up at him with tear-filled, unhappy eyes. He did not need to spell it out for her; they were convicts, their word would not be believed against that of a soldier.

"I'll 'ave ter leg it into the woods, lass," Watt said. "They'll 'ang me else. You know they will."

"I could say that I shot him, that I—I mistook him for an Indian," Jenny began, but Watt shook his grizzled head.

"No. You're young, you've got yer life ter live. I won't let yer take my blame, Jenny."

"They would not hang me. I could plead that it was self-defense."

"They'd send yer ter Norfolk Island. An' what o' Justin? No." Watt shouldered the musket. The pens, he knew, could not be saved, and with daylight the soldiers would come in search of him. He took her arm. "You go after the livestock, lass—the fence'll hold 'em. I'll pack meself up some food, an' I'll take the musket, an' maybe in a week or so I'll sneak back, just ter find out what's 'appenin'."

He passed a hand over his sweat-streaked brow, hating the thought of what he must do and of what lay before him as a hunted fugitive in the alien terrors of the bush. He asked, almost as an afterthought, "Is 'e—the lad that snake bit—is 'e alive?"

Jenny nodded. "Yes, he's alive."

"Then you'll not be alone."

"No, but—" Jenny bit her lower lip, striving to keep her tears under control. "Watt, the other soldier, the one who ran away . . . he might not lie. He might not accuse you. He—"

"That ain't likely, lass, an' you know it. 'E'll save 'is own 'ide." Watt bent to plant a light kiss on her cheek. "Take care o' my grandson, Jenny. An' now you'd best be off after them 'orses o' yours. I'll be all right, you'll see." He thrust her from him. "Go on—you gotter get them animals back."

Jenny obeyed him, feeling as if her heart were being torn from her breast. Numb with misery she set off after the horses. The mare came to her call, the foal at her heels, but it took what was left of the night to round up the rest of the livestock.

When she returned, spent and weary, Watt had gone. Little Justin and the stranger she had taken in slept on, both in blissful ignorance of the night's misfortunes.

CHAPTER IV

The leg, Dr. Thomas Arndell decided regretfully, was gangrenous and would have to come off. He was well accustomed to performing amputations and, indeed, had acquired great proficiency in this aspect of his profession, yet he hated to deprive any man—even a convicted felon—of a limb, making a cripple of the poor devil at best and, at worst, bringing his life to a premature end.

In the case of old Ben Reilly, perhaps it did not matter so much, since his active life was all but over, and if the leg he had contrived to impale with a rusty fork were not speedily removed, he would undoubtedly die a lingering and agonized death.

Arndell was a kindly man; he broke the bad news as gently as he could and was relieved when his patient grinned at him and, in a rich Irish brogue, demanded that the usual slug of rum be doubled in quantity and administered forthwith.

"Sure amn't I goin' to need, it sorr—if I'm to get over the shock o' what you're after tellin' me? You'd not want me yellin' the place down, now would you?"

"No, I would not, Ben," the young surgeon admitted. He sent an orderly to fetch the rum, and in Ben Reilly's hearing instructed him to double the dose. The old convict had come out in the *Neptune*, in the Second Fleet, and was well known to all the hospital staff, because the treatment he had received on board that evil ship had put him in the hospital for several months after his arrival in the colony and, for some complaint or other, at intervals ever since.

He was a scarecrow, just skin and bone, Thomas Arndell thought, looking down with pitying eyes at the wizened old face upturned to his. And he was seventy years of age; yet, because he had been tried and found guilty of some minor misdemeanor by the military court, he had been sentenced to labor in fetters on the road.

He sighed, containing his anger. There was, he knew, little he could do about the harsh sentences imposed by the court. When Major Grose suspended the civil magistracy, Lieutenant Macarthur had been given overall command of Parramatta and Toongabbe, with full responsibility not only for his company of the New South Wales Corps but also for the government farms and the convict labor gangs working in the area. Only the hospital in Parramatta was— in practice at least—outside Lieutenant Macarthur's control, and Thomas Arndell was determined that it should remain so. He had come out with Governor Phillip in the transport *Friendship*, with the naval rank of assistant surgeon. Having made up his mind to settle in the colony, he had taken a grant of land in the area, which was now a productive, arable farm in which he took great pride.

"Me rum, sorr," old Ben exclaimed, breaking into the surgeon's thoughts. He held out a gnarled hand for the beaker and dragged himself into a sitting position, the better to savor his unexpected treat. " 'Tis a drop o' good stuff," he added, sipping approvingly. "You'll not be in an almoighty rush to take the ould leg off me, will you, Doc?"

Dr. Arndell shook his head. "No," he answered untruthfully. "You drink it slowly and enjoy it, Ben—I've a few more patients to visit before I can come back to you." To the orderly he mouthed silently, "Have him ready in half an hour, John."

He left the male ward and strode across to the one in which the women and children were accommodated, wishing, as he always did when he made rounds, that the new hospital—intended to replace this one—were nearer completion than it was. These buildings, hurriedly erected when Governor Phillip had decided to transfer the government farm to Parramatta—then called Rose Hill—had long outlived their usefulness. Both were leaking, the roofs collapsing in places, and chinks appeared daily in the brick foundations and walls because clay had, perforce, been used in lieu of cement. Tom Macrae, the building superintendent, was an excellent craftsman and a hard worker, but Macarthur was continually taking men from his hospital building gang for some project he held to be of greater urgency than the provision of a new hospital, with the result that delay followed delay. And, Arndell reflected resentfully, only the previous week the acting governor had taken all save two of the carpenters, ordering them to Sydney to assist in completing the sloop that—brought out in frame in the *Pitt*—had been assembled there.

Admittedly a sloop in the service of the colony would be of immense advantage, but if Arndell's new hospital's completion must be delayed still further on that account, where in heaven's name was he expected to accommodate over three hundred sick? Neither Grose nor Macarthur could tell him and, to his annoyance, both appeared to treat the matter as if it were of no importance to them.

Reaching the female ward he controlled his simmering rage, examined two new admissions, chatted briefly with some of the children, and then went to collect his instruments in preparation for old Ben's amputation.

He was threading surgical needles and pinning these into the lapel of his coat when his privacy was abruptly invaded by John Macarthur. Their dislike of each other was no longer a matter for polite pretense or concealment; Macarthur offered no greeting but said in a hectoring tone, "You're needed at the Taggart holding. One of my men has been shot by an infernal convict. It's the place by the creek, four miles from here. How soon can you get out there?"

Dr. Arndell eyed him coldly. "Sometime during the afternoon, probably," he returned with deliberate casualness. "I had intended to go out there in any event—a new settler just off the *Britannia* managed to get himself bitten by a black snake. Jenny Taggart took him in. If he's still alive I'll have to treat him and—"

"Oh, for the Lord's sake, man!" Macarthur interrupted impatiently. "This is murder, don't you understand? One of my soldiers has been murdered by a convict. Your evidence as to the cause of death will be required, and you prattle on about some damned settler who's been bitten by a snake! Be so good as to bestir yourself, will you?"

"I have a hospital to run," Arndell pointed out, "and an amputation to perform in a few minutes, in order to save a man's life. And *you* prattle on about a dead soldier!"

"A *murdered* soldier," Macarthur amended. "Shot by a convict who is not permitted to carry arms. I am responsible for apprehending the miserable fellow and for seeing he's brought to justice. He's taken to the woods, of course . . . or so my sergeant tells me."

"No doubt you've instituted a hunt for him?"

"Yes, of course I have."

"Then what need is there for haste?" the surgeon asked with deceptive mildness. "If he's taken to the woods he won't stay there for long. He'll be back if the Indians don't get him first—and then you can hang him."

"It must be done legally, Dr. Arndell, as you should know by now," Macarthur retorted. "You're a justice of the peace—"

"A nonpracticing one, under the new laws, Mr. Macarthur." Having made his point, Arndell relented. "You could have your soldier's body brought here to the hospital if you really want me to pronounce on the cause of death, and I'll do so as soon as I've taken off my patient's leg. Otherwise, I regret to say, I cannot go out until this afternoon."

John Macarthur was fuming, but aware that Arndell was within his rights and certainly not a man to be coerced, he resorted to persuasion. "I'd be uncommonly obliged if you could see your way to going out there now, Doctor. I—that is, it's important that you should see the body in the exact spot where it was found. You see he—"

"What was your fellow up to when he was shot?" Thomas Arndell put in shrewdly. "Because if he was robbing a settler's farm, then he was asking for what he got, was he not? Settlers are entitled to defend their property."

"Not with firearms, if they're convicts. I want you to confirm that he was shot."

"*Has* anyone accused him of robbery, Macarthur?"

Macarthur shrugged resignedly. "The Taggart woman has, of course. But then she would, would she not? My fellow wasn't alone—he had a comrade with him who told a very different story when he reported the matter to me."

Dr. Arndell refrained from the obvious comment, much though he was tempted to make it. Instead he said briskly, "We're wasting time, and I have a poor wretch who's probably already being strapped to my operating table, so I don't intend to keep him waiting. If you'll excuse me, I—"

"You are not being very cooperative, are you?" Macarthur accused.

"My responsibility is to the sick and injured, not to the cause of what passes here for justice, sir," Arndell snapped.

"A fact that has recently been made abundantly clear to me by the acting governor. Nevertheless I am being as co-operative as I can. Either you have the body brought in to me here or I will go out to examine it in—er—in situ after luncheon. The choice is yours."

He picked up his case of instruments, and Macarthur, still glowering, made no attempt to detain him further.

Ben Reilly was, as he had anticipated, already on the table, with two orderlies in attendance, one of whom held a leather pad that when the operation began would be placed between Reilly's jaws for him to bite on. To the surgeon's relief the old man was cheerfully drunk, and Arndell guessed that he had wheedled another tot from his attendants to compensate for the delay Macarthur's visit had caused.

"All right, Ben," he promised, opening the instrument case, "I'll get this over as fast as I can."

A surgeon's skill was measured by the speed with which he could use knife and hacksaw to slice through bone and muscle, thereby reducing to an endurable minimum that which otherwise would have been unendurable. Thomas Arndell worked fast. In a matter of minutes a double flap of skin was fashioned to allow for shrinkage and muscle contraction, the gangrenous limb was severed just below the knee and discarded, ligatures tightened to control the bleeding, and the flap stitched into place in such a way as to permit drainage from the wound.

Ben Reilly was unconscious for virtually all the time the amputation took. He had struggled and given a muffled scream when the knife first bit into his flesh, but after that the shock caused him to faint, the leather pad dropped from his toothless gums, and he lay still, not even moving when a cautery was applied to his stump. With all the drink he had swallowed he probably would not remember even the initial pain when he came to, Arndell thought. That was, of course, *if* he came to. He was a tough old buzzard but suffering severely from malnutrition, which would not aid his chances of recovery.

Arndell passed a bloodstained hand across his face, from which the perspiration was dripping, and stood back from the table. He had done the best he could, now it depended on old Ben's will to live and, the surgeon reminded himself wryly, on his Maker. The orderlies carried him back to the ward and, seeing that his assistant, John Laing, was making a round, Arndell returned to his small sanctum off the dispensary. He poured himself a glass of Cape porter, sipped it with slow enjoyment, and considered the problem Macarthur had posed. Inevitably it would mean trouble for the Taggart girl.

Jenny Taggart had had her share of troubles—indeed, more than her share—and most of those undeserved. Thomas Arndell remembered her well from the voyage out, after she had transferred to the *Friendship* at Rio de Janeiro in order to care for her mother, who had beeen fatally injured in a fall. The mother had died, of course; she had broken her back and there had been no hope for her, but he remembered with what courage and self-sacrifice the girl had nursed her in the dark, malodorous confines of the transport's hold.

And she had borne an exemplary record, unlike the rest of the *Friendship*'s women. She and another girl of about her own age had stuck together through thick and thin, in spite of the appalling conditions on board and the enforced companionship of whores and brothel-keepers.

And Jenny, with her friend—what name had she gone under? Amanda, Alice—no, Amelia, Amelia Bishop—had done exceedingly well after their arrival in the colony. They had planted and cared for the best vegetable garden in Farm Cove, and both had been granted pardons. Amelia Bishop had had her sentence quashed and had gone back to England, revealed as a girl of good family who had been wrongfully convicted.

Jenny Taggart had taken a land grant and . . . Dr. Arndell set down his glass, a thoughtful frown drawing his dark brows together. The grant was small, fifty acres, but she farmed it well, irrigating her land from a creek that formed its eastern boundary. But only the previous Wednesday one of the two old convicts assigned to her had been murdered, seemingly by raiding Indians who had burned down some of her outbuildings. He had viewed the body and, like everyone else, had assumed that the killers were Indians, since as a general rule escaping convicts stole but did not indulge in arson. Only the natives did that, and now, it would appear, there had been another murder, committed by the second of Jenny Taggart's convict laborers—if Macarthur's conclusions were accurate—and the victim had been one of his soldiers.

Apparently Jenny Taggart had accused the soldier of attempting to rob her. Well, perhaps it had been an endeavor to save the second of her old laborers. But it was out of character; Jenny Taggart was not the kind to lie. There was more in this than at first met the eye.

He rose reluctantly. If he went out to the Taggart farm now, instead of waiting until later in the afternoon—when his visit would be expected—he might learn the truth. He would have to forego his luncheon, and there were two cases of dysentery he had wanted to examine before lunch, but Laing could deputize for him and could also keep an eye on Ben Reilly during his absence. Laing was himself a frail and sickly young man, who had applied for leave to return to England to recoup his health, but he was an excellent doctor and a reliable assistant who could quite safely be trusted to do his best for old Ben.

And there was the horse . . . Arndell smiled to himself. When Macrae, the building superintendent, had reported the new settler's unfortunate encounter with a black snake, he had told him that the young man had stabled two horses in his yard. He had suggested that Arndell ride out to the Taggart holding on one of them, to enable their owner to be brought back to the hospital, should it be necessary.

"Likely he'll be ower weakened tae walk, Doctor, and yon mare's a quiet creature—she would carry him gently and yourself too if you had a mind tae ride her," the Scotsman had said. And he had added, with conscious pride, that he and the blacksmith had shod both animals. "The shoes they had on them were nae use for this kind o' country, so I thocht I'd do the puir young feller a favor."

It would be good to ride a horse again, Dr. Arndell thought. In the old days, before coming out to this land peopled by strange animals and devoid of horses, he had ridden to hounds and fancied himself as a horseman. The unexpected opportunity to bestride a nice animal again would compensate for the loss of his lunch. He went in search of Dr. Laing.

* * *

Half an hour later, confidently astride the new settler's well-schooled mare, he was on his way out of Parramatta. The Taggart land was deserted when he reached it, with no sign of a scarlet coat anywhere that he could see, but Jenny Taggart, greeting him at the door of the cabin, told him in a flat, controlled voice that the search for Watt Sparrow was being undertaken by more than a score of the dead soldier's comrades.

"Mr. Macarthur instructed them to shoot to kill if Watt refused to give himself up, Dr. Arndell," she added. "But he was only trying to defend this property, and it was dark. He could not see that the man he fired at was a soldier. Neither could I because—"

"Did you witness the shooting?" Arndell put in.

She held his horse's rein while he dismounted. "Yes," she answered. "I ran out after Watt when he took the musket." In a few brief and bitter words she told him what had happened, then spread her hands helplessly. "But the other soldier, the one who was with him, said that they had surprised a party of Indians and were driving them off when Watt fired at his comrade. He claims it was deliberate and that Watt intended to kill him. And, of course, the poor old man should not have been in possession of a musket."

"Why was he, Jenny?" the doctor probed gently.

"It belonged to Mr. Dawson—the settler who suffered the snakebite. He'll confirm that, but it won't be enough, I fear. And *my* word isn't good enough."

Arndell's mouth tighened involuntarily. "This Dawson— did he see nothing?"

"He was unconscious," Jenny said. "And he still is. That is to say, he's spent most of the time asleep. He rouses when I speak to him but he . . . well, I'm afraid he does not remember anything, Dr. Arndell."

"But he's alive," Arndell said. "Thanks to you."

"Yes," she agreed. "Do you wish to see him?"

"It might be advisable. If you don't mind tying his horse up somewhere, I'll have a look at him."

"Is this mare one of his?" Jenny stroked the mare's nose, eyeing her appraisingly.

"I understand so—he left his animals in Macrae's care.

If he's fit to sit on her back, I will take him to the hospital when I return." The doctor unstrapped his instrument case from the saddle and went into the cabin's living room. The little boy, Justin, was asleep in his carved wooden cot on one side of the fireplace, his new patient occupied Jenny's own pallet bed on the other.

He had finished his examination when Jenny rejoined him, and he said, rising with a smile, "Well, you need have no anxiety on Mr. Dawson's account, Jenny. He'll be as right as rain in another twenty-four hours. He doesn't really need hospital care, but if I admit him, that will relieve you. I imagine you could do with some rest, now that you've lost both your laborers."

She inclined her head, submissive rather than grateful, and Arndell questioned her about the manner in which she had dealt with the bite, his interest quickening when she told him that she had followed the native practice and sucked out the venom after enlarging the wound with a knife blade.

"It seems to have been effective," he conceded.

"Not many of the Indians die of snakebite, Doctor."

"No . . . and our people do. I'll make a note of it for future reference."

"Will you, sir?"

Her tone mocked him and he answered, faintly nettled, "I mean it. We can learn from those who are native to this place. Damme, they've lived here longer than we have! But I'd always supposed that you got on well with them."

Jenny took his point at once. "You're thinking of the fires and poor old Reuben's death, aren't you?"

"Yes," he admitted. "Is there any reason why they should bear a grudge against you?"

"No," she said positively. "None that I am aware of, Doctor."

"Yet they appear to have made two raids on your property."

"That is the soldiers' opinion," Jenny answered. "And I suppose the one that will be given credence."

Her dignified restraint won Thomas Arndell's admiration as well as his pity. And she was right, of course. If Macarthur took a hand in the affair, her opinion would be discounted, if it were not totally ignored.

"Where is the soldier's body?" he asked, his tone deliberately noncommittal. "I have to view it."

"They moved it from where he was—that is, from where Watt and I found him. If you'll follow me, I will show you." He fell into step beside her, noting, as he passed, the burned-out buildings that had previously housed her stores and livestock. Only one now remained intact—a small animal-feed store—and it was into this that Macarthur's men had moved their dead comrade's body, leaving it unguarded but decently covered by a threadbare military greatcoat.

While Jenny waited outside in silence, Dr. Arndell did what was officially required of him. The cause of death was self-evident—a musket-ball, fired from close range, had entered just above the man's heart, passing through the left lung, from which he judged that death would have been virtually instantaneous. He recognized the dead soldier as one of the regiment's less desirable recruits: a seaman who had deserted from the *Royal Admiral* transport and who had enlisted in the corps rather than serve a punitive sentence in the colony. Arndell knew him as a heavy drinker and a troublemaker, married to a convict woman of similar character and habits. He had twice in the recent past received a flogging and been admitted to the hospital to recover.

Arndell searched his memory and the name came back to him—Heal, Private Luther Heal. Well, he was no loss to the corps and probably not to his wife either. The doctor replaced the greatcoat. He rose, conscious of a sense of deep and abiding regret at the thought that, for a man of Heal's caliber, Jenny Taggart's brave attempt to make good on her little farm was now doomed to failure. For even if she were not cast for the role of scapegoat, her convict laborer would be; she had lost old Reuben White, she would lose—what was the other old fellow called? Bird— no, Sparrow. She would lose Sparrow and would almost certainly be refused other help and a woman—even one as hardworking and determined as she was—could not do the work of two men in addition to her own. Besides, she had a child to care for. Arndell wiped his hands on a cloth he took from his medical bag and went out again into the warm noonday sunshine.

Jenny did not hear him at first; she was standing looking out across her land, and he saw that her eyes were full of tears, as if she had reached the same conclusion concerning the future as he had. He laid a hand on her shoulder, and she turned to face him, brushing away the tears, and now there was a mute and poignant question in her eyes.

Arndell answered it, "I shall have to testify that the man was shot, Jenny, and from a range of only a few yards. But you knew that, did you not?"

"Yes, I knew, Doctor. I was there. I saw what happened—I told you I did."

"Where did it happen?" the doctor asked. "Where was the man when your fellow Sparrow fired at him?"

"I'll show you exactly where," Jenny offered. She led him to the partly burned outbuilding and indicated the spot. "The thatch had just been set—that is, it had just caught alight. All I could see—all poor old Watt could see—was a dark figure. And after the attack on Reuben, we were both nervous and on edge. The stock had been driven out—the mare and foal, the pigs—I know *I* thought it was a raid. Indeed I was sure it was although, of course, I had no idea of how many men were in the stock pen, still less did I imagine that they were soldiers."

"They didn't call out, did not identify themselves, Jenny?"

"No. They did not speak."

"And it was very overcast last night," Arndell mused. "I was out, on my way back from the kangaroo hunt, so I know how dark it was." He paced out the distance between the spot on which Private Heal had fallen and that in which he estimated Sparrow must have stood when he opened fire, frowning as he did so. Jenny's story had the ring of truth whereas Macarthur's . . . He looked about him, taking in the ruined buildings and the broken padlock on the gate, and sighed.

"If they shoot poor Watt in the woods," Jenny said bleakly, "*that* will be murder, Dr. Arndell."

Indeed it would, Arndell thought; but aware that he must guard his tongue, he did not reply directly to her accusation. Instead he offered practical help in the form of two gallons of rum, to enable her to employ men to repair her buildings.

"Even if they only arrest your laborer, he'll be held for trial and you won't see him back here for a while. You'll need shelter for your stock and a store for the grain. I'll send you some good men in the charge of my farm superintendent, Jenny, to put things to rights. Pay them in liquor—they work best for that."

She thanked him in a small, choked voice that was vibrant with genuine, deeply felt gratitude, and when he had partaken of a refreshing drink of sweet tea, she helped him to lift Timothy Dawson onto the mare. Arndell climbed into the saddle behind him and set off toward Parramatta, compelled by the sheer awkwardness of his passenger to proceed at a snail's pace. Macarthur met him half a mile from the township, and the doctor was perversely pleased by the expression of dismay on his florid face when he realized that the official viewing of the dead soldier's body had been conducted in his absence.

But Macarthur quickly recovered his composure and said curtly, "Well, I trust you're satisfied that my man was shot?"

"Certainly he was," Dr. Arndell agreed. "There can be no doubt of it."

"Then you will testify—in court if required—that he was murdered?"

Thomas Arndell smiled and then, very deliberately, shook his head. "In my considered opinion, Macarthur, his death was accidental. He was mistaken for a marauder, he did not identify himself, and in the darkness it was impossible to see him for what he was. He—"

"You've permitted the Taggart girl to mislead you!" Macarthur accused. "To pull the wool over your eyes."

"No, I have not. I heard her evidence, which was that of an eyewitness, and I believe her account of what happened."

"Do you, by God! Well, we'll see what the court decides. I give you good day, Dr. Arndell."

Arndell bowed politely and continued on his way. Timothy Dawson stirred and murmured a question, his voice slurred.

"There is nothing to worry about, my friend," the doctor assured him. "Not even on your own account, unless I'm greatly mistaken. A couple of days' bed rest and you'll be as good as new."

At the hospital young Dr. Laing greeted him with the news that Ben Reilly was still clinging obstinately to life.

"Not a bad day's work, then," he said with satisfaction. "Not at all a bad day's work, John. I have the distinct impression that I have contrived to thwart one of Macarthur's ploys, although as yet I'm damned if I know what he was hoping to gain by it."

"He's a dangerous enemy," Laing warned. He helped Timothy Dawson from the saddle and, holding him upright, studied his white, shuttered face with interest. "Who's this? The fellow who was bitten by a black snake?"

"It is," Arndell confirmed. An orderly answered his summons, and he dismounted stiffly, handing the man his rein.

"His pulse is very slow and shallow, pupils dilated and cheeks puffy but . . . good heavens, Tom, he's alive! How did you manage to save him?"

"I didn't. In fact, we are going to revise our treatment of snakebite forthwith, Doctor. The native method is more effective than any we have previously employed." Arndell grinned as his colleague stared at him in perplexity. "Come on—assist me to get him into bed, and I will tell you about it." To the orderly he said, "Take that mare back to Superintendent Macrae's yard, Smollett, and rub her down well before you leave her. And you can tell him that Mr. Dawson will probably collect her from him in two or three days' time."

"You sound very confident," Laing observed.

"I am," Arndell assured him.

It was eleven days before Watt Sparrow was taken, by a party of New South Wales Corps officers returning from a kangaroo hunt organized by Lieutenant Macarthur.

Jenny heard of his capture by chance, when she trudged into Parramatta with Justin on her back to collect the week's rations. During the time Watt had spent in the bush, she had made two unsuccessful attempts to find him, but encountering the aborigine Colbee and his wife— Baneelon's oldest friends and associates—she had learned, to her intense relief, that the fugitive was safe.

Both had greeted her with their accustomed friendly

warmth; the woman Daringa, who spoke little English, using the musical-sounding word *cammarade*, which Jenny
had come to know as a term of affection.

"*Gomang alloman*, Jen-nee," the woman had said, repeating the words slowly to make sure she understood.
Gomang, which meant "grandfather," was the name they
had long since given to old Watt, and *alloman* could be
translated as implying that he had taken refuge with the
tribe.

Colbee, whose English was better, had confirmed his
wife's assertion, and taxed with the suggestion that his people had been responsible for the raid, he had hotly denied
it.

"We not burn—we not steal Jen-nee. Jen-nee *doroon-e-
nang* . . . *gomul*! Not *miyal*, not stranger." His words, despite the mixture of native and English he employed in his
indignation, had carried conviction, to Jenny at all events.
She was their friend, an adopted daughter of their tribe,
whom only a stranger from afar would dream of robbing
. . . and there had been no strangers in the area, according to Colbee. Only white men, some dressed in red coats,
who had made *gweyong* and *cadjee*—fire and smoke.

Jenny did not know how Watt had come to fall into the
officers' hands, and the storekeepers in Parramatta could
not tell her. All were convicts of good character or men
who had been granted remission, and their sympathies
were with the runaway, who was well known to them.

"Maybe the old feller got careless," one of them said.
"Or p'raps he just felt he'd had enough of living with the
Indians."

"Mr. Macarthur gave 'em a 'roo after they took 'em,"
another asserted. "Dead set on takin' 'im, it seems Mr.
Macarthur was. But I don't see as 'e can charge Watt Sparrow with murder—defendin' your property, that's all 'e was
trying ter do. Them sojers 'ad no right ter be there after
dark."

Jenny took heart from this opinion. She loaded her
stores into the small handcart Watt had made her and was
preparing to leave the store when the assistant commissary
called her into his office.

"There is a letter for you," he announced. "It came with
the mail picked up by the *Britannia* at the Cape. Been here

for a few days—I was hoping you'd call sooner." He rummaged among his papers and grunted his satisfaction when he finally ran the letter to earth. Jenny took it with scarcely a glance, her concern solely for poor old Watt Sparrow, but when she presented herself at the prison compound and asked to see him, the jailer shook his head.

"They sent 'im down ter Sydney Cove in the *Lump,* missus—first thing this mornin', on Lieutenant Macarthur's orders."

Dismayed, Jenny attempted to question him, but the jailer shrugged his broad shoulders and expressed ignorance. "I 'ardly set eyes on 'im. A couple o' sojers brought 'im in an' said 'e was to be put on board the *Lump.* All I done was put fetters on 'im, then they was off down ter the wharf with 'im. 'E wasn't in bad shape, far as I could judge, missus, but that's all I c'n tell yer."

"But surely he'll be tried here, not in Sydney?" Jenny objected. They would have to call her as a witness, she told herself. Whatever might be the charges brought against him, Watt was assigned to her and therefore legally was her responsibility. The jailer again feigned ignorance, and she left him, conscious of a growing sense of apprehension that refused to be assuaged.

Convicts accused of crimes in the Parramatta area were almost always brought to trial in the township, the court sitting in the judge advocate's house since, as yet, there was no courthouse. Only those committed on a capital charge were referred to Sydney. Was poor Watt, then, to be tried for murder? Jenny went over the possibilities in her mind as she walked back to the farm, and her anxiety increased with each plodding mile, in the awareness that both she and Watt were in danger. Her own was less predictable than his but . . . She looked back at little Justin, sleeping peacefully among the provision sacks in her handcart, and drew in her breath sharply.

She had a good friend in Dr. Arndell, it was true. The doctor had kept his word; he had sent men from his own assigned farm-labor gang under the supervision of his foreman, and they had rebuilt the burned-out pens and storehouses on her land. They had worked quickly and well, and she had rewarded them with the liquor he had so kindly supplied for the purpose, but now that was gone, and she had no means of employing any casual labor, for which the price was high. Her request that the two laborers she had lost might be replaced—if only temporarily—had been ignored, and with Dr. Arndell's men gone she was alone, with the seed wheat yet to be sown and the digging of the irrigation ditches to be completed.

True, there had been no threats or official warnings—Lieutenant Macarthur had not mentioned his desire for the creek land, but she was under no illusions on that score. What he wanted, he acquired by whatever means were at hand. The government store had supplied her with seed wheat—Justin had his head pillowed on one of the sacks, the last of her replacement, issued unasked that morning—and if she failed to sow it she would be in default and liable to forfeit her land grant.

Well, she would sow it, Jenny decided; come what may, it would all go into the ground. Just as her father and mother had toiled from dawn to dark on the land Lord Braxton had demanded they must put under wheat, she too would toil. At least it was cleared and ready . . . and the maize, which was already sprouting, would serve as a cash crop when the time came to harvest it; the proceeds would suffice to pay for the necessary casual labor.

Watt should have a home to return to—if he returned.

Reaching her cabin she carried the sleeping Justin inside and left him there, barring the door carefully behind her after unloading their ration of meat, rice, and maize flour. The seed wheat went into the newly built storehouse with her tools and the handcart, and she clicked shut the padlock Dr. Arndell had supplied, testing it, tight-lipped and grimly determined, before going about her usual evening chores.

It was dark by the time she had finished rounding up her livestock, feeding them, and locking them into their pens, and Justin was awake and crying when she returned wearily to the cabin to prepare their own evening meal. But, cheered by the sight of her, the little boy played about her feet as she coaxed the fire into life and set the stew pot to boil. He was a good child, Jenny thought, regarding him with warm affection. Of necessity he had often to be left to his own devices, but he had learned to amuse himself, was possessed of a healthy appetite, and seldom cried or made demands on her although, in Watt's absence, he lacked the companionship to which he had become accustomed.

This evening, when he had eaten, he went quite willingly to bed, and after tucking him into his cot and repeating their usual nightly prayer, Jenny was about to follow his example when she remembered the letter the assistant commissary had given her. She seated herself in Tom Jenkin's old rocking chair beside the fire, prepared to savor to the full the rare luxury of reading news from home.

It was only the second letter she had received since her arrival in the colony—the first had been from Johnny Butcher—and this she had initially supposed to have come also from him. But on opening the thin sheet of paper with its closely written, crisscrossed lines, she saw, with a leap of the heart, that it was from Andrew Hawley, dated from Plymouth six months previously.

She closed her eyes, the old, long-cherished memories flooding into her mind, evoked by the sight of his name at the foot of the page. Andrew, as she had first known him— tall, strong, a handsome, fair-haired giant, who had borne her on his shoulders into London and laughingly promised to wed her when she was old enough. She recalled her bitter distress when he had vanished into the crowd, her childish, heartbroken tears when she and her mother had searched for him in vain in Billingsgate Market, themselves penniless and starving, without a roof over their heads.

And then . . . Jenny clutched the letter to her breast, her throat tight. The miracle of their reunion on board the *Charlotte* when she had stumbled out of the foul-smelling hold in which the female convicts were confined to see him, tall and handsome as ever, in a scarlet uniform, pacing the deck. Even the dawning realization that he was a marine and she a convicted felon had not dimmed her joy at the sight of him—they had bridged the gulf between them, thanks to Sergeant Tom Jenkins's intervention and the kindness of his wife, Olwyn.

For a little while, clean and decently clothed under Olwyn's wing, she had dared to dream and to hope that she might free herself of the convict stigma, with marriage to Andrew a goal to strive for at the end of the long voyage. But the dream had faded when the fleet dropped anchor in Rio de Janeiro harbor, and in the hold of the *Friendship*, where her mother lay dying, she had learned that Andrew had been flogged for associating with her and sent back to England on Governor Phillip's orders.

And since then . . . silence. No word, save a brief message brought to her by Watt Sparrow, no letter, only the knowledge that he had been ordered to join the *Pandora* frigate when Watt had seen him. Letters were expensive, of course, and few had come, save official government dispatches, during the first two years of exile, and even these—routed by ships in the China tea trade—had taken up to a year to reach their destination. But now . . . Tears were blinding her as she looked down at the letter. Andrew had not forgotten, here at last was news of him. Impatiently, she brushed her tears away and, by the flickering firelight, started to read.

> My dearest Jenny,
>
> I had believed you lost to me, perhaps even dead, when no reply came to a letter consigned to the *Sirius* at the Cape and another, sent nearly a year later by the *Guardian*. Then I heard that both ships had been wrecked, so that it seems likely that you received neither.
>
> I sent word to you by an old convict named Sparrow, who claimed to know you, when I was on escort duty taking people to the New South Wales transports and wonder did the old fellow ever deliver it? I paid him a shilling for his service and saw him put on board of the *Matilda*, which I heard came safely to port over two years since.
>
> Then I was serving in His Majesty's frigate *Pandora* in the Indies. Maybe you heard that the poor fellows who survived the mutiny against Captain Bligh gave themselves up to our commander in Otaheite? They never made a worse mistake, for Captain Edwards was without a vestige of human compassion, and when he ran our ship onto a reef off the coast of New Holland, all would have drowned in their chains, if he had had his way. But we saved most of them and made our way in the ship's boats to Timor, taking sixteen days on our passage.
>
> There some unfortunates, who had braved the ter-

rors of the sea in a small cutter in order to make their
escape from Sydney Cove, were also given into our
captain's charge. Notwithstanding there was a young
woman and her two babes with them, they received no
mercy from Captain Edwards. The fever was bad
there and I myself succumbed to an attack of it, which
same took the lives of the convict Will Bryant and one
infant.

I was eager to make inquiries of these poor folk, but
our captain forbade all the ship's company even to
speak with them, and when we left Batavia in the
Dutch transports, he held us separate from them. So it
was not until we made port at the Cape and were removed to His Majesty's ship *Gorgon* that I was able to
arrange a meeting. My old comrades from Captain
Phillip's fleet were on board also, and Captain Tench
told me that you were well and, having merited the
governor's favorable consideration, would likely be
granted emancipation.

I learned too of the deaths of Sergeant Tom Jenkins
and his good wife with great sadness, though unable to
fathom out how it was that you were assigned servant
to the sergeant on his farm, when it was his desire, in
widowhood, to wed you. Surely . . .

The page ended at this point and Andrew had continued writing across it. Jenny peered uncertainly at the inter-
mingled lines and poked the fire, with a hand that visibly
trembled, in the hope of causing it to yield more light.

. . . so old a man could wish to wed you only in order that you might be pardoned? Tell me this was
so. . . .

The rest of the line was indecipherable.
Further on, the letter continued:

I spoke once, and alas but briefly, with the runaways
from Sydney and they told me that the life there had
been cruelly hard. All knew you and spoke well of
you, telling of the garden you had wrought in a place
they named Farm Cove. I conceived much admiration

for their enterprise and courage and especially for the skill of the man who was their navigator, name of Butcher. He said little of you but hinted, to my dismay, of a worthless convict rogue named Munday who had taken great advantage of you, after you saved his life. He said, however, that before their departure, he and his companions had made sure that Munday was paid out in his own coin. This I hope was true.

All have been tried and sent to Newgate to complete their sentences. There is much talk of a coming declaration of war with France, so I must yet again abandon my hopes of obtaining a posting to New South Wales, as I am ordered to join His Majesty's frigate *Nymphe*, with promotion to the rank of sergeant. Her commander is Captain Pellew, said to be one of the finest officers afloat, so I may count myself fortunate.

But if I live, Jenny, I will come to you. I beg you wait for me, however long it is. . . .

However long, Jenny thought, feeling tears coming once more to overwhelm her. It had already been too long and . . . there was Justin. She turned in her chair to look at him, sleeping quietly in his cot on the other side of the fireplace. His face was the mirror-image of his father's, but Johnny had—how had Andrew put it? She picked up the letter again. Johnny "had said little" of her but had hinted at her relationship with Ned. And Johnny did not know that he had a son; he was languishing in Newgate, serving out his sentence in that horror-filled prison, while Andrew went—gladly, it seemed—to war, counting himself fortunate to have exchanged a brutal captain for a fine one.

After a while the fire flickered to extinction and Jenny, still in the rocking chair, found solace from the torment of her thoughts in sleep.

The dream that came was a happy one, in which she was walking the *Charlotte*'s deck with Tom and Olwyn Jenkins and her lips curved into a welcoming smile as she saw Andrew Hawley's tall figure coming toward her.

"Oh, Andrew!" her heart cried. "It is so good to see you. . . ."

CHAPTER V

The Court of Criminal Jurisdiction had heard half a dozen minor cases when Watt Sparrow was brought into the dock.

The judge advocate, Captain David Collins, searched among the pile of depositions and witnesses' statements in front of him and, failing to find the name of the accused, glanced questioningly at Captain Foveaux, who was presiding.

Collins said, a distinct edge to his voice, "I do not appear to have examined this man, sir, or to have taken a statement from him."

Foveaux turned to Lieutenant Macarthur and, receiving a nod of affirmation, answered casually, "It is a simple case, sir, and the prisoner is pleading guilty to the charges."

Collins bristled visibly. "What charges are being made against him?"

Macarthur said, his tone as casual as that of the presiding officer, "He is charged with having run from his assigned place of labor, being absent for eleven days, and being in possession of a firearm, to wit a musket. He has confessed to stealing the musket and to firing it when Ensign Cummings called upon him to surrender himself. Ensign Cummings is, as you can see, a member of this court and can testify to the truth of my assertion. I was also present—I saw and heard the shot fired."

Very much put out, Collins opened his mouth to utter a protest and then closed it again, aware that he could count on no support from the members of the court, however unorthodox this procedure might be. He walked across to the dock, studying the prisoner with narrowed eyes. Sparrow was a white-haired little man of uncertain age and, he judged, poor physique. His skin had a healthy tan; clearly he had worked for some time at his assigned labor, and if his toil-worn hands were anything to go by, he had worked hard.

"We can save the court's time, sir," Joseph Foveaux

pointed out. "A plea of guilty surely only requires that we debate the sentence we are to impose?"

The judge advocate affected not to hear him. Facing the prisoner he asked quietly, "How say you—do you plead guilty or not guilty to the charges against you? You heard them, did you not?"

Sparrow continued to avoid his gaze, his own fixed on the floor of the dock.

"Guilty," he muttered. "I plead guilty, sir."

"Did you fully understand the charges?"

"Yessir, I understood 'em."

"And you wish to offer no defense, call no witnesses?"

The little man hesitated for a moment, biting his lower lip and, watching him, Collins found himself wondering what inducements John Macarthur had offered to persuade him to plead guilty. Probably he could have been arraigned on a more serious charge; given the choice between this and the admission that he had attempted to escape, he had decided on the lesser of two evils. . . . Most convicts did, aware that the scales were weighted against them. Collins sighed; he could do no more, and he returned to his seat, reaching for his pen in order to enter the plea on the blank charge sheet. The prisoner was marched out by his escort and Foveaux turned, as was the custom, to Ensign Piper, as the junior member of the court.

"Sentence?" he snapped.

"Deportation to Norfolk Island, sir," the boy replied instantly. He had been well briefed, David Collins thought and did not see any reason to change his mind when Piper added, "The scoundrel should be given three years, in my view, sir."

"Cummings?"

"The same, sir," Ensign Cummings answered, but he looked faintly uneasy.

"Brace?"

"I—er—I concur, sir." As a new arrival Brace was clearly anxious not to step out of line, and his glance at Foveaux clearly sought for reassurance.

Foveaux smiled at him before turning to Macarthur. "And you, John?"

"Norfolk Island certainly. But for carrying arms—

damme, for *stealing* a musket and firing on an officer in the execution of his duty, I should have thought seven years a more appropriate sentence." John Macarthur's tone was brusque.

"Edward?"

Captain Abbott raised fever-bright eyes to his questioner, his thin, sallow face devoid of expression. Poor Abbott had been suffering from an intermittent fever for the past two months, and at times, Collins suspected, he was only barely aware of what was going on around him.

Abbott said hoarsely, "I don't disagree with the other members of the court, though I must confess I should have preferred the charges against this fellow—what's his name? Er . . . Sparrow—to have been made in the proper form by the judge advocate. But since he's pleaded guilty—Norfolk Island for three years."

"Then we're in agreement," Foveaux asserted. "Bring back the prisoner for sentence if you please, Mr. Brewer."

Watt Sparrow heard his sentence with downcast eyes and without protest, but as the president prepared to dismiss him and adjourn the court, he asked hesitantly for permission to speak.

"What do you want to say?" Foveaux demanded with ill-concealed impatience. "You've had a fair trial, have you not?"

"Yessir," the little man answered. "It's jus' that . . . Jenny Taggart, sir—she's farmin' fifty acres an' wiv' me gorn an 'er other convict servant dead—killed by Indians, sir—she'll be on 'er own. Fifty acres is too much for a woman on 'er own and . . . that is, sir, I'd like to be sure she'll 'ave two other men assigned to 'er. That's all, sir."

Joseph Foveaux shrugged indifferently. "The Taggart grant is in the Parramatta area, is it not? Well, that's in Lieutenant Macarthur's jurisdiction—he is in charge of the government farms and public labor in Parramatta and Toongabbe. But I am sure that if—er—Jenny Taggart makes application to him, her request will be considered on its merits. That is so, Mr. Macarthur, is it not?"

"Of course, Captain Foveaux," Macarthur responded readily. "I'll look into the matter. But we're short of men at present—perhaps when the next transport arrives the situation will improve. Our public-work demands must be given priority, naturally, but I will do what I can." He turned to engage his neighbor in conversation, and Foveaux nodded to the escort. "Remove the prisoner. He is to be held in custody until his sentence can be implemented. The court is adjourned."

Sparrow looked as if he wanted to say more, but one of the escort grasped his arm and, acknowledging defeat, he remained silent as they led him away. David Collins frowned, still uneasy concerning the manner in which the case had been conducted. Under Governor Phillip's rule, all criminal courts had consisted of three naval and three military officers, or they had at least included one of the civilian justices of the peace. Now, on the edict of the acting governor, his corps officers held undisputed sway, and, indeed, his own position as judge advocate was being gradually undermined. He was no longer called upon to preside or, very often, even to prosecute when criminal cases were heard; the naval surgeons like Arndell, White, and Balmain were regarded as holding civil appointments, and the chaplain—who felt strongly on the subject—was constantly at loggerheads with Major Grose on this account.

Collins's frown deepened as he slowly gathered up his papers. The new arrival, young Charles Brace, departed in Foveaux's company, the two of them laughing together at some joke they did not share with the others. The sickly Abbott stumbled out on Ensign Cummings's supporting arm, looking alarmingly pale, and Piper, as was his wont, walked respectfully at John Macarthur's elbow, carrying on a low-voiced exchange that—like Foveaux's bantering remark to Brace—effectively excluded their brother officers from intimacy with them.

Collins let them go, making a show of sorting out his papers until the courtroom emptied. The provost marshal, Henry Brewer, returned a few minutes later, to slump down on the seat beside him with an exasperated sigh.

He, too, looked ill, and Collins thought how much Brewer had aged during the years he had served the new colony. He was not a young man—he admitted to being over fifty—and his pay, in the lowly naval rank of midshipman, had never been augmented, despite the responsibilities he bore and Governor Phillip's efforts to obtain a suitable emolument for the office he held.

Brewer had shipped out in the *Sirius* as captain's secretary; he had only been made provost marshal because the official designated for the post had absented himself before the first fleet sailed, and for all the governor's frequent pleas the home government had never confirmed his appointment. He lived frugally, and his shabby uniform and oft-mended shoes were a reflection of his penury, yet he seldom complained and continued conscientiously to carry out his duties for a midshipman's pittance.

David Collins, grateful for his efficiency and unfailing support, had long regarded him more as friend than subordinate, and he said now, laying a sympathetic hand on his arm, "What ails you, Henry?"

"The same as that which ails *you*, I fancy," the provost marshal returned gruffly. "The knowledge that the justice we are authorized to administer is being gravely perverted. That last case this morning is a glaring example of what is being done, seemingly with our connivance."

Collins spread his hands in a gesture of helplessness. "What can we do to prevent it if we lack the acting governor's support?"

"God knows! But you asked what ailed me—well, that is it. Everything Governor Phillip stood for, everything he achieved is going by the board." Brewer swore feelingly. "*Will* he come back, David? Because I only stayed on the hope that he would."

"I too," Collins admitted. He sighed, recalling Governor Phillip's plea that he should stay and the trust that Phillip had always reposed in him to see justice done. He had read and dispatched his chief's last letter to the Home Secretary, Sir Henry Dundas, and the wording of that letter had burned itself into his memory.

"I believe my returning to England will be the greatest service I can render this colony, independent of any other consideration," Arthur Phillip had written. "For it will put it in my power to shew what may and what may not be expected. . . ."

Later, on the eve of his departure, Phillip had given the seal of the colony into Collins's keeping. The seal was new and had only recently been delivered, and they had examined it together, remarking on the symbolism of the reverse engraving. The figure of Britannia, surrounded by a bale of wool, a beehive, a pickax, and a shovel, with a ship, a plow, three small figures of toiling laborers, and a small town. Pointing these out, the governor had questioned its meaning. *"Was he an optimist, who designed this?"* he had asked wryly. *"Or will these symbols truly represent this colony in days to come?"*

"Devil take them!" Henry Brewer exlaimed wrathfully. He brought his clenched fist down on the table in front of them with such force that a number of the papers piled on it were sent flying. "The officers are paying their men in rum, you know, or trade goods, at an exorbitant rate of profit . . . and the men, the soldiers, are selling their liquor to the convicts, also at a profit. That infernal syndicate of theirs intends to hire more ships, in addition to Raven's, as I expect you know."

"Yes, I know," Collins answered. He bent to retrieve his scattered papers, unreasonably angry with himself because he had no remedy to suggest. Dear God, he thought, back once again in memory to that last evening, when Governor Phillip had unburdened himself and confessed his fears for the future.

"Much will depend on you, David," he had said. *"You must do all in your power to prevent the officers of the New South Wales Corps from enriching themselves by private trade, as would seem to be their present objective. And they must not receive land grants whilst they are still serving in the corps."*

Wise and farsighted, Arthur Phillip had observed the danger signals and given him a warning, but Collins felt he had failed in his trust. As Henry Brewer had just reminded him, the officers of the corps were engaging in private trade, they were enriching themselves, and their commandant had seen to it that they received all the land grants they wanted. Macarthur owned more land than anyone else in the colony, and Foveaux was following his example. In Phillip's day they had been restricted to grants of a few acres, sufficient only to provide grazing for a few goats and hogs, and to grow vegetables for their own consumption. Now, under Major Grose's governorship, they were engaging in agriculture, as well as trade, without let or hindrance.

Brewer dropped stiffly to his knees, in order to aid in

picking up the last of the papers. Their eyes met and the provost marshal offered apologetically, "I'm not blaming you any more than I blame myself, David, because I've no more idea than you have as to how we can make them trim their sails. . . . Indeed, sometimes I wonder whether it isn't a waste of time even to think about it. We've no power, no real authority, and what we do have is being gradually eroded."

"What choice do we have?" Collins asked glumly.

"Very little, I'm aware. I'm tempted to offer my resignation."

As he, too, was tempted, the judge advocate thought . . . though Henry Brewer had more reason than he had and, of course, there remained the fact that he had given Governor Phillip his word he would stay.

"Perhaps, Henry," he said, "by staying in our respective offices we do dam the flood that might otherwise be unloosed on this unhappy place. We provide a form of opposition—we compel them all, even Macarthur, to pay lip service to the law. Give them a judge advocate and a provost marshal of *their* choosing and they could and would flout every law in the colony with impunity! They've clipped White's wings, Arndell's, Balmain's and the poor old chaplain's, but Dickie Atkins will fight back, and Augustus Alt's in the same position as we are. We hold the king's commission, all three of us—they cannot rid themselves of us unless we resign."

"True," Brewer conceded. "But it goes sadly against the grain, David, to stand silently by and watch these rogues destroy all we've worked so hard to build up. That case this morning—the old man, Watt Sparrow—there was more in that than meets the eye, I'd swear there was. Sparrow worked for little Jenny Taggart—"

"Ah, your paragon!" Collins put in, his tone gently mocking. "You were always an admirer of hers, my dear Henry, weren't you? Ever since she was sentenced to a week on Pinchgut!"

"A sentence that should never have been imposed on a woman," Brewer growled. He added gravely, "But yes—I do admire that young woman. She has made good. She has courage and determination beyond her years. She's an example of what this colony can offer to each and every convict who possesses a genuine desire for rehabilitation. Jenny Taggart was a mere child when she came here, but she organized that group Governor Phillip called 'the Garden Women,' and they were no angels, heaven knows. She bossed them and she set them to work, and they've all done well, largely under her influence." He shrugged his narrow shoulders and smiled, amused by his own vehemence, and added in a quieter tone, "If we had more of her kind here and fewer of John Macarthur's, this colony would be the better for it."

"You may well be right," David Collins admitted. He rose, his sheaf of papers under his arm. "Do you know more about the man Sparrow's case than was revealed in court this morning, Henry?"

Midshipman Brewer shook his head regretfully. "No—Macarthur made sure it was hushed up. But there was talk of an Indian raid on Jenny Taggart's holding—her other assigned laborer was killed, battered to death, I believe, and most of her buildings set on fire. Dr. Arndell knows about it and . . . I might have a word with him, if you approve."

"You have my approval," the judge advocate assured him. "But, if you find out anything, report to me before you mention it to anyone else, will you please?"

"Of course, sir," Brewer acknowledged formally. His smile faded. "Who else would listen?"

Henrietta Spence subjected her newly furnished withdrawing room to a critical inspection and finally gave vent to a sigh of satisfaction.

Since her return from Elizabeth Farm at Parramatta ten days earlier, she had worked hard to put the Sydney Cove house in order, aided by Mrs. O'Leary, who—although unaccustomed to the requirements of a gentleman's household—was an excellent seamstress and a tireless and willing worker.

While it was true this room would have to serve as both dining and withdrawing room and was therefore much too small, the general effect was quite pleasing, now that the curtains had been hung and carpets covered the rough brick floor. Sydney Cove, after all, was not Kensington or even Calcutta; standards were, of necessity, lower here, and

Mrs. Macarthur, for all the good taste to which she as-
pired, could not boast of a grandfather clock made by
Shannon or Bokhara carpets in every room.

Henrietta felt confident that her father, when he returned, would approve of the manner in which she had arranged their furniture and set out their Indian silver, their
fine china and glass, and the framed paintings he had purchased in London. He had chosen the land for his grant at
Portland, some three miles west of Parramatta, and he had
spent the past week there, with Seamus O'Leary and his
son, supervising the house and buildings a convict gang
was in the process of erecting.

Major Grose, he had told Henrietta, had been more than
helpful in this regard. Twenty men, with an experienced
overseer, had been allocated to the task; the house should
be completed within a few days, the sheep pens, storehouses, and stables in ample time to receive their livestock
when it arrived from the Cape. But, greatly to Henrietta's
relief, he had decided initially to install the O'Learys in the
farmhouse, while he and Henrietta took up residence in
Sydney Cove.

"It will be too primitive for you, my dear," he had said
solicitously. "Too cut off and isolated. Even at the Macarthurs' you felt that, did you not?"

She had not denied his supposition, Henrietta recalled,
although in fact she had enjoyed her stay with the Macarthurs more than she had anticipated. Her hostess, apart
from assuming a certain social superiority—to which, no
doubt, her husband's position entitled her in colonial circles—had proved very congenial. She had a young son, Edward, and a six-month-old baby daughter, to both of whom
she was devoted, and besides playing the piano and displaying a remarkable knowledge of agricultural science, she
was an entertaining companion and extremely well informed on all matters pertaining to the new colony and its
inhabitants.

Henrietta had learned much during her stay—extended
to almost a fortnight so that her father might inspect the
land and the various settlements in the area—and she had
been quite reluctant to leave when the time came. Now
that she was back in Sydney, however, with the house

properly arranged and a staff of servants engaged to keep it in order, she had come to realize her good fortune.

Sydney was the center of such social life as there was. Once her father returned, she would be able to accept invitations and, in her turn, extend them, to include small dinner parties, picnics, and whist evenings and even, perhaps, attend the plays occasionally put on by a troupe of enterprising convict theatricals. And Charles Brace, God willing, would break his inexplicable silence when he received a formal invitation to dine. She stifled a sigh, hearing the clock strike. Only two o'clock! Why, oh why, had Charles deserted her?

"You will be in great demand," Mrs. Macarthur had assured her confidently. "Especially at Government House, for few of our officers are married, and Mrs. Grose has told me often how lonely she is for female company. She has only recently come out with her family and has not really settled down as yet. Indeed, I fancy she regrets coming, although she will not admit it. Major Grose, too, at times. He covets military glory, and if there is really to be a war he will not be content to remain in what he regards as a backwater. Captain Collins is another who feels as he does—and *his* wife seems to have no intention of coming out to join him. Mr. Macarthur expects him to resign before long. I do not understand the whys and wherefores of it, but apparently his military promotion may be jeopardized if he remains here. In any event, Captain Collins was the late governor's most devoted admirer, and he does not see eye to eye with Major Grose or with my husband."

Elizabeth Macarthur had talked to her quite freely in this vein, Henrietta recalled, volunteering comments and tidbits of gossip concerning the military officers and their wives that, had they been able to overhear them, few would have relished.

Mrs. Paterson—lately returned from Norfolk Island with her husband, second in command of the New South Wales Corps—Elizabeth had described as "a dull little Scottish mouse," and Lieutenant Governor King's newlywed lady as "very frank and good-natured, but wholly lacking in intellectual accomplishments."

Elizabeth herself was well endowed with wit and shrewdness but—although her criticisms of Sydney society were often faintly tinged with malice—her actions were those of a kindly and good-hearted woman, ready to make the best of the strange new life to which fate had brought her.

It was fortunate, Henrietta reflected, that she had been able to win her hostess's esteem, for they had much in common—not least a shared love of poetry and music, which they had indulged to the full during her stay. In addition, her genuine affection for Elizabeth Macarthur's five-year-old son, Edward, her enjoyment of his company, and her patience with his flow of eager questions had further endeared her to the little boy's mother.

"You must marry, Etta dear," Elizabeth had insisted, with deep conviction, more than once. "Marry and have lots of darling little babes of your own! That is the only source of happiness and contentment for a woman in these circumstances, I am sure. You've considered the possibility, of course?"

"I . . . not really," she had replied and, even now, the answer she had given brought a blush of shame to her cheeks. "There is my father, you see. He needs me, being so recently widowed."

"But, my dear," Elizabeth had exclaimed. "You must abate such scruples! I offer myself as an instance. I was reluctant to leave my mother and my friends, and none of them, I am certain, when I married thought that either of us had taken a prudent step. I was considered indolent and inactive—Mr. Macarthur too proud and haughty for our humble fortune or expectations. Yet see how bountifully Providence has dealt with us. . . . We have our farm, our children, and in Mr. Macarthur's society I experience the tenderest affections of a husband. Etta, I can truly say that no two people on earth can be happier than we are! Can you wonder that I wish a similar state for you?"

Despite Elizabeth's evident sincerity Henrietta had still hesitated to confide the hopes she entertained concerning Charles Brace, and she was glad now that she had refrained from doing so, for Charles was proving strangely elusive. He had not called since her return to Sydney Cove—and it was impossible, in so small a community, for him not to have heard that she was there once again. True, she had paid no social calls on her own account as yet, and could not do so until her father took up residence in the Sydney house; but with Mrs. O'Leary as chaperon, there need have been no impediment to an afternoon visit from Charles. He could, had he wished, have sent a note of welcome and inquired after her health and well-being . . . but he had done nothing, and she was worried.

Elizabeth Macarthur had sought, with great delicacy, to offer a warning concerning her husband's brother officer. Henrietta smiled wryly as she recalled her new friend's efforts to cloak the warning with tactful asides and obvious evasions. What the warning amounted to was simple enough: Most of the officers, cut off from normal intercourse with females of their own class, took convict women into their quarters, ostensibly to cook and clean but—since the majority were women of easy virtue—few were employed in a purely domestic party.

Henrietta had feigned well-bred astonishment at this revelation because Elizabeth clearly expected it of her, but in fact she had been neither surprised nor shocked by the carefully worded disclosure. A similar situation had existed in India, with personable young native girls in place of the New South Wales convict women. As a child of barely twelve, she recalled, her illusions had been rudely shattered when she had become aware that her mother's delicate health had driven her father into the arms of a Hindu courtesan. She had accepted the situation while pretending ignorance of it as, she supposed, her sickly mother had also accepted it—men were men, with lusts and appetites no gently born lady, of any age, was required to gratify and still less to acknowledge. Nevertheless, faced with the possibility that Charles Brace might be tempted to engage a convict girl as housekeeper, she was beset with uneasy doubts.

His courtship during the voyage from the Cape had been ardent, though always circumspect. He had sought her company constantly and had appeared greatly to enjoy it. Convention had decreed, of course, that they could not meet unchaperoned, but there had been occasions when chance had enabled them to do so . . . on deck, in the early mornings, and once or twice under the stars, when she had gone in search of a breath of air before retiring and had found Charles there in the wind-whipped darkness.

Henrietta's cheeks burned as the memory of one such

occasion returned to torment her. He had taken her into
his arms, kissed her passionately on the lips, and whispered
of his devotion as his hands had traced the swelling con-
tours of her breasts and his hard, strong body had pressed
against hers. She had come near to swooning with ecstasy,
caught up in a heady excitement she had never before experienced, yet now . . . She shivered. Now he was holding himself aloof, seemingly indifferent to the fact that she
had come back to Sydney.

Had he meant those eagerly whispered words, she asked
herself wretchedly, or had he merely been trifling with her
affections, intending no more than to pass the long, idle
days at sea as pleasantly as he could? Or had he, perhaps,
merely found it amusing to vanquish and humiliate Timothy Dawson, who had first paid court to her before he himself had joined the ship? She did not know, and there was
no one she could ask. Elizabeth Macarthur had been kind
and friendly, and had invited confidences, but pride had
precluded Henrietta from seeking advice. Had Charles
come to Parramatta during her stay there, she might have
felt differently.

A perfunctory tap on the door heralded Mrs. O'Leary,
stout and perspiring as always but now in a state of some
excitement, wisps of untidy gray hair escaping from the
mobcap Henrietta had provided for her to wear in the
afternoons.

"Set your cap to rights, Mrs. O'Leary," Henrietta chided
her. "You know I—" but Mrs. O'Leary was not to be dis-
tracted from the news she had come to impart.

"Miss Etta, there's a ship coming in, so there is, an'
they're saying she's from Ireland! The *Boddingtons* out of
Cork, miss. The people are gathering to welcome her and
boats going out. May I have permission to go down to the
quay, if you please?"

The O'Leary family hailed from Cork, Henrietta reminded herself, and respectable though they were, it was
possible that some of the newly arrived ship's passengers
might, for all they were convicted felons, be known or even
related to them. She was about to give the requested permission when a sudden thought occurred to her—the arrival of any ship from home brought the entire population
of Sydney rushing to the quayside and the adjacent shore,

and it was probable that Charles Brace would be among them. What better than a seemingly chance meeting between herself and him to break the silence and, she hoped, ascertain its cause?

Henrietta jumped up. "You may fetch bonnets and shawls for us both, Mrs. O'Leary," she said impulsively. "I'm coming with you!"

"There'll be riffraff abounding," the Irishwoman warned. "And drunk as fiddlers'—drunk as lords, the most of them. D'ye think ye should, Miss Etta? The master—"

"We'll take Noah with us, then," the girl decided. "Tell him to arm himself with a stick or a cudgel in case some of them are troublesome. And hurry—I want to watch the ship come in!"

Mrs. O'Leary scurried off obediently. Ten minutes later, escorted by one of the new convict menservants, Noah Wright, they made for the quay, forced to make their way through a growing crowd, for even the convict labor gangs had ceased work, and the women were there in force. The ship, under a single topsail and her jibs, was nosing her way slowly into the anchorage, and Henrietta was able to make out a little group of women standing disconsolately on the after part of her upper deck, guarded by half a dozen scarlet-coated soldiers.

Drawing nearer, with the sturdy Noah clearing a path for her with his cudgel, she watched the seamen swarming aloft to take in the topsail and heard the rattle of chain cable as the anchor was let go. A ragged cheer rose from the other watchers on shore, but the *Boddingtons* had come to anchor too far out in the cove for any of them to be able to recognize the faces of those on deck, and Mrs. O'Leary cried her disappointment aloud.

"Hush!" Henrietta chided her. "Do not draw attention to yourself by such unseemly remarks. You are a free woman, not a convict, and you should remember it always."

The flustered woman apologized, her tone dutiful but her lips tightly compressed. Henrietta, however, failed to notice her unspoken resentment; ten yards from her she caught sight of Timothy Dawson and, grasping Mrs. O'Leary's arm, hastily drew her back. She had heard a rumor that he had been confined in the hospital at Parramatta following an accident, and certainly he looked thinner and a great deal paler than he had when they had landed from the *Britannia*, but he was alive and seemingly active once more, and she was anxious to avoid being accosted by him. Compelling a reluctant Mrs. O'Leary to follow her, Henrietta beat a swift retreat to where, at the summit of a grassy knoll, they could still see but were screened by a milling throng of mainly female onlookers, most of them with children.

Noah took up his position belligerently in front of them, and the women, after a few apprehensive glances in his direction, kept their distance. Several of the children, seeing—perhaps for the first time in their lives—a fashionably dressed lady, stared at her openmouthed and voiced shrill questions, but their mothers silenced them in embarrassed whispers or, if they persisted, with cuffs and curses. One, more mannerly than the rest, offered an apology before dragging her offspring out of earshot, and gradually they all moved lower down the slope, leaving Henrietta and her companions in sole possession of the knoll. Little, if anything, appeared to be happening now on board the *Boddingtons*, and losing interest and feeling the grass damp beneath her feet, Henrietta was about to tell Noah to escort them back to the house when Mrs. O'Leary gave vent to a muffled exclamation.

"There's a boat putting out from the quay, Miss Etta! A boat wiv some officers—can ye see it? One of them's Lieutenant Brace, I do believe."

Following the direction the woman had indicated, Henrietta saw that she was right. A boat *was* on its way out to the anchored transport. She shaded her eyes with a gloved hand. A dark-faced officer was seated in the stern sheets, and beside him, she recognized Charles Brace. A third and younger officer crouched at their feet.

"They are probably going out in order to arrange for the convicts to be brought ashore," she began and then broke off as a concerted howl of mingled anger and derision rose from the little cluster of women at the foot of the slope. Above the clamor a single voice shrieked in accusation. "A pox on the bloody officers! Off to choose their whores like they always do. What about us?"

Henrietta, her heart sinking, was momentarily bereft of words. Then she said with what dignity she could muster,

"It is no affair of ours, Mrs. O'Leary. Let us go back to the house—it is becoming damp and chilly."

"Very good, Miss Etta," Mrs. O'Leary answered submissively. She gestured to Noah and offered her mistress her arm. A trifle to her surprise, the offer was accepted.

The *Boddingtons'* master was waiting on his quarterdeck when the three New South Wales Corps officers, led by Captain Foveaux, presented themselves.

"Chalmers," he said. "Robert Chalmers at your service, gentlemen, although I am hopeful that you can do *me* a service—and that at your earliest convenience."

Foveaux regarded him with raised brows. "How so, Captain?"

"By providing a strong guard, sir, and removing a bunch of mutinous blackguards I have below decks," the captain answered bluntly. He was a big, powerfully built man, Charles Brace observed and, judging by his unlined face and ready smile, normally not a man who was easily perturbed or roused to anger. But he was angry now, brushing aside Foveaux's bantering suggestion that it had been their intention only to remove the women with a curt, "Hear me out, sir."

"Certainly, Captain. I am all attention," Foveaux assured him.

The captain cast him a frowning, speculative glance and, controlling himself with an almost visible effort, went on coldly, "We sailed from Cork on the fifteenth of February, having taken on board one hundred and twenty-four male and twenty female convicts . . . almost all of them sentenced for sedition. They were humanely treated, I give you my word—well fed and clothed, with a naval agent, a superintendent, and two surgeons to ensure their wellbeing, all of whom will bear me out. We have no sick, sir, and we lost only one man on the passage . . . a man we had to hang."

"Hang?" Foveaux echoed, all trace of lightness vanishing from his voice. "God in heaven, Captain Chalmers—are you telling me you had a mutiny on board?"

"An attempt to seize the ship was planned after we left Rio de Janeiro," the master returned. "And it was well planned! Before we hanged him, the ringleader—a young

rogue by the name of Conal O'Riordan—confessed that it
was their intention to murder all my officers as well as
myself, sparing only the agent, Lieutenant Bell, and Mr.
MacIver, my first mate. *They* were to be kept alive until
they had navigated the ship to a Dutch or Spanish port and
then served in like fashion to the rest of us." He shook his
head wrathfully. "Mr. Bell will confirm all I've told you,
Captain Foveaux. It was on his authority that we sentenced
O'Riordan, to make an example and stamp out the mutiny.
But in my view, there are about half a score of his cronies
as bad as he was—or even worse. He was only a lad, but
they are hard-core rebels. Some of 'em served in America
in seventy-five."

"Where are they now, sir?" Foveaux asked.

"Below in the for'ard hold," the *Boddingtons'* master
supplied grimly. "In chains, Captain Foveaux. And I want
them off my ship and in *your* custody ashore before the
women are removed and we start discharging cargo."

Foveaux nodded. To Charles Brace, in a whispered
aside, he said. "Leave me to placate this good fellow,
Charles. You and de Catteral cast your eyes over the
women."

Nothing loth, Charles Brace acted on this suggestion. He
was anxious to engage a suitable young woman to look
after his domestic needs, but the ones Foveaux's housekeeper had sent for his inspection had all proved wanting.
Several had been prostitutes, two others dumpy country
girls, unlettered and bucolic, a third, on her own admission,
prone to drink. All offended his fastidious tastes, but perhaps among the Irish women . . . He smiled to himself as
he made his way aft, young Ensign de Catteral at his heels.

The women were under guard, huddled together as if for
mutual protection, their faces uniformly sullen and unhappy. But there were a number of pretty faces among
them, he saw, and they were clean and wholesome, their
hair neatly braided, their clothing feminine. The men on
guard duty came to attention as the two officers approached; Brace addressed himself to the sergeant and
made their wants known.

"It will be to the advantage of any women to engage
themselves as domestic servants in an officer's household,"
he added, careful to observe the proprieties. "They will re-

ceive payment for their services, rations, and a clothing allowance, and they will be well treated and comfortably housed. Those engaged in the public service do not fare so well. You are, presumably, well acquainted with these women, Sergeant. Are there any you can recommend?"

To his astonishment the sergeant answered emphatically, "Nary a one, sir, and that's the gospel truth."

Brace regarded him incredulously. Then, out of the corner of his eye, he caught sight of a slim, dark-haired girl in a striped gingham dress, as she moved across to the taffrail with easy grace, her head held high. Surely she could not be . . . He turned back to the sergeant, frowning. "Are yoy saying they are *all* whores, Sergeant?"

"No sir, that's just what they're not, as we've good reason to know." The man's tone was aggrieved. He was an old soldier, one who had apparently served in convict transports before, for he went on, "They're not like the women we usually carry, sir, not by a long chalk. These are rebels, rebel bitches, sir, from Ireland, and they hate our guts. You'll have heard about the mutiny—Captain Chalmers will likely have told you?"

"Yes, he told us. But"—Brace exchanged a puzzled glance with de Catteral—"I understood it was discovered and—er—suppressed?"

"Aye, so it was, sir, just in time, before they could murder us. And 'twas these women who incited the men to try and take the ship. I'd as soon take a man-eating tiger into my house as one o' these Irish females, honest, sir. Let 'em go to the public works an' see how they like it! Maybe that'll tame 'em."

He might have said more, but receiving a peremptory summons from Captain Chalmers on the quarterdeck, he excused himself.

De Catteral asked uncertainly, "What do you think, Brace? If the sergeant's right, we'll be wasting our time with these women—or risking a knife in the back if we employ any of them. For myself I prefer an honest English whore."

Charles Brace scarcely heard him. He was watching the girl in the gingham dress with absorbed attention, taking in her youth and the classic beauty of her profile. His pulses quickened when, sensing his eyes on her, she turned to give him stare for stare, defiant and unafraid.

"Go and report to Captain Foveaux," he snapped at de Catteral. "He'll probably want to arrange for the mutineers to be put ashore. Go on—don't wait for me."

When the boy had gone, he strode purposefully across to the taffrail. There was no cage, no enclosed space for the prisoners to take their exercise, as there usually was on most convict transports. Perhaps Captain Chalmers had treated his unwilling passengers with too much humanity, he thought wryly, and thus invited them to betray his trust.

The girl in the gingham dress observed his approach calmly. She held her ground, making no attempt to avoid him, and when he came to a halt in front of her, Brace found himself at a loss for words. Her eyes, he saw, were of a deep blue, in striking contrast to her shining dark hair, and although she did not smile, she displayed no open sign of hostility. Encouraged by this he embarked clumsily on the offer of employment he had decided to make her, outlining its advantages in much the same words as he had used to explain them to the sergeant.

She heard him in silence, her lovely face expressionless. When at last she spoke, her voice was educated, with only a faint, musical lilt to it to remind him of her Irish ancestry.

"You're asking me to keep house for you, to cook and clean?"

"Yes, I—"

"And no doubt to be lady's maid to your wife?" the girl pursued.

"No. That is"—Brace could feel himself reddening—"I am not married. I've only been here for just over a month and my quarters are . . . well, in sore need of a woman's touch."

"And is it the custom here for unmarried officers to employ young convicted females to keep house for them?"

He looked at her unhappily, not certain whether her questions were intended to discomfit him or whether she genuinely sought answers to them, and finally inclined his head. "Yes, it's quite customary. Conditions are primitive. The houses—"

"I have seen the houses," the girl put in flatly. She

leaned back against the taffrail, maintaining the distance between them. "You spoke of public work. Are we required to perform hard labor? Is that the alternative to becoming a maidservant to an officer such as yourself, or, perhaps, a *married* officer?"

The emphasis she had placed on the word "married" left Brace in no doubt that she had seen through his attempt at subterfuge. Unreasonably angered by this and by the thinly veiled disdain with which she was regarding him, he listed the tasks usually allocated to female convicts.

In fact, as he was aware, little or no compulsion was exercised in order to force them to work, but they received no official issues of food or clothing if they did not. For this reason, those who were unable to find a man to provide such necessities for them usually took on some public labor . . . or became prostitutes. There was talk of establishing a tailoring factory at Parramatta, to keep the majority usefully employed and offer an alternative to prostitution, but at present, if they did not act as hut-keepers for convict labor gangs or take domestic employment with officers and superintendents, they either worked on the land or made a precarious living on piecework with their needles.

The Irish girl listened to Brace's brusque explanation of the possibilities open to her with growing anger and a sense of outrage. When he came to the end of his recital, she said in a tone of stinging contempt, "Then I shall work on the land. I would as soon herd hogs as keep house for an English redcoat. . . . All of us would!"

"Then I shall wait until you change your mind," Brace retorted, as angry as she. "Which will not take long, I'll warrant! What is your name?" When she hesitated, he added blusteringly, "I can find out easily enough from the master."

The girl shrugged. "Then I will save you that trouble, Lieutenant. I am Frances O'Riordan and—"

Brace drew in his breath sharply, remembering the name. "O'Riordan? Oh, good God, you must be—"

"Yes," the girl acknowledged bitterly. "Conal O'Riordan, the man they hanged from the yardarm of this ship, was my brother, God rest his soul."

Charles Brace eyed her with furrowed brows, feeling the hot color come flooding into his cheeks. Then he bowed to her and, turning abruptly on his heel, went to rejoin Foveaux and the master, who were now standing by the midships hatchway engaged in what sounded like an altercation.

When he had gone, Frances O'Riordan returned to lean over the taffrail, staring with unseeing eyes at the blue vista of the harbor and the distant northern shoreline astern of the ship.

Poor Conal, she thought, with infinite sadness, with his hopes and his dreams and his brave, rebellious spirit. What a waste of talent and promise his death had been! She recalled with a shudder the cruel circumstances surrounding his death, which, try as she might, she could not erase from her memory.

The ship had been alone, out of sight of land in a gray waste of storm-wracked water, eight days out from Rio de Janeiro, when they had been ordered on deck to witness punishment. The twenty women convicts had been lined up in a hollow square, separated from the men by soldiers with bayonets fixed to their muskets. Until the moment when they brought her brother from the orlop, with his hands pinioned behind his back and a rope halter about his neck, Frances had not known that he had been condemned or even that he had been found guilty of the charge of attempted mutiny.

There had been rumors, of course—the ship had been alive with whispers—but throughout the voyage the women had been kept apart from the male prisoners and permitted no contact with them. They had not been badly treated, she had to concede that—Captain Chalmers had fed them well and allowed them adequate time for exercising on deck, and their accommodation, despite the fact that it was in the bowels of the ship, had been clean and relatively dry. The health of both ship's company and prisoners had been excellent and the discipline, if rigorous, had not been harsh. She had caught glimpses of Conal and his comrades at different times, through the hatchways and occasionally on deck, and had known that he was fit and well. And there had been messages, once even a smuggled note passed to her by a sympathetic Irish seaman, which had contained a warning that an escape was being planned. But she had not been aware—none of the women had—that the escape would entail murdering the *Boddingtons*' officers.

It seemed that Conal had confessed to having conceived such a plan and to have been the moving spirit behind the mutiny attempt, which, had it succeeded, would have resulted in the seizure of the ship and the death of Captain Chalmers and probably a score of others. Even now she found this impossible to believe, for it was out of character. Conal was—*had been*—only two and twenty. He had never taken a life, never wanted to, and even after joining the secret United Irishmen's organization, he had never engaged in lawlessness or violence. True, he had helped to obtain arms—a few pistols and pikes for the Irishmen, which he had hidden in their house until they should be required. But he was studying for a law degree and, a passionate patriot, had hoped to right Ireland's wrongs through the law.

And there were wrongs to be righted, God knew, wrongs done over the centuries to Irish Catholics, with the peasants driven from their land to make room for Protestant English settlers, and the Catholic upper classes excluded from participation in the Parliament by which they were ruled and taxed, and from administering justice or holding commissions in the army.

The American colonists had set an example; they had won freedom from oppression by rebelling against the king and his redcoats—they had achieved their independence by force of arms, the arms borne and the battles fought by poor farmers and peasant exiles, like those who formed the mass of the United Irishmen. And then, four years ago, the Revolution in France had demonstrated, still more tellingly, that tyranny and injustice could be ended by resolute men and women dedicated to the ideals of liberty, equality, and freedom. . . . Frances O'Riordan expelled her breath in a long drawn sigh.

For these ideals she had been deported from the land she loved and Conal, poor young Conal, had suffered an ignominious death. She closed her eyes, seeking vainly to shut out the scene that had been enacted on the deck of this ship, only a dozen yards from where she was standing now. Weeping, she heard again the voice of the naval agent

reading from the Articles of War before announcing the
sentence, and then the master's, gruff and tinged with a
restrained bitterness, warning them that there was a price
to be paid for mutiny and rebellion.

"I have used you well," he had told them. "Unlike the
masters of some convict transports I did not withhold your
rations from you in order to profit myself by selling them
in New South Wales. You have had bedding and blankets, clean quarters—until now you have not been fettered,
you have been permitted to exercise on my decks. And you
have repaid me with treachery! For that I am compelled to
make an example of your leader, Conal O'Riordan, who
stands condemned by his own admission of guilt. And I tell
you, here and now, if there should be a repetition of your
foul treachery, you will *all* hang, as he is about to!"

There had been no priest to hear poor Conal's confession, Frances recollected; no priest to give him absolution.
One of the surgeons, Dr. Kent, had attended him and offered
a prayer on his behalf, but that was all. The boatswain had
adjusted the noose about his neck, and a seaman balanced
on the main foreyard had let down a yard rope. She had
wanted to shut her eyes then, Frances remembered dully,
but she had not been able to, lest Conal feel himself deserted. So she had gone on watching through a mist of
tears, praying in a strangled whisper as the men detailed
for the awful task took up the hauling end of the yard
rope—redcoats, under the command of their sergeant.

The boatswain had tried to place a hood over Conal's
head, but he had waved it away, and standing there, waiting for death, he had defied them to do their worst.

"God bless you," he had said. "And God bless Ireland,
my brothers! To live or die, to rise or fall—stand together,
stand together! Oh, for the living—*by* the dead, stand together, true together. . . ."

But they had allowed him to say no more. The master
had raised his hand, and the soldiers had hauled on their
rope, jerking the noose tight, choking the breath from his
thin young body. Poor Conal, swinging from the yardarm
high above the deck, had not heard them singing the song
which the United Irish had adopted as their own.

It rang and echoed in Frances's ears now, defiantly rekindling her flagging courage.

" 'Tis the green—oh, the green is the color of the true!
'Tis the color of our martyred dead—our own immortal
green! Up for the green, boys, and up for the green. . . ."

The voices sounded louder and, opening her eyes, she
saw that a dozen or so of the men, John Place—a Protestant from Tyrone—among them, were being brought up on
deck, all of them heavily chained. The soldiers' muskets
prodded them, the sergeant shouted for silence, but the
singing went on as the straggling line was herded toward
the entry port and from there into the waiting boat.

They may say they have power 'tis vain to oppose—
'tis better to obey and live than surely die as foes. . . .
But we trust in God above us, and we dearly love the
green. . . . Oh to die is far better than be cursed as
we have been!

The boat, heavily laden and low in the water, put off for
the shore, with the two young officers who had visited the
women seated in the stern. But even their brusque commands and threats of punishment to come could not silence
the singing—it went on, the fettered men roaring out the
chorus.

"And we've hearts—oh, we've hearts, boys, full true
enough, I ween . . . to rescue and to raise again our own
immortal green!"

Frances O'Riordan bit back her tears and, running to the
starboard rail, waved them farewell.

CHAPTER VI

Justin's second birthday fell on the first day of the year 1794, and for Jenny Taggart it was the most heartbreaking day she could remember since her exile had begun.

The wheat crop—which she had toiled so obstinately to sow in the land bordering the creek—had failed, its final ruin brought about by an unseasonable thunderstorm and a week of torrential rain at the end of October. Her harvesting had been delayed because the young ne'er-do-well assigned to her in Watt Sparrow's place had run off and taken to the woods, and the storm-battered sheaves had yielded barely enough to pay for the labor she had been compelled to employ to cut and thresh them. The maize and root crops had done better but . . . Looking down at Justin's sleeping face as the day drew to its close, Jenny knew that she was facing defeat.

Because the government store at Parramatta was full, she had had to sell stock in order to meet the charges for transporting her produce by boat to Sydney. The old hoy, Sydney-built and known, almost affectionately now, as the *Lump*, had failed the Parramatta settlers at last. Her bottom boards, eaten away by barnacles and river worms, had to be replaced, and she had been taken out of service, leaving the enterprising boat owners who plied for public hire to demand what prices they pleased. And their prices were high. Most of them—like the laboring convicts—insisting that payment be made in spirits. . . . Jenny bit back a tired sigh. Even the cheapest American rum cost more than twenty shillings a gallon and Jamaica half as much again. The officers of the New South Wales Corps had formed a syndicate to purchase all the available supplies, and they kept the price high so that they could sell it at a profit, but her wheat had realized only ten shillings a bushel, the maize less than seven shillings.

She was in debt; worse still, she had not been able to deliver her full quota of grain, as the law of the colony required, in exchange for the rations she drew. Even if she were assigned another laborer in place of the absent Rick

Lowe, she would, she knew, be hard put to it to feed him.

She studied her work-worn hands, with their torn nails and the scars left by cuts and blisters, and then glanced again, pityingly, at Justin's thin little face. He was a good child; he could be safely left to his own devices while she worked, he seldom cried or complained even if he had to go hungry, and he gave her a wealth of affection that, she thought bitterly, she did little to merit. But it was no life for him; she had no time to teach or train him, no energy left at the end of the day, even to play with him.

He missed Watt, of course—as, indeed, she did herself. Watt had somehow always managed to make time for Justin, to romp with him, to answer his childish questions and quell his fears. But poor old Watt, after being held in Sydney's prison since his trial, was due to leave for Norfolk Island in the newly built colonial schooner *Francis* in four or five days' time.

She had been permitted one visit to him, on Christmas Eve, and she had taken Justin with her after attending Divine Service, for the first time, in the church the Reverend Johnson had built on the east side of Sydney Cove. On her knees before the simple altar, she had prayed that by some miracle Watt's sentence might be remitted so that he could return to them, but it was New Year's Day and there had been no word of a change of heart on the acting governor's part. Already the *Francis*, just back from a testing voyage to New Zealand's Dusky Bay, was being loaded for her second, to Lieutenant Governor King's distant domain. Captain King was a good man and a fair one, it was said, but—tears came, to ache in Jenny's throat—poor frail old Watt would be put to hard labor on the island, from which there was no escape.

Justin stirred uneasily in his sleep, and choking back her tears Jenny bent to press a kiss onto his cheek. "Sleep, my baby," she whispered. "Nothing shall harm you. Your mam's here, little love."

The child snuggled down and settled once more into sleep, and half-ashamed of her moment of weakness, Jenny pulled the old rocking chair up to the open doorway and seated herself in it, taking long, deep breaths of the outside air. The day had been hot and humid, but now a cool southerly breeze had come up, rustling the feathery leaves of the big old gum tree growing at the front of the cabin, and the air was sweet with the scent of the orange trees that, at long last, had taken root in the garden.

In the outbuilding that Dr. Arndell's men had built for the purpose, she could hear old Ben Reilly contentedly singing himself to sleep. The poor old fellow, with his crutch and the rough peg-leg they had made for him in the hospital, was unable to work, of course, but he was an unexpectedly warmhearted companion, particularly to Justin, and since his arrival a week ago had proved more of an asset than the burden she had feared he might be.

She had agreed to house him out of pity for his frail health and gratitude to Dr. Arndell, who had begged it as a favor, but if she had to sell the farm, it would mean that Ben would again be homeless. There was Lieutenant Macarthur's offer, of course, to exchange her creek land for the same acreage of his, to the east . . . She frowned. In the circumstances, although hardly a generous exchange, it would enable her to continue to go on living in the cabin. She could apply all her efforts to breeding stock—pigs and goats did well throughout the colony, poultry too, and she had her mare and foal.

She would accept Mr. Macarthur's offer, she decided, grow kaffir corn on the new land and let him take the creek, the irrigation ditches, and the land that had shown her so meager a return. Watt had not wanted her to give up the creek, but Watt was no longer here, and since the alternative was either to abandon her grant altogether or sell off most of the livestock and start the uphill battle again from scratch, the choice was virtually made for her.

Tomorrow, she told herself, her spirits lifting, *tomorrow I will go into the barracks and tell Mr. Macarthur that I will make the exchange. He shall have his way.* Perhaps, she thought, hugging the idea to her, it might even be possible to persuade him to let her have two or three gallons of rum as part of the bargain, so that she could pay off her outstanding debts.

From the outhouse old Ben's voice rose to a faltering high note. He must have been drinking, Jenny decided. Probably he had consumed his entire week's spirit ration— granted him, as a special concession, from the hospital store.

She listened, puzzled by the slurred, high-pitched words. "We'll have the lash an' chain but at home they'll make it plain—we'll be a nation once again. . . ." Ben was a Liverpool Irishman who, on his own admission, had never set foot in Ireland, but he was singing an Irish rebel song, unless she was very much mistaken. There were quite a number of Irish seditionists in the colony now—the *Boddingtons* had brought one hundred fifty the previous August, the *Sugar Cane* about the same number a month later. Scarcely had both ships left the cove than there had been a spate of escapes by the prisoners they had landed.

Some had robbed settlers' farms and gardens, two were said to have been speared to death by the Indians, and one party of about a dozen had stolen a rowing boat and vanished. Jenny got to her feet, suddenly alarmed.

Suppose old Ben had misguidedly given shelter to some Irishmen on the run or had been coerced into hiding them? They were desperate people, everyone said, who had attempted mutiny during the voyage to New South Wales and who seemed bent on escape, no matter what the cost to themselves or others. All the settlers on isolated farms lived in constant fear of raids and robberies, for those who ran always stole provisions to take with them, and if their demands were refused, the Irish in particular were known to resort to violence.

The consequences of the last raid she had suffered still fresh in her mind, Jenny glanced over at the sleeping Justin and then, closing the door of the cabin behind her, made cautiously for Ben's. Officialdom had placed blame for the fire that destroyed her buildings squarely on the Indians, even naming the notorious Pimelwi and his tribe as the likely culprits but . . . Reaching the side of the outhouse, she hesitated. Ben was talking now, not singing, and she caught a word or two.

"Why sure, she'll be safe here. The missus'll not turn her in. But you'd best be off, the pair o' ye, before I tell her. She'll not want you here."

"We're away," a second voice said. "But we'll be back to slit your throat if ony harm comes to her, so we will." There were some faint thuds, a muffled curse, followed by the pad of feet and then silence.

Jenny waited in the shadows for a moment, her heart

pounding, before opening the door, and the old man greeted her with a hoarse cry of relief. There was a girl lying on the rush-covered floor, and in the dim light of the single whale-oil lamp, she appeared to be lifeless. Her face had a deathlike pallor, and her clothing was torn and covered with dark stains that looked like blood. Jenny knelt beside her, and Ben said uneasily, "I had to take her in, missus. Sure an' I couldn't leave the poor young soul to die out there in the woods, could I now?"

"No, of course you couldn't, Ben." There would be time enough to find out how the girl had come to be here and who had brought her. Now the only thing that mattered was to restore her to consciousness, get a hot drink between the cracked and bloodless lips. Or better still, a few sips of Ben's spirit ration if he had left any. Jenny covered the girl with a torn blanket from the old man's bedding, and rolling up her shawl, slipped it beneath the limp, dark head. She stirred and murmured something unintelligible, opened her eyes for a moment and then closed them again.

"I've a kettle on the hob," Ben volunteered. "An' a drop o' rum." He hobbled about the shadowed room on his crutch, clumsy but purposeful and not quite sober. But he brought the hot drink in his own chipped mug, and as she carefully spooned a few drops of the liquid into the girl's mouth, he mumbled apologetically, "I amn't a rebel, missus. The first I ever heard o' ony rebellion in Ireland was out here an' that's God's truth."

"You were singing a rebel song, weren't you?" Jenny accused without looking up from her task.

"And wasn't I tryin' to warn you?" the old man countered. "If you'd come blunderin' in, wid them boys here, why there might have bin trouble."

"They've gone, have they not?"

"Sure, they made off before you came. They said they'd bin in the woods for close on two months, but then this poor young soul took ill, so they had to find shelter for her. They promised that if we'd care for her, they would steal nothing an'—"

"Did they keep their promise, Ben?" Jenny put in anxiously. Heaven knew, they had little enough worth stealing. "*Did* they?"

The girl answered her in a soft, cultured voice with only

a hint of an Irish accent. "We don't break promises, ma'am." She said it with pride, and Jenny instinctively warmed to her.

Within an hour, revived by the rum, the fugitive was able to walk to the cabin, leaning heavily on Jenny's arm. There, crouching before the cooking fire on which a pot of gruel was warming, she gave a brief account of her wanderings. It was an oft-repeated tale, and Jenny heard it without surprise. Assigned to one of the road gangs after being moved from Sydney to Parramatta, the men of the party had rebelled against the overseers' harshness and the humiliation to which they had been subjected, and had decided to make their escape.

"We were told," the girl said wryly, "that beyond the mountains—the ones they call the Blue Mountains—we should find free settlements and friendly natives. And we believed it. Nobody told us that those mountains cannot be crossed or that the tribes we should meet with on our way would be savages." She sighed, her pale, ravaged face set in despairing lines. "Two young men were murdered by Indians, and the rest of us came perilously close to starvation. We lived on roots and berries and some fish we caught in a river. Then a party of officers from Sydney, with boats and Indian guides, almost caught us. They stumbled on our hiding place, and we had to take flight, leaving our boat for them to find and take back with them. I think that they, too, were seeking a way across the Blue Mountains, but neither we nor they were able to find one."

She talked on, dreamily, of the vain but tenacious efforts they had made, of the fast-flowing river they had endeavored to follow, only to find the way blocked by a vast chasm, down one side of which the river dropped in a spectacular waterfall.

"It is beautiful up there among the foothills. The distant peaks really do seem to be colored a rich blue, and the sunsets are—oh, they are like none I have ever seen before. It is as if the whole sky has taken fire! And the air is clean and fresh, the nights quite cool but never chilling. We could have stayed, we could have learned to live there if it had not been for the Indians, but they gave us no peace." Jenny brought her a bowl of steaming gruel, and the girl thanked her, tears in her eyes. "You are kind and this is like nectar. I—I suppose I was suffering from starvation, that was why I became ill. I—I am grateful for your kindness, yours and the old man's. Poor soul, he has lost a leg, has he not? Is he—is he your father?"

Jenny shook her head. She answered the Irish girl's questions concerning Ben, her status, and finally Justin freely and without hesitation.

"My name is Jenny Taggart," she added. "What is yours?"

"Frances O'Riordan. Tell me—have you been out here long?"

"Since the beginning. I came in the first fleet, under Governor Phillip's command."

"And you have borne it, all these years? Have you never tried to escape?"

Jenny repeated her headshake, and the other girl stared at her in unconcealed astonishment. But it was not the moment to attempt to explain or to speak of the hopes she had once cherished. She said flatly, "I am a free settler, Miss O'Riordan. My sentence was remitted—I have this cabin and a grant of land. It is not easy to—to make ends meet, and I have lost the good man who worked the land with me. Poor soul, they are to send him to Norfolk Island this week."

"The—the child's father?" Frances O'Riordan suggested, glancing across at Justin.

"No—his grandfather." The half-truth would suffice, Jenny decided. In any event, Watt had been Justin's grandfather in all but blood. She rose, holding out her hand for the now empty soup bowl. "You need rest. I will make up a bed for you and you must try to sleep. We can talk again in the morning."

The Irish girl caught at her arm. "You'll not hand me over to the soldiers, will you? You'll permit me to stay here in hiding until I am recovered?"

"Don't worry, Miss O'Riordan," Jenny assured her pityingly. "You are safe here."

"God's blessing on you! They will come for me in a few days—my friends will come. They—"

"To take you back with them, to starve in the woods? Is that what you want?"

Frances O'Riordan spread her hands in a resigned ges-

ture. "No, it is not what I want. But it is preferable to
returning to the place to which they sent me when we
landed. I was put into a hut with foulmouthed, drunken
women—whores and worse—who never gave me a moment's peace or a civil word. I—I can't go back to them. In
the woods I am with my own people, who treat me with
respect and kindness—I have known most of them since
childhood. They were my brother's friends."

"*Were?* Is your brother not with you?"

The girl shook her head. She said bitterly, "My brother
was hanged on board the ship that brought us here. Mutiny
was the charge, but he and the others were only seeking to
regain their freedom. It was claimed that they had planned
to kill the ship's officers and the soldiers, but that wasn't
true. Conal would not have killed anyone—it was not in
his nature, but they—they hanged him just the same. We're
not criminals, Mistress Taggart, none of us are. Unless it is
a crime in the eyes of God to rebel against oppression, we
are guilty of nothing."

Jenny eyed her sadly but wisely offered no comment, and
after a while the unhappy girl lay down on the rough bed
she had prepared and slept the exhausted sleep of one who
had been tried beyond her endurance. She did not waken
until almost midday, when Jenny, who had been up since
dawn caring for her livestock, came back to the cabin to
cook the usual scanty meal. But during the next few days
Frances O'Riordan began to recover her health and
strength; her face lost its alarming pallor, she bathed and
washed her clothes in the creek, braided her now shining
dark hair, and was revealed for the refined and lovely
young woman she was. She was an expert needlewoman,
and after mending her own torn garments turned her attention, unasked, to Jenny's poor wardrobe and then to Justin's, fashioning dresses and a pinafore for the little boy out
of any scraps of material on which she could lay her hands.

Justin took to her with childish eagerness. She stayed
perforce in the cabin for most of the daylight hours, and he
stayed with her, fetching and carrying for her and, curled
up at her feet as she plied her needle, listening like one
bewitched to the tales she told him and the songs she sang.

For Jenny it was also an end to loneliness. Since Melia
had left, more than two years ago, she had had no friend of

her own age and sex with whom to share the things dear to the hearts of all women, and she found a swiftly growing pleasure in the Irish girl's company.

They talked long into the night; Frances was well educated and well informed, and although much of her conversation was of Ireland and the banned organization to which she and her brother had belonged, she spoke also of the revolution in France and of the war that was ravaging the whole of Europe, in which England was now involved.

"The American colonists fought for their freedom and were victorious, Jenny, so why should we not? Ireland is treated as an English colony, garrisoned by English troops and Hessian hirelings, her people persecuted for their religious beliefs. The French showed us the way—Wolfe Tone is certain that they will aid us in our struggle."

"You surely cannot mean that Ireland will take the French side against England if there is a war?" Jenny had exclaimed, shocked to the depths of her being by the implication of Frances's words.

"There is already a war," Frances had told her. "And if the French send troops to help us to gain our freedom, as they did for the Americans during their war—then yes! We shall become their allies. What has poor Ireland to lose save her chains?"

They had argued over this question frequently, although strangely without anger. Frances was wholly committed to her beliefs, harboring no doubts as to their justification. Listening to her as intently as little Justin listened to her songs, Jenny came to understand that what had at first seemed to her to be treason was, in fact, the inevitable consequence of the tyrannical suppression of a proud and patriotic people.

"It is not only the Catholics who have become members of the United Irish movement," Frances said gravely. "The farmers and peasants throughout Ireland have joined us, many of them are Protestants, like Wolfe Tone himself. We want what the American colonists wanted and were ready to die for—independence! We are ready to die for it too, all of us."

Instead, Jenny thought, sick with pity, Frances and her fellow rebels had been condemned to exile, but even here they chose to risk falling to Indian spears or a slow death from starvation in the bush to bowing the knee to their oppressors. Her attempts to persuade the girl to remain with Justin and herself in the comparative safety of the cabin fell on deaf ears—Frances would not hear of it.

"The soldiers would find me sooner or later, Jenny," she insisted. "And that would mean trouble for you—you would be accused of harboring a fugitive."

"They do not worry too much about the women who escape," Jenny argued. "And not a great deal, now, about the men. Unless"—she thought of Watt and sighed—"unless they committed some crime and ran to avoid punishment for it. But the soldiers seldom search for them because they know that sooner or later hunger and privation force them to give themselves up. Then it's a few hours in the stocks, that's all. I should not mind being sent to the stocks for harboring you if it would prevail upon you to stay here."

"But I should not be allowed to stay with you—they would send me back to that filthy hut, with those horrible, depraved women," Frances objected. "Or force me to act as—as housekeeper to an officer. I received such an offer, even before we landed, and I refused it."

Jenny studied her thoughtfully. An idea was born, and she said cautiously, "I believe I could have you assigned to *me*, Frances. I'm not sure, but there might be a way."

It was possible, she told herself, that Lieutenant Macarthur might be disposed to view such a request favorably if she gave up her claim to the creek land. The majority of women convicts were not compelled to undertake any form of public labor, so no one worried very much if they escaped. In the past, when male escapers had been flogged, the women had received little more than a reprimand, and Frances's disappearance had in all probability not even been reported. If it had not, then even the threat of the stocks receded. Jenny's mouth tightened into a firm, resolute line.

Had she not made up her mind to yield the creek land to Mr. Macarthur before Frances had arrived at her door? Indeed, had she not planned to go to the barracks in search of him, in the hope that, if she accepted his offer of an exchange, he would assign her the labor she needed and perhaps also provide her with the means of paying off her debts to the casual workers she had been forced to employ?

She looked up and, meeting the other girl's questioning gaze, smiled in reassurance. "Frances, there *is* a way and without any risk to either of us. I need help here if you would like to stay."

"I have never worked on the land, Jenny. Besides, if you had me assigned to you, would that not mean that you would have to forgo the services of a male convict?"

"It is possible," Jenny admitted honestly. "But I think I could find a way—I am entitled to two convict workers on this land. I have none at present. Let me try, Frances. . . . Trust me to try!"

"I trust you," Frances said. "Of course I trust you but I—I gave my word to the others. I cannot desert them, can I?"

"But you are a woman! How many women went on the run with them?"

"Two," Frances conceded. "But we were separated, you see, when we reached Parramatta, so we couldn't keep in touch. And some of our girls took service on farms."

"Then why don't you?" Jenny persisted.

"You are asking me from the goodness of your heart, Jenny! I can be of so little help to you. I wasn't brought up in the country. I lived in a little town in County Wexford, and my father was a doctor there until his death. Besides, I"—Frances hesitated, her cheeks faintly tinged with embarrassed color—"I cannot take charity, even from you."

"It would not be charity," Jenny returned crisply. "I need you here, truly."

Frances's resistance seemed to be crumbling and finally, having won her agreement to this, at least, Jenny set off after their midday meal for Parramatta, intending to put her offer and her request for assigned labor to Lieutenant Macarthur.

It proved a wasted journey. At the barracks, Ensign Cummings informed her that his company commander had gone to Sydney to sit on a court-martial and would probably not return for two or three days.

"You may leave a message for Mr. Macarthur with me, if you wish, Miss Taggart," he added, his tone loftily condescending. "Or put your petition in writing if you are able to write, and I will see that he receives it."

"I am able to write, Mr. Cummings," Jenny told him. "If you will kindly provide me with pen and paper, I will do so."

The young officer eyed her with a certain disbelief, but he produced a quill and a sheet of paper and motioned her to pull up a chair so that she might compose what he persisted in referring to as her petition. He had recently taken a grant of land in the Parramatta area, she knew, and as he watched her neat and fluid penmanship, his manner warmed to her, and he began to question her concerning crop yields and other aspects of local husbandry.

Jenny answered him with confidence, while continuing to write, and when she put down the quill and folded her completed note, he observed with grudging admiration, "You appear to be well versed in the practice of agriculture, Miss Taggart."

"I have had nearly six years' experience, sir." She made to bring their interview to an end by rising, but he waved her to resume her seat.

"Then you came out with Governor Phillip?" he suggested.

"Yes, I did. We started to cultivate a vegetable garden in Farm Cove not long after we landed. But—"

"Were you one of the 'Garden Women'?" Cummings put in. There was no trace of condescension in his manner now; he seemed genuinely interested, and on receiving her assent to his question he smiled at her warmly. "Your fame has spread. The superintendent, Thomas Clarke, was telling me about that garden of yours only the other day. He claimed that you had worked a miracle, and he knows what he's talking about if anyone does. He also said that you were the first, in this area, to dig irrigation ditches to keep your wheat watered during a drought. You have a creek on your land, have you not?"

The creek she was about to abandon to Lieutenant Macarthur, Jenny thought, conscious of deep misgivings. She was tempted to ask for the return of her petition, to tear it up and somehow struggle on but . . . what was the use? Had she not worked her heart out, had she not tried and failed? It was too late now to change her mind and, besides, there was Frances O'Riordan. . . .

Sensing her sudden indecision, Ensign Cummings looked

from her face to the folded paper in his hand and said unexpectedly, "You lost your laborers, didn't you? One was killed by Indians, and the other's been deported to Norfolk Island . . . an old fellow named Sparrow, sentenced to three years?"

"Yes," Jenny confirmed. "But how did you—"

"I sat in trial on him," Cummings confessed. "He pleaded guilty to possession of a firearm and to firing it when I went to arrest him. There was another charge—he was supposed to have shot one of our men—but that was dropped, I never quite understood why." He was frowning, evidently perplexed, and Jenny, anxious that he should not probe deeper, again got to her feet. He rose with her, still holding her note in his left hand. "And you reported that another man assigned to you had run just before you started harvesting?"

"Yes—a man named Lowe. He—"

"Lowe ran before," the ensign said with emphasis. "I wonder why he was assigned to you. He was sentenced to work on a road gang, in fetters, for his last offense." He halted by the door of his small office but did not at once open it. Jenny glanced up at him apprehensively.

"Mr. Cummings, I don't think—"

He ignored the interruption. "So you had no assigned labor for your harvest?" he pursued.

"No. I had to employ men. I—"

He gestured to the paper. As if she had spoken her thoughts aloud, he said sharply, "Are you offering your holding for sale, Miss Taggart? Because if you are, I know a man who would give you a fair price for it. I could mention it to him if you wish and—"

"No," Jenny cried. "No—I'm not selling my land, Mr. Cummings. I—give my—my petition to Mr. Macarthur, if you please, as soon as he returns."

She pulled open the door and thrust past him with a mumbled apology, suddenly—for some inexplicable reason—afraid. He meant well, she knew; he was a pleasant, honest young man, but Mr. Macarthur was in command here—she could not afford to antagonize the all-powerful Mr. Macarthur.

She crossed the barrack square at a breathless run, but Ensign Cummings made no attempt to call her back, and out in the glare of Parramatta's sunbaked main street once more, she slackened her pace and set off on her homeward journey at a sober walk, her thoughts in turmoil.

Doubts and fears came alternately to plague her, and she was no longer sure that the decision she had made had been the right one. It had seemed so, when she had made it—indeed, it had seemed the best and only course to follow, for Frances's sake as well as her own and Justin's, but now it smacked of cowardice and was an admission of defeat.

Her father would have fought—her father *had* fought to keep his land from the rapacious Lord Braxton's clutches—and yet in the end he had lost not only the land but his life. Surely the lesson to be learned from poor Angus Taggart's fate was clear enough. It was foolish to fight when all the odds were stacked against you, and the laws—framed to protect the weak—were twisted by the strong in order to enhance their power and ensure their profit. Jenny expelled her breath in a sigh of frustration.

Governor Phillip had seen the danger and sought to counter it, but even under his administration the law had all too frequently been flouted and had never been impartial. She trudged on, her plodding feet kicking up the dust in choking clouds, thinking about Frances O'Riordan now and her account of the Irish struggle against oppression. Perhaps if Frances stayed the sacrifice of the creek would not be in vain. It was little enough, in all conscience, when compared with what she and her friends had lost.

When she reached the cabin Frances called out that she had a meal waiting, and Justin, beaming happily, came running to meet her, wearing the first trousers he had ever possessed with conscious pride. They had been conjured up from an old jacket of Watt's but, in the Irish girl's skilled hands, might have come from a master tailor's.

"Oh, Justin!" Strangely moved, Jenny dropped to her knees beside him. "How fine a man you make!"

She hugged him joyfully, but her joy abruptly faded when Frances indicated the two men seated on either side of the hearth—two gaunt-faced young strangers in tattered garments, one with a livid scar running from hairline to jaw, caused, Jenny did not doubt, by a glancing blow from an Indian spear.

"My people have come for me, Jenny," Frances said. Her voice was calm and resolute, but there were tears in her eyes as she added, "I must go with them. I made a vow, you see—all of us did—and I cannot break it."

She left as darkness was starting to fall, accompanied by the two young strangers, who, despite Jenny's urging, politely refused to partake of the evening meal or even to permit her to brew tea for them. The scarred youth carried a sack slung carelessly over his shoulder, and with a smile he assured her that they would all eat well that night.

Jerking his unkempt fair head toward his burden, he said, his tone mocking, "In here is a suckling pig I'd the great good fortune to come across on me way, ma'am. You'll find a wee small leg of the same animal in your stewpot, and 'tis to be hoped you'll find it tasty. You need have no fear that the owner will miss this one, for hasn't he a dozen litters of them running wild? And him a bloody redcoat officer, too!"

It could only have been Lieutenant Macarthur's farm he had robbed, Jenny realized—no one else in the area could lay claim to that number of breeding sows. She stood at the cabin door, watching the little party until they vanished into the gathering darkness.

Then, crossing to the cooking fire, she lifted the lid of the stewpot, sniffed appreciatively at the appetizing aroma arising from it, and sent Justin running to summon old Ben to join them in their unexpected feast.

The following afternoon Timothy Dawson rode out to the farm on his stallion. He had paid one brief formal call, after leaving hospital, to thank her for her prompt action when he had suffered his snakebite, but she had not seen him since. Rumor had it that he had applied for a land grant in the virtually unsettled area between Toongabbe and the Hawkesbury River, while still awaiting the arrival of his livestock from the Cape, and he confirmed this after exchanging greetings.

"The *Sugar Cane* picked up three more mares for me," he said. "But I have to continue to trespass on the kindness of Superintendent Macrae to stable them for me—an arrangement I'm compelled to make because of the present state of affairs in the Hawkesbury settlement."

"You mean Indian raids?" Jenny suggested.

Timothy Dawson inclined his head in glum assent. "Indeed I do, Mistress Taggart. I'm afraid the settlers have made matters worse by embarking on a campaign of brutal retribution. Two settlers have been killed, to my certain knowledge, and at least a dozen Indians. Three of them were young boys, who were vilely tortured by a party of settlers, and of course it led to more raids. I'd finished setting up my buildings, but only ten days ago I came back to discover my stables and stockyards burned to the ground and the men I left to guard them hopelessly drunk." He sighed in angry frustration. "It was all work wasted, Mistress, and that enrages me."

Jenny eyed him appraisingly, liking what she saw. This was a strong, determined young man, she thought, and one who would not easily be deterred by setbacks and disappointments. She found herself envying his determination, as she brewed sweet tea and set a cup beside him, listening with interest when he told her that he had had word that the rest of his stock might be expected to reach the colony within six or seven weeks, on board a storeship, the *William*.

"Which brings me to the reason for my visit," he added and hesitated, reddening a little.

"Please tell me what that is," Jenny invited.

"Well, I—I may have been misinformed, Mistress Taggart, but I heard that you've had a poor harvest and some trouble with your assigned labor."

She met his gaze without flinching. "That is true," she admitted. "And because I could not deliver my full quota of grain to the public store, Mr. Dawson, I am liable to be struck off the provision list. That means I can no longer draw rations either for myself or any labor I employ and—"

"And you have no assigned labor at present, is that not so?" her visitor put in. He smiled suddenly, the smile sympathetic and friendly. "Forgive my—my directness, but I was given to understand that this was through no fault of your own?"

Jenny found herself answering his smile, her own a trifle wry. She explained the happenings that had led to Watt

Sparrow's harsh sentence and old Reuben White's death and saw his expression harden.

"It occurred to me that we might be able to assist each other, Mistress Taggart. That is—" Again he hesitated, as if endeavoring to choose his words so as neither to hurt nor affront her, and she guessed, from the fact that he appeared to be so well informed of her circumstances, that Ensign Cummings must have spoken to him. Had he not mentioned a man who might be willing to offer her a fair price for her land? She drew in her breath in swift alarm. There was the letter she had written to Lieutenant Macarthur, her petition, as young Ensign Cummings had called it.

"Mr. Dawson," she began. "I don't think—"

He held up a big work-stained hand. "Hear me out, I beg you. I have had a good offer, a very good offer indeed, for one of my mares. Together with the money I brought with me I could pay you a good price for your land. As a free settler I am entitled to rations for a year, seed, tools, and ten laboring convicts. I would, in addition, pay you a fair wage to manage the land for me and take charge of my breeding mares . . . and I would count myself fortunate indeed, believe me, to have the services of one of your experience."

It was the answer to her prayers, Jenny thought; the answer to her most pressing problems. As a free settler Timothy Dawson would not only have the entitlements he had mentioned, he would enjoy, as of right, a status she could never attain. Mr. Macarthur could not subject a free settler to the pressure that so easily could be exerted against an emancipated convict. Besides, if she had money she could surely invest in breeding stock on her own account, perhaps, later on, even buy more land and . . . He was talking on, and she forced herself to listen. She would remain in possession of the cabin, he asserted. That would enable him to reside on his new Hawkesbury grant, instead of being compelled to leave unreliable convicts to guard it against the depredations of the Indians.

But there was still her letter to Lieutenant Macarthur. Jenny bit her lip, feeling it tremble. She started to tell him about the letter and its admission of defeat, her words tumbling out in a bitter spate, revealing more than she had intended of the persecution she had suffered, her fears and her despair.

Timothy Dawson cut her short. "Mistress Taggart, I can recover that letter before the—the officer to whom it is addressed returns from Sydney. That is, if it is your wish that I should do so. The gentleman in question need never know of its existence."

"You mean that Mr. Cummings will not tell him of it?" Jenny stared at him in wide-eyed disbelief. "Surely he—I mean—"

He laid a hand on her arm. "Mr. Cummings has become a friend to me—a good friend. I've helped him with his stock. He can be relied upon. Indeed he—he and Dr. Arndell—were the ones who informed me of your difficulties. Please, Mistress Taggart, permit me to recover your petition. I can go back to Parramatta at once, and it will be in my hands within an hour. Once that is done we can discuss our own arrangements at length and come to an agreement that, I am confident, will be greatly to our mutual advantage."

Jenny's heart leapt. She gave her assent eagerly, and he got to his feet at once.

"You may rely on my discretion," he promised gravely. "And if you will repose your trust in me, I will not fail you. After all, I owe you my life, do I not? There is the matter of my eventual marriage, but that is very much in the future and need not concern either of us now. I mention it"—once again, his tanned cheeks betrayed his embarrassment—"I mention it only so that you should not misunderstand my—my motives in making you the offer I have. I'm an honest farmer, Mistress Taggart, and not one given to promiscuity." He held out his hand, and Jenny shook it warmly.

Perhaps she could trust this man, she thought; perhaps, after all, she could find, under his protection, the life she sought for herself and Justin. If he was what he seemed, then the future augured well.

Standing by the cabin door, watching him ride away, she thought briefly of Frances O'Riordan. Then Justin came running, damp from a swim in the creek, with old Ben hobbling painfully behind him, and she went to meet them, a new lightness in her step.

CHAPTER VII

Looking down at the face of the woman lying in the hammock beside him, Andrew Hawley made a wry grimace. She was, he realized now, older than he had supposed when he had picked her from among the chattering throng of women who had come on board the *Nymphe* a few hours after she had dropped anchor in Falmouth Bay.

This was the last night the frigate would spend in the peace of the Cornish anchorage. The press gangs had done their work on shore; Falmouth was their captain's home, and he had known where to send them. Sixty-two unhappy tin miners, farm laborers, and grocer's boys had been seized and forcibly rowed out across the bay during the hours of darkness, their pleas for mercy unheeded. Together with a handful of volunteers and some twenty convicted felons, condemned by the court at Truro—who had chosen enlistment in preference to deportation or a prison sentence—they would complete the *Nymphe*'s crew, enabling her to put to sea.

It would matter little that they were untrained landsmen and that they lacked any desire to serve their country at sea—they made up the required number without which the ship could not sail. They would be attested to the king's service, supplied with clothing from the purser's slop chest, have their names entered on the watch bill, and then receive, at the hands of the petty officers and prime seamen, their harsh training in the ways of a ship of war.

And they would be fortunate if they ever again saw their womenfolk and children. They would not, in any event, see them until war with France was over. Andrew Hawley glanced once more at the woman sleeping at his side and shrugged his bare shoulders, thankful that he was unmarried and possessed no children from whom it would break his heart to part. There were always women like this to answer a man's need when the ship made port . . . women whose faces faded swiftly from memory and whose going caused no pain.

He put out a hand to rouse her, and she responded with

sleepy willingness, letting him take his pleasure of her with only the habitual endearments and the practiced skill of her profession. Her lips were dry against his, her breath sour from the rum she had swilled down so eagerly the previous evening, and when he had done, he put her from him and swung his legs onto the deck. The woman lapsed into sleep again, seemingly quite indifferent to his departure from her side, if she were even aware of it.

Accustomed by now to her kind, Andrew felt no resentment. She had given him what he had paid her for, had not cheated or tried to steal from him; but he wanted no more of her and, indeed, would be more relieved than regretful when the order came for the women to be sent ashore and the long mess deck emptied of its untidy, shrill-voiced cargo. His life—and his views on women, come to that—might have been very different, he reflected wryly, had he been permitted to continue the voyage to New South Wales and to take little Jenny Taggart to wife. But Governor Phillip had decided otherwise, and it was no use regretting the past since what was done could not be undone.

He was not unhappy, far from it. The life at sea suited him, and by any standards he had made a good career in the marines—the pipe-clayed stripes on his arm were proof of that. He smiled. His present posting was one after his own heart—Captain Edward Pellew, a man under whose command it was an honor to serve—and his memories of the *Pandora* and her vindictive and brutal captain were already beginning to fade.

From the deck above, the clanking of the pumps and the pad of bare feet on the planking told him that the duty watch had started the daily routine of holystoning and swabbing the decks. Andrew pulled on his carefully folded white breeches, thrust his feet into his boots, and buttoned his knee-length black gaiters with the speed and dexterity of long practice. Before donning stock and scarlet jacket, he ran his hand over cheeks and chin—he had shaved closely the previous evening, and satisfied that no unsightly stubble had yet had time to grow, he fastened the leather stock about his neck.

No light penetrated the closed gunports at his back, but he sensed that it wanted only a scant half-hour to dawn, and by the flickering light of the lanterns hanging at intervals from the deck beams, he saw that others were also starting to stir. The marines, of whom there were thirty in the *Nymphe*'s complement, messed and slung their hammocks separately from her seamen. Their mess deck was situated between the officers' quarters in the afterpart of the ship and the fo'c'sle, which was the domain of the seamen. This was intended—Andrew again smiled to himself—as a precaution against an outbreak of mutiny by any poor devils of pressed men, revolting against the poor food and the navy's savage discipline.

He reached for his jacket. By virtue of his rank, as a senior noncommissioned officer, he was entitled to a small, boxlike cabin on the orlop deck, beside those occupied by the gunner and the carpenter. A cabin was considered a privilege, but Andrew had hated its confinement and lack of air and had willingly relinquished his claim to the purser's clerk, a sour old man of uncertain temper, who had been displaced from his own by the captain's brother, Commander Israel Pellew. The younger Pellew had joined the ship as a volunteer and . . . The woman turned, waking from her sleep, to look about her in bleary-eyed bewilderment, and Andrew said curtly, "Bide where you are— I'm going on deck. You'll hear the pipe when it's time for you to leave."

She settled down again, drawing the blanket over her head. Andrew strapped on his pipe-clayed crossbelts and, cockaded hat tucked beneath his arm, made for the hatchway, his booted feet thudding on the deck planking as he stepped briskly between the rows of hammocks. Three bells struck as he gained the open deck. The marine sentry posted at the fore hatchway stiffened at his approach, but Andrew spared him only a cursory glance and, skirting the slowly moving line of kneeling seamen at work with sand and holystone "prayer books" on the spotless deck, he descended to the heads.

Dawn was gray in the eastern sky by the time he retraced his steps to the fo'c'sle. The swabbers had gone; only a dozen or so of the recently pressed men stood in a shivering, apprehensive group, being lectured on the various duties they would be expected to perform by a big, rawboned boatswain's mate who punctuated his remarks with a wealth of profanity. All had been hosed down with cold seawater from the pump and had had their heads drastically cropped, and now, clad in their newly issued canvas trousers and striped jerseys, their feet bare, they looked the picture of wretchedness.

Meeting Andrew's gaze the boatswain's mate raised his eyes to heaven and observed blasphemously, in a strong Irish accent, "Jaysus Christ, Sergeant, will ye look at dis miserable bunch o' dimwitted scarecrows? How am I to make sailors out o' de loikes o' thim, can ye tell me t'at? Sure an' de first puff o' wind's liable to blow the lot o' them over de side, so it is!"

Yet, for all the big Irishman's professed despair, even these men would be made into seamen of a sort, Andrew reflected grimly—the navy's brutal methods seldom failed completely. Half-starved, permitted no shore leave lest they desert, their meager pay always long in arrears and with the petty officers' rope's-end starters vying with the cat to mark their hides, some of them would even, in the fullness of time, become prime seamen. He grinned and made the bantering rejoinder that was expected of him and strode on, conscious of the eyes of the whole group on his retreating back.

From the lee side of the deck, he had a clear view of the land and the town, clustered about the harbor and spreading out along the semicircle of the bay. He watched two boats put off from among the fishing vessels and head out toward the ship—local boats, sent to take off the women, he decided. The captain, Pellew, had spent the night ashore, presumably with his family—he would want the women gone before he returned, no doubt.

The officer of the watch had seen the approaching boats too; he sang out an order and the bo'sun's mates of the watch put their calls to their lips.

"Lash up and stow! Show a leg there!"

One of them went below to repeat the pipe throughout the lower deck, and soon a bedraggled little procession of women started to gather by the entry port. The men with whom they had passed the night brought up their lashed hammocks and stowed them in the hammock netting by which the upper deck was surrounded. There, if the ship went into action, they would serve as a protective shield against grapeshot and musket-balls. Andrew watched with narrowed eyes for the scarlet jackets of his own men to appear from the hatch and ladderways. They did so, with disciplined promptitude, bringing his hammock with them, and he sent Corporal King to prepare the sideparty, ready for the expected summons when the captain's gig should be sighted.

The Falmouth boats came alongside, the bowmen in turn hooked on to the chains, and the women took their leave in virtual silence. A few called out farewells or promises, but under the eye of the officer of the watch, the men's response was muted. Andrew, looking down at the women as they clambered awkwardly into the first boat, was hard put to it to recognize his own companion of the two previous nights until she turned her face in his direction and gave him a faintly derisive wave. She *was* older than he had initially thought her, he realized, but passably good-looking, and her hair was red. Jenny Taggart had reddish copper hair, he remembered, but probably his choice had been merely a coincidence, although that did not fully account for the ache in his heart, as Jenny's small, sweet face was suddenly conjured up in memory.

The shore boats pushed off, both filled to capacity, and the women noisier now. Andrew was turning away when a scuffle broke out among the pressed men on the weather side of the deck. A thin, weedy, middle-aged man, exerting all his feeble strength, thrust the Irish boatswain's mate aside and ran frantically across the deck, shrieking to the boatmen to wait for him. He had almost gained the lee bulwark that was his objective when another of the new men—a tall, powerfully built fellow whose face was vaguely familiar—took a couple of swift paces after him and tripped him neatly. The would-be deserter collapsed sobbing on the deck, and the man who had tripped him lifted him bodily and returned him in silence to his party.

"Holy Mother of God!" the big Irishman exclaimed. He raised his starter in a fury, but as Andrew stepped forward to intervene, fearful lest the attention of any of the officers should be drawn to them, the tall man warned crisply, "Leave the poor sod be, Bo'sun's Mate!"

His tone was assured, even authoritative, and the petty officer, taken by surprise, stared at him openmouthed. But the knotted rope's-end did not descend on its intended victim, and the would-be deserter scrambled to his feet and took refuge among the others, who instinctively ranged themselves in front of him.

"And why, in the name o' God, should I lave the poor sod be?" the boatswain's mate demanded, recovering from his surprise. "Wasn't he tryin' ter jump ship, then?"

The tall man faced him unruffled, his blue eyes cold. "The first lieutenant's just come on deck. D'you want him to know you let a party of pressed men get out of hand?"

"I'll not have a bleedin' jailbird teach me my duty," the Irishman blustered. "That I will not! Damn your blood, you—"

"Please yourself, Bo'sun's Mate. But if you go running to the first lieutenant with your tale, I fancy you'll find that not one of us will back you up. We saw nothing, did we, maties?"

The sullen headshakes should have sufficed, but the boatswain's mate was angry. With an oath he turned to Andrew. "You saw what happened, Sergeant. Sure you know that little runt was tryin' to get himself into the shore boat, for wasn't he yellin' out for thim ter wait for him?"

Andrew met the tall man's gaze, and recognition dawned. Of course—hadn't Bo'sun's Mate Ryan called him a jailbird? He had filled out since the last time they had met, and his skin had lost most of its dark tropical tan, but this was one of the convict party who had sailed Governor Phillip's stolen cutter from Sydney Cove to Timor. This was the man who had been the party's navigator, the man who had known Jenny Taggart and given him news of her. He had been sent to Newgate to complete his sentence— they all had, those who had survived—but the newspapers had been full of the story of their epic voyage, and a well-known advocate, Mr. James Boswell, had interested himself in their case and endeavored to obtain pardons for them.

Andrew smiled warmly. "You're Butcher, are you not? John Butcher? Late of"—aware that Bo'sun's Mate Ryan was listening, he added—"late of His Majesty's ship *Gorgon*?"

"I go by my own name now—John Broome, at your service, Sergeant. Sergeant Hawley, if my memory does not fail me." The tall man echoed his smile. "We are well met, Sergeant!"

The boatswain's mate looked from one to the other of them, his anger slowly yielding to bewilderment. "Faith, d'ye know this fella, Sergeant?"

"Yes, I know him."

"He's a jailbird," the Irishman cautioned. "An' maybe a deserter into the bargain. I've seen him stripped, so I have, an' he bears the mark o' the cat on his back. An' d'at's not all, he——" He was interrupted by the voice of the first lieutenant, magnified by his speaking trumpet, demanding Andrew's presence on the quarterdeck.

Lieutenant Amherst Morris, like his captain, was a man after Andrew's own heart. He had been born in America, and his family had lost land and money by their adherence to the crown in the war that had brought independence to the American colonists. Morris was twenty-five, dark-haired and slightly built. He was an excellent first lieutenant and there was little that went on aboard the *Nymphe* of which he was unaware.

Acknowledging Andrew's stiff salute he said quietly, "At ease, Sergeant. Now be good enough to tell me, if you please, the reason for that—ah—altercation on the fo'c'sle."

"Altercation, sir?" Andrew questioned woodenly.

"You know what I mean, man! One of our more recent acquisitions tried to run, did he not? A man by the name of Smart who, until he entered the king's service, worked as a clerk in the town of Falmouth."

It was typical of Lieutenant Morris that he could give chapter and verse, Andrew thought glumly. "I don't know the man's name, sir," he admitted. "But he was desirous of—that is, he wanted to bid farewell to one of the women, sir. Not being aware that he should have sought permission, he made to do so, and he tripped and fell."

"From where I witnessed the incident," the first lieutenant suggested, "he appeared to have *been* tripped by another new man who, shall we say, saved him from the consequences of his own impetuosity? And who, furthermore, prevented the petty officer in charge of the party from, quite properly, laying into him . . . is that not so?"

"If you say so, sir."

"Oh, come now, Sergeant Hawley, you're not blind!"

"No, sir."

"Well, we will let that pass," Lieutenant Morris conceded. "It's the man who tripped Smart I'm interested in. Broome, John Samuel Broome . . . released from Newgate Prison on his volunteering for the king's service, and rated A.B. because he previously served in East India Company ships. You seemed to know him."

"Yes, sir, I do," Andrew admitted reluctantly.

"A deserter, perhaps?"

"No, sir, he's no deserter."

"Then tell me who he is, Sergeant."

"In confidence, sir?"

Morris shrugged his slim shoulders. "If you wish, but I have no secrets from Captain Pellew, you understand. In any event, what you tell me could well be to the man's advantage—he's more than an A.B., isn't he? Was he an officer?"

Andrew considered a further attempt at evasion and then thought better of it. His duty was clear, and he said flatly, "Broome's real name—that is the name he's best known by—is Butcher, sir. He was one of a party of convicts who made their escape from New South Wales to Timor, sir, in an open boat. There were seven or eight men, a woman and two small children, and they were close on three months at sea. Captain Edwards, of the *Pandora*—under whose command I was serving, sir—picked them up after the *Pandora* was lost in the Endeavour Strait. And at the Cape—" but he needed to say no more.

"Lord alive!" the first lieutenant exclaimed, a gleam of admiration lighting his dark eyes. "So that's who he is! I read the account of his incredible achievement in the *Chronicle*. And to think I'd rated him A.B. and had my doubts, even then, if he was up to it. But he never so much as hinted . . ." He shook his head, as if in amazement at his own lack of perception. "All right, Sergeant Hawley, carry on."

"Sir!" Andrew again came to attention.

Lieutenant Morris gave him an approving nod. "And thank you, Hawley. I shall inform the captain, of course. Why, damme, with more ships being put into commission every day and already a shortage of prime seamen to man them, a fellow of Broome's experience is worth his weight in gold. In fact we shall probably lose him to the masters' branch next time we make port." He sighed, his expression rueful, and then went on, more to himself than to Andrew. "Out of a complement of two hundred and forty, this ship has more than ninety men who have never been to sea before—or if they have it's been in fishing boats where they've never heard a shot fired. And we may well meet the enemy within a few hours of sailing! Dear God, when will our government ever learn that it's false economy to lay up ships and put good seamen on the beach to starve whenever there's a lull that passes for peace?" His voice was tense and bitter; then, recollecting his audience, he added briskly, "Well, thank God for the marines, eh, Sergeant? Perhaps you'll send Broome to see me as soon as the watch below have broken their fast."

"Sir!" Andrew saluted and left him.

Captain Pellew returned, piped aboard with due ceremony, and ten minutes later the order came to get the ship under way. With the anchor hove short and the capstan clanking, the topmen went swarming aloft to loose head and topsails and sheet home.

The new men, harried by petty officers and trained seamen and unable to comprehend the orders they were required to obey, provoked roars from Lieutenant Morris, but he handled the frigate well, and her yards braced round and courses and topgallants set, she caught the steady offshore breeze and steered northeastward for Start Point and the Channel.

The day was spent, with little pause, in exercising the entire ship's company. Under the captain's severely critical eye, sail was reefed, furled, and reset: the upper yards sent down and then swayed up again, with mast competing against mast and the hard-pressed topmen stumbling back to the deck exhausted. The ship tacked and wore a dozen times before Captain Pellew was satisfied. The landsmen, mustered with the afterguard and waisters, fought down their seasickness as the wind rose and hauled on sheets and tacks with blistered hands, urged on by the fists and starters of the boatswain's mates and the shouted curses of the men they impeded. When one watch was piped to dinner, the other manned the pumps and hosed down a supposedly blazing deck.

Then it was the turn of the guns. The marine drummer

beat to quarters, the ship's company ran to their action stations, and with sentries posted at each hatchway, the captain made a careful inspection, starting with the quarterdeck carronades and then descending to the long nine-pounders on the main gundeck.

Edward Pellew was in his mid-thirties, but he was a veteran of the American War and of a number of frigate actions still talked about in naval circles, which had won him promotion to post-rank before he was twenty-five. He was known as a taut hand and an expert on gunnery, and no detail escaped his attention as, followed by his brother, the purser's clerk, and the first lieutenant, he passed from battery to battery, questioning the crews and gun captains as to their duties and equipment and watching them go through the prescribed drill.

The *Nymphe* was well armed, mounting eight of the latest thirty-two-pounder carronades on quarterdeck and fo'c'sle, in addition to her two maindeck batteries of long nines. Marines had been detailed to serve two of the maindeck guns and the carronades on the quarterdeck, owing to the lack of trained men. Andrew, in overall charge of the larboard side carronades as well as of the marksmen normally stationed there, was sweating as freely as the rest by the time the three-hour exercise came to an end.

The guns were secured and the larboard watch piped to supper, most of them too done up even to grumble. But they had achieved a creditable rate of fire, which had finally earned the captain's praise, and even the landsmen were beginning to shake down and to look and behave more like seamen.

The lull they enjoyed was, however, all too brief. Seven bells of the middle watch had barely struck when the lookout aloft hailed the deck.

"Deck there!" His voice was excited. "Sail ahead and to loo'ard, sir! Hull down, but she's a frigate, sir, I'm sure o' that."

The midshipman of the watch, sent racing up to the foretopmast head, confirmed the lookout's sighting and added, his young voice also shrill with excitement, that the strange sail looked like a Frenchman. Within minutes Captain Pellew was on the quarterdeck, and as dawn tinged the calm June sky with pink, the *Nymphe* came round onto the starboard tack and, cramming on sail, bore up to investigate.

Andrew, roused from a deep sleep by the boatswain's stentorian bellow relaying the order to clear for action, had his men accoutered and mustered at their action stations on the quarterdeck before the lieutenant of marines came breathlessly to take command, cramming his hat on his head as he emerged from the hatchway. He was a young Welshman, known to his men—disrespectfully but with affection—as Taffy, and he said when Andrew reported to him, "Are we really giving chase to a Frenchman, Sergeant! I was thinking it was another exercise and swearing my head off!"

"It's no exercise, sir," Andrew assured him, conscious of the quickening of his heartbeat as the drummer gave a final rattle with his sticks and then, thrusting his drum onto his hip, picked up his musket and went to line up with the other men on the freshly sanded deck.

None had been in action before, and the line of tense faces reflected a wide variety of emotions as their officer completed his brief inspection and dismissed them to their posts. Two men were required to serve each carronade, sixteen had been detailed to the nine-pounders on the gundeck, and the remainder spaced themselves out along the hammock nettings, muskets loaded and primed.

The chase lasted just over an hour. Then one of the lieutenants, observing the enemy frigate from the foretopmast head, called out unexpectedly, "She's shortening sail, sir!"

"*Shortening* sail, Mr. Ross?" the captain questioned. "Are you sure?"

"Aye, sir, she's backing her tops'ls. I think she's decided to wait for us."

"Then by thunder we'll oblige her!" Captain Pellew exclaimed. "Mr. Morris, we'll haul up on her weather quarter, if you please, and give her three resounding British cheers before we open fire!"

When the two ships were within hailing distance, the French commander could be seen standing, hat in hand, at the gangway. He bowed and, speaking trumpet to his lips, he announced himself with impeccable courtesy as captain of the Republican frigate *Cléopâtre*.

"Capitaine de frégate Jean François Mullon, monsieur —à votre service!"

It was evident to Andrew, as to the other watchers on the *Nymphe*'s quarterdeck, that their own captain was enjoying himself hugely. "So chivalry is not dead in the sans-culotte navy!" he observed beaming and then added, lowering his voice, "Be ready to open fire when I lower my hat, Mr. Morris." Removing his cocked hat, he raised it high above his head and, his face still wreathed in smiles, crossed to the lee rail.

"His Britannic Majesty's frigate *Nymphe*, Captain Edward Pellew at *your* service, *monsieur!*"

The three resounding British cheers he had ordered echoed his greeting.

"Vive la nation!" the French commander responded, and his men, with less enthusiasm than their British counterparts had displayed, also cheered.

They wasted no more time in exchanging compliments; as the French frigate's yards were braced round and she began to gather way, Captain Pellew clapped his hat back onto his head and roared at the pitch of his lungs, "Fire as you bear! Braces, Mr. Morris!"

The larboard broadside struck with devastating effect seconds before the Frenchman could reply, and at little more than pistol-shot range the squat thirty-two-pounder carronades were deadly weapons. Both ships were running before the wind, but the very speed of the *Cléopâtre* proved her undoing, and as she forged ahead firing her own broadside at the *Nymphe*'s masts and rigging, her stern was exposed and the carronades raked her.

For fifteen endless minutes a furious fire was exchanged, the two ships almost hidden from each other by the swirling gunsmoke. Chain shot wreaked havoc with the *Nymphe*'s shrouds and stays, spars came crashing down in a welter of severed sheets and halyards, and grape, round shot, and canister mowed down the men on deck. One of the larboard carronades received a direct hit and exploded, killing both gunners and the powder boy running toward it with his laden bucket.

The shrieks of wounded men were drowned by the reverberating thunder of the guns, the hull shuddered beneath

Andrew's feet as he yelled to his men to reload. Beside him
the young drummer's head was taken from his shoulders by
a bouncing round shot, which went on, raising death-
dealing splinters from the deck planking. The nets, slung
for that purpose above the expanses of open deck, caught
some of the falling debris from the masts. In a momentary
break in the smoke the mainmast was seen to be swaying,
its spring stays shot away. The topgallant yard came crashing through the net, scattering the topmen who had been
preparing to go aloft to secure it.

Then a spasmodic cheer went up, to be followed by
shouts of triumph. The enemy ship hauled to the wind on
the larboard tack, and her mizzenmast went by the board.

"She's paying off!" a hoarse voice stated. "Her wheel's
gone! We've licked her, my lads, we've licked the bloody
Frenchy!"

But the *Cléopâtre* was still full of fight. She loomed
through the billowing clouds of smoke, the men on her
starboard quarter still at their guns, and a party hacked
with knives and axes at the wreckage of her mizzen hanging over her stern.

"She's going to run on board of us!" young Lieutenant
"Taffy" Jones cried in shaken tones. He grabbed Andrew's
arm. "By heaven, Sergeant, look at her!"

Grape spattered the planking in front of him, and Jones
screamed as a shower of splinters penetrated his scarlet-
coated chest. Andrew, miraculously unscathed, picked him
up and carried him to where two of the surgeon's party, in
bloodstained overalls, had just emerged from the main
hatchway.

"Take him below," he bade them thickly. "And have a
care, boys—he's badly wounded."

When he returned to his post, it was to see that the poor
young officer's prediction had been right. The *Cléopâtre*'s
chivalrous captain had done the only thing left for a brave
man to do and was making straight for his adversary. The
French frigate's jibboom passed between the *Nymphe*'s
fore and mainmasts, and for several tense minutes it
seemed that the teetering mainmast must fall, but then
with a crack like thunder the jibboom snapped off. The
two ships separated and then came together again with a
rending crash, lying alongside, head to stern, the French-

man's main topmast studding-sail boom hooked to the *Nymphe*'s main topsail leech rope and holding them locked together.

Captain Pellew roared his orders. The captain of the maintop scrambled aloft, a lone but dauntless figure, to cut the leech rope. Andrew, hearing the order for the boarders to stand by, mustered his men and, with voice and fists, lined them up by the lee rail with bayonets fixed.

"Let go the best bower, Mr. Morris!" the captain yelled through his speaking trumpet. "Out grappling irons! Look lively or she'll be away!" He put himself at the head of the assembled boarders, sword in hand, and as the seamen seized the cutlasses and axes clamped ready beside the now abandoned guns, he smiled encouragement from man to man. "Away boarders! Come on, my lads—one more effort and she's ours!"

Andrew, grasping his pike, found himself on the deck of the French ship with no clear idea of how he had reached it. He kept his men in hand for long enough to fire a disciplined volley into the advancing ranks of the defenders, and then it became a hand-to-hand battle, the clash of steel on steel, and the oaths and cries of the contestants succeeding the sound of the guns.

Somewhere among the melee he saw the limp body of the French captain lying in a pool of his own and his seamen's blood and, moved by pity, lifted it carefully to one side before returning to the fight. An ax, wielded by a giant Frenchman with a patch over one eye, caught him a glancing blow on the right shoulder and knocked the pike from his grasp. Then three others closed on him, one of whom discharged a pistol at him as he approached.

Had it been properly aimed it must have killed him. As it was it sent him crashing down to measure his length on the deck, conscious of hideous pain and a suffocating lack of breath. Teeth clamped on his lower lip to still the cry of agony that rose in his throat, he waited for his assailants to deal him the coup de grace but instead felt himself being half dragged, half lifted to his feet and propelled to the comparative safety of the *Cléopâtre*'s gangway.

His rescuer, breathing hard, bent over him, and Andrew recognized the one-time convict from New South Wales, John Broome.

"Thank you," he managed. "Thank you . . . and God bless you. I . . . dear God, I thought I was done for then!"

"You did me a good turn, Sergeant," Broome rasped cheerfully. He passed a hand over his smoke-blackened face and straightened up as the sound of cheering echoed from end to end of the fiercely contested deck of the enemy frigate. "She struck her colors! Look, they're being hauled down now—she's ours, boys! We've won our first battle." He grinned, boyishly delighted, and then, glimpsing a scarlet jacket among the cheering men, summoned the marine corporal, John Kelly, to his aid. "Lend a hand, Corporal, if you please, and let's get your sergeant to the surgeon before he bleeds to death."

Kelly came readily, and between them, as the cheers gradually faded, they carried Andrew Hawley to the *Nymphe*'s crowded cockpit to await the attentions of the surgeon. Laid out in a neat row in the waist were the bodies of a score of men for whom victory had come too late. Among them were the boatswain and five marines. The fifth marine was Lieutenant Jones, lying a little apart from the others, his round, boyish face oddly reproachful.

"The bleedin' Frenchies lost more'n we did, Sar'nt," Kelly observed callously. " 'Bout three times as many, I reckon. You should've seen their gundeck . . . talk about a shambles!" He sucked his teeth reflectively and halted by the hatchway in order to shift Andrew's weight, jarring him without warning. "The prize money'll be fair for a thirty-six-gun frigate, though, won't it?" With a sidelong glance at John Broome he added slyly, "D'you reckon jailbirds is entitled to prize money same as the rest o' us, Sar'nt?"

Before Andrew could gather his wits sufficiently to reply, Broome said, an edge to his voice, "Master's mates are, my bucko . . . and they're entitled to give orders, too. I'm giving *you* an order right now—keep moving or you won't last long enough in your rank to merit a corporal's share, I promise you!"

Corporal Kelly scowled at him and obeyed.

Broome said as he took his leave, "Maybe you'll have time for letter writing when they send you ashore, Sergeant Hawley. If you're writing to little Jenny Taggart, I'd deem it a favor if you'd remember me to her."

Well, perhaps he would write to Jenny Taggart, Andrew thought, endeavoring to shut his ears to the agonized screams of a man the surgeon was endeavoring to treat.

"All right, let's have the sergeant of marines on the table," the surgeon ordered wearily. "I can't do any more for this poor fellow."

His two mates deftly removed the body of the man who had screamed so agonizingly and in his stead lifted Andrew onto the piled sea chests that formed the operating table. One started to cut away the cloth of Andrew's tunic to expose the wound, and the surgeon inspected it critically.

"We'll need to get the ball out," he stated and reached for a probe. "This will be a mite painful, Sergeant, but we'll have you back to duty in a couple o' weeks, don't you worry."

The probe bit deep into his flesh. Andrew steeled himself to utter no sound.

"Here we are," the surgeon announced with satisfaction. His blood-caked fingers grasped the pistol-ball. "You'll be as good as new when this heals, Sergeant—ready and willing to fight the king's enemies, I'll warrant, wherever they're to be found, eh? Revolutionaries and cowardly dogs of regicides, the French, devil take them! Eh, Sergeant?"

"He's passed out, sir," one of his mates told him.

"Has he? Good God—I thought he was made of sterner stuff, by the size of him. Still"—the surgeon selected a needle from his lapel—"he's lost a lot of blood. We'll put him ashore with the serious cases, Dixon, just to be on the safe side. I've known wounds like this to turn putrid, and I don't want to keep him in our sick bay if there's any chance o' that happening. Let's have the next."

CHAPTER VIII

The *William* storeship reached Sydney on March 10, and in addition to delivering Timothy Dawson's livestock from the Cape also, to Jenny's pleasure and surprise, brought a second letter for her from Andrew Hawley.

It had taken almost seven months to reach Sydney and bore the date of July 20, 1793, by which time, it was evident, her own reply to his earlier letter had not been received.

She eagerly read,

Dear little Jenny,

I am writing this from hospital in the hope that it may merit an answer from you. But you need feel no anxiety on my account—I was wounded in an engagement with a French frigate, the *Cleopatra*, and am now fully recovered and awaiting my discharge and posting to another ship, my own having, of course, long since departed from these shores.

Address your answer to my company at Chatham, as set out above, and it will find me.

Perhaps, even in faroff Sydney Cove, you may have heard of how our ship, the *Nymphe* of 36 guns, met and defeated the Frenchman off Start Point? She was of the same size and armament as ourselves but carried a hundred more men than we, and ours had a goodly number of landsmen, pressed to serve, who had little notion of their duties. Yet within no more than one hour of battle, we had taken her! Her mizzen and her steering were shot away, her captain—a gallant officer—and over sixty seamen killed or wounded before she struck to our boarders. I was hit by a pistol shot on her deck, just before she hauled down her colors.

Our victory was well received. When we entered Portsmouth on June 21, the ships in harbor manned their yards to cheer us to our berth, and there were flags and big crowds of people gathered in the town to welcome us. Our captain is now *Sir* Edward Pellew; his brother—who was with us as a volunteer—has been made post, and our first lieutenant is advanced to the rank of commander. For us, whilst there are no promotions or honors, there will be prize money to be paid, for we brought the *Cleopatra* into port with us, sailed by a prize crew, and she is to be taken into service when the dockyard has done with her.

Once again, fate ordained that my path should cross that of the brave fellow who navigated the cutter in which the Bryant family and the other people from Sydney made their escape to Timor, John Butcher.

Just before the *Nymphe* sailed from Falmouth, my attention was drawn to this man's presence on board, and I made myself known to him.

You will be aware, no doubt, that the sentence of the court, when the survivors were tried in London, was that all must complete their original sentences in Newgate. Thanks to the intervention of Mr. James Boswell, a Scottish advocate, Mrs. Bryant was instead given a full pardon and set at liberty. Then the men were accorded the same mercy, and John Butcher— who now wishes to be known by his real name, which is Broome—volunteered to serve in the navy as a condition of his pardon.

When his name and his achievement as a navigator became known on board the *Nymphe*, he was rated master's mate, which is a rank that will give him privileges superior to the prime seamen and with which he is well satisfied.

Before I was taken ashore for my wounds to be treated in hospital, John Broome begged me to remember him to you, should I write to you, and I now do this with pleasure, for he is a fine fellow and well deserves the chance to make good on board a king's ship.

We had some talk before I left the *Nymphe* about the possibility of becoming settlers in New South Wales, and I found Broome of like mind to myself in this regard.

It is my fondest hope, dearest Jenny, that when this war is over, or if I should perhaps be invalided for my services, I may be accepted as a free settler and thus complete the voyage on which, seven years ago, I embarked.

If you are free of any legal entanglement as, for example, with the evil convict Munday, of whom Broome has told me, I may also if God spares me, cherish the hope that the plans we made on board the *Charlotte* may be—albeit belatedly—fulfilled.

I am still mindful of how pretty and sweet you were and how proud I was when you gave me your promise that we should wed.

You remain ever in my heart, dear lass, and I sign myself, as ever, your devoted Andrew.

Jenny was deeply moved by his letter, but of what use was it now to permit herself to dream of love and romance, or even of marriage? It had been so long, almost eight years since she had walked the *Charlotte*'s deck on Andrew's arm, and he had kissed her in the shadows, vowing his love to her.

Her lips twitched into a wry little smile as she recalled what those passing years had been like and the changes they had wrought in her. Did Andrew still think of her as the innocent child whom he had pledged himself to marry?

He had mentioned Ned as "the evil convict Munday" of whom Johnny Butcher—Johnny Broome—had told him, and it was clear from the tone of his letter that he liked and admired Johnny. What would he feel, what conclusions would he draw when he first set eyes on Justin—what would he think, when it dawned on him that Johnny had fathered the boy. But perhaps he never would, perhaps his talk of coming out to Sydney as a settler was just talk . . . a dream, such as her own had been, when she had taken her grant of land and seen it. In her imagination had been the home of flocks and herds, with the wheat growing tall and strong and a time of plenty following the famine they had been compelled initially to endure.

Would Andrew be capable of sharing that dream, when—if ever—he was faced with its reality? Could Johnny Broome even believe in it, when he had risked so much to escape from Sydney's servitude and found—if not freedom—at least honorable service in the navy in place of his convict's chains? It was foolish to hope that either of them would, Jenny told herself with weary resignation. She rose and started to pace the cramped living room, forcing herself to take stock of her present position, to face reality. The land was no longer hers, although she still worked it as she always had. Officially it had become the property of Timothy Dawson, and she was in his employ. She had no complaints on that score—indeed, quite the reverse. Timothy treated her as a partner in a joint and now prospering enterprise; he sought and heeded her advice, and since he himself spent most of his time on the grant he had taken near the Hawkesbury, she was free to manage this land as she saw fit; and now—she smiled with a hint of bitterness—now there was more than adequate labor force . . . Since Timothy was a free settler, he could claim his rights in this regard. Five sober, industrious male convicts had been chosen with care and assigned to work here; ten more worked the Hawkesbury grant and could be called upon at harvest time, and all, including Timothy Dawson himself, were now housed in well-constructed dwellings, the last completed a few weeks before.

Jenny looked down at the letter in her hand. She had incurred Lieutenant Macarthur's enmity, for all he had appeared to acquiesce in the agreement she and Timothy had reached. He had given no open sign of hostility, apart from questioning her need for five convict laborers, but John Macarthur, she knew, was not a man who ever forgot a slight or an injury.

She opened the letter again and returned to her seat in the open doorway, rereading the references Andrew had made to Johnny. A vision of his tanned face and defiant blue eyes floated momentarily before her. As Andrew had written, Johnny deserved the chance he had been given to make good on board a king's ship. And . . . what had he said concerning the possibility of eventual settlement in New South Wales? She turned the closely written page, seeking for the reference. Yes, here it was. . . . "We had some talk before I left the *Nymphe* . . . and I found Broome of like mind to myself in this regard."

Could Johnny really consider becoming a settler in this land that he had hated so bitterly? Surely if he made the most of his opportunities in the navy, he . . .

The sound of voices brought Jenny swiftly to her feet, peering apprehensively out into the moonlit night. Help and protection were readily at hand now—she had only to call and the men in the nearby hut would come running, she knew—but habit died hard, and the approach of strangers after dark had been for too long a cause for alarm for her to accept it with equanimity.

These strangers, however, were approaching quite openly, making no attempt at concealment, and when she hailed them, the answer came without hesitation.

"Do not be alarmed, Mistress Taggart! We are on a mission of mercy." A horseman, she saw, headed the small party, all of whom were in civilian dress, although two carried muskets and the horseman had a pistol in his belt. He removed his hat as he reined in beside Jenny's front door, revealing a head of sparse white hair and a smiling, friendly face. "I am Jasper Spence," he said, "recently settled on land to the west of here, at Portland. May I be permitted to enter your house? I have a matter to discuss with you."

At this hour? Jenny thought, but she inclined her head and the white-haired stranger dismounted from his horse, giving its rein to one of the men with him. She started to offer the whole party refreshment, but Mr. Spence held up a hand, cutting her short.

"My business will take only a few minutes." He followed her into the living room and, glimpsing Justin's fair curls in the cot on the far side of the fireplace, smiled and lowered his voice. "I won't disturb your child, Mistress Taggart."

Jenny thanked him, touched by his consideration, and he went on, eyeing her keenly, "Are you acquainted with a young woman named Frances O'Riordan, who was deported from Ireland as a seditionist and arrived here in the *Boddingtons* last year?"

Her mouth suddenly dry, Jenny stammered an assent. Poor Frances, she thought, what harm could have befallen her to send a gentleman of Mr. Spence's importance riding through the night?

"I—I know her, sir, yes. Is she—is she in trouble?"

"In sore trouble, I fear," Mr. Spence answered. "As nearly as I have been able to piece together her story, she and half a dozen or so of her countrymen, as you well know, finding their conditions of confinement and enforced labor intolerable, made their escape into the woods. For several months—she could not tell me precisely how long—they lived a hand-to-mouth existence, befriended by some of the native Indians but preyed on by others. Recently, during the course of what this poor girl described as a tribal battle, after killing each other with spears and clubs, both tribes turned on the Irish fugitives. All her male companions were brutally done to death, but she was spared; and she managed somehow to drag herself to my property, where one of my laborers found her. He, of course, brought her to me."

"Is she—is Frances very ill?" Jenny asked wretchedly. It was the outcome she had feared and concerning which she had tried to warn poor Frances; the Indians, apart from those in the immediate vicinity of Sydney, were not to be trusted. The tribal battle, which Mr. Spence had described, was a not infrequent occurrence—even Baneelon's people erupted occasionally into violence when some wrong had been done that could only be avenged in hideous bloodshed. She saw her visitor nod and drew in her breath sharply, wishing that somehow she could have persuaded Frances to stay with Justin and herself.

"She has pneumonia, I fear," Jasper Spence went on. "And after being starved for months the poor child has little resistance. She is of gentle breeding, Mistress Taggart, well spoken and clearly well educated. Whilst I am fully aware that it is my duty to hand her over to the authorities as an escaped felon, I am loath to do so. But Lieutenant Macarthur, as well as Captain Foveaux and Lieutenant Brace, are not infrequent visitors to my house—here and in Sydney Cove—so I am placed in a somewhat invidious position. Miss O'Riordan mentioned that you had given her shelter on a previous occasion, and it occurred to me that if I appealed to you, you might be willing again to take responsibility for her."

"I will, of course, sir." Jenny met his gaze steadily and was rewarded by his quick, approving smile.

"It may not be possible to move her for some days, you understand. But she is asking for you, and so I hope—that is, I should be immensely grateful if you would come back with me to my farm and do what you can for her. My own womenfolk—my daughter and the wife of my shepherd—

are in Sydney; so that, for me, caring for a very sick young woman presents its problems, as you will appreciate. Also"—his smile widened—"like those purchased on the way out here by Mr. Dawson, my sheep and horses have just been delivered by the master of the *William*, and I am anxious to settle them on my farm. So if you are willing, then—"

She could not refuse, Jenny decided. She could leave Justin with the wife of Tom Jardine—one of her assigned laborers—for two or three days, and Tom could be relied on to care for stock and land in her absence—he was a good, trustworthy man.

"I'll come, Mr. Spence," she promised. "If you can permit me a few minutes to make arrangements for my little boy to be cared for, I—"

"Bring your son with you if you wish," Jasper Spencer invited.

"No, he will be well enough here, thank you, sir."

"I'll wait for you outside. And I am grateful, believe me, Mistress Taggart."

Did he, Jenny wondered as she went to rouse the Jardines, did he realize that she was a convict? Well, perhaps he did. He was a gentleman, and he had treated her as if—she stifled a sigh—as if she were a lady. She slipped Andrew's letter into the pocket of her apron and, after explaining to Nancy Jardine the reason for her unexpected night journey, let her footsteps carry her, on impulse, to the stables. Ladies rode horses, she reminded herself, and her filly was broken to the saddle now. She saddled the pretty animal and climbed lightly onto its back, absurdly pleased by the gleam of admiration that lit Jasper Spence's eyes when she trotted across to join him.

"Your breeding, Mistress Taggart?" he questioned. "Or Mr. Dawson's?"

"Mine," Jenny told him with pride. "That is to say, sir, I bought the mare in foal, but this filly is one I broke and trained."

Jasper Spence asked numerous other questions concerning her stock and the terms on which she had accepted employment with Timothy Dawson, his interest expressed so keenly that she began to wonder what lay behind the polite but searching inquisition to which she was being subjected.

Revelation came when, entering his own, newly fenced holding, he pointed out its size and possible scope to her and then said, with unexpected frankness, "If ever you should be dissatisfied with your present employment, Mistress Taggart, I should be more than pleased to offer you an alternative in *my* service."

"In *your* service, Mr. Spence?" Jenny stared at him in openmouthed astonishment. "But why do you . . . I mean, you have your own men, have you not? Men who came out here with you?"

Spence inclined his head. "Oh, certainly I have, and they are very good men. But I am no farmer, and I have a house in Sydney Cove where, if I could find a trustworthy manager for this grant, I would more happily—and perhaps more profitably—spend the greater part of my time. So bear my offer in mind, Mistress Taggart, if you should ever feel inclined to make a change."

Jenny thanked him, gratified but still surprised. His house, when they reached it, was no larger than those of the New South Wales Corps officers' dwellings, but it was well designed and almost entirely brick-built, with a strong slate roof and what appeared, in the moonlight, to be an extensive garden surrounding it, planted with young vines and fruit trees.

The sight of Frances O'Riordan, however, drove all other thoughts from her mind. The girl was clearly very ill, her thin cheeks flushed with fever and her whole body soaked in perspiration. She looked up at Jenny without recognition, moving restlessly beneath the blankets with which she was covered and turning her head away from the candle on the table beside her, as if even its faint glow caused her pain.

Jenny stayed with her all that night and most of the following day, doing all in her power to bring down her temperature. Repeated sponging with warm water seemed to bring Frances some slight ease, as did the draught of bitter-tasting liquid that Jasper Spence offered as a remedy he had found effective in India. But it was touch and go; Frances hovered precariously between life and death, at times talking wildly in delirium, at others silent and unresponsive, seemingly resigned to whatever end fate had in store for her.

In her delirium she called her brother's name with despairing frequency, beseeching him to come to her; but when he did not, she called on others whose names Jenny did not recognize. For all its disjointedness, her wild talk was revealing, and listening to it Jenny was thankful that—apart from a once-daily visit to the sickroom—Jasper Spence left her alone with the sick girl. He had been appointed a magistrate and, with the best will in the world, would have been compelled to take note of some of Frances's disclosures and even, perhaps, report them to the authorities.

By noon on the second day, in answer, Jenny could only suppose, to her prayers, the fever abated and Frances lapsed into a deep, healing sleep. Summoned to be informed of the improvement in her condition, Mr. Spence offered warm congratulations.

"You have in truth performed a miracle, Mistress Taggart, but I wonder . . ." He was standing in the doorway of the sickroom, a strongly perfumed handkerchief held so as to cover his mouth and nose and, presumably, intended to ward off infection, and his voice sounded uneasy. "I wonder . . . that is to say, I have a cart and a newly imported pair of oxen to draw it. Would it be possible, do you think, to move the girl to your farm in that? I do not, of course, want to endanger her life by removing her prematurely, but my daughter has sent word that she wishes to join me here. I understand from her note that she will be escorted by one of the corps officers, and the O'Riordan girl's presence here will . . . well, it will require an explanation, will it not?"

Jenny was aghast. Frances was far from a full recovery; a long journey in a jolting farm cart might well cause a setback, which she had not the strength to ward off. Jenny started to say so, but Jasper Spence cut her short.

"My daughter is not due here until tomorrow. Perhaps first thing in the morning we could move the girl into my foreman's hut? It is only just across the fold yard, but Henrietta is not likely to enter it. Then, when you deem her condition warrants such a move, you could take the girl—

er—without drawing attention to her presence, needless to say, back with you to Parramatta."

Conscious of the kindness he had shown to both Frances and herself, Jenny could not but agree. The move was accomplished the following morning without apparent ill effect, and the foreman, a dark-haired, middle-aged man named Seamus O'Leary, received his unexpected guests pleasantly enough. He and his son, he assured Jenny, could sleep quite comfortably in the hay barn and take their meals with the convict laborers.

"We'll not need to trouble ye, mistress. An' when you're ready to take the poor sick child to your own place, Pat here will drive ye in the oxcart."

There was a cooking fire in the hut's small living room, a freshly filled crock of water, and an ample supply of food for their needs, the man pointed out, but if she should be in need of anything further, she had only to ask. He added apologetically, "My wife bides in Sydney Cove still, waiting on the young mistress, so you'll maybe not find the place as well cared for as you'd wish . . . but it's clean, so it is. We were up half the night scouring every room."

Henrietta Spence arrived shortly after midday, astride the horse her father had sent to the river wharf at Parramatta to meet her and escorted by an officer in uniform. Jenny glimpsed them from the window of the O'Learys' living room and was struck by the girl's dark beauty, as well as by her fashionable gown and the absurd little bonnet she had donned. Neither was suited for horseback riding, and Jasper Spence's daughter was, it seemed, aware of this, for she complained in petulant tones to her escort, as he assisted her to dismount, that it was high time carriages were put on the list of imports to the colony.

"In this heat," she exclaimed, patting delicately at her perspiring face with a scrap of cambric, "it is asking too much to expect any poor female to ride over six miles along rough and dusty roads at midday . . . truly it is! I declare I came near to swooning long before we reached our destination."

The young officer murmured something Jenny could not catch, but she saw Jasper Spence's smile of welcome fade abruptly before he stepped forward to embrace his daugh-

ter. Then they vanished into the house, leaving Pat O'Leary
to care for their two sweating horses.

Busy with Frances, Jenny kept well out of sight. The
young officer made a brief appearance in the yard with Mr.
Spence during the afternoon, and as they stood chatting
idly while their horses were being saddled, Jenny studied
Henrietta Spence's escort with casual interest.

He was tall and more than passably good-looking, and
his scarlet coatee with its distinctive yellow facings was obviously the work of an expert tailor. There was an air of
elegance about him that suggested better breeding than
could be claimed by the majority of the New South Wales
Corps officers. He rode to the manner born also, she observed when he and his host trotted out of the yard together. A fitting beau for the fashionably dressed Henrietta
and one of whom—judging by the easy intimacy of their
manner toward each other—Henrietta's father clearly approved. Mr. Spence had spoken of regular visits to his
house by Captain Macarthur and Captain Foveaux, as well
as by Lieutenant Brace, so, presumably, the young officer
who was now his guest must be Lieutenant Brace. She had
not heard his name before, which almost certainly meant
that he was a fairly recent arrival in the colony. But—she
shrugged indifferently—he was probably just the same as
the rest of them or, under their influence, would soon become so.

The day passed slowly. Frances continued to sleep, but
now the color in her cheeks was no longer the legacy of her
fever, and Jenny was able, in her occasional waking moments, to spoon water and a few drops of wine into her
parched mouth, which she swallowed gratefully.

Just before dusk, the clatter of hoofs heralded the return
of Jasper Spence and his companion, and after stabling the
horses, the foreman O'Leary came diffidently to inquire
whether she needed anything. Despite Jenny's assurance
that she did not, he lingered at the door, awkwardly shuf-
fling his feet in the dust before asking if he might enter.

"Of course, Mr. O'Leary," Jenny answered readily. "This
is your house—please come in."

"I'm not wanting to disturb the poor wee girl," the foreman began. "But—" He broke off.

"She is sleeping soundly. You won't disturb her."

"Ah, that's fine then." He took off his hat and stepped into the living room, evidently ill at ease and searching for words, and, anxious to set his mind at rest, Jenny offered encouragingly, "Is there something you want, Mr. O'Leary—something you've forgotten, perhaps?"

"No." He shook his cropped dark head. " 'Tis nothing o' that kind, mistress. 'Tis just that I—well, I'm wanting to know what do they call the wee girl?"

"Call her? You mean what is her name?"

"Aye. The master let slip she was Irish, and I was wondering—ye see, I'm from Cork meself, and I thought maybe she'd be known to me. D'ye happen to know which ship brought her out?"

Jenny smiled. Poor man, he was only seeking news from his homeland, word of relatives or friends he had left behind him to come out here. She said, still smiling, "Yes, she came out in the *Boddingtons* and her name is Frances O'Riordan, Mr. O'Leary."

Seamus O'Leary's expression changed to one of wary, even dismayed astonishment. "Mistress Frances O'Riordan!" he echoed. "Would she be the daughter of Dr. Joseph O'Riordan from County Wexford, do you know?"

Frances had spoken of County Wexford, Jenny recalled—or a place that had sounded similar—and hadn't she mentioned once that her father had been a doctor? She was about to confirm O'Leary's supposition when some instinct of caution made her hesitate. Frances was gently born, well educated, and both she and her poor dead brother had been active members of a proscribed rebel organization. What could they have in common with this rough, illiterate farm laborer, who had not been sentenced to deportation but who had come out as a bonded servant. Their religion, of course—the O'Leary family were probably Catholics—but was O'Leary also a member of the United Irishmen?

"I think, Mr. O'Leary," she said cautiously, "that you should ask Mistress O'Riordan yourself about her parents when she is sufficiently recovered to be able to talk to you."

The Irish foreman retreated instantly into his shell. "Och yes," he agreed. "Sure I'll do that, Mistress Taggart—in a couple of days, maybe. Your pardon for me intrusion. I

. . . if there's truly nothin' you need, I'll be about me own business."

He took his leave, and Jenny returned to her vigil at Frances O'Riordan's bedside. By the following morning the sick girl had regained full consciousness. Recognizing Jenny as soon as she opened her eyes, she poured out her story, going into more detail than she had when Mr. Spence had questioned her, and her voice shook with remembered terror as she described the awful slaughter that had deprived her of her companions.

"We were on the far side of the river," she whispered brokenly, "the river they call the Hawkesbury, and we believed we were safe. The Indians there were friendly, they gave us food and shelter and treated us well. We were trying to learn their ways and to help them to hunt and fish, so that we shouldn't be a burden to them. One of them, a young warrior called Bonneda, became a great friend of Danny Halloran and he took Danny's name—I think as a sign that they were brothers. You met Danny—the boy with the scarred face who came to fetch me from your house."

The boy who had brought her the stolen suckling pig, Jenny recalled, and laughingly claimed that the previous owner would feel no loss.

Frances went on, "One day it all seemed to change. The Indians became restless. They daubed their faces and bodies with hideous red and white circles and started to dance, making a weird kind of music by blowing through long wooden horns and beating clubs and spear-shafts against their shields. And then . . ." Her voice broke on a sob, and Jenny besought her to be silent.

"Don't talk about it if it distresses you. Please, Frances!"

"I want to tell you," Frances insisted. "I want you to understand that we did nothing, nothing at all to provoke them. About an hour before sunset they gathered in a huge circle, and they made Bonneda stand up in front of them with just a bark shield to protect him, and they started to throw spears at him. They wounded him quite severely, and Danny went to his aid with one of the other boys, and they . . . Jenny, the Indians killed them both! In front of our eyes they clubbed them to death, and they turned on the rest of us when we tried to save them. It was—oh, it was like a nightmare! I was clubbed, but they spared my life, and as soon as I could I ran away from them. I—I couldn't stay after what they'd done. I was afraid . . . and I didn't know why they should have turned on us."

A long time ago Colbee and Baneelon had told her of the strange code of justice practiced by the native tribes, Jenny remembered. An injury must always be avenged in blood. Any man guilty of a crime against another—even a member of the same tribe—must accept his punishment and stand, defending himself only with a shield, while the injured party's relatives and friends hurled their spears at him. No interference was permitted, but in their ignorance of native custom, Frances and her companions had unwittingly offended against tribal law.

She endeavored to explain, but the weeping girl could only shake her head in bewilderment. After a while, her sobs subsided, and she again lapsed into an exhausted sleep. Within twenty-four hours, however, she had so far regained her strength as to make the journey to Parramatta possible; anxious now to return to Justin and her own house, Jenny told Seamus O'Leary that they would be ready to start back whenever the oxcart should be available.

It was made available that evening. Neither Jasper Spence nor his daughter came to take leave of them, and their departure as the light was fading was calculated to attract no attention from any of the convict workers who were gathering in the cookhouse for their evening meal.

They reached the cabin without mishap, to a rapturous welcome from little Justin and a more subdued one from Tom and Nancy Jardine.

Tom said, when Frances was once more comfortably ensconced in Jenny's bed, with Justin curled up beside her, "We had a visit from some soldiers while you was gone, Mis' Taggart. Askin' if we'd seen any escapers—Irish, they reckoned."

"Irish?" Jenny managed somehow to refrain from glancing in Frances's direction. "What did you tell them, Tom?"

The big countryman smiled. "Why, that we'd seen neither hair nor hide of 'em. That was the truth—or as much o' the truth as I'd tell any redcoat." His smile widened. "An' Mr. Dawson sent word by young Jackie Scrope that all his stock from off of the *William* is housed an' ready to be put out to pasture. He lost eight or nine ewes on the way from Sydney Cove, but the rest are healthy an' the horses in good fettle. He didn't know you was away, of course, and he said to tell you as he'd appreciate it if you was to ride out an' look 'em over, soon as you can."

This was good news, Jenny thought, much relieved. Although the loss of the ewes was regrettable, such losses had to be anticipated as a result of the long sea journey from the Cape. And the soldiers' visit was probably just a routine one. No doubt they had heard rumors of the slaughter that had taken place beyond the Hawkesbury and, because escaped convicts had been involved, had been instructed to confirm or disprove them before the next colony-wide muster.

"I'll ride over with Jackie in a day or so," she promised. "How is Ben?" Old Ben Reilly had been ailing of late, spending more of his time on the bottle and, since Nancy Jardine's arrival, less and less with Justin.

The foreman shrugged. "Much the same, Mis' Taggart. Won't come out o' his hut 'less'n you're here to make him, and he don't seem to fancy much in the way o' food, poor old devil."

She would have to try to talk to him, Jenny knew. Perhaps if she took him his food herself, if she could persuade him to eat . . . He had usually listened to her in the past. The constant pain he had to endure from his amputated leg caused him to drink and, sadly, the drink made him sullen and short-tempered, so that even the kindly, easygoing Nancy Jardine found her tolerance strained to its limit when Ben was in one of his moods.

It was noon before Jenny was able to make time to visit the old man, but the soldiers came just as she opened the door of his hut, and hearing the rhythmic sound of marching feet and the clink of a bridle bit, she closed it again and stood beside it, wondering anxiously what this second visit might portend.

She was not left for long in doubt. The patrol of six men was under the command of the tall young officer who had escorted Henrietta Spence from Sydney, Lieutenant Brace. He halted his men and, still sitting his horse, demanded brusquely whether her name was Taggart.

"Yes, sir," Jenny acknowledged. "I am Jenny Taggart."

"I have reason to believe that you are harboring a fugitive," he accused. "One Frances Mary O'Riordan, sentenced to seven years for sedition and delivered to this colony by the *Boddingtons* transport in August last year." His tone was coldly formal, his face devoid of expression as he looked down at her. "This woman absconded from the quarters to which she had been consigned in Parramatta two months ago, with a number of her male compatriots, and has been missing ever since."

Jenny's heart sank. Who, she wondered dully, could have informed on her? Who knew that Frances had been brought here only a scant few hours ago? Not Jasper Spence, surely, for had he not gone to considerable inconvenience to give the sick girl shelter and conceal her presence on his property? Then . . . Her mouth tightened. Seamus O'Leary, his hired man . . . it could only have been he. Yet he was Irish, a fellow countryman. What possible reason could he—or his son Patrick—have had for such a betrayal?

"Well," Lieutenant Brace prompted impatiently, "where have you hidden this young woman? Or is it your intention to deny that she is here?"

Jenny shook her head. "I don't deny it, sir. But the girl is ill—ill and near to starvation. I"—aware that she must not implicate Jasper Spence if it could be avoided, she hesitated, choosing her words with care—"I gave her shelter because she was so ill. I could not turn her away. The Indians murdered her companions and—"

"Did they, by George!" Brace interrupted, a gleam in his dark eyes. He questioned her minutely concerning the killings and then said in a clipped, authoritative voice, "Very well, prepare the girl for a journey and bring her to me. At once, d'you hear? I've no time to waste."

"But she's not fit to leave her bed," Jenny protested. "Could you not let her remain here for a little while until she's well enough to travel? She—"

"And have you spirit her away?" He laughed derisively. "I shall only be taking her as far as the hospital in Parramatta, in any event—which is where she should have gone in the first place if she is really ill, as you know very well,

Mrs. Taggart. But you did not even report her arrival here to Dr. Arndell, did you?"

"She has only been here for a few hours, sir," Jenny told him quite truthfully. "I—"

"Go and get her," Brace ordered, losing patience. "I can't cool my heels around here all day."

"But, sir—"

"Damme, woman, do as I bid you! My men can make a litter for her if she's too weak to sit my horse with me. Is she?"

"I fear she may be," Jenny managed. "She—"

"You heard, Corporal," Brace said, cutting her short. "Prepare a litter for the prisoner." He jerked his head in the direction of a small pile of freshly cut fence posts lying nearby. "Use a couple of those and some sacks if you can find any. If not, take a blanket from one of the huts—it can be sent back. Go and fetch her, Mrs. Taggart."

Reluctantly, Jenny obeyed him. Frances paled when she realized that she was about to be arrested, but she offered no reproach.

"You'll be taken to the hospital," Jenny said, wrapping a blanket round her. "Dr. Arndell is a decent, kindly man. He will take good care of you. And I will apply for you to be assigned here, Frances, so do not worry. You—"

"When I have received my punishment for escaping," Frances pointed out wryly. "And what about you? Will you be punished for harboring me?"

Jenny brushed the question aside. They could prove nothing without involving Mr. Spence, who was a magistrate, and if his foreman, O'Leary, _had_ informed on Frances, he would not dare say a word against his employer. She gave the sick girl her arm, and as they moved slowly to the door of the cabin, little Justin clung wailing to her skirts. Two soldiers were waiting outside with the improvised litter, and one of them, quite gently, picked the little boy up and carried him back into the kitchen. The other, looking sheepish, assisted Frances to lie down on the litter; then, joined by his comrade, he lifted it, grinning.

"Why, you don't weigh no more'n a feather, lass! Lie still, now—we'll soon have you in the 'ospital."

It was as they were carrying their slight burden to where

Lieutenant Brace was awaiting them that old Ben Reilly emerged from his hut like an avenging fury. He was very drunk and roaring defiance at them, and before Lieutenant Brace could move out of his way, the old man was beside him, raining blows with his crutch at both horse and rider. The startled animal reared, Brace was roughly flung to the ground, and as he attempted to struggle to his feet, Ben felled him and went stumbling unsteadily toward the litter.

"Up an' run for it, girl!" he urged. "I'll not let 'em take you, that I will not!"

Poor Frances was too weak and too much afraid to attempt to heed his advice, but undeterred, Ben set about the litter bearers, both of whom had their muskets slung. They dropped the litter in an instinctive endeavor to recover the use of their weapons, and as Jenny ran frantically to Frances's aid, the flailing crutch claimed a second red-coated victim.

"Ben, for heaven's sake stop!" she cried, but her plea was shouted down by Brace.

"Get the old swine, Corporal! Get him, d'you hear me!" Brace yelled. He was on his feet at last, blood pouring from a deep cut across his cheek. "Shoot him if you have to!"

The soldiers, angry and humiliated, needed no urging. They beat old Ben into submission with their musket butts and went on beating him as he lay, helpless and defeated, on the ground. Only when Jenny, finding them deaf to her despairing cries for mercy, flung herself in front of them did they desist, to eye her sullenly before wiping the blood from their muskets on the trampled grass and turning away.

"Is the fellow dead?" Brace asked thickly. He had retrieved his horse but came on foot, leading the animal, to regard his soldiers' handiwork with shocked dismay. On receiving the corporal's nod of assent he recovered himself and rounded on Jenny. "We'll see that he's buried, Mrs. Taggart. But you must bear the burden of responsibility for his—his death. You are his assigned employer, are you not?"

Jenny rose slowly to face him. Alarmed by the hubbub Nancy Jardine came out of the cabin, white-faced and anxious. But, as always, there were no witnesses save herself and two female convicts—the men were at their work on the land, unaware of the patrol's arrival. . . . Jenny bit back the indignant words that rose to her lips and inclined her head.

"Yes. Yes, I am. That is, I was."

Brace reddened. "Then doubtless you are aware that convicts are not permitted to consume alcoholic liquor—as this man clearly had and to excess! He made an unprovoked attack on my men and myself whilst we were in the execution of our duties, and he received what he deserved in consequence. I shall make a report to this effect to my superiors. If they see fit to bring charges against you, then you will be summoned to court so that you may answer to them."

Jenny was trembling violently, and it took all the self-control she possessed to keep herself from hurling his accusations back into his face. But bitter experience had taught her over the years that defiance was to no avail. . . . Was not Ben's death further proof of it? Nancy Jardine, she saw, had gone to take the terrified Frances into her comforting arms, and she had closed the door of the cabin behind her so that Justin, at least, had seen nothing.

Jenny said, with what composure she could muster, "What charges do you propose to bring against me, Mr. Brace?"

Disconcerted by her seeming calm, he stared at her, momentarily at a loss for words. The corporal, a hard-faced veteran, prompted woodenly, "We was ordered to apprehend an escaped convict, sir, an' this woman was harborin' the fugitive. There ain't no doubt o' that, no doubt at all, sir. We was all witnesses, wasn't we?"

"Quite so, Corporal," Lieutenant Brace agreed with a confident smirk as he recalled the occasion of his first meeting with Frances O'Riordan. He would show her that it would not pay a convict whore to scorn the advances of an officer of the corps, he thought, and his smirk became a pleased smile. He remounted his horse and, from the safe vantage of the saddle, waved Jenny aside, his promise to attend to old Ben's interment forgotten—if, indeed, he had ever intended to keep it. "We'll bring the fugitive in. Form your men up, ready to march—we've wasted enough time here."

The soldiers picked up the litter and marched away at their officer's heels, Frances O'Riordan's heartbroken sobs fading at last into silence.

"No skulking there, *Mr.* Sparrow! Put yer back into it, yer mangy little cur!"

The overseer's rawhide lash curled painfully around Watt Sparrow's naked, sweat-drenched shoulders as the little man tugged and heaved on the rope to which, like beasts of burden, he and half a dozen other convicts were harnessed. The great pine came crashing down at last, sixty feet of it, and the men flung themselves to the ground, spent and breathless, to snatch a brief respite until they should be called upon to tackle the next.

But for Watt Sparrow there was to be no respite. The lash found him again, and the overseer bade him harshly, "On yer feet, Sparrow! Take an ax an' trim off them branches—you too, Mills. Jump to it, yer scurvy rogues!"

"They done their share, Brady," one of the other men protested. "Leave 'em be, can't yer?"

For answer the overseer snarled at him and plied his whip again. Newly assigned to his position of authority, Silas Brady was a loudmouthed, bullying lout, sentenced by the criminal court for a brutal assault on the woman with whom he had lived in Sydney. But on Norfolk Island, where virtually all the convicts were serving sentences for crimes committed since their arrival in the colony, Brady's was regarded as one so minor that it had proved no hindrance to his being made an overseer.

Quite early in their acquaintance Watt had incurred his enmity because he had refused to pay the "garnish" demanded of all new prisoners by those who had been on the island longest, and now that he had been afforded the opportunity to pay off his score, Brady had taken savage advantage of it. In this, Watt thought bitterly, he was no different from the rest of the men assigned to supervise the labor of their fellows. Most were bullies, many took bribes, and the island's governor, Captain Philip Gidley King—the naval officer who had founded the settlement and held the rank of lieutenant governor of New South Wales—did little to combat the evil. So long as the work was done—the roads constructed, the houses and granaries built, the na-

tive pines turned into masts for shipping, and the farming
land brought into production—Captain King appeared indifferent to the means his underlings adopted to ensure that
it was done.

He lived in some style in a recently built stone house,
much larger than his original residence, with his wife, his
three-year-old son, Phillip, and a newborn daughter. With
them were the two boys, christened Norfolk and Sydney,
whom he had fathered illegitimately by a convict woman
prior to his marriage and had now adopted, in order that
they might be educated at Thomas MacQueen's new school.

Watt had often heard Jenny Taggart and others who had
come out in the first fleet sing the praises of Governor Phillip's able lieutenant, but King, it seemed, had changed with
the passing years. His temper had become uncertain, owing, it was said, to painful attacks of gout, and his enthusiasm for the small island colony he had established appeared sadly to have waned. Or perhaps—Watt reflected
sourly as he lopped branches off the pine tree his gang had
felled—perhaps the fact that Norfolk Island was peopled
by more than eight hundred convicts whom the authorities
in Sydney wished to be rid of had given the captain ample
cause to despair of it.

Few stayed there from choice, he had learned. Many of
the island's first settlers—free men and marines who had
served under Governor Phillip—finding conditions too
hard, had sold their land grants and left. Others, during the
brief period when Major Robert Ross had been acting governor, had done the same, and faced with the major's tyranny as well as by a crop failure and the threat of starvation, even the marines of the garrison had been on the
verge of mutiny.

The island, despite its pleasant climate, was an unhappy
place, and Watt, after barely six months of it, found himself longing, with a nostalgia he had never expected to experience, for the chance to return to Sydney. Not that in
reality there was the slightest chance of such an outcome,
as he well knew. A thousand miles of the Pacific Ocean
lay between Norfolk Island and the parent settlement in
New Holland. Even if that distance could be weathered,
the launching and landing of small boats was still a hazardous undertaking, because of a heavy surf in which

even boats manned by competent naval seamen had been
known to capsize, with the loss of their entire crews.

And on an island only five miles long and three wide,
there was nowhere for an escaper to find concealment.
Watt passed a blistered right hand over his streaming face,
shifting the ax to his left. He would not live for the two
years and six months required to complete his sentence, he
thought bitterly—not if he were compelled, at his age, to
toil for most of the day under Silas Brady's merciless goad-
ing. But if he complained or stood up to the swine, he
would face an arbitrary hundred lashes, laid on by a hefty
constable. . . . He sighed and lifted the ax just as Brady's
long whiplash reached out to deal him a stinging blow
across the kidneys.

"I said you was ter lop off them branches, didn't I, yer
stinkin' little toad? Get on wi' it!"

The tree-fellers, vigorously plying their saws and axes,
had another giant ready to come down, Watt realized. A
chain had already been looped round the lower part of its
trunk, to which, in a few minutes, the rope must be attached; and then his gang must strain and haul until the
tree was brought down. Even then their work would not be
over, for each of the felled trees, roughly stripped of its
upper branches, would have to be painfully manhandled
across close to five hundred yards of rough, stump-littered
ground to join the growing pile being collected there.
He . . .

"Aw-right, you idle bastards!" Brady's hated voice broke
into Watt's thoughts. "Take a pull on yon rope! You too,
Sparrow . . . go on, take the head o' the rope, yer sniv-
elling little bleeder! Move, d'ye hear me? Move!"

The little man stumbled across in obedience to the overseer's harsh command to take up the slack of the dangling
rope. At his back a powerful young convict named Jed
Ashford whispered consolingly, "Don't 'e strain too 'ard,
Watt—leave that to me, see? And mind 'e jumps clear
when she starts to tumble!"

Watt did his best to take the big youngster's advice, but
the tree fell with less resistance than he had anticipated,
and although with Jed's help he managed to avoid the
trunk falling on him and crushing the life from his body,
the branches enveloped him, and he measured his length on

the hard, unyielding ground. They freed him, limp and barely conscious, and two of them carried him, as gently as they could, to the hospital. The assistant surgeon on duty, Dr. D'Arcy Wentworth, cleansed and dressed the cuts and scratches he had sustained and dismissed the two men who had brought him in with a confident, "Don't worry—the little fellow's not badly hurt. A week's rest in here and he'll be as good as new."

To his immediate superior, Dr. Balmain, however, Wentworth was less confident. "I'd be uncommonly obliged if you'd take a look at the poor little devil they call Sparrow. Oh, his injuries are minor, no cause for concern on that score, but the man's in his mid- or late sixties, and he's skin and bone. Men of his age should not, in my view, be put to hard labor."

"I agree wholeheartedly," Balmain said, frowning. "But how are we to prevent it—tell me that, my friend? The convicts are landed here, in accordance with their sentences, but we never see them unless they're injured or they fall sick. I'll have a word with Captain King and suggest that all newly arrived deportees over the age of, say, fifty be given a medical examination before they're put to work. But"—he shrugged and consulted his fob-watch—"I have time now, if you wish, to make a start with this fellow of yours—what's his name?"

"Sparrow," D'Arcy Wentworth supplied. "The court in Sydney sentenced him to three years for possession of a firearm and firing it at an officer of the corps who was trying to arrest him."

"Justice," Dr. Balmain remarked dryly, "is now vested in the corps and administered by the corps. You've had no experience of the corps, as yet, have you? Well, there is virtually no civil magistracy in Sydney, which was the reason, my dear D'Arcy, for my return to this place. Doubtless, should John White decide he's had enough and take passage for England, I shall be invited to become his successor. In the meantime, for all its faults, I'm happier where I am. At least King's a gentleman, with a heart and conscience, and he's not forever trying to line his own pockets, as those damned corps officers in Sydney are. We're overcrowded, and unfortunate convicts like your sixty-year-old are somehow overlooked, but . . . we've got him now,

have we not? Well, then, let's keep him in the hospital until
he's really fit. After that you can employ him on your farm
or in your household, perhaps."

Wentworth eyed him with raised brows, and William
Balmain laughed. "I have a soft spot," he confessed, "for
any man, be he convict or free, who stands up to a corps
officer. But you will not, I trust, repeat that remark to a
soul, as you value your life, D'Arcy!"

Dr. Wentworth echoed his laughter. "Most certainly not,
sir," he answered. He led the way into the ward, an
amused little smile still curving his lips. He himself was
under sentence of deportation from England, and his sympathies were with the convicts although, on the voyage out
he had struck up an acquaintance with Lieutenant Macarthur that, he thought, might later prove useful.

For Watt Sparrow, although unaware of the reason for
the favored treatment he received, the next three weeks
were the happiest he had spent since his enforced departure
from Jenny Taggart's holding. Well fed and rested, he rapidly recovered his health and his normal good humor, and
when Dr. Balmain invited him to attend the weekly theatrical performance put on by convict players, he accepted eagerly.

Having few other distractions, settlers, soldiers, and convicts alike looked forward with enthusiasm to this
Saturday-night entertainment; and the stone-built schoolhouse in which it was held was filled to overflowing when
Watt and half a dozen of his fellow hospital inmates struggled through the crowd to the places reserved for them.
The play—Farquhar's *Recruiting Officer,* now a time-
honored favorite with the performers, at least—opened under Dr. Balmain's direction to loud applause and a few ribald shouts from the packed audience.

But the atmosphere, Watt realized, was oddly tense, despite the presence of the lieutenant governor and a number
of his officers in the front row of seats. The New South
Wales Corps soldiers formed a solid phalanx in the center
of the hall, where they elbowed and jostled any settler who
attempted to pass or stand near them, and during the somewhat lengthy intermission the jostling increased, accompanied now by chants and jeers.

The settlers, distinguished by their neat homespuns and

freshly shaven cheeks, included several onetime marines, and they came in for rougher treatment than the rest. The convicts, although granted leave to attend the performance, could only do so under guard, and when they, in turn, started to jeer and bandy insults with the soldiers, Watt's apprehension grew.

"What's got into 'em?" he demanded of a neighbor. "Looks like they're spoilin' fer a fight, don't it?"

The man shrugged. "I don't rightly know, friend. But they're saying that one o' them plaguey soldiers—name o' Bannister, I believe—made a mite too free with a settler's wife an' the husband threatened to report his conduct to the guv'nor."

"Well, 'e'd a right to, 'adn't 'e?" Watt suggested.

"The soldiers don't reckon he had," his informant retorted dryly. "How long've you bin here, friend? Surely you know by this time that the corps's rights are the only rights that count in this place? Well"—he gestured to the stage—"curtain's going up on the last act. Let's hope they quieten down an' let us hear it."

But the hubbub continued, finally reaching such a pitch that Dr. Balmain angrily ordered the curtain to be lowered. Several fights broke out, and Lieutenant Governor King, rising wrathfully to his feet, shouted to the constables to clear the hall. In a loud, quarterdeck bellow he ordered the soldiers to form up outside.

"You are a disgrace to the uniform you wear and the king you purport to serve!" he told them and, turning to their commanding officer, added without attempting to lower his voice, "And the same stricture will apply to you, Captain Townson, unless you get your men in hand forthwith and march them back to their barracks!"

Some of the redcoats started sheepishly to obey him, but Watt, pressed hard against the wall, saw a little knot of grim-faced settlers make for one of them, singling him out from his comrades and, in a concerted movement, cut him off from their ranks.

"All right, Bannister," their leader threatened hoarsely. "The time o' reckoning has come. I'm going ter beat the living daylights out o' your filthy hide, so help me God I am! Watch out, you dog!"

The soldier, cornered and frightened, drew his bayonet.

"Come a step nearer and I'll kill you, Morgan! Is that slut o' yours worth dyin' for—is she? Before God, she egged me on! She . . ." Breathing hard, he retreated before the settlers, and coming to a halt beside Watt, with his back against the schoolhouse wall, he shouted to his comrades to come to his aid.

Several of them made to do so, but Captain King stopped them. "Outside!" he thundered. "Townson, take tow of your sergeants and put that soldier under arrest at once!"

Bannister suddenly lost all pretense of self-control. "You can arrest me!" he screamed. "But not before *he* gets my bayonet in his guts!"

He lunged wildly at the man he had called Morgan, and Watt Sparrow, galvanized into action, stuck out a foot, which brought Bannister crashing to the ground. Before any of the settlers had collected their wits sufficiently to move, Watt had the soldier on his feet and his own small body planted squarely in front of him.

"Get out o' here, boys," he warned the settlers urgently. "Before they try ter arrest you. Don't want no trouble, do yer?"

Clearly even Morgan did not. They vanished swiftly into the crowd, and when Captain Townson and his sergeants reached him, Watt bent to pick up the fallen bayonet from the floor and offered it with a wry grin. He said, standing aside to leave the dazed Bannister unprotected, "No 'arm done, sir."

"Oh, is there not!" Townson exclaimed furiously. "Take him away and hold him in the guardroom, Sar'nt Kane. And you, Mercer, cut along outside and get the rest of them lined up. By God, I'll have every man jack on a charge if it's the last thing I ever do! The governor's right—they're a disgrace to the uniform they wear!"

He went off fuming, thrusting his way through the straggling crowd, and Watt was about to follow him when he turned and saw that the lieutenant governor himself was beside him.

"Well done, my man," Captain King said, his smile genuinely approving as he took in Watt's frailty and his lack of stature. "Tell me your name and why you're here." Watt did so, scarlet with confusion, and King laid a hand on his arm. "I'll review your case, Sparrow. Report to me in person at noon tomorrow."

Watt's heart lifted as hope was rekindled.

Next day it was rumored that the men of the New South Wales Corps were threatening mutiny unless the governor agreed to release Bannister from arrest, and in the hospital, as well as in the prison, speculation was rife as to what the island's governor would do.

Philip King acted swiftly and decisively. He formed a unit of militia from the one-time seamen and marines who were settlers, and together with the constables and his officers, ordered them to disarm the corps and place the ringleaders of the mutiny under arrest. This was done with singularly little trouble, and when, two days later, the colonial schooner *Francis* dropped anchor inside the reef at Sydney Bay, ten soldiers of the corps were taken aboard her under guard, for trial by court-martial on the mainland.

Watt Sparrow, his sentence remitted and with a recommendation that he be granted a full pardon, was also given passage in the schooner. He wept his thankfulness as, crouched on the crowded deck of the small vessel, he watched the rocky, thickly wooded coastline of Norfolk Island vanish into the Pacific haze.

He was not going home, he reminded himself; but glory be, returning to Jenny Taggart's little farm and his adopted grandson was the next best thing and more than he had dared to hope for. If he must leave his bones in an alien land, at least he could be confident now that he would leave them where he was loved. . . .

CHAPTER IX

"We must invite the lieutenant governor and Mistress Grose," Henrietta Spence suggested, quill poised above the guest list she was compiling. "And Captain and Mistress Paterson."

"Only Captain and Mistress Paterson, Etta my dear," her father put in. "*He* is to be acting governor until Captain Hunter arrives to take up his appointment. And there are rumors of promotions—Francis Grose is now a lieutenant colonel or shortly will be. He and his family will leave for England in the *Daedalus* next week and with them Dr. White and young Dr. Laing and the corps chaplain, Reverend Bain. It is their successors you must invite."

"And who might they be?" Henrietta asked a trifle tartly. "You spend all your time out in the wilds and yet are more aware of what is happening in the colony than I am, living in Sydney Cove, Papa!"

Jasper Spence smiled. "Ah, but then Mr. Macarthur is *my* informant. Little happens that he is not apprised of within twenty-four hours. Dr. Balmain has come from Norfolk Island to take over the responsibilities of surgeon general and—"

"And I suppose," Henrietta said, her mouth tightening in distaste, "the Yorkshire blacksmith will replace Mr. Bain?"

"The Reverend Samuel Marsden, you mean—yes, my dear, he will. It's a pity you dislike him—he is a man of enterprise and character and one with whom I, for one, would not quarrel."

"He is ill-mannered and uncouth, and his wife no better, Papa," Henrietta objected. "I cannot imagine why Major Grose saw fit to appoint him a justice of the peace, truly I cannot. He is very harsh in his judgments, particularly against the Irish, who are not of his faith, after all."

"For once we must disagree, Etta," her father said, with a touch of asperity. "The Reverend Mr. Marsden is a crusading Christian, filled with the desire to spread the Lord's word among the heathen and those abandoned wretches who have no faith at all. In my view he is likely to serve this colony better than the Reverend Mr. Johnson ever has—or ever will! Mr. Johnson spends more time tending that farm of his in Canterbury and his vines and fruit trees here than he does preaching to people who, heaven knows, are in need of Christian teaching and example. He seldom opens his mouth save to complain. Indeed, one can scarcely hold converse with him before he launches into some tale of woe concerning government's failure to recompense him for the sixty-odd pounds his church cost him to build. He—"

Henrietta impatiently cut him short. "Oh, very well, Papa. . . . You needn't go on. I will add Mr. Marsden to my list. And Dr. Balmain and Mr. de Catteral. The Macarthurs are giving their own Christmas Eve dinner, you said, so I have not put them down." She read through her list, self-consciously leaving Charles Brace's name until the last. "Is there anyone else you would like me to invite?"

"Dr. D'Arcy Wentworth and his wife, if they arrive in time from Norfolk Island. He is—"

"His *wife*?" Henrietta echoed scornfully. "Elizabeth Macarthur who came out with them in the same ship, told me that Catherine Crowley was a convict, Papa! And their first child was born out of wedlock. Besides he is supposed to have fled to escape trial and to have accepted deportation instead and—"

"You must endeavor to overcome such prejudices, my dear," her father chided. "Wentworth is a man of substance now, and he will be Dr. Balmain's assistant here, as he was on Norfolk Island. However, the question of his invitation probably won't arise since he is not yet here. And—" Seeing the rebellious gleam in Henrietta's dark eyes, he hurriedly changed the subject, asking her instead about the menu.

She answered with pardonable pride, listing the dishes she had planned. "I shall need Mrs. O'Leary for at least a week before the dinner, Papa, to bake. Will you arrange for her to be sent back here?"

"Seamus and his boys won't like that, Etta. The woman's only been with them for two months. . . . You kept her much longer than they or I anticipated. Could you not manage without her?" Spence frowned. "Surely—"

Henrietta shook her head firmly. "No. Unless you expect *me* to bake pies in an earthenware oven."

"Certainly not, my dear," Jasper Spence assured her. "But I thought you were so pleased with the new girl Charles Brace found for you? What's her name . . . Frances, is it not?"

His voice was carefully level and without expression although, at the time, it had come as something of a shock when, on one of his weekend visits to the house in Sydney Cove, he had found Frances O'Riordan installed as his daughter's maidservant. Young Brace, it transpired, had arrested her as a fugitive at Jenny Taggart's farm and, while the Irish girl had escaped punishment because of her sickly condition, poor Jenny Taggart had been sentenced to a day in the stocks at Parramatta for having harbored her.

Neither had betrayed him or made any mention of the fact that he had taken her in initially. . . . Indeed Frances, he had decided, was probably quite unaware that he had been her rescuer. She had been too ill, barely conscious for most of the time she had spent at his farm, and she clearly had no recollection of having sobbed out her story to him in the darkness, before he had ridden posthaste to summon Jenny Taggart to care for her.

Not that he would have incurred any penalty had either of the young women talked of his part in the affair. His reputation, since he was a magistrate, might have suffered a little in the eyes of the corps officers, but that was all. He could have shrugged the incident off, explained it as a sudden, inexplicable impulse engendered by pity . . . as perhaps it had been, for he had believed the Irish girl to be dying. And she—

Henrietta said, breaking abruptly into his thoughts, "I *am* pleased with Frances O'Riordan, Papa. She is of gentle breeding, educated and well-mannered, and a beautiful needlewoman. She is as much a companion to me as a maid, and I'm delighted that Charles should have sent her to me. But she is not a cook and—"

"Why *did* he send her to you, my dear?" Jasper Spence asked curiously. Brace's reasons had puzzled him more than a little when he had first learned that it had been at his instigation that Frances O'Riordan had entered his daughter's employ. The girl was a beauty, and he was fully aware that most of the corps officers liked to keep such discoveries to themselves, for education and gentle breeding were rare qualities among the women deported to New South Wales.

Henrietta's reply was evasive, and he studied her face with some anxiety, wondering whether she still intended to set her cap at the Honourable Charles Windham Brace. Certainly he continued to dance attendance on her, but his courtship—if such it was—was by no means ardent, and often weeks went by when they scarcely saw him. He, too, had acquired land in the Parramatta area, and besides this, two exploratory expeditions had occupied a good deal of his time of late.

Henrietta drew herself up, flushing a little under her father's scrutiny. She said, in a impulsive burst of confidence, "Papa, I would like to marry Charles. I—"

"Has he asked you, Etta? He's said nothing to me, and he must know that I—" Jasper Spence broke off, shocked by the expression he glimpsed in her dark eyes. Her mother had sometimes looked at him as Henrietta was looking now, always when she had wanted more than was in his power to give her. He drew in his breath sharply, conscious of the old, familiar pain he had felt when he had been compelled to confess his helplessness. "Etta, my dear," he began unhappily. "Surely you—"

Henrietta interrupted, her voice strangely harsh, "No, he has not asked me. But if I had let him take Frances O'Riordan as his—his housekeeper, instead of the creature he has, he would never ask me, never in this world." She faced him, the glint of tears in her eyes, her smile forced and tremulous. "Charles did not send Frances to me . . . I took her away from him, and she was glad to come. Believe me, Papa, she was grateful for the opportunity to become my maid! And she has told me what he expected of her, what—what terms he offered."

"Frances told you *that*?"

She inclined her head, the tears flowing now without restraint. "He wanted her as his—his mistress, but I took her away. It has made him angry—with her, I think, more than with me."

"And you still want to marry him?" her father questioned, seeking vainly to conceal the sense of outrage he felt. He had tried so hard over the years to protect this beloved daughter of his, to preserve her innocence and her illusions, but like her mother before her, she demanded too much of him, and he knew that he had failed when Henrietta said in a small, choked voice, "Oh, yes. I judge him as a man, and men are not saints, are they? They have carnal lusts, they . . . even you, Papa."

"What do you mean, Etta?"

She laid a hand on his arm. "Did you think I did not know of your women . . . of the Rani Sita Devi in particular? Mamma wasn't aware of your liaison with the Rani, of course, but I was, even as a child. It was servants' gossip that at first I was too young to understand. Now that I do I would not presume to judge you, dear Papa . . . or blame you, either. The fault was mamma's, was it not?"

Jasper Spence felt the color drain from his cheeks. He managed to stammer, "Your mamma was ill, Etta, an invalid for most of her life. That was not her fault."

But, he thought dully, she had used her frailty to enslave him . . . even to ruin him. For her sake he had abused his position of trust, had squandered twenty years of dedicated industry so that he might give her the luxuries she had claimed as her due, although he had been aware that, sooner or later, the truth must be discovered and his career come to an ignoble end. Because of the Rani's involvement and in order to avoid a scandal, they had permitted him to resign, and he had retained most of the proceeds of his defection, because bribes could not be repaid or recovered even by the great John Company. He was a rich man but a man without honor and . . . He expelled his breath in a long-drawn sigh. In the penal colony of New South Wales he was a magistrate, with the power of life and death over men and women whose crimes were infinitesimal when measured against his own.

And Margaret, the wife he had loved more than life itself, was long dead . . . his secret with her. He looked at Henrietta and said abruptly, but with deep conviction, "You would be better off with young Dawson as a husband, Etta. Or one of his stamp. They are the ones who will bring prosperity to this colony because they'll work to that end. The corps officers just want to—damme, to plunder it, for their own profit!"

Her tears vanished. She said scornfully, "He is uncouth, Papa, and he smells of the stables. I know what I want . . . and that is not Timothy Dawson. I will see if luncheon is ready, if you will excuse me." At the door she turned and added spitefully, "In any event, Mr. Dawson has found himself a convict girl, has he not? One named Jenny Taggart, I'm told."

Her father did not answer her, and he made no attempt to refute her accusation. He returned to Portland next day, pleased to find that in his absence the farm's first harvest had been gathered in—despite its late sowing—with most profitable results. There would be feed and to spare for his stock through the coming winter; the grass was good, and even when seed was kept back for January sowing, Seamus O'Leary was able to point with pride to the bulging sacks in the granary that could be sold to the commissariat.

"Patrick can shift the first load wid the ox wagon tomorrow, yer honor," the foreman volunteered. "But I was thinkin' . . . they've set up a new corn mill in Parramatta that seems to be workin' well enough. Should I have a few bushels ground an' dressed for household use, here an' in yer honor's house in the cove? The miller's a convict, sorr, workin' under license, so he's not permitted to overcharge for his services."

"An excellent idea, O'Leary," Jasper Spence approved and then, mindful of his daughter's demand for Mrs. O'Leary's services, he went on, "We shall require your wife in Sydney over Christmas. I regret having to deprive you of her company during the festive season, but Mistress Henrietta particularly wants her to assist with her entertaining."

O'Leary's agreement was a trifle sullen, but he gave it, and his sullenness vanished when his employer promised a Christmas bonus in cash for himself and gave him permission to slaughter a sheep and a suckling pig for the laborers.

"Your wife can bring what we require in the way of fresh meat by boat early next week, and some of the fresh flour, also, if it's ready in time."

"I'll see to it, yer honor. Will there be ony liquor for the men, maybe? They've worked well, an' I was thinkin'—"

Jasper Spence cut him short. "They'll receive whatever is

officially permitted, O'Leary, but I want no drunkenness, you understand? You are in charge in my absence, and I shall hold you responsible for the men's behavior."

"Why, sure, yer honor, I understand that," the foreman assured him, abashed. Then, screwing up his courage, he ventured diffidently, "Dere's just one thing, sorr . . . a favor I have to ask, if yer honor will pardon the liberty."

"Well?" His employer's tone was impatient. "What is it, man?"

"Sorr—" O'Leary shuffled his feet, his gaze on the dusty tips of his worn leather boots—"I—that is, I've a few pounds put by an' wid the bonus yer honor is after promisin' me, I'd like to buy some breedin' stock on me own account. There's an ould feller sellin' up, to pay his passage home, sorr. I—that is, I could take most o' his beasts off him, his goats, an' his two breedin' sows, an' his hens as well for forty pounds. They're a bargain, sorr, an' if yer honor would allow me to keep them here, I'd be greatly beholden to you, so I would."

Jasper Spence stared at him in astonishment. How in the world, he wondered, could Seamus O'Leary have acquired such a sum? His own promised bonus was a generous one, but even so, it amounted only to five pounds, and he had intended it to be shared by the whole O'Leary family. Seamus could not have saved half the amount he was proposing to invest in livestock from his wages. He started to say so and then thought better of it. The man should be encouraged to acquire livestock on his own account, not the reverse, and with the price of breeding sows as high as ten pounds apiece, with goats between four and eight and laying hens fetching half a sovereign, he would be getting a good bargain for his forty pounds. And if he were given three or four acres and permission to erect pens and pigsties thereon, that would ensure his continued hard work and loyalty. . . .

"Certainly, O'Leary," Spence said. "Buy what stock you can afford and set the men to putting up the buildings you require in their free time . . . after Christmas, of course. And don't forget to send your wife to assist Mistress Henrietta with her dinner party. She has only your fellow countrywoman, Frances O'Riordan, to serve her at present, and there is much to be attended to."

"Mistress O'Riordan!" O'Leary echoed. "Yer honor has *Mistress O'Riordan* in your service?"

He sounded shocked, but Jasper Spence was already moving toward the door of the granary and noticed nothing amiss. "That is what I said," he returned indifferently and added, consulting his pocket watch, "I shall take luncheon in half an hour. Have the bay gelding saddled for me at three o'clock, if you please. I'll ride out to look at the land you've cleared for vines . . . and the new fenced enclosures."

"You'll find all in good order, sorr," Seamus O'Leary assured him, recovering himself. "As I'm tellin' yer honor, the men have worked well, so they have."

And indeed there was evidence to support his claim, Jasper Spence decided, after making his inspection. The dark, loamy soil had been well tilled, the timber burned off, and the fences were sturdily constructed, in readiness for the arrival of his next consignment of vines and fruit trees from the Cape. He rode back to the farmstead just before dusk, observing with approval the healthy state of his small herd of Cape sheep . . . hardy creatures that were breeding well in their new environment.

There was a handsome chestnut stallion tethered to the hitching rail at the front of the house, and he recognized it, with envy, as Timothy Dawson's. Mrs. O'Leary, answering the door to him, explained that she had shown the caller into the parlor to await his return.

"Did I do right, sir?" she asked, seeming somewhat flustered and ill at ease. "The gentleman was after sayin' he had business wid you and—"

Jasper Spence nodded. So young Dawson was rated a gentleman now, he thought cynically. . . . Or perhaps Mrs. O'Leary had failed to identify him as their fellow passenger of the *Britannia*'s passage from the Cape, the man Henrietta persisted in describing as "uncouth."

"Serve us with wine and glasses, if you please," he instructed. "A bottle of the Cape brandy will do admirably." He had bought twelve gallons of the brandy from Captain Page, master of the *Halcyon* from Rhode Island, when the ship had called in June on a voyage of speculation, and obtained it at a fair and reasonable price. Since then, however, all cargoes of spirits had been bespoken by the corps officers, who blatantly retailed their purchases at three and four times their cost. Although, to do him credit, John Macarthur had offered Spence the opportunity to add to his own stock at cost, should he wish to do so.

He smiled thinly as he divested himself of his dusty jacket and riding boots, wondering whether a similar concession had been made to Timothy Dawson and the other free settlers. It seemed unlikely, since Macarthur had stressed the fact that his offer should be regarded as a favor and the asking price kept in confidence.

Mrs. O'Leary passed him with her tray containing the decanter and glasses; Spence donned his house slippers and hesitated over the elegant gray-velvet coat she had put out for him, but it was hot, and he decided to receive the visitor in his shirtsleeves. He entered the farmhouse living room, still sparsely furnished, expecting Dawson to be similarly clad and halted in astonishment at the change in him. Gone were the rough homespuns, which Henrietta had claimed always reeked of the stable. Timothy Dawson was dressed like a gentleman born, his boots and breeches impeccable, his linen spotless, and his jacket a fashionable cutaway of lightweight green cloth.

He rose at once and, after shaking hands, politely requested his host's permission to remove his own jacket.

They talked amicably of crops and livestock as they sipped their brandy, and Jasper Spence, recalling the hours they had spent in similar fashion on board the *Britannia*, realized that he had missed the younger man's companionship during the past year, as well as his expertise and his optimism.

"You are doing well for yourself at the Hawkesbury, Tim," he suggested, rising to refill both their glasses.

"Well enough, sir," Dawson confirmed. "Very well, indeed with my horse-breeding and not badly with my sheep. But the land close to the river is prone to flooding, and all the wheat has suffered from a blight, which has reduced my crop at harvesting to ten bushels to the acre. Jenny Taggart has put me to shame on that account. . . . She has produced a bumper crop at Parramatta, and the maize there is the finest I've seen."

"Do the Indians continue to trouble you?" Spence asked curiously.

"Aye, they do, sir, sorely. We've put in request after request to have soldiers stationed near enough to our holdings to ward off the threat the Bediagal tribe present, but to no avail. Mr. Macarthur insists that he has no soldiers to spare. He's posted a corporal and six men at Toongabbe, but they are too far away to be of any assistance to us."

"Are you not able to defend yourselves?"

"A mite too well, I fear, sir." Dawson shrugged in exasperation. "The settlers take the law into their own hands. Any Indian, guilty or innocent, who shows his face near us is killed—often brutally—and they retaliate by raiding our houses and burning our crops. I've tried to get on better terms with them, but in the present climate it's useless. We need soldiers to keep the peace and, not to put too fine a point on it, sir, to hold the settlers in check. Some of them are what I can only describe as undesirables, who match the Indians in savagery and do little work on their land. They would do no good anywhere, and they're ready to sell out."

"Why do you not sell out?" Spence questioned. "And move to the Ponds or Parramatta?"

"Because the Hawkesbury land is good—the best, I dare swear, in the colony. Or it could be if we could come to terms with the Bediagal people or if the corps would furnish us with sufficient troops to prevent their raids! . . ." Timothy hesitated, eyeing his host uncertainly. "I'm looking to the future, Mr. Spence."

"As we all are, my dear boy!" his host assured him. Soon, he thought, they would come to the reason for Dawson's unexpected visit, since of a surety he had not ridden more than thirty-five miles merely in order to discuss crops and Indian raids. Smiling encouragement, he again topped up their glasses and resumed his seat.

"I need more land, sir," Dawson said. "Another fifty acres at least, though a hundred would suit me better. The grazing in the river area is really good, and I want to run more horses. Brood mares, sir, with their foals . . . farm workhorses as well as hacks. And more sheep. And I'd prefer to cultivate oats and barley for animal feed rather than wheat."

"What is to prevent you?" Spence challenged shrewdly and, still smiling, supplied his own answer. "Lack of capital? Or have the authorities refused to grant you more land?"

Dawson spread his big sunbrowned hands and wryly echoed his smile. "Both, sir. I'd have to buy the land—they won't give me any more—and I haven't the money available. But that is due to the corps officers' monopoly of the trade in spirits. . . . You do not need me to tell you that our currency here is rum. We are forced to pay our labor in rum, to sell our crops for the stuff, and only Major Grose and his cronies can buy it when it's shipped out here. The ships' masters sell it to them at five shillings a gallon, and they sell it to the rest of us for twenty, or if we trade in wheat, it costs us five bushels . . . *delivered*. The corps syndicate purchased the whole of the *Hope*'s cargo and most of the *Halcyon*'s and they've sent the old *Britannia* to the Cape solely on their behalf. They—"

"I am aware of the corps's commercial dealings, my boy," Spence pointed out mildly.

"Forgive me, sir . . . I let my indignation carry me away," Timothy Dawson apologized. "But we—the free settlers, Mr. Spence—cannot make a profit by growing food, be it wheat or livestock, and we never will, the way things are now. The officers control the prices we're paid, and Major Grose buys from us, officially on behalf of government, so that we have no redress."

"*Colonel* Grose is leaving the colony in the *Daedalus*, Tim."

"It will make no odds, sir. His place will be taken by one of the others—Captain Paterson, I heard. He will change nothing."

The chances were that he would not, Jasper Spence thought, although Macarthur was now the syndicate's organizer and its leading spirit. And he himself had a share in the enterprise, thanks to Grose, which—he frowned, studying Timothy Dawson's honest young face—which gave him, so to speak, a foot in both camps and a virtual certainty of a very handsome profit on his investment. There might be worse ways of reinvesting that profit than in Dawson, whose capacity for hard work he profoundly admired. The boy was of farming stock, he knew what he was about, and . . . dear heaven, he was infinitely to be preferred as a future son-in-law to Charles Brace!

Spence leaned forward, putting out a thin hand to touch the younger man's. "Is the purpose of your call to ask me for a loan, my dear boy?" he asked quietly.

Dawson reddened, confused by his bluntness, and then, his mouth tightening, he inclined his head. "Aye, you've read my purpose aright, sir. Only I—"

"You'd intended to come to it more circumspectly, perhaps?"

"Yes, sir, that I had." Dawson spoke ruefully. "But I brought papers with me. . . . They're here, in my coat pocket. I've set out all my assets for you to consider, and I can offer you a good collateral if that's the correct term." The papers were spread out on the table between them, and he indicated the headings to each neatly penned list. "I own the Taggart holding, but that is—it's a special agreement I made with Jenny Taggart. I gave my word that she should be free to buy her land back when she is able to afford the price. She—"

"You're not involved with the girl, are you?" Spence demanded sharply, remembering his daughter's disparaging observation.

Dawson's swift, emphatic denial was entirely convincing. "I owe my life to her, Mr. Spence. Had it not been for her prompt action and skilled nursing when I suffered the bite of a venomous snake, the day I landed here would have been my last. That is the—the basis of our relationship. I —your daughter, Henrietta, sir. As you know I—" he was stammering in embarrassment. "On board ship I asked your permission to—to pay my court to her and—"

"And I gave it, did I not?" Jasper Spence mused.

"Yes, sir. But—"

"Am I to take it that your sentiments toward my daughter remain unchanged, Tim?"

"They do, sir, yes. And always will. I'm not a man to change and I—well, I continue to cherish the hope that Henrietta may—" Timothy Dawson's voice was choked. He swallowed hard and looked up to meet his host's gaze squarely. "I'm aware that her affections are otherwise directed, Mr. Spence. But I can wait, I—I *will* wait, in the belief that my cause is not yet lost."

For a moment Jasper Spence considered issuing an invitation to him to attend Henrietta's Christmas dinner party,

but then reluctantly decided against it. Such an invitation
would be premature; Henrietta needed time to come to her
senses, and Timothy Dawson also undoubtedly needed
time—and money—to complete his metamorphosis.

He said, smiling warmly, "You shall have your loan,
Tim. But I require no collateral. Let us rather enter into a
partnership agreement. We will draft a document between
us before you leave to cover any eventuality and be binding
on us both. In the meantime, here's my hand on it."

He offered his hand, and Timothy Dawson grasped it
eagerly. "In my wildest dreams, sir, I never dared hope
that you—that is, I—" He could not go on.

"We will drink to the future, my dear boy," Spence told
him. He again refilled their glasses and raised his own.

"To our future partnership!" he said. "May it prosper in
every respect!"

The brig *Experiment* dropped anchor in Sydney Cove on
Christmas Eve, and the word swiftly spread that she was on
a voyage of speculation from Calcutta, laden with spirits
and trade goods.

The new acting governor, Captain Paterson, having engaged to purchase the spirits, gave permission to the brig's
master, Captain McLellan, to open a shop at the quayside.
Henrietta's house servant, Noah, brought news of its opening.

"There's all sorts there, mistress," the big man told her
excitedly. "Ladies' shoes an' bonnets, Indian silks an' mus-
lins, knickknacks, jewelry, copper, an' inlaid wood tables. I
ain't never seen the like, outside o' London town. You
ought ter go an' see for yourself, afore everything's sold."

Henrietta, busy with arrangements for her dinner party,
was sorely tempted but . . . She eyed him uncertainly.
Mrs. O'Leary was already in the kitchen, but she would
require supervision; it was important that everything be
done correctly, and excellent cook though the woman was,
she was not accustomed to the ways of a gentleman's
household. She turned questioningly to Frances O'Riordan.

"Noah says the *Experiment* has brought silks and mus-
lins. You are the needlewoman, Frances. Suppose you go,
and if the prices are not too high, have them put aside half
a dozen dress lengths until I can come myself to inspect

them. Shoes, too, and perhaps a bonnet . . . you know what I like. And," she added generously, "you may choose yourself a Christmas gift from me if you wish."

Frances acquiesced with delight. The *Experiment*'s trade goods were set out in a recently completed government store close to the quay, and five minutes' brisk walk brought her to the store . . . and the long queue, mainly composed of women convicts like herself, which had formed at the entrance. It was a pleasant, sunny morning, the heat tempered by a southerly breeze, and she waited without impatience for her turn to enter the dimly lit warehouse. A soldier guarded the door, and a ship's officer stood just inside, armed with a rattan cane—both there, presumably, to ensure that there was no unseemly jostling. But the crowd was orderly, and a number carried baskets of fresh vegetables and eggs with which to barter for the goods on display.

Inside at last, Frances saw that Noah had not exaggerated. The place was piled high with merchandise, resembling the descriptions she had read of Indian bazaars. Much of it was cheap-jack stuff, unlikely to be of much practical use to the impoverished settlers, who had for so long been compelled to make do with rough-hewn wooden furniture, improvised cooking and drinking vessels, and the coarse, imported issue clothing that was as drab and ill-fitting as it was uncomfortable.

There were pretty copper lamps and lanterns, fine china cups and plates, and a wealth of colorful silks and satins that were a delight to the eye, but all, she realized, so highly priced and fragile that the majority of Captain McLellan's would-be customers were—albeit regretfully—passing them by. Mindful of Henrietta's instructions, she sought among the cloth bolts and examined the ready-made bonnets and the hand-tooled Bengal leather slippers, fearing to commit herself to any definite purchases, lest she earn a reprimand for having made too frivolous a choice.

Among the copperware she found a number of pots and pans and a handsome kettle that, after lengthy reflection, she decided to ask the vendor to reserve, confident that Mrs. O'Leary would approve of them, even if Henrietta did not. Lascar seamen, dark-faced, smiling little men, were acting as salesmen under the supervision of their officers, and when she returned to the cloth stall for a second inspection, a fair-haired young apprentice came strolling across to greet her.

"Have we nothing to please your ladyship?" he demanded cheekily. "Surely this. . . ." With clumsy hands he unrolled a bale of exquisitely dyed silk and attempted to drape it about Frances's slim shouders. She backed away instinctively, and grinning, the boy held the glowing stuff against his own lanky body. "Or this. . . ." He let the bale fall and reached for another, in palest green. "Now this would set off your coloring a treat, ma'am, though I say it as shouldn't. Or maybe the peacock blue— fetch it, Bihari Lal! *Nahin*, you *ulloo ka batcha* . . . devil take you, why can't you learn to speak English?"

The lascar, beaming cheerfully, eventually selected the bale the youngster wanted, from beneath a pile of others, and Frances, for all her caution, could not repress a cry of pleasure as, between them, they spread the iridescent material across the table in front of her.

"This is the best we have," the apprentice told her. "And we're supposed to ask two pounds for enough to fashion a gown for a lady. But"—he lowered his voice to a conspiratorial whisper—"for you, and if you'll promise not to tell my captain, half price! Only a pound, ma'am, and a real bargain, because you'll look so beautiful in it."

Frances flushed. "I—I am not here to buy for myself, I—put it aside, if you please, in the name of my mistress. She—"

The boy stared at her, jaw dropping in ludicrous surprise. "Your *mistress*? You mean you're . . . damme, you're a *convict*?"

She inclined her head wretchedly, her color deepening, but finally, recovering herself, she said with dignity, "Yes, I am a convict." She gave him Henrietta's name, hurriedly chose two more dress lengths and a dozen yards of hard-wearing gingham to be put aside with the silk, and was about to make her escape from what had become an embarrassing situation, when a voice from behind her ordered her peremptorily to wait.

"Cut off five yards of that stuff—the blue silk. Yes, from that bale there . . . and here's your money."

Frances recognized the hated voice of Lieutenant Brace

and shrank from him in fear. Ever since he had arrested her at Jenny Taggart's farm she had feared him, and although not greatly enamored of Henrietta, was grateful to her—and to her father—for having saved her from being assigned to his household, which, it was now evident, had been Brace's intention. She remembered how he had approached her with his offer of what he had been pleased to call "employment," when she had just arrived in the colony, with the heartbreaking memory of her brother's death still fresh in her mind and . . . She shivered, backing still farther away from him and the grinning apprentice. Mistrust and hatred of the English redcoats and their officers had been bred in her since her early childhood; for all her father's position in the community, she had learned that in Ireland they were to be feared, even by a doctor's daughter.

"Not so fast, Frances O'Riordan," Lieutenant Brace admonished. "I wish to make you a gift." He thrust the gleaming folds of silk into her arms, head on one side as he affected to study its coloring against hers. "Splendid—it was spun for you and no one else! Accept it, I beg you, with my tender sentiments and as a token of the esteem in which I hold you."

It was a pretty speech, delivered without his customary arrogance, and Frances hesitated, torn between her instinctive mistrust of him and her reluctance to make a scene in so public a place, word of which might reach Henrietta's ears. Her mistress, as she had good reason to know, regarded Charles Brace in the light of a suitor and would undoubtedly be both hurt and angry were Frances to return to the house bearing a gift from him that, however hard she tried, she would be unable to conceal.

She said quietly, "Forgive me, sir, but I cannot accept this. I am a convict, and convicts do not dress in silks. My mistress would chide me—and with cause—were I to do so."

"If you were in *my* household, I would delight in dressing you thus!" Brace protested. "I would indulge your every whim, Frances! Come back to me, will you not?"

Frances shook her head. Poised for flight, she attempted to give him the bundle of silk, but he refused to take it. "Whether you come back to me or not, that is yours—that is my gift to you. Can you not hide it from prying eyes?

Here—" He took her basket from her and thrust the brightly hued silk into its roomy interior. "This all too severe mistress of yours, who compels you to dress in the drab trappings of servitude—damme, she won't find it now, will she?"

It was useless to argue with him, Frances thought miserably, and perhaps, after all, she could contrive a hiding place for the unwelcome gift. So long as Henrietta did not suspect the identity of the donor, she might one day even fashion herself a dress from the lovely stuff. One day, when her sentence had expired and she was free. . . . Frances drew in her breath sharply.

"I—thank you." Eyes averted, she dropped Charles Brace a curtsy and made for the warehouse entrance, her pace quickening to what was almost an undignified run as she thrust her way through the crowd, heedless now of the curious glances her haste attracted.

"What's yer hurry, lass?" a rough voice demanded. "Bin on the palming lay, 'ave yer? Let's see what yer lifted!"

Two hands grasped her firmly from behind, and Frances turned to find a heavy-jowled, unshaven face glaring down into hers. The man—an emancipated convict, by his garb—was accompanied by a thin, dark-eyed woman with a pinched mouth, who shrilly joined him in accusation.

"Gie's a cool at that basket, yer little hoister," she hissed. "Less'n yer want us ter start a jolly an' get yer nibbed!"

Frances stared at her in uncomprehending dismay. "I—I've stolen nothing," she protested, guessing at the meaning of the woman's threat. She started to open her basket, but the creature seized it from her and, with a triumphant cackle, drew out the shimmering length of silk.

"Yer didn't never come by this honestly!" the woman accused. Raising her voice to its shrillest height she invited those around her to bear witness, waving the silk over her head as evidence.

Frances, already unnerved by her encounter with Charles Brace, yielded to panic. Leaving the silk in the possession of her accuser, she turned and ran, hearing to her horror the cry of "Stop thief!" It echoed after her as, speeding blindly across the wharf, she heard others take up the cry.

Two off-duty soldiers, lounging aimlessly nearby,

brought about her downfall. One put out a booted foot to trip her, and she blundered into it, to fall heavily on the dusty ground.

"Now then, lass!" One of them dragged her, sobbing, to her feet. "Can't 'ave yer thievin' in this 'ere den of iniquity, can we?"

Frances attempted to stammer a denial, and then, to her heartfelt relief, she saw Lieutenant Brace striding toward the little group of idlers who had collected around her.

"Mr. Brace—oh, please, help me!" she besought him, and to the soldiers she added confidently, "Lieutenant Brace will explain. He know I stole nothing. The silk was his gift."

Brace had the disputed silk draped over his arm. He gave her only a cursory glance as if she were a stranger and, incredulously, Frances heard him order the soldiers to place her under arrest.

"The court is sitting," he said. "Conduct this woman there. I will have a word with the judge advocate and arrange to have the charges against her heard at once."

He went ahead of them, and as she followed, with her escort firmly gripping her by the arm, Frances stared at his retreating, red-coated back, her fears growing. Did he, she wondered dully, intend to lie about his gift, pretend that he had not made it? The shrill-voiced woman's intervention had been made purely by chance—Charles Brace could not have foreseen it, but . . . Her throat ached with tears. That he would somehow turn it to his advantage she did not doubt, and handcuffed as she waited outside the building that now housed the court, she fought back the tears and summoned the last vestiges of her courage.

The magistrates sitting, under the presidency of Captain Foveaux, in order to clear up a backlog of minor cases before the commencement of the Christmas festivities, kept her waiting for less than an hour.

"Keep yer pecker up, lass," the court jailer told her, not unkindly. "Rushin' through everything, they are, an' givin' light sentences on account o' Christmas. You're in luck, did you but know it."

But faced with the row of stern-visaged officers composing the court, Frances felt as if she were enduring a nightmare from which, God willing, she must soon awake. She had expected to be charged with theft, but, to her stunned surprise when the indictment was read to her, it accused her only of having absented herself from the labor to which she had been assigned.

"Frances O'Riordan, how do you plead?" the judge advocate asked her. He had a kindly, pleasant face, and he spoke quite gently; taking heart from this, Frances managed in a small, choked voice to say that she did not understand the charge.

Before he could reply, Lieutenant Brace rose to his feet.

"Sir," he said, addressing the president, "I believe, if you will permit me, I can save the court's time."

"You brought the charges, did you not?" Captain Foveaux suggested in a bored tone. "Then by all means save us time if you can, Mr. Brace."

Sick with despair Frances listened to his recital. Brace's claims were near enough to the truth to render them difficult, if not impossible, for her to refute; for it would, she knew, be his word against hers . . . and her word, that of a convicted felon, would inevitably be given less credence than the word of an officer, holder of the king's commission. And it seemed, from the indulgence shown him, that of a friend of the president of the court . . . She bit back a sob.

She had been assigned to him as a domestic servant, following her arrest as a runaway, Brace explained. "She is a girl of good education and presence, sir, and I confess I was moved to pity by her plight. She had been in the woods, with some ill-chosen companions, for many weeks . . . no doubt the court will recall that her companions were murdered by the native tribes beyond the Hawkesbury."

"The Irish seditionists!" one of the officers exclaimed, and Captain Foveaux, his interest kindled, asked pointedly, "Was this girl transported for sedition, Mr. Brace?"

"So I understand, sir, yes. She arrived here on board the *Boddingtons* transport. Her brother was, I believe, hanged as a ringleader of an attempted mutiny during the passage. May I continue, sir?"

"Pray do so, Mr. Brace," Foveaux invited.

Brace glossed over the manner in which Frances had al-

legedly left his employ, hinting that she had done so for
purely financial gain.

"Mr. Spence pays his domestic servants overgenerously
—much more than an officer of our corps can afford—
and doubtless the girl was tempted. I took no steps to
recover her because Mr. Spence and his daughter are personal friends, but in view of O'Riordan's past record, I did
doubt that she would be kept under sufficiently stern discipline in Mr. Spence's household. My doubts on this score
were removed this morning, sir."

"How so, sir?" the president asked. He took out his
pocket watch, to study it with a hint of impatience. "Be
brief, if you will Mr. Brace."

He had purchased a roll of silk, Brace stated, which he
had intended as a Christmas gift for a lady. Frances clasped
her handcuffed wrists in sudden fear. But surely now he
would tell the truth, surely now there was no way in which
he could lie about his gift to her? But, she realized as Lieutenant Brace went smoothly on, even the truth could be
twisted so as to make her appear to be guilty. She heard his
voice faintly, as if from a long distance, and beside her the
jailer gripped her arm with a whispered, "Bear up, my
lass—it's nearly over."

"I entrusted my gift to her," Charles Brace was saying.
"With the instruction that she deliver it to her mistress with
my respectful compliments. Instead, gentlemen, the girl apparently tried to abscond with it and was only prevented
from doing so by the intervention of two persons—a couple
by the name of Ashton—who raised a hue and cry that led
to her arrest. Both these persons and the two soldiers who
made the arrest are prepared to give evidence to this effect,
if you require them to do so, sir."

Foveaux shook his head emphatically. "Your word is
good enough, I am sure, Mr. Brace. Agreed, gentlemen?
We've wasted enough time over this case, I think and—"

"Forgive me, sir . . ." the judge advocate interrupted,
his tone no longer gentle. "If the facts are as stated by Mr.
Brace, why was the charge against this young woman not
one of attempted theft?"

Brace answered him. "Sir, I sought to spare the poor
young woman, who is, as I mentioned earlier, of good family and education, deported for a political crime. I am ask-

ing the court's indulgence on her behalf. It is Christmas, gentlemen, when the spirit of goodwill and mercy should be abroad. I brought no such charge as the judge advocate appears to consider I should have for this reason and because it is possible that the prisoner might have misunderstood the instructions I gave her regarding my gift. Sir, I—"

The president cut him short. "I accept your explanation, Mr. Brace. . . . Gentlemen?" The others inclined their heads in unison. "Good. We need not adjourn to debate the sentence or, indeed, our verdict, I think." Again, Frances saw, the heads were inclined in ready agreement, and Captain Foveaux added formally, "We find the prisoner, Frances O'Riordan, guilty as charged, and order that she return to the employment to which she was duly assigned. She is to receive one dozen lashes, but since Mr. Brace has reminded us that it is Christmas, this punishment shall not be administered unless she should again absent herself from her assigned employment. She is given into your custody, Mr. Brace, and the case is concluded."

It was not until the night of Christmas Day that Charles Brace—returning from the Spences' elaborate dinner party well primed with Cape brandy—released Frances from the room in which he had ordered her confined. He led her, white-faced but unresisting, to his own room. The roll of peacock-blue silk lay on the bed, and he gestured to it, smiling.

"You see, I didn't—didn't give it to Henrietta Spence after all. It's for you, Frances." His voice was slurred, his breath, as he bent to kiss her, reeked of brandy, but to her surprise his kiss was gentle. "Don't you understand—I've wanted you ever since I first set eyes on you," he told her thickly. "Only I have to be drunk before I can take you by force . . . and I *am* drunk, damme! But I . . . does it have to be by force, Frances?"

She faced him unhappily, yet still with a little of her old, defiant pride. "Not only by force . . . with lies, with false accusations. You—"

"Are those not a measure of how much I want you?" he protested. "And of how long I've waited for you?"

"If I had my way," Frances flung at him, "you'd wait forever!"

"That I won't do," Charles Brace asserted. His arms closed about her, and again his lips found hers, still gentle but insistent, and against her will Frances became aware of his male attraction and of the rekindling of a desire she had long kept in subjection. She endeavored to free herself, but his arms tightened about her. "I'll not be the first, will I?" he demanded, drawing her closer. "Those weeks in the woods with the Indians and the months on board the transport . . . did you not give yourself to one of your rebel countrymen?"

Swift and unbidden came a vision of Danny Halloran with his scarred young face and his eager pleading. Danny had wanted her, Frances remembered bitterly, he had loved her, cared for, and protected her and she . . . oh, dear heaven, she had felt a great tenderness for him that was close to love. She had promised to wed him, would gladly have done so, but, God rest his soul, Danny was dead, felled by an Indian spear and savagely butchered by a mob of yelling natives.

She had not given herself to Danny, for all she had been tempted to, because it would have been a sin, out of wedlock, according to the teaching of their church, but now . . . Suddenly she wished that she had disregarded the dictates of the priests and the stern injunctions that had guided her since her childhood. If sin it was for the well-brought-up daughter of a doctor, who was also a convicted rebel, then this . . . She looked up at Charles Brace in his red coat, hating what he was and all he stood for, and shook her head.

"No. I gave myself to no one, Mr. Brace. And I will not give myself to you."

"Then it's to be by force or not at all?" he challenged hoarsely. He swayed toward her, his hands reaching roughly for the fastening of her dress as he forced her back onto the bed with its covering of crumpled blue silk. "Well, so be it, you Irish witch! I told you I was drunk, didn't I? Then let us see how drunk!"

He took her brutally and without compassion, and as Frances collapsed weeping beside him when he had done, he fell into a deep sleep, his arms holding her imprisoned beneath the roll of silk.

She felt unbearably humiliated, and the fact that he

could sleep so soundly, after what he had done, pained
her more than even his assault on her body. He had taken
her as a whore is taken, and . . . She shivered in the humid
darkness. She was not a whore and her only crime had been
her love for her country which had transcended all else.
Looking down at Charles Brace's dimly seen countenance,
Frances found herself wishing that she had a weapon—any
weapon—with which she might have put an end to his life,
as well as to her own.

BOOK TWO

*Terra
Australis . . .*

CHAPTER X

"So this is your *Terra Australis*, is it, Johnny?" Midshipman Matthew Flinders exclaimed, his tone bordering on flippancy. He waved a slim brown hand in the direction of the tall, seemingly inhospitable cliffs of the coastline to leeward and smiled amusedly at his companion. "But, of course, no longer incognito to you, and His Excellency, and our revered commander. Tell me, what are your feelings now that you've come back here?"

"Be damned, I don't know, Matt." John Broome, assistant master of His Majesty's ship *Reliance* of twenty-six guns, echoed his smile a trifle wryly. South Head was in sight, a flag flying from the summit, with the *Supply* sloop tacking to bring the wind onto her starboard quarter, and he remembered with a pang the last time he had seen the rocky headland, which guarded the entrance to Port Jackson.

On that occasion—nearly five years ago—he had watched its craggy bulk vanish into the noon-heat haze from the stern of Governor Phillip's stolen cutter, and there had been joy in his heart because he had believed he was looking his last on it. Poor Will Bryant had held his little son high in his arms and cheered, while Mary had crouched in the bow, white-faced and apprehensive, her baby at her breast, and the rest of them had drunk to the colony's eternal damnation in rum supplied them by the master of the *Waak-sam-heyd*.

"I feel some responsibility," Flinders said, suddenly grave, "for having persuaded you to return."

Johnny Broome shrugged. "You need bear none. I came of my own free will—you'd not have persuaded me against my will, Matt."

And that was the truth, he knew. He had first made Matthew Flinders's acquaintance when both had joined the *Bellerophon*, a seventy-four-gun ship of the line and flagship to Rear Admiral Pasley, in the newly formed Home Fleet commanded by Lord Howe. Flinders, despite his lowly rank and his youth, had been at sea for ten years. He had learned his navigating skills when serving under Captain Bligh in the *Providence* when—following the *Bounty* mutiny—that officer had made his second and finally successful voyage to Otaheite to load breadfruit for the West Indian plantations.

Young Flinders had been an apt pupil from whom, in his turn, Johnny Broome had learned much, yet curiously it was Flinders's admiration for the open-boat voyage to Timor that was the basis for their friendship.

"Bligh is arguably the best navigator and probably the best marine surveyor living today," the midshipman had asserted more than once. "And why the deuce not, since he served his apprenticeship under the great James Cook? Certainly the way he brought the *Bounty*'s people to Timor, after the mutineers cast them adrift, was nothing short of miraculous. But he had years of experience, he had the *Bounty*'s master, Fryer, with him, and his boat's crew were all strong, healthy seamen . . . so that, in my view, his feat does not equal yours, Johnny, my friend! You sailed farther, your boat was smaller, and you had a woman and two small children as passengers—and you contrived to deliver them all to Timor alive! And I dare swear they would all be alive still had you not had the misfortune to encounter that inhuman devil Edwards at Coupang."

Perhaps this last assertion was true, Johnny reflected now, recalling it as the duty watch answered the pipe and went hurrying to their stations to bring the *Reliance* onto the other tack. Captain Edwards, late of His Majesty's ship *Pandora,* had shown no appreciation of his supposed feat. He and his fellow escapers had received the same harsh treatment at Edwards's hands as had the *Bounty* mutineers, and only he, poor young Mary Bryant, and three of the others had survived the ordeal of their passage back to England. But at least, thanks to Recorder Boswell's untiring efforts on their behalf, all had now been pardoned and set free . . . Mary with a pension, generously paid by Boswell himself.

And he was of his own volition—since he had volunteered—returning to Sydney, with the scars the place had earlier inflicted on him still, God help him, unhealed. He was returning in his own name, it was true, with a record of honorable service to his king and country behind him now. Yet the memory of the years when he had been known as Johnny Butcher, convicted felon, were too fresh in his memory to be entirely erased. Johnny Butcher had labored in chains, had been flogged within an inch of his life—dear God, the scars were there right enough, in his mind as well as on his back.

Beside him Matthew Flinders snapped his glass shut and laid a hand on his arm, as if instinctively sensing his unspoken thoughts.

"There's so much to be learned about this country, Johnny—so much to be explored and charted. I only saw a bit of it when we landed with Captain Bligh in Adventure Bay, in Van Diemen's Land, on our passage to Otaheite. But we'll make voyages of discovery, you and I and George Bass, just as we agreed we would. D'you remember when I first put forward the idea to you?"

"Aye, of course I do—how could I fail to?" In spite of his glum forebodings, Johnny laughed.

The *Bellerophon*, cleared for action, had been bearing down on the French line of battle, next astern of the van ship *Caesar*, on the morning of June 1 fourteen months ago, when Flinders, cheerful as ever, had called out to him, "If we live through this day, Mr. Broome, I've a proposal to put to you!"

He had barely heard the words for the roar and thunder of the guns and certainly had been able to make little sense of them when they were first uttered, but . . . Johnny's heart lifted at the memory. No matter what had happened before or since, that day—now called "The Glorious First of June"—was one of which he and every member of the ship's company could be proud.

It had been a Sunday, and after having his men piped to breakfast, the *Bellerophon*'s commander, Captain William Johnston Hope, had beaten to quarters. He had conducted Divine Service with his ship's guns loaded and the enemy in sight, after three days of cat-and-mouse searching for the enemy fleet and a brief but gallant engagement with a French three-decker, two days previously. The *Bellerophon* had sustained considerable damage but had kept up her fire for over an hour until, aided by the *Leviathan*, *Russell*, and *Audacious*, she had seen her one-hundred-twenty-gun adversary *Revolutionnaire* crippled and defeated.

Toiling with Flinders, parties of seamen, and men of the Queen's Royal Regiment to clear the forecastle of its welter of fallen top-hamper, Johnny had heard the captain roar to them to lie down as a broadside from an unseen ship came crashing from out of the wreathing smoke at close range.

As he obeyed, young Flinders had grinned at him and said, lips pressed against his ear in order to make himself heard, "I don't much fancy our chances now, Johnny old son, but . . . if we do live through this, promise you'll join me when the new governor sails for New South Wales. He's Captain Hunter, and I've a nodding acquaintance with his nephew. . . ." He had had time to say no more for, at that moment, the disabled foremast was brought down, crushing the boatswain, James Chapman, and half a dozen seamen beneath its welter of shattered spars and torn shrouds.

Soon after that the battle had ended. The *Latona* had contrived to take the helpless *Bellerophon* in tow, and the ship's company had turned to, setting the spritsail and rigging jury masts, repairing the blackened, shot-scarred deck timbers securing the guns . . . and burying the dead.

Johnny's mouth tightened. It had been a glorious victory, and Howe's battered ships had been cheered by great crowds when they had entered harbor with their six prizes, but the butcher's bill had been high, with more than a thousand men killed or wounded in the British fleet. But he and Flinders had survived unscathed, and the promise, made unthinkingly in the heat of battle, kept. Both of them, with Matt Flinders's boyhood friend, Assistant Surgeon George Bass, had been appointed to the *Reliance*, and now Johnny was back in the penal colony he had left as a fugitive. Back in the place he had risked his life to escape from—back to memories he had hoped to forget.

True, not all of them were bitter. There was Jenny Taggart but . . . he was reluctant to think of Jenny. She would have changed with the passing of the years, just as he had. She—

Beside him Matt Flinders snapped his glass shut and said something Johnny did not catch. Bare feet thudded on the deck as the men of the afterguard hauled on the braces, the quartermaster spun his wheel, and with her yards braced on the other tack, the frigate's head came round. Others besides themselves, who were not on watch, came crowding up on deck, and crossing to the weather side of the quarter-deck, Captain John Hunter, the newly appointed governor of New South Wales, joined the *Reliance*'s commander, Henry Waterhouse. Both turned their glasses on the *Supply*, a mile or so ahead and now wearing, preparatory to making her entry into the harbor.

The wind was southeasterly and gusting, which rendered the approach awkward, but the sloop was well handled, her topmen swarming aloft to take in sail as she came about, and Johnny, passing behind Hunter, heard the governor observe wryly, "I can remember having to beat up and down outside here for close on twenty-four hours in the poor old *Sirius*. . . . In May of eighty-nine it was, on passage from the Cape. We struck a severe gale off Van Diemen's Land, and only the intervention of Divine providence saved us then. We finally came into the harbor leaking so badly that we had to keep the pumps going continuously, and I was afraid we would founder before we could warp the poor old ship into the cove!"

"I recall that occasion very well, sir," Captain Waterhouse said, his tone equally wry. "I had succeeded poor Jamie Maxwell in command of the South Head lookout, and the first thing I noticed when you made your entry was that the figurehead—the old Duke of Berwick—had gone by the board."

"Aye, that occurred when we were embayed under Tasman's Head," Hunter confirmed. He smiled thinly. "We should change the name of the head to Berwick, perhaps, since that's where the duke now lies." Catching sight of Flinders as he sought to follow Johnny unobtrusively to the lee side of the deck, he added, his smile widening, "You will have to attend to it on my behalf, Mr. Flinders, when you commence your survey."

"Aye, aye, sir," Flinders acknowledged, touching his hat. Rejoining Johnny at the lee rail, he asked, "What was H.E. on about? He mentioned something I'm to attend to when I commence my survey, but I didn't hear what or where."

Johnny explained abstractedly, still busy with his own thoughts. Governor Hunter, he reflected, had aged a good deal since he had commanded the ill-fated *Sirius* and lost her, a year after her hazardous return from the Cape, when a great wind had driven her onto the reef in Sydney Bay, Norfolk Island, as she was unloading stores for the island's inhabitants. Her people and most of the stores had been saved, but the governor himself had been badly injured when being hauled ashore on a grating. And his voyage home in the ill-found, rat-infested Dutch snow, the *Waaksam-heyd*—which had taken thirteen months—had considerably impaired his health, already undermined by the near-starvation of the colony's early years.

He was fifty-eight, no longer a young man, and he looked much more—the once lithe, erect figure now stooping, the weatherbeaten face, with its heavy dark brows, thin and deeply lined. Hunter wore his own hair, which was steel gray, loosely tied at the nape of the neck and this—like the overgenerous cut of his uniform coat—added to the impression of a man past his prime.

Watching him now, as he paced the deck with the tall, alert Captain Waterhouse, Johnny found himself wondering, not for the first time during the voyage out, whether the new governor would be strong enough to deal with the evils that had, it seemed, beset the colony under the misrule of the two previous military lieutenant governors. There had been disquieting rumors in England concerning the powers that the officers of the New South Wales Corps had taken upon themselves since Governor Phillip's departure on a sick leave that was to be permanent. In common with most of the *Reliance*'s people, Johnny was aware that Captain Hunter had been specifically ordered to restore the civil magistracy as soon as he had been sworn in as governor.

And there were also Jenny Taggart's letters, two of which had, after long delays, eventually reached him. Both had confirmed the rumors, and although written more in sorrow than in anger, the picture they had conjured up of the present state of affairs in New South Wales had been, to say the least, an ugly one. Johnny sighed, his thoughts drifting almost against his will to Jenny. Her letters had told him so little about herself. They had been so impersonal. And he himself was reluctant to find out the truth.

Again uncannily, as if he had sensed the reason for Johnny's preoccupation, Flinders said, "There must be some people you'll be glad to see again, are there not? Or was your time here too unhappy?"

"Not all of it, Matt," Johnny confessed, "but most of it. I spent all my energies on trying to escape and in avoiding starvation."

"Wasn't there a woman?" his friend questioned curiously.

"Starving men don't think too much about women, lad. What put that idea into your head?"

The midshipman smiled. "Well, I don't flatter myself that it was entirely on my account that you decided to return here. And besides, you had letters. I seem to recall that there was one waiting for you at Spithead when the *Bellerophon* made port, and you've read it a score of times since you received it. George and I both think there's a girl waiting for you in Sydney."

Johnny shrugged. "She was a girl when I left here, but she'll be a woman now . . . married and with two or three children probably, by this time. That letter was close on a year old when it reached me."

"But would she not have told you if she had married?" Matt Flinders persisted. He was of romantic inclination, and for all his seagoing experience and his prowess as a cartographer and navigator, still boyishly naïve, and he looked disappointed when Johnny shook his head. "Did *you* want to marry her, Johnny?"

He had, Johnny thought—dear God, how much he had wanted Jenny to become his wife, to leave Sydney behind her and join the Bryants and himself in their escape attempt. But she had refused, and devil take him, there had been the unspeakable rogue Ned Munday to whom, for no reason that he had ever been able to understand, she had declared herself beholden. Well, they had cooked Munday's goose, he and Nat Lilley and Will Bryant among them, the night they had stolen Governor Phillip's cutter, and he need feel no regrets on that account.

He repeated his headshake. "No," he said untruthfully. "In any event I don't imagine she'll have waited for me. It's been more than four years."

"My love will wait for me," Matt asserted with touching conviction. "However long it may be." He expelled his

breath in a long, nostalgic sigh, and then suddenly brought
back to reality by the shrilling of the pipe and the
boatswain's mate's bellow, "Stand by to wear ship!" smothered an exclamation. "I'm due on watch in twenty minutes, damn it, and I haven't yet broken my fast! Are you
coming below?"

"No." He could not bring himself to go below now,
Johnny thought, and miss the first glimpse of the harbor.
He had stood the middle watch while young Matt Flinders
had been tucked up in his hammock, and although not on
duty for another four hours he had no intention of getting
his head down and missing the first breathtaking sight of
Port Jackson—which Governor Hunter had called the finest natural harbor in the world—opening up before them in
the bright spring sunshine.

And he was not alone in his desire, he saw, recognizing
the dark face of Baneelon emerging from the forward
hatch, his fellow Indian, Yemmerra Wannie, at his heels.
Both natives had accompanied Governor Phillip to England in the *Atlantic* in December 1792, after serving him
as interpreters and living under his roof for varying periods
during his term of office. In London, it was said, they had
been regarded as fascinating curiosities, to be feted and
pampered by the fashionable and the wealthy—noble savages, in whom even His Majesty the King, as well as Sir
Joseph Banks and members of the Royal Society had taken
the keenest interest.

Watching the eagerness with which both men were
pointing out familiar landmarks to each other, Johnny
found himself wondering a trifle cynically how long it
would be before they discarded the European clothing and
the trappings of civilization they had acquired and reverted
to their former primitive mode of life. Not long, probably,
for Baneelon was without his expensive velour hat, the
handsome, brass-buttoned coat—fashioned for him by an
expert tailor in Savile Row—was already lacking half its
buttons, and he had neglected to tie his cravat, wearing it
instead loosely round his neck. The youthful Yemmerra,
who had never wholeheartedly taken to the fashionable
London clothing that had been presented to him, was bare
of foot like the seamen and clad only in shirt and breeches.

Sydney was a far cry from the fleshpots of London town,

from visits to the theater and audiences with royalty. Johnny, whose last view of London had been from the squalid interior of Newgate Prison, decided, still cynically, that neither of Governor Phillip's dusky protégés seemed to have benefited greatly from the lavish hospitality with which they had been showered during their three-year absence from their homeland.

They were still savages, their minds in no way broadened by their travels, their knowledge of the English language, like their manner, still leaving much to be desired. Hearing the two Indians emit cries of delight on observing a shoal of mullet near the ship, Johnny turned away with ill-concealed irritation. The wind was veering again, he noticed, and the *Supply*, for all her smart handling, had failed to weather South Head and was beating back once more and taking a reef in her forecourse and topsails. It would almost certainly be late afternoon before they made port, and since there was nothing to see but a distant vista of the Heads, he might as well follow Matt Flinders's example and break his fast.

Filled suddenly with an inexplicable sense of foreboding, he went below. Devil take it, he told himself, unlike Baneelon and Yemmerra Wannie, he was not coming home. Why then had he come? What strange quirk of destiny had drawn him back across twelve thousand miles of desolate ocean to a land he had hated so bitterly?

The magnet, surely, could not have been Jenny Taggart?

Timothy Dawson rode up to the cabin soon after noon. Watt Sparrow limped out to relieve him of his horse, and in response to his inquiry, gestured in the direction of the brood mares' paddock.

"Jenny's there. The roan mare foaled this mornin'—a real nice filly foal, it is, Mr. Dawson. Goin' ter 'ave a look at 'em, are you, or shall I fix you a drink?"

Dawson shook his head to the offer of refreshment. "Thanks, I called on the Macraes in Parramatta before coming here—Annie fed me on bannocks and Indian tea. But if you could see to my animal, Watt, I'll go and inspect the new arrival. How many's that we've bred this year?"

"This 'un makes a round dozen," Watt told him proudly. "Jenny's a dab 'and wiv' them mares an' no mistake."

Watching the younger man make his way to the paddock, Watt smiled happily to himself. Since his return from Norfolk Island to find the partnership arrangement between Jenny and Dawson working so well, he had seldom missed an opportunity to sing the praises of one to the other.

Tim Dawson was the type of man he liked and even admired—shrewd, down to earth, and above all a willing and tireless worker, whose efforts were already crowned with well-deserved success. He had land on the Hawkesbury as well as Jenny's land here; he now owned more horses than anyone else in the colony, and his sheep, although fewer in number than those imported by some of the corps officers, were breeding well and had enabled him to provide fresh meat for the commissariat at a fair profit. He also grew animal fodder—kaffir grain—that did excellently on the river land and that also withstood the depredations of the numerous pests that blighted the wheat crop and ruined the maize harvest, year after year.

And—Watt's smiled widened as he watched little Justin running to meet the newcomer with shrieks of delight—and his relationship with Jenny and her small son was a happy one. He treated Jenny with consideration, respected and paid heed to her views, and with admirable good sense had entrusted to her the management of the brood mares and their foals without once attempting to interfere or question her methods. He was a regular if infrequent visitor, always courteous and pleasant, and Justin frankly adored him.

Jenny, on the other hand, was less responsive, and Watt had been unable as yet to fathom out the reason for her restraint. He had tried hard enough, the Lord knew; posing innocent-seeming questions, offering hints, and as a last resort had pointed out to her his own advancing age and increasing debility, with the observation that he would like to see her settled and her future assured before taking his final leave of her.

Indeed, only a couple of nights ago, when they had been sitting companionably on the recently completed veranda at the back of the cabin, he had taken his courage in both hands and endeavored to convince her of the advantages to be gained from putting her relationship with Dawson on a permanent basis.

"You can't tell me as Tim Dawson wouldn't make a good 'usband, lass," he had said earnestly, but her reply, delivered in a sharp, almost angry tone, had surprised as much as it had disappointed him.

"No doubt he would, for Mr. Jasper Spence's daughter . . . and she is the one he intends to wed. She is a lady, and he'll settle for no less, Watt. I'm a convict, don't forget, and Justin's what they call a Currency kid. Tim Dawson hasn't worked as hard as he has to be satisfied with *us* as his reward, you can take my word for it."

And he had had to take her word for it, Watt reflected regretfully, although watching them together now, laughing and clearly enjoying each other's company, he found it hard to do so. They were cut out for one another, and Jenny, whatever she might say about the stigma attached to her convict status, had made good out here, judged by any standard. She had worked for and gained emancipation and—Watt jerked the stallion's rein and started to lead the animal toward the stable—there wasn't a better-looking lass in New South Wales or one of better character than his little Jenny. Henrietta Spence, for all her fine clothes and her prissy manners, could not hold a candle to Jenny Taggart, and Tim Dawson was every sort of a purblind fool if he could not see it.

In the paddock, having approved the newest addition to his equine stock, Tim Dawson was explaining the reason for his visit.

"The word in Parramatta is that the new governor's ships have been sighted off the Heads, Jenny. The wind is contrary, it seems, but they're expected in the cove by this evening at the latest, according to the boatman who brought the news. I propose to ride down to Sydney and join in the welcome, and I wondered whether you and Justin would like to come with me."

Justin, at the sound of his name, seized the visitor's hand and looked pleadingly at his mother. Jenny, to his intense chagrin, shook her head.

"I cannot spare the time, and besides, my own mare's due to drop her foal at any minute, and I must be here. She's aging, poor creature, and the last time she foaled it wasn't easy for her."

"You're too conscientious," Tim reproached her. "And

anyway, it's time you ceased to refer to your stock and mine—damme, they're ours! I could never have built up this excellent little herd without you, and well you know it. Cannot Tom Jardine look after the mare?"

Jenny sighed and repeated her headshake.

"I'd rather stay with her myself, Tim. She—" Justin interrupted her with a loud sob. Visits to Sydney were rare enough for the little boy to consider them a treat, and seeing the prospect of this one about to vanish was more than he could bear.

"Please, Mam . . . oh, please, Uncle Tim! I want to go, I want to see the ships. *Why* can't you come?"

Tim Dawson, feeling the boy's small fingers tighten convulsively about his own, looked down indulgently at the ruffled fair head. "I'll take him if he cleans himself up, Jenny. What about it, young fellow? Can you make yourself look respectable in five minutes?"

" 'Course I can," Justin assured him. He glanced uncertainly at his mother. "May I go with Uncle Tim, Mam? I'll be good, I promise I will, and I *do* want to see the ships. Please, Mam."

Jenny yielded. "If you're sure he won't be a nuisance," she said to Tim. "Then I suppose—"

"I'd welcome his company. And he always behaves himself with me. Off you go, Justin lad. You'll need shoes and a jacket. Can't let the new governor see you looking like a scarecrow, can we?" As the boy sped off, Tim thought how fatherly his words had sounded and then smiled at his own thoughts. Of late he had tended to take an almost proprietary interest in Justin, concerning himself with the child's development and education, taking him to the Hawkesbury settlement and to Sydney when occasion offered and supervising his childish attempts to hunt and ride. And he was proving an apt pupil, repaying the interest with a warm, unquestioning affection that Tim had come to value highly.

His feelings for Justin's mother were more complex, colored, as he was ashamedly aware, by the fact that she was a convict . . . a barrier of which, although they never mentioned it, both were invariably conscious and that Jenny, at least, regarded as insurmountable. It made no difference to the manner in which he treated her, of course— he owed her more than he could ever repay, and from the beginning of their association he had given her the respect and the trust that were her due. But old Watt Sparrow's unsubtle hints had not been lost on him and . . . Tim sighed. Had it not been for Henrietta Spence, he might well have acted upon them. Jenny was a fine young woman who might, had she exerted herself to do so, have attracted him strongly, but she never had exerted herself, rather the reverse, in fact. Whenever he had been tempted to weaken, she had held him at arm's length until the impulse had passed, so that now . . . He repeated his sigh, watching her as she led the roan and the new filly foal into the shade of the roofed shelter at the far end of the paddock.

Now he had accepted her aloofness toward him as an integral part of their relationship, and only very occasionally—at such moments as this—did he imagine or wish that it would be changed. For there was still Henrietta and the odd promise he had made to Jasper Spence concerning his daughter—a promise he would keep, should Henrietta herself ever show any desire for him to do so. A promise he *wanted* to keep, of course, he reminded himself ruefully, whether or not Henrietta knew it or was aware of her father's views on his merits as a suitor. As he had told Mr. Spence when they had agreed on the terms of his loan, he could wait. He was a patient man, and there was still much to be done before he need give serious thought to the taking of a wife.

Jenny came back to join him, walking with the easy grace that had been the first thing he had noticed about her, at their initial—and so nearly disastrous—meeting.

She said thoughtfully, "I wonder whether the new governor will be able to improve the lot of the settlers?"

Tim did not pretend to misunderstand her meaning. "He'll have his work cut out. The corps have had it all their own way for a mite too long, I'm afraid. . . . They won't give up easily." He hesitated, frowning. "What is he like, Captain Hunter? You knew him when he was out here before, did you not?"

"I saw him often enough, but I don't think I ever spoke to him." Jenny shrugged. "He was Governor Phillip's most loyal supporter when he was here, but more often than not he was at sea in the *Sirius*. That is until she was lost at Norfolk Island. He—" Whatever she had been about to say

was lost, for at that moment Justin made his excited appearance, well scrubbed and respectfully clad, and under
his urging they returned to the cabin, where Watt Sparrow
was waiting with Tim's horse. He mounted and lifted the
boy up in front of him.

The ride to Sydney was uneventful, the tedium of it broken by the little boy's eager chatter; the guns were already
booming out their salutes when they reached their destination to find the *Supply* at anchor and the *Reliance* being
warped into the cove.

The arrival of any ship attracted a crowd, but more folk
than usual had gathered on the wharf and on the approaches to it, and with two trading vessels—the *Endeavour* and the *Fancy*—still at anchor there, Sydney Cove
must have appeared busier and more prosperous to the new
governor than in fact it was. A company of the New South
Wales Corps, spick-and-span in their scarlet, had formed
up, with the band, and as a boat put off from the *Reliance*
with Captain Hunter in the stern sheets, the band struck up
and the soldiers came to attention.

They presented arms smartly when the governor stepped
ashore, and a group of officials led by the lieutenant governor, Captain Paterson, moved forward to bid him welcome,
to the subdued cheers of some of the onlookers. Others,
Tim Dawson among them, raised their hats, but the majority maintained a sullen silence, which became more noticeable when the band came to the end of its repertoire.

"Is that him, is that the governor, Uncle Tim?" Justin
asked, his shrill young voice holding a note of disappointment. Receiving a nod of assent, he added, anxious to show
his gratitude for having been permitted to witness the new
governor's arrival, "The ships are fine, aren't they? And
they've got guns. . . . Look, on the deck there, ever so
many of them. Why do they need guns, Uncle Tim?"

"Why? Because we're at war with France," Tim answered abstractedly. He lifted the boy from his saddlebow.
"Go down and have a closer look if you want to—I'll find
you when I've arranged to bed Monarch down and for us
to stay at Superintendent Baker's overnight. I'll be about an
hour. Don't be getting into any mischief while I'm gone,
and don't leave the wharf, will you?"

"No, sir," Justin promised.

"Then off you go—only for an hour, mind." Tim moved away, edging his horse carefully through the growing throng. He had seen Henrietta Spence, with her father and a uniformed officer in attendance, on the far side of the slope leading from the west side of the cove. The officer looked younger and shorter than Lieutenant Brace, but he intended to make sure of the fellow's identity before seeking accommodation for the night. Rumor—ever active—had it that Brace had taken a convict girl as mistress, but Tim had seen no tangible evidence of this, and Brace, he knew, had recently spent a week at Jasper Spence's farm—ostensibly as a member of a kangaroo-hunting party organized by the corps officers in Parramatta.

It was odd, he reflected wryly, that no matter how often he might tell himself that he was a patient man and could afford to wait until his position justified the taking of a wife, the sight of Henrietta in Brace's company could arouse his jealous ire. Finding his way clear at last, he put his horse to a canter and started up the slope.

Justin watched his progress, puzzled but not ill-pleased. Usually when he was allowed to accompany his mother or Uncle Tim or Grandad Watt to Sydney, it was on the strict understanding that he must remain with them—or at least within their sight—but now, suddenly, Uncle Tim had permitted him an hour of freedom. A whole hour in which he was left to his own devices . . . restricted to the immediate vicinity of the wharf, it was true, but there was plenty to be seen and heard on the wharf. The sailors from the newly arrived ships, the boats in which a number of them were coming ashore now, and the crates and casks they were landing.

Some of the men, he saw as he drew nearer to the landing stage, were making for the town at a run, laughing and shouting at the tops of their voices, mocking those who remained with the boats. The town, his mother had told him, was an evil place these days, and he was forbidden to set foot in it unaccompanied. She had talked of grog shops—not to him, of course, but in his hearing—and complained that these were the property of the corps officers, run on their behalf by their women who, it seemed, were convicts. Much of what had been said had been beyond his comprehension; he did not know what grog meant or why there should not be shops in which it was sold. But . . . Justin's smooth brows met in a pucker of concentration. Had not Nancy Jardine yelled at her husband Tom like a mad thing when he had come back from Sydney town, not very long ago, with some story of a grogshop woman who had duped him?

Nancy, who was quiet and kindly and dependable, had for a few unbelievable minutes turned into a fiend, and he had run away from both of them in terror, not daring—even when the storm had passed—to ask her for an explanation. In his own mind, however, he had decided that grog and the shops that offered it for sale must be the reason for Sydney town's decline into the evil place his mother claimed it to be. Perhaps the sailors who were heading for it so gleefully did not know what it was like. They were strangers, and like Tom Jardine, it seemed likely that they, too, would be duped.

But—a voice suddenly called his name, and Justin halted, startled from his reverie. The voice, with its faint hint of an Irish accent, was familiar, but the appearance of the woman who had called out to him was not, and the little boy studied her face in polite bewilderment. She was thin, so thin that he decided she must be half-starved, and her hair, instead of being long and flowing or neatly braided, as his mother's was, had been cut short—or perhaps even shaved—and was only now starting to grow again.

He had seen shaven-headed women before, in the stocks in Parramatta, and knew that their hair had been cut to punish them for some misdeed. Once he had seen a woman tied to a cart tail and whipped, and his mother had taken him swiftly away, telling him only that what she had done must have been very bad to have merited so severe a punishment. He retreated a pace, staring in wide-eyed dismay at the poor thin creature who had called out to him. Then recognition dawned and he flung himself into her arms.

"Franny . . . oh, Franny, it's *you*!"

"Yes, Justin," she acknowledged and held him close, her cheek against his, so that Justin felt the wetness of tears coursing down her face. "You didn't know me, did you?"

"Not at first," he admitted, ashamed. "Be—because of your hair. But I'm glad to see you, truly, truly I am! I missed you *such* a lot, and Mam did too. I—" he broke off, biting his lower lip as an alarming doubt assailed him. "You *will* come back, won't you?"

And risk further humiliation, further brutal punishment. . . . *Oh, God forbid*, Frances thought bitterly, her hand trembling as she raised it to touch her shorn, disheveled hair. Had she not been trying to make her way to Jenny Taggart's cabin when they had caught her and dragged her back to receive the twelve lashes the court had ordered originally—and spared her, because it was Christmas Eve? True, she had not been compelled to return to Lieutenant Brace's service, and he had not applied for her to do so—the six months she had endured in his household had, it seemed, been enough to convince even him that coercion would not break her spirit.

He had not laid hands on her again, save when he deliberately drank himself into a state in which he was able to bring himself to do so, and that had not been often but . . . there had been other ways in which coercion could be exercised and pain inflicted. . . . all of them calculated to humiliate her and make her conscious of her convict status. Frances drew in her breath sharply, remembering, and then, conscious that Justin was pleading for her attention and near to tears, she gave him a contrite hug and released him.

"Is your Mam here, Justin?" she asked, making an effort to control her voice. The little boy shook his head. "But surely you're not alone, are you?"

"Oh, no," he assured her. "I'm with Uncle Tim—Uncle Tim Dawson," he added when Frances stared at him blankly, at a loss to know of whom he was speaking. "That's him over there on the big horse, see? He's gone to talk to some people."

Following the direction of Justin's pointing finger, Frances saw the Spences and Ensign de Catteral. Charles Brace had been on parade with his company, which had formed the guard of honor for the new governor, and had marched back with them to the barracks where, in due course, they would be dismissed. And then he, too, would join Henrietta Spence and her father for dinner, and Frances and Noah would, as usual, wait on them—for that, of late, had been the pattern of their days.

Since her release from the poor food and drudgery of the women's jail, she had been assigned officially to the Spences' service, and Charles Brace had been a frequent caller and a welcome guest at Henrietta's dinner parties. She did not know what tale he had told her employers regarding her or what excuses he had made, but never by word or look had he betrayed the fact that she was anything save a stranger to him. A servant whom he could disdainfully ignore and to whom he could hand his cloak and sword on arrival, without a word, thrusting past her into the withdrawing room as if she did not exist. She turned her head away from Justin's searching gaze, feeling tears come once more to ache in her throat.

Henrietta, too, treated her coldly now. Gone was the friendly intimacy they had once shared; she still acted as lady's maid but was more often relegated to the kitchen, where the unpleasant old convict woman who had taken Mrs. O'Leary's place bullied and harrassed her. Frances bit back her tears. . . . At least her present servitude was better than being in jail. Given time she might regain Henrietta's trust, but . . . She looked down at Justin's fair head and wished, with all her heart, that she could have responded to his invitation. In Jenny Taggart's company she had found the only happiness she had known since her arrival in this hateful place, but it had been all too fleeting. She—

Justin said excitedly, "Oh, look Franny—look at those women! They're fighting, aren't they?"

Frances instinctively grasped his hand. A mob of women, reeling drunkenly, had gathered at the end of the wharf, presumably with the intention of offering their dubious favors to the newly arrived seamen, but now they were quarreling among themselves, shrieking insults and tearing at each other's hair and clothing. The sailors started to form a ring about the contestants, laughing good-humoredly at their vicious antics and seeking to egg them on to further degrading excesses. The two sentries posted on the wharf did not intervene; they leaned on their muskets, laughing as uproariously as the rest, and a convict working party, supposedly employed in unloading baggage from the governor's boat, as if at a signal let their burdens fall and hurried across to join in the fracas.

Frances was about to lead Justin out of earshot when two officers, one a tall, good-looking man with fair hair and the other a slim, youthful midshipman, took a decisive hand in the proceedings. With fists and curses, they drove the seamen back to their boats and the convict working party to their abandoned handcarts, and the taller of the two roared impatiently to the sentries to do their duty. Startled out of their apathy, the men obeyed him, and laying about them with their musket butts, swiftly and effectively put an end to the battle. Trading obscenities with the women they started to herd them from the wharf, and Frances, seeing that order was restored, relaxed her grasp of Justin's hand.

"It's all right," she began. "It's over. They're going away—"

"They've got a puppy!" Justin exclaimed, his piping little voice shrill with shock. "A poor little puppy, and they've hurt it, Franny!"

Before Frances could attempt to stop him, he had snatched his hand from hers and was running across to hurl himself into the midst of the straggling band of angry women. And he was right, she saw, as she started after him—there *was* a little scrap of piteously yelping white fur being dragged along in their wake.

Cuffs and abuse greeted poor Justin's attempts to effect a rescue. He was too small to push his way past them, and most of the women were, in any case, too drunk to realize or care that the attack on them was being launched by a mere child. Both he and the unfortunate puppy would have been trampled underfoot had not the tall officer from the governor's ship again intervened. He strode across without hesitation to snatch up both boy and dog, and with a whimpering bundle of white fur under one arm and a bruised and sobbing Justin under the other, came to a halt in front of Frances.

"No serious harm done, I think," he greeted her. "To your boy, at all events. I am, alas, not so sure about the little dog."

He set Justin down and walked away for half a dozen paces before doing likewise with the dog. The poor creature shuddered, its tongue lolling in a gush of bloodstained froth, and then its whimpers ceased and it lay still. The officer gestured to a seaman standing nearby; the man picked up the pathetic little body and took it away, and joined by the midshipman, Justin's rescuer returned to where Frances was endeavoring to still his sobs.

"There now, that's enough, my little lad," the tall officer said crisply. "The pup's out of its misery and 'tis better so—you'd not want it to suffer, would you?"

"No, sir," Justin conceded. He gulped. "But I—"

"You did your best and it was bravely done. Your mother can be proud of you." He flashed Frances an indulgent smile and kneeling at Justin's side, brushed the dust from his clothes. "What's your name, eh?"

"It's Justin, sir." Awed by the presence of the tall, uniformed stranger, the boy's tears vanished, and he managed a tremulous smile.

"Not hurt, are you?" the stranger inquired, making to rise. The midshipman pointed to a deep gash on one small, bloodstained knee.

"He's cut his knee, Johnny. Here—use this to bind it up." A spotless kerchief was produced, and Justin submitted in silence to having the slight wound bound up; then both officers got to their feet. The taller touched his hat politely to Frances, cutting short her thanks.

"I'm glad to be of service to you, ma'am." He used the courtesy title deliberately and with deference, in patent disregard of her shorn hair and her sober servants' garb, and Frances warmed to him.

"My name is Frances O'Riordan, sir," she volunteered. "May I know to whom I—we are indebted? You are from the *Reliance*, are you not?"

"Aye, ma'am, that we are. Midshipman Matthew Flinders and Master's Mate John Broome." A glint of amusement in his very blue eyes, the tall officer doffed his hat and gallantly added, "We're proud to have made your acquaintance, Mistress O'Riordan."

It was so gratifying to be treated as a lady again that Frances would gladly have prolonged her conversation with the newly arrived officers, but Justin tugged at her arm, insisting that his uncle was waving to him, and she reluctantly took her leave, the boy clinging still to her arm.

When they were out of earshot, Matt Flinders gave vent to a guffaw of laughter.

"Why, you sly dog!" he exclaimed in mocking tones. "No wonder you wanted to come back to Sydney!"

"What in the world do you mean?" Johnny demanded, genuinely puzzled.

"Why, that boy—I could not help noticing when you had him on your knee. He's the spitting image of you, Johnny, and no mistakes. Damme, he could be your son!"

"Well, he's not," Johnny denied. "I've never set eyes on his mother before, and as you heard quite plainly, my dear Matt, she had to ask my name. So. . . ." He clapped the younger man on the back and added in friendly reproof, "A plague on your romancing! And if you are cherishing any such notions concerning the women here, you can take my word for it that there aren't many like Mistress O'Riordan. Most of them are whores of the kind you saw in that fight just now, and if you're wise you'll give them a very wide berth."

But, despite his denial, he thought suddenly of Jenny Taggart, and almost against his will found himself staring after the little boy who, if Matt Flinders were to be believed, resembled him so closely. It was impossible, of course, or at best unlikely and in any case . . . He expelled his breath in a small sigh of relief as he saw the boy lifted on the saddlebow of a mounted man who had been waiting, a few hundred yards away, on the outskirts of the crowd. His father, obviously, since they rode off together. The Irish convict girl with the shorn head did not follow them, but that signified little, for she was not mounted. A lovely, well-spoken girl with a great sadness in her eyes and probably a rebel, exiled for her political and religious beliefs, poor young soul.

"Now who's romancing?" Flinders mocked. "Are you *sure* you never set eyes on Mistress O'Riordan before, Johnny?"

"Quite sure," Johnny asserted. He grinned and added with conscious bravado, "but that's not to say I shan't see her again, is it? Or some of my one-time associates, if they are still alive. . . .

"Well, come on, Matt lad—back to the ship. Our work's done here, and we shall lose half the boat's crew if we stay any longer."

The following day, however, saw an end to the tentative

plans he had made to seek out Jenny Taggart. The *Supply*'s master had gone down with fever, and with the sloop loading for a voyage to Norfolk Island under the command of the governor's nephew, Lieutenant William Kent, Johnny was ordered to transfer to her as acting master.

This meant that Matthew Flinders and Surgeon George Bass would have to undertake their first voyage of discovery without him, but there was nothing for it save obedience to his orders. Resignedly, although conscious of disappointment, he stowed his few possessions in his sea chest, took temporary leave of his shipmates, and was rowed across the anchorage to the *Supply*.

CHAPTER XI

Captain John Hunter took the oath of office as governor of New South Wales on September 11, 1795, most of the inhabitants of Sydney—convict and free—being present to witness the ceremony.

In a brief but pertinent speech he announced a general amnesty for all who were currently held in confinement, stressed the need for continued hard work and obedience to the laws by which the colony was governed, and ordered a muster so that an exact record of the population might be compiled. This was to be taken by the commissary, at Sydney, Parramatta, and the Hawkesbury, as soon as arrangements could be made.

His official duty done, the new governor brought Captain Collins, the judge advocate, back with him for a private luncheon at Government House. They were friends of long standing, for David Collins, whose commission was in the Marine Corps, had come out to Sydney in Hunter's ship, the *Sirius*. He had served as judge advocate under Governor Phillip and, loyal to a fault, had been Phillip's secretary and closest confidant as well as his strong right hand.

From Collins, John Hunter knew, he would obtain a true and accurate assessment of the present situation of the colony, and free of protocol and safe from all danger of being overheard, he asked for and received it. Collins spoke long and earnestly, the food congealing on his plate, and apart from a few tersely worded questions, the governor heard him in tight-lipped silence. Collins spoke of the commercial interests and resulting profits of the New South Wales Corps officers, of the ships they had chartered, of the land grants they had received, and of the convict labor freely assigned to them.

"They are not military officers in the accepted sense, sir," the judge advocate said with bitterness, "since their sole concern is, with very few exceptions, the amassing of personal fortunes. They import cheap liquor in quantities sufficient to deluge the whole colony, pay their men in spir-

its, and encourage the settlers to barter their farm produce
in exchange for the stuff . . . always at a large profit. The
result, as you might expect, sir, is that this has become a
place of vice and idleness, with the destruction of order and
the almost total destruction of religious observance. Justice
is in the hands of the corps. They are the sole arbiters, and
I am powerless against them, since I must plead my cases
before a bench consisting solely of military officers. Or," he
added savagely, "of so-called military officers."

"And to think—" the governor observed when Collins
concluded his peroration—"to think, David, that Francis
Grose has been made a colonel and that his elevation and
poor Hill's tragic death at the hands of those savages at
Tate Island will mean promotions for a number of the others . . . promotions without purchase, damme! Paterson
is a major, and Macarthur and Townson have their companies. . . . Well, I shall keep back that news until it
reaches here by official dispatch, which is coming by the
Young William, if she ever gets here." He grunted wrathfully. "She was so grossly overloaded we had to leave her
behind in Rio to restow her cargo. But she's carrying six
months' supply of salt meat and sugar, and she'll be followed by the *Sovereign*. I left instructions for both masters
that they may take on livestock and provisions at the Cape
but *no* spiritous liquor."

Dave Collins smiled thinly. "The corps has two ships under charter, sir—the *Britannia* and, I believe, the *Arthur*
from Bengal. There are also a number of American ships,
whose owners are encouraged to send them here with trade
goods on what they are pleased to call 'speculation.' "

Hunter pushed his plate away, barely touched. "Who is
responsible for this appalling state of affairs, David? Grose
or Paterson?"

Collins hesitated. "Major Grose began it, and Paterson—who is at heart a decent enough fellow—allowed it to
continue. But the man actually responsible is, in my view,
John Macarthur. He exerts a very strong influence and permits no one to stand in his way, and Foveaux backs him
up. I have to say, in mitigation, however, that Macarthur
has the best and most productive farm in the entire colony."

"And the largest, I understand?" Captain Hunter said.

"With the largest convict labor force?" Collins inclined his head and the governor went on, "Well, that is one thing I intend to change, among others. Convict labor is required for government purposes and these shall, in future, be given first priority. After the musters are completed, I shall inspect all the settlements—in particular the public land and buildings—and make an assessment of what work should be put in hand. I've brought a master shipwright with me, David, and the materials to construct a small schooner and a mill . . . not to mention a clock for the town."

"And a pair of keen young explorers, I'm told, sir?"

Hunter's expression relaxed. "Three, in fact . . . though I've had to send one of them to replace Willie Kent's unfortunate master. He is an old acquaintance, of both yours and mine . . . though I think it may be best, for his sake, if his previous—er—connection with this colony isn't generally known. He is going by his own name of Broome now and holds the rank of master's mate—deservedly so, since he has served in the Royal Navy with distinction and has been granted a full pardon. But"—he smiled—"I fancy you will remember him as John Butcher. He was one of the men who escaped from here with the Bryants in Governor Phillip's cutter, aided, needless to remind you, by that old rogue Detmer Smith of the *Waak-sam-heyd*."

Collins stared at him in openmouthed astonishment. "Good God, sir! I remember Butcher very well—he was a persistent escaper and he—why, of course, he was the fellow who navigated the Bryant party from here to Timor! Well, I'll be damned! Fancy him coming back here . . . and as a master's mate, no less. He—" The governor's servant came in with coffee and brandy, and he broke off. There were two long-stemmed clay pipes on the tray, and he took a pouch from his pocket, offering it for Hunter's inspection. "Homegrown tobacco, sir—would you care to try it?"

"Certainly." Hunter opened the pouch and sniffed appreciatively at its contents. "Is this grown with official approval now?"

"Under license, sir," the judge advocate confirmed. He added, his voice carefully flat, "like the sale of liquor, licenses are granted by the civil court, which, perhaps I need hardly tell you, is composed of officers of the corps, and the licenses are only granted to those of whom they approve. And—"

"And of whom *do* they approve, David?"

"Their servants and, in particular, their female servants."

"I see." Governor Hunter, his pipe drawing to his satisfaction, leaned back in his chair. "I'm told there are grogshops now in Sydney."

Collins poured brandy into both glasses and, his face without expression, passed one to the governor. "In both Sydney and Parramatta, sir, but needless to say, brandy of this excellence is not on sale to the settlers nor, of course, to the convicts and the common soldiers. What they buy is poor-quality rum . . . and they have to pay very dearly for it in labor or produce." He quoted figures and saw the governor's mouth tighten.

"No wonder they are amassing fortunes!"

"No wonder at all, sir. Have you . . . I hesitate to ask, sir, but has the home government given you authority to put an end to these—these malpractices?"

"More than that, David. His Grace of Portland has issued me with specific instructions." Hunter sipped his brandy and then, setting the glass down, met his subordinate's anxious gaze reassuringly. "I am commanded to reinstate the civil magistracy and to suppress the illicit traffic, in rum and other goods, being carried on by the New South Wales Corps. What has been happening here is not unknown to His Majesty's government."

But David Collins, to his surprise, seemed far from reassured. He said glumly, "Sir, suppose they resist? They—"

"Resist? Devil take it, David!" Hunter was appalled. "Are you seriously suggesting that one of His Majesty's regiments would oppose His Majesty's appointed governor general?"

"They are an armed force, sir—the only armed force in the colony. The only effective way in which to put an end to their illicit trading activities would be, in my considered opinion, to replace them . . . with a regiment of marines, sir. Or a sixty-four-gun ship of the line."

He was, Hunter saw, in deadly earnest. "We are at war with the French, David," he pointed out. "Neither marines nor ships of the line can be spared. But, dear God . . . is the situation really as bad as you seem to be implying?"

Collins sighed uneasily. "Not yet, sir, no, but I feel it could become so. You invited me to speak freely and in strict confidence—"

"I expect no less of so old a friend. Carry on, if you please. You say the situation is not yet so bad that my authority might be questioned?"

"It could become so," Collins told him gravely, "if you were to carry out His Grace's instructions too—too precipitately." He hesitated and then went on, choosing his words with care. "Captain King had trouble with a detachment of the corps at Norfolk Island. He was compelled to arm a militia composed of one-time marines and other free settlers in order to put down a mutiny. But when he had the troublemakers arrested and sent here for trial, Major Grose regarded his action as an insult to the corps. The men in question received a recommendation to clemency from the members of the court-martial, and all twenty were returned to duty unpunished. And this, sir, in spite of the fact that the detachment had had to be disarmed by Captain King's militia!"

Shades of Major Ross, Hunter thought grimly, recalling how often Ross, too, had complained of insults to the honor of his corps when Governor Phillip had endeavored to restrain their excesses. . . .

"The matter did not end there, sir," David Collins continued. "Last year, having harvested a prodigious crop on the island, Captain King—under the agreement made originally by Governor Phillip that surplus grain would be purchased for the use of this colony—sent us eleven thousand bushels of maize. This arrived in excellent condition in the colonial schooner *Francis*—the ship that also brought the mutinous soldiers here for trial. Major Grose had a difference of opinion with Captain King. He objected to his soldiers being sent for trial, you see, sir, and he retaliated by refusing to sanction payment for the maize, which, as acting governor, he was required to do. The claim was in the form of bills drawn by Captain King in favor of the settlers who had grown the maize, and Captain King intimated that he had a further twenty thousand bushels ready for shipment." He paused, and the governor said, frowning, "Go on."

"Well, sir," Collins answered with restrained anger. "The results were, to say the least, unfortunate. The maize sent here was left to rot, that awaiting shipment rotted on Norfolk Island, the settlers are still unpaid, and many of them—most of the marines from the *Sirius*, sir, who took land grants on the island—sold or abandoned their holdings and either signed on passing ships or came here with like intentions. A few enlisted in the corps."

Hunter's frown lifted. "That I can rectify. See that the bills are in my hands, David, at the earliest opportunity, and I will sanction payment. And I am empowered to establish a court of justice on Norfolk Island—a deputy judge advocate, Thomas Hibbins, has been appointed and will arrive here in the *Sovereign*, bringing with him the required seal." His pipe finished, he laid it on the table and reached again for his brandy glass. It was only half-full, but he shook his head to David Collins's offer of replenishment. "No, this will suffice, thank you. I have yet to hold converse with my immediate predecessor and settle various outstanding matters. You said, if I recall, that Captain—that is, Major Paterson is at heart a decent enough fellow?"

"He is, sir," Collins affirmed. "And a particular friend of Captain King's. He served for a long time on Norfolk Island with the lieutenant governor, and their wives are, I understand, much attached to one another also."

"Then I may find in him an ally, perhaps?"

"Against his own regiment . . . that is doubtful, sir, if I am to continue to speak freely."

"Of course you are," the governor bade him with a touch of asperity. "Pray continue."

"Then, sir, he permits himself to be influenced by his officers and by John Macarthur very greatly."

"How so, David? Macarthur is a junior officer, is he not? Even with a captaincy."

David Collins spread his hands in an expressive gesture. "He has a strong and aggressive personality, sir, and can be a dangerous enemy. He quarrels bitterly with those who attempt to cross him, as a number of unfortunate individuals have found to their cost. Among them Mr. Atkins—

Richard Atkins, sir, who acts as registrar of the admiralty court—and my poor friend Henry Brewer. He—"

"Brewer?" the governor interrupted. "The provost marshal? Is he still a midshipman, or have Their Lordships seen fit, at long last, to grant him a commission?"

"They have not, sir," Collins replied. "Although, as the Lord's my witness, no one ever deserved it more! Thanks to Governor Phillip's good offices he has been given an emolument of thirty pounds a year, in addition to his naval pay, to compensate him for undertaking the duty of provost marshal. The emolument dates from two years ago and, as you know, Henry Brewer has served this colony since its inception. He is, alas, now sick and aging, sir, and would relinquish his office were he able to afford to do so."

"I'll see what can be done for him," Hunter promised. "You say he's fallen out with Captain Macarthur? Not, it would seem, on the grounds that *he* has been enriching himself by illicit trafficking in rum?"

"No, sir, decidedly not. Or Mr. Atkins either. . . ." The judge advocate gave brief details of the disagreements with Macarthur that, on the face of it, sounded trivial enough. The governor's servant reappeared to remove the tray and tidy the room, and as he was busying himself with this task, Collins volunteered, "There is one item of news that I think will interest you, sir."

"Is it good news, I trust?"

"I fancy you will find it so. Do you recall, sir, that Governor Phillip, when we first landed, set on shore some cattle he had purchased at the Cape, with which he hoped to establish a government herd?"

Hunter inclined his bewigged head. "I do indeed. About half a dozen animals, were there not? And the rogue of a convict put in charge of them suffered them all to escape?"

"Exactly so, sir," Collins confirmed. He smiled. "We believe they've been found, about forty miles southwest of Prospect Hill. Two hunters reported seeing a large herd—at least sixty, they estimated—on the far side of the Nepean River about six weeks ago. And since there are no native cattle in New Holland to the best of our knowledge, I think these must be the progeny of Governor Phillip's missing animals. If you consider it worthwhile investigating, sir, I'd be more than happy to lead a party to search the area."

"And I should be happy to accompany you," the governor assured him, "once I have dealt with the more pressing matters demanding my official attention." It would make an unexpectedly auspicious start to his governorship, he thought, if this tale proved to be true, and he questioned David Collins minutely as to the location of the herd.

"According to the hunters' report, sir, the land is well watered, the grass luxuriant, and apart from the river, they said that they came across some large inland lakes, alive with duck and black swans, and the whole area seemed to them admirably suited to agriculture. Even the hills at its extremity appeared easy of ascent."

Captain Hunter beamed his approval. "Excellent! As soon as I am able, I will go with you to examine the spot and the cattle. You know, looking back to our early days here, David, the ones I recall with most satisfaction are those we spent on exploration. 'Parties of pleasure,' that unpleasant man Major Ross used to call them, whenever poor Governor Phillip absented himself from his desk in order to join our expeditions. Well"—his smile widened into an almost boyish grin—"*this* governor has no intention of being desk-bound! No one has yet found a way to cross the Blue Mountains, I'm told."

Collins shook his head. "No, sir, not as yet. The last to try was your old quartermaster from the *Sirius*, Henry Hacking. He and two companions managed to penetrate twenty miles farther than any of us have been inland. . . ." Again he went into details, to which the new governor listened with absorbed interest.

"We must go on trying, David," he said. "By land and sea—there's so much of this great country still to be discovered. D'you remember Governor Phillip's inaugural speech? 'Here are fertile plains, needing only the labors of the husbandman to produce the fairest and richest fruits.' And . . . how did it go on?"

" 'Here are interminable pastures, the future home of flocks and herds innumerable,' " Collins finished for him.

"The damned New South Wales Corps shall not destroy that promise," Governor Hunter stated emphatically. "I'll see the lot of them in hell first, including—what's the fellow's name? Macarthur. And I shall make my intentions perfectly plain to Major Paterson. In the meantime, I think we should send Hacking out to report on that herd of wild cattle, in case I'm held up. He's a good man, Hacking, and not prone to exaggeration. See to it, will you, David?"

"Certainly, sir. And about the restoration of the civilian magistracy—"

Hunter rose to his feet. He said briskly, "Make out a list of suitable persons for me, if you please, and I'll sign the necessary papers as soon as they're prepared. I shall attend the musters and take the opportunity to inspect each of the settlements while I'm about it, as well as the government farms and livestock. I won't be too precipitate, David, but I shall let them all know who is in command here. Well"—as Collins remained cautiously silent—"no objection to that, have you?"

"I . . . no, sir, of course not. But . . ." David Collins hesitated for a long moment, reluctant to put his fears into words. As governor, Captain Hunter had the trappings of power and the best interests of the colony at heart—as indeed he had always had, in Arthur Phillip's day—and he was an upright and honest man, who would not shrink from his duty. "Sir," the judge advocate added in what was close to a plea, "Do not, I beg you, underestimate John Macarthur!"

In the street outside the recently built church at Parramatta, a crowd of convict laborers and their womenfolk had gathered. It was Sunday, and inside the church a service was in progress, conducted by the Reverend Richard Johnson.

His congregation was not large—less than half the number of those who had chosen to remain outside—and their rendering of the opening hymn, although the singing was enthusiastic enough, could not drown the ribald laughter and the sounds of revelry coming from without. Since Colonel Grose had first limited the duration of all church services to three-quarters of an hour and had then rescinded the order making attendance compulsory, religious observance throughout the colony had suffered a severe setback, which the chaplain bitterly deplored.

Grose had even added insult to injury by ordering a bu-

gle call to be sounded, to summon his soldiers to their duties, should any service continue beyond the permitted time
limit. Governor Hunter had countermanded his predecessor's instructions, it was true, but . . . The chaplain
scowled resentfully down from his pulpit at the two officers
seated with their families in the front pew.

Captain Macarthur and his wife were regular attenders,
and today they had houseguests with them in the persons of
the commandant of the New South Wales Corps and his
lady, together with their children. Yet in spite of this,
Chaplain Johnson thought, his resentment growing, the
usual mob of drunken male convicts and shrieking, foulmouthed women had been permitted to assemble in front
of the church door, to jostle and shout obscenities at him
when he had sought to enter.

And they would be there when he left, unless he timed
his departure to coincide with that of the Patersons and the
Macarthurs. The mob restrained themselves when any officers were in sight, and if he complained of their behavior—
as he frequently did—Macarthur insisted that he had seen
no evidence which would justify his taking action. Until a
few weeks ago he had exercised command of Parramatta
with an iron hand, punishing drunkenness and desecration
of the Sabbath with the utmost severity, but since the arrival of the new governor and the appointment of Mr. Atkins as inspector of public works in his stead, many
changes for the worse had taken place, all calculated to
offer proof that only military authority would suffice to
keep order. And it was the same in Toongabbe, now officially in civilian jurisdiction. . . . There had been fewer
than ever at the seven o'clock service that morning, and no
troops on parade.

Richard Johnson sighed deeply as the worshippers came
to the end of their hymn and resumed their seats. In the
sudden silence the sounds from outside could scarcely be
ignored, and heads turned apprehensively toward the door
as mothers gathered their well-scrubbed children closer to
them, whispering uneasily among themselves.

The minister delivered his sermon in loud and forthright
tones, taking as his text, "For we wrestle not against flesh
and blood, but against principalities, against powers,
against the rulers of the darkness of this world, against

spiritual wickedness in high places. . . ." He had searched his Bible for a text that would enable him to put his outraged feeling into words, and Saint Paul himself could not have uttered them with more fervor to the Corinthians or drawn more damning inferences from them. His harsh voice grated on the ears of his listeners, but Captain Macarthur, against whom his words were directed, outstared him with cool and calculated indifference, and Major Paterson, having unhooked the tight collar of his uniform coatee, dozed off after a while, still contriving to hold himself upright in his seat.

Richard Johnson's thin cheeks burned with indignant color when, his eloquence finally exhausted, he announced the number of the second hymn and himself subsided into his chair. Was his assistant, the Reverend Samuel Marsden, better able to deal with these arrogant corps officers, he wondered wretchedly—were his methods at once more subtle and more effective than his own?

Marsden, as befitted a onetime Yorkshire blacksmith, was a rough fellow, wont always to speak his mind and caring little whom he might thereby offend; he stood up to those of Macarthur's caliber instead of holding himself aloof, and they seemingly respected him for it. Certainly they listened to him. Richard Johnson repeated his sigh, belatedly rising to join in the hymn.

Samuel Marsden's heart was in the right place, he had to concede. His fellow cleric was fervent in his beliefs, a true evangelist but at the same time a realist, with his feet firmly planted on the ground. "If the corps can engage in trade, sir," he had said emphatically, "in order to enrich themselves, should not we do so, that we may enrich our church? For the good Lord knows that the church needs funds for even the barest necessities, including the provision of places of worship, yet successive governors and acting governors have refused to make money available for such purposes. Did not you yourself pay, out of your own pocket, for the building in Sydney Town, sir? And have you yet been reimbursed?"

He had not, Johnson thought with bitterness. The wattle and daub, thatched-roof church in Sydney had cost him sixty-seven pounds, and despite his repeated pleas neither Colonel Grose nor Major Paterson had been willing to authorize repayment of the money. The church here in Parramatta had admittedly been constructed from government-owned timber and with public labor, but it had been almost two years in building since the priority accorded to it had been low. In Toongabbe, services were held in the open air.

The singing petered out, the congregation, accustomed to Colonel Grose's time limit, went down on their knees, eyeing the chaplain expectantly.

Richard Johnson gave them the statutory blessing, and the church emptied with a rapidity he felt was an affront, led as it was by the two corps officers.

Outside, the Macarthurs' recently imported horse-drawn carriage awaited them, and the crowd stood, subdued if not entirely silent, while Captain Macarthur ushered the two ladies and their children into it, and Major Paterson prepared to escort them to Elizabeth Farm on horseback.

"You'll join us then, John, my dear fellow," he suggested, gathering up his reins, "as soon as you have concluded your business with—ah—Dr. Wentworth at the hospital?"

"That I will, sir," John Macarthur assured him with an affable smile. The smile faded, however, when carriage and horseman made off at a brisk trot, and the crowd, ignoring—or failing to notice—his continued presence, lapsed into its former unruliness. "Clear this scum off the street before you return to your barracks," he bade Ensign de Catteral, who was in command of the men detailed for church parade.

"Sir," de Catteral acknowledged, "I'll be glad to!" He and his men went about their task with a will, and Macarthur, leaving them to it, set off on foot for the hospital, followed by a groom leading his horse. De Catteral, he observed indifferently, was driving the mob in the direction of their huts, but as soon as the soldiers had gone, they would, he knew, straggle back to the grogshops, as was their wont on this, the only day of leisure permitted to convicts employed on public labor. And they would be joined by half the emancipists who had attended the service and others coming into Parramatta from the surrounding farms with crops to barter.

Well, it was all profit, Macarthur thought cynically and smiled as, out of the corner of his eye, he espied the chaplain come nervously to the door of the church, and finding the street deserted by the mob that had earlier jeered his arrival, go scuttling down it with almost indecent haste.

"Whither away, Chaplain?" he called out mockingly. "No need for you to run—damme, sir, have I not had the street cleared for you?"

His question was ignored, and John Macarthur shrugged and continued on his way. Johnson, he told himself contemptuously, was a fool. No lover of the depraved specimens of humanity shipped out as convicted felons, he had, nonetheless, endeavored to reform them but, lacking the common touch, had succeeded only in earning their resentment—even their hatred.

Richard Johnson had not endeared himself to the colony's officials either, or to the corps, with his endless complaints and his obsession with real or imagined affronts to his dignity . . . not to mention his self-righteous condemnation of the trading activities in which most of them were engaged. His sermon this morning had been a blatant example of his attitude. No doubt he had taken his accusations and his complaints to Captain Hunter and, devil take the new governor, would have found a ready ear for all too many of them.

And the damned fool could have feathered a comfortable nest for his old age if he had shown a modicum of sense—a precaution that surely a married man with half a dozen children to provide for *ought* to have taken. He would not be here forever, none of them would, and such opportunities as New South Wales offered to the enterprising might never be offered again.

John Macarthur quickened his pace, scowling now as he reflected on the disquieting possibility that Hunter—who had been a disciple of Phillip's—might attempt to put a stop to the opportunities that presently existed. He would have to be prevented, that went without saying; although precisely how would require considerable thought. It was for this reason that he had invited William Paterson, planning to broach the subject when his commanding officer had enjoyed a good meal and the warm and charming hospitality his dear wife, Elizabeth, was so adept at dispensing.

Even so, he would have to tread warily. Paterson, like the Reverend Mr. Johnson, had a conscience, and he was a close friend of King's, who had also been Phillip's man. It was a pity Francis Grose had gone; he had been easier to deal with than Paterson.

Macarthur, his brow still knit in a pensive furrow, reached the entrance to the hospital and halted. Paterson, damn it, had not even protested when the new governor had issued a decree restoring the civil magistracy! And he had raised only a token objection when effective command of Toongabbe and Parramatta had been given to the unspeakable Richard Atkins. Indeed, he—

"Good morning, Captain Macarthur." Dr. Wentworth made his appearance in a blood-smeared apron, which he removed, to bow politely as he recognized the caller. "Can I be of service to you?" He hesitated, his expression bland but his gray, intelligent eyes unexpectedly wary. "A glass of wine, perhaps? I was about to take one myself, so if you would care to join me, I should be honored. My room is this way—"

"I know where it is, Doctor," John Macarthur returned crisply. "If you have taken over Dr. Arndell's, I know very well where it is."

Wentworth had not been at the church service, but his wife had, with two of their children. She was a handsome young woman, neatly and soberly dressed, who had seated herself unobtrusively well away from the officers and their families, as if uncertain of her welcome. She had come out as a convict, sentenced for theft, and Wentworth—under something of a cloud himself at the time of their departure from England—had not married her until after the birth of their eldest son. Aware of this stigma, few of the Sydney or Parramatta ladies had received her socially—but that would come. Indeed, John Macarthur decided, he would endeavor to persuade his own Elizabeth to invite her to take tea at their farm, once the Patersons had gone . . . provided that her husband showed a proper willingness to make himself useful.

And he appeared to be so inclined. Since his return from Norfolk Island, young D'Arcy Wentworth had been at pains to ingratiate himself with the officers of the corps, and although the surgeon whom Governor Hunter had brought out—Dr. Leeds—would eventually supersede him as head of the Parramatta Hospital, Leeds had not yet done so because of ill health. It was, of course, on the cards that the governor might order Wentworth's return to Norfolk Island, but in the meantime, with Arndell in retirement on his farm and poor Irving recently dead, the young assistant surgeon was in a position to make himself extremely useful.

John Macarthur took his time, sizing the younger man up as he sipped a welcome glass of Cape hock and talked, in seemingly disinterested fashion, of matters of local farming interest. Wentworth, he knew, had been one of the most successful stock rearers on Norfolk Island, working two sixty-acre holdings he had purchased cheaply from disgruntled marine settlers and sold at a considerable profit on leaving the island. Undoubtedly he would apply for land here once his appointment was confirmed, and he would want to buy stock . . . so that here, too, an inducement might be offered.

Carefully, without sounding precipitate, Macarthur brought the conversation round to the prime merino herd he was planning to import from the Cape and, launching into his favorite topic, stressed the importance of keeping the breed pure, once it could be established.

"It is my intention to grow wool, Doctor. At present I have a thousand head of sheep, raised from Bengal ewes crossed with Spanish and Irish rams. These bear a mingled fleece of hair and wool. . . ." He went into details and ended, smiling, "Should I be fortunate enough to secure the flock of merinos that, I am told, will shortly be offered for sale in Capetown, I shall have quite a number of crossbreeds to dispose of, which might be of interest to anyone starting up here." Seeing a responsive gleam in the surgeon's eyes, his smile widened and he permitted his host to refill his glass.

The fish, he told himself delightedly, had risen to the bait. Now all that remained was to hook him. Still in a casual tone, he asked whether Wentworth had heard that the new governor had expressed disapproval of the number of convict laborers assigned to work on farms owned by officers of the corps.

"I did hear a rumor to that effect, sir," the surgeon admitted. "And that His Excellency was worried because so few remain to undertake necessary public work."

"Captain Hunter proposes that we should each be limited to ten convicts for agriculture and three for domestic purposes," Macarthur informed him indignantly. "And this with harvesting due to start any day now! Do you know how many I employ, Dr. Wentworth? Between thirty and forty—forty at harvest time—and I need every one. They are not a charge on the government stores since I feed and clothe them at my own expense—all they draw are their flour rations and meat only if game is scarce."

D'Arcy Wentworth eyed him with astonishment.

"But forty men, sir," he began. "Surely you—"

"I have a large holding, Doctor. Apart from my sheep, I have fifty head of cattle, about two hundred hogs, and a dozen horses. In addition, I have a thousand bushels of grain in the store, and I anticipate doubling that quantity when my land is harvested."

"You make my efforts on Norfolk Island seem paltry by comparison, sir. I—" Meeting Macarthur's intent gaze, Wentworth broke off, reddening and suddenly conscious that more was expected of him than surprise or even flattery. "I do not see of what service I can be to you, Captain Macarthur. But if—that is, if there is any way I could assist you, I'd most gladly do it."

John Macarthur did not reply directly to his halting question. Instead he posed one of his own, "You have in this hospital a number of convicts who are convalescent, do you not?"

"Oh, yes. A number. But—"

"How many?" Macarthur persisted. "On average?"

The surgeon considered, frowning. "Between fifty and sixty, I suppose."

"And they are kept on the hospital's muster roll and victualled from your stores, I take it?"

"Yes, sir"—Wentworth abandoned his pretense of misunderstanding and, shrewdly anticipating his interrogator's next question, added flatly—"for as long as the surgeon in charge deems their medical condition warrants it. Some are employed on light duties about the hospital and others, if they wish, outside."

"For which they are paid wages?"

D'Arcy Wentworth smiled thinly. "Usually liquid wages, sir, as they prefer. Our liquor ration is small, and we reserve it for the very sick."

"I imagine that we can come to an—er—equable arrangement, Doctor, don't you?" Macarthur suggested. He proceeded to outline the arrangement he proposed and, observing Wentworth's anxious hesitation, said with disarming candor, "You will not be the first to cooperate in this way, my young friend."

"Do you mean that Dr. Arndell has done so?" the surgeon queried, his anxiety fading. "I did not realize—that is, on Norfolk Island, we had no shortage of labor, so—"

John Macarthur rose, cutting him short. He neither confirmed nor denied Dr. Arndell's willingness to oblige him, brushing the query aside as he wryly recalled how often he and Arndell had been at loggerheads. It would have been as much as his commission was worth to make such a proposition to the upright Tom Arndell, but this young man was different—he had fled from England to avoid a criminal trial, and he was married to a convicted felon. In any event, Governor Hunter had brought all this on himself with his ludicrous decree and his thinly veiled determination to compel the officers of the corps to live on their meager army pay.

He held out his hand. The invitation to Wentworth's wife to call was warmly phrased and gratefully accepted, the young doctor's handshake was firm and there was, Macarthur decided, no need to warn him to guard his tongue. D'Arcy Wentworth was nobody's fool.

As they walked out together a young woman, with a child of about four or five, emerged from one of the wards. Macarthur recognized her at once as Jenny Taggart, the stubborn little emancipist who had deprived him of the creek land he had wanted for his eastern sheep pasture . . . one of Governor Phillip's overpraised Garden Women. He swore softly, and Wentworth, following the direction of his gaze, offered uncertainly. "That's Mistress Taggart, sir. She's been visiting one of her laborers, a man named Jardine, who is recovering from a fever."

"Is *he* convalescent?" Macarthur asked pointedly. Receiving Wentworth's puzzled nod of assent, he ordered, his tone one that brooked no argument, "See that the fellow's sent to me, Doctor. Tomorrow, if you can arrange it."

"But, sir—" the surgeon objected. Again John Macarthur cut him short. "Don't concern yourself, Wentworth.

You shall have him back in a couple of weeks . . . provided you can replace him. And"—he was smiling broadly now, all trace of irritation gone—"when we start harvesting, the corps officers who farm in this area will take all the convalescents you are able to furnish. I myself will need a dozen—or ten, if they're fully fit." Conscious of the irony of his last statement, he repeated it, still smiling. "You'll have to juggle your books a trifle, will you not? But so long as no convalescent is retained for more than a fortnight, the risk of—ah—discovery is small. I give you good day, Dr. Wentworth."

He waved to his groom, and when the man hurried up with his horse, swung himself lightly into the saddle, to canter past Jenny Taggart and her son with a fine disregard for the dust cloud he had raised in his wake. He did not, however, get far on his way, for as he drew level with the palisade that surrounded the barracks, Ensign de Catteral, summoned by the sentry, intercepted him.

"This was just delivered to the company office, sir," the young officer said, his tone one of barely controlled outrage. He thrust a note into Macarthur's hand. "By a *constable*, sir! He also brought with him the corporal of the guard—Britton, sir—charging him with theft and demanding that he be placed under arrest, pending trial. The letter will explain, so I thought you should have it at once."

The letter, John Macarthur saw as he perused it, was from Richard Atkins, the civilian-appointed inspector of public works. The accusations against the corporal, set out in cold legal language, were damning. According to Atkins, he had been caught red-handed in the act of stealing turnips from the governor's Rose Hill garden. In addition to being absent from his post, he was said to be inebriated and to have abused the constable who had apprehended him.

"*This is not the first instance of theft committed by your men,*" Atkins had written. "*Indeed, it has been too much the custom, for no later than two days ago, another soldier was detected in the same business.*"

White with fury John Macarthur crushed the thin sheet of paper into a ball and flung it to the ground. Damn Atkins for a lying, sanctimonious busybody, he thought . . . interfering in military matters that were not his concern! Accusing without naming names. Britton had probably asked for trouble, and he would get a flogging he would remember for allowing himself to be caught. Caught by a blasted convict constable, too . . . well, he would get an extra hundred lashes for *that*. But Atkins had not named the other man he claimed to have detected, and, by heaven, he would have to if it was the last thing he did!

Flinging his reins to de Catteral, Macarthur stormed into the barracks and, seated behind the table in his company office, ordered a startled clerk to furnish him with pen and paper. He wrote two letters, the first to Richard Atkins, which he addressed on the outside to "Mr. Richard Atkins"—deliberately denying him the courtesy title of "Esquire."

The second, which took him considerably longer to compose, was addressed to the colonial secretary, the Duke of Portland.

In this, at pains to avoid any suggestion of bias and choosing his words with extreme care, John Macarthur made what was to be the first of many such attempts to undermine the authority of Governor Hunter and his newly appointed civilian administration.

His task completed, he dispatched a messenger with Atkins's letter but pocketed that intended for the Colonial Secretary, which would, he knew, have to be confided secretly to the master of a homeward-bound vessel or one calling at the Cape. Then, whistling cheerfully, his temper fully restored, he sent for his horse and rode back through the gathering dusk to his belated dinner with his guests at Elizabeth Farm.

CHAPTER XII

Timothy Dawson was in an unwontedly angry mood when he drew rein outside the Taggart cabin. It was the end of June, the weather pleasantly cool, but his rage had simmered to white heat during the sixteen-mile ride from Sydney, and when small Justin ran out eagerly to meet him, he received a cuff for his pains.

Inside the cabin, where they had been eating their noonday meal, Watt Sparrow studied the new arrival's glowering face with mingled apprehension and surprise. Before going out to relieve him of his horse, the little man offered a low-voiced warning to Jenny.

"Tim Dawson looks in a right takin', lass . . . an' 'e's just sent poor Justin packin' wiv' a flea in 'is ear, which ain't like 'im, is it? Best pour 'im a glass o' spirit an' bide quiet till you c'n find out what's upset 'im."

Jenny took this sage advice. Watt, as she was well aware, liked Timothy Dawson and seldom, if ever, criticized him. Indeed, she herself came in for caustic comment from Justin's adopted grandfather because of her refusal to "play her cards right," as he put it. The blame for her unwed state lay at her door, according to Watt, not at Timothy's. She sighed and rose from the table, setting a clay beaker beside a small keg of Jamaica rum as Timothy stumped into the cabin.

"Please help yourself," she invited, when he offered only a curt greeting. "It would seem you need it."

"By God I do!" He splashed rum into the beaker and gulped it down as if it had been water. "Yes, by God I do, Jenny! And if I could leave this infernal colony by the next ship to depart these shores, I would. Unhappily I can't afford to."

He sounded as angry and resentful as he looked, and Jenny, heedful of Watt's admonition, returned to her seat and waited in silence for him to unburden himself.

The rum keg had been three-quarters full, but he had almost exhausted it before he spoke again. Then, in a choked voice, he burst out, "The new governor's been here

since last September—over nine months! He promised to
restore the civil administration, to curb the trading activities of those confounded rogues of corps officers, and to
see that justice was done to the settlers, did he not? And
what, *pray*, has he done? Tell me that!"

Unwisely, Jenny attempted to come to the governor's defense by reminding him that civilian justices of the peace
now administered the law in conjunction with the military.
"And," she added, "the governor has visited all the settlements in person. He—"

"Aye, when he's not chasing after wild cattle and absent-
ing himself for weeks on his 'voyages of discovery,' " Timothy retorted, unimpressed. He stared moodily into the rum
in his beaker. "Very well, I'll grant you he's a sea officer
and maybe the sea is in his blood. Perhaps some of his
discoveries may prove of value. . . . The wild cattle probably will. There may be coal in that river the shipwrecked
people from the *Sydney Cove* claim to have found and that
young surgeon, Bass, from the *Reliance* may well find a
way to cross the Blue Mountains. Plague take it, the governor himself may cross them, but of what use will any of
these discoveries be so long as all profit sticks to the fingers
of the corps officers? And when the governor, despite all
his promises, actively aids men like Macarthur!"

"I don't know," Jenny confessed. Sensing that he had not
yet revealed the true cause of his rage, she crossed to the
fireplace and, taking down the jar of homegrown tobacco,
she set it, with his pipe, beside the rum.

"Are you hoping to soothe me, Jenny?" he demanded
unsmilingly. "Well, you will not succeed. I have good reason for my indignation and, by heaven, so have the other
settlers who have sweated their guts out here for scant reward!"

Was he—Jenny wondered as, in spite of his protest, he
started from force of habit to fill his pipe—was he still indignant because the governor had ordered the settlers to
release some of their convict laborers for the performance
of urgent public work? The unloading of ships was a matter
of urgency, no one could deny that and so also, in the governor's view, was the building of a courthouse and the
completion of an enlarged jail in Sydney Town. The corps
officers, as well as the settlers, had obeyed the governor's

decree. True, those who held land had contrived to get round the resulting shortage of labor, as she knew from Tom Jardine's account, by compelling convalescents from the Parramatta Hospital to work on their farms, but that had proved a short expedient. Once Dr. Balmain and Mr. Atkins had got wind of the practice, it had ceased and—

Timothy said harshly, breaking into her train of thought, "Three ships have come here this month, Jenny—the *Britannia* and the *Ganges* with convicts from Ireland, and His Majesty's ship *Reliance* from the Cape. The *Supply* made port a few weeks earlier, in May, having been sent by the governor to procure cattle in Capetown. Prices have been favorable there since our troops took it from the Dutch, and the *Reliance* was dispatched on the same errand. . . . But for whose benefit, do you suppose?"

Jenny eyed him in some bewilderment. "Why, if the governor sent them, I suppose for the public benefit . . . to stock the government farms. I—"

"Oh, no!" Timothy interrupted, putting down his pipe with such violence that the stem snapped. "For the virtually sole benefit of Captain Macarthur! The *Reliance*'s commander, Captain Waterhouse of the Royal Navy, has delivered a herd of pedigree merino sheep purchased on his behalf from the estate of a certain Colonel Gordon. Sixty of them, including two breeding rams of the highest quality! On the books, of course, he's only written down for twenty, but the rest are in the names of corps officers— Foveaux, Brace, Cummings. I found that out when I tried to purchase some on my own account."

"And you obtained none?" Jenny asked, shocked beyond belief by what he had told her. He shook his cropped fair head. "And the government . . . surely some of the stock will go the government farms?"

"The cattle, yes—twenty-six head of inferior Cape heifers and three bulls. The sheep the *Supply* brought—about a score—were in such a bad state they're only fit for killing as mutton, and they went to the commissariat. The *Supply* had a bad passage and lost half the stock she loaded and"—Timothy shrugged impatiently—"they say she's to be condemned as unseaworthy and her cordage and canvas used for other vessels. So we're left with two ships in government service—the *Reliance* and the *Francis*. With the war in Europe, we're not likely to be sent any more, apart from convict transports and storeships. And those are chartered by Macarthur and his friends for private trade as soon as they're unloaded. Captain Raven's *Britannia* is on permanent charter to the corps, plying between here and Bengal. Do you wonder I am angry or that I despair of justice being done to the settlers, Jenny?"

"No. No, I do not," Jenny conceded. But when, she asked herself wryly, had justice ever been done to those who had been condemned to exile here, whose convict stigma clung to them, even when they had served their sentences and been given emancipation? Timothy, at least, had money with which to purchase imported stock and to buy rum for payment of his labor—the emancipists must barter their crop for everything they needed, accepting the corps's doubled and trebled prices for all imported goods. And, like herself, if they were unable to make ends meet they had to sell their land and work for the new owner. She was fortunate in having a man of Timothy's caliber as her employer; upright and honest, he had always treated her generously but . . . She bit her lower lip, feeling it tremble. For all the years she had toiled in this harsh, inhospitable land, she was not yet free.

Timothy, his face flushed and his tone still irritable, talked on, but she scarcely heard him. Suddenly, in memory, she was back on the *Charlotte*'s deck with Tom and Olwyn Jenkins and . . . Andrew Hawley. Dear Andrew, so stiff and handsome in his scarlet uniform, walking proudly beside her as he planned the new life they would build for themselves when they reached Botany Bay and she became his wife. They had dreamed of a prosperous farm, a snug house, and children . . . above all, children, for whose heritage they would gladly toil.

She had a child, Jenny thought—a fine, well-mannered, affectionate son who was the love of her life, but Justin, too, must bear the stigma of all convict stock. And he, poor lad, had never known and almost certainly never would know his father . . . although he could be proud of him. One day, quite soon perhaps, she would tell Justin about his father. Her tension drained from her, and she found herself smiling as she reached this decision. Johnny Butcher—John Broome—was a hero to the convict people of New South Wales because, refusing to yield to its tyranny, he had made an epic voyage to freedom with a skill and courage few seamen had ever surpassed.

Now, pardoned and restored to the life and the sea that he loved, he was fighting his country's battles in one of His Majesty's ships of war. . . . Andrew's letter had told her so. . . . Jenny's eyes misted. That story should be Justin's heritage. He . . .

"Captain Collins has thrown up his appointment as judge advocate," Timothy was saying. "He is taking passage home in the *Britannia* transport, and he will be a great loss. The governor has appointed Mister Atkins to succeed him—a good choice, in my view, since he is one of the few to stand up to the corps officers in general and Macarthur in particular. Mr. Spence is to replace him in the court of admiralty."

"Mr. Spence, Tim?" Jenny was all attention. "Do you mean Mr. Jasper Spence?"

His color deepened. "Aye. And that's not all. I saw him last evening at the wharf, and he told me that his daughter is to wed Lieutenant Brace."

So this, Jenny thought as she sought vainly for words of sympathy, was the real reason for Timothy's loss of temper, although typically he had not admitted that it was so.

"I am sorry, Tim," she said at last with sincerity. "For your sake. I know the feelings you entertained for Mistress Henrietta and that you hoped—"

Harshly he cut her short. "I have ceased to hope. Unhappily, though, I borrowed money from Mr. Spence in the belief that I might prevail upon the young lady to wed me, and since such an outcome is now impossible, I must repay my debt to him."

"Is he insisting that you must?"

"No, he is a good friend—he would never insist," Timothy denied. "It is I who am determined that the debt must be paid. I shall sell some of my horses to raise the required sum. Jenny"—he leaned across the scrubbed wooden table, his hand reaching for hers across it—"ride out with me to the river pasture and aid me in choosing which animals I can best spare. There's the young bay stallion, Lucifer, though I am loath to part with him. . . . He'd command a good price, it's true, but Sinbad is not getting any younger.

Or those two chestnut yearlings I gelded last month, the pair I intended to break to harness and sell as trained carriage horses at the back end of the year. But . . . oh, the devil, I cannot make up my mind! *Will* you ride out with me?"

"Now?" Jenny questioned. "Surely there's no untoward hurry if Mr. Spence isn't pressing you?"

"I want the matter settled," Timothy said obstinately. "It was for that reason I called here, though you might not think it, seeing how long it took me to impart that last bit of information. I . . . oh, I'm ashamed I suppose, and I could not bring myself to admit that one of the corps officers has bested me." He squared his broad shoulders and managed a sheepish smile. "Can you come now, this afternoon? Nancy Jardine or Watt can give an eye to Justin, can't they? And there are no mares near to foaling—please help me, Jenny."

"Yes, of course I will. But—" Jenny rose, gesturing to the remnants of the meal on the table. "You'll eat before we set off, won't you? There's a fresh bread and cheese or green bacon if you prefer it, and—"

"I'm not hungry," he assured her. "I'll saddle a horse for you while you take leave of Justin. I'm using young Jackie Scrope as a cook now—he can get a meal for us before we ride back."

He was silent during most of the ride, evidently engrossed by his own unhappy thoughts, and Jenny made no attempt to break the silence. The colony had been for a long time without rain, and the dust their horses raised was thick and choking, discouraging conversation. Most of the land on either side of the road they were following had been cleared and brought under cultivation, but since the harvest had been gathered in and the new crops—apart from maize—were not yet showing, the fields were deserted, and not until they came in sight of the government stock farm at Toongabbe did they encounter any sign of life.

There two herdsmen, resting in the shade of a clump of silver-trunked gum trees, watched over a motley but healthy-looking herd of humped Cape cattle. Pointing proudly to a group of heifers grazing nearby, one of the men, recognizing Timothy, observed that the animals' condition had improved.

"Couldn't 'ardly walk when they come ashore from the *Supply*—but you just look at 'em now, Mr. Dawson! Wouldn't know 'em as the selfsame critters, would you, sir?"

"I would not," Timothy confessed. "You've looked after them well, Jem."

"I'd need to, seein' the price they are," the convict herdsman said with a shrug. He got to his feet, eyeing Jenny's young mare with knowledgeable eyes. "Seventy an' eighty pounds an' 'ead, the last lot the *Britannia* brought from Bengal. Leastways, that's what they sold for. . . . Wouldn't 'ave made a quarter o' that back 'ome. An' a couple o' mares from the Cape—a mite too aged fer breedin' an' not a patch on that one o' yours, ma'am—why, they went for a 'undred apiece!"

After exchanging a wry glance with Jenny, Timothy said flatly, "Well, I'll be putting some of mine on the market soon, Jem. You want to have a word in your superintendent's ear. . . . They're good stock. Your grass here is about the best in the area."

"Aye." The man called Jem looked as if he wanted to say more on the subject of stock prices, but thinking better of it he kicked at the ground with a booted foot. "It's good, but we could do wiv' rain . . . an' it talks o' rain, I reckon." He gestured to a bank of heavy black clouds to the south. "You want ter watch out if you're 'eading fer the river, Mr. Dawson, 'cause when that lot breaks it'll come down in torrents, an' the ground's too dry an' bone 'ard fer it ter sink in. You could 'ave a flood in your area, like you 'ad last January."

But when they reached Timothy's holding, it was not a flood they found themselves facing—it was a fire. Jenny was the first to smell it when the buildings were still hidden from them by trees, and at her shocked warning Timothy kicked his horse into a gallop. He did not draw rein until they were at the river's edge, and cursing furiously, he pointed to half a dozen native canoes, whose occupants were paddling furiously toward the opposite bank, about eight hundred yards ahead of them. All were armed with spears and throwing-sticks, and catching sight of the two riders they waved their weapons in defiance.

"Infernal swine of Bediagal!" Timothy exclaimed.

"They've set light to the granary, the devil fly away with them! Fortunately it was all but empty—I sent my maize to Sydney last month in the *Francis*. And four men with it, in obedience to the governor's decree." He cursed again, kneeing his horse forward in the direction of the gutted building.

"Then how many have you here?" Jenny asked apprehensively. She caught her breath, glimpsing what looked ominously like a body stretched out by the side of the dwelling house. "How many men *should* you have, Timothy?"

"Three and young Jackie. But surely those savages wouldn't dare—" Timothy broke off, the ruddy color draining from his cheeks as he, too, glimpsed the recumbent form. "Oh, my God! It's Jackie. . . . Pray heaven they haven't killed the poor little devil!"

But Jackie was dead when they reached him, a spear buried deep in his chest, and Timothy's musket lay, loaded but not fired, by his side. Jenny dropped to her knees, cradling him in her arms and vainly calling his name until Timothy pulled her to her feet, with a hoarse "Leave him, Jenny lass—there's nothing you can do for him now."

"But . . ." With tears streaming unchecked, she covered the thin, blood-spattered body with her shawl. He was so young, she thought with bitterness . . . a waif of the London streets, deported six years ago at the age of perhaps seven or eight, with a life sentence to be served for stealing from a baker's stall. And here, with all the odds against him, he had made good, working on Timothy's farm and her own, acting as messenger boy between them, and lately, because Timothy had a soft spot for him, promoted to cook and granted his ticket of leave, to enable him to earn a modest wage.

Her throat tight, she remounted her mare, and at Timothy's urging, they went in search of the other men. Two, like poor Jackie, had been set on with spears and clubs and brutally hacked to death, their bodies flung beside the burning granary and charred almost beyond recognition by the flames. The third—David Leake, the foreman—was missing. His wife, a convict girl who had come to the farm only recently, emerged from the hut in which she had been hiding at the sound of their voices and came sobbing to meet them. She was heavily pregnant and so shocked that her account of what had happened was well nigh unintelligible.

They had been at their midday meal, relaxed and anticipating no trouble, when the Indians made their appearance, and although Jackie Scrope had run to the house for the musket, he had been too late.

"First off, I didn't think they meant no harm," the terrified girl whispered. She clung to Jenny, trembling as she sought to describe the ghastly scene, her voice a thin, broken whisper of sound. "They asked for food—for maize—and Davie told them we'd none to spare. Then . . . then they must have seen Jackie with the gun, Mr. Dawson. He didn't fire it or threaten them nor nothing, he just stood there. But six or seven of them ran over to the house and before we could lift a finger to—to help him, they speared him. Davie said they'd killed him, and he . . . he made me hide, so I didn't see nothing more. But I heard . . . I heard the cries, the screams and I . . . I was too scared to move. I couldn't, I just stayed where I was. And then I heard you, and—"

"Where is Davie?" Timothy demanded, controlling himself with a visible effort. "For God's sake, Molly—you must tell us!"

"I . . . I don't know." More frightened than ever by his question, the girl lapsed into a storm of weeping, covering her face with her apron and rocking to and fro in Jenny's arms, beside herself with grief. "Dead, I shouldn't wonder. . . . Like Jackie, poor young mortal! What's to become of us, Mr. Dawson? Suppose they come back—oh, God have mercy, suppose they come back? They'll kill us all!"

"Do what you can for her, Jenny." Timothy tested the priming of the musket he had taken from Jackie Scrope's side and swung himself back into the saddle. "I'll go and look for Davie. He—" But at that moment, to Jenny's intense relief, Davie himself came stumbling toward them. He was swaying and breathing hard, his shirt torn. As his wife flung herself into his arms, sobbing hysterically, he embraced her, and then, bidding her be silent, he jerked his head in the direction from which he had come.

"Them devils have fired the bush, Mr. Dawson," he gasped. "Set it alight before they made off in their canoes, the murderin' bastards! An' the wind's changin'—blowin' it this way. Quiet, Molly lass, for the Lord's sake. . . . I got ter tell Mr. Dawson. You seen what they done, ain't you, sir? To Jackie and—"

"Yes, I saw," Timothy confirmed grimly.

Davie Leake went on, struggling to regain his breath. "The young 'orses in the far paddock . . . they'll be cut off. I tried me best ter get to 'em, but . . . I was alone an' they was chuckin' spears at me, so I reckoned I'd best seek 'elp. That black fiend they call Pimelwi's leadin' them. 'Twas he started the fire."

Timothy stared at him for a moment in numb dismay.

Then, recovering himself, he ordered tersely, "You're right—go to Toongabbe for help, Davie. Saddle one of the workhorses and let the others out. Go on, man! I'll do what I can here. And take your wife with you. . . . Don't leave her here. You'd better go with them, Jenny. You—"

"No," Jenny returned. "It will take two of us to drive those horses out of the far paddock."

She was on the mare's back urging her into a canter before he could voice any objection. The best of his young stock was there, she recalled, and Timothy had prided himself on the strength and stability of the fence he had built round their pasture, using the stout timber that grew by the riverbank, instead of the brittle gum. The young horses would be caught in a trap if the woods were set alight, unable to reach the river or leap that high, all-too-solid fence.

And the woods, she realized as the mare gathered speed—the woods *were* alight. The smell of burning still lingered in her nostrils—she had supposed it was coming from the smoldering granary—but it was growing stronger, more pungent, as the flames spread. They had been without rain for so long that the trees and underbrush were tinder-dry, needing only a spark to set them ablaze. And the rain clouds—of which the herdsmen at Toongabbe had warned them—though still looming in the sky southward, showed no sign of breaking.

The mare stumbled and Jenny had all she could do to keep the weary animal on her feet, but she did not—dared not—slacken speed. The wind was not strong but it was enough, blowing from the river and, as David Leake had said, in the direction of Timothy's house and his farm buildings and bringing the fire with it. His small herd of sheep and the domestic cattle he kept should be safe. Their pasture was on the Toongabbe side of his holding, with several acres of cleared land that would act as a natural firebreak between them and the approaching danger.

She saw Timothy forge ahead of her, choking now as the billowing smoke caught at his throat. He waved to her to halt, shouting that he would go on alone, but she ignored both words and gesture, and indeed, her brain scarcely registered either. But the mare was tiring, stumbling more frequently and frightened, too, as the crackling roar of blazing brush and timber grew louder and more alarming. Flames glowed redly below the rising smoke; just ahead of her a screeching flock of parakeets took wing, seeking the safety of the upper air, and over to her right, a tall, hollow-trunked gum tree became a pillar of fire, its leafy branches disintegrating in the fierce heat. She heard the blood-chilling, half-human cry of a kangaroo that had failed to make its escape and glimpsed a score or so of others moving at incredible speed as they leaped and bounded over the dusty ground, instinctively making for the river. Their concerted rush and the strange, sobbing sounds they emitted added to the mare's reluctance to go on; she slowed to a walk, and Jenny had finally to slide from her back and lead her, using a strip torn from her skirt to serve as a blindfold.

She lost sight of Timothy but was too anxious to be conscious of fear. The horses were all that mattered, all she permitted herself to think about, and in an echo from the past she recalled the heroic efforts her father had made to save his farm workhorses when Lord Braxton's men had put a torch to the shed that housed them. Those horses had been poor Angus Taggart's livelihood—just as the young stock in the threatened paddock were Timothy's. If they were lost or injured he would be back where he had started, with five years' hard and dedicated work wasted, his capital gone, and his debt to Jasper Spence unpaid.

The house, the buildings, and the fences could be replaced if they were destroyed—the young horses could not and . . . The mare, crazed with fear, jerked her head free, and with a wild plunge that knocked Jenny to the

ground, the usually docile animal bolted, to be swiftly lost
to sight in the eddying smoke. Jenny picked herself up, sick
at heart and conscious of pain in her right ankle as she
sought to stagger on. The mare would come to no harm—
she would gallop away from the fire, like the kangaroos,
guided by instinct until she won clear of the danger, but
. . . She gritted her teeth as the pain bit deeply. Her
ankle was badly wrenched if it was not broken, and she
was still some distance from the paddock and uncertain of
which direction to take in order to find the gate. But the
fence was there, she could see it now, solid and unyielding,
twenty yards from her . . . and suddenly she saw Timothy. He had the gate open and had pulled down the top
two bars of the fence on either side of the gate, in order to
make an aperture wide enough to let the trapped animals
through.

Jenny bit back a sob. She could hear the horses, hear
their hoofbeats and their terrified neighing but could not
see them. Evidently the poor creatures were panic-stricken,
galloping this way and that in blind fear. If they were not
rounded up and driven through the opening Timothy had
managed to make in the fence, they would be destroyed
long before the fire reached the fence and destroyed it, too.

She called out to Timothy, but her mouth and throat
were too parched and dry for her words to reach him. He
turned, however, and saw her, gestured to the fence and
flung himself onto his own horse's back, to vanish a moment later as if he had never been. Jenny limped over to
the fence, and clinging to it until she could regain her
breath, she struggled desperately to continue the work he
had begun. Years of heavy toil in the fields had made her
strong, but even so, the task was beyond her, and she had
succeeded only in dragging down a small section of the
fence when the thunder of approaching hoofbeats warned
her that the horses were coming toward it.

Miraculously, it seemed, Timothy had contrived to
round them up and set some of them, at least, heading in
the right direction. She hobbled clear of the opening and,
clinging weakly to a fence post, drew a choking breath of
air into her lungs as the forerunners of the herd came tearing past her. In the smoke and dust it was difficult to count
them and, amidst the noisy pandemonium of shrill whinny-

ing and thudding hoofs, virtually impossible to pick out
and identify individual animals. But Jenny saw—or thought
she saw—a big black horse with an empty saddle leap over
the two remaining fence poles in the gap she had tried to
make to the right of the open gate.

It could only be the stallion, Sinbad, since none of the
others wore so much as a halter at pasture, and as the realization sank in, she caught her breath on a sob. If Timothy
had been thrown, then . . . oh, dear heaven! She would
have to go in search of him, she . . . The hoofbeats faded
at last into the distance, and she started to grope her way
blindly toward the onrushing flames, calling out to him a
husky, almost soundless voice.

"Tim . . . where are you? Tim—Tim, are you hurt?"

The crack of a musket shot brought her trembling to a
halt. Then, after what seemed to her an eternity, she was
able to make out Timothy's tall figure, a dark silhouette
against the burning vegetation at his back. His face smoke-
blackened and his shirt in ribbons, he lurched toward her
like a drunken man, holding himself upright by an immense effort of will. Jenny put an arm about his waist, and
together they stumbled back to the gate.

He said hoarsely, "Lucifer—my young stallion—tried to
jump the fence. He broke both forelegs, and I . . . I had
to shoot him, Jenny. But the rest . . . the rest got out,
didn't they?"

"Yes, I think so." Jenny looked up into his ravaged face,
sick with pity. "Tim, Sinbad was with them. At least I
think he was, I—"

He nodded. "I had to let him go while I went to Lucifer.
He'll lead the youngsters to safety, and they'll be easier to
round up if he's with them. Jenny, it's high time we got
away from here . . . back to the buildings. We can double
up on your mare, and then—"

"The mare's gone too," Jenny told him unhappily. "She
broke away from me. I . . . I'm sorry. She was crazy with
fear, I couldn't hold her."

"Then we'll just have to make it on foot. Come on, dear
lass, we'll head for the river. It's nearer, and we'll be safe
enough there." He took her hand, but Jenny had only
limped a few paces with him when, with a smothered excla-

mation, he turned and scooped her up into his arms. "The devil! Why didn't you tell me you were hurt?"

She was silent, leaning her head back on his shoulder, breathless and spent. Timothy muttered something she did not catch and strode grimly on. He was as exhausted as she and, half-blinded by sweat, tripped frequently over the roots and rough tussocks of grass that lay in their way. The area ahead of the fire was devoid of life. The wild denizens of the bush—kangaroos, possums, dingoes, and the like—had long since fled; the horses had vanished, and there was as yet no sign of the help that Davie Leake had gone to summon. Probably, Jenny thought wearily, it would be well after nightfall before anyone from Toongabbe could reach them, because most would have to come on foot. And the other settlers in the area would see the fire as a threat to their own livestock and property. They would first have to ensure that these were safe, before they could come to Timothy's aid.

She stifled a sigh. The soldiers, of course, would see it as their duty to capture the notorious Pimelwi and wreak vengeance on his tribe. It had been Pimelwi who had speared Governor Phillip and wounded him sorely some years before, and the soldiers had sought him ever since without success. Even Baneelon and Colbee had declared him an enemy and . . . Suddenly, unbelievably, Jenny felt a drop of moisture on her cheek. It was followed by another and another, until her whole face was wet, and glancing skyward she saw, with a swift lifting of the spirit, that the lowering gray storm clouds had broken at last.

"Oh, Tim! she cried. "Tim, it's *raining*!"

"Raining?" Timothy stopped in his tracks to gaze upward with the same incredulity that she had felt a moment before. Then, with an exultant shout, he lowered her to the ground, still retaining his grasp of her waist and supporting her against him. "You're right . . . praise be to God! This will put paid to the fire if it keeps up! We're saved, Jenny . . . By all that's wonderful, we're saved!"

It was as if the heavens had opened in response to prayer. The rain came down in torrents, blotting out the glow of the fire and the surrounding landscape, and for several minutes they stood where they were, letting the cool deluge soak their sweating and exhausted bodies and relieve their thirst.

"It's keeping up," Timothy said. "And to some tune. I reckon we ought to seek shelter, lass."

There was an odd note of alarm in his voice, and Jenny looked up at him in mute question, recalling the warning the Toongabbe herdsman had offered. Was there, she wondered anxiously, to be a flood in the wake of the fire? Had they escaped from one danger, only to be faced with a second?

But when she put her fear into words, Timothy shook his head. A vivid flash of lightning spread across the darkened sky, and thunder rolled ominously, echoed by the distant mountains.

"We've got to get under cover quickly, Jenny," he told her. "There's not time to get back to the farmhouse, but there's a feedstore not too far away, and I don't think the fire can have touched it. . . . Up you come!" Again he picked her up and started to run, ignoring her protests. "We'll make more speed this way!"

They gained their objective—a wooden shack—five minutes later, to find, as Timothy had hoped, that it was undamaged. He said as he smashed the padlock on the door with his booted foot, "I've seen these storms before and they seem to be peculiar to the Hawkesbury area. Rain, thunder, and then hail . . . with hailstones the size of pigeons' eggs. They don't last very long, but by God, they're violent while they do. There, in you go! And we're just in time, I fancy."

As if in proof of his assertion the rain ceased, and as Jenny limped painfully into the darkness of the shack, there was a loud tattoo on its roof, sounding for all the world like a hail of musket-balls. When Timothy joined her, breathing hard from his exertions, he offered two of the hailstones for her inspection on his extended palm. "You see? These can be deuced painful if a storm like this catches you in the open, and they can flatten acres of standing corn in half an hour."

Another flash of lightning briefly illuminated the interior of the feedstore, and Jenny, looking about her, identified its contents as barley—perhaps forty or fifty bushels.

"Surely"—she could not keep the surprise from sounding

in her voice—"you don't feed this to your horses? I mean, it's—"

"No." Timothy's tired, black-streaked face was lit by an amused smile. "They get grass and kaffir corn. This"—he bent to pick up a handful of whiskery grain, his smile widening—"this is my answer to Macarthur and his fellow rogues. But if I tell you about it, you'll need to keep a guard on your tongue, my dear lass, for it could get us both into serious trouble."

Jenny did not pretend to misunderstand him. "You mean you have a still?"

She asked the question with some trepidation, shocked by the risk he was taking. Malted grain, distilled into spirit by unskilled hands, produced a potent and even poisonous liquor that could be a threat to health, if not to life itself. A recent public order issued by the governor prohibited the practice, and penalties for infringements of the order were severe. But Timothy shrugged and retorted confidently that he knew what he was doing.

"I had my old friend Silas Porter, mate of the *Britannia*, procure the still for me, and Davie Leake used to work for a whiskey distiller. Our liquor is good-quality stuff, and it's a quarter of the price the infernal Rum Corps demand for theirs. I can keep my workers well satisfied, and when there's a need for them I can employ seasonal labor. For God's sake, Jenny, one has to take a few chances in this corrupt place if one is to get on, you know!"

"I know," Jenny conceded uneasily. "All the same, Tim—"

He brushed her fears aside. "Forget I ever said a word. Now lie down and let me see if I can do something to ease the pain of that ankle of yours, will you please? There's not much of my shirt left but maybe just enough to fashion a bandage. Where do you feel the pain? . . . Here, is it?"

As gently as a woman he bound up her injured ankle and then, flashing her a mischievous grin, took a flask from his hip pocket and offered it to her. "Take a sip of this to ease the pain. Go on, it's not home-produced, I promise you. It's best Cape brandy purchased from Captain Foveaux's woman, and you deserve it if anyone ever did. You've been wonderful, Jenny, and I'm grateful, believe me."

Jenny swallowed a few mouthfuls. It was heady stuff but effective, and it eased both her pain and her weariness and restored her flagging spirits. Outside the thunder echoed and reechoed, and the hail continued to beat its loud and alarming tattoo on the shingled roof of the small grain-store. Within its cramped interior it was dry and warm, however, and after a while a pleasant lassitude began to steal over her, blotting out her earlier fears.

Timothy lay stretched out beside her in tired content-ment, his eyes closed, his fingers gently massaging her in-jured ankle. In all the years she had known him he had never once attempted to take advantage of her; their rela-tionship had been one of friendship and mutual trust and liking, tempered—for herself, at any rate—by the fact that he was the owner of her land and officially her employer. She felt him move and thought of old Watt Sparrow's oft-reiterated urging that she should "play her cards right," aware that, however wise and sensible his advice, she could not take it. . . . For Tim's sake and her own.

Besides, there was Henrietta Spence. There had always been Henrietta, like a barrier between them. Although now, if it was true that she intended to marry Lieutenant Brace, the barrier was no longer there. . . . Jenny, sensing his eyes on her, instinctively drew back.

"Tim," she ventured uneasily. "Davie may have got back from Toongabbe with help. We—"

"In this?" He swore softly. "For mercy's sake, woman, they'll be taking cover, like sensible folk. The storm's not over yet, not by a long chalk."

"Yes, but we—"

Timothy ignored the interruption. He said, uncannily as if he had read her thoughts of a few minutes before, "Jenny, why did I not ask you to wed me years ago? I must have been blind! Blind or bewitched. You're a fine woman, the finest I've ever known and the bravest. Out there, fac-ing that brush fire, you never flinched! Anyone else would have run, but you didn't." He reached for her hands, im-prisoned them in his own and exclaimed wryly over their torn and blistered state. He was lying very close to her, his lithe, strong body pressed to hers, his breath warm on her cheek, and for all her stern resolve to control her emotions, Jenny's heart quickened its beat. It had been a long time since any man had desired her, but she steeled herself not to respond, again drawing away from him.

"How could I not have seen you for the woman you are?" Timothy demanded. "In all this time!"

The surprise in his voice was hurtful and pride came to her rescue. "Because of Mistress Spence," she said accusingly. "You've always been in love with her, have you not? And a friend of her father's. You've thought of no one else."

"Aye," he conceded roughly. "But she's to wed that young blackguard Brace—I told you, she's made her choice, Jenny. And that leaves me free to make mine, surely?"

"I suppose so, but I . . . Oh, leave me be, Tim, please! You'll regret this—you must consider your position. And mine." She was pleading with him now, suddenly afraid. "I'm a convict, and you know what that means here."

"Of course I know . . . and be damned to it. Do you think I care?" His arms were about her, his mouth hungrily seeking hers.

"They would make you care, the respectable ones, the officers. . . . They always do, Tim," Jenny protested. She added defiantly, "And I don't need to marry. Justin and I are well enough as we are. We . . ." A clap of thunder drowned her words. Startled by its proximity, she attempted to get to her feet, but Timothy's hands restrained her.

"Aye, there's Justin. . . . And there was Justin's father for you, was there not?" he challenged. "Well, I'd say that makes us even, save that I never laid a finger on the girl I loved. I never so much as kissed her, Jenny, once Brace came on the scene, because she would not have it."

"Yes, but you—"

"I'm a man," Timothy said without contrition. "And I won't deny that I've taken my pleasure with a few whores in Sydney Town when the chance offered. But I've wasted five years. . . . Years when I mooned around like a dumb, lovesick fool, dreaming of what I couldn't have. Well, that's over—I mean to start afresh. I want a wife and a family—I want sons like Justin to inherit what I've sweated to build up here. I want *you*, Jenny. . . . You and that lad of yours. If you wed me, lass, I swear you'll not regret it."

There were no other arguments she could use, Jenny thought—none, that was to say, to which in his present mood he would listen. Again the thunder rolled, and the flash of lightning that followed it lit Timothy's obstinately set face to an odd radiance as he reached for her and, impatient now, drew her to him.

His lips found hers, his hands caressed her breasts, moved skillfully and possessively along the line of her thighs, lifting the torn skirt that had concealed them.

Jenny ceased to struggle against him, yielding with a little sigh of mingled pain and pleasure to the swift urgency of his lovemaking.

"We'll make a good pair, my lovely lass," he whispered, his mouth against hers as, at last, passion faded to a warm contentment. "And a plague on any respectable folk who dare to say we won't."

The respectable folk would include Henrietta, Jenny reflected wryly; Henrietta and her new husband and, in all probability, her father.

"How much," she inquired apprehensively, "do you owe Mr. Spence, Tim?"

Timothy swore under his breath. "Must you remind me *now* of such matters?" He put an arm about her, drawing her head onto his shoulder. "Sleep, love. Time enough to concern yourself about my debts when we're both rested."

"I'll rest easier if I know," Jenny persisted.

"You're acting the wife already," he grumbled.

"No, truly, Tim. You've lost Lucifer, and I know what a blow that is, because you would have got a high price for him."

He sighed. "Aye, that I would. Lucifer was an animal of rare quality. But there, it would have vexed me sorely if I'd had to sell him to Foveaux or Macarthur or any of their cronies, so I'm spared that, at least, am I not?"

"How much," Jenny persisted, "do you owe Mr. Spence? Please tell me—I've a reason for asking."

He hesitated and then admitted reluctantly, "A matter of three hundred thirty pounds, with the interest." It was more, much more than Jenny had anticipated, and she could not restrain a gasp of dismay. Timothy added with a hint of sullenness, "The two chestnut geldings will have to go and maybe a couple more. . . . But I'll settle it, Jenny, so don't you fret. I've the payment for my maize still to come and having that still will be of advantage, believe me. They'll not be able to hold me to ransom by forcing me to take their rum any longer."

But they would wonder why, Jenny thought, and perhaps, suspecting the reason, make a search. . . .

"I could buy my land back from you, Tim," she offered, and then, sensing his displeasure at her well-intentioned suggestion, went on quickly, "For Justin so that he—"

"When I wed you, Justin will be my responsibility, Jenny, just as you will," Timothy put in. There was an edge to his voice, and propping himself up on his elbow he peered down at her, endeavoring to search her face in the darkness. "Do you not trust me to care for you both?"

"Oh, Tim, of course I do!" Jenny was instantly contrite. "You've never given me cause to do otherwise."

And he had not, she told herself; he had been a staunch friend and the best of masters, treating Justin with warm affection. Would he be less, would he change if she became his wife? Surely he was not the kind to change . . . and Justin was growing up. He would need a father, and his own father would not come back now, after so many years. She thought fleetingly of Johnny Butcher and then, sadly, of Andrew, stifling back a sigh.

The storm was passing, she realized, and although thunder still muttered in the distance, the hail had ceased its violent pounding on the roof of their shelter. Soon all would be peace . . . She smiled, putting out a hand to take Tim's, remembering the joy of their lovemaking with a sudden, swift lifting of the heart.

His brief anger faded. He leaned over to kiss her, and her desire flamed in response to his. . . .

Help arrived with the dawn. The dead were buried, and with half a dozen of the Toongabbe settlers Timothy set off to round up his horses. A party of soldiers commanded by Lieutenant Brace crossed the river in a boat owned by the onetime *Sirius* sailor Robert Webb, with orders to exact retribution from the Bediagal Indians, place their chief, Pimelwi, under arrest, and bring him back to Parramatta for punishment.

The military party returned twenty-four hours later, and

it was from a shocked Robert Webb that Jenny heard the story of what they had done.

"It was a bloody massacre," he told her grimly. "I don't hold with the Indians stealin' and killin' and settin' our crops and our buildings on fire, the Lord knows . . . but Brace never gave 'em a chance. True, they flung a few spears at us when we caught up with 'em, but spears are no defense against musket-balls and never will be. Brace got his redcoats into cover and then ordered them to open fire."

"But surely he parleyed with them, Rob?" Jenny was as shocked as he was. "The people who attacked and murdered Tim's men were from the other side of the river, and Davie said he saw Pimelwi with them. But that doesn't prove that the Indians Mr. Brace fired on were of Pimelwi's tribe. Did you not have an interpreter with you?"

"Aye, we had Wurgun," the onetime *Sirius* seaman confirmed. "He said the Indians claimed that the raid on this place was in retaliation for an unprovoked attack made on them ten days ago by some white men south of here. But Brace wouldn't pay any heed. He reckoned they'd admitted their guilt and that was that. Mind you, Pimelwi was with them, and they've taken him to Parramatta with six or seven musket-balls in his black hide. About a dozen others were wounded and five killed outright. A victory for the gallant Rum Corps, Jenny!" He shrugged his disgust. "Did Tim Dawson get all his stock back?"

"Yes," Jenny said flatly. "He got them back."

But at how great a cost, she wondered uneasily as Rob took his leave. The raid had been in retaliation for wrongs done them by the settlers; now with their chief seized and almost a score of others killed or wounded, the Bediagal would be out for revenge, and the whole terrible cycle would be given fresh impetus.

A feeling of great sadness swept over her, and tears were aching in her throat as she glanced across at the three newly dug graves where Jackie Scrope and his companions in misfortune lay at rest.

What heritage was this for Justin and the sons Tim and she would beget?

CHAPTER XIII

"Well?" exclaimed Surgeon George Bass as he stood stripped to the waist in the warm afternoon sunshine and looked expectantly from the half-built longboat on which he was at work. "She's going to be an improvement on the *Tom Thumb*, is she not, Matt?"

Matthew Flinders's thin young face lit with an approving smile. "Aye, that she is!" he agreed enthusiastically. "And she'll need to be."

"The *Tom Thumb*, an eight-foot-long sailing dinghy they had brought out with them in the *Reliance*, had proved too small to be practicable for the voyages of exploration they had planned. Accompanied only by the surgeon's loblolly boy, Billy Martin, they had sailed her along the coast south of Port Jackson and for many miles up the reaches of King George's River from Botany Bay, surveying, taking soundings, and preparing charts with meticulous care as they went. But their final voyage in her had come near to being their last.

A severe storm, mountainous waves, and torrential rain had threatened to swamp their cockleshell craft, and it was only by good fortune that—cold, near to starvation, and completely exhausted—they had managed to row her back to the harbor and safety.

The misadventure had not deterred George Bass. Deprived of the boat and with Flinders required for duty on board the *Reliance*, he had made a determined attempt to find a way across the Blue Mountains on foot. He had accompanied Governor Hunter, with Captain Waterhouse and Judge Advocate Collins, on the first expedition they had undertaken in search of the wild cattle in November 1795. Spurred on by what he had seen of the country beyond the Nepean River and equipped with ropes, scaling irons, and climbing hooks of his own design, he had accompanied a second expedition until the cattle were located.

Then, with Henry Hacking and the faithful Billy Martin, Bass had ascended one of the mountains to the west of the

river, which they had named Mount Hunter in honor of
the governor. It had proved a difficult climb, and from the
summit the prospect was depressing for, as far as the eye
could see, the country was wild and thickly wooded, with a
great range of mountains forty or fifty miles distant, extending in ridges from north to south.

Nevertheless, the little party had pressed on, meeting no
natives and finding only desolation, with evidence of the
high winds to which the whole area was exposed in the
shape of uprooted trees and pools of stagnant rainwater.
After fourteen days of strenuous effort their food had run
out, and they had returned, disappointed at having failed to
achieve their objective.

"I fear there is no way over those mountains from here,"
Bass confided now to Matthew Flinders. "If we are to find
out what sort of country lies beyond them, we shall have to
sail along the coast and make our approach from seaward
. . . and God knows how far we shall have to sail if we
are to make our landfall on their western side. They may
extend for thousands of miles, for all we know—or the
whole of the interior may be mountainous. Or desert," he
added wryly, "instead of the agricultural and pastoral
land the governor is hoping for."

"Which do you think it is?" Flinders questioned.

"I simply don't know," the tall young surgeon admitted.
"The place where we found the cattle is splendid grazing
land and well watered—trust those Cape cattle to find it!
But once you climb above it, the going is exceedingly
rough—an endless succession of peaks and ridges, with ra-
vines and gullies between them. Without a compass, Matt,
it's all too easy to become lost, because there are no reliable landmarks. The natural features repeat themselves like
mirror images—trees, rocks, waterfalls, cliffs, and even the
peaks. If you follow a watercourse, it suddenly vanishes
and you never find it again. And there's no one to give you
guidance—I met only one Indian in fourteen days, and he,
I fancy, was more lost than I was!"

"What of the wildlife, George?" Flinders persisted, agog
with interest.

Bass shrugged. "There was singularly little. Birds, of
course—crows, parrots, and the inevitable laughing jack-
ass, an occasional duck flying overhead. Kangaroos were

few, but I saw a colony of those odd little gray bears Major Paterson told me about—the ones the Indians call koalas—amongst the eucalyptus trees on the lower slopes. But they were too high up, and I was too done up to try and capture one. They're pretty, furry little creatures with huge ears." He talked on, in technical terms, of the bearings he had taken and the route he had endeavored to follow, and ended ruefully, "If you're not too careful, you can walk in perpetual circles up there, bewitched by the strange blue beauty of the distant peaks. Give me the sea any day!"

"My sentiments exactly," Flinders agreed. He gestured to the curved ribs of the longboat. "What is she made of, George? That looks like teak, but it's not, is it? Surely that doesn't grow here?"

"It does," George Bass assured him. "On the banks of the Hawkesbury and King George's rivers. But it has taken longer than I bargained for to have the trees felled and conveyed here by the *Francis*, because most of her deck space is taken up by settlers' grain . . . and the loggers don't exert themselves unduly. Even when the timber's here I have to find carpenters to work it—the few men with skills are in demand to build windmills and a new hospital, among other things. They say the buildings Governor Phillip had constructed are falling down because cement wasn't used in their construction."

"So you're a shipbuilder, now, as well as a sawbones?"

"Of necessity, my dear Matt." Surgeon Bass grinned. "With a single exception, none of the convict carpenters has seen a shipyard, much less worked in one. Tom Moore, the *Britannia*'s carpenter, was appointed master shipwright in Payne's place, and he's deuced good. But even he has been persuaded to give his professional assistance to the building of a tower to house the clock we brought out! So I've lost him for the time being but . . ." He shrugged his sunburned shoulders resignedly. "Our discovery vessel is taking shape, Matt. I'll launch her before the year's end, I swear."

"Hurrah!" Matt Flinders applauded. "Then she'll be ahead of the sloop they are building on Norfolk Island under Johnny's supervision." He had just returned from the island, and he launched into a description of the projected new vessel. "She'll be decked and sloop-rigged—those Norfolk pines make excellent masts, you know. And Johnny Broome's doing a fine job."

"I don't doubt he is," Bass conceded. "All the same, we could do with his skill and local knowledge here before we're much older. Matt, do you recall his telling us that when they were on their way to Timor, his party found coal in a bay they entered for shelter?"

Flinders inclined his head. "North of here, was it not? Near Port Stephens. It was the first time they made land, Johnny said."

"Well, Jack Shortland found the bay *and* the coal," Bass told him. "I went coal hunting in August at the governor's suggestion, because one of the survivors of the *Sydney Cove*—the supercargo, Clarke—who made his way here overland from one of the Furneaux Islands, reported that he had made a fire from coal found on the surface of a beach where he spent the night. Clarke left two of his companions there, the mate and the carpenter, who had not the strength to go farther. A couple of days later he and the two lascars he had with him were picked up by a fishing boat from here, in Watta Mowla Bay."

"But that's south, isn't it, George?" Flinders put in. "I thought—"

"Yes—seven leagues south of Point Solander," George Bass confirmed. "I volunteered to take a whaleboat to search for the missing men and investigate Clarke's report of coal. He and one of the lascars came with me, to act as guides. After all he'd endured, he was still willing to go back! Anyway, we found the place . . . and the bodies of the mate and the carpenter. The coal was there, too, in large quantities—a seam six feet wide and extending, as nearly as I could estimate, for eight or nine miles, some of it above the surface." Taking a scrap of paper from his pocket he drew a sketch of the bay, indicating the steep cliffs by which it was surrounded. "It is good-quality coal but in an almost inaccessible situation due to the heavy surf. However, only a couple of weeks later some rogues of Irish convicts seized possession of a decked boat, the *Cumberland*—which Moore built and which I had designs on—when she was on passage to the Hawkesbury.

"They set the cox'un and two others on the beach at Pitt Water in Broken Bay, and when they reached Sydney these men gave the alarm. Jack Shortland gave chase with two armed boats. He went as far as Port Stephens without finding any trace of the escapers, and on his way back he put into the mouth of the river Johnny talked about—ten leagues to the south, in thirty degrees of south latitude. Johnny put in at between twenty-nine and thirty, remember?"

Flinders nodded. "And he said there was an island and a reef at the entrance to the bay."

"Which Jack also found. He's named the river the Hunter and made a chart of the entrance. He said he carried three to three-and-a-half fathoms at the shoalest part and found deep water and a good anchorage within . . . and coal, in large quantities, so near the anchorage as to be easily shipped." Bass's expression relaxed. "The governor's delighted, needless to say. Indeed, he's planning to establish a settlement there, with convict working parties to dig the coal. It is now officially named Coal Harbor." Once again the surgeon went to work with pencil and paper. "This will interest our friend Johnny, I don't doubt. Tell me, did you see much of him when you were at Norfolk Island?"

"Not as much as I'd intended," Flinders said regretfully. "The poor old *Reliance* is in almost as bad a state as the *Supply*, and we were kept busy patching her up for the passage back. Johnny intimated that he was eager to return and join us, but—I don't think Major Paterson will be in a hurry to let him go. The sloop is a project very dear to his heart, and he wants Johnny to take charge of her sea trials. Poor Captain King, as you know, left in the *Britannia* to take sick leave in England, and Paterson and Abbott command the island in his absence. Paterson loves it there—it's his pride and joy, and although they've had a poor harvest, their livestock is increasing mightily. Believe this or not, George, but I feasted a dozen times on fresh roast pork during my stay!"

"Lucky devil!" George Bass mocked. "The height of my culinary enjoyment has been kangaroo at the governor's table and mutton at Foveaux's. And that black rogue Baneelon demanded—and was given—three gigantic helpings of the governor's kangaroo, to the politely restrained wrath of the rest of the company!"

Flinders chuckled appreciatively. "So he hasn't gone native after all?"

"Baneelon? Oh, yes, he has, my dear fellow—both he and Yemmerra Wannie periodically desert us in order to indulge in pitched battles with their own people. One of the young warriors stole Baneelon's wife whilst he was being lionized in London, and in the resultant fight the offender retained possession of the lady, leaving Baneelon badly mauled and in a most evil temper. I fear our attempts to civilize these people will never succeed, Matt—they are wanderers, by upbringing and nature, and savages to boot. The wood tribes are forever causing trouble. They rob and kill the settlers, particularly those on the Hawkesbury, and fire their crops and buildings. . . ." He went into details and added cynically, "Baneelon, by the way, leaves Government House naked, and then, if you please, sends for his clothes and returns, dressed in the height of London fashion, carrying his shield and his spears, and gets happily drunk on the governor's Cape brandy! The only white person for whom he appears to cherish any affection is an emancipist he calls Jen-nee, whose acquaintance he first made on Pinchgut."

"It's a very strange country," Flinders observed with resignation. "But I'm still keen to explore it, George. I am being sent in the *Francis* to bring off any of the *Sydney Cove*'s people who have survived their enforced sojourn among the Furneaux Island seals . . . and save as much of her cargo as I can. But after that I'll put in for leave, and we'll join forces again if that boat of yours is finished."

"She'll be finished," Bass promised, a note of excitement in his voice. "And, God willing, we'll solve the mystery of those westward-setting tides."

"Van Diemen's Land, you mean?"

"That's what I mean, Matt. Because I believe it is separated from New South Wales—I believe it may be an island or a whole archipelago, with water where Tasman declared there was only land. Reports from whaling skippers suggest it's there. . . ." Again, his excitement rising, Surgeon Bass illustrated his beliefs on paper, citing observations made by the governor and William Kent to back them up. Flinders's interest was swiftly kindled. They discussed the possibilities at length and became so immersed in their argument that neither noticed the sun going down. Bass thrust his scraps of paper into his pocket and stretched his cramped limbs.

"Come back to my quarters," he invited. "I've some charts the master of the *Assistance* allowed me to copy. You're the cartographer—you can take them with you to study whilst I'm gone and —"

"Gone?" Flinders turned to look at him in surprise, "Where are you off to this time?"

"I'm making the last landward survey I intend to make," Bass answered. "There's a small party going to the Cow Pasture Plain to see how the wild herd is doing—there have been reports that the Indians are killing them. I'm going with the main party as far as Mount Taurus, and then Henry Hacking and I and a settler named Dawson are going to make our way to the coast. Dawson's lending the main party some packhorses, but we'll be on foot, following the course of the Nepean River as far as we're able. A boat will pick us up five leagues to the south of Botany Bay." He clapped a hand on Flinders's shoulder. "Come with us if you like."

"I'm sitting as a member of the criminal court," the younger man said, and smiled in mock apology. "My new acting rank as lieutenant has its drawbacks! Not that I envy you. . . . You'll have a deuced long walk, George!"

Bass aimed a playful blow at him. He donned his shirt and started to pack his tools into a canvas bag.

"Nothing is safe here," he complained, "unless it's nailed down. Those rogues of convicts would steal anything—and not only boats, plague take them! The governor has ordered that no boats may be left overnight with oars, rudder, mast, or sails on board, and tools and timber must be kept under lock and key. Oblige me by closing the padlock on my store shed, would you, Matt? I cannot afford to lose my stock of precious hardwood."

Flinders obligingly fastened the padlock.

"It's mainly the Irish who steal boats, is it?" he suggested as they fell into step together and started to walk out of the yard and toward the newly built assistant surgeon's quarters behind the main wharf. "The people deported for sedition?"

George Bass nodded moodily. "Yes . . . and we're

being flooded with them—transport after transport comes here from Cork with more. The governor is deeply concerned, I understand, because they're not the kind to make settlers. Their one aim and object is escape, and the only way they can be compelled to work is if they are sent into the fields in chains."

"Do they still cling to the notion that they can escape overland to China?" Flinders asked curiously.

"Some appear to, yes. But the majority aren't criminals, like the English convicts—indeed, many are men and women of good education and breeding, who belong to a rebel society called 'The Defenders.' And they are the ones the governor doesn't want because he considers them dangerous to our security."

"And are they, do you suppose, George?"

Bass shrugged. "Few of the ships that brought them here did not suffer attempts at mutiny, so I suppose they must be regarded as dangerous. Poor souls, I can find it in my heart to pity them, though. They—"

"Pity seditionists and rebels?" Flinders questioned in surprise. "And would-be mutineers?"

"They are rebelling against tyranny," Bass argued without heat. "And defending themselves against religious persecution, Matt—I'd do the same were I in their place. But for all that, I share His Excellency's concern at the number we now have here. We need artisans and farmers in New South Wales, not ever-increasing numbers of rebels sent here because the home government doesn't know what else to do with them!"

They were passing within sight of the new jail, and George Bass gestured to it with a wry smile. It was built of logs with a thatched roof and surrounded by a high paling, also of logs, that enclosed an exercise yard and a brick building, fenced off from the main prison.

"*That* has taken virtually all the public labor gangs, Matt," he said. "Taken them from shipbuilding, from road making, and from farm work for a month past . . . and it's full! The brick building is for debtors, and I'm told that's full too. The only hopeful innovation is the establishment of a school for the children of the colony, which has an attendance of over two hundred. That, at least, augurs well for the future and for the next generation."

"Let us hope it does," Matt Flinders said, his tone significantly lacking in conviction.

"Some of them help me with the boat when school is out," Bass told him. He halted outside his quarters and, lowering the tool bag, turned to face his companion. "Matt, do you recall chaffing Johnny Broome about a little lad you declared must be a by-blow of his because he resembled him so closely?"

"The boy who tried to save a poor little dog from a mob of drunken convict women the day we landed? Yes, indeed I do. We made the acquaintance of his mother too—an Irish girl, who'd had her head shaved." Flinders laughed shortly. "One of your Defenders, I fancy. But I *was* only chaffing—it was quite evident that the girl had never set eyes on Johnny before in her life. All the same, the resemblance the boy bore to him was quite uncanny."

"Yes," Bass agreed. "I observed it also."

"Oh, then you know the boy I mean—you've seen him?"

The surgeon nodded. He shouted for his servant to admit them and added thoughtfully, "He's attending the new school and lodging with the building superintendent, Macrae, who came from Parramatta to build the monstrosity of a jail. His name, he told me, is Justin Taggart, and I see him frequently. For one of his tender years he makes himself remarkably useful about the boat . . . more so than any of the others. And—" The servant came in answer to his summons. Bass broke off to lead the way into his small living room, and sending the man for refreshments, he waved Flinders to a chair, hospitably offering his tobacco jar. "Sit down and enjoy a pipe of Toongabbe tobacco, Matt, while I show you the results of my last coastal survey. I've been comparing my charts with Cook's and Bligh's, and I think you'll find the comparisons of interest."

"Thanks—I don't doubt I shall." Flinders filled a pipe, and when they were both seated with wine and a pile of charts between them, he said, "George, before we start on your survey, answer me one question, will you?"

"Certainly, my dear fellow. Ask away."

"That boy— the one who's the spitting image of Johnny Broome—you said his surname was Taggart, did you not?"

George Bass looked up from the pile of charts he was sorting. "That's what he told me, yes."

"Well," Flinders observed. "The Irish girl's name was O-something . . . O'Rourke, O'Reilly, O'Riordan, I can't recall which, but it was definitely Irish. They were together, she and the boy, so I took it for granted that she was his mother. But I could have been mistaken—perhaps there's a woman named Taggart in the offing, who *is* the lad's mother—a woman to whom Johnny is no stranger. It's possible, is it not?"

"It certainly raises interesting possibilities," Bass conceded. He drew on his pipe, a pensive frown drawing his dark brows together as he considered the matter with evident reluctance. "But Johnny may not wish either of us to explore them, Matt. He could have done so himself, surely, had he wanted to."

"He wasn't given time," Flinders countered. "Captain Waterhouse sent him to the *Supply* just after we landed, and she was ordered to Norfolk Island within a few days of our making port here, don't you remember?"

"Yes, I remember. But"—Bass returned to his charts—"I hardly think we should interfere. We—"

"Johnny more or less admitted that there was a woman here when I quizzed him about it," Flinders put in excitedly. "But he said she was probably married by this time, with two or three children. We could find that out, could we not? If this boy Justin Taggart *is* his son, surely he would want to know? I know I would!"

"You are an incurable romantic, Matt," the surgeon retorted, his tone mildly reproving. "My advice would be to leave well alone. The boy's mother very probably *is* married by this time, and any inquiries you or I made might stir up trouble for her—and, come to that, for Johnny himself. He's not likely to want the fact that he came out here as a convict known and gossiped about, is he? It carries a stigma here, as you must be aware."

"But not for Johnny!" Matt Flinders protested. "His voyage to Timor was an epic, George. It puts him in the front rank as a navigator, and—"

"And makes him a hero to every convict in New South Wales," Bass interrupted harshly. "Though not, I can assure you, to the governor. *He* maintains that the lenient treatment the escapers received in England has served

greatly to encourage others of a like mind here. And"—he
shrugged—"Captain Hunter may be aware of Johnny's
identity—I imagine William Kent will have told him if Waterhouse didn't—but if so, he is keeping it dark. Indeed,
that may well be the reason for Johnny's lengthy stay at
Norfolk Island."

"Yes, but surely—"

"We can do nothing, Matt. In any event, what proof
have we? Besides"—Bass smiled and lifted his glass—"for
purely selfish reasons, we shall need Johnny Broome when
we tackle the Barrier Reef survey, shall we not? If he takes
up with a wife and son, he'll be lost to us. So be a good
fellow and keep your own counsel. If you do not, I shall be
sorry I ever told you about the boy."

"Why did you, George?" Flinders asked curiously. "Because the likeness made you wonder?"

Bass was spared the necessity for a reply when his servant announced a visitor. Lieutenant Shortland came into
the room at the servant's heels. A tall man of robust physique, he was clearly agitated, his cheeks pale beneath their
tan, but he did not speak until the servant had withdrawn.
Then, shaking his head to the offer of a glass of wine, he
burst out, "No, no, I haven't time. I'm on my way to the
governor with news that . . . dear God, George, news
that I pray *cannot* be true!"

Bass got to his feet, and Flinders, after a momentary hesitation, followed his example. Both were silent, Shortland's
agitation communicating itself to them. "I went out to meet
a newly arrived ship," he said in a strained voice. "She was
signaled from the South Head, and the governor wanted to
know who she was—you know he's sending all ships he
suspects of carrying liquor to Neutral Bay, to enable him to
keep control of what is landed."

His listeners nodded, and Bass prompted, "Go on, Jack."

The *Reliance's* first lieutenant drew in his breath
sharply. "She proved to be the *Deptford* brig, thirteen
weeks on passage from India. Her master, Mr. Barber, has
been here before, and I signaled him to proceed, but he
insisted I come on board. He met me at the entry port and
took me to his cabin, taking every precaution to avoid our
conversation being overheard. I thought that he had some

confidence regarding his cargo that he wished to impart, but he . . . as heaven's my witness, I still cannot believe what he told me!"

George Bass splashed wine into a glass and thrust the glass into the visitor's hand. Shortland gulped it down like a man who was still too shocked to be fully aware of what he was doing. Flinders took the empty glass from him in anxious silence, wondering as he did so whether his friend and messmate had suffered some sort of brainstorm.

But John Shortland's next words sent his heart plummeting. "Barber told me that the Channel Fleet has mutinied at Spithead, and that their example was being followed at The Nore. The seamen have hoisted the Red Flag on board king's ships and refused to take them to sea—*in time of war!* Imagine it, with England fighting for her life! I . . . God in heaven, it's beyond belief! But I . . ." He stumbled toward the door. "I shall have to tell the governor."

"I'll come with you," Bass offered and took his arm.

CHAPTER XIV

"All hands lay aft to witness punishment! Clear the lower deck! D'ye hear there, all hands!"

The pipe sounded, and the unwelcome order echoed from deck to deck of the heavily pitching ship, the stentorian voices of the boatswain's mates heard above the shriek of the wind in the rigging and the noisy clanking of the pumps.

H.M.S. *Director*, of sixty-four guns, was plowing her way homeward in the teeth of a westerly gale, at the end of a seven-week-long blockade of the Dutch fleet in the Texel and the invasion force said to be gathering there. Admiral Duncan's signal to his North Sea squadron of seventeen sail to set course for Yarmouth had come as a relief to every man on board the *Director*. She was an old ship, rat-infested and leaking badly, and her people had suffered much during the late spring blockade . . . not least from her commander's ruthless determination to instill a proper sense of discipline into her motley crew.

Captain William Bligh had won fame as a navigator, but he was a martinet who would tolerate no relaxation of the standards of efficiency he had imposed, and he used the cat mercilessly in order to enforce the demands he made on pressed men and prime seamen alike. Behind his back and knowing his record, the men called him "Breadfruit Bligh" and the "*Bounty* Bastard," and spat on the *Director*'s well-holystoned deck as they said it. But now, with the Dutch ships safely bottled up in the Wadden Zee for as long as the wind held westerly, they were on their way to their home port and, God willing, to a period of comparative peace, while their ship refitted at Sheerness and their captain spent some of his time ashore.

To Andrew Hawley, mustering with the marines in their traditional position, facing the hollow square of seamen with loaded muskets, the scene now being enacted was all too familiar . . . and he deplored it. The man awaiting punishment—a landsman named Holdman—was the eleventh to be sentenced for insubordination in as many days.

There had been a number of such incidents during the blockade, most of them too trivial to warrant flogging, and the petty officers had, for some reason known only to themselves, in any event failed to report them.

Andrew, looking to the alignment of his scarlet-coated men, was uneasy, conscious of a strange undercurrent running through the lower deck that he had never previously experienced in any ship in which he had served. It was as if some of the men were deliberately seeking to flout the captain's authority, in half a hundred covert acts of defiance—each insignificant in itself but, when added one to another, constituting a challenge. Captain Bligh was quick to pounce on any he could, his first lieutenant, McTaggart, equally so, and retribution was swiftly meted out; but even they could not flog half a watch or an entire boat's crew for what, on the face of it, could only be termed lack of effort. Or, at worst, dumb insolence.

Holdman, though, had blundered head over heels into the worst kind of trouble. He was an unwilling conscript, taken by the "press" despite his furious protestations that, as an apprentice, he was exempt. Rated a waister, he had done his work with a sullen and apparently deliberate clumsiness that had roused the first lieutenant's wrath, and then, detailed to a quarterdeck carronade crew when the guns were being exercised, he had brought himself forcibly to the captain's notice by refusing to obey an order.

The ship's surgeon completed his cursory examination, the gratings were rigged, and, impelled by a shove from the master-at-arms, the prisoner came to attention facing the captain. The charge and sentence were read and the formal question put.

"Have you anything to say on your behalf?"

Holdman, despite the advice his messmates had given him, had plenty to say, but his attempt to defend his conduct was abruptly silenced by a curt command to strip from Lieutenant McTaggart.

"Seize him up, Master-at-arms!"

Stripped to the waist, Holdman was secured to the grating, wrists and thighs firmly pinioned. He was a skinny little runt of a man, Andrew realized, seeing him thus, and all the defiance had gone out of him as he hung, limp and shivering, from the bonds that held him.

"Ship's company!" the first lieutenant shouted. "Hats off!"

Captain Bligh, his own cocked hat tucked under his arm, read briefly from the Articles of War, his voice loud and rasping. The boatswain took the cat-o'-nine-tails from its red baize bag, freed the thongs, and passed it to one of the mates standing beside him.

"Three dozen lashes, sir?" he inquired, his face expressionless.

"Three dozen," Captain Bligh confirmed. "To be laid on well. Bo'sun's Mate, do your duty!"

The marine drummer raised his sticks; the drum rolled, and the boatswain's mate stepped forward. He swung the whip behind his head and brought its knotted thongs hissing across the wretched Holdman's naked shoulders. The first stroke raised a line of ugly red weals across the tautly stretched skin and the second drew blood. It wrung a high-pitched screech of pain from the onetime tailor's apprentice. The stupid young fool had been warned not to cry out at the first few strokes; he had been provided with a leather clamp to bite on. Yet here he was, yelling his head off before the first half-dozen lashes had touched his hide! The older hands, accustomed to more stoicism on the part of those condemned to punishment, turned their heads away in disgust.

Andrew heard the mutterings. They were not the first he had heard during the past seven weeks, but the seamen kept their own counsel, meeting together in small groups below decks, that swiftly dispersed if a marine came within earshot. The strange current of unrest he had observed was confined to the seamen. . . . His men did not appear to be affected by it and, indeed, he would have been a great deal more worried if they had.

Marines were soldiers who took the king's shilling voluntarily and swore allegiance to His Majesty when they did so—they were not paid off at the end of a commission, as the seamen were, to be left ashore to starve until next a crew was wanted. And they were not pressed, dragged unwillingly from their homes and families or from East Indiamen, only lately returned from long trading voyages to China and Bengal. They . . . Andrew felt his gorge rise as

Holdman's screams faded momentarily into silence while the cat changed hands.

True, marines were flogged and they ate the same poor food, but they received their pay regularly—many seamen were kept waiting two or three years for theirs—and if he were wounded in battle a marine's pay was not stopped while he was recovering. Furthermore, military pay had recently been raised, but seamen in the king's navy still earned the same miserly pittance that had been the rate for more than a hundred years—a shilling a week for a prime topman and sixpence for a landsman.

He sighed, hearing the captain say, "Cut him down, Mr. Williams, and let the surgeon have him!"

The wretched Holdman was carried below, moaning and barely conscious. Bligh glanced with coldly appraising eyes at the ranks of men facing him, as if seeking to gauge their mood. Then he nodded to Lieutenant McTaggart and moved slowly toward the after hatchway, a stocky yet impressive figure in his blue full-dress coat with its gold lace and post-captain's epaulets.

The first lieutenant gave the order to dismiss, but to Andrew's shocked surprise, only the marines obeyed it. The seamen remained in their ranks as if they had not heard the shouted command. The captain turned and thundered, "Marines, stand steady!" He waited, watching them, as Lieutenant McTaggart repeated his order. Again it was disregarded, and from somewhere in the ranks an anonymous voice asked mockingly, "What're ye going to do, Bully Bligh? Flog the lot o' us, maybe?"

The captain's firm mouth compressed. He summoned his first lieutenant to his side with a jerk of the head and said, pitching his voice to ensure that it carried, "You may permit the officers to fall out, Mr. McTaggart. The ship's company will remain mustered at attention until I give them permission to fall out. If you need to trim or take in sail, select the men you require and send them back to their divisions when the work is done."

"Aye, aye, sir," McTaggart acknowledged, a spiteful smile curving his lips. "And the marines, sir?"

"They will remain," Captain Bligh snapped. Then, relenting, "They may stand at ease." Again his gaze went to the lines of seamen, keen and searching, as if he were endeavoring to fit a name and a face to the man who had shouted the insolent question. Finally he said, "Place Hulme under arrest and send him to my cabin under guard, if you please, McTaggart."

It was Andrew who was given the unpleasant task of escorting the man the captain had named to the great cabin. Joseph Hulme had served under Bligh in his previous ship, the *Calcutta*, and Andrew knew him both by sight and reputation. Now rated as master's mate, he was a thin, sallow-faced man of thirty or so, who paid servile lip service to the officers but was suspected of troublemaking on the lower deck. More intelligent and better educated than most, he preached the gospel expounded by Paine in *The Rights of Man*, and the seamen listened to him with increasing eagerness, particularly, Andrew imagined, when he spoke of the change of fortune the revolution in France had brought to those of their kind now serving in the enemy ships.

He said now, in a carefully lowered voice, as Andrew walked beside him in the passageway that led aft to the captain's cabin, "There'll be an end to all this tyranny when we make port, Sergeant Hawley. Great things have been happening in the fleet at Spithead, and our boys will make sure they happen at Yarmouth and The Nore, as soon as we drop our hook."

"How do you know that?" Andrew challenged.

"I know," Hulme assured him confidently. "It's been boiling up for a long time, and we've made our plans. We'll not put to sea again until the government and their bleeding Lordships o' the Admiralty give us our arrears of pay and a guarantee of better conditions—shore leave in England and better food, *and* a fairer share o' prize money into the bargain! You'll see."

"You're talking of mutiny!" Andrew exclaimed, shocked to the depths of his being by this open admission.

"You can call it that if you want," Joseph Hulme retorted, quite unabashed, although he kept his voice low. Reaching the door of the great cabin, before which a sentry paced, he halted and grasped Andrew's arm. Putting his mouth close to Hawley's ear, he whispered hoarsely, "You lobsterbacks will have to make a choice—support the officers or come in with us. I know which I'd choose if I were you. Well"—he released Andrew's arm and grinned at him defiantly as he removed his hat—"wheel me in, Leatherneck, and see me disrated to A.B. for a crime I didn't commit. But our time is coming—old Adam Duncan only delayed it by keeping us at sea for longer than he should have, make no mistake about that. And when it does come, don't say I didn't warn you!"

His words remained in Andrew's memory, gnawing at him like a painful sore, and he began to realize the truth of them soon after the squadron made port at Yarmouth on April 25. Rumors were rife concerning the mutiny that had taken place in the Channel Fleet at Spithead nine days previously, and when the *Director* reached The Nore, they were confirmed in every detail.

Lord Bridport's ships had refused to put to sea, and on Easter Sunday the men of Lord Howe's old flagship, the *Queen Charlotte*, had given the prearranged signal by an unauthorized burst of cheering. Thereafter, boats had rowed out from the flagship to pick up two delegates from each of the other anchored ships. Two days later, on April 18, when the First Lord of the Admiralty, Lord Spencer, arrived in Portsmouth, the mutineers were in command, and the Red Flag was flying in place of the Union Flag throughout the fleet.

It had seemingly been a disciplined revolt, for all that, with the officers remaining on board their ships and receiving the respect due to them, and the delegates setting out their grievances and demands in the form of a humble petition addressed to the Lords Commissioners of the Admiralty. Prefaced by assurances of their continued patriotism and loyalty, the men had requested an increase in pay for all ranks, improvements in the food supplied to the lower deck and in the treatment of sick and wounded on board His Majesty's ships, including an end to the stoppage of pay to wounded seamen and limited shore leave for those whose ships were in port.

Refusals, threats, tentative offers of compromise, and prolonged negotiations between Lord Spencer and the vice admiral, Sir Alan Gardner, had culminated in Gardner and two of his fellow admirals being put ashore by the delegates meeting on board the *Queen Charlotte*. They followed this summary dismissal from their council by a demand—again humbly phrased as a petition—for a Royal Pardon to be accorded to every seaman and marine serving in the ships of the fleet at Spithead, and they repeated their original requests. Added to these was now another to the effect that certain captains and junior officers, guilty of cruel and harsh treatment of their people, should be dismissed and replaced.

The king granted his pardon by proclamation; copies of this were read on board all the ships, and with a promise that a Seamen's Bill would be put before Parliament to enable the required increases in pay to be made, Lord Bridport hoisted his flag on board the *Royal George* and led six sail-of-the-line to St. Helens, preparatory to resuming the Channel Fleet's blockade of Brest.

At The Nore anchorage, delegates from Spithead arrived, making first for the *Sandwich,* which was being used as a receiving ship for newly pressed men. Word swiftly spread that the mutiny at Spithead was not over; they had been betrayed, the delegates claimed. Parliament had not passed the Seamen's Bill, arrears of pay had not been forthcoming, and on board the *London,* Vice Admiral Colpoys had ordered his officers to fire on his seamen when delegates from the *Queen Charlotte* had attempted to address them.

On board the *Sandwich,* on May 6, a secret meeting was held. Delegates were elected, the Sandwiches choosing a quota man, Richard Parker, as their leader and—having agreed that they, too, would mutiny within a week—sent boats to tour the anchorage and rally all the ships' companies to their support.

It was from Joseph Hulme—predictably chosen as one of the *Director*'s delegates—that Andrew learned of the decision reached on board the *Sandwich* to administer an oath to The Nore seamen, pledging their allegiance to the course on which the Channel Fleet had embarked . . . even at the risk of their lives.

"Parker's a good man," Hulme asserted. "He's served as a midshipman and an acting lieutenant previously, until some damned tyrant of a captain had him broken for insubordination. He can read and write a fair hand, and he knows how to talk to the officers, so we've elected him as president of the fleet delegates." He smiled, savoring the impressive-sounding title, before adding emphatically, "Fri-

day's the day, Hawley—Friday the twelfth o' May—when
we take over. The signal will be cheering from the *Sandwich* and the reeving of yard ropes."

"The date is settled then?" Andrew questioned uneasily.

"Aye—and there'll be no turning back," Hulme assured
him grimly. "All that aren't *for* us are *against* us, so you
bloody leathernecks had best make up your minds, one
way or t'other. Remember what that scoundrel Colpoys did
on board of the *London*. He ordered his lobsters to open
fire."

"And did they?" Andrew demanded, his throat suddenly
dry. "Did they open fire?"

"Two of 'em did," Hulme admitted. "But the rest joined
with the seamen. And the first lieutenant was lucky to escape with his life—the lads wanted to string him up from
the yardarm there and then. They had the rope round his
neck, and only one o' the *Charlotte*'s delegates, Val Joyce,
saved him . . . and that with a dozen poor sods o' seamen
lying dead or wounded on the deck!"

"Yes, but—"

Hulme produced a scrap of paper from his pocket. "This
here's the oath, Hawley. Read it and let your lads read it,
too. Only by acting together will we ever get our grievances
heard and put right—the bleeding Admiralty and the
bleeding Parliament won't listen otherwise, and you know
it."

That was true enough, Andrew reflected, glancing down
at the paper Hulme had given him. The words "I will, to
the laying down of my life, be true to the delegates at present assembled, whilst they continue to support the present
cause" caught his eye, and he looked up at his informant in
something approaching dismay.

"For God's sake, Hulme!" he exclaimed. "What if the
French come out, what if they try to launch an invasion
from Brest or the Texel? Do we just sit here, refusing to
put out to meet them?"

"Of course we don't!" Joseph Hulme was indignant.
"We're patriots, not traitors, Sergeant. If the Frogs try anything like that, we'll meet 'em and send the bastards packing, pay or no bleeding pay. But until they do, we're all
united . . . at Spithead and St. Helens, Plymouth, and
here at The Nore. We—"

"What about the North Sea squadron?" Andrew put in. Admiral Duncan, the big, towering Scotsman who commanded the squadron, had long fought both Admiralty and Parliament in his seamen's cause, and he was deservedly esteemed by every man under his command. "They're not joining, are they?"

Hulme shrugged. "There are delegates at Yarmouth, Hawley, putting our case. The only doubt concerns the *Venerable*, on the admiral's account. . . . The lads have too much respect for old Duncan to haul down his flag, see? But they'll all be with us when the time comes, and they'll not put to sea unless the sodding Dutchmen do, I can promise you that." His manner became warmer, more persuasive. "See here, Sergeant Hawley, your leathernecks don't have to sign our fraternal oath unless they truly want to. . . . All we want is a pledge that you'll not go against us if, say, we put the captain and some o' the officers ashore."

"You're surely not thinking of doing that, are you?" Andrew stared at him in disbelief. "I understood that no violence was to be offered to any of the officers. At Spithead they—"

Hulme cut him short. He said impatiently, "No violence *will* be offered. Officers will be treated with respect. But we'll be well rid o' the *Bounty* bastard and that swine Ireland. And besides"—he smiled—"we're being given the opportunity on a plate. The damned old fool of an admiral, Buckner, has convened a court-martial on board the *Inflexible* for nine-thirty on the morning of Friday the twelfth, and Bligh's on it. Couldn't be a better chance to ditch him, could there?"

There almost certainly could not, Andrew thought, his anxiety in no way lessened by his talk with Joe Hulme. He talked also with the senior sergeant of the *Director*'s marine detachment, Adam Simpson; but after a lengthy perusal of the oath Hulme wanted them to sign and an equally lengthy discussion, the gray-haired Simpson had no remedy to suggest.

"There ain't nothing we can do, Andy. Our lads won't go against their own shipmates, but by the same token, I don't fancy any of us ought to take that oath. We'll just have to keep our lads in hand, make sure they obey any reasonable orders they're given, and maintain our discipline like we always do." He met Andrew's anxious gaze with a ghost of a smile. "When you come down to brass tacks, we've got a few grievances of our own, ain't we? When did you last have shore leave and enjoy fresh meat and decent white bread? If the poor bloody navy is expected to fight the country's battles on every ocean in the world, it's only right that the lads that man the ships should get a fair rate of pay and decent food, ain't it? And shore leave, when they're in port."

He was right, Andrew was forced to concede; nevertheless, he waited with growing apprehension for the dawning of Friday, May 12. It came; Captain Bligh was rowed across to the *Inflexible* in his gig, and no sooner was the court-martial flag run up than a loud burst of cheering from the *Sandwich* heralded the start of the mutiny. The loud hurrahs from Parker's ship were echoed by those from every other ship at the anchorage, and when the order went out to reeve yard ropes and hoist the Red Flag at the mizzen peak, it was obeyed.

On board the *Director*, Joseph Hulme took command, with a seaman named MacLaurin as his deputy. When Captain Bligh returned to the ship, he was piped over the side and, to Andrew's relief, treated with respect. He went below, took possession of the keys to the arms' chests, and ordered two marine sentries to be posted outside his great cabin, instead of the usual one. Sergeant Simpson posted the two men, his weather-beaten face devoid of expression, but within an hour a delegate from the *Sandwich* presented himself at the entry port, cutlass in hand and two pistols thrust into his belt, to demand that the *Director* supply an armed boat.

"Some of our delegates are detained on board the *Clyde*," he told Hulme aggrievedly. "An' we're needin' your boat to take them off, so bestir yersel', will ye?"

Hulme, still behaving correctly, sought the captain's leave to arm and man a boat and received a brusque refusal. The *Sandwich* delegate, muttering to them to "Take his keys an' pitch the *Bounty* bastard overboard!" departed without waiting to ascertain whether or not his advice had been acted upon. But once again to Andrew's relief, it was not, and Captain Bligh, controlling his outraged feelings with an almost visible effort, was allowed to go back to his cabin with his keys intact and his authority unchallenged. The *Clyde* released the detained delegates, and her men joined the cheers of rebellion.

Later that day the delegates and the men elected to the *Director*'s committee met to decide on their future course of action. Then, having administered the fraternal oath to all save the marines, the committee went in force to seek audience with the captain. Matthew Hollister, a tough, hard-drinking seaman with ten years' service behind him, voiced the blunt demand that, for brutal and oppressive treatment of the ship's company, Lieutenant Ireland, together with Lieutenant Church and the master, should forthwith be put ashore.

Captain Bligh faced them with icy dignity.

"Since you now appear to have gained control of this ship by unlawful, treacherous, and mutinous actions, and since there are five hundred of you ranged against me, I am compelled to listen to what you have to say," he told them, an edge to his voice. "I will remove the officers you have named from the watch bill and instruct them to remain below in their own quarters . . . but I will *not* put them ashore. In their absence from duty as watchkeepers, you must accept full responsibility for the maintenance of discipline and the working of the ship—is that understood?"

Crestfallen, Hollister acknowledged that it was, and the deputation reluctantly withdrew.

"We ought to put the bleeding captain ashore—or pitch the sod overboard, like MacCarthy said," Hulme asserted angrily, "because he's not going to yield an inch." He thrust past the two silent, red-coated sentries, ignoring Andrew, who—fearing that the mutineers might bring pressure to bear on them—had hurried below to share their vigil. But beyond upbraiding them for scurvy lobsterbacks, the delegates made no attempt to persuade them to desert their post. The sentries, both young men, shuffled their booted feet uneasily, exchanging covert glances, and then one said, his tone anxious, "They'll have us for this, Sar'nt. They—"

"Are you with them, Kendrick?" Andrew snapped.

The men hesitated, and then both inclined their heads. "They reckon as any as ain't wiv' 'em is against 'em, don't they?" the second man said defensively. "Well, I ain't against 'em, no more'n Kendrick is. An' I'd as soon not let the buggers think I'm protectin' Cap'n Bligh, Sar'nt, an' that's the God's truth!"

Andrew started to remind them of their duty but broke off as both young marines came suddenly to attention, their faces reflecting dismay. The door at his back opened, and turning, he saw the captain framed in the aperture, brown eyes blazing with barely contained fury.

"Damn your blood, you infernal rogues!" he raged. "Have you no loyalty, no pride in the king's service and the uniform you wear? God's teeth, that I should see the day when the marines don't know their duty! Dismiss them, Sergeant—I want no mutinous dogs guarding me!"

Shocked by this unfortunate turn of events, Andrew obeyed him, and with a jerk of his bewigged head, Captain Bligh directed him to step into the cabin, kicking the door shut with the toe of his boot.

"It is to be hoped that *you* know your duty, Sergeant— what's your name?"

"Hawley, sir."

"And *do* you know your duty, Sergeant Hawley?"

"I believe so, sir," Andrew answered, standing stiffly to attention.

Bligh subjected him to a searching scrutiny, an ill-tempered scowl creasing his high, slightly receding brow into a maze of tiny lines. "Would you permit any of those mutinous ruffians to lay hands on me?" he rasped.

This was *Bounty* Bligh, Andrew reflected, conscious of doubt—a captain who had already driven one ship's company to mutiny. He remembered the naked, half-starved prisoners on board the *Pandora*, chained and helpless—the wretched, tortured men whom Captain Edwards would have left to drown, like rats in a trap, when the frigate sank—and drew in his breath sharply. The survivors had been brought to trial by court-martial, and although later some of them had been reprieved and pardoned, three had been hanged.

The charges had been brought against them by the officer who now faced him demanding his loyalty, his protection, as of right, but . . . had Bligh that right? Long years of service discipline had taught Andrew Hawley obedience to the orders of his superiors. The military code was a

harsh one, but he had never questioned it before . . . save
when the cries of the *Bounty* mutineers had touched his
heart and conscience and sent him back to attempt to free
them, at least, from their chains.

Did Captain Bligh, he wondered uneasily, know that he
had had a hand in saving the *Pandora*'s prisoners—did the
captain know or even remember that he had served in the
Pandora all those years ago? Probably he did not, but . . .
Andrew passed his tongue nervously over lips that were
suddenly dry. Bligh had not been present at the trial, he
had been at sea when it was convened, but it was said that
he had been outraged when, on his return from the West
Indies, he had learned of the court-martial verdicts, for he
had expected that all the men who had mutinied against
him would be hanged.

Indeed, the captain was said to have taken this as a personal affront, which even his promotion to post-rank and the
award of a thousand guineas for his services to the West
Indian planters had not mitigated and . . .

"You hesitate, Sergeant!" Captain Bligh's harsh voice
broke into his thoughts, and Andrew felt the sweat beading
his brow and upper lip. "I asked you a question—a simple
one, surely, for a man who knows his duty. But I will repeat it—would you permit any of these mutinous ruffians
to lay hands on me?"

Andrew hesitated no longer. His duty was plain and he
could not deny it. "No, sir, I would not."

"Good," the captain applauded. "Are you armed?"

Icy prickles of fear coursed down Andrew's ramrod-stiff
spine, mingling with his sweat. "I have side arms only, sir."

"Then I shall give you a pistol, Hawley." Crossing to one
of the chests of arms now stored in the cabin, Bligh unlocked it with a key he took from his breeches pocket, and
standing aside, he motioned Andrew to select one of the
weapons it contained. "You will attend me at all times," he
ordered, "when I have occasion to speak to the ship's company or any of their so-called delegates. You will keep your
pistol loaded and primed, and you will use it if and when I
command you to do so—or without an order, should any
of them offer a threat to my person. Is that understood?"

"Sir!" Andrew acknowledged woodenly. For good or ill,
he had committed himself, he thought bitterly, only too

well aware of what the consequences might be. Joe Hulme would not view his apparent adherence to the captain's cause in any save a hostile light, and probably even old Adam Simpson would condemn him for it. With the whole fleet seemingly in a state of mutiny, he could well end up swinging from the yardarm, a rope about his neck, while the man who had demanded his protection escaped scot-free. The seamen would offer no violence to their officers, he felt sure. Joe Hulme had insisted that they would not. So long as Hulme kept his word, Captain Bligh had nothing to fear from his ship's company.

If only Lord Spencer and his fellow Lords Commissioners of the Admiralty would act—and act without a delay—to put right the seamen's grievances. . . .

For the next week the situation was precarious. Shore leave was granted to any men who desired it, and predictably many did. Boatloads of seamen invaded the little town of Sheerness, where they paraded through the town wearing red revolutionary cockades and fraternized with the soldiers who had been sent to reinforce the garrison and keep order. By evening, many of them were drunk, and although they had so far only danced and sung in the streets, the townsfolk became alarmed and barred their doors against them, demanding that still more troops be dispatched for their protection.

But now came news from Spithead that the ships there had received a visit from Lord Howe and that the veteran admiral, beloved of all the seamen who had ever served under him, had acceded to the delegates' request that certain tyrannical and unpopular officers be removed from their ships and replaced by others. More than a hundred, including the hated Vice Admiral Colpoys, numerous captains and lieutenants, as well as marine officers and non-commissioned officers had been duly put ashore. Lord Howe had delivered copies of the king's pardon and had been escorted back to Portsmouth Point by the boats of the fleet, manned by cheering seamen, with their bands playing.

The delegates sent from The Nore came back two days later bringing confirmation of this news. Matthew Hollister returned on board the *Director* after making his report to the fleet president, Richard Parker of the *Sandwich*.

"It's all over bar the shoutin', lads," he announced triumphantly as the men mustered on the deck to hear him. "On the Monday morning his lordship—our own Black Dick Howe—received us on shore, an' we took a glass with him an' his lady before the lads rowed him round the fleet. He arst Charlie MacCarthy what was happenin' here, an' Charlie up an' told him. 'Me lord,' says he, 'the seamen at The Nore just want the same treatment as the Spithead people,' an' his lordship give him a copy o' the royal pardon an' the Seamen's Act. 'Show these to your people, me lad,' says he. 'And that'll make an end to it.' But our President Parker reckons the pardon don't apply to us, an' he says we must make certain-sure we get our rights afore we goes back to duty. He—"

"But you said it was all over, Matt!" a boatswain's mate protested.

" 'Bar the shoutin',' I said," Hollister corrected.

"Has the Channel Fleet sailed or ain't it?"

"Aye, it's sailed," the delegate admitted. "But Parker aims to do a mite more shoutin' afore *we* sail. We want our pay, don't we?"

"Aye, that we do!" a chorus of voices answered him.

"And," Hollister yelled at them, "we've a few score ter settle, ain't we? A few officers ter be put ashore, eh, lads? Startin' with our captain—the bloody *Bounty* Bastard!"

A roar of approval greeted his words, and Andrew's heart sank as he heard them. Captain Bligh had kept him by his side, day and night, and he was weary and dispirited, forced to snatch what sleep he could in the passageway outside the great cabin and ostracized, even by his own marines, as a "captain's man." So far they had offered him no violence, but if they put Bligh ashore . . . He stood, shoulders hunched, listening despairingly to the strident voices. The captain was on board the frigate *San Fiorenzo*, which had recently arrived at the anchorage. Her crew had not yet hoisted the Red Flag. The court-martial had been removed there that morning from the mutinous *Inflexible*, on instructions from Admiral Buckner and— there was a rush of men to the lee side of the deck and excited shouts broke into Andrew's thoughts.

"Look-ee, they've sent 'em packing! Them bloody San Fiorenzos have made the delegates' boat shove off!"

"They're makin' for *Inflexible*!"

"Now maybe we'll see some action!"

"Aye! An' we'll see what Mr. Bloody President Parker's made of! Give 'em a cheer, lads!"

They were soon to witness a measure of Richard Parker's mettle. The boatload of delegates who, evidently under threat, had been ordered away from the court-martial ship, boarded the *Inflexible*. Ten minutes later Andrew observed that the two-decker was weighing anchor. Moving slowly on the tide she ranged herself alongside the *San Fiorenzo*, and the excited voices of the *Director*'s men faded into an awed silence when the boom of a twelve-pounder echoed across the anchorage. The *Inflexible*'s gunner's aim was true—a round shot cut the footrope on the *San Fiorenzo*'s jibboom. No other threat was required; from the frigate's deck came the sound of rebel cheers, and the Union Flag came down, to be replaced by the Red Flag of mutiny.

Sickened, Andrew turned away, only to be accosted by Hulme and half a dozen of the ship's committee. All had evidently been drinking, and Hulme said, his voice slurred, "Will you take the oath, Leatherneck?"

Andrew faced him with what resolution he could summon. "You know I cannot. The captain has ordered me to guard him. I—"

Angrily Hulme cut him short. "The delegates will be here soon. As soon as Captain Bligh returns, he's to quit command of this ship and be set ashore . . . and you'll go with him, Hawley. When that's done, we'll disarm your bloody lobsterbacks unless the lot of them take the oath."

Andrew opened his mouth to protest and closed it again. There was, he thought dully, nothing he could say to sway them from their purpose.

When Captain Bligh returned to his ship, the side was not manned, and a party of delegates from the *Sandwich*, led by a man named McCann, waited for him in ominous silence on the quarterdeck. Hollister, elected as their spokesman, pulled off his hat and announced, courteously enough, "Cap'n Bligh, sir, I have to inform you as you're no longer in command of this ship. You're to hand over to the first lieutenant, sir."

The captain, Andrew realized, did not lack courage. He

drew himself up, a hand on his sword hilt, the light of battle blazing in his dark, alert eyes as he looked about him.
In waist and fo'c'sle and in the foremast shrouds, his whole
ship's company had gathered, marines mingling with seamen, and all as ominously silent as the party at Hollister's
back. One of the fo'c'sle carronades had been hauled inboard and wheeled round so that its gaping muzzle now
pointed aft. Bligh saw it but did not flinch.

"By what authority do you seek to supersede me?" he
questioned coldly. Hollister reddened.

"I'm jus' back from Spit'ead, sir, where we seen Lord
Howe," he answered, choosing his words with care.
McCann nudged him, and he went on with more confidence, "His lordship told us as all officers not approved of
by their ship's companies is to be removed. The committee
of this ship requires you to go ashore forthwith, with three
o' the young gentlemen, sir—Mr. Purdue, Mr. Blaguire,
an' Mr. Eldridge—and the sergeant o' marines, Hawley.
An' we wants the keys to the arms' chests, sir."

Captain Bligh drew a deep breath and once again looked
about him, taking in the fact that there were no sentries
posted at the hatchways. The marine officer, with his own
lieutenants, faced him glumly, and the three midshipmen
whom the delegates had named, their sea chests beside
them, stood waiting with downcast eyes for the order they
were clearly expecting him to give them.

But the captain did not give it, though his hand relinquished its grasp on his sword in an almost symbolic gesture of surrender to a force he was aware that he could not
match.

What thoughts, Andrew wondered, conscious suddenly
of pity, what emotions must be plaguing Captain William
Bligh on this, the second occasion that a mutinous ship's
company had demanded that he relinquish his command?
He was not alone this time, it was true; most of the ships at
the anchorage would obey the delegates' instruction to put
their unpopular officers ashore—it was an opportunity not
to be missed, particularly as the sanction for it appeared to
have come from Admiral Howe himself. And it had been
done at Spithead with impunity. . . .

"The keys, sir," Hollister said loudly, holding out his
hand.

Bligh eyed him with contempt, his lips compressed into a tight, unyielding line. "I will entrust them to the first lieutenant," he returned. "But to no one else." He took the bunch of keys from his breast pocket, and Lieutenant Ireland made to step forward, but Joe Hulme, his expression ugly, thrust Hollister aside and placed himself between the captain and his first lieutenant. There was a marlinespike in his hand, which he had evidently been concealing behind his back for just such an eventuality, and he raised it in blunt warning.

"Sergeant Hawley!" Captain Bligh grated. "Do your duty!"

It was the one order Andrew had been dreading, but he obeyed it instantly. The cocked pistol held steadily at Hulme's head, he interposed his own tall, scarlet-clad body between the captain and the threatening spike. If Hulme moved, he knew, he would be commanded to shoot him and, fearful of the consequences of such an action, he said urgently, "Put it down, for God's sake, Joe!"

Hulme was no fool; he, too, was aware of the consequences—not least to himself—and he lowered the spike, to Andrew's sick relief, and stepped back into the delegates' ranks. On the fo'c'sle Sergeant Simpson had, he saw, formed a line of marines in front of the menacing muzzle of the carronade to ensure that it could not be fired. The tension drained out of him, and he, too, stepped back, thrusting his pistol into his belt.

Captain Bligh gave the keys to the first lieutenant and turning, without a word, led the way to the entry port, beneath which his gig and a quarterboat were waiting. As Andrew made to follow at the rear of the small procession of officers attending him, Hulme spat on the deck at his feet.

"So help me, Hawley," he blustered. "If you ever show your face on board this ship again, I'll see you strung up, and that's a promise!"

Within twenty-four hours of being put ashore at Sheerness, Captain Bligh received a summons from Admiral Buckner. On his return he sent for Andrew.

"You are a good man, Sergeant, and I shall do my best for you," the captain told him. "I am commanded to confer with Admiral Duncan at Yarmouth and to act as liaison between Their Lordships and the North Sea fleet. I shall leave by coach as soon as I have received the First Lord's instructions—probably next week. Now here—" He put a sealed letter into Andrew's hand and fished some coins from his pocket. "This will pay your journey to Yarmouth. You are to deliver this note to the admiral on board the *Venerable*. It will advise him of my coming and request him to accept you into his marine detachment." He smiled faintly. "The Venerables are loyal, so you will be in good company. I wish you well, Hawley."

On May 26, Admiral Duncan ordered the signal for sailing to be hoisted on board his flagship. Four ships failed to obey the signal; the rest of the squadron followed him to sea, but during the next three days ship after ship backed topsails and fell astern, the Red Flag of mutiny flying defiantly in the breeze, which had now veered easterly.

By the morning of May 30 only two of his thirteen ships remained under the admiral's command—his own leaking, ill-found *Venerable,* seventy-four, and Captain William Hotham's fifty-gun *Adamant.* Admiral Duncan delayed at anchor for twenty-four hours, waiting for the reinforcements he had been promised from Spithead, but when these failed to appear he set course for the mouth of the Texel. The wind was continuing to blow easterly, and a Dutch fleet of fourteen ships of the line, eight frigates, and the invasion transports, laden with troops, had somehow to be prevented from leaving port.

The tall, white-haired Scottish admiral mustered his ship's company. His personality and powers of leadership had kept them loyal, and Andrew Hawley, lining up with the *Venerable*'s marines, felt his pride and faith renewed in the navy he served as he listened to Admiral Duncan's emotion-charged address.

"My lads, I once more call you together with a sorrowful heart," he told them. "To be deserted by my fleet in the face of the enemy is a disgrace which, I believe, never before happened to a British admiral. My greatest comfort under God is that I have been supported by the officers, seamen, and marines of this ship, for which, with a heart overflowing with gratitude, I thank you." He paused to let his words sink in, and the men raised a subdued cheer. "The duty I am charged with is to keep the Texel closed, and my lads, I intend to do that, *with* ships or *without* them. This ship shall fight till she sinks, if need be. The soundings are such that"—he waved a big hand toward the Dutch shore—"my flag will continue to fly above shoal water after the ship and her company have disappeared! But mark you well, if she survives this performance of her duty here, she is going to sail to The Nore and reduce those misguided people to obedience. D'ye understand that, my lads?"

They answered that they did, not all of them with conviction, and Admiral Duncan drew himself up to his full impressive height. "May God, who has thus far conducted you, continue to do so," he went on, his great voice carrying from end to end of the ship. "And may the king's navy, the glory and support of our country, be restored to its wonted splendor! You'll be on duty night and day till we get more ships or a change of wind. God bless you all!"

They cheered him then, many with tears in their eyes, and they kept faith with him, working the ship with a will as the old admiral bluffed the Dutch commanders by making signals to an imaginary fleet over the horizon. The Dutch admiral, deceived by Duncan's constant signaling, did not take advantage of the favorable wind. It again veered westerly three days later.

And then, in ones and twos, despite the efforts of Parker and his delegates to stop them, five of Admiral Duncan's ships hauled down their Red Flags and made their escape, many under fire from Parker's hard-core mutineers. Finally, finding themselves deserted, even these surrendered, the *Sandwich* and President Parker himself, on June 13.

More than four hundred mutineers were tried, of whom thirty-six—including Parker—were hanged. Those recommended for mercy were sentenced to transportation to New South Wales. Among them, Andrew subsequently learned, were the ten from his old ship. On board the *Venerable* on October 11, when the Dutch fleet at last came out to do battle fifteen miles from the Texel, off the village of Camperdown, he saw through the gunsmoke how nobly the *Director* and six of the once-mutinous ships redeemed themselves.

In a gallant and hard-fought action that lasted for almost three hours, eleven of the eighteen enemy ships were taken.

The leaky old *Venerable,* having battered the Dutch flagship *Vrijheid* into submission, returned to port with her
prizes in tow and Admiral de Winter on board. The British
ships, their hulls riddled with shot and some barely afloat,
limped back to Yarmouth and The Nore to a heroes' welcome and with a casualty list of 203 killed and more than
600 wounded.

But the cheers from the shore were heartfelt, for Duncan's squadron had warded off the threat of invasion and
effectively put an end to the fear of a naval mutiny.

Andrew heard them from the sick bay, as a hard-pressed
surgeon came at last to stitch up the gaping wound made
by a splinter from the deck planking, which had cut his
face and scalp almost in two.

"You're lucky not to be blinded, lad," the surgeon told
him, "but it's a clean wound—we'll soon have you back to
duty. A trifle scarred, but these are honorable scars." He
added, smiling, "They're to make our brave old admiral a
viscount, did you hear? By heaven, no one deserves it
more!"

He was right, Andrew thought, wincing as the needle,
blunted from overuse, bit into the flesh of his cheek. Admiral Duncan, in his sixty-seventh year, had kept his ship's
company to their duty and had then done his, first by outwitting the Dutch and then by defeating them.

He had given the navy back its pride and its purpose
. . . and Andrew Hawley thanked God for it.

CHAPTER XV

Pimelwi was dead, and his wild woods tribe, the Bediagal Indians, mourned their chief's passing, for they had long believed him to be immune to both the spear and the white man's firearms. He had been supposedly mortally wounded but had recovered.

Even Baneelon—who had progressed so far in the white invaders' confidence as to call their governor his father—had concurred with this belief, but . . . Pimelwi was dead. True, he had not died at the hands of the redcoat soldiers, who had tried to kill him often enough and had ironically nursed him back to health and released him. But rather one of the escaped convicts had raised a musket to his shoulder and sent a deadly metal ball deep into the old chief's entrails, from which he had, after some hours, expired.

After some ceremonial spear-throwing, Pilmelwi's people assembled to accord him the funeral his position entitled him to receive. His wives and his elder sons had predeceased the old chief, so his friend Maugodia—by virtue both of that friendship and of having slain Pimelwi's assassin—took their place. Pimelwi's body was placed on a blanket, stolen from a settler's shack, and amid noisy lamentations was borne by four young men of the tribe to the funeral pyre. This stood more than four feet high, consisting of dry logs of wood laid across a pile of twigs and light brushwood. The bearers carried bunches of grass, which they laid over the corpse until it was covered, and as the women wailed their grief, some of the men beat their clubs on hollowed-out branches, known as *tawarangs,* and drew weird, echoing music from others which they called *didgeridoos.*

When all was in readiness, Maugodia climbed a tree near the foot of the pyre, into the upper branches of which he placed the dead man's spears, his shield, and his *woomera.* Descending, he laid a log on top of the chief's grass-covered body, and as the beat of the music quickened, he applied a smoldering branch to the foot of the pyre, and the twigs and interlaced logs leaped swiftly into flames.

Only when Pimelwi's body was consumed did the Bediagals' mood change. The warriors of the tribe, their faces and bodies plastered in intricate patterns with red clay, took up their shields and spears and ran to their canoes. The chief's killing had to be avenged, and tribal honor demanded that retribution in blood must be exacted from those who had harbored his killer. The fact that the killer had been a negro, known as Caesar, with a skin blacker than their own, weighed not at all with Pimelwi's people. . . . The white men had brought him here, albeit in chains and must therefore be regarded as his kin. They manned their canoes, the women standing at the riverbank urging them on, paddled across the wide expanse of water with strong, determined sweeps of their arms, and made their landing under cover of a thick clump of ironbarks.

Within two hours they had made their presence felt. A settler and his wife were first to fall victims to their attack; leaving both dead, the Bediagals set fire to the house and farm buildings, and loping purposefully on, they burned a granary filled with stored wheat, plundered a maize field ready to harvest, and started a bushfire a mile farther on. As the fire spread they ran ahead of it, seeking more human victims for their spears.

In Toongabbe, Charles Brace observed the advancing smoke clouds and, cursing loud and long, called out his men. He had only a corporal's guard, with horses for two men besides himself, and recognizing the need for haste he ordered the corporal and a dozen men to go upriver by boat, while he led his two mounted soldiers in a wild gallop toward the Hawkesbury settlements, in the hope of cutting off the raiders before they could regain their canoes.

It was a vain hope, and in his heart he knew that he could not hope to catch them on the settled side of the river, unless some of the settlers stood their ground and were able to pin them down with musket fire. The settler most likely to do so was Timothy Dawson, who had suffered so damaging a raid five or six months ago that he now armed his workers and was himself always provided with pistols.

Brace held no brief for Dawson. Indeed, he reflected bitterly as he rode toward the first group of outlying build-

ings, he had every reason to wish the fellow in perdition
since, thanks to Jasper Spence's obvious preference for
Dawson as a future son-in-law, his present relationship
with Henrietta was, to say the least, becoming increasingly
precarious. Spence wanted a damned plowboy to marry his
daughter and run his farm for him. That was at the root of
it. And his own strait-laced, domineering old father had
made matters worse by insisting in one of his infrequent
letters that if he married "a woman from the penal colony,"
he might expect to be cut off with the proverbial ha'penny.

"Such a match," the old man had written,

> can bring only discredit to your family, Charles. So
> think well before you commit yourself to any such
> course. The young woman's father, Jasper Spence,
> may have endeavored to pass himself off as a nabob in
> the uncritical society in which you now find yourself,
> but I am informed by Sir Augustus Middleton—who
> is, as you may recall, a member of the Court of Direc-
> tors of the East India Company—that an official of
> this name left Calcutta under a cloud. Sir Augustus
> was discreet, but I understand there were certain fi-
> nancial dealings involving the ruler of a native state,
> concerning which suspicion fell on a minor official of
> the honorable company's treasury named Spence, who
> was permitted to resign, in order to avoid an unpleas-
> ant scandal.
>
> Of course, the name may be merely a coincidence,
> and an unfortunate one, but you would be well ad-
> vised to ascertain whether or not it is before embark-
> ing on matrimony.

Then had followed the thinly veiled threat to cut him
off . . . Brace scowled as a convict laborer came running
to meet him, white of face and almost inarticulate with
fear.

"Them bloody black fellows is runnin' riot again, sir,"
the man managed. "Burnin' an' killin', and the master's
maize is—"

Impatiently, Brace cut him short. "Have they been here?
Have you seen them?"

"No, sir," the convict admitted. "But they're comin' this way, ain't they? You c'n see the smoke and—"

"Where are they now, man?"

The laborer waved a vague hand. "I reckon the fire's at Mr. Dawson's place or near. An' Mr. Dawson is—"

Charles Brace waited to hear no more. He dug his spurs into his horse's heaving flanks and galloped on, his two soldiers pounding along at his heels.

Had that oaf of a laborer been trying to tell him that Dawson was not at his place after all, he wondered uneasily. Little as he liked Dawson, he was counting on his help in tackling the raiders—he and his troopers would be heavily outnumbered if Dawson wasn't there. . . . He swore under his breath. Devil take it, he ought to have made sure!

Since the woman who ran his Parramatta farm, an emancipist named Taggart, had been admitted to the hospital with a severe fever, Dawson had divided his time between the two holdings, and it was conceivable that he was in Parramatta now, not here, damn his eyes, when he was needed. He could even be at the Spence property. The infernal fellow was a frequent visitor, and Jasper Spence—ignoring Brace's own claims as Henrietta's future husband—had talked of their going into partnership. Dawson had a sizable herd of horses now, and a fair number of sheep. He had supplied Spence with three very good young riding animals and had assisted the older man with his sheep-breeding, even sharing the purchase of one of the merino rams the *Reliance* had brought back from the Cape and that Waterhouse hadn't sold to John Macarthur. But never—damn it all, not once had Jasper Spence hinted at any kind of partnership with himself, and he had been evasive concerning Henrietta's dowry, too.

"You'll be doing well enough with your regimental trading, Charles," he had said more than once. "I envy you—you have opportunities given to few young officers in His Majesty's forces, have you not?" His tone had been less envious than sarcastic. . . .

Brace drew rein, shouting out to his men to give their sweating mounts a breather while he searched the surrounding countryside with his spyglass. The opportunities of which Jasper Spence had spoken were there, right enough, but . . . He mopped at his brow and again put the glass to his eye. Of what use was a trading monopoly in rum if one had not sufficient capital to take advantage of it? Foveaux and Macarthur were coining money, so were most of the others, whereas he himself, with a miserable eighth share to their full ones, had devilish little to show for it. But perhaps if he broached the subject to Henrietta . . . His expression relaxed.

Yes, that was what he would do—explain the position to Henrietta and let her talk to her father. She was eager enough to wed him, but thanks to her father, a day for their nuptials had not yet been named, and . . .

"Sir, look—over to yer right, sir!" one of the troopers exclaimed. "There're the black bastards! Makin' for the river, I do believe!"

The man was right, Brace saw, turning the glass in the direction to which he had pointed. Half-hidden from them by the feathery leaves of the gum trees, a large party of Indians moved stealthily toward the river. It was difficult to count them as they flitted from tree to tree like shadows, but some were weighed down with sacks of stolen maize and several others had donned European hats and jackets, also stolen, no doubt, and these burdens slowed them down. All were daubed with red clay and all carried weapons. Brace searched the river for some sign of the corporal's boat party but could see none. There was time, he realized, to get between the raiders and the river, but even at a rough guess there must be forty or fifty of them. He and his two troopers might pick off half a dozen if they lay in wait under cover and took them by surprise, but after that . . . He drew in his breath sharply. After that the three of them would not stand a chance—sheer weight of numbers would overwhelm them, unless the corporal's party joined up with them very rapidly . . . and probably the idiots were taking their time. It was a long pull, from this point, and the corporal would not hurry unduly on the march to the river. . . . It was too hellish hot.

One of the troopers, guessing his thoughts, offered apprehensively, "We can't stop the swine, sir, not just the three o' us. I reckon there's close to an 'undred o' the bastards."

He had exaggerated, Brace knew, but for all that, what

he said was true. "We'll cut across to Mr. Dawson's," he decided. "And collect some reinforcements."

"He's only got four men now, sir," the second trooper reminded him. "The guv'nor called in 'arf the settlers' laborin' convicts. An' I seen 'is foreman, the one they call Davie Leake, come through Toongabbe early this mornin' wiv' a pair o' 'orses. On 'is way ter Parramatta wiv' 'em, he said."

Which left three—four, if Dawson himself was there—hardly, Brace told himself wryly, the size of the reinforcements he had hoped for. And there had been no shooting, as might have been expected, if the men were on the alert. Either they had been taken by surprise and murdered, or they were in hiding, waiting somewhere in the woods until the Indians recovered their canoes and made off, back to their own side of the river. The fires were still a long way off, he saw, and dying out. It looked as if the blacks had contented themselves with burning crops and buildings. They had not set the bush alight, waiting, no doubt, to use that ploy to cover their retreat across the river. Or else the settlers, with more energy than they usually displayed, had managed to extinguish the flames.

"Ride back to the river as fast as you know how, Ruffler," he ordered. "And signal Corporal Partridge to cross to the far bank. He can take cover and fire on the black fellows as they're trying to paddle their canoes across."

Trooper Ruffler thankfully obeyed, and his comrade asked anxiously, "What about us, sir? 'Adn't we best take cover as well, seein' as there's the whole tribe of 'em down there?"

"We'll keep them under observation, Larra," Brace returned. "From that clump of trees over there." He kneed his horse into a trot, heading for a thick clump of gums about two hundred yards to his right, but before they had covered half the intervening distance, a single shot rang out, followed an instant later by a high-pitched scream of pain. Brace reined in and listened intently, but neither shot nor scream were repeated. Both appeared to have come from the trees they had been making for, and he jerked his head at the trooper, signing to him to circle round to his right. They separated, Trooper Larra with evident reluctance walking his horse as slowly as he dared in the direc-

tion his officer had indicated, while Brace himself rode
on at a brisk canter, inclining to his left, where the ground
rose in a series of hillocks twenty yards or so above the
trees.

Even from the summit of this vantage point he saw nothing calculated to alarm him. After pausing briefly with his
glass to his eye, he pocketed the glass, attended to the
priming of his pistol, and, with the weapon in his right
hand, entered the wood. The trees grew more thinly than
he had anticipated, among lank grass and stony hillocks,
with a small stream running down to the river—now so dry
that it was little more than a trickle—descending from a
cleft in the rocks above him and to his left.

He moved on, looking about him cautiously, and found
the first body a moment later. It was that of a white man—
one of Dawson's field workers—and Brace did not have to
dismount to ascertain that the unfortunate man was dead,
for a well-aimed native spear was deeply embedded in his
back, and the grass about him heavily stained with his
blood. A musket lay beside him, and about twenty paces
beyond, the clay-daubed Indian he had shot had died as he
sought vainly to crawl to safety among the rocks. The musket shot and the scream he had heard must, Brace decided, have come from here . . . the scream, probably,
from the convict laborer, who would not have died as in-
stantaneously as his black adversary. The rest of the raiders
had gone—making, as he had first supposed, for their canoes, which would no doubt be hidden among the man-
groves growing at the river's edge.

It was to be hoped that Corporal Partridge would have
received his orders and be in position waiting to receive the
swine and . . . Brace stiffened, hearing an odd sound he
could not at first identify. A bubbling, faintly hissing sound,
as of water boiling . . . He listened, every sense alert. It
was coming from the cleft in the rocks from which the tiny
rivulet emerged . . . yes, coming unmistakably from
there. Anticipating what he would find if he traced the
sound to its source, he flung himself from his saddle, tied
his horse's rein to the branch of a nearby tree, and—the
Indian raiders forgotten—started to climb the low escarp-
ment, his boot toes slipping on the damp stone.

There was a cave halfway up, running back for ten or

eleven yards, and when he finally reached it, his excitement knew no bounds. Inside was, as he had guessed, an illicit still, a maze of metal tubing and glass cylinders, bubbling away and emitting a thin cloud of steam, although—its custodian being dead—the fire that activated it was also dying. Charles Brace did not have to search far for the product of the contraption's metallic hissing—three full and two empty wooden kegs were lined up against the moist rock wall, and his nostrils told him plainly enough what the full ones contained.

So this, he thought, was the reason for Timothy Dawson's prosperity, this was why he could afford to buy more imported horses and share in the cost of a damned Spanish ram! The blackguard was distilling his own liquor from the corn he grew, instead of paying the corps's price for rum and, rot him, instead of bartering his wheat and barley for the corps's trade goods or selling it to the commissariat at the government-controlled price! Did Henrietta's father know of his activities? Did he suspect that the man he proposed to take into partnership was a lawbreaker, a rogue who was flouting the governor's official order that forbade such practices as this?

His hands trembling, Brace thrust the bung back into the mouth of the keg he had opened. The penalties Dawson would suffer when the presence of the still was reported would, he knew, be severe. Confiscation of the apparatus itself and its destruction, a heavy fine, and, quite possibly, confiscation of his stock or of some of his land if he had not the cash to pay the fine imposed on him. His social pretensions would meet with a setback also, no doubt of that. Jasper Spence, as a magistrate, would cease to receive him. Dear heaven, this chance discovery could ruin Dawson or go a pretty fair way to doing so if he reported it. *If* . . . For the Lord's sake, what was he thinking of? There was no "if" about it, for his duty was inescapable.

He was an officer of the corps, and the corps did not take kindly to those who broke the rules or who attempted in any way to interfere with or threaten their jealously guarded monopoly in the supply of liquor to the colony. Brace glanced uneasily at the now-cooling still. Had not the governor himself endeavored to put a curb on their trading and failed dismally? The corps officers, led by John

Macarthur, had defied him and were working, behind his
back, poor devil, to engineer his recall. They would probably succeed in the end since Macarthur boasted openly of
the correspondence he was conducting with the Duke of
Portland and other influential members of the home government the object of which was to discredit Governor
Hunter and have him replaced by one of their own kind.

Brace got to his feet. He *had* to report the still even
though it was possible that Timothy Dawson would be willing to pay him to keep silent and . . . Almost as soon as
it occurred to him, he banished the thought. Much as he
needed money, the risk would be too great, and in any
event, there would undoubtedly be some benefit to himself
arising from Dawson's exposure—from the corps and perhaps even from Jasper Spence.

He moved to the cave entrance, only to halt there, horrified. He had heard nothing, but now he saw about a dozen
Indians were standing, spears and throwing-sticks poised,
at the foot of the rocks he had climbed so incautiously ten
minutes before. They were waiting for him and had, he
supposed miserably, been waiting ever since he had made
his discovery of the still.

He raised his pistol and started to retreat into the cave,
hearing the fusillade of musketry coming from the river.
Corporal Partridge's ambush must have been successful although, Goddamn it, the Indians below him did not move.
One, a graybeard with a hideous clay-daubed face, stepped
from their ranks and hurled his spear, straight and true,
into Brace's scarlet-jacketed chest. His pistol exploded in
his nerveless hand, but the ball ricocheted harmlessly off
the roof of the cave as he slumped, screaming his agony
aloud, into a limp heap beside the still.

From the cover of the trees, thirty yards away, Timothy
Dawson opened fire. He got off two shots, neither of which
found a mark, before Trooper Larra galloped up and flung
himself down beside him, musket to his shoulder. Whether
alarmed by their unexpected attack or by the sound of firing from the river, Timothy could not afterward have said
with any certainty, but the little party of natives made off,
the trees giving them concealment, the plunder they had
taken abandoned on the grass.

Larra made no attempt to pursue them. He said with an odd lack of emotion, "They got 'im, didn't they? They got Mr. Brace."

"I fear they did," Timothy returned, "but they may not have killed him. We'd best go and see."

His conscience troubled him as he led the way to the cave, motioning the trooper to wait at the foot of the rocks. He had heard the first shot and poor Rick Larkin's cry of pain and had galloped to the scene while Brace was still a hundred yards off, searching the area with his glass. Then, God forgive him, he had taken up his position to guard the still, and in a torment of indecision had watched Brace's approach and discovery of the cave, knowing only too well what that discovery would mean to him.

Sweat broke out on his palms as he dragged himself up the rocks, slipping as his hold dislodged a small boulder. He had seen the aborigines' stealthy arrival and could have warned Brace. By firing a single shot he might have put the raiding party to flight. Even if he had failed to do so, even if they had held their ground, Charles Brace would have been put on his guard and been given a chance to defend himself.

But he had done nothing. God in heaven, he had not only done nothing, he had allowed the raiders to solve his problem for him. He . . . Timothy reached the cave mouth and dropped to his knees beside the man he had left to his fate. Charles Brace was dead, the barbed spearpoint in his heart, his scarlet jacket stained a deeper red, its yellow facings spattered with his life's blood. His face seemed very young as he lay there, but his sightless eyes were reproachful, almost as if . . . oh, God, almost as if he knew. Timothy closed the lids and, after pulling out the spear, lifted the body and handed it down to the waiting trooper.

"'E's dead," Larra pronounced. "Dead as a doornail." There was no pity in his voice, and he did not look up, clearly quite unsuspicious of the secret the darkness of the cave concealed. The fire had burned out, the water, off the boil now, made no sound. . . . The risk of discovery had passed.

Timothy mopped the sweat from his face and clambered down to where the trooper waited.

"I'll get 'is 'orse, sir. Best take 'im in, I reckon, an' your convict's body too, 'adn't we?" Larra hesitated and then said, an edge of malice to his tongue, " 'Tis justice, in a way, them black fellers killin' Mr. Brace. I was wiv' 'im when 'e ordered us ter firé on a bunch of 'em we'd tracked down after a raid—back in June it was. Mr. Brace shot their chief—the one they call Pimelwi. Ought to 'ave died, but 'e didn't."

"He's dead now, I imagine," Timothy told him. "That is probably the reason for his tribe crossing over here in such numbers—they wanted to avenge him. But"—he gestured toward the river, from whence a few isolated shots still echoed—"your fellows appear to be dealing with them."

"Oh, aye," Larra agreed. "Corporal Partridge is commandin' the boat party, and 'e 'ates their guts. Used to be a convict, Partridge did, 'fore 'e enlisted in the corps—come out in the *Scarborough* wiv' Guv'nor Phillip. 'E went on the run in them early days, an' the black fellers treated 'im a mite rough. Well"—he grinned sheepishly—"I'll get the 'orses, sir. Ain't nothin' more we can do 'ere, is there?"

There was not, Timothy thought, his conscience again tormenting him. It had all been done. He looked down once more at the dead face of the man who had been his rival for Henrietta Spence's affections and realized then, with a sense of profound shock, that their rivalry was over. Lieutenant the Honourable Charles Windham Brace would not go to the Chaplain Johnson's wooden church on the east side of Sydney Cove as Henrietta's bridegroom. He would be carried there in his coffin by men of the corps, who would fire a volley over his grave and, in due course, erect a headstone to his memory . . . one of a growing number in the new cemetery.

There to be forgotten. But . . . He caught his breath. Could *he* forget Charles Brace after what had happened here today? Would Henrietta forget the man who was to have been her husband, the bridegroom of whom he had robbed her?

Timothy turned, hearing the clip-clop of horses' hoofs as Trooper Larra led Brace's horse and his own to where he was standing.

"I'll put 'im across the saddle, Mr. Dawson, if you'll give me an 'and," the man suggested. "They're rowin' back to this side o' the river now, Corporal Partridge's party. I reckon it's just about over."

The firing, Timothy noticed then, had ceased. He helped to lift both bodies onto Brace's horse, securing them with the stirrup leathers and, with Larra at his heels leading the other two horses, started to make his way to the river.

Partridge met them there, his smoke-blackened face wearing a triumphantly savage grin.

"We showed the black bastards, Mr. Dawson," he shouted. "Must've killed about a score of 'em!"

And the blacks, Timothy reflected wryly, could claim Charles Brace . . . He sighed and gestured to the body.

Governor Hunter sat at his desk, paper and inkwell in front of him and a quill in his hand. As yet the paper bore only two words—*Your Grace*—and he had spent fully half an hour considering with infinite care what words should follow these.

The truth, he told himself, it was always best to speak and certainly to write the truth, with whomsoever one might be dealing but particularly when dealing with authority. And, so far as he was concerned, His Grace of Portland was, in his ministerial capacity, the ultimate authority, but . . . of what use to attempt to reveal the truth when the mind of the man to whom he was appealing had already been poisoned by a tissue of lies? It was unlikely that he would be believed, even were he to write frankly, for the harm had been done and his credibility almost wholly destroyed, although he had only recently become aware of the fact.

John Hunter heaved an exasperated sigh and, taking a handkerchief from his breeches pocket, mopped his face and brow. God in heaven, it was hot! He let the quill fall and picked up a sheet of coarse paper from the desk, his mouth tightening as he reread it. It was not the first lampoon holding him up to public ridicule that had been distributed in Sydney and Parramatta, but it was by far and away the most scurrilous.

He knew only too well from whom this and most of the previous pamphlets had emanated as, of course, he knew for what purpose they were being so widely circulated. His attempts to break the corps's control of the trade in liquor were beginning at last to succeed, and for this reason, his recall was being demanded. Before long, if the pamphleteer had his way, even the settlers and the emancipists—whom he was endeavoring to protect and aid—would be deceived into joining the officers in their demand, and the Duke of Portland would advise him to resign the governorship of the colony.

Hunter repeated his sigh, and crushing the offending scrap of paper into a ball, he threw it from him. An honest and high-principled man who had always put duty before his own personal interests, he found it difficult to combat deceit, more especially when this was being practiced by a man devoid of scruples. John Macarthur did not hesitate to employ dishonest tactics—he won support by a mixture of low cunning, bullying, and cajolery and, when opposed, by defending himself by means of legal injunctions and appeals to the civil court that, even when denied, proved a useful threat against the fainthearted.

He himself was no faintheart, Hunter reflected. He was ready to do battle, but the only weapons at his command would not suffice, and he scorned those to which his opponent resorted. Not for the first time in the past few soul-destroying months, he found himself regretting Arthur Phillip's decision to resign his governorship, as well as the departure of David Collins and the death of poor Henry Brewer, that loyal, snowy-haired midshipman who had served the colony so long and with such loyalty as provost marshal. Phillip was now deservedly a rear admiral and again hoisting his flag at sea, but—Hunter sighed. He had left a great gap behind him.

Richard Atkins had acted as judge advocate immediately after Collins had sailed for home, but his quarrels with Macarthur had been too acrimonious and too public, amounting almost to a scandal, for him to be permitted to remain permanently in office. And his heavy drinking and his impulsive nature made him less an ally than a liability, for he provided fuel for Macarthur's all-too-ready pen. A government-appointed successor to Collins, Richard Dore, had only lately arrived in the *Barwell* and—a shrewd judge of character—the governor had felt an instinctive mistrust of his glib tongue and overingratiating manner.

Dore, he reminded himself now, was not one with whom he could talk over the situation or discuss the problems posed by Captain John Macarthur and his unprincipled brother officers in their determination to preserve their commercial interests intact. And it was, of course, entirely because of Macathur's infernal machinations that Dore had been sent out to supersede Atkins, devil take him!

Hunter picked up his quill and started to write.

"I am of the opinion," he wrote with conscious bitterness,

> that were every restless, speculative, troublesome, or dissatisfied individual in this or any distant colony encouraged to consider himself of sufficient importance to take the liberty of corresponding with His Majesty's Ministers upon the public concerns of that colony, and wholly independent of the Governor, it would soon occasion such a variety of opinions as could only serve to embarrass the judgement of government, and would generally be found to be directed more to the private interests of the several schemers than that of the public. . . .

He hesitated, quill poised, wondering even now whether he would not be well advised to avoid personalities. But Macarthur had made his attack a personal one; a list of complaints he had sent to the Duke of Portland two years ago lay on the desk, forwarded to him by His Majesty's minister with the request that they be answered by the colony's governor—in detail and forthwith. It was not enough to reply in general terms—as governor, he must answer the charges leveled against him, and when he did so, make it plain that he was aware of the identity of the complainant. Hunter's strong brown fingers closed about the quill and his jaw hardened. God roast the impudent young upstart! He should have his reply, and the truth of the situation should be revealed without fear or favor.

For almost an hour he wrote furiously. Macarthur had had the effrontery to complain of the licentiousness and drunkenness that prevailed throughout the colony, and to this Governor Hunter made withering reply.

These conditions are due to the military oligarchy and to nothing else. The officers had chartered the *Britannia* during the period when their commanding officer, Colonel Grose, was acting as Governor of the Colony and prior to my arrival. Following this a trade began with the settlers and lower orders of the people, the effect of which will long be felt, and this alone was the ruin of many industrious people, the destruction of all moral order.

And this officer—Your Grace's correspondent—who purports to be so strenuous an advocate for such order and good management was himself one of the most extensive dealers in the colony, a role he continues, for his own profit, to play. For this reason and, indeed, for the sole purpose of thwarting my endeavor to carry out the orders and instructions of His Majesty's Government in regard to the trading activities of the New South Wales Corps, Captain Macarthur forwards his unsubstantiated complaints to Your Grace.

I consider this officer's conduct to be impertinent, indiscreet, and highly censurable interference in the duties and department of the Governor of this Colony. . . .

There was much more he could have said—perhaps more that he would be compelled to say, but . . . His heavy dark brows met in a frown. Would his words have more effect, would Portland be more inclined to believe them if he resigned his office and went home, to report to the Colonial Office in person? He had been maligned, his honor was at stake, and . . . Hunter looked down, still frowning, at the crumpled lampoon.

Damn them, he did not want to run away; he wanted to stay and fight them, with God's help, for had he not a duty to the colony he had helped to found? A duty to Arthur Phillip, who had cherished such high hopes of what Sydney could become, given good government and justice, even for those banished from their own country for . . . He smiled, recalling a ditty the convict actors at Sydney's playhouse had recently sung. "True patriots all; for be it understood,/we left our country for our country's good. . . ." Well, he owed them a duty too, those poor wretches sent out in chains against their will to become colonists in an alien land, to labor in their chains, to build roads, houses, hospitals, and even a prison, to till the soil, harvest its produce, and reseed its hungry acres. He owed a duty to the industrious among them, but perhaps most of all, he owed it to the weak and the intractable to save them from further corruption by those of Macarthur's kind who, appointed their guardians, were bent on abusing their trust so that they might line their own pockets. But could he do his duty if he stayed here? It seemed to him a matter for doubt—unless they were removed.

Governor Hunter ended his letter with a strongly worded plea for a picked regiment of marines to be sent out to replace the corps. He was signing his name to the letter when Richard Dore made his appearance.

"Forgive me for disturbing Your Excellency," the new judge advocate offered, his tone, as always, overly respectful and, to Hunter's mind, unctuous.

"Well, what is it?" the governor snapped. Thanks to goverment parsimony, Dore—as had Collins before him—combined the office of judge advocate with that of secretary. Nevertheless, Hunter was careful to conceal his recently finished letter from the younger man's curious gaze. Richard Dore, he was certain, would, if allowed even to glimpse its contents, at once carry a warning to Macarthur—the two were already as thick as thieves.

"Well?" he prompted impatiently. "Why have you disturbed me, Mr. Dore?"

"A vessel has just come to anchor in the cove, sir. I had supposed you might wish to be informed of her arrival." Dore sounded hurt, but the governor made no attempt to placate him. He was aware of the so-called vessel's impending arrival since the signal on the South Head had been hoisted five or six hours earlier, and Captain Townson—in command at Norfolk Island since William Paterson had gone to England on leave—had sent word that the island-built sloop might soon be expected in Sydney. He grunted noncommittally and busied himself, to his secretary's obvious chagrin, with the sealing of his letter.

Dore went on, his tone once again overly respectful, "She is quite a small—er—decked vessel, sir, and although

I know little about—er—nautical matters, she looks to
me as if she's had a rough passage."

"Oh?" Still bent over his letter the governor did not look
up. Neither, as his secretary had supposed he would, did he
cross to the window in order to inspect the new arrival.
"What makes you think so, eh?"

"Well, sir, her—her pumps are going, which suggests she
must have—er—sprung a leak or something of that kind."

"Unfortunate," Hunter observed. "But she got here." He
pushed his sealed letter across the desk. "This is to be forwarded by the next ship to depart from here. Be so good as
to lock it up, would you?"

"Most certainly, sir." Dore, left with no excuse to remain, took his dismissal resignedly. When he was gone the
governor rose and made his way to the upper floor. From
his bedroom window he subjected the latest addition to his
seagoing command to a long and critical scrutiny. William
Paterson had been enthusiastic about the sloop, aware that
the colony was much in need of some small, handy vessels
capable of carrying stores and passengers between Sydney
and Norfolk Island. Paterson, the governor reflected, was
the best of the corps officers—the best by a long chalk—
and he made sincere efforts to serve the colony's interests
and support the governor in virtually all he did. Even—he
smiled grimly—even, at times, against Macarthur and his
cronies, but the poor fellow was no seaman.

The island-built sloop's maiden voyage had, it was evident, tested her severely and found her wanting—Dore had
been right about that. It was a pity, for he had intended to
give command of her to young Matt Flinders and send
him, with his friend Bass, to search for the strait both were
convinced lay between Van Diemen's Land and what they
were now pleased to call the mainland of *Terra Australis*.

While Flinders had gone with the colonial sloop *Francis*
to pick up the master and other survivors of the ill-fated
Sydney Cove, the intrepid Bass had taken his longboat,
with a small crew of volunteers from the *Reliance*, to sail
westward from *Cape Howe* in furtherance of his search.
The young surgeon had been unfortunate in his weather—
indeed, Hunter reminded himself, he had only survived by
a miracle. He had returned after a twelve-week absence,
having explored some six hundred miles of coast, discov-

ered a good harbor southwest of *Port Hicks*, and rescued a party of escaped convicts, who had been near to death from starvation.

Bass had reported that there was every evidence of a strait between the latitudes of 39° and 40° South, and he had pleaded for a better boat to enable him to complete his investigation and confirm his belief that Van Diemen's Land was, in fact, an island or a group of islands. And Flinders had supported his plea with impassioned fervor. . . . The governor smiled to himself, remembering with approval the enthusiasm both young officers had displayed for an enterprise that might well cost them their lives.

They deserved the best boat he could give them, heaven knew, but there *was* only this new Norfolk Island pine sloop available. The *Francis* could not be spared; the *Reliance* was undergoing a much-needed refit, before sailing for the Cape to purchase more cattle, and . . . He saw the *Reliance*'s commander, Henry Waterhouse, come striding up to the front door of Government House, obviously in search of him. He waved and, cramming his hat onto his head, went down to join him, pointedly ignoring his secretary's obsequious attempts to attract his attention.

After exchanging greetings the governor and his senior naval officer fell into step together and walked at a brisk pace toward the quay. Reaching it, both stood for some minutes in silence, studying the new arrival with critical eyes.

Her design, the governor decided, was by no means ill-conceived. Flush-decked and with a sharp-raked stem, her single mast was tall, and she carried a jib and staysail, in addition to her loose-footed gaff mainsail. But she had a distinct list to larboard and, he saw, her hands were still at the pumps. He glanced in mute question at his companion, and Henry Waterhouse shrugged.

"I went out to meet her, sir, soon after the signal was hoisted," he volunteered. "Broome—you may remember him, sir, as one of my master's mates in the *Reliance*—"

"Broome?" Governor Hunter echoed with feeling. "Now that I have learned his identity, by God, how could I forget him? Is *he* in command?"

Waterhouse nodded. "Aye, sir, he is. And he designed

her and supervised her construction. But he told me that,
for the want of the proper facilities at Norfolk Island, she
had to be launched from the shore, and the commandant
ordered him to take her directly to sea." He repeated his
shrug. "Broome said he wasn't satisfied with her caulking
and she had sprung a couple of planks during the launching, but Captain Townson wouldn't hear of any delay. He
said repairs would have to be made here. And they will
have to be, sir, before she'll be of use to Bass and Flinders."

"Even so, she should be an improvement on the longboat young Bass built, should she not?"

"Well, she's bigger, sir," the *Reliance*'s captain conceded. "She'll be able to carry more provisions and a crew
of about eight."

"How long was she on passage?" Hunter asked. "Did
Broome tell you?"

Waterhouse permitted himself a sly smile. "She made a
fast passage, sir," he answered. "Twelve and a half days,
running before a nor'easterly gale." His smile widened. He
was aware of the governor's feelings concerning John
Broome since the revelation of his previous history, but the
onetime convict had proved himself not once but ten times
over, and he added with conviction, "Broome is a fine seaman, sir, and a first-rate navigator—he told me he had
only a quadrant he himself made on the island, as an aid to
his reckoning. And he had to keep the pumps going throughout his passage. Her bottom's worm-eaten as well as being
poorly caulked—he did well to bring her here."

"I grant you that," Hunter allowed. "But for all that, the
fellow's caused me more trouble than anyone else in the
colony . . . with the exception of Macarthur. Always with
the exception of Macarthur, Henry! However, I fancy I've
devised a means of curbing *his* excesses. . . ." He went
into the details of his letter and added grimly, "If His
Grace will not believe the written word, I shall request they
appoint Philip King in my place, and I'll go home—damme
if I won't. I'll put my case to the whole of His Majesty's
government and to Their Lordships in person if I have to.
Admiral Phillip will bear me out. They'll have to listen
then. And it may be the only way I can save the colony

from these money-grubbing traders who dare to call themselves officers in His Majesty's service!"

Waterhouse stared at him, his blue eyes reflecting his dismay. "You cannot mean that, sir, surely?"

John Hunter reverted to the thick Scottish accent of his boyhood. "Laddie, ye ken fine I do!" he exclaimed vehemently. "For 'twill be the infernal Rum Corps or ma'sel'—ma heid on a plate or Jack Boddice's!" He controlled himself with a visible effort and went on more calmly, dropping the accent, "There's no limit to that man's vile deceit, Henry. He writes to the Duke of Portland that the people of this colony are suffered by *me* to indulge in licentiousness, drunkenness, and every abominable act of dissipation. I grant the truth of his assertion in regard to the people's behavior, but it was thus when I came here after two years under the corps's administration. If it exists, they, not I are responsible for it—their misrule destroyed in two short years all that Governor Phillip had worked for and achieved. You know that to be so."

"Most certainly I do, sir," Henry Waterhouse affirmed without hesitation. "But surely His Grace will not believe it otherwise?"

"It's to be hoped he'll not, but I daren't count on it." Hunter gave vent to an exasperated sigh. "We came here to inspect Norfolk Island's first attempt at shipbuilding, did we not? Perhaps we should confine ourselves to that."

Sensing his inner bitterness and resentment, Waterhouse shook his head. "The sloop can wait, sir. The question of your resigning office cannot. It would be a disaster if you were to do so, truly, sir."

"Would it? Have you seen the lampoons that are being circulated about me?"

"I've seen them, yes. But—"

The governor cut him short. "Henry, do you realize that the Duke of Portland sent me Macarthur's venomous accusations with his official dispatches and invited me to answer them—damme, to *defend* myself against them! For that's what it amounts to. I fancy I've answered them—my letter was explicit, the Lord knows. But will Portland believe me?"

"He must, sir. You are the governor."

Hunter shook his head morosely. "Henry, Macarthur

had the sheer effrontery to infer that I *allow* the clergy to be insulted in the street, without receiving any redress. But what, I ask you, did this—damn his eyes—this pretended advocate for the moral conduct of the people . . . what action did *he* take when the poor chaplain's cherished place of worship was burned to the ground? He was in command, I was absent at Parramatta—and his men were gathered outside, engaged in cardplaying, drinking, and leering at the women. They could have saved the church, but Macarthur gave them no orders and they let it burn."

Henry Waterhouse shook his head somberly. He, too, had been absent from Sydney when the church and later the new jail had been set on fire. The jail, being built of more robust materials, had not been entirely destroyed and had now been repaired, but the church, built with such labor by poor Johnson, was a charred ruin, and Divine Service was once again held in the open.

"He'll accuse me of permitting arson next," the governor asserted wrathfully. He started to pace up and down, hands clasped behind his back and heavy dark brows furrowed. "The devil take it, Henry, I'm a post captain in His Majesty's navy, and a damned tradesman masquerading as a king's officer is seeking to cause me to be recalled! I've a mind not to wait for my recall. They've made Paterson a lieutenant colonel, and he's supposed to be returning here to take command of the corps. I'll let *him* deal with Macarthur, and I'll go home. There's a war raging in Europe—Their Lordships will give me a command, and I'll take it as soon as I've made Portland see the truth. Thanks be to God, the mutiny is over and the seamen are doing their duty, as British seamen should. Old Adam Duncan proved it at Camperdown, and Sir John Jervis and Nelson off Saint Vincent." A fugitive gleam of envy lit his eyes as he turned his gaze on Waterhouse again. "We're in the wrong place here, you and I, Henry—guarding convicts, when we might be fighting the king's enemies!"

"Is not Macarthur, sir?" Henry Waterhouse suggested with a wry smile. "Why not send him to England and let him have a taste of campaigning?"

"That thought had crossed my mind," Governor Hunter admitted. "But I fear he would merely advance his own interests were I to do so. The only campaign he would take part in would be the encompassing of my ruin by gaining the ear of His Grace of Portland . . . and Pitt himself, given the chance." He laughed shortly. "*I* intend to gain the duke's ear, and, believe me, I shall make use of it, for this colony's salvation."

Waterhouse started to voice objections, but the governor turned and gestured toward the anchorage.

"The sloop is putting out a boat," he said. "Let's go and greet Mr. Broome. If she can be put in good order, I shall give command of her to Flinders, and if you can furnish him with a crew, he shall take her to search for Bass's strait. Indeed"—he had recovered his good humor and was smiling at his subordinate—"Flinders's orders shall be to sail right through the strait if it's there and circumnavigate Van Diemen's Land!"

Henry Waterhouse again fell into step with him. He said, as they walked briskly toward the landing stage, "I can furnish a crew, sir, without any trouble. Er—what about Broome, sir? I fancy Matt Flinders would like to have him, and—"

To his surprise the governor shook his head. "I think not, Henry. He can rejoin the *Reliance*. You can make use of him, can you not?"

"Of course, sir," the *Reliance*'s captain agreed, "if that's your wish."

He did not argue and Hunter, relenting, said gruffly, "I'm a mite prejudiced. If young Flinders wants him, he can ask, can he not?"

The small, two-oared boat, fashioned of Norfolk pine like the sloop, came smartly alongside the landing stage, and Master's Mate Broome stepped ashore, hat in hand.

"His Majesty's sloop *Norfolk*, at your service, sir," he told the governor. "But in need, I deeply regret to say, of repair before she can enter Your Excellency's service."

Governor Hunter eyed him thoughtfully. Finally he said without enthusiasm, "I'll inspect her, Mr. Broome."

"Sir," Johnny Broome acknowledged and added, greatly daring, "She's better than Governor Phillip's cutter, sir."

"Which, I'm given to understand, you had ample time and experience to ascertain?" Hunter suggested.

But he was smiling as he stepped down into the sloop's boat.

CHAPTER XVI

"The only way in which we can ensure our survival, Tim," Jasper Spence said with emphasis, eyeing the younger man searchingly, "the only way is if the colony's free settlers present a united front, in order to *demand* fair prices for our crops and livestock. If we do not, Macarthur and his infernal Rum Corps will *ruin* us!"

Timothy Dawson met his gaze with a faintly puzzled frown. For a long time, he was aware, his host had had a foot in both camps; he had held a share in the corps's trading ventures and had helped to defray the costs of the various ships they had chartered, in particular those sent on speculation to Calcutta, where he still had influence with the Bengal merchants. Recently, however, Spence had fallen out with Lieutenant Piper. Then an acrimonious wrangling between Macarthur and Spence over a lost cargo had resulted in their appearance, on opposite sides, in the civil court. The legal battle had proved costly, and Henrietta's father, bested by his opponent and still smarting under his defeat, had found himself joined in an unexpected alliance with Richard Atkins and the two surgeons, Balmain and Arndell, against whom Macarthur was also engaged in litigation.

Timothy waited, thoughtfully sipping his second glass of Cape brandy. Since Charles Brace's death he had avoided all personal contact with the Spences; a note of condolence, addressed to Henrietta in carefully formal terms, had been the only indulgence he had permitted himself. And, in truth, he reflected, he had had little time for social calls—with poor Jenny confined for weeks in hospital, he had been hard put to it to cope with the work on their two holdings, aided only by Davie Leake at the Hawkesbury farm and old Watt Sparrow and the Jardines at Parramatta.

Governor Hunter, in a well-intentioned desire to repair and add to the existing buildings in Sydney and enlarge the prisoners' accommodation at Parramatta and Toongabbe, permitted far fewer convict laborers to the settlers than had Governor Phillip or Colonel Grose. And . . . Timothy drained his glass and sighed. While he applauded the governor's motives and thoroughly approved of his recent decision to issue liquor licenses to selected emancipists, the resultant shortage of agricultural labor was, to say the least, a source of much inconvenience to himself and others like him. True, most of the convict transports now reaching the colony came from Ireland, and the Irish rebels were difficult to control and reluctant to work. There was a high proportion of the better educated among them, people who were, in any case, unsuited to manual labor and untrained for anything more skilled. And the Catholic priests who accompanied them into exile were forever inciting them to further acts of rebellion or abortive attempts to escape.

He had been fortunate in being allocated a wizened little carpenter from County Wexford in place of the unfortunate Rick Larkin. . . . Timothy smiled to himself in quiet amusement, recalling with what eagerness old Seamus O' Hagen had worked to acquire Rick's more productive skills. He . . .

"You smile," Jasper Spence observed, his tone reproachful. "But surely you must agree with me, Tim? Macarthur is doing all in his power to force the governor to resign or even to scheme his recall. If he succeeds, then we might as well pack our bags and sell up."

Timothy shrugged. "The governor is His Majesty's representative, sir, and Macarthur a—damn it—a mere captain in a far-from-honored corps! How can he possibly hope to succeed?"

"He has money and a good deal of land. He also exercises a strong—I might almost describe it as malign—influence over most of his brother officers. Poor Hunter has no power, no troops to back him up. If it were to come to a trial of strength, the governor and the crew of the *Reliance*, if he called them to his support, would not stand a chance. Besides"—Jasper Spence reached for the brandy bottle and moodily refilled both their glasses—"the colony is full of malcontent Irishmen. You know as well as I do that at the first sign of trouble between the governor and the corps, the whole lot of them would break out in rebellion."

This, Timothy knew, was an ever-present danger, with or without any trouble with the corps to spark it off. There were rumors of clandestine meetings in Toongabbe and Parramatta, of the gathering of arms and inflammatory speeches by the Irish priests and leaders of the so-called Defenders and the—how did they style themselves? United Irishmen . . . those same treacherous rogues who had sought French aid and whose leader, Wolfe Tone, was said to have been on board the Dutch flagship at Camperdown, wearing French uniform, preparatory to an invasion of Ireland. Admiral Duncan's epic victory had, it seemed, prevented the planned invasion, but Tone's defeat had not cooled the ardor of those of his persuasion who had been deported to New South Wales.

He nodded thoughtfully. "There's talk of forming militia units from among the settlers and selected emancipists," he began, but Spence irritably cut him short.

"Yes," he snapped. "To assist in controlling the Irish rebels—*not* to curb the damned Rum Corps! If Hunter's forced to go, they'll do what they damned well please."

"He would not go before a new governor was appointed, surely, sir?" Timothy objected.

"The British government is preoccupied solely with prosecuting the war. Whoever they appointed would have to come out here, and in the interim the senior officer of the corps would act as governor." Jasper Spence spread his hands despairingly. "Captain King is said to be coming back, but there's no definite word as to when he may be expected, and Colonel Paterson is still in England. Which leaves us with Foveaux, and as you don't need me to tell you, he's in the Macarthur camp."

Timothy waited, expecting more, since clearly Jasper Spence had not sent for him solely in order to air vague complaints of the corps's trading activities in general and those of Captain Macarthur in particular. But the complaints were aired at some considerable length before his host, having again refilled their glasses, came to the reason for his summons.

"Tim," he said earnestly, "there is only one way to deal with Macarthur—apart, of course, from giving the governor our unstinted support—and that, in my opinion, is to beat him at his own game."

"What exactly do you mean, sir?"

Spence smiled thinly. He answered the question with another. "How has that blackguard gained the influence, dammit, the power he enjoys? By the simple expedient of owning more land and more livestock than any other individual in the colony and by controlling the trading ventures of his brother officers."

That, Timothy thought grimly, was true, but he listened in silence while his host enlarged on the theme, pointing out that the average free settler's holding seldom exceeded two hundred acres.

"We're not united by any bond save that of necessity," Jasper Spence went on. "Each landowner makes his own bargain with the commissariat, but he's compelled to bargain with the corps officers or their representatives for liquor and household goods—even for his clothing and his shoe leather! If he has to pay laborers, he must do so in rum, and Macarthur and his cronies control virtually all the supplies coming in—the governor does his best, but he's powerless to stop their trafficking. Legally his hands are tied, because the cargoes are bought and paid for—he cannot confiscate them without paying compensation, and he has no government funds he can use for that purpose."

"He can buy our grain, sir," Timothy put in. "And he has. He—"

Again Spence cut him short. He said angrily, "Poor Hunter made a bad error there. He took all the grain the settlers could supply—far and away too much for the commissariat's needs. Now more than half of it is rotting, consumed by weevils and rats and useless for human consumption . . . and the home government is unlikely to approve of the costs he incurred. Haven't you seen the latest lampoons?"

"I've seen some, yes. But—"

"They are scurrilous, but there's a certain truth in the allegations they make. And you may be sure that some of them have found their way into the English mailbags."

Jasper Spence heaved a frustrated sigh and again reached for the brandy bottle, only to find that it was empty. He rose and, opening the door, called softly, "Frances . . . could you bring us another bottle of the Cape brandy, my dear?" His voice, Timothy realized with some surprise, held a note almost of affection in it, and when a slim, good-looking young woman came in a few

moments later with the bottle he had asked for, Spence
took it from her with effusive thanks. She withdrew, and he
said as he uncorked the bottle, "That girl, Frances O'Riordan, is one of the better—er—imports from Ireland, Tim.
She's of a good family. Her father was a physician, and her
brother a lawyer, until, poor fellow, he allowed himself to
get mixed up with a bunch of wild seditionists, which cost
him his life."

Timothy remembered the name then. The girl was the
one whom Jenny had befriended when she had fallen ill
and come in from the woods after an abortive escape attempt. He had seen her at the cabin, a frail, sickly wraith
with scarcely the strength to lift her head from the pillow.
But now . . . He swiftly suppressed a smile, realizing that
his host was watching him with an odd intentness, as if
challenging him to question the girl's presence in his house.
Frances O'Riordan had been employed as Henrietta's maid.
Jenny had told him that and had been pleased that such
congenial employment had come the Irish girl's way. If she
had improved her status by becoming mistress to Henrietta's father, then good luck to her, although . . . His lips
twitched involuntarily. It was a common enough practice
out here, but he did not imagine that her father's indulging
in it would meet with Henrietta's approval since Frances,
whatever her family background, was a convict.

Jasper Spence resumed his seat. "Tim, my boy," he exclaimed with sudden vehemence, "I have a mind to return
to the partnership we once envisaged, if you are willing."

Taken by surprise, Timothy stared at him, reddening.
When Henrietta had announced her betrothal to Charles
Brace, he had felt honor bound to repay the money Spence
had lent him and to dissolve the proposed partnership.
With bitterness, he recalled what that repayment had cost
him. His host talked on, emphasizing the advantages that
would accrue from the amalgamation of their landholdings,
the capital sums he was prepared to make available for the
import of stock and the purchase of more land.

"I am no farmer, Tim, but farming is in your blood.
Together our holdings would equal Macarthur's, and if I
were able to entrust all the land management to you, I
could devote my energies to a field of enterprise in which I
have experience, for I'm a merchant at heart. And I still

have some influence, some valuable contacts in Calcutta. I'd go there in person, buy goods and charter ships and—"

"In opposition to the Rum Corps, sir?"

"Why not, if I can do so with official approval. The governor would welcome it."

Perhaps he would, Timothy thought, if only because it would afford a challenge to the corps's monopoly. This evidently was what Spence had meant when he had talked of beating Macarthur at his own game. He listened, only sipping at his brandy now and uncomfortably aware that he had consumed more than enough of the potent liquor already. His host, too, was beginning to show the effects of their afternoon's drinking; his thin, angular face was flushed and his voice was more than a little slurred.

"Of corsh"—Jasper Spence corrected himself quickly—"of *course* the—ah—the arrangement I am suggesh . . . suggesting would only be possible if we were related, Tim. That is to say, if you were my son-in-law, my dear boy, and the—ah—the partnership a family concern, if you take my meaning."

It was out, Timothy thought wryly—the real reason for his summons was now made plain. The opportunity he was being offered—the dazzling opportunity, the chance to expand his agricultural interests until he could rival Macarthur . . . devil take it, these were his for the asking if he married Henrietta! And had he not always wanted Henrietta for a wife? He drew a long breath, more than ever aware of the fumes of alcohol clouding his brain as Spence asked, a sharp edge to his voice, "You've not changed your mind, have you? You still desire to take my daughter to wife?"

"She's given me no encouragement, sir," Timothy stammered awkwardly. He drained his glass. "That is, she—"

"The situation is now radically altered," the older man retorted. "Poor young Brace is dead, as you know."

Indeed he did know, Timothy told himself, the all-too-familiar pangs of conscience returning once again to plague him. He had killed Henrietta's intended bridegroom as surely as if he had put a pistol to his head . . . he had watched Brace die, without lifting a finger to save him. He felt the hot, betraying color rise to flood his cheeks as Spence added, with conviction, "I can assure you, Tim my boy, Henrietta is ready to listen to you now, and she is aware that a—ah—a match between you would meet with my unqualified approval. I want to see her settled—a natural desire, on the part of any father, is it not?" He refilled both their glasses and smiled. "Eh?"

"Yes, of course, sir." For all his hesitation, Timothy felt his pulses quicken at the thought of what marriage to Henrietta Spence would mean. He gulped down the contents of his glass, his thoughts running riot on lines it had never previously occurred to him to consider. The unattainable would be his—the lovely girl who had for so long despised and scorned him would be his wife, his to possess, dependent on him, her pride humbled at last. Socially there would be advantages too; with Henrietta as his wife and Jasper Spence as his father-in-law, the doors of Sydney society would no longer be closed to him. He would dine at the governor's table, meet John Macarthur and his lady on equal terms, while setting up in opposition to them.

An appealing prospect, but there was Jenny Taggart—Jenny, to whom he had given his word and to whom he owed so much. He had intended to wed her and would have done so long since, had it not been for her illness and her long sojourn in hospital. But she had returned only a week or two ago, a shadow of her hardworking, competent self, and his desire for her, which he had supposed would be sharpened by her absence, had not been rekindled. This had not caused him serious concern, for he had recognized that it was a passing phase brought about by her weakness and the sickly state that had left her pale and listless, incapable of passion. He had sought to bed her only once since her discharge from the hospital and . . . He passed his tongue over his dry lips, recalling Jenny's own sad comments.

Jenny Taggart would not stand in the way of his advancement, he told himself. Had she not expressed her own doubts of the wisdom of his marrying a convict—had she not warned him that he would regret it if he took her to wife? Being the woman she was, she would not hold him to his promise and . . . he would provide for her, for her and young Justin. They should have the Parramatta holding and the stock they had bred there, free of all ties.

"Well?" Jasper Spence prompted with a hint of impatience. He hiccoughed behind his hand, eyeing Timothy with shrewdly appraising eyes. "Will you address yourself to my daughter?"

Timothy hesitated no longer. "With your permission, sir, I shall be honored to do so. She—Mistress Henrietta is in Sydney, is she not?"

Henrietta's father inclined his white head.

"She prefers to remain there, and she has O'Leary's wife to look after her. That is why I have brought Frances O'Riordan here to keep house for me. A man needs a woman's touch, and since losing my own dear wife, I . . . well, I've felt the loss increasingly, I don't mind telling you, Tim."

"I don't doubt that, sir," Timothy said, again aware of the older man's searching gaze. Jasper Spence started to speak and then thought better of it. He splashed brandy into both glasses and raised his own solemnly. "To our future relationship, dear boy . . . and in the hope that it may prosper!"

"I'll gladly drink to that, sir." Their glasses clinked, and Timothy added, "If it will be convenient to you, I will call on Mistress Henrietta next Sunday." The die was cast, he reflected; he had committed himself and there could be no turning back. But he owed it to Jenny Taggart to tell her of his intentions before he made his promised call on Henrietta and . . . now was as good a time as any to make the final and irrevocable break between them. Now, while his future father-in-law's good brandy might be expected to assuage any twinges of conscience he might feel on Jenny's account or, come to that, on poor dead Brace's as well.

He rose and, swaying a little, took his leave, Frances O'Riordan making him a demure curtsy as she handed him his hat and cane at the door.

It was late afternoon by the time Timothy drew rein outside the cabin Jenny occupied and, in response to his shouted summons, she came to the door looking listless and pale.

"I had not expected you, Tim," she began. "But come in, if you wish. Tom can take your horse and—"

Timothy shook his head. He dismounted, his horse's rein looped over his arm, and said abruptly, "I've come to ask you if you will free me, lass. I'll make reparation to you, of course—to you and Justin. You shall have the deeds to this place and I'll hand over the stock to you, free of all claim."

She stared at him, shocked into silence for a moment and finally managed in a flat, expressionless voice, "That is . . . good of you."

"It is no more than you deserve, lass," he returned gently, trying to make amends.

Jenny drew herself up, her emotions now under stern control. "You . . . that is, you want to marry Henrietta Spence, is that it?"

Timothy nodded. He felt ashamed, unable to meet her gaze, his own on the scuffed dust at his feet. The effects of the brandy he had drunk had worn off, and he found himself wishing, quite unreasonably, that Jenny would offer him more of the stuff. But, under her quiet probing, he revealed the opportunity Henrietta's father had put before him, stressing the advantages of their proposed partnership.

"And you've always loved her, have you not?" Jenny put in without bitterness. "Henrietta is the one you've always wanted to wed—not me?"

"I care for you a great deal, Jenny," he answered awkwardly. "And I owe you so much, I—"

She cut him short. "Then there is no more to be said, is there? Of course you are free, Tim—I would not try to hold you to any promise. A match with Mistress Spence, partnership with her father . . . you must grasp such chances with both hands! If you wed me, you'd be wedding a convict. . . . I told you that when you first asked me, didn't I?"

"Aye," he agreed gruffly "Aye, you did, but—"

"It's the truth," Jenny stated gravely. "I wish you well, Tim, truly I do, with all my heart!"

"I believe you do," Timothy said. He took her hand, raised it to his lips and then from his saddlebag he took the title deeds to the holdings they had shared, thrust them at her as if the touch of them were repugnant to him.

"Thank you, lass, and God bless you. I . . ." His voice broke, and turning away to hide his face from her, he flung himself into the saddle and rode away in a cloud of choking dust.

* * *

Jenny sat in the old rocking chair Tom Jenkins had made, and with eyes that saw nothing of its spectacular beauty, she watched the sun go down in a golden blaze of glory.

On her lap were the deeds to the holding—Tim's parting gift to her—but to this, too, she was blind. As her restless fingers toyed with the roll of parchment, she was conscious only of relief because Watt Sparrow and Justin were in Sydney and, in consequence, neither had been witness to her humiliation. She would have to tell Watt, of course, and the old man would be upset—angry on her behalf and resentful on Justin's. He had set so much store by her marriage to Tim Dawson, had talked of little else since her return from the hospital, incessantly urging her to set a date for the ceremony, and she . . . Jenny caught her breath on a sob.

Had it been instinct, she wondered, instinct or a premonition that had made her hold back, waiting for Tim to make the first move? Had she sensed, even then, that he had regretted his impulsive proposal and had thought better of wedding a convict? She looked down at her hands, noticing for perhaps the hundredth time how thin and weak they had become. Her whole body was thin—skin and bone, old Watt had said, when she had slipped out of her shawl that first day, following her discharge from the hospital, and stumbled over, exhausted, to the rocking chair, unable to hold herself upright.

She was lucky to be alive, the doctors had told her, and she knew that they were right—she had come near to death, had felt its ghostly presence hovering over her when the fever reached its climax and each breath she drew had been an agony. But she had not died; she had fought for her life, for Justin's sake and, ironically, for Tim's, in the belief that they needed her. Well, Justin did still, but Tim . . . Tim no longer cared whether she lived or died. She flexed the flaccid fingers gripping the roll of parchment he had thrust into them barely half an hour before, and tears filled her eyes, bitter and burning.

They were tears of weakness, of self-pity, of defeat . . . tears for a lost dream. Jenny sat up, letting the parchment fall, her hands clenched into fists. There was still that other dream, she reminded herself, the dream Gover-

nor Phillip had inspired—his vision of the future in which,
throughout the long years of her exile, she had forced herself to believe.

The colony's first governor had proclaimed that here
were, and she remembered his words exactly: ". . . the
fertile plains needing only the labor of the husbandman to
produce in abundance the fairest and richest fruits. Here are
interminable pastures, the future home of flocks and herds
innumerable."

That dream was within sight of fulfillment, Jenny reminded herself as, each year, more land was discovered,
surveyed, and opened for settlement. The Cow Pasture—
that well-watered land bordering the Hawkesbury River—
provided acres of fine grazing between Prospect Hill and
Mount Hunter and to the east of King George's River. The
flocks of imported sheep, the horse and cow herds were
breeding and increasing, and her own small holding—hers
again, now—produced wheat, maize, tobacco, kaffir corn,
grapes, and kitchen vegetables in abundance as well as
grass for the brood mares and their foals.

Besides, there was Justin. Jenny blinked back the tears,
conscious of an aching pride in her son. Justin was devel-
oping into a fine boy; his education—interrupted by the
destruction of the church in Sydney, in which school was
held—was now to be resumed, the governor having allocated a newly constructed building for the purpose. Watt
had taken him back to his lodgings that morning—the reason for their providential absence from the cabin during
Timothy Dawson's call—and, happily installed with the
Macraes, who doted on him, the boy could take one more
step toward the future she had planned for him.

The future . . . Jenny smiled to herself. The future on
which Justin himself had set his heart, ever since she had
told him his father's story. She had bred no farmer but, it
seemed, a seaman, determined to pit his seven-year-old wits
against the problems posed by astral navigation and the in-
tricacies of the sextant and marine compass—the rudiments
of which, he assured her gravely, had been explained to
him by Surgeon Bass of the *Reliance*.

Well, if the thirst for knowledge kept the boy dutifully at
his desk, it could not fail to be to his advantage, Jenny
thought, and remembered then that Tim had talked of

making a farmer of him. Perhaps, after all, it was an ill wind that blew nobody any good, she told herself wryly and, conscious of a sudden chill in the air, rose stiffly to her feet and went into the cabin to prepare a meal for Watt on his return.

The morning of Wednesday, October 7, dawned fair and clear, with a brisk southeasterly breeze. For the four seagoing ships in Sydney Cove the change of wind was what they had been waiting for, and first the two American trading ships—the *Semiramis* and the *Argo* schooner, their cargoes disposed of—weighed anchor and made sail, their destination China.

Matthew Flinders, eager to follow in their wake, went below to supervise the stowage of two extra water-casks in the cramped storage space of his new command, and it was then that, quite by chance, he discovered the presence of a stowaway. Dragged by the scruff of his neck from his hiding place, the boy faced him shamefacedly, his lower lip tremulous.

"Please, sir—*please,* Mr. Flinders, I want to come with you. I'll make myself useful—Dr. Bass'll tell you I can, sir. He's been teaching me. Please, sir, let me stay. I—"

Flinders cut him short "You're Justin, are you not—Justin Taggart?" he demanded severely. The boy nodded. "Should you not be in school?" the *Norfolk*'s commander persisted. Once again, the fair, tousled head was bowed. The lad offered no excuses, and Flinders relented. Reverting to the intimate speech of his own boyhood, he asked quite gently, "How old art thou, Justin?"

"I'm . . . that is, I'll be ten very soon, sir," Justin answered. To cover the lie he went on, his words falling over each other in his anxiety to carry conviction, "You take boys to sea at ten years in His Majesty's Navy, don't you, sir? To train them and—"

"Aye, some we do—*if* they're ten years old and have their parents' consent. Not if they are playing truant from school and lie about their age, though. *How* old art thou, Justin?"

"Nearly seven," Justin admitted reluctantly.

"Hast thou the consent of thy parents, lad?"

"No, sir. My father's not here—he is serving in the

king's navy. And my mother . . . well, she . . ." The boy broke off, a natural tendency to tell the truth struggling against his eagerness to be permitted to sail with the *Norfolk* on her voyage of discovery. Before the burning of the Reverend Richard Johnson's church had compelled his return to the farm at Parramatta, he had helped Surgeon Bass with the building of the longboat, and the kindly surgeon had talked of the projected voyage, even allowing the boy to study the charts of the area he and Lieutenant Flinders had made.

"I know where you're going, sir, and I know why. You're looking for a strait to the west of the Furneaux Islands. . . ." Quoting from his memory of Surgeon Bass's charts, Justin gave him chapter and verse, the measurements of latitude and longitude tripping from his tongue as easily and fluently as the names given to areas of coast, which he had seen when the ink on the charts had been barely dry.

Flinders stared at him in stunned surprise.

"What dost thou know of Twofold Bay and Ninety Mile Beach, lad? Or come to that Wilson's Promontory, for any sake?"

"I know where they are, Mr. Flinders," the little boy assured him. "Truly I do. Dr. Bass showed me his charts and described them, and I remembered. I want to go to sea, sir, and—"

Reluctantly, Matt Flinders waved him to silence. Time was passing. The brig *Nautilus* was to sail in company with the *Norfolk* to the Furneaux Islands. Her master, Bishop, impatient to get under way, had catted his anchor even before the arrival of the *Norfolk*'s water casks. . . . Flinders sighed, wishing that Johnny Broome could have heard young Justin's plea. The boy looked like him—damn it, he was, as George Bass had said, the spitting image of Johnny. There had to be a relationship, but . . . Johnny was on board the *Nautilus* to aid her navigation, and he would have no opportunity even to speak to him until they reached the Furneaux group and Johnny rejoined the *Norfolk*. He had to put the boy ashore.

"I'm sorry, lad," he said with genuine regret. "But thou art too young—I cannot take thee. But grow a mite and work at thy studies, and I give thee my word—thou shalt come on my next voyage if God grants me a ship to command. Now take thyself off. I must take this ship to sea."

Justin did not question his decision. Flinders saw him into the water scow, which still had not returned to shore, with a shouted injunction to the boatman to deliver him to the school, and then ordered the *Norfolk*'s anchor hove up.

CHAPTER XVII

Henrietta Spence's marriage to Timothy Dawson took place on New Year's Day 1799. It was not the ceremony she had dreamed of; her bridegroom, although dressed elegantly enough, was in civilian clothes, and there was no scarlet-clad guard of honor to make an archway of drawn swords as the newlywed couple left the church.

Even the church was a disappointment. The foundations of an extensive stone building had been laid out at the end of the previous year, but its walls stood barely two feet above the ground, and the converted granary that, of necessity, served the dual purpose of schoolhouse and place of worship was, to Henrietta's critical eye, all too reminiscent of its originally intended function. She had caused its dimly lit interior to be filled with flowers—the native wattle and a profusion of greenery—but in the humid heat even those swiftly wilted for lack of air, and the blossoms from her bridal bouquet of carefully nurtured English roses were falling before she entered the church.

The guest list, however, compiled with much thought, delighted her. The governor had accepted the elaborate, handwritten invitation, together with the newly promoted commandant of the New South Wales Corps, Colonel Paterson, who, with Captain Abbott and their two ladies, had returned to the colony in November. The other corps officers and their naval counterparts would be well represented, and the Macarthurs had promised to come in from Parramatta, with their growing family, at her insistence— her father's quarrel with Captain Macarthur in temporary abeyance.

Since the day heralded not only her nuptials but the last year of the old century, it was an auspicious occasion, and, Henrietta reflected as she glided demurely up the improvised aisle on her father's arm, if the surroundings fell short of her expectations, this glittering gathering had never previously been equaled in Sydney Town . . . and it would probably be a very long time before it was excelled.

She was aware that she presented a vision of dignified beauty—the gasps and comments of the crowd that had collected outside the church had told her that. True, they were the usual riffraff who seemed perpetually to throng the streets—ill-clad convict women, unemployed emancipists, off-duty soldiers, their number swelled by some seamen from the whalers, who had lately come into port in their evil-smelling ships . . . and few of them were sober. Henrietta's nose wrinkled in distaste. It was a regrettable fact that even during the hours of daylight most Sydney crowds were noisy, drunken, and foulmouthed. At night they were infinitely worse, although then they kept to the less salubrious areas like the Rocks where, in its jumble of malodorous houses, liquor was sold and, she had heard it hinted, prostitution flourished.

Nevertheless, the comments had been flattering. Henrietta smoothed the shimmering folds of her skirt as the recently imported harmonium-player brought an air by Handel to an end, and Timothy stepped purposefully to her side, a welcoming smile curving his lips. He looked well, she thought, in his gray cutaway coat—tall and tanned and strong, a man . . . a *husband* of whom she had no reason to feel ashamed. Already, under her tutelage, he had mellowed and his manners had improved; he might not possess poor Charles Brace's charm or the same air of breeding, but he had other qualities, of equal, if not greater value in a community such as this. Her father, a shrewd judge of character, approved of him warmly and, indeed, had forecast that within a few years he would be one of the largest and most successful landowners in the colony . . . Henrietta glanced up into her bridegroom's face, and her heart quickened its beat.

Timothy's courtship, as she had no need to remind herself, had been a revelation to her during the past weeks. It had been ardent and arousing, quite unlike poor Charles's correct and, at times, almost reluctant wooing. But Charles, she knew, had taken his physical pleasures elsewhere. Frances O'Riordan had told her as much or hinted at it. False, ungrateful creature that she was, Frances could never be trusted to tell the complete truth, and for all her Irish blarney she had hated Charles.

The Reverend Richard Johnson, looking ill and tired,
started to intone the opening words of the marriage service.

"Dearly beloved, we are gathered here in the sight of
God . . ." Henrietta made a conscious effort to listen, but
his voice was flat, lacking inspiration. A weary, disillu-
sioned voice, she thought resentfully, which reflected his
whole personality. He was said to be one of the best agri-
culturists in the colony and certainly his Sydney garden,
with its acres of flourishing vines and fruit trees, appeared
to bear out this claim. As the colony's chaplain, he was
neither successful nor popular, but faced with a choice between himself or the Reverend Samuel Marsden, Henrietta
had asked for him to perform her wedding service, unable
to bear the thought of Samuel Marsden's booming Yorkshire voice in the confined space of the converted granary.

Yet Mr. Johnson's glum tones were almost as bad, and
because he had been asked to officiate at the service, he
and his sharp-tongued, ever-critical wife had had to be invited to the reception and could be expected to bring with
them as many of their numerous children as they could
suitably clothe for the occasion. It was rumored that the
Johnsons intended to sell out and return, in the near future,
to England, but . . .

"Wilt thou, Timothy John, take this woman to be thy
wedded wife, to have and to hold from this day forward,
for richer, for poorer, in sickness and in health, until death
do you part?"

The question was posed without looking up from his
prayer book; Chaplain Johnson waited, with resigned patience, for the expected reply, and Timothy's response, uttered loudly and forcefully, seemed to startle him out of his
apathy. There was more feeling in his voice when he turned
to address Henrietta, who answered with a subdued, "I
do."

The ceremony proceeded. Dr. Arndell, who was acting
as best man, offered the ring for the traditional blessing,
and Henrietta blushed becomingly and stood with downcast
eyes as Timothy slipped the thin gold band onto the third
finger of her left hand.

"With this ring I thee wed," he declaimed in ringing
tones. "With my body I thee worship, and with all my
worldly goods I thee endow!"

"I now declare thee man and wife," the Reverend Johnson mumbled, returning his gaze to his prayer book.
"Those whom God hath joined together, let no man put
asunder."

He left them kneeling side by side in front of the improvised altar and, with more enthusiasm than he had hitherto
displayed, began his address. It was, Henrietta thought indignantly, more suited to the convicts he usually joined in
matrimony than to people of breeding, and his chosen text
from Saint Paul's Epistle to the Romans—"Be kindly affectioned one to another . . . in honor preferring one another"—came close to being insulting. She shut her ears to
his ranting, her fingers smoothing the folds of her skirt
once again, fearful lest it be crushed.

Her bridal gown was lovely, emphasizing the erect slim-
ness of her body and the soft, shapely curves of her bosom.
She had been compelled, much against her better judgment, to enlist the services of Frances O'Riordan in the
fashioning of the gown. Frances had wormed her way into
her father's household at his farm and, Henrietta now suspected, into his bed; but the Irish girl was still the most
accomplished needlewoman in the colony, and in any
event, keeping her at work on the dress in Sydney during
the past few weeks had also kept Frances away from her
father.

She had been in the crowd outside the church with all
the convict riffraff, which should have put her in her place,
for the time being. At the reception, which was to be held
in a borrowed marquee erected at the rear of the house,
Frances would again be visible only in her capacity as a
domestic servant. Perhaps when he witnessed this, her father might come to his senses. Frances looked less alluring
in a print dress and apron than she contrived to look when
she was working at the Portland Place farmhouse, and besides . . .

The Reverend Johnson came, at last, to the end of his
address. Timothy touched her arm, and she rose, a trifle
stiffly, to her feet. The signing of the marriage register
completed, Henrietta turned, smiling, to her husband. He
kissed her ardently on the cheek and offered her his arm;
side by side, they walked slowly toward the bright square

of sunlight shining through the open doorway as the organist, perspiring freely, thumped out some chords on his unmelodious instrument to speed them on their way.

But as they reached the door Henrietta realized to her dismay that some sort of altercation had broken out among the crowd. A constable was holding a struggling, fair-haired boy by the scruff of the neck with one hand and a lathered horse—far too large for so young a boy—with the other. Women screeched abuse at him, a man yelled at him to release his captive, but the constable was deaf to their demands.

"Be off with you, you little rogue!" he ordered. "Or I'll put you in charge for disturbin' the peace—an' that'll mean a tannin' from the corporal o' the guard. Don't you know there's a weddin' in the church an' all the quality there?" Turning to see the bridal couple he added apologetically, "I'm sorry sir—ma'am. But this young rascal says as he must see a Mr. Dawson, and—"

The boy interrupted him. Recognizing Timothy, he jerked himself free of the constable's grasp and called out in a high-pitched treble, "Uncle Tim—Mam sent me to find you! Please, Uncle Tim, you *must* listen!" He fell, tripped by the constable's foot.

"It's young Justin Taggart," Timothy said unnecessarily, for Henrietta had guessed the boy's identity, and her mouth tightened ominously as her bridegroom dropped to his knees in the dust to gather the ill-dressed, mud-spattered urchin to him. "What is it, Justin lad? Is there something wrong?"

"It's the river, Uncle Tim," Justin blurted out breathlessly. "The drought's broken, there's been a storm, and we got word that the river's in flood. It—it had risen twenty feet in less'n two hours, one man said. Mam's gone out with Gran'pa Watt and Tom Jardine to help round up the stock, but she said you'd have to be told—even though it's your wedding day. She said I had to find you."

There were dark clouds over to the northwest, Henrietta saw—distant but clearly bearing out the boy's assertion—and she knew, for both her father and Timothy had often talked of it, that the Hawkesbury area was subject to sudden, violent rainstorms. But surely Timothy . . . She waited, holding her breath, for her husband's reply. When it came, it did not surprise as much as it angered her.

"I'll come at once, lad," he promised, springing to his feet. "Bring the horse over." He turned to Henrietta with a wry smile, but before he could utter any excuses, she clutched at his sleeve, forcing him to look at her.

"Timothy, this is our wedding day . . . and there's the reception! The governor will be there and the Patersons, the Macarthurs—all our guests. You *cannot* go!" It would also be their wedding night, she thought, her heart sinking . . . surely that must mean more to him than a few sheep and horses! The emancipist woman, the boy's mother, was capable enough—had she not managed the holding at Parramatta for him until with regrettable quixotism Timothy had deeded it to her? Let Mrs. Taggart and the convict laborers earn their keep, let *them* wade through the rising waters and secure the stock. Let *them* take boats and load up any grain that might be threatened by the floods . . . that was what they were there for, surely?

She said as much, too upset to lower her voice, and retaining her grasp of Timothy's arm, aware that her father and Dr. Arndell, hearing the hubbub, had come to the door of the church to ascertain its cause. In a few moments, the governor would come also, and . . .

"I'm sorry, my dear," Timothy said brusquely. "I must go—it's my livelihood. Try to understand. Jenny Taggart would not have sent for me if it hadn't been necessary, I promise you." His tone softened. "You . . . that is please, I beg you, entertain our guests in my—my absence. Explain to them what has happened, and . . . my dearest love, I'll be back as soon as I possibly can."

His lips brushed her cheek; he held her to him for a moment, then, stripping off his elegant gray cutaway, he thrust it into her arms and strode over to where her father and Dr. Arndell were waiting. They accepted his explanation without question; she heard the doctor shouting for his horse and watched, through unhappy, tear-filled eyes, as Timothy vaulted into the saddle of Justin Taggart's mount, the boy seated behind him as he trotted off.

He did not look back, did not even wave, and the crowd swallowed him up, some of them running after him, and all

WILLIAM STUART LONG

of them shouting at the top of their voices, passing the news on to those who had not heard it.

"The bloody river's in flood!"

"Aye, the Hawkesbury—bin rainin' cats an' dogs out there, seemingly!"

"A lot o' livestock'll be lost unless they look slippy!"

Henrietta turned away, stifling her impulse to call after Timothy in futile appeal. He father came to her and took her arm; the governor and Colonel Paterson offered their commiserations.

"We will hold the reception, Captain Hunter," Henrietta said, recovering her poise. "I hope, sir, you will honor us with your presence, despite the absence of my—my husband."

"That will be my pleasure, Mistress—ah—Mistress Dawson," Hunter answered gallantly, "as soon as I have made arrangements for boats to be sent up to the Hawkesbury. I trust that your husband will not be delayed for too long."

All things considered, the reception was a success. Henrietta, a lovely dignified figure in her wedding dress, contrived to make light of her bridegroom's absence, accepting the sympathy of her guests with a mixture of gratitude and courage that won the approval of all. Governor Hunter proposed the toast; the assembled company drank to the newlyweds' future and Henrietta thanked them with proper modesty and decorum, on her own and her husband's behalf.

Inwardly, she was deeply hurt, regretting the death of Charles Brace more now than when the news of it had reached her. *He* would not have abandoned her on their wedding day, she thought bitterly. Charles, God rest his soul, had been a gentleman, with a proper awareness of a gentleman's obligations and of the relative importance of matters of this kind, to which Timothy was seemingly blind. Yet recalling the sensitivity of her husband's proposal, her bitterness was in part assuaged.

"I love you, Henrietta," Timothy had said, "truly and with all my heart . . . you are my love, before all others. If you will wed me, you will make me the happiest man alive!" Sobbing herself to sleep, she prayed for his safe re-

turn. But it was three days before her prayer was answered
and Timothy at last rode back to Sydney Town, weary,
unshaven, his eyes red-rimmed from lack of sleep. They
had saved most of his stock, but half his newly harvested
grain had been lost and about a dozen sheep drowned, the
maize crop ruined.

Henrietta, with bitter memories of her wedding night
spent alone, could not find it in her heart to reproach him,
although, for all her attempts to forget the episode, some of
its bitterness lingered on.

Timothy's lovemaking was perfunctory and gave her no
pleasure, and when he finally slept, his big body slumped
beside her in the marriage bed that had been her parents',
she wept for her lost illusions and for the aristocratic young
soldier to whom—but for his tragically premature death—
she might have been married. Charles would have displayed more finesse, she told herself miserably. However
exhausted he was he would never have permitted his good
manners to desert him—or come to her bed with the sweat
of his exertions at the river still on him, as Timothy had
done. And he would not now be snoring like a—like an
animal.

"Be kindly affectioned one to another," the chaplain had
enjoined them as they had knelt in front of his altar a few
minutes before the untimely appearance of the convict
woman's son. "In honor preferring one another . . ." She
would try, Henrietta decided, and God helping her, she
would adhere to her marriage vows. The man lying at her
side was her husband. . . . She caught her breath. Her
husband, whom she had pledged herself to love, honor, and
obey . . . She raised herself on one elbow and, leaning
across Timothy's recumbent body, pressed her lips against
his half-open mouth.

She had intended it as a gesture of forgiveness, a light
and gentle kiss calculated not to waken him, but he stirred,
and lifting her head she saw, in the moonlight shining in
through the curtained window, that he was smiling. He
captured her hand and murmured sleepily, "Ah, Jenny
love, it's good to be with you . . . but let me sleep a while
longer, will you, lass? Because I'm done up, I—"

Henrietta recoiled from him, hurt and sickened, the tears

streaming down her cheeks unchecked, as the implication of his words sank in.

So that was the way of it, she thought dully—that was why, at the behest of a wretched, emancipated convict woman, Timothy had deserted her on her wedding day! It had not been the stock that mattered or the flooded river— Jenny Taggart had sent her son to demand his presence, and he had gone without a moment's hesitation . . . and gone to her bed, it would seem, as he was in the habit of doing.

She did not know the Taggart woman and, to the best of her knowledge, had never even set eyes on her, but suddenly Henrietta Dawson found an object for all the bitterness and resentment that was in her, and when Timothy, roused by the sound of her sobbing, sought to take her into his arms, she held him off, weeping hysterically, her clenched fists beating against his chest.

He scarcely heard the accusations she flung at him, and finally losing patience with her he imprisoned her slight, trembling body beneath his own and took her with an angry passion that belied his earlier restraint.

Her response was instinctive, drawn from her almost against her will but born of a long hunger that would not be denied. When it was over, Henrietta clung to him weakly, hiding her tear-drenched face against his naked chest, and Timothy whispered soft endearments as he held her to him.

"You are my wife and I love you, Henrietta," he told her. "No other woman—only you, my dearest—now and always. From the very moment I met you, it was you I wanted for my wife, believe me."

She wanted with all her heart to believe him, to forget the name he had uttered in his sleep so short a time ago, but it remained, a faint yet disturbing memory when, her questions still unanswered, she, too, drifted into sleep, with Timothy's arms about her.

On the morning of Tuesday, January 12, the flag was hoisted at the South Head and word spread swiftly throughout Sydney that it heralded the return of the *Norfolk* sloop.

A crowd had already assembled to witness the execution of a man convicted of theft and the flogging of two Irish rebels, whose persistent refusal to work and defiance of authority had led the magistrates of the criminal court to order that an example be made of them. A last-minute pardon at the foot of the scaffold deprived the watchers of the drama they had anticipated and, floggings being commonplace, most of them drifted away to take up positions of vantage round the cove, there to await the arrival of Lieutenant Flinders and his crew.

Justin Taggart heard the news at his desk in the schoolhouse, but it was not until the ordained hour for play that the master permitted his pupils' release from their books. By that time, to his intense disappointment, Justin learned that the pilot boat had long since departed, and a rapid inspection of the anchorage revealed that no others were being manned.

Disconsolate, the boy wandered over to where the floggings were taking place, a line of red-coated soldiers drawn up along the seaward side of the parade ground obscuring his view of both cove and prisoners. He squirmed past them and, to his surprise, recognized Frances O'Riordan standing a few yards away on the edge of the diminishing crowd of spectators. It was a long time since he had seen her—apart from a brief glimpse outside the church when he had been sent to summon Uncle Timothy because of the Hawkesbury flood—and he ran to her eagerly.

"Franny—oh, Franny, how are you? Mama said you—" She cut him short with a curt, angry "Quiet, Justin!" that was both hurtful and unexpected. He was about to run on, lower lip trembling, when she grasped his arm and drew him to her side. "Listen," she bade him. "And you'll hear what a brave man has to say for Ireland's Defenders."

Justin waited in obedient silence, puzzled by her intensity and not quite clear as to whom it was she wanted him to listen. Most of those who were publicly flogged were criminals—thieves and escapers, his teacher had told him—and it was unusual for any save a man about to end his life on the gallows to be permitted to address the watching crowd.

"There," Frances whispered. "That is him, that is Brian

McCormack." She indicated a tall, red-haired man who was being led to the triangles by two soldiers. He stood head and shoulders above his escort, blue eyes blazing defiance, and when they attempted to seize him up, he broke from them with an almost contemptuous display of strength and, leaving one spread-eagled on the ground and the other clutching a twisted arm, mounted the steps to the gallows. Balanced lightly halfway up to the platform, he turned to face the startled crowd and announced in a deep, commanding voice, "Hear me, you misbegotten children of Satan."

The watchers fell silent, initially as bewildered as Justin, but then, realizing that the prisoner's act of defiance had thrown the soldiers into confusion, a few spasmodic cheers broke the silence, interspersed by jeering abuse as a sergeant attempted vainly to dislodge the Irishman by prods from his pike.

"I'll come down when I've had my say," the big Irishman promised. "And without your encouragement," he added, kicking the pike from the sergeant's hands. The people laughed, delighted by the red-faced soldier's discomfiture, and began cheering wildly.

From his lofty perch the prisoner waved them again to silence. "On behalf of the United Irishmen," he thundered, "I'd have you all know that Ireland has severed all connection with England and King George! We have been sent here unjustly, convicted and sentenced by a government that has no power over us or our country and that has no claim to our loyalty. Ireland is in allegiance with France, and France is at war with England! We are fighting for Ireland's freedom and our own liberty! None of us who are here are to be considered as convicts nor treated as such, for we—"

The crack of a musket brought his impassioned tirade to an abrupt conclusion, and Justin stared in horror as the ball found its mark and the big man, bleeding from a wound in the fleshy part of his right leg, came crashing to the ground.

A surgeon examined him, pronounced him unfit to receive punishment, and he was carried off, none too gently, by two of the soldiers. Justin had seen enough. He took his leave of Frances, who seemed scarcely aware of his presence, and leaving her in the midst of a small group of vociferously angry women, he retraced his steps to the boatyard, relieved—since hitherto everything had gone wrong with his day—to find Tom Moore, the head shipwright, at work there.

Moore was a kindly man, with a soft spot for all youngsters who helped him in the yard and, in particular, for Justin, who displayed more ability than most of the others, and he greeted the boy's arrival with a genial smile.

"Well, young feller-me-lad, come to give us a hand, have you?" He paused, mopped his heated brow and then consulted a big turnip watch, which he took from the pocket of his breeches. "Hey, now—school ain't due to come out for another two or three hours! What're you doing—playing hooky, is it?"

Justin glumly inclined his head. "The *Norfolk*'s on her way in, Mr. Moore."

"Aye, so I heard. Be a while yet, though, with this sou'easterly, won't it, lad?"

"The pilot boat went out more than two hours ago," Justin reminded him. "I was promised I could go, but Mr. Finch kept us in school. I did want to go out to meet them, Mr. Moore. You see, Mr. Flinders said he'd take me on his next voyage, and I—"

"You wanted to show willing, is that it?" Moore suggested, his tone not unsympathetic. "Well, too bad old Finchy kept you in, but seeing there's nothing to be done about it, and you're playing hooky anyway, you might as well help me for a couple of hours, eh? Fetch me over that adz, there's a good lad."

Justin did as he was asked. He looked around the yard, which was deserted save for a deaf old convict carpenter who was always there, working away with maddening slowness but considerable skill on the cabin fittings for the sloop Tom Moore was assembling. The timber had been sent out from England, but it was inferior stuff, not properly seasoned, and Mr. Moore, he knew, was always complaining of the difficulties in which its use had involved him.

"Haven't you anyone here, except old Mr. McCann?" he

asked, deftly upending a plank as the shipwright plied his adz to its edge.

"No," Moore grunted. "The miserable Irish fellow they sent me refused to work, and the others were needed to set up the shingles on the roof of the new hospital building. I had to let 'em go, I wasn't given no choice. Hold that plank steady now!"

"Yes, sir, I will." Justin worked willingly for almost half an hour before he nerved himself to make the request he had planned. "You wouldn't let me have the loan of your skiff, would you, Mr. Moore?" he inquired diffidently.

"To go out and meet the *Norfolk*, is it?"

"Yes, sir."

"The answer's no, lad," Moore said with finality. "Give me the hammer—it's over on the larboard side o' this monstrosity, I fancy. But if not, then—"

"It's here," Justin told him. He held out a wooden canister of nails, anticipating the next demand, and asked, as Moore crammed his mouth with half a dozen nails, "Why does the answer have to be no, Mr. Moore? I'd take good care of the skiff, and—"

"You're too small to handle it," Moore retorted uncompromisingly. He plied his hammer dexterously. "Only wants a squall to blow up, and you'd be swamped."

"I wouldn't," Justin argued. "Truly I wouldn't, sir."

"Dead keen, ain't you, lad? Well, I tell you what I'll do. . . ." The hammer thudded. "You give me a couple of hours, and I'll take you out in the skiff meself, seeing you're so set on it. How's that, eh? A bargain?"

It was the best offer he could hope for, and Justin assented gleefully. "It's a bargain, Mr. Moore. Thank you, sir."

"You're a good boy," Tom Moore told him, smiling. "And I owe you a favor. But two hours, mind—and no slackening. Reckon you can sort out that mess o' cordage over there before we knock off for a bite o' dinner?"

"I can sort it," Justin assured him and went at once to work.

They shared the old shipwright's meager repast at midday, and at two o'clock, true to his word, Moore locked up his tools and, with the oars slung over his shoulder, led the way to where his skiff was moored. They rowed out of the cove, giving a wide berth to the newly arrived transport *Minerva*, which was unloading the last of her batch of convicts. All of them were heavily shackled, and Moore growled disparagingly as he watched them being herded into the ship's boats. They were Irish.

Reminded of the spectacle he had witnessed earlier that morning with Frances O'Riordan, Justin described what he had seen and heard. "He was a brave man, that Brian McCormack, standing up to the soldiers the way he did."

"I don't doubt they're brave enough, lad," Tom Moore conceded. "But they're all damned rebels, the lot of 'em, and we can do without their kind here. What this colony needs is skilled and willing workers, not men who have to be flogged into earning their keep. You'll do well to learn a skill, Justin lad, to practice when you're grown."

"I'm going to be a sailor when I'm grown, sir," the little boy said with conviction.

"It's a hard life, seafaring—and I should know, for I spent fifteen years in the king's service." Moore rested on his oars, eyeing his passenger thoughtfully. "I wouldn't recommend it. Why're you so set on going to sea, eh?"

"My father's in the navy," Justin asserted proudly. "Mam told me all about him. He—" The *Norfolk* came into sight at that moment, about two miles down the harbor, and he broke off, gesturing excitedly. "There she is, Mr. Moore—there's the *Norfolk*!"

Moore glanced over his shoulder. "Aye," he agreed. "There she is right enough. And I'll wager that when we come up to her, we'll find her pumps going just like they did when she come across from Norfolk Island. She's an unseaworthy craft, Justin."

"Is she, Mr. Moore?" Justin queried. Eyes shaded with his free hand, he watched the graceful sloop come about on the starboard tack, showing them her counter. "She looks beautiful—like a seabird swooping over the water."

"Her design's fair enough, lad," the shipwright admitted, again pausing in his rowing to glance astern. "It's the timber they built her with that's at fault." He went into technical details, frowning as he spoke and forgetful of the fact that his listener was only a slip of a boy who could scarcely be expected to understand the points he made. He added, resuming his slow, rhythmic strokes of the skiff's oars, "It is a miracle young Mr. Flinders has brought her back safely—I, for one, did not think he would. And if he and Dr. Bass have found the strait they were looking for into the bargain—well, that'll be an even greater miracle, I tell you!"

Justin held his peace, aware that it was seldom of much use to argue with Tom Moore, who, in any case, where ships and the sea were concerned, was usually right. The sloop tacked again, heading toward them now as her big gaff mainsail filled, and her headsail came smartly round. But Justin could hear the pumps going, as his companion had predicted. From her deck Matthew Flinders recognized the fair-haired lad crouching in the stern sheets of the skiff, and he grinned delightedly as he gave the order for his command to bring to.

"Your son's coming aboard, Johnny," he said, his grin widening. "And our friend Tom Moore, who saw fit to prophesy that we'd founder long before we ever had sight or sound of the Bass Strait! We'll take his boat in tow, and George and I will make him eat his words while you make your peace with the boy."

Johnny Broome's face was pale beneath its coating of tan as he lifted Justin onto the sloop's narrow deck. Matt Flinders had made the most of his story of the boy's attempt to stow away when they had left Sydney three months before, and both he and George Bass had amused themselves at Johnny's expense by teasing references to Justin's striking likeness to him. He saw this as he held the boy in his arms and caught his breath, in a momentary surge of emotion, on recognizing the truth of their claim. The boy *was* like him, with his tousled fair hair and blue eyes, and there was a look of Jenny about the curve of his chin and the warm, shy smile.

He left Flinders and Bass to tell old Tom Moore the triumphant story of their circumnavigation of Van Diemen's Land and carried the boy to the lee side of the deck.

"I can walk, sir," Justin protested indignantly, squirming free. "I'm not a child."

"I know you're not, lad," Johnny assured him, "but I want to talk to you." He felt oddly tongue-tied and embarrassed but nerved himself to ask the first, all-important question. "Your name's Justin, is it not—Justin Taggart?"

"Yes, sir." The blue eyes met his in some surprise. "Sir—did you find the strait? Did you sail round Van Diemen's Land?"

"Aye, that we did, Justin . . . and you'll hear all about it in due course. But first—tell me, is your mother's Christian name Jenny?"

More puzzled than ever, Justin nodded. Under Johnny's prompting he described the land grant at Parramatta and conceded that his mother worked the land with the aid of his grandfather and a convict couple named Jardine. There was no mention of a husband, and Johnny asked brusquely, "What of your father, lad? Do you know aught of him?"

"Indeed I do, sir," Justin returned. "My father is serving in the king's navy, fighting the French." With pride, he asserted, "And he's a brave man, sir, and a good one, even though they sent him out here as a convict, like my Mam. My father did what nobody else ever did—he escaped and sailed to Timor in an open boat, much smaller than this sloop, sir."

Unmanly tears ached in Johnny's throat as he heard the boy describe his father's exploits with a wealth of detail that Jenny had somehow contrived to piece together, and even a warning yell from Flinders to haul in the jib had twice to be repeated before he could gather his scattered wits sufficiently to carry out the order.

That this boy was his son he could no longer doubt. He had guessed it when he had rejoined the sloop's crew from the *Nautilus* off Preservation Island, and Flinders had told him that Justin's surname was Taggart. But now, with the boy himself here to confront him in person, he was suddenly a prey to wildly conflicting emotions, uncertain whether to reveal their relationship or to say nothing until he could consult with Jenny.

She had given her son an idealized picture of his father, an image from which, Johnny thought uneasily, he must inevitably fall a long way short. He was no hero, and the voyage to Timor in the stolen cutter—although magnified now into an epic—had, in reality, been no more than an exercise in . . . damn it, in self-preservation! He and the others had gone on because they had had no choice. The risk of dying at sea had been no greater than the risk of being hanged, had they returned to the colony, and to them all it had seemed preferable.

So where was the heroism? Mary Bryant might, perhaps, deserve the heroic accolade for her loyalty to her husband and the selfless care she had given to their two poor little infants, but . . . He sighed, looking down into Justin's small, eager face, seeing the pride in it and hating himself because he, however inadvertently, had inspired it. He and the rest of them had sought only to save their own skins, and they had quarreled bitterly among themselves during the long, perilous voyage when survival had so often been in doubt. He recalled the differences he had had with Jamie Cox and Lilley and the occasion when, losing his temper, he had beaten Nat Lilley into resentful obedience on some unnamed beach off the Great Barrier Reef. And then . . .

"We're nearly in, sir," Justin exclaimed, jerking him from his abstraction. "And just look at the crowd on shore! The governor's there, too, and the kids from school . . . I reckon they'll be green with envy when they see me standing here with you!"

Would they have cause to envy his son, Johnny wondered, or would they pity him if the truth were known? The cheers of the waiting crowd were tumultuous as the battered sloop came to anchor, her pumps still continuing their monotonous, metallic cranking, and a boat put out with Governor Hunter in the stern sheets, his hat raised above his head in salute.

"Man the side, Mr. Broome," Flinders sang out, and moving to obey him, Johnny reached a decision.

He said softly, a hand on the little boy's thin, bony shoulder, "I'd be obliged if you would take me out to visit your mother tomorrow forenoon, Justin. Can you do that?"

"Why, yes, Mr. Broome, of course I can," Justin assented, taken by surprise. "I—I'm sure she'll be honored, sir."

Jenny was on her way to the cabin from the brood mares' paddock when she heard Justin's shrill young voice calling to her. She turned, puzzled by his unexpected arrival when he was supposed to be in school. Her heart missed a beat and then began to pound like a living thing in her breast when she saw and instantly recognized his companion. He had not changed, she thought, although in the smart, brass-buttoned uniform he cut a more dignified figure than he had done in his ragged convict garb. And he was smiling.

"Johnny!" she cried, suddenly so pleased to see him that the intervening years fell away. That was an illusion, she knew; she was no longer a girl, no longer even a good-looking woman, for her illness had taken its toll of her, but . . . this was Johnny Butcher, the father of her son, who all those years ago had loved and sought to wed her. Gathering up her skirts she ran to meet him. "Oh, Johnny, it's so good to see you again!"

"And you, Jenny lass!" He clasped both her hands in his, and Justin, who had been rehearsing his introduction of the visitor, stared from one to the other in ludicrous astonishment.

"You know each other!" he exclaimed when he could find his tongue. "Mam, you *know* each other! But Mr. Broome never said, and I thought . . ." He broke off as comprehension slowly dawned. "Mam, he's—Mam, is he . . . is he *my father*?"

Jenny's gaze, mutely questioning, met that of the new arrival. She read his assent in both eyes and smile and answered, after a barely perceptible hesitation, "Yes, Justin, this is your father."

There was a moment of uncertain silence as they both waited for the boy's reaction, but then the silence was broken by Justin himself. He held out a small hand, and as Johnny took it he said gravely, "I'm pleased you've come back, sir. You . . ." He did not finish whatever he had meant to say but let out an excited and undeniably triumphant yell. "I must tell Gran'pa Watt! *He'll* be pleased . . . and just wait till I tell the boys at school. They won't have to call me a Currency kid anymore, will they?"

He was off as fast as his legs would carry him in search of old Watt, and Johnny said, looking down at his boots, "You didn't marry then, lass?"

"No," Jenny answered, absurdly conscious of the wave of shamed color that flooded her cheeks. "No, I didn't marry."

"No more did I." Still he did not look at her. "What of Munday, Jenny?"

"He's dead," Jenny told him, her voice devoid of expression. "The soldiers shot him the night Justin was born—they claimed he was trying to escape. But he wasn't escaping—poor fellow, he went to fetch the midwife."

"He was no loss to you, was he?"

"No," she admitted. "No loss, really. But I was sorry for him, Johnny."

"You always had too soft a heart," Johnny gently reproached her. He glanced about him, taking in the cabin, twenty yards away, with its flourishing garden, the brood mares with their foals in the paddock beside the creek, and, in the distance, the cleared ground from which a wheat crop had recently been harvested. "You've done what you said you would," he observed. "You've made your home here. Is this land yours, Jenny?"

"Yes." She looked up at him then, still a trifle uneasy in his company, still unsure of his motives in coming to seek her out. She would have to tell him how she had acquired her land and tell him about Tim Dawson, too, but . . . there was time enough for that, and Tim was married to Henrietta now. He . . . Johnny reached for her hand.

He said, a catch in his voice, "It's a long time since I asked you to wed me, Jenny lass—and you refused me then. Would you still say no to me if I were to ask you now?" He grinned and it was the old devil-may-care grin she remembered so well. "We've a son, and by the looks of him, he's one we can both be proud of and . . . devil take it, lass, I want to claim him as my son and give him my name! My *own* name of Broome, not the one on the felons' roll. What do you say, Jenny? Will you wed a seafaring man who's kept your memory in his heart for a tidy number of years? Aye"—he drew her to him, the grin fading—"and it must be said . . . a man who came looking for you, and then when he got here, lacked the courage to seek you out for fear you'd changed."

"I have changed, Johnny," Jenny whispered.

"No," Johnny denied. "I don't believe you have. From what the boy's told me of you on the way up here, I reckon you're not much different from the lass you used to be. A few years older, that's all. . . . But we're both that, aren't we?" He held her close, and Jenny knew that there was only one answer she could give him, for her own sake and not only for Justin's.

"I'm pleased you've come back," she told him, using Justin's words. "So pleased, and . . . I'll be proud to wed you, Johnny. I'll be truly proud!"

She was holding her head high as they walked together to the cabin, with her hand in his.

BOOK THREE

A
Host of
Good Thieves . . .

CHAPTER XVIII

The rhyming lampoons that had so enraged John Hunter during the last years of his governorship had started again—but aimed now, more vindictively than ever, against himself, Philip King thought . . . and for the same underlying reason.

Like his predecessor and friend he had endeavored to curb the trading activities of his military officers, and the corps had reacted to his efforts precisely as they had to Hunter's—with closed ranks and open defiance. And with venomous ridicule in the form of crude "pipes," which they saw to it were widely circulated.

Frowning, he read one of the sheets that Richard Atkins had brought to his attention.

> My power to make great,
> O'er the laws and the state—
> Commander-in-chief I'll assume!
> Local rank, I persist,
> Is in my own fist,
> To doubt it who shall dare presume?
>
> On Monday, keep shop,
> In two hours' time stop,
> To relax from such *Kingly* fatigue,
> To pillage the store,
> and rob government more
> Than a host of good thieves—by intrigue!

It was—or purported to be—the work of an uneducated person, and the cartoon of a bloated officer in naval uniform dishing out government stores to which outrageous price labels were attached was, to say the least, a gross impertinence.

Philip King bristled but forced himself to read the second of his traducer's attempts to discredit him in the public mind. This took the form of a long, ill-scanning poem, and the final verse summed up its sentiments.

> The brig be damned, the crew and all the meat!
> Fresh beef and sheep are what I like to eat.
> A Royal Mandate brings them from Toongabbe—
> Expecting only what are sick and scabby.

The foul thing was printed, the governor realized; and since there was only one printing press in the colony, and that the property of government, it was evident that some kind of official double-dealing must have taken place to enable the copies to be made.

Well, these and some other equally unpleasant examples should be sent to the colonial office with his next dispatch, he decided, and before heaven he would see that the officer responsible for their distribution was swiftly brought to trial and made to answer for his insolence. His identity was no secret. This, he knew, was Macarthur's work although his crony, Captain Anthony Kemp, was in charge of the press and would therefore have to be the one to face charges.

He expelled his breath in an exasperated sigh. Hunter had warned him that while John Macarthur was the evil influence and the organizer of the campaign of vilification, he was careful to keep in the background—"Well out of the line of fire," as Hunter had expressed it—so that it was seldom possible to take action against him. Macarthur used the law for his own ends, yet never fell foul of it himself—a tactic that up till now had paid him handsomely.

"He's a dangerous rogue," Arthur Phillip had said when King had visited the colony's first governor while on sick leave in England. "And John Hunter will need all the support you can give him when you go back, Philip." He had said much more, King recalled, and offered much sage advice, but neither of them had, of course, anticipated that he—King, not Hunter—would now be acting as governor of the colony and by virtue of his new office be cast for the role of Macarthur's chief opponent.

Philip King repeated his sigh. He had come back to Sydney in April 1800, having taken a lengthy and uncomfortable passage in the transport *Speedy,* which, belying her name, had taken more than six months to reach her destination.

He had found poor Hunter in a state bordering on desperation, induced as much by the home government's failure to support his authority as by the corps officers' opposition to it.

"Macarthur defies me at every turn, Philip," Hunter had asserted wearily. "And the rest of them dance to whatever tune he calls, with the sole exception of William Paterson, who is, I think, a well disposed and honest man. But he lacks the strength of character to go against Macarthur."

He had talked bitterly of the devious methods to which the corps officers had resorted in order to render his task impossible and, King recalled, had stated with conviction that Macarthur had gone to unprecedented lengths to bring about his dismissal.

"The damned fellow has friends well placed in the colonial office," Hunter went on. "Through them he has contrived to destroy His Grace of Portland's confidence in me—to the extent that my only recourse is now to return to London in order that I may defend my reputation against the slurs he has cast upon it. You, God willing, may be able to succeed where I have failed, Philip. At least you will start with Paterson's friendship and a full awareness of what and whom you are up against. My considered advice to you is that you find some excuse to send Macarthur away from here—home to face charges if you can contrive sufficient reason to do so. With his damned intrigues he is a danger to any governor, and if he's not sent packing, he will one day set this colony in flames. . . . That is my greatest fear."

Hunter had gone, a broken and disheartened man, in September, taking passage in H.M.S. *Buffalo*, and with him the Reverend Richard Johnson and his family and his nephew and aide, William Kent.

The corps had given him a royal send-off, with an arrogant parade in full strength, the firing of salutes from the new battery that had been established on the point where Baneelon had once had his hut, and the ironic cheers of officers and men ringing in his ears. Few in the watching crowds had been aware that on relinquishing his office John Hunter had called out his enemy, but Macarthur, devious as ever, had refused the challenge, offering instead a meaningless apology for "any offense he might unwittingly have given the late governor."

Philip King rose from his chair and limped to the window. His gout troubled him greatly and, he reminded himself wryly, at times rendered him exceedingly short of temper. His wife, gentle, kindly creature that she was, did her best to soothe and cosset him. Indeed, were it not for her restraining influence and the care she took to restrict so many of his more burdensome callers to the times when he was best able to cope with them, he, too, might well have flung a challenge at one of his tormentors, meeting with no more success than poor John Hunter.

But Macarthur would make a mistake, sooner or later, he felt certain—no man was infallible—and when he did, that would be the time to take Hunter's advice and send the unprincipled rogue packing. In the meantime . . . There was a soft knock on the door, and his wife came in bearing a tray that she set on his desk with a smiling invitation to him to drink a glass of porter and sample the cakes she had made for him.

"Rock cakes, Philip dear—you used to say you liked them. And you must eat, you know."

"Yes. Yes, of course. Thank you, my dearest. It was good of you to take the trouble."

The governor resumed his seat, making a determined effort not to let her see that he was limping. She missed her children, he knew—young Phillip, named after his old chief, and little Anna Maria, both of whom they had left behind in England to enable them to be properly educated. The two were with good and reliable friends who would take excellent care of them, but all the same . . . King laid an affectionate hand on his wife's arm. She had their two adopted sons, Norfolk and Sydney, and her babies, the three-year-old Elizabeth, and the tiny, frail Mary; but her social life was inevitably affected by his own, somewhat strained relations with most of the corps officers.

"It is shameful," Anna King said, her quick intuition enabling her to guess at his thoughts. "The way these—these gentlemen see fit to use you." She glimpsed the lampoons, and her lips tightened in distaste. "More of the scurrilous things, Philip?"

"Yes," he admitted, biting into one of the rock cakes without appetite. "More of them."

"Can you not put a stop to them? Can you not make sure that whoever is responsible for them is reprimanded?"

"I can have Captain Kemp and Lieutenant Bayley court-martialed," the governor answered wearily, "and probably the insubordinate Lieutenant Hobby as well. But it will profit me little if I do, since the court that tries them will consist of their fellow officers." He forced a smile. "These cakes are deuced good, my dear."

"Please, Philip," his wife begged, her smooth cheeks unhappily flushed. "Do not try to spare my feelings. I know what you are going through, and I saw what Captain Hunter had to endure. It is—oh, it's quite monstrous! You are the governor—these creatures who call themselves king's officers owe you obedience and respect, yet they give you neither . . . and they publish these!" She gestured indignantly to the lampoons. "There are no bounds to their insolence."

"Or to their avarice, my dear," Governor King put in, his tone dry. "I stand in the way of their profits, and—excepting William Paterson—God knows they are making profits! Before I sent him to Norfolk Island, Major Foveaux sold his land and his stock for two thousand pounds sterling. And the buyer, the wealthy Captain Macarthur, paid that sum without a qualm."

"I regard the Patersons as friends," Anna King said, "as you well know, Philip. But surely, surely it should be possible to have the corps replaced by a—a reliable regiment?"

"John Hunter will do all in his power to recommend such a measure to the Colonial Office, and I have Arthur Phillip's promise that he will lend his backing to the recommendation," her husband assured her. "I can only pray that the home government will agree to it, but the war makes heavy demands on what you are pleased to call 'reliable regiments.'"

"And on reliable naval officers and their ships," Anna King exclaimed with more than a hint of bitterness in her normally quiet, controlled voice. "It was a sad day for the colony when Captain Waterhouse and Mr. Flinders went home."

It was indeed, the governor reflected glumly. She left him with an apologetic, "I think I hear Baby crying, dear," and he took a draft of porter and went on munching the hard little cakes without enjoyment. Young Flinders and his friend George Bass were a great loss—and not only because of the loyal support they had given to both Hunter and himself. Their voyages of discovery had been of immense value. Their exploration of Van Diemen's Land had resulted in the prospect of founding a new settlement there; one that, with the accessible harbors, good rivers, and equable climate, might well replace that on Norfolk Island, should the convict population expand. Landings on Norfolk were difficult, as he knew only too well, and it was small and really too distant to serve the purpose for which it had originally been designed.

It would go against the grain for him to abandon the island—he had been founder and first governor, but . . . the convict ships kept coming, to spew out their cargoes of felons indiscriminately on Sydney's wharfs. There had to be a suitable place where the recalcitrant and the rebellious could safely be confined, and Norfolk could hold and feed few more. He drained his porter and pushed the remaining cakes on the plate away, swearing under his breath as he again felt a savage twinge of pain in his gouty foot.

Flinders's last voyage in the *Norfolk* had been made before Hunter's departure and at the late governor's behest, and that, too, had been valuable. Without Bass—who had taken passage home to recoup his health—young Matthew had taken a master's mate named Broome to assist in navigation. It had not been until their return six weeks later that Broome's identity had been made known to him. Despite his pain, the new governor smiled. . . . For Broome, it seemed, had been retracing the route he had taken with the Bryant party, ten years before, when they had made their escape to Timor in a stolen cutter. And a good job he and Flinders had made of the charts they had brought back after following Cook's route north from Port Jackson to Moreton Bay. Measuring and surveying, sounding and investigating rivers and areas of coast, they had filled gaps in the original sketchy charts made when Cook's *Endeavour* had sailed hurriedly toward the strait named after her. They had completed Kent's survey in Coal River, confirming its possibilities as the source of good-quality coal and as an excellent natural harbor. Hunter had dispatched the first nucleus of a working convict settlement there before his departure.

Made restless once more by his pain, Governor King

heaved himself out of his chair and again crossed to the window to look out over the anchorage in the cove. The *Porpoise*, the naval vessel that had now replaced Waterhouse's splendid *Reliance*, swung to her anchor in the light, offshore breeze, the duty watch of her seamen engaged in drying out canvas after her long voyage. The *Francis* was moored beyond her, listing heavily from the pounding she had taken on passage from Norfolk Island with her foremast sprung, but the *Norfolk* had returned in comparatively good condition, having weathered the same storm. Her temporary commander, Flinders's friend Broome, had evidently handled her well . . . or else had been exceptionally lucky. And he, at least, was staying in the colony—he had married the Taggart girl, of whom, as one of his "Garden Women," Arthur Phillip had thought highly. She had a grant in the Parramatta area, but despite his marriage Broome had stated his intention to continue to serve at sea when required, and he would be useful . . . prime seamen always were, in virtually any capacity.

But, as King's wife had remarked, it had been a sad day for the colony when Waterhouse and Flinders had departed for home, their last service a spirited refusal to permit an innocent emancipist named Isaac Nichols—who had incurred Macarthur's displeasure—to be condemned on perjured evidence by the military court, of which both had been members. With James Grant, then commander of the brig *Lady Nelson*, they had stood out against the three corps members and the then judge advocate, Richard Dore—now dead of a fever and succeeded once more by Atkins—and the sentence of fourteen years' transportation to Norfolk Island that had been imposed. They . . . A knock on the door interrupted his train of thought.

"Come in, come in," the governor called out testily and stumped back to his desk, wincing as he caught his foot on the leg of his chair.

"Mr. Atkins, Your Excellency," his secretary, William Chapman, announced. Unbidden, he placed a bottle of Madeira and two glasses on the desk and withdrew.

Richard Atkins came storming in, his long, lugubrious face aflame with indignation, his hands trembling visibly. The corps had opposed his reappointment, but the Colonial Office had confirmed it, and Atkins remained judge advo-

cate—to the governor's relief. He waved the visitor to a
seat, and filling a glass, passed it to him across the desk.
Atkins drained it thirstily and then burst out, "They have
triumphed again, sir!"

King stared at him stonily. "Are you telling me that
John Marshall has been adjudged guilty of the—damme,
the preposterous charges brought against him?"

"That is precisely what I am telling you, sir," Atkins
answered. "Only Mr. Grant and I dissented from the
court's findings. The five corps officers brought in a verdict
of guilty."

"Dear God!" the governor's control was shaken. John
Marshall, a naval lieutenant, had earlier quarreled with
Macarthur and, considering himself insulted by accusations
of dishonesty leveled against him, had challenged his accuser to a duel. The challenge had been accepted, but Captain Abbot, Macarthur's second, had refused to proceed
with the duel on the grounds that Marshall's appointed second—a young storekeeper named Jefferies—was not his social equal, according to the rules of dueling.

Despite Marshall's assurance that he would accept any
second the two corps officers chose to name, neither Abbott nor Macarthur had presented themselves at the time
and place appointed. Furious at what he claimed was Macarthur's cowardice, John Marshall had somewhat foolishly
taken the law into his own hands and made what Abbott
asserted was an unprovoked assault on his person, accompanied by threats against his principal.

And Macarthur, predictably, had charged him with assault, demanding that he be put on trial before the criminal
court.

"Mr. Marshall," Atkins went on, "objected to the five
corps officers hearing the case against him on the grounds
of prejudice—grounds, sir, that I fully supported—but his
objection was summarily overruled." He looked down at
his empty glass, his expression woebegone, and the governor refilled it resignedly. Colonel Paterson, he recalled, was
one of the members of the court—only James Grant had
represented the navy. Small wonder if Marshall *had* objected to its composition. If the corps closed ranks, as they
usually did, in support of John Macarthur, he could not
hope for a fair hearing.

"Pray continue, sir," King invited, feeling rage catch at his throat but making a great effort to control his voice. "Give me chapter and verse, if you please."

The judge advocate shuffled the papers he took from his brief case. "I instructed the clerk to take down Mr. Macarthur's address to the court verbatim," he said. "And I have to tell you, sir, that I have never heard so extraordinary a combination of malice and exaggeration . . . even from Macarthur. Ah, here it is. . . ." He found the papers for which he had been searching. "Permit me to read it to Your Excellency."

"By all means do so, Mr. Atkins."

In a flat, expressionless voice Atkins began his recital. "Referring to Mr. Marshall, sir, Macarthur said, and I quote: 'Let me entreat you to look upon this man, view his gigantic stature and . . . imagine that you see him advancing, as it has been sworn to you he did, intoxicated with fury, breathing mischief, and you will be able to form some idea of the danger of my situation.' "

A grunt of disgust, which he could not suppress, escaped the governor's tightly pursed lips. "He spoke in such terms, for God's sake?"

Richard Atkins raised his faintly bloodshot eyes from the paper in his hand. "These are the clerk's notes, sir, taken down as the words were spoken. And there is more." He went on reading, " 'Who is there who saw his advance, armed as he was, and who had witnessed or heard of his attack on Captain Abbott, but supposed I must immediately be crushed beneath his arm? Such was my own expectation and great was my astonishment to observe my drawn sword instantly operating on this ferocious savage, like the wand of a necromancer or the talisman of a magician to see it, in a moment, taming him from the excess of offensive fury into unconditional surrender and coward-like submission. To find him suddenly frightened into the attitude of a suppliant, with his weapon dropped to the ground and asking in a tremulous tone, of mingled terror and entreaty, whether I would run him through the body—' "

"Enough!" Governor King interrupted, sickened. "I can listen to no more of such—such unmitigated hypocrisy! D'you mean to tell me that the court—that Colonel Paterson permitted Macarthur to address them in such terms?"

"They did, sir."

"Dear God in heaven! And what reply—presuming they allowed him to reply—did Marshall make?"

"I have a note of that too, sir," the judge advocate said, again searching through his papers. "Lieutenant Marshall stated, and I quote: 'I cannot avoid expressing my astonishment at the effrontery of Captain Macarthur in my presence, in the presence of any man of honor, attempting to justify his late conduct. He would fain persuade you, gentlemen, that I am the coward, but you know perfectly well from your own and from the world's knowledge of that man, and the circumstances which have appeared before you, as well as those upon record in the history of this colony, which of the two of us shrunk from his engagement . . . I will say from his claim, if a man so acting *has* any claim, to honor.' "

"Evidence concerning Macarthur's failure to meet his challenge was before the court?" King questioned.

"Yes, indeed, sir. Mr. Marshall presented that evidence most ably."

"And they still found against him?"

"He was found guilty of assaulting Captain Abbott, sir. In the case of Captain Macarthur, a special finding was made to the effect that Lieutenant Marshall's conduct was threatening, but the court declined to determine whether such conduct amounted in law to a punishable assault. The sentence—"

"Ah!" There was a wrathful gleam in the governor's dark eyes. "And what sentence did they have the gall to pass, Mr. Atkins?"

Atkins swallowed hard. "A year's imprisonment and a fine of fifty pounds, sir."

Unable to contain himself, Philip King got to his feet, cursing blasphemously and oblivious to pain as he paced from desk to window and back again to his chair. "I shall remit that sentence if I have to," he grated. "But it will leave poor Marshall with an undeserved stain upon his character if I do. Mr. Atkins, I want the case reopened, and—"

"On what grounds, sir?" the judge advocate ventured uncertainly. "The court can only be convened in order to hear fresh evidence, and—"

"Then for pity's sake, man, reconvene it for that purpose! The whole trial was a damned travesty of justice, and you know it! Macarthur should never have been allowed to bring such charges in the first place."

"He claimed that he had brought them on your—er—on your personal advice, sir," Atkins volunteered. He avoided the governor's eye, but his glance at the bottle between them was ignored.

"In court?"

"No, sir, to me—er—to me privately."

"So he seeks to involve me in his dirty dispute, does he? Well, he shall not, the devil take his impudence!" King contrived, somehow, to restrain his rising fury. He remembered other cases and the depths to which Macarthur had delved in his attempt to influence the courts. He leaned across the desk, reaching for the small brass bell with which he summoned his secretary and ringing it impatiently.

When Chapman entered, he said curtly, "I wish to see Colonel Paterson on a matter of urgency. Send someone to inform him, if you please."

"Does Your Excellency wish to see him at once?" Chapman queried.

The governor relented. William Paterson was a friend, he reminded himself, a loyal and trusted friend, and ever since their early Norfolk Island days, his kindly little Scottish wife had been Anna's closest companion and confidante. It would be a grave error to regard Paterson in the same light as Macarthur or to blame him for what was not his doing. He shook his bewigged head. "No, not at once, boy. Request that he and Mistress Paterson should dine with us . . . and see that my wife is told "

"Very good, sir." Chapman sped off on his errand, and after another vain glance at his empty glass, Judge Advocate Atkins rose reluctantly to take his leave.

"See to it, Mr. Atkins," the governor called after him, "that the court is reconvened tomorrow morning. I want the matter settled without delay."

"I will do my best, sir," Atkins promised, but his voice lacked conviction. He had crossed swords with John Mac-

arthur too often in the past to be sanguine as to the result
of any demand he might make on the governor's behalf.
Against all the odds, Macarthur had won the verdict he
wanted, and he was not the man to permit his victory to
elude him.

"I consider, sir," John Macarthur said forcefully, "that
this affair touches our regimental honor."

"It is a delicate matter," Colonel Paterson conceded.
"But, in my view, one best forgotten."

"It is more than that—the devil take it, Colonel, we *cannot* just forget it! It was the unanimous decision of the
court that Marshall's case should *not* be reopened." Macarthur was working himself up into a fine rage, his pendulous lower lip aggressively pouting, and he waved aside
his commanding officer's protest with the contempt he
clearly considered that it deserved. "That infernal drunken
blackguard Atkins uttered no objection, nor did Grant,
so technically the decision was unanimous. Besides—"

"You are splitting hairs, John," the colonel put in.

"I'm not. But if you insist, the decision was by a majority of five to two. There was no fresh evidence—therefore,
legally, our conviction and the sentence we imposed should
stand. But the governor, it seems, considers himself above
the law. He has no right to quash the sentence, but that's
what he's done. That ruffian Marshall goes free!"

"Oh, come now," Paterson protested. "As governor he
had every right."

"After *he* advised me to bring charges?" Macarthur
countered, his tone cold.

"I find that rather hard to credit. Oh, no doubt it suited
your book to imply in court that the governor offered you
such advice, John. But be good enough, if you please—"
Paterson's tone was equally cold, "to spare *me* your his-
trionics."

"Are you calling me a liar, Colonel?"

"Oh, for the Lord's sweet sake, of course I'm not! But
can you substantiate your claim?"

John Macarthur smiled. It was an odd smile, Paterson
thought, wholly lacking in amusement. "I put it in writing
to His Excellency, and I assure you, if he denies having
advised me, then he is a liar."

"What does it matter to you, in any event?" Paterson asked reasonably. "Marshall is leaving the colony—the incident is over, finished, and as I told you, it is surely best forgotten."

"*You* may forget it, but I shall not. It was I who suffered the damned fellow's assault, and Ted Abbott with me. And," the younger man added with emphasis, "it was *my* honor he impugned. He implied publicly that I was afraid to face him, did he not?"

Wisely, Colonel Paterson did not argue the point. John Macarthur, as he knew from bitter experience, was an implacable enemy. His anger was always controlled, and expressed not in curses but in calculated vituperation, designed to wound and to provoke those against whom it was directed. But, devil take the fellow, he must not be permitted to cause dissension in the regiment, which was clearly what he was endeavoring to do. In the absence on leave of George Johnstone, Macarthur was second-in-command of the corps, and unhappily he had most of the officers—and virtually all the other ranks—behind him, because he put money into their pockets . . . and rum in their bellies.

But . . . The colonel drew himself up to his full impressive height. *He* was in command, his authority not to be questioned by a mere captain. However wealthy his damned trading ventures had made him, John Macarthur was still a comparatively junior officer and, as such, subject to military discipline.

"I've heard enough," he snapped. "The matter is closed. You—"

"No, it is *not* closed." The interruption was sharp, and the manner of it verging on insubordination. Macarthur went on, still in the same sharp, dictatorial tone, "As I mentioned to you just now, I consider that the affair touches our regimental honor, Colonel . . . and my brother officers agree with that conclusion. No—" as Paterson attempted to speak. "Hear me out, if you please. Governor King has overstepped the mark. In reversing the findings of a legally constituted court he has abused his powers and, as I said, set himself above the law—aided and abetted by Atkins. The officers of the regiment are therefore resolved to ostracize the damned governor. Save in the direct course of our military duty, none of us will address him, and neither we nor our wives will, in future, accept invitations to Government House. Do I make myself clear, sir?"

He paused, letting his words sink in, and Colonel Paterson stared at him in disbelief, so angry that he was momentarily deprived of words. Before he could find his tongue, Macarthur said, with icy deliberation, "Since the honor of the regiment is at stake, I am deputed by the other officers to request that you, sir, will join us in this expression of our united disapprobation of Governor King's action."

"By God, sir, I will not!" For all his determination not to allow himself to be provoked, Paterson was shaking with barely restrained fury. "Who are you, that you set yourself up as an arbiter of what does or does not concern the honor of the regiment under my command? Answer me that, sir!"

"The role has been forced upon me," Macarthur returned smoothly, "since you, as commanding officer, appear reluctant to assume it. I can only in fairness suppose that your enjoyment of Captain King's friendship is the reason for your reluctance, sir. But would His Excellency continue to invite you to dine with him were he to be made privy to your correspondence with Mr. Marsden—answer *me* that, sir, if you can!"

William Paterson lost his temper. "You are an insolent rogue, Macarthur!" he stormed, recalling with dismay the possibility that one of the letters he had exchanged with the Reverend Samuel Marsden might be open to misinterpretation. He *had* written in critical terms of the governor. . . . Furiously he returned to the attack. "A perfidious villain! Even in this regiment, which is officered by damned tradesmen, who have never heard a shot fired in anger, you are unworthy to hold a commission . . . and I shall see to it that yours is forfeited with as little delay as possible. I'll see you broken, sir, by God I will!"

"Will you, by God, sir!" Macarthur sneered. "Aided, no doubt by Marsden and the governor!"

"You are insubordinate. You—"

"There are no witnesses, Colonel. Without them you could not prove any charges concerning my conduct here this morning. But"—coolly, a smile again playing about his lips, John Macarthur took a glove from his pocket and flicked it insultingly across his commanding officer's flushed cheek—"I am calling you out, sir. I trust you will receive my second when he calls upon you. The choice of weapons is, of course, yours."

His parting thrust, as he turned insolently to take his leave, was doubly wounding to the corps's commandant as, he decided ruefully, it was intended to be.

"I fear, Colonel, that you may have to seek for a second from the ranks of the navy, since I take leave to doubt that you will find any officer in your regiment who is willing to act for you on this occasion," Macarthur said. He bowed. "This is an engagement from which you need have no fear that I shall shrink. I give you good day, sir."

It had been so theatrical—matching the man's performance at the Marshall trial—that, when he had calmed down sufficiently to think about the encounter, William Paterson decided that the whole thing had been deliberately planned, down to the last detail. Macarthur's demand that he end his friendship with the governor, his insults and accusations—even the single glove he had taken from his coat pocket were means to an end, one of the devious ploys in which he now frequently engaged.

He, more than anyone else, had brought about Governor Hunter's recall. Was his intention now to bring about King's? Paterson's dark brows met in a worried frown. His first impulse was to seek out the governor and inform him of all that had passed between Macarthur and himself, but he dismissed the thought as soon as it entered his head. Dueling between officers of His Majesty's forces was officially forbidden; it took place, of course, but of necessity in secret, and if he informed the governor of the challenge he had received, his action might be misconstrued . . . even, perhaps, regarded as cowardice on his part. There was Marshall's example before him; he, poor devil, had been the unhappy victim of one of Macarthur's challenges. Had he not complained to the court that John Macarthur had sought to persuade them that *he* was the coward? What had he said? Paterson's frown deepened as he recalled the words: *You know perfectly well from your own and from the world's knowledge . . . which of the two of us shrunk from his engagement. . . .*

Yes, he knew now, but at the time and to his shame he

had believed Macarthur's account of the affair and had concurred in the verdict.

Well, there should be no shrinking from this engagement, by heaven, and there was no need to warn Philip King who knew, if anyone did, of what his enemies were capable. The duel, provided Macarthur did not shrink from it, might well be the means the governor was seeking to rid himself of his most dangerous and resourceful enemy.

Jack Boddice, his commanding officer reflected vengefully, like the majority of his comrades in arms, had never gone into battle against his country's foes, and he might yet regret this morning's unprovoked challenge. He himself, as a young ensign in the famous "Scotch Regiment"—the 73d—could recall with pride the campaigns he had fought under Sir Eyre Coote in the Carnatic. He had been in action at Porto Novo, Pollilore, and Sholinghur against the French-officered Mahratta armies of Hyder Ali and Tipu Sultan, and had seen the Mysore ruler's defeat at Arnee. For God's sake, he told himself, what had he to fear from a damned tradesman's son . . . a rogue who should never have been permitted to hold a king's commission?

But the duel, when it took place soon after dawn in a small, tree-girt clearing a few hundred yards from the Parramatta road, did not turn out as Colonel Paterson had confidently expected. Macarthur made his appearance at the agreed hour, swaggering arrogantly beside his second, Captain John Piper of the corps, who carried a velvet-lined case containing a pair of matched dueling pistols. These he offered for cursory inspection, with a clipped, "I trust these weapons are satisfactory to you, sir," and then, without waiting for a reply, he gave the case to Macarthur. Both officers turned their backs and, suspecting that—contrary to the accepted laws of dueling—Macarthur was loading his own pistols, the colonel started to voice a protest, but thinking better of it, shrugged and accepted one of the proffered pieces in constrained silence.

For the sake of secrecy it had been agreed that—apart from Dr. Harris, the corps's surgeon—only their two seconds should be witnesses to the engagement, and Paterson experienced an odd uneasiness as he met Harris's anxious eyes. His heartbeat quickened and he felt bile rising in his throat, but it was too late now to back down; his honor demanded that he see the miserable affair through to its conclusion.

The distance between himself and his antagonist was paced out, both turned on the shout command, pistols cocked. Paterson aimed for his opponent's left arm and missed, the ball falling short. An instant later he found himself spread-eagled on the camp ground, coughing up blood and conscious of excruciating pain as he sought vainly to draw breath.

Surgeon Harris ran over and dropped to his knees beside him, turning him carefully onto his back.

"God in heaven, Macarthur!" the colonel heard him exclaim. "You've killed him!"

Those were the last words he heard clearly, but as a black mist blotted out the dawn sky, the sound of a laugh penetrated his agony, and he heard—or imagined he heard—John Macarthur say coldly, "He would have betrayed us to his friend King. His wife wrote as much to mine. Dammit, I saw the letter . . . *and* what he wrote to Samuel Marsden! He . . ."

The voice faded into silence and with it, momentarily, his pain.

Richard Atkins, supported by the colony's surgeon general, Dr. William Balmain, brought news of the duel to the governor. Both men had suffered at Macarthur's hands—Balmain, in his capacity as a civil magistrate, as a result of the corps officers' virtual monopoly of the administration of justice—and their account of the affair was, the governor expected, heavily biased in Colonel Paterson's favor. Nevertheless, the facts were beyond dispute, and he listened with growing satisfaction and relief, realizing that John Macarthur had finally made the mistake for which he had prayed. It was a pity that it had had to be at poor William Paterson's expense, but . . .

"How is Colonel Paterson?" he asked, addressing Balmain.

The doctor spread his blunt, capable hands in a resigned gesture. "He is very severely wounded, sir—the ball struck him full in the chest, and there is hemorrhage from the lungs. Fortunately young Harris was present, and he acted most promptly in obtaining a wagon from the Brickfields and conveying him at once to the hospital. I do not despair of the colonel's life, sir, but only the next twenty-four hours will tell."

"It is tana—tantamount to murder, sir," Atkins asserted. He had fortified himself with a liberal dose of brandy, the governor guessed, before coming here, and his voice was slurred. "Will Your—Your Exshell—Your Excellency give me authority to order Captain Macarthur's arrest on that charge?"

Giving careful consideration to his reply, Governor King said firmly, "Certainly Captain Macarthur is to be placed under arrest, Mr. Atkins . . . and with him the two officers who acted as seconds. But the charge must be for engaging in a duel, contrary to king's regulations and the Articles of War, and all three should be held in house arrest only. They are not to be confined in the jail with common felons."

"But surely you will order Macarthur's trial in the criminal court, sir?" the judge advocate insisted, waxing indignant. "If Colonel Paterson dies—"

"God willing, the skill of the surgeons may save him," King countered. "And even were it not to do so—which God forbid—do you for one moment imagine that the officers of his regiment, who constitute the majority of our judiciary, would administer justice impartially were their patron, who is the source of their prosperity, to be brought to trial either by a court-martial or in the criminal court? No." He answered his own question, aware that the opportunity to rid the colony of John Macarthur's evil influence was, at long last, there for the taking. "*No,*" he repeated, with heavy emphasis. "Captain Macarthur shall be sent to England to stand his trial there."

"A wise decision, sir," Dr. Balmain applauded, a gleam in his eyes. "Without wishing to appear vindictive, I have just come from William Paterson's sickbed. I have witnessed his pain and the extreme distress of the gentle and affectionate lady who is his wife, and by heaven, sir, I feel most strongly that Macarthur, who is the cause of both, should not escape retribution. And he might well do so if he were permitted to remain here."

"He'll demand a court-martial," Atkins predicted glumly. He hiccoughed, and the governor flashed him a reproving glance.

"He may make what demands he pleases, Mr. Atkins. I assure you, I shall be deaf to all of them. Captain Macarthur shall be held in house arrest until a ship can be found to remove him. And," King added, "I shall see to it that the Colonial Office is fully informed of every detail of his misconduct during the time he has been here. My report shall be delivered to His Grace of Portland by Lieutenant Grant, and I shall arrange his passage in the *Anna Josepha* when she sails for the Cape."

Beginning at last to appreciate the governor's strategy, Atkins, too, expressed his approval.

"Shall I give instructions for the arrests now, sir?" he offered.

"Without delay," Governor King confirmed. He rose to his feet, signifying dismissal. "And I shall compile my dispatch with equal celerity."

True to his word he started work on it at once and, during the next week, had little time to spare for anything else. Save for two visits to Colonel Paterson he was at his desk all day and far into the night, and even when the surgeons pronounced the commandant's life to be out of danger, Governor King permitted himself no respite.

Aided by his secretary and the judge advocate, he copied out court records and supported his charges against John Macarthur with irrefutable and fully documented evidence. To preface the bulky report he wrote, under the date of November 5, 1801:

I have no other means of restoring and insuring the tranquility of this colony than by sending Captain John Macarthur, of the New South Wales Corps, to England under arrest.

From the circumstances of the officers of his corps being so much involved in the events I have detailed, recourse could not be had to the General Court-Martial demanded by Captain Macarthur. Therefore, as he did not choose to quit his arrest unless tried by a General Court-Martial, I judged it necessary and indispensable to direct that he be sent to England, there to answer for his conduct in the preceding transactions, and more particularly on the representations I have very reluctantly been obliged to make—viz., of his having endeavored to create a dissension between me and Lieutenant Colonel Paterson.

Should any further proof be wanting of the turbulent and restless conduct of Captain Macarthur beyond what are mentioned in the accompanying statement and proofs, I must require that the evidence of the late Governors Phillip and Hunter be procured which, with many documents now in the Secretary of State's Office, will fully bear out my assurance that Captain Macarthur's misconduct has not been confined to the present moment.

Of Piper, he wrote:

Captain Piper's conduct in going out with an officer against their commanding officer, and against a man who had always acted towards him as a father and friend, and departing so much from the rules of propriety—if I may so term it—as to allow Captain Macarthur to load his own pistols, were circumstances that excited my most serious reprimand. As he had nothing to offer in reply, I ordered him to return to his confinement and prepare for being sent to England.

The lengthy task finally completed and copies made of all the documentary evidence, the governor ordered the papers placed in his dispatch box, and under his personal supervision Atkins and Chapman locked the box, placing it for safety in a locked drawer in his office.

Atkins, ever pessimistic, observed when this had been done, "This evidence of his guilt will ensure that Macarthur never returns here, sir, and he's well aware of it. I've heard a rumor—which may, of course, prove false—that he's offered a large reward to anyone who will steal it."

"You've *what?*" Philip King stared at him in shocked incredulity, and when the judge advocate repeated his assertion, raised his eyes to heaven.

"I swear not even Macarthur would stoop so low!"

"The rumor is very persistent, sir," the young secretary, Chapman, said diffidently.

"Rumors in Sydney are always persistent," the governor returned cynically. "And who knows, perhaps, even Captain Macarthur has enemies who are responsible for starting this one? How do they propose to steal my dispatch box—does the rumor reveal that?"

"I heard—er—at sea, sir," Chapman supplied. "I beg you to take it seriously."

King laughed shortly. "Very well, then—I shall take it seriously. I shall myself place the box in Lieutenant Grant's hands, with both of you to witness that I've done so. And we'll give him an escort to the wharf . . . oh, no, better still, he shall be rowed out in a naval boat after the *Anna Josepha* has weighed anchor. Does that satisfy you, eh?"

"It might also be as well, sir," Atkins advised, "since the brig is privately owned, to cause her master, Mr. Meehan, to give a bond which he would forfeit should either Lieutenant Grant or your dispatch box be interfered with. I can arrange that if you wish, sir."

Governor King suppressed a weary yawn. "Very well," he conceded. "If you deem it necessary, Mr. Atkins. I'm done up, and I have to visit Parramatta tomorrow, so I must get some sleep." He flexed his stiff limbs and yawned again, this time without attempting to suppress the evidence of his exhaustion. "In the meantime, Willie my boy," he added, addressing the young secretary, "since the damned box must remain here until Meehan is ready to sail, you had better arrange for a guard. My cox'un, in the circumstances, perhaps, in addition to the corps sentry."

His tone was again cynical, and when he had gone, Chapman looked uncertainly at the judge advocate. "Do you suppose His Excellency meant that, Mr. Atkins?"

"About his coxswain?" Atkins, too, was tired, and he shook his head. "I hardly think so. It would take a very daring thief to attempt to rob Government House. And the reward would have to be exorbitantly high to persuade even a penniless convict to risk his neck in such an enterprise. If an attempt *is* made, it will be at sea, I'm quite sure, when there's only Grant to deal with. Captain Meehan's reputation is not of the highest, but I'll set his bond at five hundred pounds, which should suffice to keep him honest."

"It would be little short of a disaster if Macarthur reaches home ahead of the governor's report," Chapman said anxiously.

"He won't, boy," Atkins assured him. "This time his goose is well and truly cooked. His passage is not even arranged yet, and the *Anna Josepha* is a fast ship. You may take my word for it, Willie boy, we shall not see Jack Boddice's face in Sydney again, thanks be to God! Freed of his malign influence and his infernal intrigues, this colony may yet prosper."

He clapped the young secretary on the shoulder and bade him a gruff good night. Then, fortified by a long draft from his hip flask, he set off across the Government House garden in the direction of his own residence at the end of George Street.

The sentry at the gate saluted him.

CHAPTER XIX

"Name this child," the Reverend Samuel Marsden's booming Yorkshire voice invited.

"William John," Johnny Broome supplied when Annie Macrae, who was acting as sponsor, hesitated, momentarily confused and uncertain of the order in which the names should go.

The chaplain took the baby in his arms, dipped two fingers into the font, and intoned, "William John, I baptize thee in the name of the Father, and of the Son, and of the Holy Ghost. Amen."

The ceremony was, of necessity, brief; a line of parents and godparents had stretched the length of the aisle when the service began, headed by those families who passed as gentry in New South Wales. Johnny's rank—he was now a full-fledged master, in command of his own sloop—would have entitled his small party to a place close to the front of the procession as, indeed, would Superintendent Macrae's. But Jenny, anxiously scanning the small crowd, had recognized Timothy Dawson, with his wife and two small daughters, and, realizing that the younger was also a candidate for admission to the Christian Church, had insisted with rare obstinacy that they themselves should join the convict families at the rear.

Such niceties worried Johnny not at all. What, he asked himself, did it signify if the three-month-old William John had to wait in the company of the colony's so-called Currency kids and, having approached the fine new font at a somewhat slower pace than he had anticipated, demonstrated the strength of his lungs—and of his disapproval—by yelling louder than any of them when holy water was splashed over his face?

William John was a lusty little fellow, who might one day prove as great a source of joy and pride to him as his firstborn was. He smiled, letting his hand rest lightly on Justin's shoulder as they followed Jenny and the two elderly Macraes into a vacant pew. Justin was a lad after his own heart, and he thought, with a shame that still lingered,

that left to himself he might never have known that he had
a son . . . or that his first love, who had borne him,
would be willing to become his wife.

He glanced at Jenny, and his smile widened as he
watched the baby snuggle into her arms, his crying stilled
now that she was holding him again. His wife was a rare
woman. . . . Dear God, how lucky he had been! Unlike
most wives she had not complained when he had told her
he wanted to stay at sea, and even when he had told her he
wanted young Justin to come with him, Jenny had raised
no objections, sensing the affinity that was already growing
up between them.

"Take good care of him, Johnny," was all that she had
asked. "Remember that he is only a little boy still. And
don't let him miss too much of his schooling . . . because
I want him to command his own ship one day, if the sea's
to be his life instead of the one I'd thought to raise him to."

The christening ceremony came finally to an end. The
Reverend Samuel Marsden dried his damp hands on his
surplice and, presumably in the hope of drowning out the
noisy clamor of crying babes, announced a hymn before
launching into the customary address. Johnny rose to his
feet with the rest, amused by the odd contrast to his
thoughts as he joined in the opening verse.

"We plow the fields and scatter the good seed on the
land. . . ."

Well, that was what most of these people did—including
Timothy Dawson. It was what they had to do in New
South Wales in order to survive, and whether they plied
their hoes under the overseer's lash or, without compulsion,
on their own small grants, they were still slaves to the demands of the land. As he had been when he had first come
out, a rebellious and bitter prisoner in the hold of one of
Governor Phillip's convict ships. But it would be different
for Justin, God willing, as it was now for himself. And for
Jenny and their little one . . .

The hymn over, Chaplain Marsden began his address.
His words and the tone in which they were uttered were
reminiscent of his appearances on the magistrates' bench
when he gave his approval to savage sentences and ex-
horted the malefactors to reform, and wearying of the hectoring, Johnny let his mind wander.

Justin, he thought, had shaped well on his first voyage. Matt Flinders, true to his promise, had readily agreed to permit the boy to enroll as a member of the *Norfolk*'s crew. It was a small crew, a mere half-dozen volunteers from the *Reliance* because the sloop could accommodate no more; but from the outset, despite his age, Justin had more than held his own. And there had been Flinders's young brother, Samuel, also making his first voyage of discovery, with whom to establish a new and lasting friendship.

For himself, on the voyage northward, following the course he had set with Will Bryant in the stolen cutter, there had been the relics of a half-forgotten fear. They had come near to disaster so often in the cutter, and the same strong winds and wayward currents, the same heavy seas and pounding surf were still to be met with and overcome, just as they had been before. Johnny caught his breath, remembering. The same hostile Indians had watched the sloop's progress from beach and clifftop and had waited with spears and throwing-sticks poised when any of them went ashore.

This time, however, there had been many differences. The *Norfolk*, although of only twenty-five tons burthen, was much larger and more seaworthy than Governor Phillip's cutter. She had been well overhauled and properly caulked following her return from Van Diemen's Land; she was manned by a disciplined, experienced crew; she had carried adequate provisions for her six weeks' voyage; and her men were armed.

The muskets and a native boy named Bongree, who accompanied them as interpreter, had rendered the threat of a surprise attack almost negligible. Only once, in the mangrove-grown swamps in the Moreton Bay area, had they met with serious resistance, and a few shots from the landing party had been sufficient to keep the Indians at a distance. Flinders named the scene of their encounter Skirmish Point, and he added other names like Shoal Bay, Break Sea Spit, Curlew Islet, and Sugarloaf Point as he worked assiduously at his charts—sounding, sketching, measuring, and correcting latitudes that, in his haste to journey farther northward, the great navigator Cook had been compelled to base on dead reckoning by the sun.

Justin, his father reflected with satisfaction, had learned much from Matt Flinders during those six weeks, and the lad had revealed a skill and a comprehension of mathematical calculation that Samuel Flinders could not match, despite his extra years. By day, when landings had been made, Justin had reveled in the freedom to roam the unexplored bays and inlets of the eastern coast; he had learned to identify the different birds and to distinguish among the peppermint, myall, and cedar trees and the various species of the ever-present gum—from the giant whitebarks to the smaller reds and blues of the endless inland forests.

At night, when the sloop had lain at anchor, they had talked of Admiral Horatio Nelson's great victory over the French in Aboukir Bay, of which news had reached Sydney just before they sailed, and discussed Sir Adam Duncan's courage at Camperdown, comparing that triumph to those off Saint Vincent and Copenhagen. Justin had been less interested in tales of battles than in his study of the stars glowing in the clear night skies, and . . . Johnny, only half-hearing Reverend Marsden's "Let us pray," dutifully dropped to his knees though his thoughts still wandered.

He had been conscious of a strange nostalgia, a restlessness that would not be assuaged, during those nightly discussions on the *Norfolk*'s crowded deck, and at times he had longed to be back on board the *Nymphe* or the old *Bellerophon* instead of where he was. With England at war and the navy so desperately engaged, New South Wales, with its convicts and its ruffian garrison of deserters and misfits from fighting regiments, seemed to him less desirable than it had ever been . . . even in his own convict days. He would gladly have gone with the *Reliance* when she sailed for home and most willingly have given up his promotion and command of the *Norfolk*, had it not been for Jenny and his newfound son. He glanced over at his wife's bent head and the child in her arms and, from them, to Justin's bright fair head, also dutifully bowed in prayer, and stifled a sigh.

He had committed himself to them, he reminded himself, and because of them, to the colony . . . there could be no second escape, no running away for Johnny Broome. His future was here with Jenny and his sons, and . . . His expression softened as he took in the barely perceptible signs of his wife's new pregnancy. And with their yet unborn children too . . .

"The Peace of God, which passeth all understanding, be with you and remain with you," the Reverend Samuel Marsden boomed. Gathering his surplice about his ample frame, he made for the vestry, and the congregation began slowly to file out, the gentry, as before, taking precedence over the humbler convict families. Old Watt Sparrow, showing the signs of his advancing years, had dozed off on the aisle side of the pew, and waking suddenly without any clear idea of where he was, he started to shuffle out, inadvertently impeding Henrietta Dawson, who was holding her elder child by the hand.

Jerked back by her mother the toddler slipped and set up a piteous wailing. Before Johnny could intervene to stop him, old Watt, touched by the little girl's distress, scooped her up in his arms and bore her out of the church on his shoulders. He had a way with children, and she was crowing with delight, her tears forgotten, when they emerged into Parramatta's main street, followed by Henrietta and Frances O'Riordan, who was carrying the Dawson baby at her mistress's heels.

There was a look of tight-lipped resentment on Henrietta Dawson's face, but although he observed this and wondered at it, Johnny was taken by surprise when Jenny gave her own small William to Annie Macrae and thrust past him without explanation or apology. Puzzled but not alarmed, he took his time, waiting to shepherd Annie out with her charge and laying a restraining hand on Justin's arm when he sought to run after his mother.

"Mind your manners boy," he said sternly. "You . . ." But the boy broke away from him, dodging through the slowly moving procession of people after flinging a hoarse, "I have to go with Mam!" to him over his shoulder.

Emerging into the street at last, Johnny was horrified to see that a heated argument was taking place, with the hitherto well-behaved congregation joining vociferously in the fracas. He caught only a word here and there, and was at a loss to account for the strong feelings being expressed by the crowd until he glimpsed Watt Sparrow, very white of face and shocked, and saw that Jenny had her arm about his bowed shoulder and was clearly attempting to soothe him.

The Dawsons had come in an imported chaise drawn by a pair of Timothy Dawson's matched chestnuts, and as this drew away with his wife and family and Frances O'Riordan seated behind the coachman, a man in the crowd picked up a stone and hurled it viciously at the departing vehicle. His action was the signal for a barrage, although insults and coarse jibes outnumbered the stones. Dawson himself, who had stood his ground until then, flung himself onto the back of his own horse and spurred after the carriage.

He called out something that sounded like "Forgive me, Jenny!" but his words were lost in the thud of hoofs. Johnny, when he was able to thrust his way to Jenny's side, was shocked to see that the tears were streaming unchecked down her flushed, unhappy face. He besought her to tell him what had happened, but she was silent, and it was Justin who answered him, his voice choked.

"Mistress Dawson told Gran'pa Watt to put the little girl down, because she wasn't going to let a—a filthy old convict like him lay hands on her child. Mam went to take the girl from him. . . . She was trying to help, Dad, that was all, and Mistress Dawson turned on her. I didn't hear half of what she said, but I could see how upset Mam was, and I—I called out to Uncle Tim to stop her. And then . . ." For all his brave attempt to speak calmly, Justin's control deserted him. "Mistress Dawson said he wasn't my uncle, and I was to call him 'sir' and—and keep my place, because I"—he gulped—"because I was a bastard and the —the son of a convict whore, whose father could—could have been anyone. But it's not true, Dad, is it? Tell me it's not true!"

"Of course it's not true, son—how could it be?" Johnny held the boy to him, feeling his pain more keenly than if it had been his own and furiously angry. Fool that he was, he reproached himself, not to have seen what was brewing, not to have gone with his wife and son when they left the church! He looked down at Jenny and a knife twisted in his heart when he saw that Justin's distress was mirrored in her eyes. But still she did not speak; rising, she took old Watt's arm and, her expression frozen, led him toward the street.

Two constables, Johnny saw, were halfheartedly starting to disperse the crowd. It was evident that they wanted no trouble and had not the slightest interest in inquiring into the reasons for the disturbance. The owners of drays and the only other carriage had piled into them and gone; a solitary ensign of the corps—a new arrival, judging by the expression of shocked bewilderment on his face—was making off on foot for the barracks, as anxious as were the two custodians of the law to avoid involvement. For the rest, the excitement over, there was a concerted movement in the direction of Parramatta's licensed premises, where the heads of the newly christened babes could be wetted, as tradition decreed, and the insults—to which, in any event, most of them were inured—could be spoken of briefly and then forgotten.

But Jenny would not forget them, or old Watt, or, God help him, poor little Justin . . . a plague take Timothy Dawson! If he could not control his wife's venomous tongue, at least he should have stayed to offer a proper apology for the hurt she had caused. Her attitude was typical of the colony's respectable class; there was and, Johnny thought bitterly, there probably always would be a great gulf between the free settlers and the convicts and emancipists, with the corps officers setting themselves above them all.

He frowned, wishing that he did not have to return to his ship that evening, but . . . at least he would be taking Justin with him, for the boy had to return to school. On the way by the ferryboat to Sydney he could talk to him, reassure him, and, God willing, restore his pride and confidence. And Jenny would not be left alone to brood over what had happened—she would have faithful old Watt and the Macraes for overnight company. Annie Macrae, bless her kind heart and staunch cheerfulness, would not permit anyone to yield to despondency for long.

Johnny's anger gradually faded. They drank baby William's health in porter and Cape brandy at the cabin, and Jenny took leave of him with composure, refusing to talk about the morning's happenings, although he attempted twice to bring up the subject. She said only that the baptismal service had been well conducted and then added, as she always did when he was going back to sea, "Take good

care of yourself, Johnny. And don't let Justin persuade you
into letting him go with you . . . he must finish his
schooling."

"Aye, I know," he agreed and kissed her with more than
his usual tenderness. "It's just Norfolk Island with mail and
stores and a few poor devils of convicts. I'll be back before
you know it, lass. God bless you!"

"And you, my dear," she echoed and then, evading his
embrace, gave Justin's school bag into his care and reminded him, unnecessarily, that in the Macraes' temporary
absence, the boy was to lodge with the schoolmaster.

Justin talked volubly as they plodded the four miles to
the Parramatta wharf, but like his mother he steered cautiously clear of any mention of Mrs. Dawson's cruel taunts,
and it was only when the ferryboat was in sight of the flickering lights of Sydney town that he said, after a sudden and
prolonged silence, "You *are* my father, aren't you?"

"Aye, that I am, Justin," Johnny answered. He was
tempted to say more, even to tell the story of his courtship,
but feeling the boy reach for and grip his hand, he knew
that it was not necessary—the bond between them was as
strong as he could wish for.

"I'm glad," Justin said softly.

"So am I, lad. Glad and proud."

As the boy tied up at the Public Wharf the convict rowers
thankfully shipped their oars, the lugsail came down, and
they stepped ashore with the rest of the old ferry's passengers. The Public Wharf was on the west side of the cove,
immediately below the hospital garden and the Market
Place, and as they swung along side by side in the direction
of the schoolmaster's house in the High Street, Justin
pointed out the building immediately ahead of them.

"That used to be Lieutenant Kent's house, but now he's
gone it's to be the new school—the Orphan School, Dad.
But we're to have lessons there when it suits." He glanced
sideways at his father and added, a note of deeply felt relief
in his shrill young voice, "I'm glad I'm not an orphan. But
when Mistress Dawson said I was a—a bastard I . . .
well, I was just a mite afraid, you see. Because most of the
orphans are bastards, aren't they. . . . Currency kids, they
call them, when they're trying to taunt them. But I gave
the last boy who called me that a bloody nose!"

"Good lad," Johnny approved, his voice not quite steady. He parted from his son at the schoolmaster's house with a more than usually warm embrace, and as his lips brushed the boy's thin cheek, he tasted the salty bitterness of tears and held him close, wondering wretchedly whether—for all his good intentions—he had failed him.

He was still wondering, still going over the day's events in his mind as he crossed the old stone bridge over the Tank Stream and passed the darkened block of government offices that lined the narrow, stone-chip road that led to Government House and thence, skirting the governor's extensive garden, to the naval storeyard and wharf where his boat was under regulation lock and key. The main guardhouse was situated at the corner of this road—Bridge Street—at the point where it had been widened to permit oxcarts to draw into the commissariat bakehouse and deliver wheat to the recently constructed windmills for grinding. A sentry was normally posted at the yard entrance, with two more at the Government House gateway, a hundred yards or so farther on, but Johnny was surprised to see that the wooden sentry box was empty.

He peered into it, puzzled, aware that Commissary Palmer, fearful of hungry thieves, maintained a strict watch on both grain store and bakery at all times, but a sudden gale of ribald laughter coming from the guardhouse partially explained the sentry's absence. He swore disgustedly. The plaguey Rum Corps was living up to its name, he decided as, nearing the building, a chorus of drunken voices assailed his ears. They were singing the cynical ditty made popular by Sydney's convict players and singing it with hiccoughing gusto and some added obscenities its original composer had never intended.

> From distant climes, o'er widespread seas we come,
> Though not with much eclat or beat of drum;
> True patriots all—for be it understood
> We left our country for our country's good!
> And none will doubt but that our immigration
> Has proved most useful to the British nation. . . .

Another voice, louder than the rest, broke into the singing. "Nah, then, me lucky lads, let's 'ave three cheers fer

our benefactor, shall we? Fer the best bloody officer in the
New South Wales Corps an' the soddin' Botany Bay Rang-
ers—Cap'n John Macarthur 'isself! Hip, hip . . . come
on, boys, raise them rafters! Let the cap'n know as we appreciate 'is generosity. Hip, hip, hip . . ."

The cheers were deafening.

Johnny stood where he was for a moment, his earlier
disgust succeeded by a choking anger. These were the
swine who were entrusted with the colony's security, he
thought furiously. These were the men who took their pay
in liquor and sold it for ten times its worth to the wretched
convicts they guarded, or traded the stuff to the settlers for
their hard-won wheat and maize at even greater profit.
Most of them had themselves been felons, convicted of
both civil and military crimes, but now, dressed in the
king's uniform, they drank and gambled and indulged their
lecherous desires without a thought for their duty or the
oath of service they had sworn.

Then, as the cheers faded and a fiddler struck up another tune, he tensed, recalling that the officer they had
cheered so enthusiastically—Captain Macarthur—had been
placed under house arrest by the governor. He was to be
sent back to England for trial by court-martial, after the
duel with Colonel Paterson, but . . . what had that
drunken sod said when he had called for his infernal cheers
for "the best bloody officer in the New South Wales
Corps?"

Hadn't he told his fellows to let the captain know that
they appreciated his generosity? And . . . good God,
could Macarthur have supplied them with the liquor they
were swilling? Johnny instinctively started to run, making
for the gate of Government House where, under standing
orders, two sentries should be posted. He approached the
gate without making the smallest attempt at concealment,
but no red-coated soldier challenged him and none when
he reached it stepped forward to bar his way. . . . And
the sentry boxes were empty, as the one outside the commissariat grain store had been.

The governor, he knew, was in Parramatta with his family—he had seen them that morning on their way to inspect
the new weaving looms at the factory for women convicts,
in which Mrs. King was taking an interest. Jenny had told

him this and she had said that they were going on to Toongabbe for . . . He stiffened, glimpsing a light coming from behind one of the shuttered windows of Government House. It was the merest pencil of light, and it was only by chance that he saw it—a faint flicker, no more, as if a candle had been lit and then extinguished in one of the ground-floor rooms.

There would be servants in the rambling, two-story house, of course, even in the governor's absence, but they had their own quarters in some buildings at the rear and would have no occasion, surely, to enter the room the governor used as an office. It was in his office that the light had appeared, Johnny realized—he had entered it several times since taking over command of the *Norfolk* from Matt Flinders, and he had no difficulty in locating the position of its window. He hesitated, staring up at the façade of the house, uncertain whether or not he ought to investigate further since, in the absence of the two sentries, it was possible that a robbery was in progress. If so, it was his duty to give the alarm, but . . . The light did not reappear, and he began to wonder if he could have imagined it.

Then, so suddenly that he was taken completely by surprise, the front door opened and a uniformed sergeant of the corps appeared in the aperture. He stood at the head of the short flight of steps leading to the door, looking about him; assuming that he was the official guardian in the governor's absence, Johnny was about to continue on his way, his mind now at ease, when the man saw him and beckoned him over to reveal himself as Whittle, the corps's senior NCO.

"What are you doing here?" Whittle demanded. His tone was suspicious, his manner edgy and unexpectedly nervous. "Got no call to go prowling about His Excellency's garden at this time o' night, have you? That's to say, unless you . . ." He broke off, recognizing Johnny's uniform. "Bloody matelot, are you? You from the brig?"

"What brig, Sergeant Whittle?" Johnny countered, his own suspicions returning. The sergeant had a musket, and that, too, was unusual since, at his rank, he would not normally stand guard. But perhaps he . . . From the shadowed hallway at his back a voice said sharply, "He's not one of ours—get him quick!"

Sergeant Whittle moved fast. The butt of his musket wa
raised, and before Johnny could move or attempt to war￼
off the blow, it struck him on the side of the head. Hi
knees buckled and he sank down, half on, half off the steps
and as he crouched there helplessly the musket butt struc￼
him again, this time on the back of the head, depriving hin
of his senses, and he collapsed without a sound.

From the door of Government House three me￼
emerged. The first put out a hand to stay the sergeant'
arm as he was lifting his musket with the intention of de
livering a final blow.

"No need to kill the fellow—he saw nothing."

"He saw *me*," the sergeant grunted.

"You've split his skull—he won't remember his ow￼
name, much less your face." The speaker knelt briefly a￼
Johnny's side and then, rising, issued his orders. To one o
his companions he said curtly, "All right, cracksman—you
did what we paid you for, so be off and make sure you'r￼
seen a mile away from here. And keep a still tongue ir
your head, or I'll see you hang if it's the last thing I eve￼
do!" The man he had addressed obeyed him instantly an￼
without argument, slipping away into the shadowed garder
to vanish as if he had never been.

"You sure he's to be trusted?" Sergeant Whittle aske￼
nervously. He was sweating, his lean, pockmarked fac￼
drained of all color; looking down at the man he had s￼
savagely injured, reaction set in and he shuddered. "Gawd
that bloody matelot's a mess, ain't he, sir? I must've hit hin
harder than I thought."

"We'll deal with him—douse him with a few gills of run
and dump him on the steps down to the jetty. They'll thin￼
he got drunk and fell down 'em. He—"

"He's a naval man, sir." The third member of the party
was examining the buttons on Johnny's watch jacket
"Master, by his rig—must be off the *Porpoise*. Well
they've got a few hard drinkers, I don't reckon they'll as￼
too many questions when they find him." He took a flas￼
from his coat pocket and emptied its contents over John
ny's unconscious face, spilling it onto his jacket and th￼
front of his shirt. "He's ready—shall we dump him, sir?'

"In a minute," the leader of the party snapped. H￼

turned to Whittle. "Give us five minutes to get clear—no, better make it ten, he's a big man—and then you know what to do, don't you?"

Sergeant Whittle wiped his face with the back of his hand. "Aye—I'm to go to the guardhouse and give them hell for dereliction of duty, sir. And then—"

"Then," the leader of the party reminded him, "you're to allow yourself to be persuaded *not* to report them . . . and you can make your own conditions." He smiled, his dark, high-boned face expressing genuine amusement. "You'll earn twice what we've paid you if you play your cards right, Whittle, you damned rogue!"

The sergeant took no offense. He, too, was smiling now. "You think of everything, don't you, Mr. Fitz?"

"I try to, Sergeant. And I don't gamble unless I'm pretty sure I'm putting my money on a winner . . . and in this case, I know I have. Make sure you have sentries posted outside my revered superior's granary as well as at the governor's gate, won't you? Right, Smith my lad, heave up this mass of bleeding flesh and let's get rid of it. After that you can go and report to your master that the deed is done. Tell him that all His Grace of Portland will receive in His Excellency's dispatch box is a packet of old English newspapers . . . that will make him laugh." The man addressed as Fitz added reflectively, "As it makes me. My one regret is that I shall not be present in the Colonial Office to see the Secretary of State's face when he unlocks his precious box. It should be a sight worth seeing!"

He was still in high good humor when, twenty minutes later, he and the man called Smith allowed Johnny Broome's limp body to slither down the steps of the government jetty and lie precariously at its foot.

Johnny returned to a dazed awareness of his surroundings to find Surgeon Balmain bending over him.

"Well, well, Mr. Broome . . ." The surgeon's voice appeared to be coming from a great distance, echoing through his head and causing him to wince with pain. "You would seem to have hit the bottle a mite too hard! Were it not for the extraordinary thickness of your skull, I should have grave doubts of your survival. But as it is . . ." He shook his head in simulated wonder. "I fancy you are going to confound my initial prognosis. Do you have any recollection of what happened to you?"

Johnny stared up at him blankly. "No," he managed hoarsely. "No . . . except that a sergeant of the corps was . . ." A face, dimly remembered, floated tantalizingly between himself and the ceiling, pockmarked and leathery, with lackluster dark eyes. Then it faded before he could put a name to it. "No, sir. I don't recollect anything."

"Never mind," Dr. Balmain said consolingly. He straightened up. "Your wife and son are here, and after a week's anxiety on your behalf I'm sure they will be overjoyed to find you once more conscious and in the land of the living. I will send them to you."

They came; Jenny red-eyed but bravely composed, and Justin scarcely able to contain his relief. Johnny held out his hands to them and somehow contrived to twist his stiff lips into a smile of welcome. Then, without warning, he was back in limbo, his head aching unmercifully and his eyes unable to focus. He heard Jenny's voice but could not answer her, and his hand holding hers involuntarily relaxed its grip.

Dr. Balmain ushered the visitors away. He said gravely, when they were out of earshot of the occupants of the crowded hospital ward, "Your husband has a fractured skull, Mistress Broome—indeed, it's a miracle he's still alive, as I told you when he was first brought in here. But"—his shrug was resigned—"if men will drink themselves into a stupor, they've no one to blame save themselves."

"My husband is not a drinking man, sir," Jenny asserted, with so much conviction that the surgeon eyed her in surprise.

"Well, perhaps he ran into some convivial companions when he got to Sydney and decided to make a night of it. I can assure you, he reeked of spirits when he was admitted."

Jenny shook her head. "I am sure he did not do anything of the kind, Dr. Balmain. He had been given command of the *Norfolk* sloop and was due to sail the very next day for Norfolk Island. He was not likely to fail in his duty. And besides, he had just left our son at the schoolmaster's house, and . . ." She appealed to Justin. "He was on his way back to his ship, was he not, Justin?"

Dr. Balmain listened thoughtfully to Justin's account of his return to Sydney with his father.

"I confess," he conceded, when the boy came to the end of his recital, "that the nature of the head wounds he received did puzzle me a little."

"They puzzled you, sir?"

"Yes. They were not consistent with a fall, even onto the stone steps of the jetty. However"—he repeated his shrug—"unless your husband can remember the events of the night, we shall never know how he came to be so severely injured. Possibly he was set on and robbed, which, alas, is no uncommon an occurrence in Sydney these days."

"Do you think he will remember?" Jenny asked, biting her lip to still its trembling.

Dr. Balmain would not commit himself. "He may, Mistress Broome, given time. He knew you, did he not, and the boy? But I must emphasize that his injuries are very severe. He will not be fit to go back to sea for some considerable time."

"For how long, Doctor?"

"I cannot say, Mistress Broome. Six months, even a year, perhaps. And he will require careful nursing when he is discharged from here." The doctor went into details. "You have a land grant, have you not?"

"Yes, sir, at Parramatta," Jenny answered.

"And you breed horses, I believe? Well . . ." Dr. Balmain smiled encouragement. "Try to arouse his interest in that or, better still, in arable farming, good food, and very light work on the land to enable him to recoup his strength. If he went back to the sea, it might kill him. That fractured skull has to heal. I'll arrange sick leave for him, and the rest will be your responsibility."

"I understand, sir." Jenny spoke firmly, her eyes on Justin in mute question. The boy inclined his head without hesitation.

It was six weeks before Johnny was discharged from the hospital, to find a greatly changed life awaiting him.

Jenny took him back in a borrowed dray to a new farm on the Hawkesbury River, its pleasant house a solidly built log cabin constructed from local hardwood, situated above a bend in the river, with a view of Richmond Hill a scant two miles to the north. Good buildings and a hundred and fifty acres of fine arable land and sheep pasture constituted the holding, and it was only when he searched in vain for her brood mares that Johnny understood the sacrifice his wife had made.

"I sold them," she confessed. "The price they commanded and the sale of the Parramatta land sufficed to buy this. The man who owned it was heavily in debt—he lost heart because of the floods and the native raids, and his wife was afraid to stay here."

"And you are not?" Johnny questioned.

"No," Jenny said, with confidence. "I have always got on with the Indians, and I have two of them working here—Bediagal boys. They will leave us be, Johnny, if they know that we shall not harm them."

"And the floods, my love?" His tone was wry.

Jenny met the doubt in his eyes with a quiet, "The land is good because of the floods, Johnny . . . and the river does not flood every year. When it does—well, that is the price we must pay for good, productive years. And the Hawkesbury gives warning. Besides, we are on high ground." She took his arm and led him toward the farmhouse. "The late owner has taken a licensed tavern in Sydney. He bought it lock, stock, and barrel, so he left us his furniture, all handmade. It was an amicable arrangement, and the house is sound and in good repair."

The old rocking chair she had always treasured stood in the inglenook beside the stone-built fireplace, Johnny saw, with William in his cot nearby, a smiling Nancy Jardine hovering over him, and old Watt Sparrow in the background.

"Is Justin here?" he asked.

Jenny shook her head. "No. He has apprenticed himself to Tom Moore in the shipyard. It was his wish, Johnny . . . and he will continue his schooling in the evenings. He promised me that."

So his son, too, had made sacrifices for him, Johnny thought, feeling oddly humbled. Justin would learn to build ships, but the lad could not go to sea until he himself could take him. Or perhaps until Matt Flinders returned with his ship of discovery and the scientists Sir Joseph

Banks had promised him. Matt would not come back, as George Bass had recently done, bent only on trading ventures and profits for his shareholders . . . Johnny drew in his breath sharply, his gaze on Jenny's thickening figure.

There would be another child soon, and this was to be his home and theirs. It would be churlish and ungrateful were he to refuse what was now being offered to him.

He said softly, reaching for Jenny's hand, "God grant I may deserve all you've done for me, lass."

CHAPTER XX

Happiness, Jenny reminded herself, did not last, and she knew that the happiness she had enjoyed for almost a year past was at an end when the colonial schooner *Cumberland*, built in Tom Moore's yard, delivered her son Justin to the bosom of his family from the Hawkesbury wharf.

The boy was beside himself with excitement and so clearly the bearer of momentous news that, when he asked for his father—insisting that he must be present before he could impart the tidings he had brought—she gave in with a good grace.

"He is out in the sheep pasture, Justin. I'll send Nanbaree to fetch him, and you shall eat whilst you're waiting. If you can spare the time, your brother and sister would like to see you, I am sure."

Justin made a face and then relented, grinning. He was well grown for his eleven years, Jenny thought with pardonable pride, a handsome, sturdy boy who resembled his father more with every passing year. His schoolmaster spoke well of him, the Reverend Marsden—a stern teacher—praised his grasp of mathematics, and old Tom Moore took an almost personal pride in his achievements in the building yard. But . . . She bit back a sigh, as she watched her firstborn subject his baby sister Rachel to an initially cautious inspection, followed by the tickling of her bare pink toes that, although awkward and even a trifle overboisterous, set her crowing with delight.

Justin's attitude to the younger members of his family was that of an adult rather than a child. . . . He was grown prematurely to responsibility, already a skilled craftsman and earning a small wage, and little William's disappointed howls, when he was ignored on the baby's account, merited only a tolerant smile. His elder brother continued with the toe-tickling, and William trotted away, sulky and abashed, to console himself by playing with the puppies to which the half-bred collie bitch had recently given birth.

Jenny busied herself setting food on the table, and when Justin drew up his chair, she chided him gently.

"Willie looks forward to your coming home, love. You could spare some notice."

"He's a crybaby, Mam," Justin answered defensively. "And you spoil him." He helped himself to damper, breaking off a hunk of it to dip in his broth. "You never spoilt *me*, did you?"

Perhaps she didn't, Jenny was forced to concede, her conscience pricking her. But when Justin had been William's age, she had been virtually alone, working the small grant at Parramatta with only old Watt's help and hard put to it to care for both child and stock.

"You're none the worse for it, are you?" she countered and was rewarded by an affectionate hug.

"No, of course not. I just thought young Willie could do with a dose of what I had. Dad mollycoddles him, too. Is there any tea, Mam?"

She poured a generous mugful for him, adding milk and sugar . . . more luxuries Justin had not known during his childhood.

"I saw that blackfellow you used to talk about," Justin volunteered, pushing his bowl away. "Baneelon—the one Governor Phillip took to England with him, and who came back in the *Reliance* all dressed up in London clothes. Poor devil, he must have been in an almighty battle—he's lost an eye and his whole body is scarred. He was begging outside the grogshops, claiming that he was a friend of King George, and His Majesty would be upset if he was allowed to die of starvation. But it wasn't food he wanted . . . it was rum. He made quite a hit with the French sailors and ended up in the gutter, drunk as a lord."

Poor Baneelon, Jenny thought. . . . How different it might have been for Governor Phillip's protégé had he never set eyes on England or been permitted to kiss the king's hand! Yemmerra Wannie, who had gone with him, had been speared in some tribal affray not very long ago, and Baneelon's wife—her onetime friend Barangeroo—tired of waiting for her lord and master's return, had deserted him for a younger suitor. Or so Jenny had heard. She poured herself a beaker of tea, and recalling Justin's mention of French sailors, looked at him inquiringly.

"What French sailors do you mean, Justin?"

"Men off the *Géographe* and the *Naturaliste*, Mam. They came into port ten days ago, in a very bad way, half of them down with scurvy. We had to tow the *Naturaliste* in from the Heads—she had only half a dozen fit men on board, and—"

"But I thought France was at war with us." Jenny demurred.

"Not any more." Justin bit hungrily into his third hunk of damper. "There's been some kind of treaty—the Treaty of Amiens or something like that. These ships, the Frenchmen, had been on a voyage of scientific discovery along the south coast of New Holland, with official permission from the British Admiralty, like—" He broke off, shrugging his slim shoulders. "I'll tell you more about it when Dad comes in."

Once again scenting danger, Jenny eyed her elder son suspiciously, replying to his questions regarding the farm without enthusiasm. It had prospered, there could be no denying that, and Johnny, after the first two months of convalescence, had worked like two men to make it so. The small flock of hardy Bengal sheep, purchased with the farm, had virtually doubled in number, and few lambs had been lost in spite of winter storms and a cold spell at the beginning of the month. Pigs, too, bred well and could be fattened at small cost; they had three house cows and some beef stirks, a fine stock of poultry to provide both eggs and meat, and the arable—which Johnny and Tom Jardine tended—was coming on, the virgin land starting to fulfill its promise.

She missed the horses still, but Johnny had bought her a young mare of her own breeding, which Tim Dawson had put up for sale at Christmas, and the animal was in foal to his newly imported Cape stallion. In any event she had little time for breaking horses now, with two small children to care for and poor old Watt Sparrow to nurse through a bad attack of fever. Besides, she . . . Justin jumped to his feet, spilling his half-empty teacup in his eagerness to get to the door.

"Dad's here now!" he exclaimed and left her at a run.

They came into the room together, looking so pleased to see one another that Jenny's fears grew. Justin, she told herself, had come to entice his father away, back to the sea, and she was conscious of no surprise when Johnny said, his eyes bright with longing, "Justin came to tell me that Matt Flinders. is back in Sydney, Jenny love . . . a captain now, and in command of a ship that's worthy of him. His Majesty's ship *Investigator*!"

It all came out then, in Justin's excited words. Sir Joseph Banks, the famous botanist who had landed with Cook and named the place of their landing Botany Bay, had inspired the venture, and Captain Flinders—for all he had married a few weeks before sailing—had left his bride in England in order to make another voyage of discovery.

"I saw him, Mam," Justin boasted. "Saw him and talked to him, and he told me what he had done and where he had been. He let me study his charts. Since December of last year, when the *Investigator* made Cape Leeuwin, Mr. Flinders—Captain Flinders, I mean—has been exploring the southern coast. He's found new rivers and harbors, and they're all named and measured and marked on his charts. . . ." The boy prattled on, quoting the new names and describing the new discoveries with a wealth of detail, for all the world, Jenny thought numbly, as if he had been present when Flinders's ship had sighted them.

Over Justin's bent fair head, as he started to illustrate the course the explorers had followed, she met Johnny's gaze and, with a sinking heart, saw it drop before her own.

"They are here to refit and provision," Justin went on. "Then they will go on with the *Lady Nelson* in company to survey the west coast and the Great Barrier Reef, then pass through the Strait of Endeavour and into the Gulf of Carpentaria to the Dutch Islands. And . . ."

But Jenny was not listening. They would follow the same route that Johnny had taken with the Bryants, and now it was she who could not, dared not look at him, fearing the longing she knew would be in his blue seaman's eyes. The pleading . . . She choked back the tears that had come to ache in her throat. Justin would go, of course—that went almost without saying, for the boy was already dreaming of it and, no doubt, had already made his plea to Captain Flinders. But Johnny . . . The tears she had tried to suppress ran down her cheeks, salt as the sea.

"Captain Flinders is without a sailing master," Justin

was saying, looking up at his father. "Mr. Thistle and six men were caught in a tide-rip and drowned, when their boat foundered in Spencer Gulf. Captain Flinders named the place Cape Catastrophe, and Samuel said—"

"Is young Samuel with them?" Johnny asked, speaking for the first time after a lengthy silence.

The boy nodded. "He's a full-blown watchkeeper now, and there's a friend of his, a midshipman named John Franklin, who fought in the Battle of Copenhagen under Lord Nelson. He was on board the *Polyphemus*, Dad, a sixty-four, and he told me—"

For the second time, his father interrupted him. "You say they've no master? What about the ships in harbor—could one of them not supply a master?"

"They're convict transports, sir," Justin returned, his tone contemptuous. "The *Atlas* lost sixty poor devils of convicts on passage—she's a stinking old tub, Dad, with a drunken crew. And the *Hercules* had a mutiny—the master, Captain Betts, was charged with murder, and the admiralty court fined him five hundred pounds. One of his mates volunteered, but Captain Flinders said that . . ." He flashed an anxious glance at Jenny. "Mam, he—"

"Is Surgeon Bass not in Sydney?" Johnny put in.

"Why, no, Dad." Justin sounded surprised. "I thought you knew—he sailed for Otaheite two months ago."

It was no use, Jenny thought, the two of them talking this way, avoiding the issue. It was not hard for her to guess what Captain Flinders had said and why, although a mate from a transport had volunteered to join the *Investigator*, her commander had hesitated before accepting him. And if Matthew Flinders could leave his bride of a few weeks behind him, what chance had she of keeping Johnny?

She said, her voice flat and devoid of feeling, "How long will Captain Flinders be away, Justin?"

"He is taking twelve months' provisions on board, Mam." Justin's eyes, as blue as his father's, searched her face as he answered her. "He has a four-year commission, he told me. But he'll be coming back here, to Port Jackson, because his orders are to sail right round—that is circumnavigate—what he calls *Terra Australis*. It . . . oh, Mam, it's a chance that may never come our way again! A chance to make discoveries like Captain Cook did. Captain Flinders has Cook's own chronometer on board the *Investigator*. . . . He showed it to me, and he said that Sir Joseph Banks had entrusted it to him. Mam, it is a wonderful chance, isn't it?"

"For you, Justin?" Jenny managed. "Or for you and your father? Is that what you're trying to say?"

Johnny intervened, seeking to spare the boy. "Matt Flinders needs a sailing master, Jenny. And he—"

"And he's your friend?"

"Yes," Johnny agreed. "But you're my wife. I'll only go with your consent, my love."

There was, Jenny knew, no more she could say. He was fit and strong. Matt Flinders's wife had let him go, aware that it would be four years before she saw him again, and she was being asked for only one of those years. She smiled, putting a brave face on it as she looked from her husband to her son. "Oh, off you go then," she bade them. "Both of you—I'll not stand in your way."

She heard William set up an injured howl and thankfully, hiding her tears, she went to comfort him.

"Captain Bligh, Sir Joseph," the footman announced and stood aside to permit the stocky uniformed figure of William Bligh to precede him.

Sir Joseph Banks rose courteously from his desk by the wide, mullioned window to receive the visitor, and waved him to a chair before resuming his own seat. The footman brought in a tray laden with cut-glass decanters and long-stemmed wine glasses, set it at his master's side, and silently withdrew. Bligh settled himself into a brocaded wing chair.

"Be pleased to help yourself, my dear fellow," his distinguished host invited. "Madeira, brandy, or may I recommend the hock, if your throat is dry?"

"Thank you, sir." His throat was indeed dry, the captain reflected ruefully—a lengthy wait in the First Lord's anteroom at the Admiralty and a brief, noncommittal interview with Lord Spencer was enough to give a man apoplexy, never mind a thirst. He helped himself to a glass of hock, raised it in Sir Joseph's direction, and drank gratefully, while at the same time seeking, by a covert study over the rim of his glass, to gauge his host's mood.

Their acquaintance stretched back a long way. Sir Joseph Banks, Baronet, Privy Councillor, and now President of the Royal Society, had been one of those responsible for the decision of His Majesty's government to found a penal colony in New South Wales, his evidence as to its advantages for the purpose having tipped the scales when the House had considered the question.

Now nearing his sixty-first year, Sir Joseph was still regarded by the British government as a leading authority on antipodean matters—since he had landed with Cook at Botany Bay in 1768. He had continued to concern himself with the colony's administration and development, Bligh was aware, particularly in regard to exploration in the area.

Rich and influential, with financial interests in the West Indian sugar plantations as well as in the City, the patronage of such a man as Sir Joseph Banks was of inestimable value to a junior lieutenant who possessed none of these advantages, and he had sought eagerly to justify the famous scientist's confidence in him . . . only, Bligh recalled bitterly, to be thwarted by Fletcher Christian.

The loss of the *Bounty*, although a subsequent courtmartial had exonerated him from blame, might well have robbed him of his patron's trust—but miraculously it had not. Sir Joseph had offered him a second chance, and this time there had been no mutiny, no sniveling rogue of a Fletcher Christian to incite his ship's company to mutiny. He had delivered Sir Joseph's healthy breadfruit plants to their destination and brought the *Providence* and the brig *Assistant* safely back to England. And his patron had seen to it that he was handsomely rewarded, with promotion to post-rank, fellowship of the Royal Society, and the society's coveted gold medal to mark his achievement.

Yet—he was now without a command, despite the great Admiral Nelson's praise of his recent conduct at the victory over the Danes at Copenhagen. Bligh frowned, the memory of his interview with the First Lord still rankling.

"What have they offered you, William?" Sir Joseph's deep, pleasant voice broke into his thoughts, and William Bligh forced a smile.

"There is a possibility of my being given the *Warrior*,

sir," he answered, deciding to put as good a face on the matter as he could.

"How strong a possibility?"

"Lord Spencer did not commit himself. He—"

Sir Joseph put in, leaning forward to refill his guest's glass, "If Their Lordships do not give you a command, would you consider New South Wales? Or, perhaps, even if they do?"

Taken completely by surprise, Bligh could only echo the question blankly. "New South Wales, Sir Joseph? But I thought that Captain King was—that is to say, if you are talking of the governorship, I had understood that he . . ." He broke off, lost for words.

"It is *my* understanding that King is tired of his station," Sir Joseph Banks said. "And well he may be, poor fellow! He has endeavored to carry into effect certain reforms—at the behest, I may say, of His Majesty's government—and these have conflicted with the interests of the military garrison of the colony who, by all accounts, are a ruffianly set, engaged in lining their own pockets. King is, in consequence, disliked and much opposed, and he has asked leave to return."

"I . . . see, sir," Bligh acknowledged uncertainly. "But I scarcely imagine that I—"

He was cut short. "In my considered view," Sir Joseph told him, "neither King nor Hunter possess the qualities necessary to bring the colony to order. I've talked to poor John Hunter, and he's admitted as much. The appointment requires a man of great integrity, with a mind capable of providing its own resources in difficulties, without leaning on others for advice. He must be firm in maintaining discipline, and not one to whimper and whine, but to act, if need be with severity, when that is required in order to deal with emergencies. I believe that you would be an admirable choice, William."

Flattered, as much as astonished by this assessment, Bligh was again at a loss for words. But Banks, it seemed, expected no reply. He went on, almost as if he were talking to himself, "I cannot in all honesty claim that the colony is near to my heart, but by the same token I do have it on my conscience that it exists at all, and, as God is my witness, I should like my initial hopes for it to be realized. To that end—and since both His Majesty and Mr. Addington, our esteemed Prime Minister, have sought my advice concerning the appointment of a successor to the present governor—it behooves me to offer my opinion, does it not?"

He paused then, looking with bright, inquiring eyes at his guest, and Bligh nerved himself to express guarded agreement.

"The governor's salary is at present one thousand pounds per annum, but I fancy that it could be increased— perhaps even doubled, if I have a word in the right quarter," Sir Joseph informed him with a faint smile. "And the pension is fixed at a thousand . . . some inducement, perhaps to a man with a wife and family dependent on him."

It would be, Bligh thought—dear God, indeed it would be. But Britain and France were again at war, after the ending of the short-lived Treaty of Amiens, and Nelson was leading the navy to even greater glory. New South Wales was thousands of miles from the theater of war and would offer little opportunity for the promotion of flag rank that he so greatly coveted.

Sir Joseph put in shrewdly, as if Bligh's last thought had been spoken aloud, "It is understood that whoever is appointed governor will not lose naval seniority. Arthur Phillip is now a rear admiral, as I am sure you know." Again he did not wait for a reply. "It is a pity that the war precludes the replacement of the New South Wales Corps by marines, as both Hunter and King requested, for that regiment—or at any rate its officers—appear to be the root cause of the dissension in the colony. The present commandant, William Paterson, is an excellent fellow and a remarkably fine botanist, with whom I have corresponded for a number of years. He brought me some beautiful specimens for the garden at Kew when he last came home on leave . . . and sent me sketches, also, of immense interest. I have some of them here, depicting creatures that exist only in the antipodes."

He took the bulging portfolio from a drawer in his desk and, opening it at random, displayed several of the meticulously executed sketches. Bligh had seen kangaroos and black swans in the course of his own voyages in the area and, listening to Sir Joseph's expert descriptions of some even stranger denizens of the vast New Holland forests, his interest was swiftly rekindled.

"But I digress," his host said, after some twenty minutes had been spent examining the sketches. He replaced them carefully in his desk and went on, with a noticeable change of tone, "There is a . . . what can I call him? A representative of the New South Wales Corps here in London, by the name of Macarthur—Captain Macarthur who, I am told by John Hunter, is an unprincipled rogue, who has amassed a fortune by means of a trade in rum. This, it appears, is the main, if not the sole, activity of his regiment."

"Good God!" Bligh exclaimed, shocked to the depths of his being by his host's statement.

"That is by no means Mr. Macarthur's only crime," Sir Joseph told him. "I am given to understand that he called out my friend Colonel Paterson—his commanding officer, mark you—and wounded the poor fellow so gravely that he almost expired. The governor, Captain King, sent him back here for trial by court-martial—in the hope, I imagine, that the villain would be cashiered and forbidden to return to New South Wales to enjoy his ill-gotten gains. But—"

"Don't tell me, sir, that he's *not* been cashiered? Surely no court in this country could possibly exonerate him?"

"He has not even been brought to trial, William . . . and therein hangs a most curious tale. Shall I recount it to you?"

"If you please, Sir Joseph. I—that is"—Bligh met the scientist's keen gaze and reddened a trifle—"it is undoubtedly something I should be cognizant of, in the event that, through your good offices, sir, I might be considered as Governor King's successor in the—er—the not too distant future."

"Quite so, my dear fellow," Banks agreed affably. But his tone was harsh as he went on, "King's complaints concerning this rogue Macarthur and the evidence against him, intended to be revealed at his trial, were sent in a locked dispatch box addressed to the Duke of Portland, and entrusted to a lieutenant of your service—one James Grant. He delivered the box to the Colonial Office where—when it was opened by Lord Camden, our present Secretary for the Colonies—it was found to contain a bundle of newspapers several years old. Clearly," Sir Joseph added, forestalling his listener's question, "it must have been broken into and its contents stolen before it left the colony. Grant swears the box was not tampered with when it was in his charge, and he is seemingly a conscientious and reliable officer."

William Bligh's brows met in a thoughtful frown. "I presume, sir, that Captain King retained copies of his documents, and—"

"And if he did," the older man interrupted, "when they eventually reach these shores, Macarthur will have left them . . . he's been permitted to sell his commission. And he has convinced the members of the Privy Council, before whose committee he gave sworn evidence, that New South Wales offers a unique opportunity for the development of a fine wool industry. Indeed, he has proposed that he should form a company from among our London merchants, assuring them of excellent profits and wool for manufacture that will be superior to the Spanish!" He sighed. "I have details of his proposals here."

Bligh, anger catching at his throat, listened in brooding silence to the proposals. The sheer effrontery of the man Macarthur was, in itself, astonishing enough. . . . To come back to England with ruin staring him in the face and then to turn the unenviable situation in which he found himself to his advantage was . . . good heavens, it was unprecedented!

"But surely, sir," he began when Sir Joseph Banks put down the papers he had been consulting. "Surely Lord Camden—"

"Lord Camden has added his recommendation to that of the Privy Council. Mr. Macarthur is to return to Sydney, freed of his arrest by the Horse Guards and with a letter from his lordship directing the governor to grant him ten thousand acres of land for the pasturage of sheep. Furthermore, he is to be permitted to take back with him a number of purebred Spanish Merinos from the royal herd, to enable him to improve the breed."

Sir Joseph Banks smiled thinly and once again anticipated Bligh's question. "The rogue has the luck of the devil, William. The vessel in which he left Sydney met a typhoon in the South China Sea and, dismasted, sought shelter at Amboyna. There Mr. Macarthur made the acquaintance of Sir Robert Farquhar and, it would seem, did him some service. Sir Robert gave him an introduction to his son, who is physician to His Royal Highness the Prince of Wales, who whispered the right word into his royal patient's ear. And, if that were not enough, he was recommended to the good offices of Lord Camden's private secretary, a certain Mr. Watson Taylor. What more could any man, in Macarthur's position, possibly want?"

What more indeed, Bligh reflected sourly. As Sir Joseph had said, the fellow had the devil's own luck. Instead of the disgrace and the ruin he had deserved, he was to return to the colony with the blessing of the Colonial Office and the Privy Council, and—

"And in his own ship," Sir Joseph asserted. "He has bought the *Argo* from the Hullets. I believe she's fitting out now, with accommodation for a nephew of His Royal Highness's physician and one of Macarthur's and . . . a specially commissioned figurehead. A Golden Fleece, no less!"

"The man is arrogant," Bligh said, making no attempt to conceal his disgust.

"Oh, yes, he is all of that. He called on me, William, soon after he reached London . . . without prior notice or an invitation from me. The urgency of his mission was his excuse."

Moodily, Sir Joseph poured himself a second glass of wine. He gestured to the tray.

"Don't stand on ceremony, my dear fellow. Take a glassful when you are ready—talking's thirsty work. But . . . to return to this fellow Macarthur. He came from Amboyna in an Indiaman that called at St. Helena, where Lord Valentina entrusted him with some valuable botanical specimens to deliver to me. To save himself trouble when he landed, the fool had crammed the whole consignment into three small wooden boxes. He offered no apology but instead, damn his impudence, talked to me of sheep! His specimens of wool were better packed than my plants."

The resentment in his patron's voice was not lost on Bligh. Understanding the reason for it, he sympathized while reflecting, with a sense of almost vindictive satisfaction, that justice might yet be served. The conniving Captain Macarthur had made one serious mistake—he might have Lord Camden and the Privy Council eating out of his hand, but he had offended Sir Joseph Banks, founding father of the colony of New South Wales, whose wealth and influence exceeded that of any mere politician.

As if to bear him out in this belief, Banks added forcefully, "I pointed out to Lord Camden that ten thousand acres is too vast a grant if it's to be given to one man for a sheepwalk. I have reason to suppose that the grant is now to be halved and that it will also be conditional—government may reclaim ownership should the land be required for other purposes."

Bligh was tempted to smile, but a glance at Sir Joseph's sternly set face caused him to think better of it.

"It is not," his patron said, weighing his words with care, "that I am any less anxious than the Privy Council or the London Chamber of Commerce to see New South Wales produce good wool for the home market. But not, I feel very strongly, for the sole benefit of one man—and he the villainous and insubordinate officer who shot poor William Paterson! The Horse Guards may see fit to release him from his arrest, and Camden permit—nay, encourage—his return to Sydney, without even waiting until Governor King's charges against him are received, but I"—his clenched fist came down on to the polished surface of the desk—"I, damme, I consider Macarthur an unmitigated rogue and a liar to boot!"

These were so much his own sentiments regarding the unknown Captain Macarthur that William Bligh nodded vigorously.

"It's a pity the regiment cannot be replaced, sir," he observed.

"It is, William. They've earned themselves the disgraceful title of the Rum Corps," Banks said, his lips curling in distaste. "The military garrison of the colony has never acquitted itself well—the excellent Governor Phillip experienced trouble with the marines he took out with him. But these men have gone much further, and if Captain Hunter is to be believed—and I am sure he is—it is largely due to the evil influence of our bête noire Macarthur." He waved his hand to the scattered papers on his desk. "I have had countless letters on the subject—from Captain King, from

William Paterson, and even from the chaplain, Samuel Marsden. They tell me that Sydney has become a veritable den of iniquity, filled with whores and drunkards—the worst of the drunkards being soldiers in the king's uniform, who rob the settlers and indulge in violence toward the civil officials. It must be stopped, William, if the colony is to prosper . . . indeed, if it is to survive."

He paused, eyeing Bligh expectantly. "The rule of law must be restored, and these—these liquor traders who masquerade as king's officers put in their place. In my opinion, *you* are the man to do what is required, as I told you. Now wait . . ." and as Bligh started to voice his feelings; "I have mentioned only the debit side. There is much going on in our antipodean possessions that is richly promising and in which you could play a distinguished part. You know, of course, that we dispatched young Matthew Flinders, with a goodly team of young scientists, to survey the southern coast of New Holland from Cape Leeuwin to Van Diemen's Land, and thence north to refit at Port Jackson?"

Bligh inclined his head. He was aware that not only Sir Joseph Banks's scientific interests were being served by the dispatch of Flinders's expedition. A passport had been reluctantly granted to two French ships, *Le Géographe* and *Le Naturaliste*, under the command of Commodore Baudin, to voyage in the same waters and for a similar purpose, and the British government—ever suspicious of French intentions in regard to the land Cook had claimed—had hastened to send Flinders after them. He had sailed from Spithead in the middle of July 1801 in the sloop *Investigator*—an old convoy escort vessel, previously H.M.S. *Xenophon*—with orders to circumnavigate the whole continent or archipelago of *Terra Australis* . . . and to keep a weather eye open for the Frenchmen. But Sir Joseph Banks, waxing enthusiastic concerning the likelihood of the discovery of new rivers and harbors, talked rather of future settlement than of any possibility of French treachery.

"Coal has been found north of Port Jackson," he went on, "and a convict mining camp set up there. I hear also that Governor King is considering the abandonment of Norfolk Island, which has become too small to house the number of recalcitrant felons exiled there from Sydney. In its stead he has suggested the establishment of a larger penal colony in Van Diemen's Land, at the head of one of the rivers Flinders and Bass discovered four or five years ago. Or alternatively one could be established on the south coast of what, I suppose, must now be termed the mainland. Colonel David Collins, who was Phillip's judge advocate, has volunteered to establish one there if Flinders is able to report favorably as to a site. And there's Princess Royal Harbor, which George Vancouver claimed for the Crown. The colony can grow, William—it must grow and expand! The wilderness must be reclaimed and filled with industrious settlers . . . and there are still Arthur Phillip's Blue Mountains to be crossed, for who knows what fine pasture land may lie beyond them?"

His eyes were very bright now, bright and filled with the light of dreams, and William Bligh, almost against his will, found himself responding to the challenge.

For challenge it was, irresistible to an ambitious man. A corrupt military hierarchy had first to be brought to order, its evil genius rendered submissive to authority or, if necessary, crushed and destroyed. He thought suddenly of the *Bounty* and of Christian and his fellow mutineers, and his expression hardened. The memory of his lost ship would always haunt him, for it smacked of failure, of a lack of firmness in himself. . . . But he had learned his lesson, learned it at The Nore and at Camperdown and Copenhagen. There was no fatal weakness in him now; he knew how to command obedience, how to suppress rebellion.

The rogue Macarthur, as yet personally unknown to him, was another Fletcher Christian. He might have defeated Hunter and defied King, and bamboozled the Privy Council and the Colonial Secretary, but, by heaven, in William Bligh he would meet his match! The challenge was irresistible indeed. . . .

"Shall I be given a king's ship, sir?" he asked, scarcely realizing that he had spoken the words aloud until his host's hand clapped his epauleted shoulder in warm approval.

"I feel sure that could be arranged, William—if it means you'll be willing to go out to the colony in King's place. Does it?"

Bligh's hesitation was momentary. "If I am offered the appointment, Sir Joseph, I'll accept it gladly. I am more grateful to you than words can express, and I assure you, sir, I shall do all in my power to prove worthy of your confidence in me."

"I don't doubt you will, my dear fellow." Sir Joseph Banks raised his glass in pleased salute. "Not a word about the matter yet, though—not until King's resignation is accepted. When it is, you may count on my recommending you in the highest terms."

Outside in Soho Square, twenty minutes later, William Bligh was conscious of a sense of heady elation. A governorship, a munificent salary and a pension, his own king's ship and her company to support his authority, and a newly discovered country ripe for development . . . As he had sat cooling his heels in the First Lord's anteroom that morning, he had hoped only to be given a ship. But now . . . God in heaven, in his wildest dreams he had envisaged nothing to compare with what he had been promised!

Betsy, his beloved, patient wife, must be told. Her health might preclude her from accompanying him on the long voyage to Port Jackson, but bless her heart, she would be overjoyed for his sake and free, for the first time during their married life, of financial worries. He would bring his daughter Mary with him—Mary, and her husband, Charles Putland, at present languishing on a lieutenant's half-pay ashore. And . . . He raised his white-gloved hand to call his chair.

And there was the marine sergeant, Hawley, who had served him so well during the fleet mutiny at The Nore. He had gone to Admiral Duncan's flagship *Venerable*—the only one of the North Sea line-of-battle ships to keep her record clean and her people loyal . . . well, it should not be too difficult to find Hawley and offer him the chance to go to New South Wales. A loyal, dependable Royal Marine sergeant might well prove worth his weight in gold to a new governor pledged to restore the military garrison to a state of proper discipline . . . and rid it of officers of Macarthur's caliber.

A sudden idea occurred to him and, as he stepped into his hired chair, William Bligh was smiling. He could pro-

cure Hawley a commission in the colony's regiment—
before heaven, a noncommissioned officer in the Royal
Marine Corps with a fine war record behind him could
hold his own with officers like Macarthur, tradesmen's
sons, and the misfits from fighting regiments. Besides, the
promise of such a. promotion would be an inducement,
should Hawley prove reluctant to transfer from his own
proud corps to . . . What had Sir Joseph called Macarthur's regiment? The Rum Corps . . . His smile widened and, as his chairmen moved slowly through the
crowded streets, he faced the long journey by coach to
his lodgings in Southsea with less than his usual impatience.

A week later a brief communication from the Admiralty
informed him that he had been appointed to command the
Warrior, a third-rate, now in her twenty-first year of service in the Royal Navy.

Johnny Broome felt a lifting of the heart when he saw
the flag run up on Port Jackson's South Head on the morning of June 9, 1803. He murmured a prayer of thankfulness
as H.M.S. *Investigator* limped into the harbor with her
pumps going, her hull leaking badly, and eighteen of her
crew down with scurvy or the aftermath of fever. The sloop
had been away for just over eleven months, and in spite of
her unseaworthy state and her depleted crew, Matt Flinders had sailed her five thousand miles in forty-eight days
since leaving Timor . . . and brought them back alive.

Not all of them, alas. Johnny gripped the wheel with
rawly ulcerated hands, aware that, of the eighteen sick, one
at least was dying . . . and he now a close and valued
friend after the months of shared endeavor—the botanist
and gardener Peter Good.

It had been, in many respects, a disastrous voyage, he
knew, although its purpose had been achieved. Flinders's
cramped cabin was piled high with newly compiled charts
of the eastern coast, the Barrier Reef, and the vast, empty
Gulf of Carpentaria to the north of the great continent he
had named Australia. Islands had been explored and
named; they had braved Pandora's Passage with a leadsman in the chains calling out depths, taken more soundings
in the Torres Strait, and held off attack by dark-skinned

pirates paddling swift-moving native *prahus*, under the pretext of trading their coconuts for axes and nails.

With monsoon storms in the offing and the sloop's bottom rotting beneath them, they had careened her on the burning yellow sand of a deserted beach and made what repairs they could to her peeling copper and barnacle-encrusted timbers, with time running out and food and fresh water in short supply.

Sir Joseph Banks's artists and botanists had made sketches and gathered plants and seeds for their patron, but sometimes in their enthusiasm they had come under attack from hostile natives. A young mate named Whitewood had died under a shower of spears, and the artist William Westall had barely escaped with his life a few days later.

They had made at last for Timor, in the hope of replenishing their provisions, and for Johnny the return to Coupang had been a strangely moving experience. He had seen again the white-walled house of the Dutch officials, the palm-thatched hospital where he and the Bryant party had first been lodged and nursed back to health . . . and then, almost unwillingly, his gaze had gone to the fort to which, on Captain Edward Edwards's instructions, they and the unhappy survivors of the *Bounty* mutiny had been removed, to swelter in chained misery in its malodorous dungeons.

Justin, remarkably lively and fit, and eager to explore in spite of the heat and the flies, had begged him for details of his earlier stay, but Johnny had brusquely bade the boy hold his tongue. The day before they had sailed, however, he had gone with Surgeon Bell and some of the youngsters, with Justin at his heels, to the European cemetery and had seen there the headstone of the Dutch governor, Timotheus Wanjon, the man who had given him into Edwards's brutal custody. Yet still, as the others read the names of the *Bounty*'s botanist, David Nelson, and those of *Le Géographe*'s lost scientists—all victims of Coupang's fatal fever—he had held his peace.

Timor had been his goal, the destination he and the men of Will Bryant's party had dreamed of reaching when they had planned their escape from Sydney; and for all its evil reputation, to him it was—and would always be—the safe haven they had sought for and found. Timor had meant

freedom, and the Dutch would have given it to them with
the same hospitable willingness they had shown in supplying Flinders's needs, despite being themselves short of all
provisions, save rice and fruit. Only their own countryman,
Captain Edwards, had demanded that he and his companions must be given up, so that they might be brought to
trial in England, together with his tortured captives from
the *Bounty*. Governor Wanjon had yielded to that demand,
but he had done so with reluctance, and . . . Johnny's
swollen lips twitched into a wan smile as he remembered.

An odd sentimental impulse had sent him—when Surgeon Bell and the others had wandered off—back to the
lonely, overgrown grave with a handful of jungle orchids,
which he had laid at the foot of Timotheus Wanjon's cross.

"Put your helm up, Johnny!" Matt Flinders's voice was
a harsh croak as he gave his orders, and the *Investigator*
sluggishly came about. Like the rest of them Matt was suffering from dysentery, and the lack of antiscorbutics during
the past month had affected them all in varying degrees
. . . although Matt refused to admit being ill. He was
standing now on the quarterdeck in full uniform, his sword
at his side, ready to go ashore and pay his respects to
Governor King, a thin, pale shadow of himself but in-
domitable as ever.

The courses were taken in; the topmen dragged themselves up the shrouds, and young Midshipman Franklin supervised the firing of the signal gun's salute. Her pumps
still cranking dismally, the battered *Investigator* came to
anchor in Sydney Cove, dwarfed by the three East Indiamen already at anchor there.

Justin, thin as a rake but still in high spirits, came on
deck laden with the charts Flinders had said he wanted for
the governor's inspection. He grinned at his father, elated
because he had been chosen to accompany his captain
ashore—albeit as the humble bearer of the rolls of precious
records.

Flinders, Johnny was aware, was his son's new hero, the
sea the life he now wanted, and he wondered, with the first
stirrings of uneasiness, how Jenny would view the offer
Flinders had made to take the boy into the navy under his
patronage. It was, of course, a splendid offer for a Currency kid from the penal colony of New South Wales, since

Matt Flinders would almost certainly rise to the height of his profession and any protégé of his would rise with him. Even in the nominal berth of captain's servant, Justin would have the status of an embryo deck officer, and once he reached England he would be eligible to apply for midshipman's rate on board any king's ship to which his patron was appointed. His own prospects, in the masters' branch, would always be limited, Johnny thought wryly. Masters came through the hawsehole from the lower deck and were very rarely granted commissions, but for Justin, if he followed Matt Flinders's star, promotion to a lieutenancy was bound to come. And in the fullness of time, if he acquitted himself well, he might even command a king's ship. But . . . there was Jenny. For her it would mean the ultimate sacrifice.

He went to aid the lowering of the launch, saw the first batch of sick men packed carefully into it, and bade a sad farewell to Peter Good, who lay motionless, wrapped in his blankets on the bottom boards, the mark of death already on his white, agonized face. Poor Peter would never see his beloved Kew again, Johnny thought bitterly, and the plants he had so assiduously tended would have to be cared for by others now.

Three of the seamen had the same mark as he, manifested in a weary lassitude, and they had all been fine young men when he had first known them, in the prime of their lives. The sea took its toll, he reminded himself, and he was again conscious of misgiving as he watched Matt Flinders's gig put off for the governor's wharf, with Justin seated proudly beside him.

They were gone for almost four hours. There was much to be done in their absence; the scientists were starting to pack up their specimens, but in a desultory fashion, aware that it might be days before they could transfer them to the shore or to another ship, for the *Investigator* would be unable to take any of them back to England. Like the poor old *Supply*, she would almost certainly have to be condemned and end her days—like the *Supply*—as a dismasted hulk.

Johnny occupied himself with the duties of the ship, his mind not on the familiar chores he had performed so often, but rather thinking now of Jenny and, with eagerness, of his younger son and daughter—babies he scarcely knew—and of the rolling acres of the farm he had left so light-heartedly. It was cold after the tropical heat to which they had all become accustomed, and he shivered as a heavy rain squall slashed across the deck, blotting out the Sydney shoreline and wringing curses from the sailmaker's crew, who had been spreading some of their stained canvas out to dry.

It was dark when the gig tied up to the *Investigator's* starboard chains, and they all gathered around, avid for news, when Flinders hoisted himself to the deck. He had much to tell and mail to distribute. To the seamen he said only, "Shore leave for the larboard watch tomorrow, lads, and starboard watch the day after. There are fresh provisions in the boat—hoist them inboard, and she'll go back for more." Smiling, he added, "His Excellency the governor wishes me to convey his warmest thanks and congratulations to you all, both ship's company and distinguished passengers. He has told me, gentlemen, that we have written the most inspiring page in the history of this colony, and has promised that a full account of our discoveries will be published in the newssheet known as the *Sydney Gazette*, as soon as I can furnish it."

To subdued cheers from the weary men, their commander—no less weary, Johnny felt certain, than they—limped below to his cabin, and for the next half hour did his best to pass on to his officers what local and home news he had contrived to glean from the governor.

There was belated confirmation that a peace of sorts had been made with France, under the Treaty of Amiens, which was not expected to last.

"But Captain King is wary of French colonial ambitions in this part of the world," Flinders qualified. "He has sent Lieutenant Bowen in the *Lady Nelson* to establish a settlement in Van Diemen's Land, at the mouth of our Derwent River. And there is the possibility of another at Port Phillip under Colonel Collins—the bay to the west of Wilson's Promontory, to which our friend Murray beat us to the naming. And, come to that, to the claiming . . . it is situated in thirty-eight degrees of south latitude and one hundred and forty-five of east longitude, in case any of you have forgotten. And"—he laughed—"our good Dr. George, who, alas, is again on passage to Otaheite in his *Venus,* is to have the strait between Van Diemen's Land and the mainland *officially* named after him—their lordships have confirmed it! I have been given the northernmost island in the Furneaux group—the sealers' paradise—for posterity to remember me by."

They all joined in his laughter and Robert Fowler, the first lieutenant, asked cautiously, "Are we to be given passages home, sir? And leave?"

"Leave, yes, Robert," his commander assured him. "As to passages, the governor has promised to do his best for us. I've told him that this poor old ship is no longer fit to put to sea, and he says he will have her inspected as soon as he can. They managed to patch up the *Lady Nelson* after we sent her back."

"They'll not be able to patch up our ship," Fowler returned with conviction. "I wish they could!"

Flinders inclined his head. He looked unbearably tired and ill, Johnny saw, but still he talked on, giving them what gossip Sydney could provide. "The infamous Captain Macarthur has been sent home under arrest, and the governor hopes he'll never show his face here again, for it seems Sydney is a better place without him. But the Rum Corps continues to plague the poor governor, even in Macarthur's absence. He ordered three corps officers to be tried by court-martial for issuing lampoons, calculated to libel him, but Major Johnstone—who's in temporary command— terminated the proceedings by arresting the deputy judge advocate, Dr. Harris. Mr. Atkins replaced him and . . . all three officers were acquitted! His Excellency is in such despair he's talking of requesting that he be relieved."

"Do you think he will, sir?" Surgeon Bell asked.

"I don't know," Flinders admitted. "But I felt intensely sorry for him when he told me how Johnstone had behaved to him. Poor Colonel Paterson is still unable to return to duty, and he may take sick leave. If he does, I don't fancy the governor will stay. It's a damnable pity. Captain King and Captain Hunter—*both* of them—are fair-minded, honest gentlemen who've done all in their power to serve the best interests of this colony. It's iniquitous to see them persecuted—there's no other word for it—by a set of ruffians who wouldn't last a day in *our* service! Mistress King is—

oh, she's heartbroken, poor lady." He sounded at once angry and despairing. "I hope to God, though," he added, "that we haven't opened up the continent of Australia for their kind!"

Later, when the evening meal—freshly killed mutton, courtesy of the governor—had been eaten with rare appetite by the whole ship's company, Flinders called Johnny into his cabin.

"You've talked of that farm of yours on the Hawkesbury, Johnny, and young Justin's talked about it too. You'll be going back there, I presume?" His tone was casual but his eyes were oddly bright.

"Indeed I will!" Johnny confirmed. "The instant my captain sees fit to grant me leave."

"Your captain will oblige at the earliest possible moment . . . and he'd like to come with you, if your wife can put up with a miserably sick man for a week or two."

Johnny stared at him and then grasped him warmly by the shoulders. "I'd like nothing more, Matt. And Jenny will welcome you with open arms, however sick you are."

Flinders smiled and gestured to the letters spread out on his chart table. "From my wife, from my beloved Annette. Reading them has made me . . . Oh, I'll not be able to stomach Sydney and the infernal Rum Corps. A home with children in it, that's what I crave. And time to—to recover, Johnny. To forget responsibilities."

"That I can promise you," Johnny assured him.

"Thanks. I . . . one other thing. Justin told me this afternoon that he's decided not to take my offer. He says he wants to stay here, and—I'm glad."

For a moment, Johnny was too astonished to take it in. Then he grinned. "By God, Matt, so am I! The boy's a fool, but I'm damned glad."

"I'd give a great deal," Matt Flinders told him, a catch in his voice, "if Annette and I could have a fool like that for a son."

CHAPTER XXI

"I'm after saddling the bay gelding for ye, mistress," Seamus O'Leary said, his manner toward her, as always, faintly resentful. Frances thanked him without warmth and, avoiding his proffered assistance, swung herself gracefully onto the bay's back. The two pistols she was carrying concealed beneath her cloak made a slight metallic clink, but looking anxiously down at the farm foreman's face, she decided that if he had heard it the sound had had no significance for him.

She gathered up the reins, impatient to be on her way, but O'Leary detained her, his hand on the horse's noseband.

"Will ye be late back?" he asked.

"I may be," Frances evaded. "But you need not put yourself out, Mr. O'Leary—I can stable the horse without troubling you."

" 'Tis no trouble, mistress," O'Leary retorted with mock servility. "Amn't I here to serve you?"

Frances dug her single heel into the bay's side and, settling herself comfortably into the beautiful leather sidesaddle Jasper Spence had imported for her, left O'Leary staring balefully after her.

Her recent marriage to Jasper Spence had not only antagonized Henrietta, she reflected wryly; it had set the O'Leary family against her as well. And she had neither expected nor asked for marriage. Jasper Spence had been the kindest and most considerate of masters, treating her always as his social equal and going to immense pains to obtain her emancipation, so as to enable them to marry.

Besides—her lips twisted into an ironic little smile as she put her horse into a canter—contrary to Henrietta's belief, she had never been Jasper's mistress; his had been a patient and selfless courtship, conducted with a circumspection that he had supposed would placate his daughter and allay her suspicions. Indeed, it had not been until a year after Henrietta's marriage to Timothy Dawson and the birth of their first child that he had asked her whether she would accept Frances as her stepmother. Predictably, of course, Henrietta had refused, and there had been further delays while poor Jasper had wrestled with his conscience, and finally—driven to it largely by loneliness—he had proposed to her.

And—Frances expelled her breath in a longdrawn, regretful sigh—she was happy, fond and admiring of the man she had married, grateful to him too, if not in love with him; but her conscience, like his, continued to trouble her, although not on Henrietta's account. Jasper's spoiled, self-willed daughter might—and often did—endeavor to humiliate her convict stepmother, but she had been compelled to accept the relationship. Timothy had seen to that. And Henrietta herself, for all her reluctance to admit it, was so deeply in love with Timothy Dawson that she was wax in his hands. Besides, there were the children. She had always had a way with children, Frances thought in all humility. Starting with little Justin, Jenny Broome's son, she had realized that she could win their trust and enjoy their company, and the two little Dawson girls, to whom she had acted as nursemaid before her marriage, had given her their complete devotion.

The bay gelding, unaccustomed to being ridden without the company of other horses and riders, shied at a shadow and gave vent to a nervous whinny. Frances calmed him, a hand gently caressing his cropped mane. Was it, she wondered uneasily, her imagination, or was there another rider, hidden behind the clump of straggling gum trees she had just passed? She pulled up and listened, glancing over her shoulder but unable to discern any sign of pursuit.

Chiding herself for her lack of courage, she rode on. Who, in any case, would trouble to follow her? Surely not Seamus O'Leary? In Jasper's absence—her husband had gone to Sydney with Timothy to buy horses—the foreman had plenty to occupy him without wasting valuable time prying into her affairs . . . however curious he might be. And there was no denying that he *was* curious; he had asked questions the last time she had ridden out alone, in an attempt to find out for what purpose and where she had gone. As if it were any business of his; but conscious of the weight of the two pistols against her thigh, Frances put out a hand to shift them, her conscience again tormenting her.

Before her marriage she had subscribed to only one loyalty and had felt no qualms on that account, since it had been loyalty to the United Irish and the Defenders' cause that brought her to New South Wales as a convicted felon. And it had been for that sacred cause that her brother had forfeited his life, God rest his gallant soul! In the fading light she crossed herself, seeing again in memory Conal's limp, broken body swinging from the *Boddingtons'* yard-arm.

The terrible, vindictive treatment of her countrymen was still going on, she thought despairingly. One of the transports that had anchored in Sydney Cove only a few months ago—the *Hercules*—had been carrying Irishmen to exile, men sentenced to transportation for life, after the bloody suppression of the rebellion Wolfe Tone had inspired. The ship's master had hanged a score of them (just as the *Boddingtons'* master had hanged poor Conal) claiming that they had attempted mutiny. But at least the ship's master had been brought to trial and heavily fined, for what had amounted to murder. And the survivors, sick and emaciated, suffering from the brutal floggings he had administered, had been driven ashore in chains and put to work on the roads.

How could she desert the Defenders' cause now, even if, thanks to Jasper Spence, she was free and the wife of a landowner and magistrate? Frances's fingers closed about the hilt of one of the pistols. Brian McCormack, that brave, red-headed giant who had defied the soldiers when they tried to flog him, had asked for weapons, and Father Dixon, when she had sought his guidance, had assured her that she would be guilty of no sin were she to accede to his request. She had brought him a musket on her first visit to the Defenders' secret meeting place outside Parramatta

It was an old and rusty weapon she had found discarded in one of the farm buildings, but the pistols were in good condition, and they belonged to Jasper, as also did the powder and shot with which to arm them. Despite Father Dixon's assurance, she felt guilty because she had taken them, although . . . She caught her breath sharply.

All Brian McCormack wanted was to be set free . . . he and the rest of her poor, tortured countrymen. They would throw off their chains, leave the wretched prison huts in which they were confined, and make their way in a body to Sydney, there to petition the governor for a ship to take them back to Ireland. There would be no violence, unless the soldiers of the Rum Corps opposed them—and the chances were that they would not, since many of them had been convicts and quite a number were Irish. The Irish in Sydney, free as well as convict, would join them, Brian McCormack had confidently predicted, and faced with their united appeal, Governor King—who was not an unjust man—would give them what they asked.

Father James Dixon, whose brother had fought so gallantly in Wexford for the Cause, had added that another hero of the '98 Rebellion, Joseph Holt from County Wicklow, who had held the rank of general, would take command and act as intermediary in the negotiations with the governor.

"You'll see, Frances, my child," he had said earnestly. "We will get our way here without bloodshed. It'll not be as it was in Wexford. But we shall need weapons, just to put the fear of God and our Irish patriots into the drunken bullies who call themselves King George's soldiers. If you can help, then God's blessings on you, my daughter, for a loyal Irishwoman!"

Frances thought about his words as she rode on into the gathering darkness, faltering a little in her resolution as she considered the possible consequences. Father Dixon had said there would be no violence; Father Harrold and Father O'Neill had confirmed his statement. They were priests of God, and she could not doubt their sincerity.

The lights of the Parramatta township were shining out of the darkness when the bay horse whinnied again and Seamus O'Leary, astride one of the young workhorses, came trotting up to join her.

"What do you want, Mr. O'Leary?" Frances demanded, startled and more than a little alarmed by his unexpected appearance. "Have you been following me?"

Seamus O'Leary doffed his hat. "Come now, Mistress O'Riordan," he countered, giving her, almost insultingly, her maiden name. "Did you t'ink dat you were de only patriot among us? Sure an' amn't I Irish like yourself, den, an' ready an' willing to fight for de Cause?" He gestured to the pitchfork and the two reaping hooks that hung from his saddle and waved her to precede him.

"So you see, yer honor, dere's good reason to suppose dey'll rise up, under arms, wid'in de next twenty-four hours. Maybe even tonight, sorr."

The nasal Irish voice was intended to be ingratiating, but Captain Abbott, commanding the Parramatta company of the New South Wales Corps, eyed its owner with barely concealed dislike. He despised traitors and in particular those who betrayed their comrades in the hope of reward.

"And where, pray, do these rebels plan to launch their insurrection?" he questioned coldly.

"Dey'll gather at King's Town an' Castle Hill, yer honor."

"And then?"

"Why, dey'll march to Sydney, Captain, where dey're countin' on others to join dem. 'Tis a ship dey say dey're wantin', but 'tis my belief dey plan to murder de governor and de officers, and—"

"And take over the colony, I suppose?" Edward Abbott snapped. "Armed with pitchforks and axes and homemade pikes?"

"A few have muskets, sorr, an' pistols."

"And what do they imagine they can achieve against five hundred trained soldiers? Not to mention a king's ship at anchor in the cove?" Abbott's tone was derisive. He dismissed his informant with scant ceremony, not even troubling to ask his name.

When the man had gone, however, he decided to take out a patrol to reassure himself that all was well in the Castle Hill area, and before doing so he wrote a brief report of what his visitor had told him and sent it, by the hand of a mounted trooper, to Major Johnstone in Sydney. In the continued absence, on sick leave, of Colonel Paterson, George Johnstone was acting commandant of the corps, and it was up to him to decide whether or not to take the warning seriously.

The damned Irish were always making trouble, he thought irritably. Successive governors had complained repeatedly to the Colonial Office concerning the number being sent out, but to no avail. In Governor Phillip's day they had had only English felons to contend with, but now every infernal seditionist of Irish or Scottish nationality was bundled into a transport and decanted, still bitter and rebellious, to swell the number already here. The so-called Scottish martyrs had been reasonable enough, but the Irish were beyond reason, plague take them!

Captain Abbott shouted to his orderly to saddle a horse for him, and swearing under his breath, he buckled on his sword belt and saw to the loading of a pair of pistols before stumping out into the night.

A settler and his wife, both in their nightclothes and clutching whimpering children by the hand, met the patrol on the outskirts of the King's Hill hamlet. Their smallholding had been robbed by a band of armed Irishmen, the man said, quaking with remembered terror, and a number—which he estimated at several hundred—were running amok all over the scattered settlement, pillaging and looting.

Abbott directed them to seek shelter in the Parramatta Hospital and dispatched a second mounted trooper to inform Major Johnstone of what was afoot. He had horses for only eight men besides himself, and his company was depleted by the need to furnish garrisons in outlying areas; two of his mounted troopers were on their way to Sydney, which left him with six. He was debating whether to continue on his way to the scene of the riot or to go back for infantry reinforcements when the Reverend Samuel Marsden made his appearance, mounted on a gray cob.

"I'm thankful I caught up with you, Captain Abbott," the chaplain said breathlessly as he drew rein.

"What can I do for you, sir?" Abbott inquired, still refusing to regard the outbreak as cause for serious alarm . . . although Marsden, he observed, was very much alarmed and, for a man of God, greatly enraged.

"I hold no brief for Captain Macarthur, as you well know," the Yorkshireman told him, "but he's out of the country and his wife and children are alone and unprotected, save for their servants. And if the convicts are rebelling, then convict servants are probably not to be relied upon. I think, sir, that you should send a guard to Elizabeth Farm and—"

"But they are in no more danger than anyone else, Mr. Marsden," Abbott began. "They—"

"I fear they are, sir," Marsden interrupted, his tone one to brook no argument. "I have it from an informant—a *trusted* informant—that there's a plan afoot to raid the Macarthur property. These villains intend to burn the place to the ground!"

"My information is that they will make for Sydney. But . . ." Edward Abbott broke off, frowning. John Macarthur would never forgive him if any harm came to his wife and family, he was aware, and Macarthur could be an implacable enemy. Abbott shrugged. Since the Reverend Marsden, who had even less reason than most to seek protection for Macarthur's wife and property, was the man to ask for it, he could hardly refuse the request.

"Are you going to Elizabeth Farm?" he asked.

The stout chaplain nodded. "I was on my way there to warn Mistress Macarthur. But then I was told you were out with your troops, and so I came in search of you, hoping to enlist your aid. I trust I do not appeal to you in vain, Captain Abbott?"

"No," Abbott assured him. "Take four of my troopers, sir. I'll ride back to barracks and call out my foot soldiers. I'd probably need them in any case if the mob is as large as I've been led to believe. I've sent for Major Johnstone from Sydney. . . . He'll almost certainly meet the rebels on his way here, if they *are* making for Sydney."

Major Johnstone, on receiving his company commander's report, lost no time in answering it. After sending a message to the governor he mustered forty of his men, ordered sixteen of them to Castle Hill, and himself led the remainder by the more direct route to the Northern Boundary, hoping to catch the rebels between two fires.

He came up with them at ten-thirty next morning, near the Ponds settlement, guided there by the smoke and flames of looted buildings and the riotous shouts of the raiders. Receiving word that his second detachment was in position under the command of Lieutenant Davis, he ordered his own to follow him and take cover outside the settlement, and he himself rode forward, with a single mounted trooper as escort, to parley with the Irishmen's leaders. All was, however, in confusion, the leaders seemingly nowhere to be found, and those to whom he addressed himself answered him with insolent catcalls, mingled with threats, and a refusal to surrender.

Returning to his main body, which had now caught up with him, Major Johnstone told his second-in-command, "The scoundrels are insolent, and I can talk no sense into them. We'll give them half an hour to find their leaders, and then I'll talk to them again. I don't want to open fire on them if it can be avoided, but if needs be, I shall have to."

"I think they're determined to make a fight of it, sir," the tall quartermaster, Lieutenant Laycock, called back from his vantage point in the branches of a tree. "They're pulling back to the foot of that low hill over to our right—Castle Hill, it's called, I believe. And they're taking up defensive positions. But Brabyn's party should have them covered if he moves right-handed."

Johnstone dismounted and joined him, field glass in hand. There were, as nearly as he could judge from a swift survey, now upward of two hundred ragged, unkempt Irishmen milling about at the edge of the burning houses. As Laycock had said, they appeared to be preparing to defend themselves against attack, and voices were raised, urging them to take up their positions behind the scrub and scattered rocks of the spur of raised ground he had identified as Castle Hill. Johnstone glimpsed the dull gleam of a musket barrel here and there among the straggling ranks; he saw one man wielding a cutlass, but for the most part their weapons appeared to be a motley collection of agricultural implements, with pitchforks predominating.

Poor, misguided wretches, he thought, momentarily pitying them; but then his resolution hardened and he gave orders to his own men to form up in two ranks, with their muskets primed, still keeping under cover.

"I will try to persuade them to surrender," he said to Lieutenant Brabyn, who had moved to the right at Laycock's suggestion. "If the leaders refuse after I've parleyed with them, then I shall ride them off and drive them toward you if I can. Without their leaders they will probably go to pieces and run. If they do, pick off one or two and then call on the rest to give themselves up. But understand, we don't want a wholesale massacre—arrest, don't shoot them."

Brabyn looked disappointed, but he acknowledged his understanding, and Major Johnstone again rode forward with his single escort. This time two men came to meet him, a slim young priest and an impressive red-haired giant with a noticeable limp.

"Are you the leaders of this insurrection?" the major asked them uncompromisingly.

"We are representing the United Irishmen, sir," the red-haired man said. His tone was courteous and his voice educated, belying his mud-stained rags and wild, long hair. The severed end of a chain fetter hung from one of his wrists, and when he turned to shout to one of his fellows, Johnstone saw, through the torn and filthy shirt, his back bore the half-healed lacerations of a recent flogging. Clearly this man had reason to rebel, for even in New South Wales it was unusual to force convicts with education to perform manual labor in one of the chain gangs . . . or, indeed, to flog them.

The priest started to speak, attempting in a few impassioned words to give reasons for the uprising, but conscious of his duty, Johnstone interrupted him.

"I must remind you both," he told them, "of the impropriety of your conduct. To bear arms is contrary to the laws of this colony when you are under sentence for having committed a felony in your country of origin, and—"

"It is no felony," the priest exclaimed angrily, "to defend the rights of freeborn Irishmen against foreign tyranny and oppression! And that is all we are doing now, sir. We do not recognize the justice of English courts, nor are we subject to English laws. In the name of God, let us pass, sir, without hindrance. We—"

"No!" Johnstone roared, losing patience. "To avoid bloodshed I am offering you the chance to lay down your arms and surrender. If you do not, then I shall be compelled to order my men to open fire on you. The decision is yours, Master Priest—consider carefully before you give me your answer."

"We will not surrender, Major," the red-haired man replied without hesitation. "If you open fire on us, we shall return your fire."

Johnstone nodded to the trooper, and they both swung their horses around, cutting off the Irishmen's retreat. A pistol to the head of the priest, Johnstone propelled him with a booted foot in the direction of his waiting detachment, and as the mounted trooper followed his example, half a dozen foot soldiers ran out from their concealment and dragged the two captives, struggling violently, back to their lines.

From the hill, a single musket blazed abortive defiance, and Brabyn, as soon as his company commander was out of his line of fire, yelled to his detachment to open up.

The battle, such as it was, lasted for barely fifteen minutes. Then, with sixteen of their number dead and as many more wounded, the Irish broke and fled. Lieutenant Davis's detachment caught them in the planned cross fire as they sought vainly to escape, and leaving his two subalterns to join Abbott and continue the pursuit, Major Johnstone accepted the surrender of more than a score and marched back with them to Sydney. Surgeon Harris and two assistants remained to care for the wounded.

Retribution was swift and salutory. Within two days of the battle, a military court presided over by Captain Abbott assembled to try ten of the ringleaders. They were charged with having, on March 4, 1804, riotously assembled at Castle Hill, armed with offensive weapons, with an intent to overthrow the government.

All were found guilty . . . eight of them sentenced to death, and the two who were reprieved to receive five hundred lashes and hard labor at Coal River. Charles Hall, Samuel Himes, and John Place were hanged at Parramatta on March 8; William Johnston, John Neale, and George Harrington at Castle Hill on the same day. On the tenth, at Sydney, John Brennon and Timothy Hogan met their end on the gallows, and John Burke and Brian McCormack received two hundred of their five hundred lashes.

Frances heard this unhappy news from Henrietta, who paid her an unexpected visit accompanied by her two small daughters, her baby son, Alexander, and their new convict nursemaid, a subdued and frightened little London seamstress named Abigail Mullins.

Henrietta complained of fatigue after the drive by carriage from Sydney, and while she reclined with closed eyes on a chaise longue, Frances made tea and assisted Abigail to ply her two little charges with refreshments. The children, as always, were delighted to see her; four-year-old Julia insisting on being taken onto her knee, despite the fact that her sister, pert, pretty little Dorothea Rose, was already seated there.

Conscious of their mother's unspoken resentment toward her, Frances bustled them off to rest, in the nursemaid's charge, as soon as they had finished eating and Henrietta roused herself to ask for tea. Sipping delicately from a bone china cup, she described the Sydney hangings with a wealth of grim detail.

"I did not witness them, of course, but Timothy and my father did, and they said that both of the condemned made full confession and pleaded for forgiveness on the scaffold. What deluded, wicked fools they were to imagine that they could overcome the garrison and seize possession of the colony! Do you not think they were justly condemned for their crimes, Frances?"

Aware of the searching scrutiny to which she was being subjected, Frances strove to retain her customary composure, her face pale but carefully devoid of expression. She murmured a vague denial, and Henrietta seized on it with unconcealed eagerness.

"You don't agree? Well, of course, they were your countrymen, were they not? Did you, by any chance, know any of them?"

Too proud to lie, Frances answered flatly, "Some of them, yes, from home, from Wexford. And Father Dixon was a friend of my brother's. He—"

"The priests have not yet been tried," Henrietta put in. "But they say in Sydney that their cloth will not save them if they are found guilty of conspiracy. They will be sent to Norfolk Island or Coal River—or even to the new penal settlement in Van Diemen's Land, if Lieutenant Bowen sends word that he can take them. And that man Holt, the one who was supposed to be an Irish general . . ." Her glance at Frances was frankly malicious. "My father says that he's to be banished to Norfolk Island because he knew about the uprising long before it took place but did not inform Major Johnstone."

Joseph Holt, Frances thought bitterly, had nevertheless betrayed his fellow Defenders. They had counted on him to lead them, had waited for him at Castle Hill long after the agreed hour, but he had gone, instead, to the New South Wales Corps adjutant, Lieutenant Cox—on whose farm he acted as overseer—and aided him to put his house in a state of defense in case the rebels launched a raid on it. Those same rebels who had trusted him with their lives, made him privy to all their plans, and who . . .

Henrietta passed her cup. "Pour me some more tea, will you? It was so dusty, driving here—my throat's quite sore." She accepted the refilled cup without acknowledgment and went on, "They are searching the convicts' huts for arms, and I heard that Mr. Marsden found pikes and swords in the homes of some *English* emancipists in Toongabbe. Imagine the English allying themselves with Irish traitors! But what can you expect of people who came out here as convicted felons?"

The last observation was, Frances knew, intended to provoke her, but she resolutely ignored it, although her hands were visibly trembling as she helped herself to tea from the tray between them.

Disappointed by her lack of response Henrietta talked idly of improvements that Timothy was making to the farmhouse at the Hawkesbury and then returned to the subject of the Irish uprising.

"I expect you know that there was no love lost between Mr. Marsden and Captain Macarthur . . . and small wonder, in the circumstances, is it? But perhaps you *don't* know that the good chaplain—when he learned that the Irish rebels planned to raid the Macarthurs' farm and burn it to the ground—went out there himself with some soldiers to offer Elizabeth Macarthur his protection?"

"I did not know that," Frances confessed and forced herself to add, "It was very—very Christian of him."

"Yes, was it not? I used to consider him rather coarse and ill-bred, but he has mellowed since he came out here, and he works tirelessly in the colony's interests." Henrietta consulted the pretty pendant-watch hanging about her neck—a gift from Timothy on the occasion of little Dorothea Rose's birth—and stifled a yawn. "I hope they will not be too late arriving here. It will be a nuisance if we have to stay the night." Meeting Frances's bewildered gaze, she laughed. "Didn't my father send you word? He and Timothy have concluded their business in Sydney."

"You mean they've bought the horses? But I had supposed that—"

"They did not buy horses—the ones that arrived were in poor condition, hardly worth importing, Timothy said." Henrietta laughed again. "Does my father tell you nothing, in spite of having married you?"

Resentful color came to burn in Frances's cheeks. It irritated her that Henrietta always spoke of "my father," never of "your husband," but it was true, she was forced to concede, that Jasper seldom told her of his commercial dealings. He and Tim were in partnership, and Tim, it seemed, had no secrets from his wife. . . . Or else Henrietta was better able than she to wheedle such details from him. But it was strange that Jasper, who was considerate where domestic matters were concerned, had not sent word to warn her of his impending return . . . or even of Henrietta's visit.

Unless . . . Her smooth brow creased into a thoughtful pucker. Unless he had sent a message by Patrick O'Leary, who had gone with him to Sydney, and Seamus O'Leary had neglected to pass on his son's message to her. Seamus had, of late, begun to take liberties, to treat her disrespectfully, hinting that they were fellow conspirators and therefore on terms of equality, and she found herself wondering, not for the first time, whether he was to be trusted. True, he had supplied the Defenders with a few weapons, as she had herself, but he had taken no part in the uprising, pleading his freeman's status as the reason, and his explanation had been accepted, even by Brian McCormack and Father Dixon. He was from New Ross, on the Wexford county border, and had told her he was a Catholic. She had, surely, no real reason to mistrust him? He could hardly denounce her for supplying the weapons without implicating himself, and yet . . . Her frown deepened into one of perplexity.

The sound of horses' hoofs and raised voices broke into her thoughts and brought Henrietta impatiently to her feet.

"They're here!" she exclaimed. "Tim and my father are back! Tell O'Leary to put the horses back in the carriage, will you, Frances? I want to get home before dark."

But there was no sign of either Jasper or Timothy when Frances went to the door. Instead, four mounted troopers met her startled gaze, and she saw that one of them—a sergeant—was talking to Seamus O'Leary.

"What brings you here?" she inquired with no smallest premonition of trouble. "How can we help you, Sergeant?"

The sergeant, a big, red-complexioned man whose face was vaguely familiar, came striding over to confront her.

"Frances O'Riordan?" he said, and then, evidently recognizing her, his slack mouth twisted into a grin. "Why, o'course you are! I arrested you once before, at a settler's farm over in Parramatta. You was a fugitive then, I recollect."

"I am Mrs. Spence," Frances told him with what firmness she could muster as she, too, recalled the occasion of her last meeting with the big, red-faced soldier. He had come with Lieutenant Brace to Jenny Taggart's farm, and the poor old one-legged cripple whom Jenny had also been sheltering had been killed when he had tried to protect her. . . .

She shrank back involuntarily. "My husband is Mr. Jasper Spence," she began. "And he—"

The sergeant cut her short. "It don't matter a tinker's cuss what name you're goin' under, missus. I got my orders, and my orders is ter bring you into Parramatta fer questionin'. Come now—you ain't goin' ter resist arrest, are you?"

"But *why* are you arresting me? I've done no wrong, and my husband—" but he would not let her finish.

"Information has bin laid against you," he retorted, "in connection with the recent uprisin' o' certain Irish rebels against His Majesty's forces. You're accused o' supplyin' them wiv' arms."

Frances could feel the color draining from her cheeks. She looked around for Seamus O'Leary, but he had vanished. Only Henrietta stood framed in the open front door of the farmhouse, and—although she could not have failed to hear what the sergeant had said—she made no attempt to intervene. Meeting Frances's mute, appealing glance, she turned and went back into the house, shutting the door behind her.

"Well?" the sergeant challenged. "You comin' peaceable, or have I got to put the fetters on you?"

She could achieve nothing by resisting. . . . Biting her lip, Frances nodded, and the sergeant waved to the man who was holding her horse.

"You c'n ride on my crupper," he told her, and lifted her slight form into the saddle. "If you're innocent o' the charge you'll just have ter tell Cap'n Abbott so. . . . Or maybe your husband c'n speak up fer you. Is he convict or free?"

"He is a free settler," Frances answered with dignity. "And a magistrate, Sergeant. Mr. Jasper Spence."

The name struck a chord this time, and the sergeant whistled his surprise as he slowly got up behind her. "Is he now? Well, maybe there's bin a mistake, but . . . I got my orders. Bring in Frances O'Riordan, sentenced fer sedition, I was instructed. An' you *are* Frances O'Riordan. . . . I reckernise you from 'way back, that time at Parramatta. The late Loo'tenant Brace was in command, an' I was still a two-striper—it was you, wasn't it?"

"Yes," Frances admitted. "And I expect you remember the poor old cripple you killed—Ben Reilly?"

"No, can't say as I do, ma'am. There's so many of 'em— escapers, drunks, bloody Irish rebels. I—" he broke off, evidently recalling her claim to be the wife of a magistrate and added apologetically, "If the charge is false an' if you really are Mrs. Spence, why, all you'll have ter do is explain ter Cap'n Abbott an' he'll let you go." He put his horse into a shambling trot, and the escort fell in behind them, wooden-faced.

"Who made the charge, Sergeant?" Frances asked. She held her breath, tense and anxious, fearing that he would not answer her, but it seemed he had no compunction about revealing her accuser's identity.

"Why, 'twas Mr. Spencer's foreman—a feller named O'Leary. It was he gave Cap'n Abbott the first warnin' o' the uprisin' at Castle Hill. If you are Mrs. Spence, I reck-on you know him, don't you?"

"Yes, I know him," Frances managed, filled suddenly with bitter, choking anger. She said no more during the uncomfortable ride to Parramatta, her mind in torment. It had been her fault, she told herself. . . . She and no one else had been to blame for the betrayal, for had she not brought O'Leary to the Defenders' meeting place the night he had followed her? Deceived by the weapons he had been carrying and believing his declaration of loyalty to the Cause, she had introduced—nay, vouched for—a traitor. The troops had been warned, and they had been there waiting to shoot her countrymen down, to take them prisoner, *to hang them.*

God forgive me, she prayed silently, as they reached the barracks at last. *Merciful Father, forgive me, for I cannot forgive myself. . . .*

To an agitated Captain Abbott, who came apologetically to order her release, Frances said with quiet firmness, "I am guilty of the charge, sir. You will have to keep me here."

"Guilty?" Abbott echoed, stunned. "But that is . . . good heavens, Mrs. Spence, my sergeant was an idiot. He should never have arrested you! Didn't you tell him who you were?"

"Yes, I told him. But—"

"The charge was laid against Frances O'Riordan, not Mr. Jasper Spence's wife. I don't know how the—the mistake occurred. But if you will accept my sincere apology and permit me to arrange conveyance back to Portland Place, I—I"—Edward Abbott was stammering in his anxiety to avoid offending her—"I beg you, Mrs. Spence. . . ."

Frances eyed him sadly. "But I have told you, sir, I am guilty of the charge. I furnished the Irish Defenders with arms—I gave them pistols and ammunition, and I am ready to stand my trial."

"It will not—not be necessary, ma'am. As the wife of a civil magistrate, to stand trial on such charges would be . . . it would cause a scandal and—ah—weaken the authority of the judiciary. The governor would not hear of it, I am sure. His Excellency is—"

"But if I were Frances O'Riordan still," she persisted bitterly, "I should be sent to the pillory and my head would be shaved—or I should be deported to Norfolk Island."

"Perhaps," Abbott conceded. He shuffled the papers on his desk with nervous fingers, avoiding her gaze. The sergeant came in and spoke in a low voice, gesturing behind him, and Abbott nodded, looking immensely relieved. "I understand that Mr. Spence is on his way here, and I've sent Sergeant May to intercept him. If you will be good enough to wait here, I—I'll return to you when I have spoken to him. Er—I will have wine sent in, so that you . . . that is, excuse me, Mrs. Spence."

It was half an hour before Jasper came into the small, dimly lit office. He offered no reproach, simply took her in his arms and asked, quite gently, "Frances, my dear, is it true—did you give the Irishmen arms?"

"Yes," Frances admitted. "Yes, I . . ." She told him the truth, sparing herself nothing, the tears she had held back for so long suddenly overwhelming her.

"And O'Leary informed on you? He made the charge against you to Captain Abbott?"

"Yes. That is, the sergeant said so."

"He also claimed a reward, I understand, for giving warning of the rebellion. They paid him twenty pounds." Frances felt her husband's arms tighten about her. "I will deal with Seamus O'Leary . . . and with you, my dear."

"I ought to stand my trial," Frances whispered. "Please try to understand. My conscience—"

"It would cause too great a scandal," Jasper Spence told her. "You will have to learn to live with your conscience, just as I have had to . . . and believe me, that is punishment enough, Frances."

"You?" she stared at him incredulously. "*You* have such a—such a secret on your conscience? But—"

He met her shocked gaze gravely. "Oh, yes, my dear. The crime of which I was guilty is far more heinous than those for which most of the poor wretches of convicts were sent out here. They stole, all too often, because they were starving, whereas I . . . I had other motives."

"For stealing, Jasper?" Still Frances could not believe it.

"It is known by another name." He smiled faintly. "Abuse of trust, I think, best describes it, and it is not punished because it is difficult to prove. Or, as in your case, my dear, because it would cause too great a scandal. Even O'Leary will not really be punished. . . . I shall dismiss him, of course, but he has his own land and the stock he's been building up. He'll become a free settler."

"But I . . . Jasper, I don't understand. You speak as if—"

"I speak as a prisoner of my own conscience," he answered gently. "But by an odd coincidence, my dear, yesterday I took the first step to free myself of its intolerable burden. I bought a share in a trading vessel from Mr. Campbell's agent. I shall use her to establish an honest trade with certain merchants in Bengal. An honest trade, Frances. It will prove an indirect means of making reparation, God willing, and when I go back to Calcutta I shall be able to go with my head held high." He took Frances's arm and tucked it beneath his own. "I had not intended to make the first voyage in my new purchase, but in the circumstances I think that it would be advisable if I were to do so—and if you were to accompany me. We shall be absent for—oh, I suppose for the better part of a year, and by the time we return, all the unhappy business in which you were involved will, I trust, have been forgotten."

"I shall not forget it," Frances said uncertainly.

"No," her husband conceded. "You no more than I. But . . . let us go home. There is much to arrange. Tim will have to manage my farm, and I must find a new foreman. And," he added, with a touch of severity, "you will, in the future, have to behave not as Frances O'Riordan but as Mrs. Jasper Spence. You will have to become—what did Captain Flinders propose to call this continent? Australia, was it not? You will have to become Australian . . . you and your compatriots. *That* is how to throw off your chains!"

Frances followed him in silence to where a servant waited with two horses in the barrack square. For all the torment of her conscience, her strongest emotion, as she mounted behind the man she had married, was one of deep and abiding gratitude.

From the barracks gate Captain Abbott bowed them on their way with unconcealed relief.

There would be no scandal; a magistrate's wife was going free, which was as it should be in a penal colony, and he had Mr. Spence's assurance that they would both be absent on a trading mission to Bengal, as soon as his ship was ready for sea. First thing tomorrow morning a chas-

tened Sergeant May could be sent to arrest the miserable
Irish rogue who had laid information against his employer's
wife . . . and against his own people. Although . . .
Returning to his office, he searched for the handwritten
note in which the denunciation of Frances O'Riordan had
been made.

Finding it, Edward Abbott studied it with thoughtfully
puckered brows. The handwriting was clear, the note itself
without an error of grammar or spelling, and . . . Seamus
O'Leary, on his own admission, was illiterate. He had
signed his first deposition, written out for him by a clerk,
with the cross of an unlettered man. And this writing, with
its carefully crossed *t*'s and dottied *i*'s, looked to him like a
woman's. True, O'Leary had delivered the note, but . . .
perhaps it would be best to delve no deeper.

He summoned May. "No need to bring in Mr. Spence's
foreman, Sergeant," he said. "I don't doubt the bird will
have flown the coop long before you could ride out there."

"I could find him, sir," the sergeant offered. "He's got
stock and a family—he won't be able to go far."

"You can look for him in the Hawkesbury area in a couple of weeks' time," the garrison commander told him.
"Probably he'll be on Mr. Dawson's property. All you need
do will be to put the fear of God into him and then leave
him be—d'you understand?"

"Yessir," Sergeant May assured him woodenly. He did
not understand, but it was not for him to question an officer's order. He saluted and withdrew.

CHAPTER XXII

All day, in groups of half a dozen or so, the aborigines of the Cammeragal and Gweagal tribes had been gathering on a patch of cleared land a mile above Farm Cove. There, by tradition, the Cammeray people held their initiation ceremonies and, on occasion, did bloody and savage battle with their rivals or—when honor demanded it—with each other.

The overseer of a convict road gang reported the gathering, and a military patrol was dispatched to ensure that no harm was likely to result from the influx of natives from Botany Bay and the North Shore.

"They're just singin' an' dancin', sir," the sergeant in command of the patrol assured the duty officer. "They've painted theirselves so's they don't look 'uman, but they ain't fightin'. I don't reckon they'll make trouble, and they're keepin' well away from the gardens an' the settlers' land."

"Then we'll leave them be," the officer decided, relieved. "You may dismiss your men, Sergeant—but better have another look at what's going on in the morning. That's the time they start their battles, as a rule."

Until sunset the Indians continued to sing and dance; then, exhausted, most of the performers flung their grotesquely daubed bodies onto the bare earth and slept, as and where they found themselves. Only Baneelon, who had come from the governor's house in Sydney just before dusk, held aloof.

He had come arrogantly, wearing the garments made for him in London, and he had not discarded them as he watched the frenzied posturing and stamping of his people in disdainful silence—as if the age-old stories they were enacting so graphically no longer had any meaning for him.

His attitude roused no little resentment among the older men of both tribes, and they muttered angrily. Did Baneelon, they asked each other, now consider himself as one of the "men from afar," one of the white *tulanis* who had come in ever-increasing numbers to wrest possession of the land from its native inhabitants? With their great sailing canoes and their fire-sticks—the dreaded *gooroo-beeras,* which could kill from a far greater distance than the most skilled warrior could throw his spear—the white invaders now held all the tribes in thrall.

The white people had seized the fishing grounds, denuded the woods of wild game, and cut down trees. Worse, they had fenced in great acres where once the Cammeragal had hunted, driving the *patagaran* and the *bagaray* farther and farther afield in order to replace them with strange, four-legged creatures of their own . . . few of which were ever killed for food.

If Baneelon chose to ally himself to these invaders, then he should face the spears of the Gweagal warriors alone, one old graybeard threatened angrily. It had been Baneelon's attempt to seize a Gweagal woman and take her to wife that had led to this gathering, and since he had caused the rift between the two tribes by clubbing the girl to death, it was only fit and proper that he—and he alone—should take the consequences when the new day dawned.

Surely, the old man reasoned, the white people among whom Baneelon moved so freely should have provided him with a *deein*—a wife. . . . Were they not his friends?

Several others, darting accusing glances at the silent offender in his alien clothes, echoed the graybeard's words. Even Colbee, for all he was Baneelon's bosom friend and the companion of years, said no word in his defense. Following the premature death of his first wife, Barangaroo, Baneelon had sought to recover his second—a young *deein* named Goobaroo, who had taken up with Colbee during her husband's absence in the place the white people called England. He had failed. In a subsequent contest Colbee had proved much the stronger, and Baneelon's injuries had been severe. Since then, while jealously guarding Goobaroo, Colbee's affection for his onetime friend had cooled.

Questioned now by one of the Cammeragal elders, Colbee raised his eyes to the darkening vault of the heavens, by this negative gesture letting it be understood that he would abide by whatever decision the elders might reach. After a brief discussion and with no dissenting voice, the tribal council agreed that Baneelon had forfeited his right to Cammeray support. . . . He must stand alone against however many warriors the Gweagal might choose to pit against him.

Their decision reached, the old men composed themselves for sleep, and it was not until day dawned that Baneelon was informed of his fate. Never anything but courageous, he accepted the elders' verdict stoically. Aided by Yemmerra Wannie—his companion in London—he divested himself of the threadbare cutaway jacket of which he had been so proud and, slipping out of waistcoat, shirt, and knee breeches, folded all his European garments carefully and laid them beside his discarded Hessian boots.

Naked now, as were his companions, he permitted two of the women to smear his heavily scarred, obese body with clay and ash, and Yemmerra Wannie to paint the red and white patterns on face and torso that were the mark of a Cammeray warrior seeking battle. While this was being done, both Gweagal and the Cammeragal women, in separate parties, stamped out a flat square of earth with their bare feet, singing in muted voices as they toiled, each party at pains to avoid physical contact with the other, their eyes pointedly averted when the two lines chanced to come face to face.

The mother of the Gweagal girl who had died, following Baneelon's attempt to club her into accepting his advances, came forward at the head of the five warriors of her tribe who had elected to take vengeance in blood on the dead girl's behalf. In a stream of vituperative words, screeched at the pitch of her lungs, the bereaved mother hurled accusations and curses at Baneelon, who heard her in dignified silence, offering no reply. His elder son, Dilboong, gave him his shield—the only defense, by tradition, that he was permitted—and Baneelon strode to the square of flattened earth prepared for the contest.

Aware that only by a miracle could he expect to survive his opponents' combined assault, he showed no fear and, indeed, felt none. If this was the hour when the Dreamtime Snake came to coil itself about his vitals, then so it must be. The mother of the Gweagal *deein* had "sung him"—she had invoked the Snake and death was inevitable for him. There could be no escape and he would seek none. He would die with honor, as a warrior should, here on the *Yoolong*, with his own people around him, and by the manner in which he died he would give them proof that he was flesh of their flesh, blood of their blood . . . a Cammeragal, not an alien.

When it was over, his sons, with Colbee and Yemmerra Wannie, would attend his last rites. They would see to it that his earthly body was consumed by the flames. They would build his funeral pyre high, so that his *mawn*, his ghost, should not linger, but his spirit be borne on the wings of the strong south wind, the *pukara*, back into clouds from whence he had come, as a puling infant, many moons before.

His people would forget then that he had deserted them for the white invaders' settlement, and that he had allowed himself to be seduced by their promises, their food and drink, their garments. Perhaps, in time, his exploits would become legend, of which the old men would sing as they gathered about the *gooyoung* fires. In time they might even boast that one of their number had sailed the far-flung oceans in a great, bird-winged *korong* and had journeyed to the place the white invaders of their land had called "Home." . . . Baneelon drew in his breath sharply, as memories returned to flood his mind.

He had seen sights they could not comprehend—vast cities, teeming with life, tall buildings, war-*korongs* larger and more powerful than any of those that had come here. . . . He grasped his shield firmly, delaying the moment when he must place it in position to guard against the Gweagal spears. His people had judged him, they had condemned him, but . . . they did not understand, for they had not seen what he had seen. He and Yemmerra Wannie were the only ones. . . He turned to look once again at the faces of Yemmerra Wannie, of Colbee, and of the young Dilboong, who was more Colbee's son than his now, because Colbee had adopted him when he had taken Goobarro. All three looked back at him sternly. Suddenly aware that even they doubted him, Baneelon spun around, the wooden shield held before him, inviting attack.

The first spear came hurtling through the air toward him. He fended it off easily and, bending, contemptuously threw it back, so that his opponents might use it again. Its owner did so, leading a shower of spears launched with great speed and accuracy from the Gweagal warriors' throwing-sticks. Baneelon deflected the barbed points with his shield, and he continued to do so for almost an hour, his skill born of long practice and the experience of many similar contests.

But years of overindulgence in his white friends' liquor had weakened his once sinewy frame and dulled the speed of his reactions. He was visibly tiring, the sweat pouring off him as he turned and twisted to avoid the spearpoints. Although he still returned his opponents' missiles, he was doing so now without his initial contempt, and most fell short of their target.

The Gweagal men came closer, shouting in derision, and the murdered girl's mother urged them on, reiterating her curse. To the watching military patrol, concealed behind the trees that screened the battleground on the seaward side, the uneven contest was mystifying.

"Why don't the stupid bugger fight back?" one of the men demanded of his sergeant. "Look at 'im . . . 'e's just chuckin' 'em their bloomin' spears back, 'e ain't aimin' at 'em!"

"They're all crazy savages," the sergeant returned. "I've seen 'em act like this before. . . . I reckon it's their way of punishin' any of their fellows as commits a crime. The poor sod that's found guilty ain't allowed ter fight back. 'E just 'as ter stand there an' take it fer as long as they c'n 'and it out."

"But they'll kill 'im, Sar'nt!" another man exclaimed. He gestured to the little pile of folded Europen clothing at the edge of the clearing. "Ain't 'e the one they calls Banny Long, the one Gov'ner Phillip took 'ome wiv' 'im?"

"They all look alike ter me, lad," the sergeant confessed. "But—" He subjected the naked, sweat-drenched figure to a frowning inspection, shading his eyes with his hand. "You could be right."

"Them's 'is clobber," the soldier asserted. "I've seen the black sod wearin' them boots often enough, when I've been on guard duty at Gov'ment House."

A chorus of voices confirmed his statement, and the sergeant's frown deepened as he saw the beleagured native drop to his knees and then rise, with stubborn courage, to face his assailants once more. But he was swaying, his strength ebbing fast, and one of the spears at last found its mark. Blood poured from the man's thigh as he wrenched the barb from his lacerated flesh, and a second spear struck his ribs a glancing blow when he relaxed his grip on the shield.

"They'll kill 'im for sure, Sar'nt," the young soldier who had first noticed the clothing repeated. "What's the guv'ner goin' ter say if they do? 'Adn't we oughter stop 'em? If it is Banny Long, the guv'ner sets a lot o' store by 'im, don't 'e?"

Undoubtedly the governor did but . . . The sergeant hesitated and finally shook his head. "There's six of us an' over two 'undred of them," he said unanswerably. "Nothin' we can do. An' our orders was not ter interfere unless they made trouble wiv' the settlers or tried ter damage growin' crops—and they ain't doin' nothing like that, are they?" He rose to his feet and shrugged his scarlet-clad shoulders resignedly. "Best thing we can do is withdraw an' leave 'em to it, not go stirrin' up no soddin' 'ornets' nest. Anyways, that poor bloody Banny Long brought what's comin' to 'im on 'imself an' 'e knows it . . . else why's 'e standin' there givin' 'em their weapons back? On your feet, my lads, an' let's get out o' here."

His men obeyed him, and the patrol slipped away virtually unnoticed by the milling throng of tribesmen, from whose throats rose a savage murmur as they sensed that the end of the contest was near.

Blinded by sweat and bitterly aware that he had reached the limit of his endurance, Baneelon stooped yet again to pick up an ill-aimed spear. He saw suddenly, in memory, a vision of the lined and kindly face of the man he had venerated and trusted above all others. The leader of the strangers from afar, Governor Phillip, the man he had called *beanna*—father, in his native tongue—for whose sake he had left his people and his homeland and given his friendship to an alien race.

Unmanly tears came to join the sweat flooding his eyes, but he blinked them back, lifting his head proudly as another remembered face floated before him. This, too, was white . . . the face of Jennee, the woman whose name, in his language, meant laughter.

"Jennee-bi!" His parched lips formed the word soundlessly. Then he lifted the spear—a *billar*, with a single barb cut from the wood—and, holding it at shoulder height, he aimed it carefully and let it go. The weapon was propelled, straight and true, to land at Colbee's feet.

"Ki-yah!" Baneelon roared at him defiantly and lowered his shield. He could feel the Dreamtime Snake gnawing at his vitals now, turning his blood to water, but he did not flinch when Colbee responded to his appeal and sent the barbed spear winging its way to his heart. . . .

The transport *Tellicherry* lay at anchor in Sydney Cove, a squat, broad-beamed old barque that had seen better days.

Boats laden with convicts were plying between the ship and the Public Wharf, Governor King saw, and his own pinnace was tied up to her larboard chains, waiting to take delivery of mail. He gave vent to a resigned sigh. Mail from home these days seldom brought him anything calculated to afford him pleasure or an easing of the heavy burden of responsibility he bore. He looked forward to the ill-spelled missives from his elder son and daughter, it was true, but his official mail tended invariably to depress him.

The new Colonial Secretary, Lord Hobart—in spite of being honored by having the new settlement in Van Diemen's Land named after him—appeared to be as ill-informed and critical of the colony's affairs as his predecessor in office had been. And Lord Camden, heaven knew, had caused trouble enough by his partiality in the Macarthur affair. . . . Philip King repeated his sigh, conscious of a deep and abiding sense of injustice.

The rogue he had sent home in disgrace to face his trial by court-martial had returned in his own ship and, armed with letters bearing the seal of the Colonial Office and a directive from the Secretary of State, had arrogantly demanded a grant of five thousand acres of land for himself and two thousand for his protégé, Walter Davidson. Not just any land—or even land contiguous to his original grant at Parramatta . . . only the best, it seemed, was good enough for John Macarthur. The new grant had to be in the area known as Cow Pastures, where the wild cattle that had escaped soon after Governor's Phillip's landing had bred and prospered during the intervening years . . . the finest grassland in the colony.

He had resisted the demand, King thought resentfully. He had delayed, argued, explained, and even threatened, but all to no avail. Armed with his official directive, Macarthur had refused to be deterred or browbeaten. He had the Privy Council and the London Board of Trade behind him, the fellow had boasted, and furthermore, he was now a civilian and a free settler and fully within his rights. In Sydney itself, of course, he had the support of Major Johnstone and the corps officers, to which was now added that of Garnham Blaxcell, the new holder of the office of secretary of the colony. Faced with such opposition the governor had no alternative but to haul down his colors and give Macarthur what he wanted . . . and even then he was not satisfied.

Controlling himself with an effort, Philip King reached for the note that had been delivered by hand an hour ago.

> Dear Sir:
> I received the Cow Pasture grants all safe yesterday, with Harper's emancipation, for which I beg to return you my sincere thanks.
> Expecting to see you at Parramatta, I delayed sending my return of convicts in my employment; but I now enclose it, for my wants are become so urgent, that unless you have the goodness to give me some immediate assistance, it will be impossible even to take care of my present flocks of sheep and consequently all idea of increasing them must be abandoned as impracticable—I hope you will not consider me troublesome upon this subject, for I assure you were it possible to hire free men or in any other way to get forward with my business, I would forbear to pester you with applications of such a nature. . . .

The letter, signed *Your Obliged & Faithful Humble Servant*, ended with solicitous inquiries concerning the health of the governor's lady, and the governor's hand shook as he replaced it on his desk. Macarthur already had four times as many convict laborers as anyone else—and at least half a dozen free men in addition to the newly emancipated Harper—working for him, and he had more than a thousand acres in Parramatta. . . . Was there to be no end to his avarice? Rumor had it that he intended to call his new holding Camden, and . . . King swore loudly and blasphemously. The infernal fellow would be asking for a military guard at Camden next, to protect his thrice-damned sheep from pillage by Indians, and no doubt Johnstone would give him one.

Restless and angry he returned to his vantage point at the window, to see that the pinnace, laden with mail sacks, was putting off from the *Tellicherry*'s black-painted side. Chapman, his secretary, was seated in the stern sheets, which meant that all too soon the official correspondence would be piled up on his desk, demanding his attention. The old transport was the only ship at present in the anchorage, apart from two small Sydney-built sloops and the old *Francis*.

The *Venus*, owned jointly by George Bass and Henry Waterhouse and captained by Bass, had failed to return from a projected voyage to South America and must now be presumed lost at sea. The *Calcutta*—his only ship of war—had had to be sent to Port Phillip to convey David Collins and his ill-fated settlers to Van Diemen's Land. Collins, for all he had been one of Governor Phillip's officers, had proved a poor pioneer. After only three months he had condemned Port Phillip as totally unfit for settlement, and he and his three hundred convicts, with their marine guard, had been granted permission to transfer themselves, lock, stock, and barrel, to Van Diemen's Land. There they would join Lieutenant Bowen's small tented establishment on the Derwent River estuary . . . probably, the governor reflected, to poor young Bowen's discomfiture, since as a recently promoted colonel, the colony's first judge advocate would assume command. But here again he had been left with no alternative.

Matthew Flinders had reported on the prospects of the development of Port Phillip in glowing terms; so had John Murray when he had laid claim to it, and Grimes had charted the course of a fine river there. But—Colonel Collins would have none of it. He had complained of lack of fresh water, poor pasturage, and a dry, sandy soil, and had dismissed the harbor as a "deep and dangerous bight" in which his accompanying storeship, the *Ocean*, had come near to foundering.

With frowning brows the governor started to pace the floor of his office. Flinders, he thought with keen regret, was now as lost to the colony as his friend and fellow explorer, the intrepid Surgeon Bass. He had given Flinders passage to England in the *Porpoise*, and she had sailed the previous July in company with two Indiamen, intending to take the Torres Strait route to the Dutch East Indies and Bengal. When some eight hundred miles from Sydney, both the king's ship and one of the Indiamen had run onto a reef in darkness, and Flinders had returned in the *Porpoise*'s cutter to seek help for the survivors, whom the other Indiaman, for no reason that he could explain, had abandoned to their fate.

Fortunately, King recalled, he had had a ship to send to their rescue, but he had been compelled to give Flinders the home-built *Cumberland* to speed him on his belated way to England. She was small for such a voyage, but Matt Flinders was impatient, and Tom Moore had built her well—Flinders deemed the risk worth taking. He had accompanied the *Rolla* to the wrecks, and after seeing the castaways safely on board the transport and saving what he could of Sir Joseph Banks's botanical specimens, had parted company and sailed . . . only to vanish.

News that the Treaty of Amiens was at an end and England was once more at war with France had reached Sydney too late to warn him, but . . . Flinders had had his safe conduct, so it seemed unlikely that he could have been sunk or captured by an enemy man o' war. Therefore . . . Governor King bit back a frustrated sigh. The only conclusion to be reached was that somewhere in the Timor Sea or the Indian Ocean the twenty-six-ton *Cumberland* had encountered a tropical storm and foundered, with the loss of her captain and her company. It was a tragic end for a young officer of great promise, who had bidden fair to emulate—if not even to surpass—James Cook as both explorer and cartographer.

A knock on the door interrupted the governor's train of thought. His secretary came in, the expected bundle of mail and the Colonial Office dispatch box borne carefully in his blue-clad arms.

"The English mail, Your Excellency," he announced unnecessarily and deposited his burdens on the desk. He unlocked the box and stood back expectantly, but the governor waved him away.

"I'll call for you when I want you," he said and limped across to the desk, oddly reluctant, now that the time had come, to peruse the mass of official documents the dispatch box contained. But there were letters from young Phillip and little Anna among the bundles of ordinary mail, and his wife—confined to her room with a feverish chill—would be eager to have them. He gave them to William Chapman. "Be so good as to have these delivered to Mrs. King, William. And inform her that I will join her as soon as I've dealt with the Colonial Office dispatches."

Chapman departed obediently, and when the door had closed behind him, Governor King picked up the first letter, which, he saw, bore Lord Hobart's personal seal. He himself had written at considerable length to the new Secretary of State, setting out in detail the uncooperative and biased attitude of the New South Wales Corps officers, when all or any of them were required to sit in judgment on their fellows—or others of like persuasion—in the courts. In particular he had cited Major Johnstone's high-handed arrest of the deputy judge advocate, when he had ordered Captain Kemp to be court-martialed for permitting the libelous lampoons to be distributed—lampoons that impugned his honor—and the court's subsequent dismissal of his charges.

This probably was in reply to his accusations against the corps and to his request for leave of absence, enabling him to vindicate himself in person to His Majesty's ministers. . . . He had worded his request very strongly, he recalled, describing the authors of the infamous jingles as "the dark and concealed assassins" of his character and reputation. He glanced at the date on the head of the Colonial Secretary's letters. . . . Yes, this was the reply. Unfolding the thin sheet of paper, he started to read.

"His Majesty's Government has deemed it advisable," the letter began,

> to relieve you of the Office of Captain-General and Governor of the Colony of New South Wales . . . in view of the unfortunate differences which have so long

subsisted between Your Excellency and the Military Officers of the Colony. . . .

The words blurred before Philip King's eyes.

No leave of absence, this, he realized—it was dismissal, without justification, without even apology, permitting him no chance to defend himself. Macarthur had done his work well, lying, unprincipled villain that he was! He choked, a savage anger catching him by the throat and momentarily depriving him of breath, so that he was compelled to limp to the window and stand there drawing great gulps of air into his lungs.

Jack Boddice, the tradesman's son, the rum-purveyor, had challenged the authority of the governor appointed by the king—no, the devil take him, he had challenged Hunter's authority, too, and that of his own commanding officer and defeated them all. Hunter had been permitted to resign and had gone; and William Paterson, poor devil, had been reduced to a cipher, in so much pain from the wound Macarthur had inflicted on him that he was drinking himself to death and demanding to be sent to Van Diemen's Land. And now he himself was to be dismissed, in view of . . . The governor stumbled back to his desk reaching blindly for Lord Hobart's letter.

In view of the unfortunate differences which have so long subsisted between Your Excellency and the Military Officers of the Colony . . .

Did Hobart really believe that the differences were solely of *his* making? Before heaven, how could a minister of the British Crown take the word of an upstart officer, in a discredited regiment, before that of a naval post-captain who had served the colony for nearly twenty years and whose record was impeccable? Foveaux was in England, of course—he had applied for sick leave, and Piper had relieved him at Norfolk Island—and, in addition to being a close friend of Macarthur's, Foveaux had influence. It was possible that the new Colonial Secretary had been swayed by both men if each had supported the other's mendacious claims, but . . . damn it, there were Phillip and Hunter, also in England, also available for consultation! Why had his infernal lordship not sought the opinion of two of the colony's past governors? Or, come to that, why had his predecessor, Lord Camden, failed to do so?

Governor King slumped into his chair, the painful twinges from his gouty foot adding to his smoldering rage. He skimmed through the rest of the Colonial Secretary's letter, scarcely taking in the courteously phrased, meaningless observations. Beyond the fact that Hobart wished him to remain in the colony until he was replaced, it made little impact on him until, turning to the second page, he saw that it was His Majesty's intention to replace him by "an officer competent to exercise the duties" of governor, who would be "free from the spirit of party which has reached such an alarming height."

But then he saw the name of his successor, hastily scribbled into a postscript, and gasped in audible astonishment. . . . Captain William Bligh was to be offered the appointment. Bligh of the *Bounty* . . . on the recommendation, no doubt, of Sir Joseph Banks.

Well, at least the next governor would be a naval officer, Philip King reflected, following in the tradition of the colony, but it was to be hoped that Bligh would be given a regiment of Royal Marines or of the line to replace the Rum Corps. If he were not, then . . . Another, rather nervous, tap on the door interrupted his thoughts, and he called out with deliberate lack of welcome, "Yes, yes . . . what do you want?"

William Chapman entered, looking as apprehensive as his knock had sounded. "Sir, I hesitate to disturb you, but . . . Major Johnstone, sir, is in the anteroom. I told him that you were engaged in reading the Colonial Office dispatches, but he insisted he must see you. On a matter of some urgency, he said, sir."

The acting commandant of the New South Wales Corps, following hard on the secretary's heels, gave the governor no chance to refuse him an interview. Johnstone came striding in, borne on the tide of his own indignation, his slightly pale bulbous eyes blazing. Without the courtesy of a greeting he launched at once into the reason for his call.

"Sir, I must protest most strongly against your order—of which I have only now been informed—authorizing the reenrollment of what you are pleased to call, sir, the *Loyal* Associations. There is no occasion for the recruitment of any such bodies. Damme, sir, the New South Wales Corps, in which I have the honor to serve, is more than capable of maintaining public order! And of enforcing a curfew in Sydney, Parramatta, Greenhills, or the Hawkesbury settlements, if you deem it advisable to proclaim one . . ." He ranted on, his manner deliberately offensive, and Governor King listened in constrained silence.

The recruitment of the colony's free inhabitants into an armed voluntary militia had only been opposed by the corps's officers, mainly on the ground that the majority of the free inhabitants were emancipated convicts, but . . . King's mouth tightened ominously. He had received the home government's authority to encourage recruitment some weeks previously, and—he thought resentfully— nothing that George Johnstone said was likely to deter him from exercising that authority.

Each township should have its volunteers, drilled and properly disciplined and under the command of reliable officers, to act in support of the constables, patrol the streets when called upon, and prevent another rebellion, such as the Irish Defenders had attempted. True, the corps and, in particular, Johnstone himself, had been instrumental in quelling the Irish outbreak and bringing the rebels to justice. . . . He had taken official cognizance of their zeal, in his dispatches to the Colonial Secretary, and given praise where it had been deserved. But, King's hands clenched into fists beneath the desk top, since then, there had been too many clandestine raids on the premises of licensed liquor retailers and ale houses and even one daring attempt, during the hours of darkness, to burn the new brewery he had set up at Parramatta, in the hope of weakening the convicts' dependence on corps-imported rum by supplying them with beer.

The raiders had not been traced, of course, but their identity was not hard to conjecture, and if the home government was unable—or unwilling—to replace the corps with an untainted regiment, then the Loyal Associations would provide an armed backing for such countermeasures as the imposition of a curfew, which he had recently ordered.

He would leave them, the governor told himself wryly, for his successor . . . as a valuable bequest.

"And, sir," Johnstone said, winding up his tirade at last, "I must insist that I do not look upon convicts conditionally emancipated as being amenable to the Articles of War, or on a footing with those who are considered to be the *respectable* inhabitants of this colony. Indeed, sir, I don't imagine that I could justify my conduct were I to sanction such a measure, damme if I do!"

"Your own corps has enlisted a number of convicts in its ranks," Philip King pointed out, controlling his rising temper with some difficulty. "Upwards of seventy, I believe."

"They are under military discipline at all times, sir, whereas these so-called free men, whom you propose to entrust with arms, would only be so when called up for drills and the like. . . ." Johnstone was launched on another catalogue of complaints, and the governor was unpleasantly reminded of Major Ross who, heaven knew, had tried poor Arthur Phillips's patience sorely—and his own, during their time together on Norfolk Island.

Johnstone had been a Royal Marine officer, one of the original garrison who had served under Ross's command. In those days, however, as a comparatively junior lieutenant, he had been one of the best, conscientious in the performance of his duties and a favorite of Phillip's, to whom, for a time, he had acted as secretary. Had Macarthur's malign influence changed him? Governor King wondered, studying the face of his protagonist with frowning concentration. Certainly he and Macarthur were intimate friends, acting in concert, backing one another in both military and civil matters, and despite the fact that Macarthur had sold his commission prior to returning to Sydney, he was always present at such regimental functions as mess dinners—presumably at the invitation of the corps's acting commandant.

And . . . King's lips twitched into a reminiscent smile. When he had sent the master of the *Manila* schooner packing, with his entire cargo of spirits and tobacco—on the grounds that he had not shipped the cattle required by his manifests—George Johnstone had been louder in his protests than any of the other officers. Which suggested, if it did not actually prove, that Phillip's one-time trusted secretary was now as deeply involved in his regiment's liquor trading as Kemp, Abbott, and Macarthur himself.

"You betray a bias against the corps, Captain King," Johnstone accused—his accusation, the governor remembered, was one that Ross had frequently flung at both Phillip and himself.

King's smile abruptly faded, and he said, a distinct edge to his voice, "Then doubtless you will be pleased to know, Major, that I shall very soon be relinquishing the reins of office."

Major Johnstone stared at him, taken by surprise, his jaw dropping in disbelief. "You mean, sir, you . . . you're resigning the governorship? But surely you—"

"That is precisely what I mean," Phillip King snapped. Feeling that, for the first time since their one-sided interview had begun, he held the advantage, he added crisply, "My successor has been named as Captain William Bligh."

"Bligh? Good God!" The corps acting commandant visibly taken aback. "Bligh of the *Bounty—Breadfruit Bligh*?"

"I believe malicious tongues have named him thus, Major. It might, however, behoove *you* to remember that Mr. Bligh is a post-captain in His Majesty's Navy, who has served with distinction in two fleet actions against the French and their allies." The governor's tone was tinged with sarcasm, but Major Johnstone seemed scarcely to notice it. Clearly the announcement of the new governor's name had upset him; his round, oddly cherubic face was suffused with color, and he stuttered unintelligibly, as if vainly seeking to control his sense of outrage.

Finally he said, with a restraint that cost him dearly, "You—you're sure of this, sir?"

"I am quite sure," King returned. He gestured to the Colonial Office dispatch box, suddenly glad, when earlier he had felt wounded, by the news it had contained. It would be a relief to end his governorship, he thought, a merciful relief, and God in heaven, if his recall was an indication that he had failed in the task assigned to him, then he was failing in good company. If *he* had failed, then so had John Hunter and, perhaps, even Phillip before him, because . . .

Johnstone exclaimed indignantly, "Why have they chosen Bligh . . . *why*, for God's sake? Did you know he was court-martialed and severely reprimanded—found guilty of behaving in an oppressive and tyrannical manner to one of his lieutenants in the *Warrior*? The trial took place when I was still in England. A young cousin of mine was serving under Bligh's command in the *Warrior*—he told me about the trial and what an arrogant swine the man is. And Keltie—you remember the excellent Mr. Keltie, who was out here as master of the *Sirius*, do you not? Well, let me tell you, sir, he gave evidence at the trial—*against* Captain Bligh, not for him."

"Is that so?" This time it was the governor who was surprised, for James Keltie had, indeed, been an excellent man and the most loyal of subordinates.

"I can only suppose," Johnstone went on sourly, "that this appointment has been made to enable their lordships to rid themselves of a captain they no longer wish to employ in the fleet. Damme, there can be no other reason for it!"

"You go too far, Major Johnstone," Governor King reproved him coldly. "Have the goodness to withdraw that remark. This is not the place to air such views, as you very well know."

The acting commandant's color deepened, but choking over the words, he apologized and took his leave, his objections to the reenrollment of the Loyal Associations forgotten in his dismay at the news of William Bligh's appointment. No doubt Johnstone was off, posthaste, to acquaint Macarthur with what he had learned. The governor, meanwhile, pondered what had transpired and found himself in a more cheerful frame of mind than he had been in for a very long time as he, too, went to tell his wife that he was to be relieved of office . . . and that his successor had been named.

Perhaps an oppressive tyrant was what was needed in the colony, and perhaps in Bligh of the *Bounty* even John Macarthur would meet his match. . . . Philip King smiled, heartened by the prospect.

It came as no surprise to him when his wife wept for joy on hearing that his governorship would soon be at an end.

Jenny was with Tom Jardine and old Watt in the river pasture when six-year-old William came running excitedly to tell her that the colonial sloop *Phillip* had been sighted approaching the Hawkesbury settlers' wharf.

"That's Dad's ship, ain't it?" the boy asked. "And he'll likely have Justin with him, won't he?"

"Yes," Jenny responded, feeling her heart lift. "I hope so." Belatedly she reproved, "You shouldn't say *ain't*, Willie. Don't you learn anything at school?"

William made a face at her. "No," he asserted. "We don't. Only dull things like reading an' 'rithmetic. But it's better when Mr. Marsden gives us lessons, 'cause he tells us 'bout his travels an' places like New Zealand. He says the Indians there are worse than the ones here . . . proper savages, he reckons. But one day he says he's going to teach 'em to be Christians, an' I said I'd go with him an' help him."

But Jenny was not listening, and he broke off, eyeing her sullenly. It was always the same, he thought—when his Dad and Justin came home, his mother had no ears for anyone else. And when his Dad had brought Captain Flinders to stay with them and recoup his strength, it had been worse. . . . Old Grandpa Watt had been the only one who had given him the time of day, and he was so deaf now he couldn't hear much anyway.

He said, raising his voice and determined to be heard, "If you want to go an' meet the ship, Mam, I can round up those ewes for you. Me an' Frisky." He pointed proudly to his dog—an ugly half-breed, with a walleye, which he had been endeavoring to train as a sheep-herd for the past six months—and was gratified when his mother nodded.

"All right, Willie love—thank you. You can help Tom." She turned to Watt in mute question, and the old man shook his head.

"I'll stay, lass. Give 'em a word o' welcome from me."

"Yes, of course I will, Watt." Jenny laid an affectionate hand on his stooped shoulder and set off in the direction of the farmhouse, her pace brisk and eager.

Johnny had been given command of the *Phillip* soon after Matt Flinders's departure in the *Cumberland*—now almost three years ago. The *Phillip* was the largest and, according to her captain, the best vessel Tom Moore had built. A sturdy, brig-rigged sloop of some forty tons burthen, she carried a crew of between twelve and twenty, depending on her destination and the purpose of her voyage. Her greatest achievement—and Johnny's—had been the salvaging of H.M.S. *Porpoise* from the reef on which she had so unfortunately foundered with the *Investigator*'s company on board, but for the most part the sloop plied between Sydney and Norfolk Island and thence to Port Dalrymple, in Van Diemen's Land, carrying convicts.

Following the harvest—as she was now—she was pressed into service to load grain and timber from the Hawkesbury settlements, a task the aging *Francis* could no longer solely perform. But, Jenny thought contentedly as she halted by the door to her small stable, at least a spell on the river meant that for a few precious weeks her family could be reunited. Robert Webb, who knew the Hawkesbury better than anyone else, was usually available to act as Johnny's relief and to permit him to take leave and play the farmer for a while.

The two-year-old colt she had bred came whinnying to the half-door of his box; she saddled him and, mounted on his skittish back, rode him at a smart canter toward the wharf. Her saddle was a homemade affair, fashioned out of three layers of Parramatta factory-woven blanket, with leather stirrups secured to the girth, which compelled her to ride astride. Timothy Dawson and his father-in-law had imported sidesaddles for their wives; even so, neither Henrietta nor Frances Spence could match Jenny's skill and seemingly had no desire to do so, for only six months ago Timothy had come, cap in hand, to ask her to aid him with his horsebreaking.

Since Mr. Spence's purchase of a ship, Timothy's stock had been virtually doubled. They had imported a score of Indian-bred mares from Bengal, as well as sheep and oxen—the latter finding a ready sale as beasts of burden—and both men were well on the way to becoming wealthy landowners, whereas she . . . Jenny's smile faded. Her farm was doing well enough, she told herself, despite Johnny's lengthy and enforced absences, but unlike the corps's officers and the free settlers, who appeared able to obtain additional land when and wherever they wished, her applications for grants were invariably refused.

Perhaps, had they been made by Johnny the result might have been different, but Johnny was never there to put his signature to the documents, and hers, it seemed, bore the stigma of her emancipist status. The officers and, she had recently learned, Timothy himself extended their holdings by the simple expedient of fencing in pasture land that bordered on their grants and nothing was said—possession, in their case, being nine-tenths of the law. And rumor had it that Captain Macarthur and the relatives he had brought back with him had been granted several thousand acres of the so-called Cow Pastures, on the authority of the home government—and this in spite of Governor King's efforts to retain the land for public use.

She sighed and, glimpsing the *Phillip*'s stumpy topmasts through a break in the trees, slowed her pace to a trot. Frances O'Riordan—Frances *Spence*—had called on her soon after returning from the voyage she and Mr. Spence had made to Bengal and China and, full of the wonders she had seen in those far-off, exotic places, had suddenly buried her face in her hands and wept.

"I do not deserve what I've been given, Jenny," she had whispered brokenly. "For I betrayed the cause poor Conal died for, and I . . . oh, it breaks my heart to be safe and happy and rich when the others are slaving their lives away at Coal River and in Van Diemen's Land. They've even sent poor General Holt to Hobart, I was told, and Brian McCormack has died from the flogging they inflicted on him. He was accused of planning an attack on the garrison at Coal River. . . ."

There had been a good deal more on these lines, but mystified by it all, Jenny had offered what consolation she could and seen the girl depart, dry-eyed but still conscience-stricken, for the fine home her elderly husband had had built for her during their absence overseas. Frances, she reflected wryly as she came in sight of the crowded wharf, did not know how lucky she was . . . and not least because she was able to accompany her husband when he went to sea.

But all such faintly envious reflections were forgotten when she saw Johnny on the deck of his ship, tanned and smiling, his hand upraised in greeting, and Justin standing beside him proudly wearing the brass-buttoned jacket of a master's mate.

The explanation came when he joined her on the wharf. A board composed of officers of His Majesty's ship *Calcutta* had, her son told her breathlessly, examined him in navigation while detained in port at the new Hobart settlement, and he had passed with flying colors.

"I'm in the navy now, Mam," he said, his eyes searching her face a trifle anxiously for signs of disapproval. "I've been accepted for the masters' branch as a volunteer, subject to Their Lordships' confirmation. It's not quite as good as if I'd been able to obtain a mid's berth in a king's ship," he added with painful honesty. "But out here, when I've put in the sea time and I'm eighteen, I can expect a warrant. And one day, if I'm lucky, I can get to be a master like Dad and command my own ship. Are you—are you pleased, Mam?"

What could she say, Jenny thought, save that she was pleased . . . however much her heart might fail her. He had worked so long and so hard to achieve his ambition, given up the chance Captain Flinders had offered him, for her sake, and lost the midshipman's berth he might have had. . . . She hugged her tall young son in his ill-fitting, obviously borrowed uniform and managed huskily, "Oh, Justin, of course I'm pleased! Pleased and proud of you, love."

And then Johnny was taking her into his arms, holding her close, his blue eyes tender, his skin, as always, smelling of the sea, as if there were salt in his veins instead of blood.

"The lad looks well, does he not? That's an old uniform of John Bowen's he's wearing, with the mid's patches cut off. And young Franklin gave him his dirk—he insisted, so that Justin could show himself off to you in all his glory." He walked with her to where she had tied her horse and lifted her back into the saddle. "This, the colt—what did you call him? Baneelon, wasn't it, after Governor Phillip's Indian?"

"Yes," Jenny confirmed. "He's dead, you know, the real Baneelon. But I wanted to remember him." She looked down into Johnny's face, seeing the happiness in it, and her own smile woke in answer. "Will you be long? The children will be eager to see you."

"A couple of hours, lass. Rob Webb's not here yet, so I'll have to make a start on stowing cargo." He jerked his head toward the piled sacks of wheat and maize on the wharf. "Looks as if you've had a good harvest."

"We have. The best since we've been here, I think."

Jenny started to give him details, but sensing his lack of interest, broke off. Johnny was no farmer, and for all his trying he never would be. . . . Even old Watt, London Cockney though he was, was a better hand than her seafaring husband. But she offered no reproach; she answered his inquiries for William and Rachel and, in her turn, questioned him about his passage from Van Diemen's Land and the new settlement of Hobart.

The colt stirred restlessly, startled by the excited shrieks of a bunch of settlers' children playing on the riverbank below the wharf, and she gathered up her reins. "I'd best let you get on with your work, Johnny."

"All right, my love." He hesitated and then said in a low, oddly strained voice, "I heard some bad news in Sydney."

"Bad news? Oh, Johnny, what?"

"Governor King's resigning. . . . Captain Bligh's to be our new governor."

"Is he?" Jenny frowned, wondering why the name sounded familiar.

"*Bounty* Bligh, lass," Johnny supplied, tight-lipped. "And there's still no word of Matt Flinders and the poor old *Cumberland*. I'd hoped there would be, but all anyone's talking about in Sydney town is what things will be like under Captain Bligh. The Rum Corps are worried, so maybe that's a good sign—although I, for one, won't welcome him. I . . . oh, there's Rob. I'll need to go, Jenny love, but I'll be home as soon as I can."

It was dusk by the time he reached the farmhouse with Justin, and both of them received a rapturous welcome from five-year-old Rachel and a slightly more restrained one from William, in whom the appearance of his elder brother in uniform provoked a certain envious sullenness. Old Watt boxed his ears, and when Justin came heatedly to William's defense, harmony was restored, and Watt, grinning hugely, retired to his corner at the fireside to doze until the evening meal was ready.

It was a festive meal, for all it consisted of the usual broth and damper rounded off with cheese and the first of a crop of homegrown apples. Jenny had made a cake with flour ground by one of the windmills now changing the face of the landscape in Toongabbe, as well as in Sydney and Parramatta, and a hoarded bottle of Cape brandy was old Watt's contribution. The two Jardines were invited to share this, and Tom, his round, red face suffused with smiles, invited the assembled company to drink to his expected emancipation.

When pipes had been lit and the remnants of the meal cleared away, the men gathered round the fire, and Johnny observed thoughtfully, "On our way upriver I noticed fences on the Dawson property, enclosing two horse paddocks. It looked to me as if he had increased his holding by a couple of hundred acres."

"He has, Mr. Broome," Tom Jardine confirmed. "And it's the same on the south side, too, where he runs his sheep."

"Did he buy the land?" Johnny pursued. "Or obtain it in grants?"

Watt and Tom answered him together, with a wry "No," and Watt added succinctly, " 'E jus' took it, Johnny."

"*Took* it?"

"Aye—'e squatted on it an' put up 'is fences. Claimin' squatters' rights, they call it."

"And nothing was done to stop him?"

Jenny, returning to the firelit living room after putting her two younger children to bed, heard Johnny's last, puzzled question and replied to it with an emphatic headshake.

"They are all doing the same in this area, and a blind eye is turned—provided the squatters are officers of the corps or free settlers. Emancipists are bound by the terms of their original grant leases."

"On what grounds, love?" Johnny wanted to know.

"As I understand it," Jenny answered, "on the grounds that they were conveyed here at the expense of the home government and were supplied with seed, stock, and tools and commissariat rations during their first year." She went into details, explaining the refusals with which her applications for more land had been met and glad that at last Johnny had given her the opportunity to speak to him of such matters.

He was in a thoughtful mood for the remainder of the evening, and when they retired to bed he made love to her with a strange mixture of passion and tenderness. Later, lying with her in his arms, he said softly, "I'm a selfish oaf,

Jenny my love. . . . Damme, I don't deserve you! I'm away for months on end, leaving you the work of this farm, the care of our little ones, and all the responsibilities that go with both. I've even taken Justin away from you, at an age when, if I'd left him here, he would have been a help to you."

"I don't mind." Jenny, her head on his shoulder, sleepy and fulfilled, was in no mood to argue with him. "If you are happy—you and Justin—that is all that matters. And that you should come back to me, Johnny . . . that you should *want* to come back whenever you can."

"You know I'll always come back, love." Johnny's hands caressed her slender, naked body, drawing her closer to him. "You're my wife . . . and my woman! There'll be no other woman for me."

"Yes, I know . . . and I thank God for it." She smiled in the warm darkness. "And you've no call to worry about Justin. He was never cut out to be a farmer, any more than you were. He's happy to be with you."

"Aye, and he's done well. I was sorry for his sake that he decided not to go to England with Matt Flinders. But now, of course, I'm thankful he stayed."

Jenny, wakeful now, raised herself on one elbow to look down at him. "Because you believe that poor Matt and his people are lost, that they went down in the *Cumberland* in a storm? That's what people seem to think, isn't it?"

"Aye," Johnny conceded. "But I'll never believe the *Cumberland* foundered. She was my ship, remember, and I sailed with Matt. . . . He's a fine seaman, the best I ever knew. She could have run onto a reef, like the *Porpoise*, but even if she did, Matt would have saved his people." He sighed. "There's no doubt about George Bass, I'm afraid. The wreck of his *Venus* was seen and reported in Dusky Sound, on the sou'west coast of New Zealand. But there's been word that Matt reached Timor, and if the little *Cumberland* made it that far, I reckon the chances are that Matt got the hang of her, for all his complaints about her 'roaches and her Sydney rats. He'd have taken her on."

"What do you think happened to her?" Jenny asked. Johnny shrugged.

"I don't know. . . . No one knows, and there's been no word since she left Coupang. But it'd be my guess that the damned Frenchies took her. . . . Maybe they sank her. Their privateers are all over the Indian Ocean, preying on our shipping, in revenge for being thrown out of Pondicherry. If they took her, then I'm truly thankful that Justin wasn't on board."

Jenny shivered, conjuring up a mental vision of the stout little sloop slithering beneath the waves, under fire from a squadron of French privateers. She had carried no guns and would have been unable to defend herself against attack. Matt had depended on his safe conduct to save him from molestation, just as the French Commodore Baudin had done . . . and his ships and their crews had been hospitably treated in Port Jackson. So surely no French man o' war would have sought to sink or capture the unarmed *Cumberland* with her depleted cargo of botanical specimens and her scientists.

As if he had read her thoughts, Johnny said gravely, "Privateers are a law unto themselves, lass—indeed, pirates would be a better name for the villains."

"Poor Matt," Jenny whispered. "I liked him very much, you know, when he was here."

"Aye . . . and Dr. Bass." Johnny drew her down beside him "I thought the world of them both . . . as I do of you. You're a wonderful woman, Jenny, my love. If this colony prospers, it will be thanks to men like Bass and Flinders . . . and women like you."

"I've done nothing," Jenny countered wryly. "Except work to keep starvation at bay. For nearly eighteen years, Johnny! I'll soon be thirty-four years old, and what have I achieved?"

"You've made a home," Johnny told her. He kissed her and added forcefully, "First thing tomorrow, I'm going to take Tom and the boys and fence in that new pasture land you want. And I'll not go back to the *Phillip* until the job's done, I promise you. Hell's teeth, if Dawson and Spence and the Rum Corps can squat on land, so can we! And if *Mr.* Macarthur can run sheep on the best land in the colony, with the government's blessing, then we'll run ours up to the foot of Richmond Hill without it, and be damned to them! Aye, and for good measure, a plague take *Bounty* Bligh!"

CHAPTER XXIII

It started to rain when Johnny, aided by Tom Jardine, Justin, and William, began fencing in the virgin grazing land at the foot of Richmond Hill. They toiled steadily for two days, the rain never ceasing, and when he returned to the wharf to ascertain what progress Rob Webb had made, Johnny found the older man seriously alarmed by the flooded state of the river.

"It's the old Hawkesbury trouble," he said disgustedly. "Months o' drought leaves the land bone hard an' then, when the bloody rain does come, it comes down in torrents—like it's doing now—and the water can't sink in. I've been ten mile up river, Johnny, an' it's the same story everywhere . . . a rise of over forty foot an' still risin'. I reckon we're in for another bad one this time, an' we'll likely lose most o' the wheat from the outlyin' farms, less'n it's stored under cover. The rust got at the early crop, an' this infernal plaguey rain is spoilin' what the farmers have stacked out o' doors."

"How much have you been able to bring down?" Johnny asked, glumly squeezing the wet from his sodden jacket.

"I ain't been up higher than ten mile, like I said," Rob confessed. "No point goin' farther, was there, wi' all the cargo space filled? An' the decks cluttered up, so's we can hardly work the ship." He gestured to the piled grain sacks about him, which occupied every available foot of the sloop's open deck, under coverings of sailcloth. In reply to Johnny's question he listed the farms he had visited and the quantities of produce he had taken on board from each. There was only one wharf; the outlying farmers had to have their grain transported by boat, which was a time-consuming procedure, as they both knew from past experience. But this had been a bumper harvest, Johnny realized, with yields in some cases doubled; in particular the Dawson holding had shipped more than twice the previous year's total of wheat and coarse barley.

"The quality ain't so good," Webb told him. He opened the mouth of one of the sacks. "Weevils, see, an' blight an'

smut. . . . This damp won't improve it neither. I'd
thought maybe we could store some o' it here in the granary an' cart the rest to Toongabbe wi' oxen, but . . ." He
shrugged despondently. "It'll rot if it's left too long. By
rights we should ship it straight to Sydney, so's it can be
milled right away an' most of it'd be saved, then."

"Aye, so it might, Rob. But"—Johnny looked anxiously
up at the lowering sky—"that would mean over a week's
delay in getting to the upper river and outlying settlements,
would it not?"

"It would, yes," Rob conceded. They both knew, without
the need for words, what a week's delay would mean to the
outlying settlers, particularly if the rain failed to slacken
off. But Rob's idea of discharging his cargo into the grain
store at the rear of the wharf could not be considered, for if
the river burst its banks—as it had done several times in the
past few years—both wharf and granary would, in all probability, be flooded. And there was no time to send for carts
and oxen from Toongabbe. . . . Johnny scowled at the
swift-flowing water below him.

"Assistant Commissary Fitz was here las' night," Rob
went on. "He said I was to take what we've got on board
down to Sydney today. But I told him I'd have to get your
permission first."

"And what did Mr. Fitz say to that?" Johnny demanded
sharply. He did not like Robert Fitz, who was one of the
Macarthur faction and, on his own account, was one of
the leading traffickers in rum . . . although behind the
screen of emancipist licensees.

"He said he'd have no choice—he'd have to condemn
the whole lot," Rob answered unequivocally.

"Then we've no choice, have we? You'll have to take it
to Sydney. And I'll have to man all the boats I can lay my
hands on and make for the upper river."

"Aye. Likely there'll be folk to be saved as well as crops,
Johnny, if this goes on," Rob warned. He gestured to the
far end of the wharf. "You c'n take my boat, for a start.
I've rigged a lugsail on her, and she's pretty sound. You
and young Justin could handle her with one other man."

"Any other boats that you know of?" Johnny asked.

"Aye. Mr. Biggers has a sizable craft—she's under sail
too. And there's about three others—oared boats." Rob

enumerated them. He added, scuffing his feet on the lit-
tered deck and avoiding Johnny's eye, "You could take the
Phillip down river, Johnny, an' leave the boats to me, if
you'd sooner."

Johnny shook his head. "No, you'd lose your pay if I
did. We'll stick to our usual arrangements. Anyway, I have
a vested interest in this cargo—my wife's wheat crop is on
board." He clapped a hand on Rob's broad shoulder. "Cast
off right away—I'll go and find Biggers. All I ask is you get
back here as soon as you can. If this wharf's flooded, we'll
stow whatever we're able to save in Dawson's granary—it's
on high ground and should be safe enough."

Within an hour of the *Phillip*'s departure he had the
available boats manned, and leaving the oared boats to
tackle the nearer farmers' holdings, he and the middle-aged
settler John Biggers hoisted the dingy canvas of the luggers and began to work their way upstream in the teeth of
a driving rainstorm.

By midafternoon it became evident that the flooding of
the Hawkesbury's upper reaches had reached danger level,
with acres of arable and pasture land feet deep in the
spreading tide of turbulent river water. Wheat stacks
floated sluggishly downstream, retaining for a time a recognizable shape; all too soon these were followed by half-
drowned cattle, dead sheep and hogs and, two or three
times, by human bodies. Between them the two luggers
saved over a hundred stranded settlers, plucking them to
safety from the roofs of their flooded homes, from the precarious tops of trees, and from the water itself.

Biggers went back, with most of the survivors huddled
together in jam-packed misery above and below the flush
deck of his small vessel, and Johnny went on in Rob
Webb's sturdy craft, guided through the rain-obscured
darkness by the shouts and cries of terrified people trapped
by the deluge and long despairing of rescue.

A wind got up just before dusk, compelling them to
lower the sail lest the overcrowded boat capsize, and
Johnny and a man from the *Phillip*'s crew—an emancipist
named Reuben Hale—took over the two pairs of oars, leaving Justin to steer as best he could. They rowed throughout
the night, occasionally relieved by men they had plucked
from the flood, and finally drifted downstream on the point

of exhaustion as the dawn of a new day was heralded by a violent thunderstorm.

The crash of thunder echoed from peak to peak of the distant mountains, and flashes of forked lightning illuminated the gray, ominous clouds overhead, causing some of the children in the boat to scream their fear aloud. But the wind had veered and lost its savagery, and Johnny hoisted the sail again with blistered hands, to hunch himself over the tiller and mutter hoarsely to Justin, "Rest, lad, while you've the chance."

"I can't," Justin protested. For the first time there was angry doubt in his eyes as he looked at his father. "What of Mam? Whilst we've been saving these people, have you thought of her?"

"Long Wrekin's on high ground, most of it," Johnny answered wearily. "The house may be cut off, but it won't be under water. And your mam has a boat and Tom Jardine and the others, if she's in need of help."

For all his optimistic words, anxiety for his own family had been tormenting him throughout the seemingly endless night. But the farm—which Jenny had called Long Wrekin after the one that had been her father's—and its buildings were on high ground, the risk to human life far less than that run by the settlers on the outlying holdings to which he had taken his boat. Many were small, worked by a man and his wife without the aid of convict labor for which they could not pay, and of the holders of small, far-flung grants, all too few were country folk with experience of the land.

Their need, as he had told himself repeatedly, was greater than Jenny's or, come to that, the Dawsons'. Tim Dawson knew the river's vagaries; he had suffered flooding before and, like Jenny, possessed a boat and horses to make flight possible, if it became necessary, for his family and his workers. The loss of stock was inevitable for them all, but at least those nearest to the wharf had saved their harvest. . . . Johnny swore softly as another batch of half-submerged and waterlogged wheat stacks floated past the boat's counter, the current carrying them toward the far bank. Some of the poor devils they had picked up would have lost their all, he thought, seeing a year's backbreaking work destroyed in a single night—and they would in all probability, when they eventually went back to their holdings, find that the swollen river had swallowed up the flimsy wattle and daub huts they had called home.

Justin said something, his tone aggrieved, and Johnny harshly bade him hold his tongue.

"Mr. Biggers will have passed in sight of your mother's farmhouse," he began. "And—"

"In darkness?" Justin countered. He waved to the wilderness of water about them and to the submerged trees, which had previously marked its banks. "In *this*, Dad?"

"We'll go back," Johnny promised, relenting, "as soon as we've set these poor folk safely on shore."

But it was another four hours before this could be done. Overnight the wharf and the grain store had vanished beneath the advancing flood; like Biggers before them they had to go on until, to their heartfelt relief, a bend in the river revealed a small cluster of oared boats tied up to the anchored *Phillip* and the old *Francis* at the mouth of a creek that, miraculously, appeared almost at its normal autumn level.

Rob Webb had waited, defying Commissary Fitz's warning, and the master of the *Francis*—good man that he was—had chanced her barnacle-encrusted timbers when word had reached him of the serious extent of the flood.

"There's more help on the way, Johnny," Rob shouted as they came within hailing distance of the sloop. "The governor's sending boats. We'll take your people back to Port Jackson as soon as they get here." He added, when Johnny maneuvered the boat alongside, "To hell with my pay if you want to take over the *Phillip*."

"No, thanks." Johnny shook his head. "As Justin has reminded me, I'd best see after my own family now. But if you can oblige me with a drink and a couple of fresh hands, I'd be grateful, because it's liable to be a long, hard pull with this wind."

It proved longer and harder even than he had anticipated, with both wind and current against them, but the rain slackened off at last into a thin drizzle. With the coming of darkness it ceased altogether, and with it the buffeting wind. By dint of tacking they made the final passage upriver under sail to find, as Johnny had expected, that the Long Wrekin farmhouse—although surrounded and cut off—was itself clear of the flood water.

Jenny welcomed the return of her husband and eldest
son with tears of thankfulness, but it was evident from her
tear-reddened eyes and constrained manner that all was not
well, and she said in answer to Johnny's anxious question,
"It's William . . . he's gone, Johnny—just vanished
with that dog of his. He—"

"Vanished?" Johnny put in, his throat suddenly tight.
"For God's sake, when did you last see him?"

"Not since the night before last. I went to rouse him in
the morning, and"—Jenny caught her breath on a sob—
"he wasn't in his bed. He shares the loft room with Rachel,
and she told me he had gone away in the night, but, poor
little mite, she can't say exactly when. Tom and the other
men took the horses and as many of the other stock as they
could round up and drove them to Toongabbe as soon as
we realized how bad the flooding was. I knew they might
not be able to get back, and I told them not to try, that
we'd be all right. But this morning I . . ." She was sobbing
openly now, and Johnny took her into his arms, laying his
gaunt, unshaven cheek on hers.

"There, love, there . . . don't take on so. We'll find
him, Justin and I. We—"

"It's not only William," Jenny whispered, vainly trying
to stem her tears. "It's Watt, too. He took the oared boat
and went to look for William, and he—he hasn't come
back. He was alone—I think he was afraid I'd try to stop
him, poor old man, if he told me what he meant to do. But
because he took our only boat, Johnny, I couldn't go in
search of either of them, and I . . . I've just had to stay
here, waiting and praying. I . . ."

"*We* should have been here," Justin said bitterly, "instead of worrying about other folk. But Dad—"

Johnny cut him short. "We're here now," he countered
brusquely. "And we have a boat and four of us manning it.
We'll go and search for them at once. Off with you to the
cookhouse, Justin, and pick up some bread and cheese for
the men and any spirits you can find. A keg of rum if there
is one." The boy left on his errand, and he turned to Jenny
again. "Jenny love, have you any idea what William was
trying to do—where he was going? It'll be like looking for
a needle in a haystack—it's a wilderness out there. But it

would help to narrow the search if we knew which direction the little lad took."

Jenny shook her head helplessly. "I just don't know, Johnny. Perhaps Watt did—William was with him yesterday. But we . . . there was so much to do, you see. And I—I don't mean yesterday, I mean the day before yesterday. He's been gone for two days." She was shaking, her voice choked with sobs, but she made a valiant effort to keep her fears in check. "He . . . he took his dog, Johnny."

"His dog?" Impatient to begin the search, Johnny hesitated. "He always did take the dog, did he not?"

Jenny looked up into his anxious face, her own lighting with sudden hope. "The sheep!" she exclaimed. "He was upset when I said—to Tom, I think it was—that we should have to lose the sheep in the river pasture. And he's been trying to train that dog of his to work sheep. . . . Johnny, perhaps he went out to try and save the sheep! To—to drive them onto that high ground the three of you fenced before the river burst its banks. He could have got there two days ago."

"It's worth trying, Jenny love." Johnny drew her to him and his lips brushed hers lightly in farewell. "We'll be back, God willing, with the little lad and old Watt. Have a meal waiting for us, will you? They'll both be ready for it, and so shall we."

The moon, riding serene once more in a cloudless sky, aided their search, and they found the small, oared boat less than a mile from the farmhouse. It had drifted into a grove of trees, to be held fast there, as if in a vice, by a mass of flotsam carried down by the flood. The current had carried away the oars, and old Watt Sparrow sat hunched in the stern, half buried beneath the canopy of leaves and the branches he had torn down in what had evidently been a frantic effort to drag the boat clear of their encumbrance.

The effort had killed him, and, Johnny judged when he touched the old man's ice-cold cheek, he had probably died ten or twelve hours before, any cries for help he might have uttered unheard for the tumult of running water by which he and his frail craft were surrounded.

"Are you just going to leave him there?" Justin demanded when Johnny fended their own boat off and motioned the oarsmen away. "That's Gran'pa Watt, and he—"

"Yes," Johnny grated, conscious of an unreasoning anger against his firstborn but reluctant to put it into words. "We'll pick his body up on the way back. First we have to find your brother if we can. He'll be wet and cold and hungry, poor little fellow."

"If he's alive," Justin muttered rebelliously.

Johnny was silent. He thought, sick with pity, of the small six-year-old boy who had gone out with his half-trained dog to try to rescue the sheep he had helped to tend. Then, his throat tight, he thought of old Watt—old Grandpa Watt—to whom his children had been kith and kin and for whom the old man had risked his life. Risked and given it, because he himself had not been there, and there had been no one else.

"We shouldn't have left them," Justin said, a catch in his voice.

"I don't need you to remind me," Johnny returned coldly. He bent to his oar and, head lowered, pulled with such power and frustrated anger that the man on the thwart behind him swore in protest.

"Hell's teeth, Mr. Broome—we bin at these oars all day. Have a heart, will yer?"

It was a heart that Justin seemed to imagine he lacked. Johnny thought resentfully, but he eased the stroke and Justin, unbidden, started to dole out rum to their weary companions.

Their search ended, as Jenny had predicted it would, when they came in sight of the newly fenced hill pasture an hour later. William was there, with his dog, guarding a flock of some twenty Bengal ewes, dim white blurs in the fitful moonlight but identified by their plaintive bleating. The sheep were spread out over the high ground, and as the boat approached, Johnny saw the dog dash out, at its master's shrill whistle, to bring in some stragglers that had wandered too far from the rest. A born shepherd, William, he thought with a pang and, cupping his hands about his mouth, called out to the boy that they were coming.

The water became shallower as the ground rose and the boat's keel touched bottom, to be held in glutinous mud some sixty or seventy yards from where William had taken refuge. The dog, scenting the prospect of food and human companionship, came splashing out to meet them, and William rose to his feet with the obvious intention of following suit.

"Stay where you are, lad!" Johnny bade him. "I'm coming to get you."

"I'll get him," Justin volunteered. He had a leg over the boat's side when Johnny grasped him by the scruff of the neck and yanked him unceremoniously back to sprawl helplessly among the oarsmen's legs. He picked himself up, furious with his father for the humiliation inflicted on him. One of the men laughed at the spectacle he made and said teasingly, "You ain't the commander yet, me young cock—whatever you think o' yerself. An' I'll tell you somethin' else . . . it'll be a while before you're half the man your father is, so jus' put that in yer pipe an' smoke it!"

His fellows joined in his laughter. Both were convicts serving in the *Phillip*'s crew, and Justin rounded on them. But the angry words he had been about to fling at them were never uttered, for suddenly a thunderous roar from out of the darkness froze them on his lips. Boulders came rolling down from the hillside to splash into the water ahead of the boat's bow, initially few in number and small in size but gathering in momentum as part of the lower slope seemed almost to disintegrate. Tons of sodden earth and uprooted trees cascaded down, dimly seen where the moonlight struck them, but their menace unmistakable.

"It's a—it's a bleedin' landslide!" the man who had laughed at him gasped, and Justin screamed out a high-pitched warning to his father, which was lost in the tumult of the tumbling earth.

Johnny was facing the hill. He saw and realized what was happening, watched the blurred white shape of the sheep, bunched together in terror, vanish beneath the welter of falling debris as if they had never been . . . and he saw William glance over his shoulder and start to run. Waist deep in water, his feet caught and held by the clinging mud, Johnny struggled toward his son. Reaching him an instant before the oncoming landslide struck the water, he picked the boy up and, exerting the last ounce of his failing strength, flung him toward the boat.

He did not fling him clear, but it was far enough to enable the boy's small body to escape with a few buffetings and then—miraculously caught up in the branches of a shattered tree—to float near enough for Justin and one of the oarsmen to haul him to safety.

But where their father had been there was now a dark mound, rising three or four feet above the water, the threshing struggles of a bleating ewe the only sign of life in its vicinity. Even these ceased when the poor creature abandoned her fight for survival and slid into the murky depths below, as the mound spread out and flattened.

A few more boulders rolled slowly down but in virtual silence, and within minutes the avalanche was over, with the same stunning suddenness with which it had begun. The little dog came paddling alongside the boat; they dragged it on board, and with sodden tail wagging it crept over to where William was lying, still gasping and choking on the water he had swallowed, and started to lick his face. The little boy clasped it in his arms and lapsed into childish tears.

Justin harshly told him to be silent and, having secured the boat by its painter, he and the two men from the *Phillip* waded across to the mound to commence their hopeless search. With their bare hands they tore at the unyielding mass of earth and trees and boulders, concentrating on the spot where they had last seen Johnny standing upright. But under the pressure of the flood water the whole mass was breaking up and disintegrating, like the hillside from which it had originated; Justin was coming close to despair when a shaft of moonlight fell on his father's white, barely recognizable face a few inches below the surface of the water.

He tugged frantically and, sobbing, brought the big, crushed body out from beneath the uprooted gum that had held it there, aided by the man who had compared him, so unfavorably and contemptuously, with his father. And it was true, he told himself with bitter self-reproach—he was not half the man his father was and never would be.

"Help me," he gritted hoarsely. "Help me get him to the boat, will you?" He grasped his father's wrist and felt the puckered scars left by the fetters that had once held Johnny Broome in hated convict servitude, and his control broke.

"Leave him to us, lad," the older of the two seamen urged with gruff pity. "We'll see to 'im an' yer gran'pa too. You take care o' the little feller—he's cryin' fit ter bust hisself. An' you're all he's got now . . . you an' yer Ma."

Justin gulped and did as he had been told, but the man's words haunted him and he recalled them, almost with a sense of shame, when the boat returned to Long Wrekin with its sad cargo and it fell to him to tell his weeping mother of what had happened.

"I'll be here, Mam," he promised her. "From now on, whenever you need me, I'll be here. I'll not go to sea again, that . . . that's over."

Jenny laid her hand on his shoulder and then turned away, unable to speak. Finally she said, in a flat, controlled voice, "See that the men are fed, Justin. There's a meal ready in the kitchen, as your Dadda asked—and you must eat something too. You and William. I . . . I'd like a little time . . . alone. I haven't taken it in yet, I . . . if I'm by myself for an hour or two, perhaps I'll be able to bear it, to—to understand why God has let this happen. Can you—can you manage without me?"

Justin nodded and left her by herself as the men carried in his father's body.

CHAPTER XXIV

The convoy bringing Captain William Bligh to the colony entered Port Jackson on a cool, sunlit August afternoon of the year 1806. It was headed by the transport *Lady Madeleine Sinclair*, with three convict ships astern of her and the old government sloop H.M.S. *Porpoise,* bringing up the rear.

The signal had been hoisted at South Head the previous morning so that, with ample time to prepare for his coming, an impressive reception awaited the new governor's arrival. The New South Wales Corps had paraded with colors flying and the fifes and drums playing, their scarlet-clad ranks flanked by a full company of the Loyal Association of Sydney, proudly bearing arms as defenders of the colony under their own mounted officers.

Saluting cannon boomed from the shore batteries in answer to those fired by the *Madeleine Sinclair* as she dropped anchor in the cove, and standing on her quarter-deck William Bligh turned his glass on the small uniformed party now assembling on the wharf in front of Government House.

Governor King was there, easily recognizable in his gold-laced, naval full dress; his wife and two of his children stood with a group of officers' and settlers' families a little distance away in the Government House garden, where a marquee had been erected. There were sentries posted at the gates and at the approaches to the wharf, the blue-uniformed constables held the crowds of convict and emancipist inhabitants in rigid check, when necessary enforcing order with blows from the long staves they carried.

Bligh said, lowering his glass as he turned to his daughter, "This is quite a welcome, Mary my dear. I confess I hadn't expected anything on this scale."

Mary Putland smiled thinly. "It is well organized, Father, but very . . . military."

"It's a convict colony. The military presence is inevitable." The new governor again raised his glass. "And it's quite a sizable town. The buildings are unimaginative, perhaps, and there's a sameness about them, but I like the

windmills on the skyline. And the harbor is magnificent.
. . . As Admiral Phillip said, the whole British fleet could
anchor here in perfect safety. It's a wonder the French did
not try to wrest it from us."

"Since Trafalgar the French navy is a spent force," his
son-in-law, Charles Putland, asserted. "We'll be safe
enough here, sir, for the next twenty years."

"It's to be hoped for longer than that," Bligh grunted.
"But that upstart Bonaparte has to be beaten first." He let
his glass range along the shore. "They have a shipyard, by
God! That augers well. I can see two small vessels on the
stocks, and it looks as if they have one more fitting out.
Captain Hunter said they had found hardwood, the equal
of teak, growing naturally in several areas, and . . ." His
voice was lost as the *Porpoise* brought to and commenced
to fire the traditional salute. "That infernal villain!" he
added vehemently when the guns fell silent at last. "Don't
forget what I told you, Charles—Mr. Short is to be placed
under arrest the instant he steps ashore."

"Aye, aye, sir," Lieutenant Putland acknowledged unhappily. "You—er—you'll inform the governor of the—
er—the circumstances, will you not, prior to the arrest?"

"Certainly I shall inform Captain King. But"—his
father-in-law eyed him coldly—"from the moment I step
ashore, *I* am the governor in all but name. And I have
logged Short's misconduct, which, as you know, took place
when we were at sea. It does not concern this colony,
Charles, or come under colonial jurisdiction. It's merely
convenient to arrest Short here. At the first opportunity I
shall send him back to England for trial by a naval court-
martial. Damme, you know all that! Do I need to repeat
myself?"

"No, sir." Charles Putland's thin, pale face was suffused
with embarrassed color. He was a sick man, suffering from
a severe infection of the lungs, and William Bligh had frequently regretted his daughter's choice of a husband. But
. . . the poor devil *was* married to his much loved Mary,
and in the hope that the warm climate of New South Wales
might improve his condition, the new governor had appointed him as his aide.

They both looked at Mary now, Putland's glance appealing for her support, and she ventured uncertainly, "Papa

dear, it does seem very hard on Captain Short's wife and their two little children. I mean—they had intended to settle here, had they not? To take land and farm it, they—"

William Bligh interrupted brusquely, "I will thank you not to interfere in matters that do not concern you, my dear. For the sake of naval discipline, I cannot overlook an act of gross insubordination by a junior officer. Short should have considered the consequences to his family, as well as to himself, when he chose to behave as he did."

"Yes, but his wife should not be punished for it, Papa," Mary protested.

"She does not have to be," her father snapped. "She'll be at liberty to stay here or go home with Short, as she chooses. For God Almighty's sake, he's another Fletcher Christian! Though I dare swear that Christian would not have disputed my command with me *and* gone to the length of firing a shot across the bow of a ship wearing a commodore's broad pennant, as Joseph Short saw fit to do. Devil take it, Mary, I am a post-captain and he's a mere lieutenant!"

"Yes, I know, Papa. But I still think that if you could be merciful, if you could overlook Cap—Lieutenant Short's behavior, then . . ." Her husband, recognizing the light of anger blazing in the new governor's eyes, grasped her arm and drew her away. He whispered something that William Bligh did not catch, and he started after them, his anger swiftly controlled.

"Charles, my dear boy, I—"

"She does not understand," Charles Putland put in. "Leave her to me, sir, and I'll explain." Thankfully he saw a boat put off from the government wharf and, forestalling the officer of the watch, drew Captain Bligh's attention to it. "Do you wish us to come ashore with you, sir?"

"Yes, of course I do, Charles. Governor King's married—Mary must pay her respects to his wife. They seem to have set up a marquee in the Government House grounds—I imagine they intend to wine and dine us there after I've inspected the troops. Ah . . ." He lowered his voice. "I don't want Short dining with us. Make a signal to the *Porpoise* instructing him to remain on board."

"Aye, aye, sir." Putland knew better than to argue. Retaining his light, comforting grasp of his wife's arm, he asked woodenly, "Is that all, sir?"

"Yes . . . no! Tell them to send Hawley to hold him in arrest." Captain Bligh turned away, to watch the approaching boat with a critical eye wondering, as he did so, what Philip King's feelings were. It must be damned unpleasant to be relieved in this manner, he thought—unpleasant and . . . yes, humiliating. He had been well briefed by Lord Hobart and, of course, by Sir Joseph Banks and was fully aware of the official reasons for King's recall. He frowned, remembering. Sir Joseph had told him, not mincing words, where the trouble lay, and he knew that he would have to break the power of the Rum Corps if he himself were not to suffer King's fate.

The Rum Corps and Captain John Macarthur—the one-time officer whom King had described as *"the dark and concealed assassin of my character and reputation"* in a letter to the Colonial Office. He braced himself as the boat came alongside, and the bowman hooked his boathook to the *Madeleine Sinclair's* chains.

On the wharf Governor King waited with ill-concealed impatience for his successor's arrival. He had ordered the reception and the marquee, but he had not invited either Macarthur or his wife to join the official parties. Yet Macarthur he saw mounted on a handsome chestnut horse with Major Johnstone at the head of the corps. His wife, Elizabeth—with whom, it was true, he and Anna had remained on friendly terms during Macarthur's absence in England—was in the marquee, and she had brought her children with her, in the care of a convict nursemaid.

None of the children—his own included—were expected to stay for dinner, which was to be an exclusively male affair, but his ever-hospitable wife was, he knew, planning to serve them with an evening meal at Government House. And she had gathered a number of settlers' wives about her, and their children. The garden was echoing with their shrill cries. It would be pandemonium for hours, the governor thought sourly, and the rooms would all be in disarray when finally he was able to repair there with the new governor, to whom he had so much advice to offer and so many warnings to impart.

"Oh, Governor, how delightful to see you. . . . I give you good day!"

Philip King recognized the voice and he turned without enthusiasm to respond to Mrs. Dawson's effusive greeting. He liked Timothy Dawson well enough and could not but applaud his achievements, since this was the result of hard work and an intelligent acceptance of conditions as they were in the colony. But his wife . . . He sighed, restraining himself, as Henrietta Dawson moved on with queenly dignity toward the lawn where the other children were disporting themselves, her own small daughters, impeccably dressed and bonneted, following in docile procession at her heels, her little son grasped firmly by the hand.

The sight of her reminded him of what he wished he could forget. The disastrous Hawkesbury flood of five months ago was still, to him, a haunting reproach with its appalling toll of lost lives and ruined crops. The Dawsons, he recalled, had fled the scene at the outset, Dawson prudently taking his breeding stock and his laborers with him, probably as a result of his wife's urging—because he had come back on his own to give what aid he could, when the area was beyond aid. They, virtually alone amongst the Hawkesbury settlers, had sustained no irreparable loss—their wheat, as well as their horses, had been saved, thanks to its having been loaded aboard the *Phillip* before the river had risen a full, devastating ninety feet above its normal level.

Most of the smaller farmers had found themselves facing ruin, with their stock drowned, their dwelling places and other buildings destroyed, and their crops so much flotsam, borne down on the turgid river water to Broken Bay and the sea. And some—like the poor Broome woman—had lost husbands and children in the disaster. He had done what he could for them, the governor reflected, but it was little enough. Even the remission of their quit rents for a year could not compensate for what Hawkesbury River had taken from them. And worst of all, perhaps, had been the effect the flood had had on their morale, for they had been robbed of hope.

There was a slight stir in the knot of people gathered on the wharf, and Governor King saw the judge advocate, Richard Atkins, thrust his way toward him. Breathing hard, as if from running, Atkins said angrily, "Is Your Excellency aware of who are the signatories to the Address of Welcome from the free settlers?"

Address of Welcome . . . of course, this was to be presented to the new governor; he recalled there had been talk of it, but . . . He shook his head, puzzled by Atkins's wrath. "No, I only know there's to be one. Who *has* signed it, then?"

"John Macarthur!" the judge advocate exploded. "He has also signed your Farewell Address—again on behalf of the free inhabitants—and he intends to present it to you in person!"

This was too much to take, even from Macarthur, Philip King thought wearily, but he was at a loss to know how he could possibly prevent its delivery.

"Who else has signed?" he asked.

"No one else, sir. I signed on behalf of the civil authorities, and Major Johnstone for the military. The wording of the Farewell Address is . . . good God, I scarcely know how to tell you because—oh, damme, because Macarthur composed it! Naturally I refused to add my name—we're organizing another, but I doubt if there will be time to make the substitution."

"Spare yourself the trouble, Mr. Atkins," the governor bade him, a distinct edge to his voice. "But tell me the gist of it, so that I may be prepared."

Atkins took a crumpled sheet of paper from his pocket. "The gist is, sir, that they thank you for your services in— and I quote—'discharging an office arduous and difficult beyond what can easily be imagined by any person unacquainted with the peculiar problems which beset this colony.' There is more on the same lines, but I should have to quote it from memory—I had no time to take a written note."

"That will more than suffice," King said, contriving by a great effort of will to speak calmly. "Thank you, my friend. The warning is timely."

He felt sick with fury, his stomach churning. Macarthur's sheer effrontery was calculated to enrage him, the so-called Farewell Address worded so as to ensure his humiliation. Bile rose in his throat, and he tasted its bitterness as he swallowed, aware that it was the bitterness of defeat. John Macarthur had challenged and bested him, as he had bested Hunter. But . . . The boat, with the new governor seated in the stern sheets, came alongside the wharf. The crew tossed their oars smartly, and as he walked toward it, Philip King remembered his conversation with Major Johnstone.

Bligh had recently been tried by court-martial, Johnstone had said, charged with oppressive tyranny to certain of the officers under his command. Well, if there was any justice in the world, Bligh would display something of that tyrannical spirit here and direct it against Johnstone and his iniquitous Rum Corps. Before heaven, it would be no more than they deserved. He removed his cocked hat and bowed to his successor, who returned the salute and then turned, smiling, to hand his daughter from the boat and courteously effect the necessary introductions.

"Mistress Putland," King said pleasantly, extending his hand, "my wife is receiving in the marquee and is, I know, eager to make your acquaintance. Perhaps, ma'am, you will permit my secretary to escort you there. Willie, my boy, your arm for Mistress Putland. William Chapman, ma'am, my secretary."

"And mine, sir," Captain Bligh offered. "Edmund Griffin . . . and my son-in-law, Charles Putland."

The introductions completed and Mrs. Putland on her way to the marquee, the past and future governors covertly took stock of one another. They had not met before, but each was aware of the other's record in the service, William Bligh's being at once the more notorious and the more distinguished. He had been one of Nelson's captains at the battle of Copenhagen and, in proof of this, wore the gold medal awarded for that victory about his neck with conscious pride. The news of Nelson's tragic death at the greater victory off Cape Trafalgar had recently reached the colony and this, in a subtle way, seemed to add something to Bligh's distinction.

They exchanged a few polite if meaningless words, and Philip King was agreeably surprised by the understanding sympathy he read in his successor's dark eyes when Major Johnstone advanced arrogantly to present the Address of Welcome, introducing himself as lieutenant governor and acting commandant of the corps. The address was read by

Richard Atkins, the scroll ceremoniously handed over, and Johnstone, without waiting for permission, brought John Macarthur forward to be formally presented as the third signatory to the address.

"Now, sir, if it would please you," the acting commandant said. "My troops are ready for Your Excellency's inspection."

William Bligh turned pointedly to the man he was to relieve, ignoring the question. "It is not usual here, Your Excellency," he inquired with deceptive mildness, "for the recipient of an Address of Welcome to make reply?"

"Indeed it is, Captain Bligh," King assured him, matching his tone. "I am certain that the people would be most gratified were you to reply. Shall we move to where you can best be heard?"

As the new governor made to follow him, he saw Macarthur look up from the Farewell Address he had been about to read, visibly taken aback by the turn events had taken, and found himself smiling at his enemy's discomfiture. The infernal fellow would almost certainly insist on reading his address—he was nothing if not tenacious—but it might be best, in the circumstances, if he were permitted to do so at the conclusion of this evening's formal dinner. He said as much, in a low voice, to Atkins and saw the judge advocate's smile echo his own as he, too, prepared to follow the small procession now forming up at Bligh's back.

Reaching the chosen vantage point—a low rise just beyond the Government House garden fence—Bligh took a folded paper from the pocket of his blue tailcoat, studied it for a moment in frowning concentration, and then started to read. The new governor was plainly no orator, but he had a strong, forceful delivery, which carried as clearly to the waiting crowd of free and convict inhabitants as it did to the soldiers.

"I have come from England and from the fleet at war," he announced, "to relieve your present governor who, like myself, has the honor to serve in His Majesty's Navy. You will no doubt have heard—although you are many thousands of miles from the theater of war—of the glorious victories our fleet has won. The most recent and the most glorious—the naval battle fought off Cape Trafalgar in Oc-

tober of last year—was won at the cost of the life of our
most revered and famous admiral . . . the late Lord Nelson, under whose command I am proud to tell you that I
have served. On that day the might of the French and
Spanish navies was utterly destroyed. . . ."

His listeners cheered, but the corps officers' applause
was merely lukewarm, for the implications of his words
had not escaped them. They were soldiers who were many
thousands of miles from the theater of war. They bore arms
and had paraded in the king's scarlet, but they had fought
none of their country's battles, and the new governor had
as good as told them so.

Bligh paused, looking searchingly at the faces about him,
and then he plunged in, stating unequivocally what he intended to do when the reins of government were in his
hands. Standing stiffly at his side, Philip King paid silent
tribute to his courage when Bligh spoke of the "proper regulations" he would introduce for the purpose of encouraging the merchant and the industrious settler.

"I have my instructions, set out under His Majesty's sign
and seal, and in order to ensure that these are implemented, I intend to exercise a close superintendence over
the colony. I shall pay particular attention to the inculca-
tion of the Christian religion and Christian standards of
morality throughout the length and breadth of the land on
which you have settled and built your homes. I shall make
it my task to encourage Christian marriage and to see that
religious instruction is provided, together with a sound general education for all the children born here. I shall give
my wholehearted support to the Orphan School founded by
your present governor's lady, for you are all as much aware
as I am, I feel sure, that it is upon your children that the
future happiness and prosperity of this colony will depend. . . ."

The officers, who had given merely token approbation to
his mention of the naval victory at Tafalgar, applauded
with more enthusiasm, although both Johnstone and Abbott—who were standing near him—looked visibly apprehensive, Governor King saw. Thus far, apart from his reference to proper regulations as yet unspecified, William
Bligh had expressed only platitudinous sentiments in which
they could all concur, but . . . He heard his successor

draw a deep breath and then continue, the pitch of his voice that of a commander accustomed to shout his orders from the quarterdeck of a ship at sea.

"His Majesty's ministers have instructed me to exercise a rigid control over the illegal trade in liquor, which is said to flourish here to the detriment of morality and good order. This I most certainly intend to do, and when I have assumed office as governor I shall issue an Order of Prohibition in accordance with my instructions."

He had flung down the gauntlet, Philip King thought, elated—he had offered a challenge to those whose trading monopolies had enriched them. His own efforts, heaven knew, had been directed to that end, and had he been given the home government's support, he might well have seen them succeed. But Bligh seemingly had been promised full support; he had his royal instructions and had declared his determination to implement them without fear or favor, and whoever had the temerity to oppose him would need to count the cost.

He glanced, almost without realizing he had done so, at John Macarthur and observed that he had reddened. But the colony's largest landowner gave no other outward sign of his feelings and, indeed, appeared to be avoiding Johnstone's eye.

Captain Bligh went on, declaring his interest in the repair and completion of all public buildings and, in particular, of Sydney's church, and hinting at new regulations that would restrict private buildings in the town and the granting of long leaseholds. These, because they were measures that were unlikely to affect them to any great extent, were received with comparative indifference. . . . In any event, Philip King reflected glumly, the Macarthur faction already owned all the Sydney leaseholds they wanted. Lord Camden had seen to that. . . .

Bligh ended with a pledge to introduce a stable currency in the near future, and then, folding his notes, he turned to the man standing beside him.

"Has Your Excellency anything further for me to add?"

Governor King hesitated and then inclined his head. "We have had a disastrous flood in the Hawkesbury River area, which has left the settlers there with ruinous losses. Perhaps Your Excellency might feel it advisable to pledge government aid in the replacement of stock, as soon as it can be arranged? I have already revoked their rents and supplied them with commissariat rations, but more help is needed if the people there are to recoup their losses."

Bligh thanked him and delivered the pledge with so much feeling that the settlers cheered him.

"I will visit the Hawkesbury settlements," he promised, "at the first opportunity that Governor King can afford me."

This brought renewed cheers from a large section of his audience, but it was evident from their expressions that very few of his observations and promises had found favor with the officers of the corps. The acting commandant escorted him to make his belated inspection of the troops on parade, his manner icy, and even genuine praise for the smartness of their turnout brought no relaxation on Johnstone's part.

Philip King said when, the inspection over, Bligh joined him, "That was a notable beginning, and I should like to offer my congratulations."

"I've made enemies, have I not, sir?" the new governor suggested wryly. "Rather sooner than later, perhaps."

"They would have been enemies whatever you had said," King returned with bitterness. "As they have been mine and John Hunter's in the past. But you have also made friends, Mr. Bligh, and I trust, sir, that if you will permit me to introduce you to my wife and her guests, that you will make many more friends here. Step this way, sir."

Halfway to the marquee Captain Bligh halted, brows knit in a frown. "There is one small matter I must bring to your notice, Mr. King. The commander of my escort vessel—Lieutenant Short. I've ordered him to remain on board the *Porpoise* for the time being, but as soon as a passage can be arranged for him, I want him sent home for trial by a naval court-martial."

Philip King stared at him in unconcealed surprise. He was, he thought suddenly, seeing a different side to William Bligh—very different from the one he had presented a short while before, when he had faced the hostility of the Rum Corps with dignity and courage. This was *Bounty* Bligh, the captain who had provoked a mutiny by his ship's company and hounded the survivors with merciless persistence, damning even those who had been acquitted at their trial, in print and in person. He listened in embarrassed silence as his successor listed the charges he intended to bring against the unfortunate Short, but on the face of it the *Porpoise*'s commander had acted foolishly, and if Bligh insisted, he would have to be sent home.

"Very well, sir," he agreed resignedly. "I shall be taking the *Buffalo* to England, when she returns from the Cape. Mr. Short and his family can accompany me if that is your wish."

"It is," Bligh answered uncompromisingly. "I'll not tolerate insubordination when I'm in command—damme if I will!—from whomsoever it may come, and that, between you and me, Captain King, applies to Mr. Macarthur and the—ah—the officers and men of the New South Wales Corps as much as it does to Lieutenant Short."

It was to be hoped, Governor King reflected as they again fell into step together—indeed, it was devoutly to be hoped—that where insubordination on the part of the corps was concerned, the new governor would stick to his guns and refuse to tolerate any manifestation of it.

He himself, when the old *Buffalo* returned from her cattle buying at the Cape, would go back to his homeland in the company of a number of others who had once thought as he did and had endeavored in the past to cross swords with the insubordinate John Macarthur. Colonel Paterson, broken in health and spirit, had already gone to recuperate in Van Diemen's Land—and he had volunteered to go with a most indecent haste. His wife would, in all probability, decide on the *Buffalo* and England, so would the Reverend Samuel Marsden, Surgeon Harris, and perhaps even Judge Advocate Atkins—and they would officially only be going on leave. But how many of them would return if Governor Bligh failed to keep the promises he had made today?

Philip King stifled a sigh and led his guest into the marquee.

In obedience to Captain Bligh's orders, Andrew Hawley was rowed across the anchorage to the *Porpoise*. The orders were far from being to his liking, but it had been many years since he had questioned the orders of a superior officer—the last time, in fact, had been in his clash

with Lieutenant Leach, on board the *Charlott*e of Governor
Phillip's fleet.

And that deviation from his duty had cost him his corporal's stripes, a flogging, and . . . Jenny Taggart. He stared
across at the receding shoreline and at the regimented rows
of convicts' huts, haphazardly spaced public buildings,
windmills, and gardens—all he had so far seen of Sydney
town—and fell to wondering what his situation might have
been had Governor Phillip not sent him back to England
nineteen years ago.

He would have married Jenny—that much, at least, was
certain—and neither Leach nor old Sergeant Jenkins nor,
come to that, Governor Phillip himself would have stopped
him. They would have settled on a grant of land, reared a
family and stock, and, by heaven, if the reports he had
heard were true, he would have been a wealthy man by
now, as all the military garrison were. More traders than
soldiers, by all accounts, which would have gone against
the grain in his case, for he was proud of his profession.

As things had turned out, though, he could not regret
Governor Phillip's arbitrary decision, Andrew decided.
True, he had neither wife nor family; the women in his life
had been transient and unloved, few of them even remembered. He had no money save his pay, but he had fought
his country's battles and been advanced to commissioned
rank, not by favor or patronage but on his own merits.

He touched the scar on his cheek. After Camperdown
the surgeon who had stitched up the gaping wound had told
him that it would heal and added philosophically, "And if
it does not, these are honorable scars of which you need
not be ashamed."

Probably he was right, for all that particular scar was
unsightly, lending his face a curiously sardonic look, it had
caused him much less pain than the wound he had received
in the left thigh when serving in the *Vanguard*, Admiral
Nelson's flagship, at the battle of Aboukir Bay. He winced
involuntarily, recalling how close he had come to losing his
leg. It had kept him ashore and out of action for the best
part of a year, but then he had been sent to the *Superb*,
and after the action off Algeciras against the Dons, he had
been commissioned on the recommendation of her commander, Captain Keats.

Thereafter he had taken part in Admiral Nelson's long, abortive chase to the West Indies in pursuit of the combined French and Spanish fleets, transferring to the *Belleisle* when the old *Superb,* battle-scarred and leaking, had paid off to refit. He had come through the final reckoning at Trafalgar without a scratch, although his ship had been dismasted and had suffered more than a hundred and thirty casualties.

He had, Andrew told himself, much to be grateful for when the assessment was made. He was thirty-nine years old and as fit as any man of his age; the new governor of the colony of New South Wales had invited him to join his staff, and in promising his patronage had assured him that his transfer from the Royal Marines to the New South Wales Corps could be arranged, if he should wish to make it, without loss of rank. He was free to settle here, to apply for a grant of land, and even to marry if . . . He sighed, wondering again about Jenny Taggart. It had been a long time since he had received a letter from her—years, in fact—and he knew that she would have changed, probably out of recognition, from the pert, pretty little lass he had borne on his shoulders into London Town half a lifetime ago and found again on board the convict transport *Charlotte.*

But her image was enshrined in his heart, and he supposed it always would be, even if she were now a mature woman with a husband and children and a life of her own. Although perhaps if she had married old Tom Jenkins, in his widowerhood, she might be free, and . . .

The boat pulled alongside the *Porpoise,* the coxswain responding to the hail of the officer on watch, and he hauled himself up to the entry port with the ease of long practice.

Her commander, Joseph Short, met him on the quarterdeck, his plump, good-natured face wearing an anxious frown. The sloop was his first command, and aware that he would probably be relieved of it, he asked with bitterness, "Does your arrival mean what I fear it does, Captain Hawley?"

"I am commanded by Commodore Bligh to place you under arrest, sir," Andrew told him. He added with genuine sympathy, "I regret the necessity, Captain Short."

"Not as much as I do!" Short exclaimed ruefully. "I've

already received a signal instructing me to remain on board, so your appearance is not unexpected. But you'll be missing the welcome ceremony and all the festivities ashore on my account, I'm afraid. I can only apologize."

Andrew glanced over his shoulder at the crowds gathered at every vantage point on the distant shore and shrugged philosophically. "It's no matter, sir. I shall get there soon enough."

"They tell me that the town of Sydney is a sink of iniquity," Short observed. "Awash on a sea of rum, so perhaps neither of us is missing much. But I'm sorry for my wife. . . . She was looking forward to setting foot on dry land and making the acquaintance of the other officers' ladies. Poor sweet soul, she is far from well—this voyage has tried her sorely. And now . . ." He broke off, frowning, and Andrew offered quickly, "I have no instructions concerning Mrs. Short or your children. My boat is still here if she would care to make use of it."

"No, she would not hear of it unless I go with her," the *Porpoise*'s commander said decisively. He gestured to the hatchway. "Come below to my cabin, Hawley. At least we can celebrate our safe arrival, can we not? I have some capital Maderia or Cape hock, if you prefer it. Have the goodness to precede me or . . . should I first yield up my sword to you?"

"I don't deem it necessary, sir," Andrew assured him. "You're scarcely likely to make an escape from here, are you?"

Short managed a hollow laugh. Reaching his cabin he shouted for his steward to bring them brandy and the wine he had promised, and when the man had served it and withdrawn, he raised his glass, "Well, to our safe arrival, shall it be? Or to New South Wales's new governor? And may the colonists have joy of him!" Andrew drank without answering, and his host refilled their glasses. "I'm sorry, Hawley—I shouldn't have said that, should I? Better if I keep a rein on my tongue, eh?"

"It's always prudent, sir," Andrew suggested mildly. "I've found it so."

"Of course, you're a leatherneck, and leathernecks are prudent fellows. Disciplined body, His Majesty's Marine Corps—dependable . . . the officer's safeguard if the seamen attempt mutiny." Short, Andrew decided, studying his flushed face and over-bright eyes, had been drinking before he came aboard—and probably brandy, not Madeira. Well, it was understandable—the poor devil was facing the possible ruin of his career as well as the loss of command.

"We swear an oath of allegiance, Captain Short," he supplied flatly.

"Oath of allegiance?" The captain drained his glass and slopped more wine into it, his hand not steady. "Ah, yes, of course—you came through the hawsehole, did you not? And you were with Mr. Bligh at The Nore someone said . . . saved his life or his dignity when the *Director*'s people wanted to string him up during the fleet mutiny. Is that not so, Captain Hawley?"

Andrew got to his feet. "I think, sir, if you will permit me, I will go on deck."

"No, no, for God's sake!" Joseph Short was instantly contrite. "I did not mean to offend you. It is just that . . . oh, the devil! Any adherent of Captain Bligh is anathema to me. The man *is* a tyrant, as the people in this colony will find out very soon. And . . . I imagine you've heard what he intends to do with me?"

"I heard a rumor," Andrew admitted cautiously. Compassion for the *Porpoise*'s young captain brought him back to his seat to accept the topping up of his glass.

"I'm to be packed off home," Short told him, "for court-martial, charged with insubordination. But, damme, Hawley, *I* was given command of the convoy by Their Lordships. I was to take the course from Captain Bligh but nothing more, and when he altered course and headed the convoy in the *Sinclair* without advising me, what choice had I?"

Recalling the occasion, Andrew sighed. "Was it necessary—or prudent—to fire on him?"

"That word again—prudent!" Joseph Short grated. "Hell's teeth, I only fired a shot across his bows to attract his attention . . . and Charlie Putland actually gave the order, I didn't tell him to direct his fire at the damned *Sinclair*! But I'll wager he hasn't had the guts to admit the truth to his precious father-in-law."

He probably had not, Andrew thought, but he refrained from saying so. Short tipped another glass of brandy down his throat and reached again for the bottle. "I'm not a drinking man, Hawley," he offered apologetically, "in normal circumstances. But these are not normal circumstances, are they? I'm to be relieved of my command, sent back to England, and deprived of the chance I was promised by Their Lordships to take a land grant here and settle. Do you wonder I'm trying to drown my sorrows? And," he added aggrievedly, "I was in the right, plague take it! The commander of a convoy is responsible—he is required to keep his ships on course together. He . . ."

From the deck above, the officer of the watch called out a warning.

"Captain, sir—boat approaching from the shore!"

Captain Short lumbered to his feet with a smothered curse and stumbled across to the stern window. He said thickly, "There are damned redcoats in the boat—two of them and an officer! They've come to arrest me, I fancy. . . . Well, you'll be relieved of your charge, Hawley my friend, and that should please you."

Andrew remained silent, but he was apprehensive. It was one thing to keep the *Porpoise*'s commander under open arrest on board his own ship, but . . . He drew in his breath sharply. If Captain Bligh had sent the boat to take Joseph Short ashore, in his present mood the young commander might well attempt to resist the order, with dire consequences.

He said, gripping the younger man's arm, "I beg you, sir, to comply with whatever instructions the boat commander may bring . . . in your own best interests, sir."

Short turned on him, his eyes blazing, but then, recognizing the hopelessness of his situation, he controlled himself. "That's sound advice, Captain Hawley. So long as they provided suitable quarters for my wife and family ashore, I'll go . . . for their sake. And . . . thank you."

"Boat's coming alongside, sir!" came the second warning hail from the deck.

"Escort the officer to my cabin," Short ordered. He looked at Andrew and shrugged; then, his features carefully composed, he resumed his seat.

The corps officer who entered the cabin a few minutes later was young, a sallow-faced individual with dark, close-set eyes and an unpleasantly rasping voice, and to Andrew's dismay he appeared to be enjoying the errand on which he had been sent. Clearly it was not every day that an ensign of the New South Wales Corps was afforded the opportunity of arresting a senior naval officer, and his announcement to this effect was less than tactfully phrased. Addressing the *Porpoise*'s captain as "mister," he reeled off his instructions without pause for breath.

"I am instructed to tell you, sir, that you are to hand over command of this ship to your second-in-command and accompany me ashore forthwith. You will be so good, if you please, to hand me your sword. My men will escort you to my boat."

Short restrained himself with a visible effort, his face scarlet with indignation. "From whom, sir, did you receive these instructions?" he demanded hoarsely.

"From Major Johnstone, acting commandant of my regiment," the ensign returned. "And now if you—"

Short interrupted him. "And from whom did your major receive his instructions?"

With less assurance the young officer was compelled to confess that he did not know. "I presume from the governor, sir, but I was not told." He glanced at Andrew in silent appeal. "I—er—your sword, sir. My orders are to ask for your sword."

"Lest I use it to resist arrest?" Joseph Short taunted. He unbuckled his sword and laid it on the cabin table. "Have quarters been arranged for my wife and family on shore?"

"I understand that the wife of our commandant—Mrs. Paterson, sir—has offered hospitality to your family," the ensign supplied. He added, with what appeared to be an attempt at a placatory tone, "I am to return to the ship after I have taken you ashore, sir, in order to wait on your lady and escort her to the commandant's house when she is ready."

Short turned to Andrew. "It seems I must submit, Captain Hawley. But may I ask, as a favor, that you will remain on board until a boat is sent for my wife and children? And that you will accompany them when they are taken ashore? I hesitate to ask, but this will be a shock to my poor wife, and—I'd be grateful to you."

"Of course, Captain Short," Andrew answered readily. He felt acutely sorry for the unhappy young captain, but there was little more he could do. When the boat had put off for the distant shore, he requested that a message be sent to Mrs. Short, but before it had been delivered, she herself appeared in the cabin, weeping and distraught, to ply both himself and the first lieutenant with anxious questions.

Both did their best to reply and to offer sympathy, but the poor young woman seemed scarcely to take it in. She was clearly in poor health, her cheeks devoid of color and her eyes red and swollen with weeping, and Joseph Short's second-in-command confided to Andrew in a whisper that—as her husband had said earlier—the long voyage had tried her sorely.

"She will be better off ashore and the children, too," the first lieutenant added, his tone angry and resentful. "You saw them in Rio and Capetown, did you not, Captain Hawley? The picture of health, they all were then, but it was the cold and those ice-laden winds we struck on the passage from the Cape. Fifty-one days of that and look at the poor gentle soul! Captain Bligh will be—damme, he'll be guilty of murder if he insists on sending her back with the captain! And I fear he will, the devil take him."

This was insubordinate language, but Andrew offered no denial. He was, he thought, constantly seeing a new side to the man he was pledged to serve, and little of it was to his liking.

The boat returned at last. The arrogant young ensign had brought a stout, motherly woman servant from Mrs. Paterson's household to assist in caring for the two small children, and at the sight of the sickly, distraught wife of the man he had arrested, his manner changed. He showed her every solicitude, assisting her into the boat, wrapping his own cloak round her, and even taking one of the infants on his knee as he, in turn, endeavored to answer her questions concerning her husband's fate.

The band was still playing, and as the boat neared the wharf Andrew saw that the crowds of people who had turned out to bid welcome to their new governor had not dispersed. They were there in their hundreds, a noisy, ribald mob whose somber, government-issue clothing lent them a drab uniformity that was belied by their lack of order and their vociferous chatter.

Many of the convicts wore fetters on their wrists and

ankles, but as today had been declared a holiday, none were working, and a large proportion appeared to be drunk. Andrew watched the milling throng with some alarm, wondering how the unhappy Mrs. Short and her children would fare if they attempted to walk past some of the groups of convict women who, he saw, were shamelessly importuning the seamen from the newly arrived ships. But as the boat tied up to the wharf, he realized with relief that Mrs. Paterson had not merely sent a carriage for her unexpected guests but had come in person to receive them. She was a plump, dowdily dressed woman of uncertain age, but her smile was warm and her manner kindly and concerned as she ushered Mrs. Short into the carriage and then held out her arms to the ensign, who placed the child he had been holding into them.

The carriage moved away; the crowd parted to give it passage, and the ensign said, mopping his brow, "Praise be to God that's over! They'll be in good hands with Mistress Paterson, who is the best and kindest of ladies. The commandant's house is over there"—he pointed—"across the bridge over the Tank Stream and facing on to the High Street, if you have it in mind to call on the poor lady."

"Thank you," Andrew acknowledged. He hesitated. "You spoke this morning of your *acting* commandant, did you not?"

"Major Johnstone . . . yes." There was an odd look on the youthful officer's face, at once wary and contemptuous. "He is in effective command. Colonel Paterson was injured in a duel with one of our other officers, now retired— Captain Macarthur. I haven't been out here very long, so I'm not conversant with the ins and outs of the affair. Colonel Paterson is in command of a new settlement in Van Diemen's Land—Port Dalrymple, I believe."

Puzzled by his tone, Andrew looked at him in mute question, and the boy went on, "As I mentioned, I haven't been out here long, but . . . there is bad blood between Governor King and Major Johnstone, that I do know. And between the governor and Captain Macarthur. The regiment, of course, supports its officers, as might be expected. That is . . ." He broke off, and eyed Andrew uncertainly, as if fearing that he might inadvertently have said too much. "What I've told you is—well, it's common gossip.

Er—you are on the new governor's staff, are you not, sir?"

"Yes," Andrew confirmed guardedly. "My name is Hawley."

"Sir . . . and mine is Bell, Archibald Bell." As if this belated introduction had reminded him of his social duties, Ensign Bell offered politely, "There is a reception being held in the marquee on the Government House lawn, and it's to be followed by a dinner in the new governor's honor. If you would care to go up there now, Captain Hawley, I should be more than pleased to escort you and—er— present some of our officers to you."

Andrew glanced toward Government House, with its parading sentries and the lawn crowded with the socially elite families of Sydney, and shook his head. There was, he told himself, no chance that Jenny Taggart would be on the governor's lawn, but there was a possibility that she might be somewhere among the milling throng beyond those august confines, and . . . He expelled his breath in a long-drawn sigh. It had been so many years since he had first dreamed of setting foot on these shores with Jenny on his arm . . . so many years, and yet the dream had persisted. It would be like looking for a needle in a haystack, he knew; he might pass her by without recognition, she might not even be here—there were settlements outside Sydney Town, farms and homesteads, agricultural land being developed miles beyond, at Parramatta and along the Hawkesbury, and, he had been told, at a place called Coal River and in Van Diemen's Land.

His might be a futile quest, but he must begin it, and in any case . . . He smiled wryly. . . . The reception held no appeal for him; for God's sweet sake, there would be time enough to meet Major Johnstone and Captain John Macarthur and perhaps, on Captain Bligh's account, become embroiled in their feuds and differences.

"I will attend the dinner," he told Ensign Bell, "but now I want to have a look at the town; so if you will forgive me, I'll take my leave."

"There's little enough to see," Bell warned him. "Save dirt and depravity and convict strumpets touting for custom. But if that's your pleasure . . ." He shrugged, in willful misunderstanding. "I will see you later, sir."

The boy had been right, Andrew realized at the end of

an hour's tramping round the drab hovels and the unkempt
streets, fending off the clamorous, ill-clad whores, whose
drunken advances sickened him. There were whores in
plenty in Plymouth and Sheerness, in Portsmouth and Yarmouth town when the ships came in, but none as unwhole-
some and shameless as these. And—perhaps because it was
a public holiday—the taverns and grogshops were filled to
overflowing, with pitched battles being fought in and
around their premises and, to his disgust, drunken soldiers
joining in the fray.

God in heaven, he thought, had Jenny had to spend the
intervening years here? Had she been compelled to waste
her youth and her beauty in such surroundings as these?
But in her letters she had written of working the land,
growing wheat and maize and grapes; she had written contentedly, never railing against her lot, telling him sometimes about the hardships, but more often of the rewards.
And of her horses . . . she had written at length about
them, of the foals she had bred and broken and of good
people among whom she had made a new life.

But not here, surely not here! Jenny was country bred,
not like the sluts from the London gutters who haunted
these mean streets, making the night hideous with their
foulmouthed imprecations, their cackling laughter, and
their wanton invitations.

He trudged on, heading now for the part of town where
the officers of the corps and the civil officials had their
homes, and already the air felt cleaner, the atmosphere
less oppressive. The houses were built of brick—locally
produced, he knew—of a pleasing light-brown color, with
matching shingled roofs. Those wholly or partially constructed of wood had been covered with pipe-clay bleached,
over the years, to a dazzling white by the sun. They were
commodious dwellings, many with verandas reached by
short flights of wooden steps from sloping lawns, and the
gardens, although most were of the kitchen variety, were
extensive and well kept, set behind neat timber fences.

It was not yet dark, and passing the straggling hospital
buildings Andrew climbed to the top of a grassy knoll and
witnessed the breathtaking spectacle of the great harbor as
the last rays of the setting sun turned its waters to molten
gold. Below him, in the cove, the ships lay at anchor—

those of his own convoy dwarfing the small sloops and cutters rocking gently inshore of them—and, as lanterns started to spring to life to illuminate their decks and shine through their open ports, he suddenly found himself caught and held by the beauty of the scene, the drab degradation of the town momentarily forgotten.

Ahead of him he could make out a dockyard, the ribs of a ship on the stocks starkly silhouetted against the glow of the sunset; as he approached to take a closer look at the half-built vessel, he was surprised to hear the sound of steady hammering and to see that a man was at work there. As he watched, the solitary toiler descended from his perch and, whistling cheerfully, went in search of a lantern that, after several attempts, he lit. By its flickering glow, Andrew saw that he was a boy of perhaps fifteen or sixteen summers, with a tanned young face and a mop of unruly fair hair. The face and the lad's slim, well-proportioned body reminded him of someone, but unable to recall who it was, he halted and called out a greeting.

"Who . . . oh, good evening, sir. I beg your pardon—I had not heard you coming."

"Your hammering drowned my footsteps," Andrew said. "But why, when the rest of Sydney is on holiday, are you at work? Did you not greet the new governor?"

The boy's smile faded. He took in Andrew's uniform, and his tone was guarded as he answered, "I can cheer him as well from here as from the other side of the cove."

"Aye, I suppose you can. That's not a bad-looking vessel you are building." Offering some technical comments, Andrew found himself rewarded by a return of the young shipbuilder's smile. The boy supplied details, displaying a knowledge of his craft and a readiness to argue the merits of construction and design that was astonishing in one of his years.

"You'll not be able to see much of her in this light, sir," he said apologetically. "But she's the type of vessel best suited to the needs of the colony—of light draft, so that we can use her for river work, but stout enough to make the passage between here and Norfolk Island and Van Diemen's Land. She'll carry two masts and be brig-rigged, capable of being worked by a small crew, decked and with ample cargo space. We've the masts out of Captain Flinders's ship *Investigator* and her spare suit of sail."

"The *Investigator*? Is she here? I mind her sailing from Sheerness. Was she not once called *Xenophon*?"

"She was condemned here, but Mr. Moore and I salvaged her masts, against the time we'd built a ship capable of taking them." Something in the boy's voice, a note of genuine sadness, startled Andrew. He asked quietly, "Were you at sea in her?"

"Yes, I was, sir. With Captain Flinders and my father too. My father was sailing master. . . ." The story came out then, under some judicious prompting, told without boasting, although it was evident that the boy took pride in telling, and Andrew warmed to him. Dear heaven, there was hope for the colony if it could breed lads of this caliber, he told himself, even if they came of convict stock.

"Captain Flinders took my father's ship—a small sloop we built here, the *Cumberland*, of twenty-six tons burthen—for the voyage back to England. But they never got there. It's said that the *Cumberland* foundered, only my father never believed that. He used to say that the French took her, and—"

Memory stirred, and Andrew gripped the boy's arm. "The French *did* take her—we had word, I recall it now. Captain Flinders and his ship's company are alive, but they are interned as prisoners of war in the Ile de France."

The boy stared at him, an odd mixture of joy and anger in his blue eyes. "I'm glad they're alive, more than glad, sir, but . . . Captain Flinders had a passport from the French, a safe conduct. They had no right to take him or the ship, no right at all. My father told me that because Governor King honored the French commodore's safe conduct when the *Naturaliste* and the *Géographe* called here, then Captain Flinders ought to be able to count on the same treatment from them, in spite of the war. But he'd served against them, and he always said you could not trust the French. My father's fear was that a French privateer attacked the *Cumberland* before she could identify herself and—"

"Wait!" Once again memory stirred as Andrew studied the boy's face in the faint glow from the whale-oil lantern. Convict stock, he had supposed, taking it for granted that, in a penal colony, this was what he had sprung from. But he had described his father as Flinders's sailing master and the *Cumberland* as his ship, and there was a look about him . . . God in heaven, was it possible? He asked tensely, "What is your father's name, lad? It's not Broome, by any chance, is it? *John Broome?*"

"Yes," the boy answered with a catch in his voice. "That was his name. But . . . he's dead, sir. He was drowned in the Hawkesbury floods five months ago. He"—a sob escaped him—"that's why I'm here. I—I'm paid for working here, and there was nothing I could do on the land until our seed corn can be replaced. I thought if I could earn some money I'd be able to buy stock—pigs and goats maybe. But . . ." Andrew's question had unnerved him, and he was talking at random, the control he had imposed on his grief suddenly shattered. He recovered his composure and asked with a swift change of tone, "Did you know my father, sir? Did you serve with him?"

"Aye, that I did, lad. But it was a while ago, and we lost touch. You . . . are you named John, after him?"

"No, sir, my name is Justin. Justin Angus, after my grandfather . . . my mother's father, Angus Taggart, sir. He had a farm in Yorkshire . . ." The boy was talking eagerly now, pleased at the unexpected revelation that the strange marine officer who had accosted him was, after all, no stranger. "Our farm on the Hawkesbury is called Long Wrekin, after his. My mother . . ."

He talked on, but Andrew did not hear what he was saying. Justin's mother was Jenny Taggart, his mind registered, and his search was over, but . . . There was a chill about his heart. Jenny was Johnny Broome's wife . . . his widow, recently widowed, too, and this was her son, hers and Johnny Broome's. He stirred restlessly, and Justin sensed that all was not well. He asked diffidently, "May I know your name, sir? My mother would be pleased to welcome you, I know, if you were a friend of my father's."

Andrew was silent, his emotions as chaotic in that moment as they had been, nineteen years before, when Lieutenant Leach had accosted him, with Jenny in his arms, in the cramped cabin on board the *Charlotte*. She had been his then, the girl he purposed to marry, but now . . . He drew a deep breath and said with unintended bitterness,

"I'd not wish to intrude on her grief. But you can tell her Andrew Hawley sends his regards."

Justin looked disappointed. "Is that all, sir—Captain Hawley?"

"Yes . . . oh, for God's sake, no! Of course it's not. I knew your mother when she was no older than you are, Justin. Tell her . . ." Again he hesitated, at a loss to know how to put his feelings into words. "Tell her that I'm at her service, in any way she may desire. I . . ." Belatedly he recalled the governor's dinner, which it was his duty to attend. Captain Bligh was a stickler for duty and would notice his absence. From somewhere a considerable distance away he heard a clock strike, and he realized with relief that, although it was now quite dark, it wanted an hour to the accustomed time for such dinners to begin.

He took his leave of Jenny Taggart's son and strode back through the darkness at a brisk pace, following the path that skirted the cove.

CHAPTER XXV

Jenny came to terms with her grief, finding assuagement in the sheer, grinding toil required to restore her flooded land to something approaching its former fruitfulness.

There had been floods before and fires, outbreaks of blight and rust and pestilence, but nothing as bad as the scene of devastation the March storm had left in its wake. Granaries, cattle shelters, outbuildings, and fences had been lost beneath the spreading river water and, apart from the horses and a small herd of cattle from the home pasture—which Tom Jardine had driven to safety—all her livestock had been swept away and drowned. Their pathetic corpses were revealed as the river water slowly receded—sheep, goats, hogs, and even hens, barely recognizable beneath the mud and slime.

Little William's rescue attempt, which had cost his father his life, had been the salvation of a scant half-dozen ewes. But there was no time for heartbreak, no time to think or weep, and Jenny worked from first light to dusk and uttered no word of reproach. Johnny and poor old Watt Sparrow had simply gone, with the stock and the burgeoning heads of maize, the stored animal fodder, the haystacks, and the grass . . . a part of the terrible toll the Hawkesbury River had exacted from those who had settled and sought to husband its banks.

The new governor acted decisively. He had visited the settlements within a few days of his arrival, and profoundly shocked by this insight into the suffering the flood had caused and the extent of the damage it wrought, he had spared no effort to send aid to the stricken farmers.

Boats came upriver, loaded with timber and sacks of seed wheat and corn from the holds of the *Lady Sinclair* and the other transports. He dispatched carpenters and convict labor gangs with them, demanding that the corps officers and free settlers in unaffected areas release half their workers for urgent relief projects, which were energetically pursued. When the *Buffalo* returned from the Cape, all the livestock she had on board were allocated to the Hawkesbury settlers, together with breeding animals from the government stock farms at Parramatta and Toongabbe . . . and Governor Bligh would listen to no complaints from members of the corps syndicates when he issued compulsory purchase orders for cargoes they had chartered.

The corps officers saw their consignments of liquor seized and retailed at a price little above cost under government license and were compelled, not only to relinquish half their laborers but also to pay, in money, those whose services they retained a fixed wage. By means of another order the voluntary donation of every eleventh bushel of corn ground by the government-owned mills was required—and was complied with generously by all the free settlers—for the purpose of flood relief.

Jenny, toiling with the rest, was deeply moved by the stoic courage of her neighbors and by the kindness shown to them all by those whose holdings had escaped the devastation. Frances Spence came in person, in her husband's ox-drawn dray, with gifts of food, clothing, and the offer to take Rachel back with her to the luxurious house at Portland Place, for a stay of indeterminate duration.

"I am caring for Henrietta's children," she explained persuasively. "And they would be company for each other, Jenny. Besides, it would leave you free, would it not? And"—she had added, anticipating Jenny's doubts—"Henrietta will not be with us. She insists on staying here to aid Tim."

In the end Frances had taken both Rachel and William and the little dog, from which he was inseparable. Justin—at his own suggestion—had gone back to Sydney in the *Phillip*, to resume his work under Tom Moore at the shipyard, once the more urgent repairs had been completed.

Somehow, for all her devotion to them, Jenny found life easier without her children. True, it was lonely, the house empty of their shrill voices and their eager, running footsteps, but in their absence she had no longer to pretend, to keep up the brave front she had assumed for their benefit to hide her heartbreak. The days passed swiftly, each marked by the progress made—a few acres resown, the arrival of a young ram from the government farm, the gift of a plow, the purchase—at a bargain price—of an aging workhorse trained to its use. The two aborigine boys she

had previously employed, who had fled when the river
had started to rise, returned without explanation or apology, to continue herding the remaining ewes as if they had
never been away . . . and Jenny welcomed them as a
sign that life had resumed its accustomed course.

There were rumors that Governor Bligh was engaged in
a series of acrimonious disputes with the corps officers concerning their trading activities and the free convict labor
most of them looked upon as their right, but the agricultural interests of the free and emancipist settlers were being
accorded official priority, and few lamented the corps's discomfiture.

Ten days before Christmas, Timothy Dawson called,
bearing an Address to the Governor for which he was collecting signatures. He had called several times in the intervening months, but never with Henrietta; Jenny had been
grateful for his visits, since each had been for the purpose
of offering practical help, and she greeted him warmly
now.

Over a meal in the firelit kitchen he promised to arrange
transport for the return of their two families from Portland
Place in time for the Christmas festivities, and then he
drew her attention to the address.

"We want to express our gratitude to the governor for
his prompt and effective aid during the recent calamity in
this area, Jenny, and to pledge him our unstinted support,
The Sydney and Parramatta settlers are preparing a similar
address, but"—he smiled—"theirs is to be prefaced by a
statement to the effect that they did not authorize John
Macarthur to present the Address of Welcome on their behalf on the occasion of the governor's arrival here. And
they've pulled no punches!"

"What do you mean?" Jenny questioned uncertainly.

Timothy laughed in genuine amusement. "It was my
father-in-law's idea, but I venture to suggest that it originated from Frances! They've placed the blame squarely
where it belongs for once. . . . But wait, I have the text of
it here." He read aloud, still smiling, " 'We beg to observe
that had we authorized anyone, John Macarthur would not
have been chosen by us, we considering him an unfit person to step forward on so auspicious an occasion, as we

may chiefly attribute the rise in the price of mutton to his withholding a large flock of wethers he now has, to make such price as he may choose to demand now.' "

Jenny looked at him, wide-eyed and incredulous. "Do you really mean they are including such a—such a statement in their Address to the Governor, Tim? It's hard to credit."

"It happens to be true," Timothy asserted, "and there are one hundred and thirty-five signatures to witness its truth."

"Yes, but—"

"Jenny, this governor is making a most far-reaching and determined attempt to curb the corps's trading monopoly. Our address is designed to make it plain that we approve of the measures he is taking and to invite him to press ahead with what we believe are necessary reforms, for the greater good of the colony as a whole. We have formed a committee amongst ourselves to set out the terms of the reforms we want to see implemented." Timothy unfolded the papers he had brought and spread them out on the table between them. Jenny glimpsed the number of names signed at the foot of the document and was amazed.

"There must be more than a hundred who have signed, Tim."

"Nearer two hundred," Timothy amended, disclosing two more sheets. "And I'm counting on more signatories—including you. What this amounts to is . . . well, I suppose you could almost call it a bill of rights. We are asking for freedom of trade, with the right to buy and sell commodities in open market, and we want the existing monopolist syndicates suppressed . . ." He read from the address. " 'Justice should, in future, be administered not only by the military but also, in equal part, by the free inhabitants of the colony . . . and magistrates appointed from among the emancipated settlers of proven good character and exemplary record.' "

"The corps will never permit that!" Jenny exclaimed.

"They may be compelled to," Timothy countered. "But at all events it is set down as a hope for the future, and I feel confident that Governor Bligh will view it thus. We are also petitioning that all debts shall be made payable in a

stable currency, whether constituted by coins or orders on
government—to be legally recognized at its full nominal
value—in the sale and purchase of every article of merchandise, land, property, or livestock . . ." He read on,
and while not fully comprehending the legal terms, Jenny
felt her spirits lift.

It was, she knew, inevitable that the corps officers would
raise objections, since such reforms—if the governor did
decide to implement them—must result in the curtailment
of their power. They had made high profits from their ex-
tortion; they all owned good land, and the barter system,
by means of which they paid their soldiers as well as their
laborers, operated unjustly in their favor. She heard Timothy read on.

"Here is the crux of it, Jenny, and you should listen
carefully before you sign. *'Under a just and benign Government, we wish to assure our Excellency that we will be
ready at all times, at the risk of our lives and properties, to
give our support to the above mentioned reforms.'* "

Jenny met his gaze without flinching. The memory of
Governor Phillip's speech, made when they had landed in
Sydney Cove nineteen years before, came crowding into
her mind. Had she not built her whole life on the promise
of the future that his words had held out?

> Here are fertile plains, needing only the labors of the
> husbandman to produce in abundance the richest and
> fairest fruits. Here are interminable pastures, the fu-
> ture home of flocks and herds innumerable . . .

Here, in this land that Matthew Flinders had called Australia . . . a barren, hostile land, inhabited by savages
until the coming of Governor Phillip's convict fleet. The
land was productive now, the flocks were there—surely
there must be hope, surely the toil of people like herself
over the long years must be the basis for that hope?

Jenny caught her breath on a sob. Under a just and benign government, the address had stipulated, with the
Rum Corps's evil influence ended at last . . . was that not
worth any risk, of stock, of property, of life itself? Had
Johnny not given his life already, as hostage to the future
for his son's sake—and old Watt too?

"I will sign, Tim," she said, and pushing her empty plate away, set quill and ink in place of it.

"We are also pledging ourselves to supply grain at the price fixed by the governor at the next harvest," Timothy told her, "to repay the debts we have all incurred as a result of the flood and the aid we have been compelled to accept. That is the least we can do, or at any rate, it was the feeling of the committee. One or two members feared making a long-term contract, although it was suggested, so we compromised and have stipulated one of just a year's duration. But you understand, don't you, Jenny, that it could be renewed voluntarily?"

"Yes," Jenny assured him. "I understand. And I'll gladly sign."

She added her name to the list of signatories at the foot of the page.

"Captain Macarthur, sir," Secretary Griffin began. "He has a request to put before Your Excellency. I understand that it is urgent—" He was thrust unceremoniously aside, and Governor Bligh found himself confronting an angry John Macarthur.

"Your manners, sir," Bligh said coldly, before the unexpected caller could give vent to his rage, "leave much to be desired, but if the matter is urgent, pray be seated."

Red of face, his pendulous lower lip drooping with its characteristic sullenness, Macarthur scornfully disregarded the invitation.

"I have come to demand my rights, sir!" he stated explosively. "Rights to the land I was granted by the British Colonial Office—grazing land for my sheep. You may not be aware, sir, that I possess the finest—indeed the only—flock of purebred Merino sheep in the colony. On the recommendation of His Majesty's Privy Council, I was to have ten thousand acres of grazing land on which to rear them. The Secretary of State himself assured me that I—"

William Bligh cut him short, his own temper rising. "Damn the Privy Council—and damn the Secretary of State too! He commands at home, *I* command here, and you would do well to remember that!"

"But my sheep," Macarthur protested. "My cattle . . . plague take you, sir, you deprive me of my labor, my herdsmen and shepherds, as well as of the land I need for them!"

"What have I to do with your sheep, sir?" the governor countered wrathfully. "What have I to do with your cattle? Are you to have such flocks of sheep and herds of cattle as no man ever heard of before? Are you to employ more labor than anyone else in this colony? I have heard of your concerns, sir. You have got five thousand acres of land in the finest situation in the whole country, but by God, sir, you shan't keep it!"

The color drained from John Macarthur's face. "Is that a threat, sir?" he asked, his tone ominously quiet.

"If you choose to take it as such."

"I fancy you may live to regret having threatened me," Macarthur warned.

Bligh shrugged. He contained his anger with a visible effort and motioned his caller to the door. "If that is all you have to say to me, Mr. Macarthur, I give you good day."

Macarthur held his ground. "Are you refusing my legitimate application for the land to which I am entitled?"

"You will get no more whilst I am governor," Bligh returned uncompromisingly, "in fairness to the rest of the community, for whose well-being I am also responsible."

"And my laborers—the men you took from me six months ago for flood relief?"

"They are still required for essential public works, sir. And now—"

John Macarthur bowed stiffly. "Is that your last word on the matter?"

"It is, Mr. Macarthur."

Macarthur strode across to the door. Reaching it, he turned briefly to face the governor. "It remains to be seen, Mr. Bligh," he sneered, "for how long you will remain governor, does it not? I shall apply to the courts for justice since I cannot obtain it from you. If necessary, sir, I shall bring the matter to the attention of His Majesty's government, who may well see fit to order your recall. It is not without precedent that earlier governors have been recalled, is it? And now, sir, I will give you good day!"

William Bligh waited until the door closed behind him and then reached for pen and paper. Heading his letter

"Your Lordship" he wrote rapidly and decisively for almost an hour. Finally, the letter concluded, he summoned his secretary. "This is to go by the first ship bound for England, he said. "See it it, will you?"

EPILOGUE

The children returned and the house began to live again. Jenny's sad heart melted when Rachel came running toward her with arms outheld and a glad cry of "Mam!" on her lips, with William close behind her, walking more sedately, the collie dog, as always, at his heels.

They had much to tell her of their stay at Portland Place and evidence of the Spences' kindness to offer for their mother's inspection. Nancy Jardine, who had accompanied them in the role of nursemaid, had a similar tale to tell. They had been to Sydney numerous times. They had witnessed the arrival of the new governor and the parade, and although they had not been invited to join Henrietta and her children on the Government House lawn, they had enjoyed themselves hugely in Frances's lively company and had been royally entertained in the Spences' Sydney drawing room.

"We saw Justin," William supplied, "but he wouldn't come with us. He was working on some old ship at the yard and said he didn't care about the parade. But it was grand, Mam, truly it was." He had much to tell her of his exploits—he had helped to break a young horse and had been the first to ride it; he had gone with the Spence workers to round up sheep and brand the new lambs, and his dog, he assured her solemnly, was now a perfectly trained shepherd.

"I'll be a help to you now, Mam," the little boy added eagerly. "A real help when Justin goes back to sea."

Jenny caught the last words and bit back a cry. Justin had promised, she thought; surely William's childish imagination had conjured up the idea that Justin intended—or even wanted—to go back to sea? She questioned him cautiously but then desisted. Justin himself would be here soon; he had sent word that he would come up river in the *Phillip*, and the sloop was due within a day or so, bringing a final gift of Christmas cheer from the governor.

"He's working for a Mr. Lord now," William told her, his tone casual, as if Justin's change of employment were of

little consequence. "Not for Mr. Moore. He gets better pay,
he said. Mam, can I go out with Tom now and show him
how good Frisky is with the sheep?"

Jenny let him go. Later, when both children were asleep,
she and Nancy talked far into the night in the lamp-lit
kitchen, but apart from general gossip—with which Nancy
was well primed—she learned little, save that the new governor was becoming increasingly popular with the free settlers . . . and much less so with the corps.

"It's almost like there are two sets o' folk in the colony
now," Nancy said. "With us—that's the emancipists—an'
the free settlers on one side an' the corps and some o' the
commissariat on the other. *I* say good luck to Governor
Bligh, but Mr. Spence reckons as he may be heading for
trouble."

As Timothy Dawson had also hinted, Jenny recalled,
and, she supposed, as the address she had signed had implied. Had it not stated the willingness of the Hawkesbury
settlers, free and freed, to support the governor's reforms,
even at the risk of their lives and properties? Well, they
had reason to be grateful to Governor Bligh, all of them
had, including herself, and . . . Nancy Jardine put her
thoughts into words when she added shrewdly, " 'Tis a
pity, in my opinion, Mistress Broome, that the New South
Wales Corps can't be sent back to England. There's a war,
ain't there? Well, let them go and fight in it an' bad cess to
them!"

Major Ross's marines had gone, Jenny thought; perhaps,
in time, the home government would see fit to recall the
corps and either replace them with an exemplary regiment
or permit the Loyal Associations to guard the colony and
those convicts who required guarding.

She asked about Mr. Lord, anxious concerning Justin's
new employer, but beyond expressing the belief that Mr.
Simeon Lord was heavily involved in the rum trade and
was building ships in order to further his interest in that
regard, Nancy knew little.

"He's an emancipist," she stated. "Or so they say, but
he's mixed up with two brothers by the name o' Blaxland,
who have just come out here and don't seem to be too well
thought of. Accordin' to Mr. Spence there's a right gang o'
them, all hand in glove with the corps officers, an' they're

plannin' to start a distillery to get around the governor's new licensing laws. That's to say, if Governor Bligh stops them importin' liquor, they reckon to produce it right on his back door."

It was a disquieting thought, and Jenny worried about Justin's possible involvement with the mysterious Mr. Lord and his associates. His desire for more pay was understandable—even laudable, since he wanted money in order to buy additions to her depleted livestock—but if, in order to earn it, he had taken employment with one of the liquor traffickers, then there was reason for concern.

Going about her daily chores she became increasingly anxious, despite the distraction afforded by her younger children's return. The *Phillip* was sighted the following morning, but when she rode to the wharf it was to learn that Justin was not on board. Rob Webb, who was in command, shook his head to her question.

"He said he might take passage with me a week or so back, but he never showed up an' I couldn't wait. I'm sorry, Jenny lass—you were countin' on having him back home fer Christmas, wasn't you? But I'm afraid I don't know where he's got to, the young rogue."

He went off to supervise the unloading of his cargo, and Jenny was about to return, disconsolately, to her tethered horse when the white gleam of a sail some distance downriver caught and held her gaze.

It was tacking across from the far bank, a small, graceful cutter that, it was evident even to her uncritical eyes, was being expertly handled. She watched it for several minutes, reminded of the skimming, dipping flight of the birds known as Mother Carey's Chickens that she had watched with the same fascination, years before, from the icy deck of the *Lady Penrhyn*, as Governor Phillip's fleet approached the coast of Van Diemen's Land.

That had also been at Christmas—the first Christmas of her exile, she thought, and then, glimpsing a redcoat in the cutter's bows, she turned away, suddenly, inexplicably blinded by tears and unable to watch any longer. Rob came after her, as she was swinging herself back into Baneelon's saddle, to thrust a sack into her hands.

"Compliments o' His Excellency the Guv'nor, Jenny," he told her. "Indian tea, a pound o' the best, fresh-ground flour, a keg o' molasses—an' a ham, from me an' Charlotte, spice-cured, wi' our best wishes. Here, I'll lay it across yer saddlebow, shall I? Be easier fer you to manage that way."

Deeply touched by his generosity, Jenny thanked him, the tears flowing unashamedly down her cheeks. Rob grinned at her, muttering sheepishly that it was nothing and that Charlotte had never forgotten her, and then he strode off, back to the wharf and to the ship Johnny had once commanded. In memory she saw Johnny on the narrow deck, with Justin beside him in his shabby, ill-fitting brass-buttoned uniform, and caught her breath on a sob.

Johnny would never walk the *Phillip*'s deck again, and Justin, for all he had discarded his naval uniform, had not come to spend Christmas with his family because he was planning to go to sea again. . . .

She rode back to Long Wrekin, the sack of provisions bumping awkwardly on her horse's neck and her heart close to breaking. . . .

Justin made his appearance two hours later. He was in shirt and breeches, not in his uniform jacket, and he had brought gifts for all of them, which he listed proudly: a crate of hens and a pair of breeding ewes, to be brought from the wharf in daylight; a beautifully carved shepherd's crook for William; a wooden doll, fashioned by his own hands, for Rachel; a shawl for Nancy Jardine; and tobacco for Tom.

"You saw me coming up river in the *Matthew Flinders*, Mam," he added, his tone faintly reproachful. "Rob told me you were watching her—but you didn't wait."

"No," Jenny acknowledged, searching his thin young face. "No, I did not realize it was you, but—Justin, did you build her for Mr. Lord?"

He shook his head. "No, for myself. I only used his yard because Tom Moore hadn't space—the sloop we were working on takes up all there is. William told you, I suppose? Well, he got it wrong, as usual. I'm my own man now; I've completed my apprenticeship, and I'll take any man's contract if he pays me. But the *Flinders* is mine."

"Is she"—Jenny's brow was furrowed as she searched her memory for the right words—"is she seagoing?"

"Yes." He gave her no details, offered no explanation, and her doubts and fears grew. He had brought no gift for her, she realized, no personal gift. There were the hens, of course, and the two ewes, but he had brought her nothing that he had fashioned with his own hands, and . . . there had been a soldier with him in the cutter. She had seen the red jacket, as its owner had gone forward to attend the jib. That had been when she had turned away and ceased to watch the boat, for which her son had reproached her.

She studied him anew, noticing almost with surprise how tall he was—a head taller than herself and almost as tall now as his father had been. And he resembled his father; the blue, restless eyes were as much Johnny's as the tanned, handsome young face. The eyes were those of a seaman, just as his father's had been, with that faraway gaze that, an instant before, she had characterized in her thoughts as restless. But they were restless because they sought far horizons. . . . Matt Flinders's eyes had held the same look, and once when he had been with them he had talked of the land as a prison.

"Give me the sea," Matt had said more than once in her hearing. "For that is freedom!"

Jenny forced a smile. She said gently, "Oh, Justin—I do understand, you know. I'll not try to keep you if you do not want to stay. And I'll hold you to no promises if you find them hard to honor . . . you need never fear that."

Justin let out his breath in a pent-up sigh, and suddenly his arms were round her and he was hugging her with all his old, eager affection. For a long moment he said nothing but simply held her, his cheek on hers, and feeling its roughness, she knew that her son was no longer a boy but a man.

It was William who broke the silence. He came in, an expression of alarm on his round, chubby face. "Mam, there's a soldier outside—an officer. I asked him what he wanted, and he said that Justin would tell you. He—"

Justin cut him short. "And so I will, if you'll hold your tongue, you miserable little blabbermouth!" He turned to Jenny. "Mam, I brought an old friend to spend Christmas with us."

"An officer—a *corps* officer?" Jenny exclaimed, unable

to keep the bitterness from sounding in her voice. "An old friend of *yours*, Justin?"

"No, Mam—of yours. Yours and my father's. He's a captain of marines who fought under Nelson at Trafalgar," Justin told her. "He knew you in the old days in Yorkshire when you were a child. He says he carried you into London, pickaback, and . . . he wouldn't come in lest you—"

Jenny stared at him incredulously. "Andrew . . . Justin, are you saying that *Andrew Hawley* is outside? Outside, when surely he must know how glad I'll be to see him . . . how truly glad! Don't stand there, son—bring him in!"

"I'll bring him in, Mam," William offered eagerly. "He's playing with Rachel, and—" Justin grabbed him by the collar.

"No, Willie. It's Mam's place to bid him welcome." He gave Jenny a gentle push, still holding the indignant William. "It's you he's waiting for, Mam . . . *you* invite him in."

Jenny went hesitantly to the door, feeling as if she were dreaming, and a tall stranger in a gold-laced red coat turned at the sound of her footsteps and came to meet her, with Rachel clinging to his hand.

There was a puckered scar on his face, flecks of white in his neatly tied hair, and uncertainty in his eyes as he halted in front of her. But before he could speak, Rachel's small face puckered and she started to cry. Smiling, Andrew bent to pick her up and hoist her onto his shoulders, and as her sobs turned to whoops of delight, he carried her into the house, a stranger no more.

Jenny followed him, her heart lifting. The wheel had turned full circle, she thought, and when he set Rachel down and turned again to face her with both hands outheld, she ran to take them in her own.

"Oh, Andrew," she told him in a choked voice. "It's so good to see you again—so very, very good!"

"Perhaps," Andrew suggested with gentle mockery, "this will make up for losing you on London Bridge . . . or was it in Billingsgate?"

"It was on London Bridge," Jenny said. "But you've come back to Long Wrekin."

"Aye," he acknowledged. "And to you. . . ."

The Traitors, Book Three in the magnificent six-book series *The Australians,* continues the story of Jenny Broome; Frances O'Riordan Spence; Andrew Hawley; Jenny's son, Justin; and many of the other men and women you have met in *The Settlers.*

In *The Traitors* you will meet Abigail—passionate daughter of a former gambler—who stops at nothing to defend what she holds dearest in life. You will also follow the struggles of Governor William Bligh, of *Mutiny on the Bounty* fame, who fights to end the terrible rum traffic engaged in by officers of the notorious New South Wales Corps—the "Rum Corps"—during one of the most turbulent eras in Australian history.

Here is a stirring look at the action in *The Traitors*, to be published by Dell early next year, © 1980 by Book Creations, Inc. Produced by Lyle Kenyon Engel.

The sound of martial music, on fife and drum, brought Sydney's inhabitants crowding into the dusty, ill-kept streets.

At first, few were aware of what was afoot; men turned in bewilderment to their neighbors in the crowd, asking in anxious voices for answers no one could supply. Then from the brothels and taverns came a surging mob, egged on by a handful of soldiers—the notorious Sergeant Major Whittle at their head—and drunken cries of "Down with the tyrant!" and "Death to *Bounty* Bligh!" became ominously audible.

A band of Simeon Lord's seamen, holding flaming torches above their heads, came in a wild rush from the warehouses on the west side of the Cove and, well primed with rum, added their voices to the din. The occupant of a house opposite the jail opened the door and seeing the disorderly scene hurriedly closed it again, only to be subjected to a storm of abuse from the seamen, who hammered with their fists on the door until he consented to join them. Others, in adjacent houses, soon followed his example in response to the seamen's shouted threats, and several bonfires—evidently prepared in advance—were lit at strategic points along the route from Barrack Row to the High Street.

The troops, some three hundred strong, swung smartly to the right to cross the Tank Stream Bridge. Major George Johnstone, mounted on a roan charger, rode at their head, showing no obvious sign now of the injuries resulting from his fall, which had earlier precluded his attendance on the governor.

At his back, an ensign carried the Colors of the Corps, his escort marching with measured tread and bayonets fixed, to be greeted with applause from the crowd, as the band struck up "The British Grenadiers" and the redcoated ranks advanced steadily toward their objective. Realizing that this was Government House, the crowd fell momentarily silent, but then a few bolder spirits took up the cry of "Down with the tryant!" once more and it was soon echoed by the mob.

At the gate of Government House, a single, small intrepid figure barred their way. It was the governor's daughter, Mary Putland. The shawl slipping from her shoulders and hair blown into disarray by the wind, the slender woman faced the corps and its commander without flinching.

"You traitor!" she flung at Johnstone as he reined in beside her. "You rebels! You have just walked over my husband's grave—have you now come to murder my father?"

The accusation, bravely delivered in a shrill, carrying voice, stung as it was meant to and gave even Johnstone pause. Then he recovered himself and motioned to the sentry to take the governor's daughter in charge.

"Mr. Bligh will come to no harm," he stated coldly. "We intend only to place him under arrest."

Mary Putland broke away from the sentry's halfhearted grasp and ran, weeping, back to her father's official residence.

A mocking taunt followed her from somewhere in the close-packed crowd, the words drunkenly slurred but their meaning clear enough to the distraught girl as she stumbled up the steps to safety.

"Down with the tyrant! Death to the tyrant!"

Panic-stricken by the temper of the crowd, Mary Putland flung herself into the hall of Government House. "Papa, Papa, where are you?" she cried brokenly.